A master storyteller, Sidney Sheldon is the author of eighteen novels (which have sold over 300 million copies), over 200 television scripts, twenty-five major motion pictures and six Broadway plays, ranking him as one of the world's most prolific writers. His first book, *The Naked Face*, was acclaimed by the *New York Times* as 'the best first mystery novel of the year' and subsequently each of his highly popular books have hit No. 1 on the *New York Times* bestseller list. His latest bestseller, *Are You Afraid of the Dark?*, cements Sheldon's reputation as the master of the unexpected.

For more about Sidney Sheldon, visit his website at www.sidneysheldon.com.

For automatic updates on Sidney Sheldon visit HarperCollins.co.uk/sidneysheldon and register for AuthorTracker.

SIDNEY SHELDON

Master of the Game

If Tomorrow Comes

HarperCollins*Publishers*

HarperCollins*Publishers*
77–85 Fulham Palace Road,
Hammersmith, London W6 8JB

www.harpercollins.co.uk

This omnibus edition published in 2006 by HarperCollins*Publishers*

A catalogue record for this book is
available from the British Library

ISBN 0 00 777775 2

Set in Sabon by
Palimpsest Book Production Limited, Polmont, Stirlingshire

Printed and bound in Great Britain by
Clays Ltd, St Ives plc

Master of the Game

For my brother,
Richard
the Lion-Hearted

My appreciation goes to Miss Geraldine
Hunter for her endless patience and assistance
in preparing this manuscript.

'And hence one master-passion in the breast,
Like Aaron's serpent, swallows up the rest.'
— ALEXANDER POPE
Essay on Man, Epistle II

'Diamonds resist blows to such an extent that an iron hammer may be split in two and even the anvil itself may be displaced. This invincible force, which defies Nature's two most violent forces, iron and fire, can be broken by ram's blood. But it must be steeped in blood that is fresh and warm and, even so, many blows are needed.'
— PLINY THE ELDER

PROLOGUE

Kate

1982

The large ballroom was crowded with familiar ghosts come to help celebrate her birthday. Kate Blackwell watched them mingle with the flesh-and-blood people, and in her mind, the scene was a dreamlike fantasy as the visitors from another time and place glided around the dance floor with the unsuspecting guests in black tie and long, shimmering evening gowns. There were one hundred people at the party at Cedar Hill House, in Dark Harbor, Maine. *Not counting the ghosts*, Kate Blackwell thought wryly.

She was a slim petite woman, with a regal bearing that made her appear taller than she was. She had a face that one remembered. A proud bone structure, dawn-grey eyes and a stubborn chin, a blending of her Scottish and Dutch ancestors. She had fine, white hair that once had been a luxuriant black cascade, and against the gracefolds of her ivory velvet dress, her skin had the soft translucence old age sometimes brings.

3

I don't feel ninety, Kate Blackwell thought. *Where have all the years gone?* She watched the dancing ghosts. *They know. They were there. They were a part of those years, a part of my life.* She saw Banda, his proud black face beaming. And there was her David, dear David, looking tall and young and handsome, the way he looked when she first fell in love with him, and he was smiling at her, and she thought, *Soon, my darling, soon.* And she wished David could have lived to know his great-grandson.

Kate's eyes searched the large room until she saw him. He was standing near the orchestra, watching the musicians. He was a strikingly handsome boy, almost eight years old, fair-haired, dressed in a black velvet jacket and tartan trousers. Robert was a replica of his great-great-grandfather, Jamie McGregor, the man in the painting above the marble fireplace. As though sensing her eyes on him, Robert turned, and Kate beckoned him to her with a wave of her fingers, the perfect twenty-carat diamond her father had scooped up on a sandy beach almost a hundred years ago scintillating in the radiance of the crystal chandelier. Kate watched with pleasure as Robert threaded his way through the dancers.

I am the past, Kate thought. *He is the future. My great-grandson will take over Kruger-Brent, Limited one day.* He reached her side, and she made room for him on the seat beside her.

'Are you having a nice birthday, Gran?'

'Yes. Thank you, Robert.'

'That's a super orchestra. The conductor's really *bad*.'

Kate looked at him in momentary confusion, then her brow cleared. 'Ah. I presume that means he's good.'

Robert grinned at her. 'Right. You sure don't seem ninety.'

Kate Blackwell laughed. 'Just between the two of us, I don't feel it.'

He slipped his hand in hers, and they sat there in a contented silence, the eighty-two-year difference between them giving them a comfortable affinity. Kate turned to watch her granddaughter dancing. She and her husband were without doubt the handsomest couple on the floor.

Robert's mother saw her son and grandmother seated together and she thought, *What an incredible woman. She's ageless. No one would ever guess all she has lived through.*

The music stopped, and the conductor said, 'Ladies and gentlemen, it's my pleasure to present young Master Robert.'

Robert squeezed his great-grandmother's hand, stood up and walked over to the piano. He sat down, his face serious and intent, and then his fingers began to race across the keyboard. He played Scriabin, and it was like the rippling of moonlight on water.

His mother listened and thought, *He's a genius. He'll grow up to be a great musician.* He was no longer her baby. He was going to belong to the world. When Robert finished, the applause was enthusiastic and genuine.

Earlier, dinner had been served outdoors. The large and formal garden had been festively decorated with lanterns and ribbons and balloons. Musicians played from the terrace while butlers and maids hovered over tables, silent and efficient, making sure the Baccarat glasses and Limoges dishes were kept filled. A telegram was read from the President of the United States. A Supreme Court justice toasted Kate.

The governor eulogized her. '. . . One of the most remarkable women in the history of this nation. Kate Blackwell's endowments to hundreds of charitable causes around the world are legendary. The Blackwell Foundation has contributed to the health and well-being of people in more than fifty countries. To paraphrase the late Sir Winston Churchill, "Never have so many owed so much to one person." I have had the privilege of knowing Kate Blackwell . . .'

Bloody hell! Kate thought. *No one knows me. He sounds like he's talking about some saint. What would all these people say if they knew the real Kate Blackwell? Sired by a thief and kidnapped before I was a year old. What would they think if I showed them the bullet scars on my body?*

She turned her head and looked at the man who had once tried to kill her. Kate's eyes moved past him to linger on a figure in the shadows, wearing a veil to conceal her face. Over a distant clap of thunder, Kate heard the governor finish his speech and introduce her. She rose to her feet and looked out at the assembled guests. When she spoke, her voice was firm and strong. 'I've lived longer than any of you. As youngsters today would say, "That's no big deal." But I'm glad I made it to this age, because otherwise I wouldn't be here with all you dear friends. I know some of you have travelled from distant countries to be with me tonight, and you must be tired from your journey. It wouldn't be fair for me to expect everyone to have my energy.' There was a roar of laughter, and they applauded her.

'Thank you for making this such a memorable evening. I shall never forget it. For those of you who wish to retire, your rooms are ready. For the others, there will be dancing in the ballroom.' There was another clap of thunder. 'I suggest we all move indoors before we get caught in one of our famous Maine storms.'

Now the dinner and dancing were over, the guests had retired and Kate was alone with her ghosts. She sat in the library, drifting back into the past, and she suddenly felt depressed. *There's no one left to call me Kate*, she thought. *They've all gone.* Her world had shrunk. Wasn't it Longfellow who said, 'The leaves of memory make a mournful rustle in the dark'? She would be entering the dark soon, but not yet. *I still have to do the most important thing of my life*, Kate thought. *Be patient, David. I'll be with you soon.*

'Gran . . .'

Kate opened her eyes. The family had come into the room. She looked at them, one by one, her eyes a pitiless camera, missing nothing. *My family*, Kate thought. *My immortality. A murderer, a grotesque and a psychotic. The Blackwell skeletons. Was this what all the years of hope and pain and suffering had finally come to?*

Her granddaughter stood beside her. 'Are you all right, Gran?'

'I'm a little tired, children. I think I'll go to bed.' She rose to her feet and started towards the stairs, and at that moment there was a violent roar of thunder and the storm broke, the rain rattling against the windows like machine-gun fire. Her family watched as the old woman reached the top of the stairway, a proud, erect figure. There was a blaze of lightning and seconds later a loud clap of thunder. Kate Blackwell turned to look down at them and when she spoke, it was with the accent of her ancestors. 'In South Africa, we used to call this a *donderstorm*.'

The past and present began to merge once again, and she walked down the hallway to her bedroom, surrounded by the familiar, comfortable ghosts.

BOOK ONE

Jamie

1883–1906

ONE

'By God, this is a real *donderstorm*!' Jamie McGregor said. He had grown up amid the wild storms of the Scottish Highlands, but he had never witnessed anything as violent as this. The afternoon sky had been suddenly obliterated by enormous clouds of sand, instantly turning day into night. The dusty sky was lit by flashes of lightning – *weerlig*, the Afrikaners called it – that scorched the air, followed by *donderslag* – thunder. Then the deluge. Sheets of rain that smashed against the army of tents and tin huts and turned the dirt streets of Klipdrift into frenzied streams of mud. The sky was aroar with rolling peals of thunder, one following the other like artillery in some celestial war.

Jamie McGregor quickly stepped aside as a house built of raw brick dissolved into mud, and he wondered whether the town of Klipdrift was going to survive.

Klipdrift was not really a town. It was a sprawling canvas village, a seething mass of tents and huts and wagons crowding the banks of the Vaal River, populated by wild-eyed dreamers drawn to South Africa from all parts of the world by the same obsession: diamonds.

Jamie McGregor was one of the dreamers. He was barely eighteen, a handsome lad, tall and fair-haired, with startlingly light grey eyes. There was an attractive ingenuousness about him, an eagerness to please that was endearing. He had a lighthearted disposition and a soul filled with optimism.

He had travelled almost eight thousand miles from his father's farm in the Highlands of Scotland to Edinburgh, London, Cape Town and now Klipdrift. He had given up his rights to the share of the farm that he and his brothers tilled with their father, but Jamie McGregor had no regrets. He knew he was going to be rewarded ten thousand times over. He had left the security of the only life he had ever known and had come to this distant, desolate place because he dreamed of being rich. Jamie was not afraid of hard work, but the rewards of tilling the rocky little farm north of Aberdeen were meager. He worked from sunup to sundown, along with his brothers, his sister, Mary, and his mother and father, and they had little to show for it. He had once attended a fair in Edinburgh and had seen the wondrous things of beauty that money could buy. Money was to make your life easy when you were well, and to take care of your needs when you were ailing. Jamie had seen too many friends and neighbours live and die in poverty.

He remembered his excitement when he first heard about the latest diamond strike in South Africa. The biggest diamond in the world had been found there, lying loose in the sand, and the whole area was rumoured to be a great treasure chest waiting to be opened.

He had broken the news to his family after dinner on a Saturday night. They were seated around an uncleared table in the rude, timbered kitchen when Jamie spoke, his voice shy and at the same time proud. 'I'm going to South Africa to find diamonds. I'll be on my way next week.'

Five pairs of eyes stared at him as though he were crazy.

'You're goin' chasing after diamonds?' his father asked. 'You must be daft, lad. That's all a fairy tale – a temptation of the devil to keep men from doin' an honest day's work.'

'Why do you nae tell us where you're gettin' the money to go?' his brother Ian asked. 'It's halfway 'round the world. You hae no money.'

'If I had money,' Jamie retorted, 'I wouldn't have to go looking for diamonds, would I? Nobody there has money. I'll be an equal with all of them. I've got brains and a strong back. I'll not fail.'

His sister, Mary, said, 'Annie Cord will be disappointed. She expects to be your bride one day, Jamie.'

Jamie adored his sister. She was older than he. Twenty-four, and she looked forty. She had never owned a beautiful thing in her life. *I'll change that*, Jamie promised himself.

His mother silently picked up the platter that held the remains of the steaming haggis and walked over to the iron sink.

Late that night she came to Jamie's bedside. She gently placed one hand on Jamie's shoulder, and her strength flooded into him. 'You do what you must, Son. I dinna ken if there be diamonds there, but if there be, you'll find them.' She brought out from behind her a worn leather pouch. 'I've put by a few pounds. You needn't say nothin' to the others. God bless you, Jamie.'

When he left for Edinburgh, he had fifty pounds in the pouch.

It was an arduous journey to South Africa, and it took Jamie McGregor almost a year to make it. He got a job as a waiter in a workingman's restaurant in Edinburgh until he added another fifty pounds to the pouch. Then it was on to London. Jamie was awed by the size of the city, the huge crowds, the noise and the large horse-drawn omnibuses that raced along at five miles an hour. There were hansom cabs everywhere, carrying beautiful women in large hats and swirling skirts and dainty little high-button shoes. He watched in wonder as the ladies alighted from the cabs and carriages to shop at Burlington Arcade, a dazzling cornucopia of silver and dishes and dresses and furs and pottery and apothecary shops crammed with mysterious bottles and jars.

Jamie found lodging at a house at 32 Fitzroy Street. It cost ten shillings a week, but it was the cheapest he could find. He spent his days at the docks, seeking a ship that would take him to South Africa, and his evenings seeing the wondrous sights of London town. One evening he caught a glimpse of Edward, the Prince of Wales, entering a restaurant near Covent Garden by the side door, a beautiful young lady on his arm. She wore a large-flowered hat, and Jamie thought how nice it would look on his sister.

Jamie attended a concert at the Crystal Palace, built for The Great Exhibition in 1851. He visited Drury Lane and at intermission sneaked into the Savoy Theatre, where they had installed the first electric lighting in a British public building. Some streets were lighted by electricity, and Jamie heard that it was possible to talk to someone on the other side of town by means of a wonderful new machine, the telephone. Jamie felt that he was looking at the future.

In spite of all the innovations and activity, England was in the midst of a growing economic crisis that winter. The streets were filled with the unemployed and the hungry, and there were mass demonstrations and street fighting. *I've got to get away from here*, Jamie thought. *I came to escape poverty*. The following day, Jamie signed on as a steward on the *Walmer Castle*, bound for Cape Town, South Africa.

* * *

The sea journey lasted three weeks, with stops at Madeira and St Helena to take on more coal for fuel. It was a rough, turbulent voyage in the dead of winter, and Jamie was seasick from the moment the ship sailed. But he never lost his cheerfulness, for every day brought him nearer to his treasure chest. As the ship moved towards the equator, the climate changed. Miraculously, winter began to thaw into summer, and as they approached the African coast, the days and nights became hot and steamy.

The *Walmer Castle* arrived in Cape Town at early dawn, moving carefully through the narrow channel that divided the great leper settlement of Robben Island from the mainland, and dropped anchor in Table Bay.

Jamie was on deck before sunrise. He watched, mesmerized, as the early-morning fog lifted and revealed the grand spectacle of Table Mountain looming high over the city. He had arrived.

The moment the ship made fast to the wharf, the decks were overrun by a horde of the strangest-looking people Jamie had ever seen. There were touts for all the different hotels – black men, yellow men, brown men and red men frantically offering to bear away luggage – and small boys running back and forth with newspapers and sweets and fruits for sale. Hansom drivers who were half-castes, Parsis or blacks were yelling their eagerness to be hired. Vendors and men pushing drinking carts called attention to their wares. The air was thick with huge black flies. Sailors and porters hustled and halloaed their way through the crowd while passengers vainly tried to keep their luggage together and in sight. It was a babel of voices and noise. People spoke to one another in a language Jamie had never heard.

'Yulle kom van de Kaap, neh?'
'Het julle mine papa zyn wagen gezien?'
'Wat bedui' di?'
'Huistoe!'

He did not understand a word.

Cape Town was utterly unlike anything Jamie had ever seen. No two houses were alike. Next to a large warehouse two or three storeys high, built of bricks or stone, was a small canteen of galvanized iron, then a jeweller's shop with hand-blown plate-glass windows and abutting it a small greengrocer's and next to that a tumble-down tobacconist's.

Jamie was mesmerized by the men, women and children who thronged the streets. He saw a kaffir clad in an old pair of 78th Highland trews and wearing as a coat a sack with slits cut for the arms and head. The kaffir walked behind two Chinese men, hand in hand, who were wearing blue smock frocks, their pigtails carefully coiled up under their conical strat hats. There were stout, red-faced Boer farmers with sun-bleached hair, their wagons loaded with potatoes, corn and leafy vegetables. Men dressed in brown velveteen trousers and coats, with broad-brimmed, soft-felt hats on their heads and long clay pipes in their mouths, strode ahead of their *vraws*, attired in black, with thick black veils and large black-silk poke bonnets. Parsi washerwomen with large bundles of soiled clothes on their heads pushed past soldiers in red coats and helmets. It was a fascinating spectacle.

The first thing Jamie did was to seek out an inexpensive boarding-house recommended to him by a sailor aboard ship. The landlady was a dumpy, ample-bosomed, middle-aged widow.

She looked Jamie over and smiled. *'Zoek yulle goud?'*

He blushed. 'I'm sorry – I don't understand.'

'English, yes? You are here to hunt gold? Diamonds?'

'Diamonds. Yes, ma'am.'

She pulled him inside. 'You will like it here. I have all the convenience for young men like you.'

Jamie wondered whether she was one of them. He hoped not.

'I'm Mrs Venster,' she said coyly, 'but my friends call me "Dee-Dee".' She smiled, revealing a gold tooth in front. 'I have a feeling we are going to be very good friends. Ask of me anything.'

'That's very kind of you,' Jamie said. 'Can you tell me where I can get a map of the city?'

With map in hand, Jamie went exploring. On one side of the city were the landward suburbs of Rondebosch, Claremont and Wynberg, stretching along nine miles of thinning plantations and vine-yards. On the other side were the marine suburbs of Sea Point and Green Point. Jamie walked through the rich residential area, down Strand Street and Bree Street, admiring the large, two-storey buildings with their flat roofs and peaked stuccoed fronts – steep terraces rising from the street. He walked until he was finally driven indoors by the flies that seemed to have a personal vendetta against him. They were large and black and attacked in swarms. When Jamie returned to his boardinghouse, he found his room filled with them. They covered the walls and table and bed.

He went to see the landlady. 'Mrs Venster, isn't there anything you can do about the flies in my room? They're –'

She gave a fat, jiggling laugh and pinched Jamie's cheek, '*Myn magtig*. You'll get used to them. You'll see.'

The sanitary arrangements in Cape Town were both primitive and inadequate, and when the sun set, an odoriferous vapour covered the city like a noxious blanket. It was unbearable. But Jamie knew that he would bear it. He needed more money before he could leave. 'You can't survive in the diamond fields without money,' he had been warned. 'They'll charge you just for breathin'.'

On his second day in Cape Town, Jamie found a job driving a team of horses for a delivery firm. On the third day he started working in a restaurant

19

after dinner, washing dishes. He lived on the left-over food that he squirrelled away and took back to the boardinghouse, but it tasted strange to him and he longed for his mother's cock-a-leekie and oatcakes and hot, fresh-made baps. He did not complain, even to himself, as he sacrificed both food and comfort to increase his grubstake. He had made his choice and nothing was going to stop him, not the exhausting labour, nor the foul air he breathed, nor the flies that kept him awake most of the night. He felt desperately lonely. He knew no one in this strange place, and he missed his friends and family. Jamie enjoyed solitude, but loneliness was a constant ache.

At last, the magic day arrived. His pouch held the magnificent sum of two hundred pounds. He was ready. He would leave Cape Town the following morning for the diamond fields.

Reservations for passenger wagons to the diamond fields at Klipdrift were booked by the Inland Transport Company at a small wooden depot near the docks. When Jamie arrived at seven a.m., the depot was already so crowded that he could not get near it. There were hundreds of fortune seekers fighting for seats on the wagons. They had come from as far away as Russia and America, Australia, Germany and England. They shouted in a dozen different tongues, pleading with the besieged ticket sellers to find spaces for them. Jamie watched as a burly Irishman angrily pushed his way out of the office onto the sidewalk, fighting to get through the mob.

'Excuse me,' Jamie said. 'What's going on in there?'

'Nothin',' the Irishman grunted in disgust. 'The bloody wagons are all booked up for the next six weeks.' He saw the look of dismay on Jamie's face. 'That's not the worst of it, lad. The heathen bastards are chargin' fifty pounds a head.'

It was incredible! 'There must be another way to get to the diamond fields.'

'Two ways. You can go Dutch Express, or you can go by foot.'

'What's Dutch Express?'

'Bullock wagon. They travel two miles an hour. By the time you get there, the damned diamonds will all be gone.'

Jamie McGregor had no intention of being delayed until the diamonds were gone. He spent the rest of the morning looking for another means of transportation. Just before noon, he found it. He was passing a livery stable with a sign in front that said MAIL DEPOT. On an impulse, he went inside, where the thinnest man he had ever seen was loading large mail sacks into a dogcart. Jamie watched him a moment.

'Excuse me,' Jamie said. 'Do you carry mail to Klipdrift?'

'That's right. Loadin' up now.'

Jamie felt a sudden surge of hope. 'Do you take passengers?'

'Sometimes.' He looked up and studied Jamie. 'How old are you?'

An odd question. 'Eighteen. Why?'

'We don't take anyone over twenty-one or twenty-two. You in good health?'

An even odder question. 'Yes, sir.'

The thin man straightened up. 'I guess you're fit. I'm leavin' in an hour. The fare's twenty pounds.'

Jamie could not believe his good fortune. 'That's wonderful! I'll get my suitcase and –'

'No suitcase. All you got room for is one shirt and a toothbrush.'

Jamie took a closer look at the dogcart. It was small and roughly built. The body formed a well in which the mail was stored, and over the well was a narrow, cramped space where a person could sit back to back behind the driver. It was going to be an uncomfortable journey.

'It's a deal,' Jamie said. 'I'll fetch my shirt and toothbrush.'

When Jamie returned, the driver was hitching up a horse to the open cart. There were two large young men standing near the cart: one was short and dark, the other was a tall, blond Swede. The men were handing the driver some money.

'Wait a minute,' Jamie called to the driver. 'You said *I* was going.'

'You're all goin',' the driver said. 'Hop in.'

'The *three* of us?'

'That's right.'

22

Jamie had no idea how the driver expected them all to fit in the small cart, but he knew he was going to be on it when it pulled out.

Jamie introduced himself to his two fellow passengers. 'I'm Jamie McGregor.'

'Wallach,' the short, dark man said.

'Pederson,' the tall blond replied.

Jamie said, 'We're lucky we discovered this, aren't we? It's a good thing everybody doesn't know about it.'

Pederson said, 'Oh, they know about the post carts, McGregor. There just aren't that many fit enough or desperate enough to travel in them.'

Before Jamie could ask what he meant, the driver said, 'Let's go.'

The three men – Jamie in the middle – squeezed into the seat, crowded against each other, their knees cramped, their backs pressing hard against the wooden back of the driver's seat. There was no room to move or breathe. *It's not bad*, Jamie reassured himself.

'Hold on!' the driver sang out, and a moment later they were racing through the streets of Cape Town on their way to the diamond fields at Klipdrift.

By bullock wagon, the journey was relatively comfortable. The wagons transporting passengers from Cape Town to the diamond fields were large and roomy, with tent covers to ward off the blazing winter sun. Each wagon accommodated a dozen passengers and was drawn by teams of horses or mules. Refreshments were provided at regular stations, and the journey took ten days.

The mail cart was different. It never stopped, except to change horses and drivers. The pace was a full gallop, over rough roads and fields and rutted trails. There were no springs on the cart, and each bounce was like the blow of a horse's hoof. Jamie gritted his teeth and thought, *I can stand it until we stop for the night, I'll eat and get some sleep, and in the morning I'll be fine.* But when nighttime came, there was a ten-minute halt for a change of horse and driver, and they were off again at a full gallop.

'When do we stop to eat?' Jamie asked.

'We don't,' the new driver grunted. 'We go straight through. We're carryin' the mails, mister.'

They raced through the long night, travelling over dusty, bumpy roads by moonlight, the little cart bouncing up the rises, plunging down the valleys, springing over the flats. Every inch of Jamie's body was battered and bruised from the constant jolting. He was exhausted, but it was impossible to sleep. Every time he started to doze off, he was jarred awake. His body was cramped and miserable and there was no room to stretch. He was starving and motion-sick. He had no idea how many days it would be before his next meal. It was a six-hundred-mile journey, and Jamie McGregor was not sure he was going to live through it. Neither was he sure that he wanted to.

By the end of the second day and night, the misery had turned to agony. Jamie's travelling companions were in the same sorry state, no longer even able to complain. Jamie understood now why the company insisted that its passengers be young and strong.

When the next dawn came, they entered the Great Karroo, where the real wilderness began. Stretching to infinity, the monstrous veld lay flat and forbidding under a pitiless sun. The passengers were smothered in heat, dust and flies.

Occasionally, through a miasmic haze, Jamie saw groups of men slogging along on foot. There were solitary riders on horseback, and dozens of bullock wagons drawn by eighteen or twenty oxen, handled by drivers and *voorlopers*, with their *sjamboks*, the whips with long leather thongs, crying, 'Trek! Trek!' The huge wagons were laden with a thousand pounds of produce and goods, tents and digging equipment and wood-burning stoves, flour and coal and oil lamps. They carried coffee and rice, Russian hemp, sugar and wines, whiskey and boots and Belfast candles, and blankets. They were the lifeline to the fortune seekers at Klipdrift.

It was not until the mail cart crossed the Orange River that there was a change from the deadly monotony of the veld. The scrub gradually became taller and tinged with green. The earth was redder, patches of grass rippled in the breeze, and low thorn trees began to appear.

I'm going to make it, Jamie thought dully. *I'm going to make it.*

And he could feel hope begin to creep into his tired body.

They had been on the road for four continuous days and nights when they finally arrived at the outskirts of Klipdrift.

Young Jamie McGregor had not known what to expect, but the scene that met his weary, blood-shot eyes was like nothing he ever could have imagined. Klipdrift was a vast panorama of tents and wagons lined up on the main streets and on the shores of the Vaal River. The dirt roadway swarmed with kaffirs, naked except for brightly coloured jackets, and bearded prospectors, butchers, bakers, thieves, teachers. In the centre of Klipdrift, rows of wooden and iron shacks served as shops, canteens, billiard rooms, eating houses, diamond-buying offices and lawyers' rooms. On a corner stood the ramshackle Royal Arch Hotel, a long chain of rooms without windows.

Jamie stepped out of the cart, and promptly fell to the ground, his cramped legs refusing to hold him up. He lay there, his head spinning, until he had strength enough to rise. He stumbled towards the hotel, pushing through the boisterous crowds that thronged the sidewalks and streets. The room they gave him was small, stifling hot and swarming with flies. But it had a cot. Jamie fell onto it, fully dressed, and was asleep instantly. He slept for eighteen hours.

Jamie awoke, his body unbelievably stiff and sore, but his soul filled with exultation. *I am here! I have made it!* Ravenously hungry, he went in search of food. The hotel served none, but there was a small, crowded restaurant across the street, where he devoured fried snook, a large fish resembling pike; carbonaatje, thinly sliced mutton grilled on a spit over a wood fire; a haunch of bok and, for dessert, *koeksister*, a dough deep-fried and soaked in syrup.

Jamie's stomach, so long without food, began to give off alarming symptoms. He decided to let it rest before he continued eating, and turned his attention to his surroundings. At tables all around him, prospectors were feverishly discussing the subject uppermost in everyone's mind: diamonds.

'. . . There's still a few diamonds left around Hopetown, but the mother lode's at New Rush . . .'

'. . . Kimberley's got a bigger population than Joburg . . .'

'. . . About the find up at Dutoitspan last week? They say there's more diamonds there than a man can carry . . .'

'. . . There's a new strike at Christiana. I'm goin' up there tomorrow.'

So it was true. There were diamonds everywhere! Young Jamie was so excited he could hardly finish his huge mug of coffee. He was staggered by the amount of the bill. Two pounds, three shillings for one meal! *I'll have to be very careful*, he thought, as he walked out onto the crowded, noisy street.

A voice behind him said, 'Still planning to get rich, McGregor?'

27

Jamie turned. It was Pederson, the Swedish boy who had travelled on the dogcart with him.

'I certainly am,' Jamie said.

'Then let's go where the diamonds are.' He pointed. 'The Vaal River's that way.'

They began to walk.

Klipdrift was in a basin, surrounded by hills, and as far as Jamie could see, everything was barren, without a blade of grass or shrub in sight. Red dust rose thick in the air, making it difficult to breathe. The Vaal River was a quarter of a mile away, and as they got closer to it, the air became cooler. Hundreds of prospectors lined both sides of the riverbank, some of them digging for diamonds, others meshing stones in rocking cradles, still others sorting stones at rickety, makeshift tables. The equipment ranged from scientific earth-washing apparatus to old tub boxes and pails. The men were sunburned, unshaven and roughly dressed in a weird assortment of collarless, coloured and striped flannel shirts, corduroy trousers and rubber boots, riding breeches and laced leggings and wide-brimmed felt hats or pith helmets. They all wore broad leather belts with pockets for diamonds or money.

Jamie and Pederson walked to the edge of the riverbank and watched a young boy and an older man struggling to remove a huge ironstone boulder so they could get at the gravel around it. Their shirts were soaked with sweat. Nearby, another team loaded gravel onto a cart to be sieved in a cradle. One of the diggers rocked the cradle while another poured buckets of water into it to wash away the silt. The large pebbles were then emptied onto an improvised sorting table, where they were excitedly inspected.

'It looks easy,' Jamie grinned.

'Don't count on it, McGregor. I've been talking to some of the diggers who have been here a while. I think we've bought a sack of pups.'

'What do you mean?'

'Do you know how many diggers there are in these parts, all hoping to get rich? Twenty bloody thousand! And there aren't enough diamonds to go around, chum. Even if there were, I'm beginning to wonder if it's worth it. You broil in winter, freeze in summer, get drenched in their damned *donderstormen*, and try to cope with the dust and the flies and the stink. You can't get a bath or a decent bed, and there are no sanitary arrangements in this damned town. There are drownings in the Vaal River every week. Some are accidental, but I was told that for most of them it's a way out, the only escape from this hellhole. I don't know why these people keep hanging on.'

'I do.' Jamie looked at the hopeful young boy with the stained shirt. 'The next shovelful of dirt.'

But as they headed back to town, Jamie had to admit that Pederson had a point. They passed carcasses of slaughtered oxen, sheep and goats left to rot outside the tents, next to wide-open trenches that served as lavatories. The place stank to the heavens. Pederson was watching him. 'What are you going to do now?'

'Get some prospecting equipment.'

In the centre of town was a store with a rusted hanging sign that read: SALOMON VAN DER MERWE, GENERAL STORE. A tall black man about Jamie's age was unloading a wagon in front of the store. He was broad-shouldered and heavily muscled, one of the most handsome men Jamie had ever seen. He had soot-black eyes, an aquiline nose and a proud chin. There was a dignity about him, a quiet aloofness. He lifted a heavy wooden box of rifles to his shoulder and, as he turned, he slipped on a leaf fallen from a crate of cabbage. Jamie instinctively reached out an arm to steady him. The black man did not acknowledge Jamie's presence. He turned and walked into the store. A Boer prospector hitching up a mule spat and said distastefully, 'That's Banda, from the Barolong tribe. Works for Mr van der Merwe. I don't know why he keeps that uppity black. Those fuckin' Bantus think they own the earth.'

The store was cool and dark inside, a welcome relief from the hot, bright street, and it was filled with exotic odours. It seemed to Jamie that every inch of space was crammed with merchandise. He walked through the store, marvelling. There were agricultural implements, beer, cans of milk and crocks of butter, cement, fuses and dynamite and gunpowder, crockery, furniture, guns and haberdashery, oil and paint and varnish, bacon and dried

30

fruit, saddlery and harness, sheep-dip and soap, spirits and stationery and paper, sugar and tea and tobacco and snuff and cigars . . . A dozen shelves were filled from top to bottom with flannel shirts and blankets, shoes, poke bonnets and saddles. *Whoever owns all this*, Jamie thought, *is a rich man.*

A soft voice behind him said, 'Can I help you?'

Jamie turned and found himself facing a young girl. He judged she was about fifteen. She had an interesting face, fineboned and heart-shaped, like a valentine, a pert nose and intense green eyes. Her hair was dark and curling. Jamie, looking at her figure, decided she might be closer to sixteen.

'I'm a prospector,' Jamie announced. 'I'm here to buy some equipment.'

'What is it you need?'

For some reason, Jamie felt he had to impress this girl. 'I – er – you know – the usual.'

She smiled, and there was mischief in her eyes. 'What is the usual, sir?'

'Well . . .' He hesitated. 'A shovel.'

'Will that be all?'

Jamie saw that she was teasing him. He grinned and confessed. 'To tell you the truth, I'm new at this. I don't know what I need.'

She smiled at him, and it was the smile of a woman. 'It depends on where you're planning to prospect, Mr –?'

'McGregor. Jamie McGregor.'

'I'm Margaret van der Merwe.' She glanced nervously towards the rear of the store.

'I'm pleased to meet you, Miss van der Merwe.'

'Did you just arrive?'

'Aye. Yesterday. On the post cart.'

'Someone should have warned you about that. Passengers have died on that trip.' There was anger in her eyes.

Jamie grinned. 'I can't blame them. But I'm very much alive, thank you.'

'And going out to hunt for *mooi klippe*.'

'*Mooi klippe?*'

'That's our Dutch word for diamonds. Pretty pebbles.'

'You're Dutch?'

'My family's from Holland.'

'I'm from Scotland.'

'I could tell that.' Her eyes flicked warily towards the back of the store again. 'There are diamonds around, Mr McGregor, but you must be choosy where you look for them. Most of the diggers are running around chasing their own tails. When someone makes a strike, the rest scavenge off the leavings. If you want to get rich, you have to find a strike of your own.'

'How do I do that?'

'My father might be the one to help you with that. He knows everything. He'll be free in an hour.'

'I'll be back,' Jamie assured her. 'Thank you, Miss van der Merwe.

He went out into the sunshine, filled with a sense of euphoria, his aches and pains forgotten. If

Salomon van der Merwe would advise him where to find diamonds, there was no way Jamie could fail. He would have the jump on all of them. He laughed aloud, with the sheer joy of being young and alive and on his way to riches.

Jamie walked down the main street, passing a blacksmith's, a billiard hall and half a dozen saloons. He came to a sign in front of a decrepit-looking hotel and stopped. The sign read:

R-D MILLER, WARM AND COLD BATHS.
OPEN DAILY FROM 6 A.M. TO 8 P.M.,
WITH THE COMFORTS OF A NEAT
DRESSING ROOM

Jamie thought, *When did I have my last bath? Well, I took a bucket bath on the boat. That was* – He was suddenly aware of how he must smell. He thought of the weekly tub baths in the kitchen at home, and he could hear his mother's voice calling, 'Be sure to wash down below, Jamie.'

He turned and entered the baths. There were two doors inside, one for women and one for men. Jamie entered the men's section and walked up to the aged attendant. 'How much is a bath?'

'Ten shillings for a cold bath, fifteen for a hot.'

Jamie hesitated. The idea of a hot bath after his long journey was almost irresistible. 'Cold,' he said. He could not afford to throw away his money on luxuries. He had mining equipment to buy.

The attendant handed him a small bar of yellow lye soap and a threadbare hand towel and pointed. 'In there, mate.'

Jamie stepped into a small room that contained nothing except a large galvanized-iron bathtub in the centre and a few pegs on the wall. The attendant began filling the tub from a large wooden bucket.

'All ready for you, mister. Just hang your clothes on those pegs.'

Jamie waited until the attendant left and then undressed. He looked down at his grime-covered body and put one foot in the tub. The water was cold, as advertised. He gritted his teeth and plunged in, soaping himself furiously from head to foot. When he finally stepped out of the tub, the water was black. He dried himself as best he could with the worn linen towel and started to get dressed. His pants and shirt were stiff with dirt, and he hated to put them back on. He would have to buy a change of clothes, and this reminded him once more of how little money he had. And he was hungry again.

Jamie left the bathhouse and pushed his way down the crowded street to a saloon called the Sundowner. He ordered a beer and lunch. Lamb cutlets with tomatoes, and sausage and potato salad and pickles. While he ate, he listened to the hopeful conversations around him.

'. . . I hear they found a stone near Colesberg weighin' twenty-one carats. Mark you, if there's *one* diamond up there, there's plenty more . . .'

'. . . There's a new diamond find up in Hebron. I'm thinkin' of goin' there . . .'

'You're a fool. The big diamonds are in the Orange River . . .'

At the bar, a bearded customer in a collarless, striped-flannel shirt and corduroy trousers was nursing a shandygaff in a large glass. 'I got cleaned out in Hebron,' he confided to the bartender. 'I need me a grubstake.'

The bartender was a large, fleshy, bald-headed man with a broken, twisted nose and ferret eyes. He laughed. 'Hell, man, who doesn't? Why do you think I'm tendin' bar? As soon as I have enough money, I'm gonna hightail it up the Orange myself.' He wiped the bar with a dirty rag. 'But I'll tell you what you might do, mister. See Salomon van der Merwe. He owns the general store and half the town.

'What good'll that do me?'

'If he likes you, he might stake you.'

The customer looked at him. 'Yeah? You really think he might?'

'He's done it for a few fellows I know of. You put up your labour, he puts up the money. You split fifty-fifty.'

Jamie McGregor's thoughts leaped ahead. He had been confident that the hundred and twenty pounds he had left would be enough to buy the equipment and food he would need to survive, but the prices in Klipdrift were astonishing. He had noticed in Van der Merwe's store that a hundred-pound sack of Australian flour cost five pounds. One pound of sugar cost a shilling. A bottle of beer cost five shillings. Biscuits were three shillings a pound, and fresh eggs sold for seven shillings a dozen. At that rate, his money would not last long. *My God*, Jamie thought, *at home we could live for a year on what three meals cost here.* But if he could get the backing of someone really wealthy, like Mr van der Merwe . . . Jamie hastily paid for his food and hurried back to the general store.

Salomon van der Merwe was behind the counter, removing the rifles from a wooden crate. He was a small thin man, with a thin, pinched face framed by Dundreary whiskers. He had sandy hair, tiny black eyes, a bulbous nose and pursed lips. *His daughter must take after her mother*, Jamie thought. 'Excuse me, sir . . .'

Van der Merwe looked up. '*Ja?*'

'Mr van der Merwe? My name is Jamie McGregor, sir, I'm from Scotland. I came here to find diamonds.'

'*Ja?* So?'

'I hear you sometimes back prospectors.'

Van der Merwe grumbled, '*Myn magtig!* Who spreads these stories? I help out a few diggers, and everyone thinks I'm Santa Claus.'

'I've saved a hundred and twenty pounds,' Jamie said earnestly. 'But I see that it's not going to buy me much here. I'll go out to the bush with just a shovel if I have to, but I figure my chances would be a lot better if I had a mule and some proper equipment.'

Van der Merwe was studying him with those small, black eyes. '*Wat denk ye?* What makes you think *you* can find diamonds?'

'I've come halfway around the world, Mr van der Merwe, and I'm not going to leave here until I'm rich. If the diamonds are out there, I'll find them. If you help me, I'll make us both rich.'

Van der Merwe grunted, turned his back on Jamie and continued unloading the rifles. Jamie stood there awkwardly, not knowing what more to say. When Van der Merwe spoke again, his question caught Jamie off guard. 'You travel here by bullock wagon, *ja?*'

'No. Post cart.'

The old man turned to study the boy again. He said, finally, 'We talk about it.'

They talked about it at dinner that evening in the room in the back of the store that was the Van der Merwe living quarters. It was a small room that served as a kitchen, dining room and sleeping quarters, with a curtain separating two cots. The lower half of the walls was built of mud and stone, and the upper half was faced with cardboard boxes that had once contained provisions. A square hole, where a piece of the wall had been cut out, served as window. In wet weather it could be closed by placing a board in front of it. The dining table consisted of a long plank stretched across two wooden crates. A large box, turned on its side, served as a cupboard. Jamie guessed that Van der Merwe was not a man who parted easily with his money.

Van der Merwe's daughter moved silently about, preparing dinner. From time to time she cast quick glances at her father, but she never once looked at Jamie. *Why is she so frightened?* Jamie wondered.

When they were seated at the table, Van der Merwe began. 'Let us have a blessing. We Thank Thee, O Lord, for the bounty we receive at Thy hands. We thank Thee for forgiving us our sins and showing us the path of righteousness and delivering us from life's temptations. We thank Thee for a long and fruitful life, and for smiting dead all those who offend Thee. Amen.' And without a breath between, 'Pass me the meat,' he said to his daughter.

The dinner was frugal: a small roast pork, three boiled potatoes and a dish of turnip greens. The portions he served to Jamie were small. The two men talked little during the meal, and Margaret did not speak at all.

When they had finished eating, Van der Merwe said, 'That was fine, Daughter,' and there was pride in his voice. He turned to Jamie. 'We get down to business, *ja*?'

'Yes, sir.'

Van der Merwe picked up a long clay pipe from the top of the wooden cabinet. He filled it with a sweet-smelling tobacco from a small pouch and lighted the pipe. His sharp eyes peered intently at Jamie through the wreaths of smoke.

'The diggers here at Klipdrift are fools. Too few diamonds, too many diggers. A man could break his back here for a year and have nothing to show for it but *schlenters*.'

'I – I'm afraid I'm not familiar with that word, sir.'

'Fool's diamonds. Worthless. Do you follow me?'

'I – Yes, sir. I think so. But what's the answer, sir?'

'The Griquas.'

Jamie looked at him blankly.

'They're an African tribe up north. *They* find diamonds – big ones – and sometimes they bring them to me and I trade them for goods.' The Dutchman lowered his voice to a conspiratorial whisper. 'I know where they find them.'

'But could you nae go after them yourself, Mr van der Merwe?'

Van der Merwe sighed. 'No. I can't leave the store. People would steal me blind. I need someone I can trust to go up there and bring the stones back. When I find the right man, I'll supply him with all the equipment he needs.' He paused to take a long drag on his pipe. 'And I'll tell him where the diamonds are.'

Jamie leaped to his feet, his heart pounding. 'Mr van der Merwe, *I'm* the person you're looking for.

39

Believe me, sir, I'll work night and day.' His voice was charged with excitement. 'I'll bring you back more diamonds than you can count.'

Van der Merwe silently studied him for what seemed to Jamie to be an eternity. When Van der Merwe finally spoke, he said only one word. *'Ja'*

Jamie signed the contract the following morning. It was written in Afrikaans.

'I'll have to explain it to you,' Van der Merwe said. 'It says we're full partners. I put up the capital – you put up the labour. We share everything equally.'

Jamie looked at the contract in Van der Merwe's hand. In the middle of all the incomprehensible foreign words he recognized only a sum: *two pounds*.

Jamie pointed to it. 'What is that for, Mr van der Merwe?'

'It means that in addition to your owning half the diamonds you find, you'll get an extra two pounds for every week you work. Even though I know the diamonds are out there, it's possible you might not find anything, lad. This way you'll at least get something for your labour.'

The man was being more than fair. 'Thank you. Thank you very much, sir.' Jamie could have hugged him.

Van der Merwe said, 'Now let's get you outfitted.'

It took two hours to select the equipment that Jamie would take into the bush with him: a small tent, bedding, cooking utensils, two sieves and a washing cradle, a pick, two shovels, three buckets and one change of socks and underwear. There was an axe and a lantern and paraffin oil, matches and arsenical soap. There were tins of food, biltong, fruit, sugar, coffee and salt. At last everything was in readiness. The black servant, Banda, silently helped Jamie stow everything into backpacks. The huge man never glanced at Jamie and never spoke one word. *He doesn't speak English*, Jamie decided. Margaret was in the store waiting on customers, but if she knew Jamie was there, she gave no indication.

Van der Merwe came over to Jamie. 'Your mule's in front,' he said. 'Banda will help you load up.'

'Thank you, Mr van der Merwe,' Jamie said. 'I –'

Van der Merwe consulted a piece of paper covered with figures 'That will be one hundred and twenty pounds.'

Jamie looked at him blankly. 'W – what? This is part of our deal. We –'

'*Wat bedui'di?*' Van der Merwe's thin face darkened with anger. 'You expect me to *give* you all this, and a fine mule, and make you a partner, and give you two pounds a week on top of *that*? If you're looking for something for nothing, you've come to the wrong place.' He began to unload one of the backpacks.

Jamie said quickly, 'No! Please, Mr van der Merwe. I – I just didn't understand. It's perfectly all right. I have the money right here.' He reached in his pouch and put the last of his savings on the counter.

Van der Merwe hesitated. 'All right,' he said grudgingly. 'Perhaps it was a misunderstanding, neh? This town is full of cheaters. I have to be careful who I do business with.'

'Yes, sir. Of course you do,' Jamie agreed. In his excitement, he had misunderstood the deal. *I'm lucky he's giving me another chance*, Jamie thought.

Van der Merwe reached into his pocket and pulled out a small, wrinkled, hand-drawn map. 'Here is where you'll find the *mooi klippe*. North of here at Magerdam on the northern bank of the Vaal.'

Jamie studied the map, and his heart began to beat faster. 'How many miles is it?'

'Here we measure distance by time. With the mule, you should make the journey in four or five days. Coming back will be slower because of the weight of the diamonds.'

Jamie grinned. '*Ja.*'

When Jamie McGregor stepped back out onto the streets of Klipdrift, he was no longer a tourist. He was a prospector, a digger, on his way to his fortune. Banda had finished loading the supplies onto the back of a frail-looking mule tethered to the hitching post in front of the store.

'Thanks.' Jamie smiled.

Banda turned and looked him in the eye, then

silently walked away. Jamie unhitched the reins and said to the mule, 'Let's go, partner. It's *mooi klippe* time.'

They headed north.

Jamie pitched camp near a stream at nightfall, unloaded and watered and fed the mule, and fixed himself some beef jerky, dried apricots and coffee. The night was filled with strange noises. He heard the grunts and howls and padding of wild animals moving down to the water. He was unprotected, surrounded by the most dangerous beasts in the world, in a strange, primitive country. He jumped at every sound. At any moment he expected to be attacked by fangs and claws leaping at him from out of the darkness. His mind began to drift. He thought of his snug bed at home and the comfort and safety he had always taken for granted. He slept fitfully, his dreams filled with charging lions and elephants, and large, bearded men trying to take an enormous diamond away from him.

At dawn when Jamie awakened, the mule was dead.

TWO

He could not believe it. He looked for a wound of some kind, thinking it must have been attacked by a wild animal during the night, but there was nothing. The beast had died in its sleep. *Mr van der Merwe will hold me responsible for this*, Jamie thought. *But when I bring him diamonds, it won't matter.*

There was no turning back. He would go on to Magerdam without the mule. He heard a sound in the air and looked up. Giant black vultures were beginning to circle high above. Jamie shuddered. Working as quickly as possible, he rearranged his gear, deciding what he had to leave behind, then stowed everything he could carry into a backpack and started off. When he looked back five minutes later, the enormous vultures had covered the body of the dead animal. All that was visible was one long ear. Jamie quickened his step.

It was December, summer in South Africa, and the trek across the veld under the huge orange sun was a horror. Jamie had started out from Klipdrift with a brisk step and a light heart, but as the minutes turned into hours and the hours into days, his steps got slower and his heart became heavier. As far as the eye could see, the monotomous veld shimmered flat and forbidding under the blazing sun and there seemed no end to the grey, stony, desolate plains.

Jamie made camp whenever he came to a watering hole, and he slept with the eerie, nocturnal sounds of the animals all around him. The sounds no longer bothered him. They were proof that there was life in this barren hell, and they made him feel less lonely. One dawn Jamie came across a pride of lions. He watched from a distance as the lioness moved towards her mate and their cubs, carrying a baby impala in her powerful jaws. She dropped the animal in front of the male and moved away while he fed. A reckless cub leaped forwards and dug his teeth into the impala. With one motion, the male raised a paw and swiped the cub across the face, killing it instantly, then went back to his feeding. When he finished, the rest of the family was permitted to move in for the remains of the feast. Jamie slowly backed away from the scene and continued walking.

It took him almost two weeks to cross the Karroo. More than once he was ready to give up. He was not sure he could finish the journey. *I'm a fool. I should have returned to Klipdrift to ask Mr van der Merwe for another mule. But what if*

Van der Merwe had called off the deal? No, I did the right thing.

And so, Jamie kept moving, one step at a time. One day, he saw four figures in the distance, coming towards him. *I'm delirious*, Jamie thought. *It's a mirage.* But the figures came closer, and Jamie's heart began to thud alarmingly. *Men! There is human life here!* He wondered if he had forgotten how to speak. He tried out his voice on the afternoon air, and it sounded as if it belonged to someone long dead. The four men reached him, prospectors returning to Klipdrift, tired and defeated.

'Hello,' Jamie said.

They nodded. One of them said, 'There ain't nothin' ahead, boy. We looked. You're wastin' your time. Go back.'

And they were gone.

Jamie shut his mind to everything but the trackless waste ahead of him. The sun and the black flies were unbearable and there was no place to hide. There were thorn trees, but their branches had been laid to waste by the elephants. Jamie was almost totally blinded by the sun. His fair skin was burned raw, and he was constantly dizzy. Each time he took a breath of air, his lungs seemed to explode. He was no longer walking, he was stumbling, putting one foot in front of the other, mindlessly lurching ahead. One afternoon, with the midday sun beating down on him, he slipped off his backpack and slumped to the ground, too tired to take another step. He closed his eyes and dreamed he was in a giant crucible and the sun was a huge, bright diamond blazing down on him, melting him. He awoke in the middle of the night trembling from the cold. He forced himself to take a few bites of biltong and a drink of tepid water. He knew he must get up and start moving before the sun rose, while the earth and sky were cool. He tried, but the effort was too great. It would be so easy just to lie there forever and never have to take another step. *I'll just sleep for a little while longer*, Jamie thought. But some voice deep within him told him he would never wake up again. They would find his body there as they had found hundreds of others. He remembered the vultures and thought, *No, not my body – my bones*. Slowly and painfully, he forced himself to his feet. His backpack was so heavy he could not lift it. Jamie started walking again, dragging the pack behind him. He had no recollection of how many times he fell onto the sand and staggered to his feet again. Once he screamed into the predawn sky, 'I'm Jamie McGregor, and I'm going to make it. I'm going to live. Do you hear me, God? I'm going to live . . .' Voices were exploding in his head.

You're goin' chasin' diamonds? You must be daft, son. That's a fairy tale – a temptation of the devil to keep men from doin' an honest day's work.

Why do you nae tell us where you're gettin' the

money to go? It's halfway 'round the world. You hae no money.

Mr van der Merwe, I'm the person you're looking for. Believe me, sir, I'll work night and day. I'll bring you back more diamonds than you can count.

And he was finished before he had even started. *You have two choices*, Jamie told himself. *You can go on or you can stay here and die . . . and die . . . and die . . .*

The words echoed endlessly in his head. *You can take one more step*, Jamie thought. Come on, Jamie boy. One more step. One more step . . .

Two days later Jamie McGregor stumbled into the village of Magerdam. The sunburn had long since become infected and his body oozed blood and sera. Both eyes were swollen almost completely shut. He collapsed in the middle of the street, a pile of crumpled clothes holding him together. When sympathetic diggers tried to relieve him of his backpack, Jamie fought them with what little strength he had left, raving deliriously. 'No! Get away from my diamonds. Get away from my diamonds . . .'

He awakened in a small, bare room three days later, naked except for the bandages that covered his body. The first thing he saw when he opened his eyes was a buxom, middle-aged woman seated at the side of his cot.

'Wh – ?' His voice was a croak. He could not get the words out.

'Easy, dear. You've been sick.' She gently lifted

his swathed head and gave him a sip of water from a tin cup.

Jamie managed to prop himself up on one elbow. 'Where – ?' He swallowed and tried again. 'Where am I?'

'You're in Magerdam. I'm Alice Jardine. This is my boarding-house. You're going to be fine. You just need a good rest. Now lie back.'

Jamie remembered the strangers who tried to take his backpack away, and he was filled with panic. 'My things, where – ?' He tried to rise from the cot, but the woman's gentle voice stopped him.

'Everything's safe. Not to worry, son.' She pointed to his backpack in a corner of the room.

Jamie lay back on the clean white sheets. *I got here. I made it. Everything is going to be all right now.*

Alice Jardine was a blessing, not only to Jamie McGregor, but to half of Magerdam. In that mining town filled with adventurers, all sharing the same dream, she fed them, nursed them, encouraged them. She was an Englishwoman who had come to South Africa with her husband, when he decided to give up his teaching job in Leeds and join the diamond rush. He had died of fever three weeks after they arrived, but she had decided to stay on. The miners had become the children she never had.

She kept Jamie in bed for four more days, feeding him, changing his bandages and helping him regain his strength. By the fifth day, Jamie was ready to get up.

'I want you to know how grateful I am to you, Mrs Jardine. I can't pay you anything. Not yet. But you'll have a big diamond from me one day soon. That's a promise from Jamie McGregor.'

She smiled at the intensity of the handsome young boy. He was still twenty pounds too thin, and his grey eyes were filled with the horror he had been through, but there was a strength about him, a determination that was awesome. *He's different from the others*, Mrs Jardine thought.

Jamie, dressed in his freshly washed clothes, went out to explore the town. It was Klipdrift on a smaller scale. There were the same tents and wagons and dusty streets, the flimsily built shops and the crowds of prospectors. As Jamie passed a saloon, he heard a roar from inside and entered. A noisy crowd had gathered around a red-shirted Irishman.

'What's going on?' Jamie asked.

'He's going to wet his find.'

'He's what?'

'He struck it rich today, so he stands treat for the whole saloon. He pays me for as much liquor as a saloon-full of thirsty men can swallow.'

Jamie joined in a conversation with several disgruntled diggers sitting at a round table.

'Where you from, McGregor?'

'Scotland.'

'Well, I don't know what horseshit they fed you in Scotland, but there ain't enough diamonds in this fuckin' country to pay expenses.'

They talked of other camps: Gong Gong, Forlorn Hope, Delports, Poormans Kopje, Sixpenny Rush . . .

The diggers all told the same story – of months doing the back-breaking work of moving boulders, digging into the hard soil and squatting over the riverbank sifting the dirt for diamonds. Each day a few diamonds were found; not enough to make a man rich, but enough to keep his dreams alive. The mood of the town was a strange mixture of optimism and pessimism. The optimists were arriving; the pessimists were leaving.

Jamie knew which side he was on.

He approached the red-shirted Irishman, now bleary-eyed with drink, and showed him Van der Merwe's map.

The man glanced at it and tossed it back to Jamie. 'Worthless. That whole area's been picked over. If I was you, I'd try Bad Hope.'

Jamie could not believe it. Van der Merwe's map was what had brought him there, the lodestar that was going to make him rich.

Another digger said, 'Head for Colesberg. That's where they're findin' diamonds, son.'

'Gilfillans Kop – *that's* the place to dig.'

'You'll try Moonlight Rush, if you want my opinion.'

*   *   *

At supper that night, Alice Jardine said, 'Jamie, one place is as big a gamble as another. Pick your own spot, dig in your pickaxe and pray. That's all these other *experts* are doing.'

After a night of sleepless self-debate, Jamie decided he would forget Van der Merwe's map. Against everyone's advice, he decided to head east, along the Modder River. The following morning Jamie said goodbye to Mrs Jardine and set off.

He walked for three days and two nights, and when he came to a likely-looking spot, he set up his small tent. Huge boulders lay along both sides of the riverbank, and Jamie, using thick branches as levers, laboriously moved them out of the way to get at the gravel that lay beneath.

He dug from dawn until dusk, looking for the yellow clay or the blue diamondiferous soil that would tell him he had found a diamond pipe. But the earth was barren. He dug for a week without finding a single stone. At the end of the week, he moved on.

One day as he walked along, he saw in the distance what looked like a silver house, glowing dazzlingly in the sun. *I'm going blind*, Jamie thought. But as he got closer, he saw that he was approaching a village, and all the houses seemed to be made of silver. Crowds of Indian men, women and children dressed in rags swarmed through the streets. Jamie stared in amazement. The silver houses glistening in the sun were made of tin jam pots, flattened out, fastened together and nailed over the crude shacks. He walked on, and an hour later, when he looked back, he could still see the glow of the village. It was a sight he never forgot.

Jamie kept moving north. He followed the riverbank where the diamonds might be, digging until his arms refused to lift the heavy pick, then sifting the wet gravel through the hand sieve. When it got dark, he slept as though drugged.

At the end of the second week, he moved upstream again, just north of a small settlement called Paardspan. He stopped near a bend in the river and fixed himself a meal of carbonaatje, grilled on a spit over a wood fire, and hot tea, then sat in front of his tent, looking up at the wheeling stars in the vast sky. He had not seen a human being in two weeks, and an eddy of loneliness washed over him. *What the hell am I doing here?* he wondered. *Sitting in the middle of a blasted wilderness like a bloody fool, killing myself breaking rocks and digging up dirt? I was better off at the farm. Come Saturday, if I don't find a diamond, I'm going home.* He looked up at the uncaring stars and yelled, 'Do you hear me, damn you?' *Oh, Jesus,* he thought, *I'm losing my mind.*

Jamie sat there, idly sifting the sand through his fingers. They closed on a large stone, and he looked at it a moment, then threw it away. He had seen a thousand worthless stones like it in the past weeks. What was it Van der Merwe had called them? *Schlenters*. Yet, there was something about this one that belatedly caught Jamie's attention. He rose, went over to it and picked it up. It was much larger than the other stones and of an odd shape. He rubbed some of the dirt off it against the leg of his trousers and examined it more closely. It *looked* like a diamond. The only thing that made Jamie doubt his senses was the size of it. It was almost as large as a hen's egg. *Oh, God. If it is a diamond* . . . He suddenly had difficulty breathing. He grabbed his lantern and began searching the ground around him. In fifteen minutes he had found four more like it. None of them was as large as the first one, but they were large enough to fill him with a wild excitement.

He was up before dawn, digging like a madman, and by noon he had found half a dozen more diamonds. He spent the next week feverishly digging up diamonds and burying them at night in a safe place where no passers-by could find them. There were fresh diamonds every day, and as Jamie watched his fortune pile up, he was filled with an ineffable joy. Only half of this treasure was his, but it was enough to make him rich beyond anything he had ever dared to dream.

At the end of the week, Jamie made a note on his map and staked out his claim by carefully marking the boundaries with his pick. He dug up his hidden treasure, carefully stored it deep down in his backpack and headed back to Magerdam.

The sign outside the small building read: DIAMANT KOOPER.

Jamie walked into the office, a small, airless room, and he was filled with a sudden sense of trepidation. He had heard dozens of stories of prospectors who had found diamonds that had turned out to be worthless stones. *What if I'm wrong? What if –?*

The assayer was seated at a cluttered desk in the tiny office. 'Somethin' I can do for you?'

Jamie took a deep breath. 'Yes, sir. I would like to have these valued, please.'

Under the watchful eye of the assayer, Jamie started laying the stones on his desk. When he was finished, there was a total of twenty-seven and the assayer was gazing at them in astonishment.

'Where – where did you find these?'

'I'll tell you after you tell me whether they're diamonds.'

The assayer picked up the largest stone and examined it with a jeweller's loupe. 'My God!' he said. 'This is the biggest diamond I've ever seen!' And Jamie realized he had been holding his breath. He could have yelled aloud with joy. 'Where –' the man begged, 'where did these come from?'

'Meet me in the canteen in fifteen minutes,' Jamie grinned, 'and I'll tell you.'

Jamie gathered up the diamonds, put them in his pockets and strode out. He headed for the registration office two doors down the street. 'I want to register a claim,' he said. 'In the names of Salomon van der Merwe and Jamie McGregor.'

He had walked through that door a penniless farm boy and walked out a multimillionaire.

The assayer was in the canteen waiting when Jamie McGregor entered. He had obviously spread the news, because when Jamie walked in there was a sudden, respectful hush. There was a single unspoken question on everyone's mind. Jamie walked up to the bar and said to the bartender, 'I'm here to wet my find.' He turned and faced the crowd. 'Paardspan.'

Alice Jardine was having a cup of tea when Jamie walked into the kitchen. Her face lighted up when she saw him. 'Jamie! Oh, thank God you're back safely!' She took in his dishevelled appearance and flushed face. 'It didn't go well, did it? Never you mind. Have a nice cup of tea with me, dear, and you'll feel better.'

Without a word. Jamie reached into his pocket and pulled out a large diamond. He placed it in Mrs Jardine's hand.

'I've kept my promise,' Jamie said.

She stared at the stone for a long time, and her blue eyes became moist. 'No, Jamie. No.' Her voice was very soft. 'I don't want it. Don't you see, child? It would spoil everything . . .'

When Jamie McGregor returned to Klipdrift, he did it in style. He traded one of his smaller diamonds for a horse and carriage and made a careful note of what he had spent, so that his partner would not be cheated. The trip back to Klipdrift was easy and comfortable, and when Jamie thought of the hell he had gone through on this same journey, he was filled with a sense of wonder. *That's the difference between the rich and the poor*, he thought. *The poor walk; the rich ride in carriages.*

He gave the horse a small flick of the whip and rode on contentedly through the darkening veld.

THREE

Klipdrift had not changed, but Jamie McGregor had. People stared as he rode into town and stopped in front of Van der Merwe's general store. It was not just the expensive horse and carriage that drew the attention of the passers-by; it was the air of jubilation about the young man. They had seen it before in other prospectors who had struck it rich, and it always filled them with a renewed sense of hope for themselves. They stood back and watched as Jamie jumped out of the carriage.

The same large black man was there. Jamie grinned at him. 'Hello! I'm back.'

Banda tied the reins to a hitching post without comment and went inside the store. Jamie followed him.

Salomon van der Merwe was waiting on a customer. The little Dutchman looked up and smiled, and Jamie knew that somehow Van der Merwe had already heard the news. No one could explain it, but news of a diamond strike flashed across the continent with the speed of light.

When Van der Merwe had finished with the customer, he nodded his head towards the back of the store. 'Come, Mr McGregor.'

Jamie followed him. Van der Merwe's daughter was at the stove, preparing lunch. 'Hello, Margaret.'

She flushed and looked away.

'Well! I hear there is good news.' Van der Merwe beamed. He seated himself at the table and pushed the plate and silverware away, clearing a place in front of him.

'That's right, sir.' Proudly, Jamie took a large leather pouch from his jacket pocket and poured the diamonds on the kitchen table. Van der Merwe stared at them, hypnotized, then picked them up slowly, one by one, savoring each one, saving the largest until last. Then he scooped up the diamonds, put them in a chamois bag and put the bag in a large iron safe in the corner and locked it.

When he spoke, there was a note of deep satisfaction in his voice. 'You've done well, Mr McGregor. Very well, indeed.'

'Thank you, sir. This is only the beginning. There are hundreds more there. I don't even dare think about how much they're worth.'

'And you've staked out the claim properly?'

'Yes, sir.' Jamie reached in his pocket and pulled out the registration slip. 'It's registered in both our names.'

Van der Merwe studied the slip, then put it in his pocket. 'You deserve a bonus. Wait here.' He started towards the doorway that led into the shop. 'Come along, Margaret.'

She followed him meekly, and Jamie thought, *She's like a frightened kitten.*

A few minutes later, Van der Merwe returned, alone. 'Here we are.' He opened a purse and carefully counted out fifty pounds.

Jamie looked at him, puzzled. 'What's this for, sir?'

'For you, son. All of it.'

'I – I don't understand.'

'You've been gone twenty-four weeks. At two pounds a week, that's forty-eight pounds, and I'm giving you an extra two pounds as a bonus.'

Jamie laughed. 'I don't need a bonus. I have my share of the diamonds.'

'Your share of the diamonds?'

'Why, yes, sir. My fifty percent. We're partners.'

Van der Merwe was staring at him. 'Partners? Where did you get that idea?'

'Where did I –?' Jamie looked at the Dutchman in bewilderment. 'We have a contract.'

'That is correct. Have you read it?'

'Well, no, sir. It's in Afrikaans, but you said we were fifty-fifty partners.'

The older man shook his head. 'You misunderstood me, Mr McGregor, I don't need any partners. You were working for me. I outfitted you and sent you to find diamonds for me.'

Jamie could feel a slow rage boiling up within him. 'You gave me nothing. I paid you a hundred and twenty pounds for that equipment.'

The old man shrugged. 'I won't waste my valuable time quibbling. Tell you what I'll do. I'll give you an extra five pounds, and we'll call the whole thing quits. I think that's very generous.'

Jamie exploded in a fury. 'We'll nae call the whole thing quits!' In his anger his Scottish burr came back. 'I'm entitled to half that claim. And I'll get it. I registered it in *both* our names.'

Van der Merwe smiled thinly. 'Then you tried to cheat me. I could have you arrested for that.' He shoved the money into Jamie's hand. 'Now take your wages and get out.'

'I'll fight you!'

'Do you have money for a lawyer? I own them all in these parts, boy.'

This isn't happening to me, Jamie thought. *It's a nightmare.* The agony he had gone through, the weeks and months of the burning desert, the punishing physical labour from sunrise to sunset – it all came flooding back. He had nearly died, and now this man was trying to cheat him out of what was his.

He looked Van der Merwe in the eye. 'I'll not let you get away with this. I'm not going to leave Klipdrift. I'll tell everybody here what you've done. I'm going to get my share of those diamonds.'

Van der Merwe started to turn away from the fury in the pale grey eyes. 'You'd better find a doctor, boy,' he muttered. 'I think the sun has addled your wits.'

In a second, Jamie was towering over Van der Merwe. He pulled the thin figure into the air and held him up to eye level. 'I'm going to make you sorry you ever laid eyes on me.' He dropped Van der Merwe to his feet, flung the money on the table and stormed out.

When Jamie McGregor walked into the Sundowner Saloon, it was almost deserted, for most of the prospectors were on their way to Paardspan. Jamie was filled with anger and despair. *It's incredible*, he thought. *One minute I'm as rich as Croesus, and the next minute I'm dead broke. Van der Merwe is a thief, and I'm going to find a way to punish him. But how?* Van der Merwe was right. Jamie could not even afford a lawyer to fight his case. He was a stranger there, and Van der Merwe was a respected member of the community. The only weapon Jamie had was the truth. He would let everyone in South Africa know what Van der Merwe had done.

Smit, the bartender, greeted him. 'Welcome back. Everything's on the house, Mr McGregor. What would you like?'

'A whiskey.'

Smit poured a double and set it in front of Jamie. Jamie downed it in one gulp. He was not used to drinking, and the hard liquor scorched his throat and stomach.

'Another, please.'

'Comin' up. I've always said the Scots could drink anybody under the table.'

The second drink went down easier. Jamie remembered that it was the bartender who had told a digger to go to Van der Merwe for help. 'Did you know Old Man Van der Merwe is a crook? He's trying to cheat me out of my diamonds.'

Smit was sympathetic. 'What? That's terrible. I'm sorry to hear that.'

'He'll nae get away with it.' Jamie's voice was slurred. 'Half those diamonds are mine. He's a thief, and I'm gonna see that everybody knows it.'

'Careful. Van der Merwe's an important man in this town,' the bartender warned. 'If you're goin' up against him, you'll need help. In fact, I know just the person. He hates Van der Merwe as much as you do.' He looked around to make sure no one could overhear him. 'There's an old barn at the end of the street. I'll arrange everything. Be there at ten o'clock tonight.'

'Thanks,' Jamie said gratefully. 'I won't forget you.'

'Ten o'clock. The old barn.'

The barn was a hastily thrown-together structure built of corrugated tin, off the main street at the edge of town. At ten o'clock Jamie arrived there. It was dark, and he felt his way carefully. He could see no one around. He stepped inside. 'Hello . . .'

There was no reply. Jamie went slowly forwards. He could make out the dim shapes of horses moving restlessly in their stalls. Then he heard a sound behind him, and as he started to turn, an iron bar crashed across his shoulder blades, knocking him to the ground. A club thudded against his head, and a giant hand picked him up and held him while fists and boots smashed into his body. The beating seemed to last forever. When the pain became too much to bear and he lost consciousness, cold water was thrown in his face. His eyes fluttered open. He thought he caught a glimpse of Van der Merwe's servant, Banda, and the beating began anew. Jamie could feel his ribs breaking. Something smashed into his leg, and he heard the crunch of bone.

That was when he lost consciousness again.

His body was on fire. Someone was scraping his face with sandpaper, and he vainly tried to lift a hand to protest. He made an effort to open his eyes, but they were swollen shut. Jamie lay there, every fibre of his being screaming with pain, as he tried to remember where he was. He shifted, and the scraping began again. He put out his hand blindly and felt sand. His raw face was lying in hot sand. Slowly, every move an agony, he managed to draw himself up on his knees. He tried to see through his swollen eyes, but he could make out only hazy images. He was somewhere in the middle of the trackless Karroo, naked. It was early morning, but he could feel the sun starting to burn through his body. He felt around blindly for food or a billy can of water. There was nothing. They had left him there for dead. *Salomon van der Merwe. And, of course, Smit, the bartender. Jamie had threatened Van der Merwe, and Van der Merwe had punished him as easily as one punished a small child. But he'll find out I'm no child*, Jamie promised himself. *Not anymore. I'm an avenger.* They'll pay. They will pay. The hatred that coursed through Jamie gave him the strength to sit up. It was a torture for him to breathe. How many ribs had they broken? *I must be careful so they don't puncture my lungs.* Jamie tried to stand up, but fell down with a scream. His right leg was broken and lay at an unnatural angle. He was unable to walk.

But he could crawl.

Jamie McGregor had no idea where he was. They would have taken him to some place off the beaten track, where his body would not be found except by the desert scavengers, the hyenas and secretary birds and vultures. The desert was a vast charnel house. He had seen the bones of men's bodies that had been scavenged, and there had not been a scrap of meat left on the skeleton. Even as Jamie was thinking about it, he heard the rustle of wings above him and the shrill hiss of the vultures. He felt a flood of terror. He was blind. He could not see them. But he could smell them.

He began to crawl.

* * *

He made himself concentrate on the pain. His body was aflame with it, and each small movement brought exquisite rivers of agony. If he moved in a certain way, his broken leg would send out stabbing pains. If he shifted his position slightly to favour his leg, he could feel his ribs grinding against each other. He could not stand the torture of lying still; he could not stand the agony of moving.

He kept crawling.

He could hear them circling above, waiting for him with an ancient, timeless patience. His mind started to wander. He was in the cool kirk at Aberdeen, neatly dressed in his Sunday suit, seated between his two brothers. His sister, Mary, and Annie Cord were wearing beautiful white summer dresses, and Annie Cord was looking at him and smiling. Jamie started to get up and go to her, and his brothers held him back and began to pinch him. The pinches became excruciating shafts of pain, and he was crawling through the desert again, naked, his body broken. The cries of the vultures were louder now, impatient.

Jamie tried to force his eyes open, to see how close they were. He could see nothing except vague, shimmering objects that his terrified imagination turned into feral hyenas and jackals. The wind became their hot, fetid breath caressing his face.

He kept crawling, for he knew that the moment he stopped they would be upon him. He was burning with fever and pain and his body was flayed by the hot sand. And still, he could not give up, not as long as Van der Merwe was unpunished – not as long as Van der Merwe was alive.

He lost all awareness of time. He guessed that he had travelled a mile. In truth, he had moved less than ten yards, crawling in a circle. He could not see where he had been or where he was going. He focused his mind on only one thing: Salomon van der Merwe.

He slipped into unconsciousness and was awakened by a shrieking agony beyond bearing. Someone was stabbing at his leg, and it took Jamie a second to remember where he was and what was happening. He pulled one swollen eye open. An enormous hooded black vulture was attacking his leg, savagely tearing at his flesh, eating him alive with its sharp beak. Jamie saw its beady eyes and the dirty ruff around its neck. He smelled the foul odour of the bird as it sat on his body. Jamie tried to scream, but no sound came out. Frantically he jerked himself forwards, and felt the warm flow of blood pouring from his leg. He could see the shadows of the giant birds all around him, moving in for the kill. He knew that the next time he lost consciousness would be the last time. The instant he stopped, the carrion birds would be at his flesh again. He kept crawling. His mind began to wander into delirium. He heard the loud flapping wings of the birds as they moved closer, forming a circle around him. He was too weak now to fight them off; he had no strength left to resist. He stopped moving and lay still on the burning sand.

The giant birds closed in for their feast.

FOUR

Saturday was market day in Cape Town and the streets were crowded with shoppers looking for bargains, meeting friends and lovers. Boers and Frenchmen, soldiers in colourful uniforms and English ladies in flounced skirts and ruffled blouses mingled in front of the bazaars set up in the town squares at Braameonstein and Park Town and Burgersdorp. Everything was for sale: furniture, horses and carriages and fresh fruit. One could purchase dresses and chessboards, or meat or books in a dozen different languages. On Saturdays, Cape Town was a noisy, bustling fair.

Banda walked along slowly through the crowd, careful not to make eye contact with the whites. It was too dangerous. The streets were filled with blacks, Indians and coloureds, but the white minority ruled. Banda hated them. This was his land, and the whites were the *uitlanders*. There were many tribes in southern Africa: the Basutos, Zulus, Bechuanas, the Matabele – all of them Bantu. The very word *bantu* came from *abantu* – *the people*. But the Barolongs – Banda's tribe – were the aristocracy. Banda remembered the tales his grandmother told him of the great black kingdom that had once ruled South Africa. *Their* kingdom, *their* country. And now they were enslaved by a handful of white jackals. The whites had pushed them into smaller and smaller territories, until their freedom had been eroded. Now, the only way a black could exist was by *slim*, subservient on the surface, but cunning and clever beneath.

Banda did not know how old he was, for natives had no birth certificates. Their ages were measured by tribal lore: wars and battles, and births and deaths of great chiefs, comets and blizzards and earthquakes, Adam Kok's trek, the death of Chaka and the cattle-killing revolution. But the number of his years made no difference. Banda knew he was the son of a chief, and that he was destined to do something for his people. Once again, the Bantus would rise and rule because of him. The thought of his mission made him walk taller and straighter for a moment, until he felt the eyes of a white man upon him.

Banda hurried east towards the outskirts of town, the district allotted to the blacks. The large homes and attractive shops gradually gave way to tin shacks and lean-tos and huts. He moved down a dirt street, looking over his shoulder to make certain he was not followed. He reached a wooden shack, took one last look around, rapped twice on the door and entered. A thin black woman was seated in a chair in a corner of the room sewing on a dress. Banda nodded to her and then continued on into the bedroom in back.

He looked down at the figure lying on the cot.

Six weeks earlier Jamie McGregor had regained consciousness and found himself on a cot in a strange house. Memory came flooding back. He was in the Karroo again, his body broken, helpless. The vultures . . .

Then Banda had walked into the tiny bedroom, and Jamie knew he had come to kill him. Van der Merwe had somehow learned Jamie was still alive and had sent his servant to finish him off.

'Why didn't your master come himself?' Jamie croaked.

'I have no master.'

'Van der Merwe. He didn't send you?'

'No. He would kill us both if he knew.'

None of this made any sense. 'Where am I? I want to know where I am.'

'Cape Town.'

'That's impossible. How did I get here?'

'I brought you.'

Jamie stared into the black eyes for a long moment before he spoke. 'Why?'

'I need you. I want vengeance.'

'What do you –?'

Banda moved closer. 'Not for me. I do not care about me. Van der Merwe raped my sister. She

71

died giving birth to his baby. My sister was eleven years old.'

Jamie lay back, stunned. 'My God!'

'Since the day she died I have been looking for a white man to help me. I found him that night in the barn where I helped beat you up, Mr McGregor. We dumped you in the Karroo. I was ordered to kill you. I told the others you were dead, and I returned to get you as soon as I could. I was almost too late.'

Jamie could not repress a shudder. He could feel again the foul-smelling carrion birds digging into his flesh.

'The birds were already starting to feast. I carried you to the wagon and hid you at the house of my people. One of our doctors taped your ribs and set your leg and tended to your wounds.'

'And after that?'

'A wagonful of my relatives was leaving for Cape Town. We took you with us. You were out of your head most of the time. Each time you fell asleep, I was afraid you were not going to wake up again.'

Jamie looked into the eyes of the man who had almost murdered him. He had to think. He did not trust this man – and yet he had saved his life. Banda wanted to get at Van der Merwe through him. *That can work both ways*, Jamie decided. More than anything in the world, Jamie wanted to make Van der Merwe pay for what he had done to him.

'All right,' Jamie told Banda. 'I'll find a way to pay Van der Merwe back for both of us.'

For the first time, a thin smile appeared on Banda's face. 'Is he going to die?'

'No,' Jamie told him. 'He's going to live.'

Jamie got out of bed that afternoon for the first time, dizzy and weak. His leg still had not completely healed, and he walked with a slight limp. Banda tried to assist him.

'Let go of me. I can make it on my own.'

Banda watched as Jamie carefully moved across the room.

'I'd like a mirror,' Jamie said. *I must look terrible*, he thought. *How long has it been since I've had a shave?*

Banda returned with a hand mirror, and Jamie held it up to his face. He was looking at a total stranger. His hair had turned snow-white. He had a full, unkempt white beard. His nose had been broken and a ridge of bone pushed it to one side. His face had aged twenty years. There were deep ridges along his sunken cheeks and a livid scar across his chin. But the biggest change was in his eyes. They were eyes that had seen too much pain, felt too much, hated too much. He slowly put down the mirror.

'I'm going out for a walk,' Jamie said.

'Sorry, Mr McGregor. That's not possible.'

'Why not?'

'White men do not come to this part of town, just as blacks never go into the white places. My neighbours do not know you are here. We brought you in at night.'

'How do I leave?'

'I will move you out tonight.'

For the first time, Jamie realized how much Banda had risked for him. Embarrassed, Jamie said, 'I have no money, I need a job.'

'I took a job at the shipyard. They are always looking for men.' He took some money from his pocket. 'Here.'

Jamie took the money. 'I'll pay it back.'

'You will pay my sister back,' Banda told him.

It was midnight when Banda led Jamie out of the shack. Jamie looked around. He was in the middle of a shantytown, a jungle of rusty, corrugated iron shacks and lean-tos, made from rotting planks and torn sacking. The ground, muddy from a recent rain, gave off a rank odour. Jamie wondered how people as proud as Banda could bear spending their lives in a place such as this. 'Isn't there some –?'

'Don't talk, please,' Banda whispered. 'My neighbours are inquisitive.' He led Jamie outside the compound and pointed. 'The centre of town is in that direction. I will see you at the shipyard.'

Jamie checked into the same boardinghouse where he had stayed on his arrival from England. Mrs Venster was behind the desk.

'I'd like a room,' Jamie said.

'Certainly, sir.' She smiled, revealing her gold tooth. 'I'm Mrs Venster.'

'I know.'

'Now how would you know a thing like that?' she asked coyly. 'Have your men friends been tellin' tales out of school?'

'Mrs Venster, don't you remember me? I stayed here last year.'

She took a close look at his scarred face, his broken nose and his white beard, and there was not the slightest sign of recognition. 'I never forget a face, dearie. And I've never seen yours before. But that don't mean we're not going to be good friends, does it? My friends call me "Dee-Dee". What's your name, love?'

And Jamie heard himself saying, 'Travis. Ian Travis.'

The following morning Jamie went to see about work at the shipyard.

The busy foreman said, 'We need strong backs. The problem is you might be a bit old for this kind of work.'

'I'm only nineteen –' Jamie started to say and stopped himself. He remembered that face in the mirror. 'Try me,' he said.

He went to work as a stevedore at nine shillings a day, loading and unloading the ships that came into the harbour. He learned that Banda and the other black stevedores received six shillings a day.

At the first opportunity, Jamie pulled Banda aside and said, 'We have to talk.'

'Not here, Mr McGregor. There's an abandoned

warehouse at the end of the docks. I'll meet you there when the shift is over.'

Banda was waiting when Jamie arrived at the deserted warehouse.

'Tell me about Salomon van der Merwe,' Jamie said.

'What to you want to know?'

'Everything.'

Banda spat. 'He came to South Africa from Holland. From stories I heard, his wife was ugly, but wealthy. She died of some sickness and Van der Merwe took her money and went up to Klipdrift and opened his general store. He got rich cheating diggers.'

'The way he cheated me?'

'That's only one of his ways. Diggers who strike it lucky go to him for money to help them work their claim, and before they know it Van der Merwe owns them.'

'Hasn't anyone ever tried to fight back?'

'How can they? The town clerk's on his payroll. The law says that if forty-five days go by without working a claim, it's open. The town clerk tips off Van der Merwe and he grabs it. There's another trick he uses. Claims have to be staked out at each boundary line with pegs pointing straight up in the air. If the pegs fall down, a jumper can claim the property. Well, when Van der Merwe sees a claim he likes, he sends someone around at night, and in the morning the stakes are on the ground.'

'Jesus!'

'He's made a deal with the bartender, Smit. Smit sends likely-looking prospectors to Van der Merwe, and they sign partnership contracts and if they find diamonds, Van der Merwe takes everything for himself. If they become troublesome, he's got a lot of men on his payroll who follow his orders.'

'I know about that,' Jamie said grimly. 'What else?'

'He's a religious fanatic. He's always praying for the souls of sinners.'

'What about his daughter?' She had to be involved in this.

'Miss Margaret? She's frightened to death of her father. If she even looked at a man, Van der Merwe would kill them both.'

Jamie turned his back and walked over to the door, where he stood looking out at the harbour. He had a lot to think about. 'We'll talk again tomorrow.'

It was in Cape Town that Jamie became aware of the enormous schism between the blacks and whites. The blacks had no rights except the few they were given by those in power. They were herded into conclaves that were ghettos and were allowed to leave only to work for the white man.

'How do you stand it?' Jamie asked Banda one day.

'The hungry lion hides its claws. We will change all this someday. The white man accepts the black man because his muscles are needed, but he must also learn to accept his brain. The more he drives us into a corner, the more he fears us because he knows that one day there may be discrimination and humiliation in reverse. He cannot bear the thought of that. But we will survive because of *isiko*.'

'Who is *isiko*?'

Banda shook his head. 'Not a *who*. A *what*. It is difficult to explain, Mr McGregor. *Isiko* is our roots. It is the feeling of belonging to a nation that has given its name to the Great Zambezi River. Generations ago my ancestors entered the waters of the Zambezi naked, driving their herds before them. Their weakest members were lost, the prey of the swirling waters or hungry crocodiles, but the survivors emerged from the waters stronger and more virile. When a Bantu dies, *isiko* demands that the members of his family retire to the forest so that the rest of the community will not have to share their distress. *Isiko* is the scorn felt for a slave who cringes, the belief that a man can look anyone in the face, that he is worth no more and no less than any other man. Have you heard of John Tengo Jabavu?' He pronounced the name with reverence.

'No.'

'You will, Mr McGregor,' Banda promised. 'You will.' And Banda changed the subject.

Jamie began to feel a growing admiration for Banda. In the beginning there was a wariness between the two men. Jamie had to learn to trust a man who had almost killed him. And Banda had to learn to trust an age-old enemy – a white man. Unlike most of the blacks Jamie had met, Banda was educated.

'Where did you go to school?' Jamie asked.

'Nowhere. I've worked since I was a small boy. My grandmother educated me. She worked for a Boer school-teacher. She learned to read and write so she could teach me to read and write. I owe her everything.'

It was on a late Saturday afternoon after work that Jamie first heard of the Namib Desert in Great Namaqualand. He and Banda were in the deserted warehouse on the docks, sharing an impala stew Banda's mother had cooked. It was good – a little gamey for Jamie's taste, but his bowl was soon empty, and he lay back on some old sacks to question Banda.

'When did you first meet Van der Merwe?'

'When I was working at the diamond beach on the Namib Desert. He owns the beach with two partners. He had just stolen his share from some poor prospector, and he was down there visiting it.'

'If Van der Merwe is so rich, why does he still work at his store?'

'The store is his bait. That's how he gets new prospectors to come to him. And he grows richer.'

Jamie thought of how easily he himself had been

cheated. How trusting that naive young boy had been! He could see Margaret's oval-shaped face as she said, *My father might be the one to help you.* He had thought she was a child until he had noticed her breasts and – Jamie suddenly jumped to his feet, a smile on his face, and the up-turning of his lips made the livid scar across his chin ripple.

'Tell me how you happened to go to work for Van der Merwe.'

'On the day he came to the beach with his daughter – she was about eleven then – I suppose she got bored sitting around and she went into the water and the tide grabbed her. I jumped in and pulled her out. I was a young boy, but I thought Van der Merwe was going to kill me.'

Jamie stared at him. 'Why?'

'Because I had my arms around her. Not because I was black, but because I was a *male*. He can't stand the thought of any man touching his daughter. Someone finally calmed him down and reminded him that I had saved her life. He brought me back to Klipdrift as his servant.' Banda hesitated a moment, then continued. 'Two months later, my sister came to visit me.' His voice was very quiet. 'She was the same age as Van der Merwe's daughter.'

There was nothing Jamie could say.

Finally Banda broke the silence. 'I should have stayed in the Namib Desert. That was an easy job. We'd crawl along the beach picking up diamonds and putting them in little jam tins.'

'Wait a minute. Are you saying that the diamonds are just lying there, on top of the sand?'

'That's what I'm saying, Mr McGregor. But forget what you're thinking. Nobody can get near that field. It's on the ocean, and the waves are up to thirty feet high. They don't even bother guarding the shore. A lot of people have tried to sneak in by sea. They've all been killed by the waves or the reefs.'

'There must be some other way to get in.'

'No. The Namib Desert runs right down to the ocean's shore.'

'What about the entrance to the diamond field?'

'There's a guard tower and a barbed-wire fence. Inside the fence are guards with guns and dogs that'll tear a man to pieces. And they have a new kind of explosive called a land mine. They're buried all over the field. If you don't have a map of the land mines, you'll get blown to bits.'

'How large is the diamond field?'

'It runs for about thirty-five miles.'

Thirty-five miles of diamonds just lying on the sand . . . 'My God!'

'You aren't the first one to get excited about the diamond fields at the Namib, and you won't be the last. I've picked up what was left of people who tried to come in by boat and got torn apart by the reefs. I've seen what those land mines do if a man takes one wrong step, and I've watched those dogs rip out a man's throat. Forget it, Mr

81

McGregor. I've been there. There's no way in and there's no way out – not alive, that is.'

Jamie was unable to sleep that night. He kept visualizing thirty-five miles of sand sprinkled with enormous diamonds belonging to Van der Merwe. He thought of the sea and the jagged reefs, the dogs hungry to kill, the guards and the land mines. He was not afraid of the danger; he was not afraid of dying. He was only afraid of dying before he repaid Salomon van der Merwe.

On the following Monday Jamie went into a cartographer's shop and bought a map of Great Namaqualand. There was the beach, off the South Atlantic Ocean between Lüderitz to the north and the Orange River Estuary to the south. The area was marked in red: SPERRGEBIET – Forbidden.

Jamie examined every detail of the area on the map, going over it again and again. There were three thousand miles of ocean flowing from South America to South Africa, with nothing to impede the waves, so that their full fury was spent on the deadly reefs of the South Atlantic shore. Forty miles south, down the coastline, was an open beach. *That must be where the poor bastards launched their boats to sail into the forbidden area*, Jamie decided. Looking at the map, he could understand why the shore was not guarded. The reefs would make a landing impossible.

Jamie turned his attention to the land entrance

to the diamond field. According to Banda, the area was fenced in with barbed wire and patrolled twenty-four hours a day by armed guards. At the entrance itself was a manned watch-tower. And even if one did somehow manage to slip past the watchtower into the diamond area, there would be the land mines and guard dogs.

The following day when Jamie met Banda, he asked, 'You said there was a land-mine map of the field?'

'In the Namib Desert? The supervisors have the maps, and they lead the diggers to work. Everybody walks in a single file so no one gets blown up.' His eyes filled with a memory. 'One day my uncle was walking in front of me and he stumbled on a rock and fell on top of a land mine. There wasn't enough left of him to take home to his family.'

Jamie shuddered.

'And then there's the sea *mis*, Mr McGregor. You've never seen a *mis* until you've been in one in the Namib. It rolls in from the ocean and blows all the way across the desert to the mountains and it blots out everything. If you're caught in one of them, you don't dare move. The land-mine maps are not good then because you can't see where you're going. Everybody just sits quietly until the *mis* lifts.'

'How long do they last?'

Banda shrugged. 'Sometimes a few hours, sometimes a few days.'

'Banda, have you ever *seen* a map of those land mines?'

'They're closely guarded.' A worried look crossed his face. 'I'm telling you again, no one can get away with what you're thinking. Once in a while workers will try to smuggle out a diamond. There is a special tree for hanging them. It's a lesson to everybody not to try to steal from the company.'

The whole thing looked impossible. Even if he could manage to get into Van der Merwe's diamond field, there was no way out. Banda was right. He would have to forget about it.

The next day he asked Banda, 'How does Van der Merwe keep the workers from stealing diamonds when they come off their shifts?'

'They're searched. They strip them down mother-naked and then they look up and down every hole they've got. I've seen workers cut gashes in their legs and try to smuggle diamonds out in them. Some drill out their back teeth and stick diamonds up there. They've tried every trick you can think of.' He looked at Jamie and said, 'If you want to live, you'll get that diamond field off your mind.'

Jamie tried. But the idea kept coming back to him, taunting him. Van der Merwe's diamonds just lying on the sand waiting. *Waiting for him.*

The solution came to Jamie that night. He could hardly contain his impatience until he saw Banda.

Without preamble, Jamie said, 'Tell me about the boats that have tried to land on the beach.'

'What about them?'

'What kind of boats were they?'

'Every kind you can think of. A schooner. A tugboat. A big motorboat. Sailboat. Four men even tried it in a rowboat. While I worked the field, there were half a dozen tries. The reefs just chewed the boats to pieces. Everybody drowned.'

Jamie took a deep breath. 'Did anyone ever try to get in by raft?'

Banda was staring at him. *'Raft?'*

'Yes.' Jamie's excitement was growing. 'Think about it. No one ever made it to the shore because the bottoms of their boats were torn out by the reefs. But a *raft* will glide right over those reefs and onto the shore. And it can get out the same way.'

Banda looked at him for a long time. When he spoke, there was a different note in his voice. 'You know, Mr McGregor, you might just have an idea there . . .'

It started as a game, a possible solution to an unsolvable puzzle. But the more Jamie and Banda discussed it, the more excited they became. What had started as idle conversation began to take concrete shape as a plan of action. Because the diamonds were lying on top of the sand, no equipment would be required. They could build their raft, with a sail, on the free beach forty miles south of the *Sperrgebiet* and sail it in at night, unobserved. There were no land mines along the unguarded shore, and the guards and patrols only operated inland. The two men could roam the beach freely, gathering up all the diamonds they could carry.

'We can be on our way out before dawn,' Jamie said, 'with our pockets full of Van der Merwe's diamonds.'

'How do we get out?'

'The same way we got in. We'll paddle the raft over the reefs to the open sea, put up the sail and we're home free.'

Under Jamie's persuasive arguments, Banda's doubts began to melt. He tried to poke holes in the plan and every time he came up with an objection, Jamie answered it. The plan *could* work. The beautiful part of it was its simplicity, and the fact that it would require no money. Only a great deal of nerve.

'All we need is a big bag to put the diamonds in,' Jamie said. His enthusiasm was infectious.

Banda grinned. 'Let's make that *two* big bags.'

The following week they quit their jobs and boarded a bullock wagon to Port Nolloth, the coastal village forty miles south of the forbidden area where they were headed.

At Port Nolloth, they disembarked and looked around. The village was small and primitive, with shanties and tin huts and a few stores, and a pristine white beach that seemed to stretch on forever. There were no reefs here, and the waves lapped gently at the shore. It was a perfect place to launch their raft.

There was no hotel, but the little market rented a room in back to Jamie. Banda found himself a bed in the black quarter of the village.

'We have to find a place to build our raft in secret,' Jamie told Banda. 'We don't want anyone reporting us to the authorities.'

That afternoon they came across an old, abandoned warehouse.

'This will be perfect,' Jamie decided. 'Let's get to work on the raft.'

'Not yet,' Banda told him. 'We'll wait. Buy a bottle of whiskey.'

'What for?'

'You'll see.'

The following morning, Jamie was visited by the district constable, a florid heavy-set man with a large nose covered with the telltale broken veins of a tippler.

'Mornin',' he greeted Jamie. 'I heard we had a visitor. Thought I'd stop by and say hello. I'm Constable Mundy.'

'Ian Travis,' Jamie replied.

'Headin' north, Mr Travis?'

'South. My servant and I are on our way to Cape Town.'

'Ah. I was in Cape Town once. Too bloody big, too bloody noisy.'

'I agree. Can I offer you a drink, Constable?'

'I never drink on duty.' Constable Mundy paused, making a decision. 'However, just this once, I might make an exception, I suppose.'

'Fine.' Jamie brought out the bottle of whiskey, wondering how Banda could have known. He poured out two fingers into a dirty tooth glass and handed it to the constable.

'Thank you, Mr Travis. Where's yours?'

'I can't drink,' Jamie said ruefully. 'Malaria. That's why I'm going to Cape Town. To get medical attention. I'm stopping off here a few days to rest. Travelling's very hard on me.'

Constable Munda was studying him. 'You look pretty healthy.'

'You should see me when the chills start.'

The constable's glass was empty. Jamie filled it.

'Thank you. Don't mind if I do.' He finished the second drink in one swallow and stood up. 'I'd best be gettin' along. You said you and your man will be movin' on in a day or two?'

'As soon as I'm feeling stronger.'

'I'll come back and check on you Friday,' Constable Mundy said.

That night, Jamie and Banda went to work on the raft in the deserted warehouse.

'Banda, have you ever built a raft?'

'Well, to tell you the truth, Mr McGregor, no.'

'Neither have I.' The two men stared at each other. 'How difficult can it be?'

They stole four empty, fifty-gallon wooden oil barrels from behind the market and carried them to the warehouse. When they had them assembled, they spaced them out in a square. Next they gathered four empty crates and placed one over each oil barrel.

Banda looked dubious. 'It doesn't look like a raft to me.'

'We're not finished yet,' Jamie assured him.

There was no planking available so they covered the top layer with whatever was at hand: branches from the stinkwood tree, limbs from the Cape beech, large leaves from the marula. They lashed everything down with thick hemp rope, tying each knot with careful precision.

When they were finished, Banda looked it over. 'It still doesn't look like a raft.'

'It will look better when we get the sail up,' Jamie promised.

They made a mast from a fallen yellowwood tree, and picked up two flat branches for paddles.

'Now all we need is a sail. We need it fast. I'd like to get out of here tonight. Constable Mundy's coming back tomorrow.'

It was Banda who found the sail. He came back late that evening with an enormous piece of blue cloth. 'How's this, Mr McGregor?'

'Perfect. Where did you get it?'

Banda grinned. 'Don't ask. We're in enough trouble.'

They rigged up a square sail with a boom below and a yard on top, and at last it was ready.

'We'll take off at two in the morning when the village is asleep.' Jamie told Banda. 'Better get some rest until then.'

But neither man was able to sleep. Each was filled with the excitement of the adventure that lay ahead.

At two a.m. they met at the warehouse. There was an eagerness in both of them, and an unspoken fear. They were embarking on a journey that would either make them rich or bring them death. There was no middle way.

'It's time,' Jamie announced.

They stepped outside. Nothing was stirring. The night was still and peaceful, with a vast canopy of blue overhead. A sliver of moon appeared high in the sky. *Good*, Jamie thought. *There won't be much light to see us by.* Their timetable was complicated by the fact that they had to leave the village at night so no one would be aware of their departure, and arrive at the diamond beach the next night so they could slip into the field and be safely back at sea before dawn.

'The Benguela current should carry us to the diamond fields sometime in the late afternoon,' Jamie said. 'But we can't go in by daylight. We'll have to stay out of sight at sea until dark.'

Banda nodded. 'We can hide out at one of the little islands off the coast.'

'What islands?'

'There are dozens of them – Mercury, Ichabod, Plum Pudding . . .'

Jamie gave him a strange look. *Plum Pudding?*

'There's also a Roast Beef Island.'

Jamie took out his creased map and consulted it. 'This doesn't show any of those.'

'They're guano islands. The British harvest the bird droppings for fertilizer.'

'Anyone live on those islands?'

'Can't. The smell's too bad. In places the guano is a hundred feet thick. The government uses gangs of deserters and prisoners to pick it up. Some of them die on the island and they just leave the bodies there.'

'That's where we'll hide out,' Jamie decided.

Working quietly, the two men slid open the door to the warehouse and started to lift the raft. It was too heavy to move. They sweated and tugged, but in vain.

'Wait here,' Banda said.

He hurried out. Half an hour later, he returned with a large round log. 'We'll use this. I'll pick up one end and you slide the log underneath.'

Jamie marvelled at Banda's strength as the black man picked up one end of the raft. Quickly, Jamie shoved the log under it. Together they lifted the back end of the raft and it moved easily down the log. When the log had rolled out from under the back end, they repeated the procedure. It was strenuous work, and by the time they got to the beach they were both soaked in perspiration. The operation had taken much longer than Jamie had anticipated. It was almost dawn now. They had to be away before the villagers discovered them and reported what they were doing. Quickly, Jamie attached the sail and checked to make sure everything was working properly. He had a nagging feeling he was forgetting something. He suddenly realized what was bothering him and laughed aloud.

Banda watched him, puzzled. 'Something funny?'

'Before, when I went looking for diamonds I had a ton of equipment. Now all I'm carrying is a compass. It seems too easy.'

Banda said quietly, 'I don't think that's going to be our problem, Mr McGregor.'

'It's time you called me Jamie.'

Banda shook his head in wonder. 'You *really* come from a faraway country.' He grinned, showing even white teeth. 'What the hell – they can hang me only once.' He tasted the name on his lips, then said it aloud. 'Jamie.'

'Let's go get those diamonds.'

They pushed the raft off the sand into the shallow water and both men leaped aboard and started paddling. It took them a few minutes to get adjusted to the pitching and yawing of their strange craft. It was like riding a bobbing cork, but it was going to work. The raft was responding perfectly, moving north with the swift current. Jamie raised the sail and headed out to sea. By the time the villagers awoke, the raft was well over the horizon.

'We've done it!' Jamie said.

Banda shook his head. 'It's not over yet.' He trailed a hand in the cold Benguela current. 'It's just beginning.'

They sailed on, due north past Alexander Bay and the mouth of the Orange River, seeing no signs of life except for flocks of Cape cormorants heading home, and a flight of colourful greater flamingos. Although there were tins of beef and cold rice, and fruit and two canteens of water aboard, they were too nervous to eat. Jamie refused to let his imagination linger on the dangers that lay ahead, but Banda could not help it. He had been there. He was remembering the brutal guards with guns and the dogs and the terrible flesh-tearing land mines, and he wondered how he had ever allowed himself to be talked into this insane venture. He looked over at the Scotsman and thought, *He is the bigger fool. If I die, I die for my baby sister. What does he die for?*

At noon the sharks came. There were half a dozen of them, their fins cutting through the water as they sped towards the raft.

'Black-fin sharks,' Banda announced. 'They're man-eaters.'

Jamie watched the fins skimming closer to the raft. 'What do we do?'

Banda swallowed nervously. 'Truthfully, Jamie, this is my very first experience of this nature.'

The back of a shark nudged the raft, and it almost capsized. The two men grabbed the mast for support. Jamie picked up a paddle and shoved it at a shark, and an instant later the paddle was bitten in two. The sharks surrounded the raft now, swimming in lazy circles, their enormous bodies rubbing up close against the small craft. Each nudge tilted the raft at a precarious angle. It was going to capsize at any moment.

'We've got to get rid of them before they sink us.'

'Get rid of them with what?' Banda asked.

'Hand me a tin of beef.'

'You must be joking. A tin of beef won't satisfy them. They want *us*!'

There was another jolt, and the raft heeled over.

'The beef!' Jamie yelled. 'Get it!'

A second later Banda placed a tin in Jamie's hand. The raft lurched sickeningly.

'Open it halfway. Hurry!'

Banda pulled out his pocketknife and pried the top of the can half open. Jamie took it from him. He felt the sharp, broken edges of the metal with his finger.

'Hold tight!' Jamie warned.

He knelt down at the edge of the raft and waited. Almost immediately, a shark approached the raft, its hugh mouth wide open, revealing long rows of evil, grinning teeth. Jamie went for the eyes. With all his strength, he reached out with both hands and scraped the edge of the broken metal against the eye of the shark, ripping it open. The shark lifted its great body, and for an instant the raft stood on end. The water around them was suddenly stained red. There was a giant thrashing as the sharks moved in on the wounded member of the school. The raft was forgotten. Jamie and Banda watched the great sharks tearing at their helpless victim as the raft sailed further and further away until finally the sharks were out of sight.

Banda took a deep breath and said softly, 'One day I'm going to tell my grandchildren about this. Do you think they'll believe me?'

And they laughed until the tears streamed down their faces.

Late that afternoon, Jamie checked his pocket watch. 'We should be off the diamond beach around midnight. Sunrise is at six-fifteen. That means we'll have four hours to pick up the diamonds and two hours to get back to sea and out of sight. Will four hours be enough, Banda?'

'A hundred men couldn't live long enough to spend what you can pick up on that beach in four hours.' *I just hope we live long enough to pick them up . . .*

They sailed steadily north for the rest of that day, carried by the wind and the tide. Towards evening a small island loomed ahead of them. It looked to be no more than two hundred yards in circumference. As they approached the island, the acrid smell of ammonia grew strong, bringing tears to their eyes. Jamie could understand why no one lived here. The stench was overpowering. But it would make a perfect place for them to hide until nightfall. Jamie adjusted the sail, and the small raft bumped against the rocky shore of the low-lying island. Banda made the raft fast, and the two men stepped ashore. The entire island was covered with what appeared to be millions of birds; cormorants, pelicans, gannets, penguins and flamingos. The thick air was so noisome that it was impossible to breathe. They took half a dozen steps and were thigh deep in guano.

'Let's get back to the raft,' Jamie gasped.

Without a word, Banda followed him.

As they turned to retreat, a flock of pelicans took to the air, revealing an open space on the ground. Lying there were three men. There was no telling how long they had been dead. Their corpses had been perfectly preserved by the ammonia in the air, and their hair had turned a bright red.

A minute later Jamie and Banda were back on the raft, headed out to sea.

They lay off the coast, sail lowered, waiting.

'We'll stay out here until midnight. Then we go in.'

They sat together in silence, each in his own way preparing for whatever lay ahead. The sun was low on the western horizon, painting the dying sky with the wild colours of a mad artist. Then suddenly they were blanketed in darkness.

They waited for two more hours, and Jamie hoisted the sail. The raft began to move east towards the unseen shore. Overhead, clouds parted and a thin wash of moonlight paled down. The raft picked up speed. In the distance the two men could begin to see the faint smudge of the coast. The wind blew stronger, snapping at the sail, pushing the raft towards the shore at an ever-increasing speed. Soon, they could make out the outline of the land, a gigantic parapet of rock. Even from that distance it was possible to see and hear the enormous whitecaps that exploded like thunder over the reefs. It was a terrifying sight from afar, and Jamie wondered what it would be like up close.

He found himself whispering. 'You're sure the beach side isn't guarded?'

Banda did not answer. He pointed to the reefs ahead. Jamie knew what he meant. The reefs were more deadly than any trap man could devise. They were the guardians of the sea, and they never relaxed, never slept. They lay there, patiently waiting for their prey to come to them. *Well*, Jamie thought, *we're going to outsmart you. We're going to float over you.*

The raft had carried them that far. It would carry them the rest of the way. The shore was racing towards them now, and they began to feel the heavy swell of the giant combers. Banda was holding tightly to the mast.

'We're moving pretty fast.'

'Don't worry,' Jamie reassured him. 'When we get closer, I'll lower the sail. That will cut our speed. We'll slide over the reefs nice and easy.'

The momentum of the wind and the waves was picking up, hurtling the raft towards the deadly reefs. Jamie quickly estimated the remaining distance and decided the waves would carry them in to shore without the help of the sail. Hurriedly, he lowered it. Their momentum did not even slow. The raft was completely in the grip of the huge waves now, out of control, hurled forwards from one giant crest to the next. The raft was rocking so violently that the men had to cling to it with both hands. Jamie had expected the entrance to be difficult, but he was totally unprepared for the fury of the seething maelstrom they faced. The reefs loomed in front of them with startling clarity. They could see the waves rushing in against the jagged rocks and exploded into huge, angry geysers. The entire success of the plan depended on bringing the raft over the reefs intact so that they could use it for their escape. Without it, they were dead men.

They were bearing down on the reefs now, propelled by the terrifying power of the waves. The roar of the wind was deafening. The raft was suddenly lifted high in the air by an enormous wave and flung towards the rocks.

'Hold on, Banda!' Jamie shouted. 'We're going in!'

The giant breaker picked up the raft like a matchstick and started to carry it towards shore, over the reef. Both men were hanging on for their lives, fighting the violent bucking motion that threatened to sweep them into the water. Jamie glanced down and caught a glimpse of the razor-sharp reefs below them. In another moment they would be sailing over them, safe in the haven of the shore.

At that instant there was a sudden, tearing wrench as a reef caught one of the barrels underneath the raft and ripped it away. The raft gave a sharp lurch, and another barrel was torn away, and then another. The wind and the pounding waves and the hungry reef were playing with the raft like a toy, tossing it backwards and forwards, spinning it wildly in the air. Jamie and Banda felt the thin wood begin to split beneath their feet.

'Jump!' Jamie yelled.

He dived over the side of the raft, and a giant wave picked him up and shot him towards the beach at the speed of a catapult. He was caught in the grip of an element that was powerful beyond belief. He had no control over what was happening. He was a part of the wave. It was over him and under him and inside him. His body was twisting and turning and his lungs were bursting. Lights began to explode in his head. Jamie thought, *I'm drowning.* And his body was thrown up onto the sandy shore. Jamie lay there gasping, fighting for breath, filling his lungs with the cool, fresh sea air. His chest and legs were scraped raw from the sand, and his clothes were in shreds. Slowly, he sat up and looked around for Banda. He was crouching ten yards away, vomiting seawater. Jamie got to his feet and staggered over to him.

'You all right?'

Banda nodded. He took a deep, shuddering breath and looked up at Jamie. 'I can't swim.'

Jamie helped him to his feet. The two men turned to look at the reef. There was not a sign of their raft. It had been torn to pieces in the wild ocean. They had gotten into the diamond field.

There was no way to get out.

FIVE

Behind them was the raging ocean. Ahead was unbroken desert from the sea to the foothills of the distant, rugged, purple mountains of the Richterveld escarpment, a world of kloofs and canyons and twisted peaks, lit by the pale moon. At the foot of the mountains was the Hexenkessel Valley – 'the witch's cauldron' – a bleak wind trap. It was a primeval, desolate landscape that went back to the beginning of time itself. The only clue that man had ever set foot in this place was a crudely printed sign pounded into the sand. By the light of the moon, they read:

VERBODE GEBIED
SPERRGEBIET

Forbidden.

There was no escape towards the sea. The only direction left open to them was the Namib Desert.

'We'll have to try to cross it and take our chances,' Jamie said.

Banda shook his head. 'The guards will shoot us on sight or hang us. Even if we were lucky enough to slip by the guards and dogs, there's no way to get by the land mines. We're dead men.' There was no fear in him, only a resigned acceptance of his fate.

Jamie looked at Banda and felt a sense of deep regret. He had brought the black man into this, and not once had Banda complained. Even now, knowing there was no escape for them, he did not utter one word of reproach.

Jamie turned to look at the wall of angry waves smashing at the shore, and he thought it was a miracle that they had gotten as far as they had. It was two a.m., four hours before dawn and discovery, and they were both still in one piece. *I'll be damned if I'm ready to give up*, Jamie thought.

'Let's go to work, Banda.'

Banda blinked. 'Doing what?'

'We came here to get diamonds, didn't we? Let's get them.'

Banda stared at the wild-eyed man with his white hair plastered to his skull and his sopping trousers hanging in shreds around his legs. 'What are you talking about?'

'You said they're going to kill us on sight, right? Well, they might as well kill us rich as poor. A miracle got us in here. Maybe a miracle will get

102

us out. And if we do get out, I damned well don't plan to leave empty-handed.'

'You're crazy,' Banda said softly.

'Or we wouldn't be here,' Jamie reminded him.

Banda shrugged. 'What the hell. I have nothing else to do until they find us.'

Jamie stripped off his tattered shirt, and Banda understood and did the same.

'Now. Where are all these big diamonds that you've been talking about?'

'They're everywhere,' Banda promised. And he added, 'Like the guards and the dogs.'

'We'll worry about them later. When do they come down to the beach?'

'When it gets light.'

Jamie thought for a moment. 'Is there a part of the beach where they *don't* come? Someplace we could hide?'

'There's no part of this beach they don't come to, and there's no place you could hide a fly.'

Jamie slapped Banda on the shoulder. 'Right, then. Let's go.'

Jamie watched as Banda got down on his hands and knees and began slowly crawling along the beach, his fingers sifting sand as he moved. In less than two minutes, he stopped and held up a stone, 'I found one!'

Jamie lowered himself to the sand and began moving. The first two stones he found were small. The third must have weighed over fifteen carats. He sat there looking at it for a long moment. It was incredible to him that such a fortune could be picked up so easily. And it all belonged to Salomon van der Merwe and his partners. Jamie kept moving.

In the next three hours, the two men collected more than forty diamonds ranging from two carats to thirty carats. The sky in the east was beginning to lighten. It was the time Jamie had planned to leave, to jump back on the raft, sail over the reefs and make their escape. It was useless to think about that now.

'It will be dawn soon,' Jamie said. 'Let's see how many more diamonds we can find.'

'We're not going to live to spend any of *this*. You want to die *very* rich, don't you?'

'I don't want to die at all.'

They resumed their search, mindlessly scooping up diamond after diamond, and it was as though a madness had taken possession of them. Their piles of diamonds increased, until sixty diamonds worth a king's ransom lay in their torn shirts.

'Do you want me to carry these?' Banda asked.

'No. We can both –' And then Jamie realized what was on Banda's mind. The one caught in actual possession of the diamonds would die more slowly and painfully.

'I'll take them,' Jamie said. He dumped the diamonds into the rag that was left of his shirt, and carefully tied it in a knot. The horizon was light grey now, and the east was becoming stained with the colours of the rising sun.

What next? That was the question! What was the answer? They could stand there and die, or they could move inland towards the desert and die.

'Let's move.'

Jamie and Banda slowly began walking away from the sea, side by side.

'Where do the land mines start?'

'About a hundred yards up ahead.' In the far distance, they heard a dog bark. 'I don't think we're going to have to worry about the land mines. The dogs are heading this way. The morning shift is coming to work.'

'How soon before they reach us?'

'Fifteen minutes. Maybe ten.'

It was almost full dawn now. What had been vague, shimmering patterns turned into small sand dunes and distant mountains. There was no place to hide.

'How many guards are on a shift?'

Banda thought for a moment. 'About ten.'

'Ten guards aren't many for a beach this big.'

'*One* guard is plenty. They've got guns and dogs. The guards aren't blind, and we're not invisible.'

The sound of the barking was closer now. Jamie said, 'Banda I'm sorry. I should never have gotten you into this.'

'You didn't'

And Jamie understood what he meant.

They could hear voices calling in the distance.

Jamie and Banda reached a small dune. 'What if we buried ourselves in the sand?'

'That has been tried. The dogs would find us and rip our throats out. I want my death to be quick. I'm going to let them see me, then start running. That way they'll shoot me. I – I don't want the dogs to get me.'

Jamie gripped Banda's arm. 'We may die, but I'll be damned if we're going to *run* to our deaths. Let's make them work for it.'

They could begin to distinguish words in the distance. 'Keep moving, you lazy bastards,' a voice was yelling. 'Follow me . . . stay in line . . . You've all had a good night's sleep . . . Now let's get some work done . . .'

In spite of his brave words, Jamie found he was retreating from the voice. He turned to look at the sea again. *Was drowning an easier way to die?* He watched the reefs tearing viciously at the demon waves breaking over them and he suddenly saw something else, something beyond the waves. He could not understand what it was. 'Banda, look . . .'

Far out at sea an impenetrable grey wall was moving towards them, blown by the powerful westerly winds.

'It's the sea *mis*!' Banda exclaimed. 'It comes in two or three times a week.'

While they were talking, the *mis* moved closer, like a gigantic grey curtain sweeping across the horizon, blotting out the sky.

The voices had moved closer, too. '*Den dousant!* Damn this *mis*! Another slowdown. The bosses ain't gonna like this . . .'

'We've got a chance!' Jamie said. He was whispering now.

'What chance?'

'The *mis*! They won't be able to see us.'

'That's no help. It's going to lift sometime, and when it does we're still going to be right here. If the guards can't move through the land mines, neither can we. You try to cross this desert in the *mis* and you won't go ten yards before you're blown to pieces. You're looking for one of your miracles.'

'You're damned right I am,' Jamie said.

The sky was darkening overhead. The *mis* was closer, covering the sea, ready to swallow up the shore. It had an eerie, menacing look about it as it rolled towards them, but Jamie thought exultantly. *It's going to save us!*

A voice suddenly called out, 'Hey! You two! What the hell are you doin' there?'

Jamie and Banda turned. At the top of a dune about a hundred yards away was a uniformed guard carrying a rifle. Jamie looked back at the shore. The *mis* was closing in fast.

'You! You two! Come here,' the guard yelled. He lifted his rifle.

Jamie raised his hands. 'I twisted my foot,' he called out. 'I can't walk.'

'Stay where you are,' the guard ordered. 'I'm comin' to get you.' He lowered his rifle and started moving towards them. A quick look back showed that the *mis* had reached the edge of the shore, and was coming in swiftly.

'Run!' Jamie whispered. He turned and raced towards the beach. Banda running close behind him.

'Stop!'

A second later they heard the sharp crack of a rifle, and the sand ahead of them exploded. They kept running, racing to meet the great dark wall of the fog. There was another rifle shot, closer this time, and another, and the next moment the two men were in total darkness. The sea *mis* licked at them, chilling them, smothering them. It was like being buried in cotton. It was impossible to see anything.

The voices were muffled now and distant, bouncing off the *mis* and coming from all directions. They could hear other voices calling to one another.

'Kruger! . . . It's Brent . . . Can you hear me?'

'I hear you, Kruger . . .'

'There're two of them,' the first voice yelled. 'A white man and a black. They're on the beach. Spread your men out. *Skiet hom!* Shoot to kill.'

'Hang on to me,' Jamie whispered.

Banda gripped his arm. 'Where are you going?'

'We're getting out of here.'

Jamie brought his compass up to his face. He could barely see it. He turned until the compass was pointing east. 'This way . . .'

'Wait! We can't walk. Even if we don't bump

into a guard or a dog, we're going to set off a land mine.'

'You said there are a hundred yards before the mines start. Let's get away from the beach.'

They started moving towards the desert, slowly and unsteadily, blind men in an unknown land. Jamie paced off the yards. Whenever they stumbled in the soft sand, they picked themselves up and kept moving. Jamie stopped to check the compass every few feet. When he estimated they had travelled almost a hundred yards, he stopped.

'This should be about where the land mines start. Is there any pattern to the way they're placed? Anything you can think of that could help us?'

'Prayer,' Banda answered. 'Nobody's ever gotten past those land mines, Jamie. They're scattered all over the field, buried about six inches down. We're going to have to stay here until the *mis* lifts and give ourselves up.'

Jamie listened to the cotton-wrapped voices ricocheting around them.

'Kruger! Keep in voice contact . . .'

'Right, Brent . . .'

'Kruger . . .'

'Brent . . .'

Disembodied voices calling to each other in the blinding fog. Jamie's mind was racing, desperately exploring every possible avenue of escape. If they stayed where they were, they would be killed the instant the *mis* lifted. If they tried moving through the field of mines, they would be blown to bits.

'Have you ever seen the land mines?' Jamie whispered.

'I helped bury some of them.'

'What sets them off?'

'A man's weight. Anything over eighty pounds will explode them. That way they don't kill the dogs.'

Jamie took a deep breath. 'Banda, I may have a way for us to get out of here. It might not work. Do you want to gamble with me?'

'What have you got in mind?'

'We're going to cross the mine fields on our bellies. That way we'll distribute our weight across the sand.'

'Oh, Jesus!'

'What do you think?'

'I think I was crazy for ever leaving Cape Town.'

'Are you with me?' He could barely make out Banda's face next to him.

'You don't leave a man a lot of choice, do you?'

'Come on then.'

Jamie carefully stretched himself out flat on the sand. Banda looked at him a moment, took a deep breath and joined him. Slowly the two men began crawling across the sand, towards the minefield.

'When you move,' Jamie whispered, 'don't press down with your hands or your legs. Use your whole body.'

There was no reply. Banda was busy concentrating on staying alive.

They were in a smothering, grey vacuum that made it impossible to see anything. At any instant they could bump into a guard, a dog or one of the land mines. Jamie forced all this out of his mind. Their progress was painfully slow. Both men were shirtless, and the sand scraped against their stomachs as they inched forwards. Jamie was aware of how overwhelming the odds were against them. Even if by some chance they did succeed in crossing the desert without getting shot or blown up, they would be confronted by the barbed-wire fence and the armed guards at the watchtower at the entrance. And there was no telling how long the *mis* would last. It could lift at any second, exposing them.

They kept crawling, mindlessly sliding forwards until they lost all track of time. The inches became feet, and the feet became yards, and the yards became miles. They had no idea how long they had been travelling. They were forced to keep their heads close to the ground, and their eyes and ears and noses became filled with sand. Breathing was an effort.

In the distance was the constant echo of the guards' voices. '*Kruger . . . Brent . . . Kruger . . . Brent . . .*'

The two men stopped to rest and check the compass every few minutes, then moved on, beginning their endless crawl again. There was an almost overwhelming temptation to move faster, but that would mean pressing down harder, and Jamie could visualize the metal fragments exploding under him and ripping into his belly. He kept the pace slow. From time to time they could hear other voices around them, but the words were muffled by the fog and it was impossible to tell where they were coming from. *It's a big desert.* Jamie thought hopefully. *We're not going to stumble into anyone.*

Out of nowhere, a large, furry shape leaped at him. It happened so swiftly that Jamie was caught off guard. He felt the huge Alsatian's teeth sinking into his arm. He dropped the bundle of diamonds and tried to pry open the dog's jaw, but he had only one free hand and it was impossible. He felt the warm blood running down his arm. The dog was sinking its teeth in harder now, silent and deadly. Jamie felt himself begin to faint. He heard a dull thud, and then another, and the dog's jaw loosened and its eyes glazed over. Through the mist of pain, Jamie saw Banda smashing the sack of diamonds against the dog's skull. The dog whimpered once and lay still.

'You all right?' Banda breathed anxiously.

Jamie could not speak. He lay there, waiting for the waves of pain to recede. Banda ripped off a piece of his trousers and tied a strip tightly around Jamie's arm to stop the bleeding.

'We've got to keep moving,' Banda warned. 'If there's one of them around, there are more.'

Jamie nodded. Slowly he slid his body forwards, fighting against the terrible throbbing in his arm.

He remembered nothing of the rest of the trek.

He was semi-conscious, an automaton. Something outside him directed his movements. *Arms forwards, pull . . . Arms forwards, pull . . . Arms forwards, pull . . .* It was endless, an odyssey of agony. It was Banda who followed the compass now, and when Jamie started to crawl in the wrong direction Banda gently turned him around. They were surrounded by guards and dogs and land mines and only the *mis* kept them safe. They kept moving, crawling for their lives, until the time came when neither man had the strength to move another inch.

They slept.

When Jamie opened his eyes, something had changed. He lay there on the sand, his body stiff and aching, trying to remember where he was. He could see Banda asleep six feet away, and it all came flooding in. The raft crashing on the reefs . . . the sea *mis* . . . But something was wrong. Jamie sat up, trying to figure out what it was. And his stomach lurched. *He could see Banda! That was what was wrong. The mis was lifting.* Jamie heard voices nearby. He peered through the thin mists of the dissipating fog. They had crawled near the entrance to the diamond field. There was the high guard tower and the barbed-wire fence Banda had described. A crowd of about sixty black workers was moving away from the diamond field towards the gate. They had finished their shift and the next shift was coming in. Jamie got on his knees and crawled over to Banda and shook him. Banda sat up, instantly awake. His eyes turned to the watch-tower and the gate.

'Damn!' he said incredulously. 'We almost made it.'

'We *did* make it! Give me those diamonds!'

Banda handed him the folded shirt. 'What do you –?'

'Follow me.'

'Those guards with the guns at the gate,' Banda said in a low voice, 'they'll know we don't belong here.'

'That's what I'm counting on,' Jamie told him.

The two men moved towards the guards, drifting between the line of departing workers and the line of arriving workers who were yelling at one another, exchanging good-natured catcalls.

'You fellas gonna work your asses off, man. We got a nice sleep in the *mis* . . .'

'How did you arrange for the *mis*, you lucky bastards. . . . ?'

'God listens to me. He ain't gonna listen to you. You're bad . . .'

Jamie and Banda reached the gate. Two huge armed guards stood inside, herding the departing workers over to the small tin hut where they would be thoroughly searched. *They strip them down mother-naked and then they look up and down every hole they've got.* Jamie clutched the tattered shirt in his hand more tightly. He pushed through the line of workers and walked up to a guard. 'Excuse me, sir,' Jamie said. 'Who do we see about a job here?'

Banda was staring at him, petrified.

The guard turned to face Jamie. 'What the hell are you doin' inside the fence?'

'We came in to look for work. I heard there was an opening for a guard, and my servant can dig. I thought –'

The guard eyed the two ragged, disreputable-looking figures. 'Get the hell back outside!'

'We don't want to go outside,' Jamie protested. 'We need jobs, and I was told –'

'This is a restricted area, mister. Didn't you see the signs? Now get the hell out. Both of you!' He pointed to a large bullock wagon outside the fence, filling with the workers who had finished their shift. 'That wagon'll take you to Port Nolloth. If you want a job, you have to apply at the company office there.'

'Oh. Thank you, sir,' Jamie said. He beckoned to Banda, and the two men moved out through the gate to freedom.

The guard glared after them. 'Stupid idiots.'

Ten minutes later, Jamie and Banda were on their way to Port Nolloth. They were carrying with them diamonds worth half a million pounds.

115

SIX

The expensive carriage rolled down the dusty main
street of Klipdrift, drawn by two beautiful matched
bays. At the reins was a slender, athletic-looking
man with snow-white hair, a white beard and
moustache. He was dressed in a fashionable
tailored grey suit and ruffled shirt, and in his black
cravat was a diamond stickpin. He wore a grey
top hat, and on his little finger was a large,
sparkling diamond ring. He appeared to be a
stranger to the town, but he was not.

Klipdrift had changed considerably since Jamie
McGregor had left it a year earlier. It was 1884,
and it had grown from a camp to a township. The
railway had been completed from Cape Town to
Hopetown, with a branch running to Klipdrift, and
this had created a whole new wave of immigrants.
The town was even more crowded than Jamie
remembered, but the people seemed different.
There were still many prospectors, but there were
also men in business suits and well-dressed matrons

116

walking in and out of stores. Klipdrift had acquired a patina of respectability.

Jamie passed three new dance halls and half a dozen new saloons. He drove by a recently built church and barbershop, and a large hotel called the Grand. He stopped in front of a bank and alighted from the carriage, carelessly tossing the reins to a native boy.

'Water them.'

Jamie entered the bank and said to the manager in a loud voice, 'I wish to deposit one hundred thousand pounds in your bank.'

The word spread quickly, as Jamie had known it would, and by the time he left the bank and entered the Sundowner Saloon, he was the centre of interest. The interior of the saloon had not changed. It was crowded, and curious eyes followed Jamie as he walked up to the bar. Smit nodded deferentially. 'What would you like, sir?' There was no recognition on the bartender's face.

'Whiskey. The best you have.'

'Yes, sir.' He poured the drink. 'You're new in town?'

'Yes.'

'Just passin' through, are you?'

'No. I've heard this is a good town for a man looking for investments.'

The bartender's eyes lighted up. 'You couldn't find better! A man with a hundred – A man with money can do real well for hisself. Matter of fact, I might be of some service to you, sir.'

'Really? How is that?'

Smit leaned forwards, his tone conspiratorial. 'I know a man who runs this town. He's chairman of the Borough Council and head of the Citizen's Committee. He's the most important man in this part of the country. Name of Salomon van der Merwe.'

Jamie took a sip of his drink. 'Never heard of him.'

'He owns that big general store across the street. He can put you on to some good deals. It'd be worth your while to meet him.'

Jamie McGregor took another sip of his drink. 'Have him come over here.'

The bartender glanced at the large diamond ring on Jamie's finger, and at his diamond stickpin. 'Yes, sir. Can I tell him your name?'

'Travis. Ian Travis.'

'Right, Mr Travis. I'm sure Mr van der Merwe will want to meet you.' He poured out another drink. 'Have this while you're waitin'. It's on the house.'

Jamie sat at the bar sipping the whiskey, aware that everyone in the saloon was watching him. Men had departed from Klipdrift wealthy, but no one of such obvious wealth had ever arrived there before. It was something new in their experience.

Fifteen minutes later, the bartender was back, accompanied by Salomon van der Merwe.

Van der Merwe walked up to the bearded, white-haired stranger, held out his hand and smiled. 'Mr Travis, I'm Salomon van der Merwe.'

'Ian Travis.'

Jamie waited for a flicker of recognition, a sign that Van der Merwe found something familiar about him. There was nothing. *But then, why should there be?* Jamie thought. There was nothing left of that naïve, idealistic, eighteen-year-old boy he had been. Smit obsequiously led the two men to a corner table.

As soon as they were seated, Van der Merwe said, 'I understand you're looking for some investments in Klipdrift, Mr Travis.'

'Possibly.'

'I might be able to be of some service. One has to be careful. There are many immoral people around.'

Jamie looked at him and said, 'I'm sure there are.'

It was unreal, sitting there carrying on a polite conversation with the man who had cheated him out of a fortune and then tried to murder him. His hatred for Van der Merwe had consumed him for the last year, his thirst for vengeance was all that had sustained him, kept him alive. And now Van der Merwe was about to feel that vengeance.

'If you don't mind my asking, Mr Travis, how much money were you planning on investing?'

'Oh, around a hundred thousand pounds to begin with,' Jamie said carelessly. He watched Van der Merwe wet his lips. 'Then perhaps three or four hundred thousand more.'

'Er – you should be able to do very well with

that, very well, indeed. With the right guidance, of course,' he added quickly. 'Do you have any idea what you might want to invest in?'

'I thought I'd look around and see what opportunities there were.'

'That's very wise of you.' Van der Merwe nodded sagely. 'Perhaps you would like to come to dinner tonight and we can discuss it? My daughter's an excellent cook. It would be an honour to have you.'

Jamie smiled. 'I'd enjoy that, Mr van der Merwe.' *You have no idea how much I'd enjoy that*, he thought.

It had started.

The journey from the diamond fields of Namib to Cape Town had been uneventful. Jamie and Banda had hiked inland to a small village where a doctor treated Jamie's arm, and they had gotten a lift on a wagon bound for Cape Town. It was a long, difficult ride, but they were oblivious to the discomfort. At Cape Town, Jamie checked into the ornate Royal Hotel on Plein Street – 'Patronized by HRH, the Duke of Edinburgh' – and was escorted to the Royal Suite.

'I want you to send up the best barber in town,' Jamie told the manager. 'Then I want a tailor and a bootmaker up here.'

'At once, sir,' the manager said.

It's wonderful what money can do, Jamie thought.

* * *

The bath in the Royal Suite was heaven. Jamie lay back in the hot water, soaking the tiredness out of his body, thinking back over the past incredible weeks. Had it been only weeks since he and Banda had built that raft? It seemed like years. Jamie thought about the raft sailing them to the *Sperrgebiet*, and the sharks, and the demon waves and the reefs tearing the raft to pieces. The sea *mis* and the crawling over the land mines, and the huge dog on top of him . . . The eerie, muffled cries that would ring in his ears forever: *Kruger . . . Brent . . . Kruger . . . Brent . . .*

But most of all, he thought of Banda. His friend.

When they had reached Cape Town, Jamie had urged, 'Stay with me.'

Banda smiled, showing his beautiful white teeth. 'Life's too dull with you, Jamie. I have to go somewhere and find a little excitement.'

'What will you do now?'

'Well, thanks to you and your wonderful plan about how easy it is to float a raft over the reef, I'm going to buy a farm, find a wife and have a lot of children.'

'All right. Let's go to the *diamant kooper* so I can give you your share of the diamonds.'

'No,' Banda said. 'I don't want it.'

Jamie frowned. 'What are you talking about? Half the diamonds are yours. You're a millionaire.'

'No. Look at my skin, Jamie. If I became a millionaire, my life would not be worth a tickey.'

'You can hide some of the diamonds away. You can –'

'All I need is enough to buy a morgen of farm-land and two oxen to trade for a wife. Two or three little diamonds will get me everything I'll ever want. The rest are yours.'

'That's impossible. You can't give me your share.'

'Yes, I can, Jamie. Because you're going to give me Salomon van der Merwe.'

Jamie looked at Banda for a long moment. 'I promise.'

'Then I'll say good-bye, my friend.'

The two men clasped hands.

'We'll meet again,' Banda said. 'Next time think of something *really* exciting for us to do.'

Banda walked away with three small diamonds carefully tucked in his pocket.

Jamie sent off a bank draught amounting to twenty thousand pounds to his parents, bought the finest carriage and team he could find and headed back to Klipdrift.

The time had come for revenge.

That evening when Jamie McGregor entered Van der Merwe's store, he was gripped by a sensation so unpleasant and so violent that he had to pause to regain control of himself.

Van der Merwe hurried out of the back of the shop, and when he saw who it was, his face lighted up in a big smile. 'Mr Travis!' he said. 'Welcome.'

'Thank you, mister – er – sorry, I don't remember your name . . .'

'Van der Merwe. Salomon van der Merwe. Don't apologize. Dutch names are difficult to remember. Dinner is ready. Margaret!' he called as he led Jamie into the back room. Nothing had changed. Margaret was standing at the stove over a frying pan, her back to them.

'Margaret, this is our guest I spoke of – Mr Travis.'

Margaret turned. 'How do you do?'

There was not a flicker of recognition.

'I'm pleased to meet you,' Jamie nodded.

The customer bell rang and Van der Merwe said, 'Excuse me, I'll be right back. Please make yourself at home, Mr Travis.' He hurried out.

Margaret carried a steaming bowl of vegetables and meat over to the table, and as she hurried to take the bread from the oven Jamie stood there, silently looking at her. She had blossomed in the year since he had seen her. She had become a woman, with a smouldering sexuality that had been lacking before.

'Your father tells me you're an excellent cook.'

Margaret blushed. 'I – I hope so, sir.'

'It's been a long time since I've tasted home cooking. I'm looking forward to this.' Jamie took a large butter dish from Margaret and placed it on the table for her. Margaret was so surprised she almost dropped the plate in her hands. She had never heard of a man who helped in woman's work. She lifted her startled eyes to his face. A broken nose and a scar spoiled what would otherwise have been a too-handsome face. His eyes were light grey and shone with intelligence and a burning intensity. His white hair told her that he was not a young man, and yet there was something very youthful about him. He was tall and strong and – Margaret turned away, embarrassed by his gaze.

Van der Merwe hurried back into the room, rubbing his hands. 'I've closed the shop,' he said. 'Let's sit down and have a fine dinner.'

Jamie was given the place of honour at the table. 'We'll say grace,' Van der Merwe said.

They closed their eyes. Margaret slyly opened hers again, so that she could continue her scrutiny of the elegant stranger while her father's voice droned on. 'We are all sinners in your eyes, O Lord, and must be punished. Give us the strength to bear our hardships on this earth, so that we may enjoy the fruits of heaven when we are called. Thank you, Lord, for helping those of us who deserve to prosper. Amen.'

Salomon van der Merwe began serving. This time the portions he served Jamie were more than generous. They talked as they ate. 'Is this your first time out this way, Mr Travis?'

'Yes,' Jamie said. 'First time.'

'You didn't bring Mrs Travis along, I understand.'

'There is no Mrs Travis. I haven't found anyone who'd have me.' Jamie smiled.

What fool of a woman would refuse him? Margaret wondered. She lowered her eyes, afraid the stranger might read her wicked thoughts.

'Klipdrift is a town of great opportunity, Mr Travis. *Great* opportunity.'

'I'm willing to be shown.' He looked at Margaret, and she blushed.

'If it isn't too personal, Mr Travis, may I ask how you acquired your fortune?'

Margaret was embarrassed by her father's blunt questions, but the stranger did not seem to mind.

'I inherited it from my father,' James said easily.

'Ah, but I'm sure you've had a lot of business experience.'

'Very little, I'm afraid. I need a lot of guidance.'

Van der Merwe brightened. 'It's fate that we met, Mr Travis. I have some very profitable connections. Very profitable, indeed. I can almost guarantee that I can double your money for you in just a few months.' He leaned over and patted Jamie's arm. 'I have a feeling this is a big day for both of us.'

Jamie just smiled.

'I suppose you're staying at the Grand Hotel?'

'That's right.'

'It's criminally expensive. But I suppose to a man of your means.' He beamed at Jamie.

Jamie said, 'I'm told the countryside around here is interesting. Would it be an imposition to ask you

125

to let your daughter show me around a bit tomorrow?'

Margaret felt her heart stop for a second.

Van der Merwe frowned. 'I don't know. She –'

It was an iron-clad rule of Salomon van der Merwe's never to permit any man to be alone with his daughter. In the case of Mr Travis, however, he decided there would be no harm in making an exception. With so much at stake, he did not want to appear inhospitable. 'I can spare Margaret from the store for a short time. You will show our guest around, Margaret?'

'If you wish, Father,' she said quietly.

'That's settled then.' Jamie smiled. 'Shall we say ten o'clock in the morning?'

After the tall, elegantly dressed guest left, Margaret cleared away the table and washed the dishes, in a complete daze. *He must think I'm an idiot.* She went over and over in her mind everything she had contributed to the conversation. Nothing. She had been completely tongue-tied. Why was that? Hadn't she waited on hundreds of men in the store without becoming a stupid fool? Of course they had not looked at her the way Ian Travis had. *Men all have the devil in them, Margaret. I'll not let them corrupt your innocence.* Her father's voice echoed in her mind. Could that be it? The weakness and trembling she had felt when the stranger had looked at her? Was he corrupting her innocence? The thought of it sent a delicious thrill through her body. She looked down at the plate she had dried three times and sat down at the table. She wished her mother were still alive.

Her mother would have understood. Margaret loved her father, but sometimes she had the oppressive feeling that she was his prisoner. It worried her that he never allowed a man to come near her. *I'll never get married*, Margaret thought. *Not until he dies.* Her rebellious thoughts filled her with guilt, and she hurriedly left the room and went into the store, where her father sat behind a desk, working on his accounts.

'Good night, Father.'

Van der Merwe took off his gold-framed spectacles and rubbed his eyes before he raised his arms to embrace his daughter good night. Margaret did not know why she pulled away.

Alone in the curtained-off alcove that served as her bedroom, Margaret studied her face in the small, round mirror that hung on the wall. She had no illusions about her looks. She was not pretty. She was interesting-looking. Nice eyes. High cheekbones. A good figure. She drew nearer to the mirror. What had Ian Travis seen when he looked at her? She began getting undressed. And Ian Travis was in the room with her, watching her, his eyes burning into her. She stepped out of her muslin drawers and camisole and stood naked before him. Her hands slowly caressed the swell of her breasts and felt her hardening nipples. Her fingers slid down across her flat belly and his hands became entwined with hers, moving slowly downward. They were between her legs now, gently touching, stroking, rubbing, harder now, faster and faster until she was caught up in a frantic whirlpool of sensation that finally exploded inside her and she gasped his name and fell to the bed.

They rode out in Jamie's carriage, and he was amazed once more at the changes that had taken place. Where before there had been only a sea of tents, now there were substantial-looking houses, constructed of timber with roofs of corrugated iron or thatch.

'Klipdrift seems very prosperous,' Jamie said as they rode along the main street.

'I suppose it would be interesting for a newcomer,' Margaret said. And she thought, *I've hated it until now.*

They left the town and drove out towards the mining camps along the Vaal River. The seasonal rains had turned the countryside into an enormous, colourful garden, filled with the luxuriant bush Karroo, and the spreading Rhenoster bush and heaths and diosmas plants that could be found nowhere else in the world. As they drove past a group of prospectors, Jamie asked, 'Have there been any big diamond finds lately?'

'Oh, yes, a few. Every time the news gets out, hundreds of new diggers come pouring in. Most of them leave poor and heartbroken. Margaret felt she had to warn him of the danger here. 'Father would not like to hear me say this, but I think it's a terrible business, Mr Travis.'

'For some, probably,' Jamie agreed. 'For some.'

'Do you plan to stay on a while?'

'Yes.'

Margaret felt her heart singing. 'Good.' Then added quickly, 'Father will be pleased.'

They drove around all morning, and from time to time they stopped and Jamie chatted with prospectors. Many of them recognized Margaret and spoke respectfully. There was a warmth to her and an easy friendliness that she did not reveal when she was around her father.

As they drove on, Jamie said, 'Everyone seems to know you.'

She blushed. 'That's because they do business with Father. He supplies most of the diggers.'

Jamie made no comment. He was keenly interested in what he was seeing. The railroad had made an enormous difference. A new combine called De Beers, named after the farmer in whose field the first diamond discovery was made, had bought out its chief rival, a colourful entrepreneur named Barney Barnato, and De Beers was busily consolidating the hundreds of small claims into one organization. Gold had been discovered recently, not far from Kimberley, along with manganese and zinc. Jamie was convinced this was only the beginning, that South Africa was a treasure-house of minerals. There were incredible opportunities here for a man with foresight.

When Jamie and Margaret returned, it was late afternoon. Jamie stopped the carriage in front of Van der Merwe's store and said, 'I would be honoured if you and your father would be my guests at dinner tonight.'

Margaret glowed. 'I'll ask Father. I do so hope he'll say yes. Thank you for a lovely day, Mr Travis.'

And she fled.

The three of them had dinner in the large, square dining room of the new Grand Hotel.

The room was crowded, and Van der Merwe grumbled, 'I don't see how these people can afford to eat here.'

Jamie picked up a menu and glanced at it. A steak cost one pound four shillings, a potato was four shillings and a piece of apple pie ten shillings.

'They're robbers!' Van der Merwe complained. 'A few meals here and a man could eat himself into the poorhouse.'

Jamie wondered what it would take to put Salomon van der Merwe in the poorhouse. He intended to find out. They ordered, and Jamie noticed that Van der Merwe ordered the most expensive items on the menu. Margaret ordered a clear soup. She was too excited to eat. She looked at her hands, remembered what they had done the night before and felt guilty.

'I can afford dinner,' Jamie teased her. 'Order anything you like.'

She blushed. 'Thank you, but I'm – I'm not really very hungry.'

Van der Merwe noticed the blush and looked sharply from Margaret to Jamie. 'My daughter is a rare girl, a rare girl, Mr Travis.'

Jamie nodded. 'I couldn't agree with you more, Mr van der Merwe.'

His words made Margaret so happy that when their dinner was served, she could not even eat the soup. The affect Ian Travis had on her was incredible. She read hidden meanings into his every word and gesture. If he smiled at her, it meant he liked her a lot; if he frowned, it meant he hated her. Margaret's feelings were an emotional thermometer that kept going up and down.

'Did you see anything of interest today?' Van der Merwe asked Jamie.

'No, nothing special,' Jamie said casually.

Van der Merwe leaned forwards. 'Mark my words, sir, this is going to be the fastest-growing area in the world. A man would be smart to invest here now. The new railway's going to turn this place into a second Cape Town.'

'I don't know,' Jamie said dubiously. 'I've heard of too many boomtowns like this going bust. I'm not interested in putting my money into a ghost town.'

'Not Klipdrift,' Van der Merwe assured him. 'They're finding more diamonds all the time. And gold.'

131

Jamie shrugged. 'How long will that last?'

'Well, nobody can be sure of that, of course, but –'

'Exactly.'

'Don't make any hasty decisions,' Van der Merwe urged. 'I wouldn't like to see you lose out on a great opportunity.'

Jamie thought that over, 'Perhaps I am being hasty. Margaret, could you show me around again tomorrow?'

Van der Merwe opened his mouth to object, then closed it. He remembered the words of Mr Thorenson, the banker: *He walked in here and deposited a hundred thousand pounds, cool as you please, Salomon, and he said there'd be a lot more comin'.*

Greed got the better of Van der Merwe. 'Of course she could.'

The following morning, Margaret put on her Sunday dress, ready to meet Jamie. When her father walked in and saw her, his face turned red. 'Do you want the man to think you're some kind of fallen woman – dressin' up to attract him? This is business, girl. Take that off and put on your workin' clothes.'

'But, Papa –'

'Do as I say!'

She did not argue with him. 'Yes, Papa.'

* * *

132

Van der Merwe watched Margaret and Jamie drive away twenty minutes later. He wondered if he could be making a mistake.

This time Jamie headed the carriage in the opposite direction. There were exciting signs of new developments and building everywhere. *If the mineral discoveries keep up*, Jamie thought – and there was every reason to believe they would – *there is more money to be made here in real estate than in diamonds or gold. Klipdrift will need more banks, hotels, saloons, shops, brothels* . . . The list was endless. So were the opportunities.

Jamie was conscious of Margaret staring at him. 'Is something wrong?' he asked.

'Oh, no,' she said, and quickly looked away.

Jamie studied her now, and noticed the radiance about her. Margaret was aware of his closeness, his maleness. He sensed her feelings. She was a woman without a man.

At noon Jamie drove off the main road down to a wooded area near a stream and stopped under a large baobab tree. He had had the hotel pack a picnic lunch. Margaret put down a tablecloth, unpacked the basket and spread out the food. There was cold roast lamb, fried chicken, yellow saffron rice, quince jam and tangerines and peaches and *soetekoekjes*, almond-topped spice cookies.

'This is a banquet!' Margaret exclaimed. 'I'm afraid I don't deserve all this, Mr Travis.'

'You deserve much more,' Jamie assured her.

Margaret turned away, busying herself with the food.

Jamie took her face between his hands. 'Margaret . . . look at me.'

'Oh! Please. I –' She was trembling.

'Look at me.'

Slowly she lifted her head and looked into his eyes. He pulled her into his arms, and his lips found hers and he held her close, pressing his body against hers.

After a few moments she struggled free, shook her head and said, 'Oh, my God. We mustn't. Oh, we mustn't. We'll go to hell.'

'Heaven.'

'I'm afraid.'

'There's nothing to be afraid of. Do you see my eyes? They can look right inside you. And you know what I see, don't you? You want me to make love to you. And I'm going to. And there's nothing to fear, because you belong to me. You know that, don't you? You belong to me, Margaret. You say it. I belong to Ian. Go on. I – belong – to – Ian.'

'I belong – to Ian.'

His lips were on hers again, and he began to undo the hooks on the back of her bodice. In a moment she stood naked in the soft breeze, and he lowered her gently down to the ground. And the tremulous passage from girlhood to womanhood became an exciting, soaring experience that made Margaret feel more alive than she had ever felt in her life. *I'll remember this moment forever*, she thought. The bed of leaves and the warm caressing breeze on her naked skin, the shadow of the baobab tree that dappled their bodies. They made love again, and it was even more wonderful. She thought, *No woman could ever love anyone as much as I love this man.*

When they were spent, Jamie held her in his strong arms, and she wished she could be there forever. She looked up at him and whispered, 'What are you thinking?'

He grinned and whispered back, 'That I'm bloody starving.'

She laughed, and they rose and had their lunch under the shelter of the trees. Afterwards they swam and lay down to let the hot sun dry them. Jamie took Margaret again, and she thought, *I want this day to go on forever.*

That evening, Jamie and Van der Merwe were seated at a corner table at the Sundowner. 'You were right,' Jamie announced. 'The possibilities here may be greater than I thought.'

Van der Merwe beamed. 'I knew you were too clever a man not to see that, Mr Travis.'

'What exactly would you advise me to do?' Jamie asked.

Van der Merwe glanced around and lowered his voice. 'Just today I got some information on a big new diamond strike north of Pniel. There are ten

135

claims still available. We can divide them up between us. I'll put up fifty thousand pounds for five claims, and you put up fifty thousand pounds for the other five. There are diamonds there by the bushel. We can make millions overnight. What do you think?'

Jamie knew exactly what he thought. Van der Merwe would keep the claims that were profitable and Jamie would end up with the others. In addition, Jamie would have been willing to bet his life that Van der Merwe was not putting up one shilling.

'It sounds interesting,' Jamie said. 'How many prospectors are involved?'

'Only two.'

'Why does it take so much money?' he asked innocently.

'Ah, that's an intelligent question.' He leaned forwards in his chair. 'You see, they know the value of their claim, but they don't have the money to operate it. That's where you and I come in. We give them one hundred thousand pounds and let them keep twenty percent of their fields.

He slipped the twenty percent in so smoothly that it almost went by unnoticed. Jamie was certain the prospectors would be cheated of their diamonds and their money. It would all flow to Van der Merwe.

'We'll have to move fast,' Van der Merwe warned. 'As soon as word of this leaks out –'

'Let's not lose it,' Jamie urged.

Van der Merwe smiled. 'Don't worry, I'll have the contracts drawn up right away.'

In Afrikaans, Jamie thought.

'Now, there are a few other deals I find very interesting, Ian.'

Because it was important to keep his new partner happy, Van der Merwe no longer objected when Jamie asked that Margaret show him around the countryside. Margaret was more in love with Jamie every day. He was the last thing she thought of when she went to bed at night, and the first thing she thought of when she opened her eyes in the morning. Jamie had loosed a sensuality in her that she had not even known existed. It was as though she had suddenly discovered what her body was for, and all the things she had been taught to be ashamed of became glorious gifts to bring pleasure to Jamie. And to herself. Love was a wonderful new country to be explored. A sensual land of hidden valleys and exciting dales and glens and rivers of honey. She could not get enough of it.

In the vast sweep of the countryside, it was easy to find isolated places where they could make love, and each time for Margaret was as exciting as the first time.

The old guilt about her father haunted her. Salomon van der Merwe was an elder of the Dutch Reformed Church, and Margaret knew if he ever found out what she was doing, there would be no forgiveness. Even in the rough frontier community where they lived, where men took their pleasures where they found them, there would be no understanding. There were only two kinds of women in the world – nice girls and whores – and a nice girl did not let a man touch her unless she was married to him. So she would be labelled a whore. *It's so unfair*, she thought. *The giving and taking of love is too beautiful to be evil.* But her growing concern finally made Margaret bring up the subject of marriage.

They were driving along the Vaal River when Margaret spoke. 'Ian, you know how much I –' She did not know how to go on. 'That is, you and I –' In desperation she blurted out, 'How do you feel about marriage?'

Jamie laughed. 'I'm all for it, Margaret. I'm all for it.'

She joined him in his laughter. It was the happiest moment of her life.

On Sunday morning, Salomon van der Merwe invited Jamie to accompany him and Margaret to church. The Nederduits Hervormde Kerk was a large, impressive building done in bastard Gothic, with the pulpit at one end and a huge organ at the other. When they walked in the door, Van der Merwe was greeted with great respect.

'I helped build this church,' he told Jamie proudly. 'I'm a deacon here.'

The service was brimstone and hellfire, and Van

der Merwe sat there, rapt, nodding eagerly, accepting the minister's every word.

He's God's man on Sunday, Jamie thought, *and the rest of the week he belongs to the devil.*

Van der Merwe had placed himself between the two young people, but Margaret was conscious of Jamie's nearness all through the service. *It's a good thing* – she smiled nervously to herself – *that the minister doesn't know what I'm thinking about.*

That evening, Jamie went to visit the Sundowner Saloon. Smit was behind the bar serving drinks. His face brightened when he saw Jamie.

'Good evenin', Mr Travis. What will you have, sir? The usual?'

'Not tonight, Smit. I want to talk to you. In the back room.'

'Certainly, sir.' Smit scented money to be made. He turned to his assistant. 'Mind the bar.'

The back room of the Sundowner was no more than a closet, but it afforded privacy. It contained a round table with four chairs, and in the centre of the table was a lantern. Smit lit it.

'Sit down,' Jamie said.

Smit took a chair. 'Yes, sir. How can I help you?'

'It's you I've come to help, Smit.'

Smit beamed. 'Really, sir?'

'Yes.' Jamie took out a long, thin cigar and lighted it. 'I've decided to let you live.'

An uncertain look flickered over Smit's face. 'I – I don't understand, Mr Travis.'

'Not Travis. The name is McGregor. Jamie McGregor. Remember? A year ago you set me up to be killed. At the barn. For Van der Merwe.'

Smit was frowning now, suddenly wary. 'I don't know what –'

'Shut up and listen to me.' Jamie's voice was like whiplash.

Jamie could see the wheels turning in Smit's mind. He was trying to reconcile the face of the white-haired man in front of him with the eager youth of a year before.

'I'm still alive, and I'm rich – rich enough to hire men to burn this place down and you with it. Are you with me so far, Smit?'

Smit started to protest his ignorance, but he looked into Jamie McGregor's eyes and saw the danger there. Smit said cautiously. 'Yes, sir . . .'

'Van der Merwe pays you to send prospectors to him so he can cheat them out of what they find. That's an interesting little partnership. How much does he pay you?'

There was a silence. Smit was caught between two powerful forces. He did not know which way to jump.

'How much?'

'Two percent,' he said reluctantly.

'I'll give you five. From now on when a likely prospect comes in, you'll send him to me. I'll finance him. The difference is that he'll get his fair share and you'll get yours. Did you really think

Van der Merwe was paying you two percent of what he made? You're a fool.'

Smit nodded. 'Right, Mr Trav – Mr McGregor. I understand.'

Jamie rose to his feet. 'Not completely.' He leaned over the table. 'You're thinking of going to Van der Merwe and telling him about our little conversation. That way, you can collect from both of us. There's only one problem with that, Smit.' His voice dropped to a whisper. 'If you do, you're a dead man.'

SEVEN

Jamie was getting dressed when he heard a tentative knock at the door. He listened, and it was repeated. He walked over to the door and opened it. Margaret stood there.

'Come in, Maggie,' Jamie said. 'Is something wrong?' It was the first time she had come to his hotel room. She stepped inside, but now that she was face to face with him, she found it difficult to speak. She had lain awake all night, wondering how to tell him the news. She was afraid he might never want to see her again.

She looked into his eyes. 'Ian, I'm going to have your baby.'

His face was so still that Margaret was terrified that she had lost him. And suddenly his expression changed to such joy that all her doubts were instantly wiped out. He grabbed her arms and said, 'That's wonderful, Maggie! Wonderful! Have you told your father?'

Margaret pulled back in alarm. 'Oh, no! He –'

She walked over to the Victoria green-plush sofa and sat down. 'You don't know Father. He – he would never understand.'

Jamie was hurriedly putting on his shirt. 'Come on, we're going to tell him together.'

'Are you sure everything will be all right, Ian?'

'I've never been surer of anything in my life.'

Salomon van der Merwe was measuring out strips of biltong for a prospector when Jamie and Margaret strode into the shop. 'Ah, Ian! I'll be with you in a moment.' He hurriedly finished with the customer and walked over to Jamie. 'And how is everything this fine day?' Van der Merwe asked.

'It couldn't be better,' Jamie said happily. 'Your Maggie's going to have a baby.'

There was a sudden stillness in the air. 'I – I don't understand,' Van der Merwe stuttered.

'It's very simple. I've gotten her pregnant.'

The colour drained from Van der Merwe's face. He turned wildly from one to the other. 'This – this isn't true?' A maelstrom of conflicting emotions whirled through Salomon van der Merwe's head. The terrible shock of his precious daughter losing her virginity . . . getting pregnant . . . He would be the laughing stock of the town. But Ian Travis was a very wealthy man. And if they got married quickly . . .

Van der Merwe turned to Jamie. 'You'll get married immediately, of course.'

Jamie looked at him in surprise. '*Married?* You'd

allow Maggie to marry a stupid bairn who let you cheat him out of what belonged to him?'

Van der Merwe's head was spinning. 'What are you talking about, Ian? I never –'

'My name's not Ian,' Jamie said harshly. 'I'm Jamie McGregor. Dinna you recognize me?' He saw the bewildered expression on Van der Merwe's face. 'Nae, a course you don't. That boy is dead. You killed him. But I'm not a man to hold a grudge, Van der Merwe. So I'm giving you a gift. My seed in your daughter's belly.'

And Jamie turned and walked out, leaving the two of them staring after him, stunned.

Margaret had listened in shocked disbelief. He could not mean what he had just said. *He loved her!* He –

Salomon van der Merwe turned on his daughter, in the throes of a terrible rage. 'You whore!' he screamed. '*Whore! Get out! Get out of here!*'

Margaret stood stock-still, unable to grasp the meaning of the awful thing that was happening. Ian blamed her for something her father had done. Ian thought she was part of something bad. *Who was Jamie McGregor? Who –?*

'Go!' Van der Merwe hit her hard across the face. 'I never want to see you again as long as I live.'

Margaret stood there, rooted, her heart pounding, gasping for breath. Her father's face was that of a madman. She turned and fled from the store, not looking back.

* * *

144

Salomon van der Merwe stood there watching her go, gripped by despair. He had seen what happened to other men's daughters who had disgraced themselves. They had been forced to stand up in church and be publicly pilloried and then exiled from the community. It was proper and fitting punishment, exactly what they deserved. But his Margaret had been given a decent, God-fearing upbringing. *How could she have betrayed him like this?* Van der Merwe visualized his daughter's naked body, coupling with that man, writhing in heat like animals, and he began to have an erection.

He put a Closed sign on the front door of the store and lay on his bed without the strength or the will to move. When word got around town, he would become an object of derision. He would be either pitied or blamed for his daughter's depravity. Either way, it would be unbearable. He had to make certain no one learned about it. He would send the whore out of his sight forever. He knelt and prayed: *O, God! How could you do this to me, your loyal servant? Why have you forsaken me? Let her die, O Lord. Let them both die . . .*

The Sundowners Saloon was crowded with noon trade when Jamie entered. He walked over to the bar and turned to face the room. 'Your attention, please!' The conversation tapered off into silence. 'Drinks on the house for everybody.'

'What is it?' Smit asked. 'A new strike?'

Jamie laughed. 'In a way, my friend. Salomon

van der Merwe's unmarried daughter is pregnant. Mr van der Merwe wants everybody to help him celebrate.'

Smit whispered, 'Oh, Jesus!'

'Jesus had nothing to do with it. Just Jamie McGregor.'

Within an hour, everyone in Klipdrift had heard the news. How Ian Travis was really Jamie McGregor, and how he had gotten Van der Merwe's daughter pregnant. Margaret van der Merwe had fooled the whole town.

'She doesn't look like the kind, does she?'

'Still waters run deep, they say.'

'I wonder how many other men in this town have dipped their wick in that well?'

'She's a shapely girl. I could use a piece of that myself.'

'Why don't you ask her? She's givin' it away.'

And the men laughed.

When Salomon van der Merwe left his store that afternoon, he had come to terms with the dreadful catastrophe that had befallen him. He would send Margaret to Cape Town on the next coach. She could have her bastard there, and there was no need for anyone in Klipdrift to know his shame. Van der Merwe stepped out into the street, hugging his secret, a smile pasted on his lips.

'Afternoon, Mr van der Merwe. I hear you might be stockin' some extra baby clothes.'

'Good day, Salomon. Hear you're gonna get a little helper for your store soon.'

'Hello there, Salomon. I hear a bird watcher just spotted a new species out near the Vaal River. Yes, sir, a stork!'

Salomon van der Merwe turned and blindly stumbled back into his shop, bolting the door behind him.

At the Sundowner Saloon, Jamie was having a whiskey, listening to the flood of gossip around him. It was the biggest scandal Klipdrift had ever had, and the pleasure of the townspeople took in it was intense. *I wish*, Jamie thought, *that Banda were here with me to enjoy this*. This was payment for what Salomon van der Merwe had done to Banda's sister, what he had done to Jamie and to – how many others? But this was only part payment for all the things Salomon van der Merwe had done, just the beginning. Jamie's vengeance would not be complete until Van der Merwe had been totally destroyed. As for Margaret, he had no sympathy for her. She was in on it. What had she said the first day they met? *My father might be the one to help you. He knows everything*. She was a Van der Merwe too, and Jamie would destroy both of them.

Smit walked over to where Jamie was sitting. 'Kin I talk to you a minute, Mr McGregor?'

'What is it?'

Smit cleared his throat self-consciously. 'I know

a couple of prospectors who have ten claims up near Pniel. They're producin' diamonds, but these fellas don't have the money to get the proper equipment to work their claim. They're lookin' for a partner. I thought you might be interested.'

Jamie studied him. 'These are the men you talked to Van der Merwe about, right?'

Smit nodded, surprised. 'Yes, sir. But I been thinkin' over your proposition. I'd rather do business with you.'

Jamie pulled out a long, thin cigar, and Smit hastened to light it. 'Keep talking.'

Smit did.

In the beginning, prostitution in Klipdrift was on a haphazard basis. The prostitutes were mostly black women, working in sleazy, back-street brothels. The first white prostitutes to arrive in town were part-time barmaids. But as diamond strikes increased and the town prospered, more white prostitutes appeared.

There were now half a dozen sporting houses on the outskirts of Klipdrift, wooden railway huts with tin roofs. The one exception was Madam Agnes's, a respectable-looking two-storey frame structure on Bree Street, off Loop Street, the main thoroughfare, where the wives of the townspeople would not be offended by having to pass in front of it. It was patronized by the husbands of those wives, and by any strangers in town who could afford it. It was expensive, but the women were young and uninhibited, and gave good value for the money. Drinks were served in a reasonably well-decorated drawing room, and it was a rule of Madam Agnes's that no customer was ever rushed or short-changed. Madam Agnes herself was a cheerful, robust redhead in her mid-thirties. She had worked at a brothel in London and been attracted to South Africa by the tales of easy money to be picked up in a mining town like Klipdrift. She had saved enough to open her own establishment, and business had flourished from the beginning.

Madam Agnes prided herself on her understanding of men, but Jamie McGregor was a puzzle to her. He visited often, spent money freely and was always pleasant to the women, but he seemed withdrawn, remote and untouchable. His eyes were what fascinated Agnes. They were pale, bottomless pools, cold. Unlike the other patrons of her house, he never spoke about himself or his past. Madam Agnes had heard hours earlier that Jamie McGregor had deliberately gotten Salomon van der Merwe's daughter pregnant and then refused to marry her. *The bastard!* Madam Agnes thought. But she had to admit that he was an attractive bastard. She watched Jamie now as he walked down the red-carpeted stairs, politely said good night and left.

When Jamie arrived back at his hotel, Margaret was in his room, staring out of the window. She turned as Jamie walked in.

'Hello, Jamie.' Her voice was atremble.

'What are you doing here?'

'I had to talk to you.'

'We have nothing to talk about.'

'I know why you're doing this. You hate my father.' Margaret moved closer to him. 'But you have to know that whatever it was he did to you, I knew nothing about. Please – I beg of you – believe that. Don't hate me. I love you too much.'

Jamie looked at her coldly. 'That's *your* problem, isn't it?'

'Please don't look at me like that. You love me, too . . .'

He was not listening. He was again taking the terrible journey to Paardspan where he had almost died . . . and moving the boulders on the river-banks until he was ready to drop . . . and finally, miraculously, finding the diamonds . . . Handing them to Van der Merwe and hearing Van der Merwe's voice saying, *You misunderstood me, boy. I don't need any partners. You're working for me. . . . I'm giving you twenty-four hours to get out of town.* And then the savage beating . . . He was smelling the vultures again, feeling their sharp beaks tear into his flesh . . .

As though from a distance, he heard Margaret's voice. 'Don't you remember? I – belong – to – you . . . I love you.'

He shook himself out of his reverie and looked at her. *Love.* He no longer had any idea what the word meant. Van der Merwe had burned every emotion out of him except hate. He lived on that. It was his elixir, his lifeblood. It was what had kept him alive when he fought the sharks and crossed the reef, and crawled over the mines at the diamond fields of the Namib Desert. Poets wrote about love, and singers sang about it, and perhaps it was real, perhaps it existed. But love was for other men. Not for Jamie McGregor.

'You're Salomon van der Merwe's daughter. You're carrying his grandchild in your belly. Get out.'

There was nowhere for Margaret to go. She loved her father, and she needed his forgiveness, but she knew he would never – could never – forgive her. He would make her life a living hell. But she had no choice. She had to go to someone.

Margaret left the hotel and walked towards her father's store. She felt that everyone she passed was staring at her. Some of the men smiled insinuatingly, and she held her head high and walked on. When she reached the store, she hesitated, then stepped inside. The store was deserted. Her father came out from the back.

'Father . . .'

'*You!*' The contempt in his voice was a physical slap. He moved closer, and she could smell the whiskey on his breath. 'I want you to get out of this town. Now. Tonight. You're never to come near here again. Do you hear me? Never!' He pulled some bills from his pocket and threw them on the floor. 'Take them and get out.'

'I'm carrying your grandchild.'

'You're carrying the devil's child!' He moved closer to her, and his hands were knotted into fists. 'Every time people see you strutting around like a whore, they'll think of my shame. When you're gone, they'll forget it.'

She looked at him for a long, lost moment, then turned and blindly stumbled out the door.

'The money, whore!' he yelled. 'You forgot the money!'

There was a cheap boardinghouse at the outskirts of town, and Margaret made her way to it, her mind in a turmoil. When she reached it, she went looking for Mrs Owens, the landlady. Mrs Owens was a plump, pleasant-faced women in her fifties, whose husband had brought her to Klipdrift and abandoned her. A lesser woman would have crumbled, but Mrs Owens was a survivor. She had seen a good many people in trouble in this town, but never anyone in more trouble than the seventeen-year-old girl who stood before her now.

'You wanted to see me?'

'Yes. I was wondering if – if perhaps you had a job for me here.'

'A job? Doing what?'

'Anything. I'm a good cook. I can wait on tables. I'll make the beds. I – I'll –' There was desperation in her voice. 'Oh, please,' she begged. 'Anything!'

Mrs Owens looked at the trembling girl standing

there in front of her, and it broke her heart. 'I suppose I could use an extra hand. How soon can you start?' She could see the relief that lighted Margaret's face.

'Now.'

'I can pay you only –' She thought of a figure and added to it. 'One pound two shilling eleven pence a month, with board and lodging.'

'That will be fine,' Margaret said gratefully.

Salomon van der Merwe seldom appeared now on the streets of Klipdrift. More and more often, his customers found a Closed sign on the front door of his store at all hours of the day. After a while, they took their business elsewhere.

But Salomon van der Merwe still went to church every Sunday. He went not to pray, but to demand of God that He right this terrible iniquity that had been heaped upon the shoulders of his obedient servant. The other parishioners had always looked up to Salomon van der Merwe with the respect due a wealthy and powerful man, but now he could feel the stares and whispers behind his back. The family that occupied the pew next to him moved to another pew. He was a pariah. What broke his spirit completely was the minister's thundering sermon artfully combining Exodus and Ezekiel and Leviticus. 'I, the Lord thy God, am a jealous God, visiting the iniquity of the fathers upon the children. Wherefor, O harlot, hear the word of the Lord. Because thy filthiness was poured out, and thy nakedness discovered through thy whoredomes with thy lovers . . . And the Lord spake unto Moses, saying, 'Do not prostitute thy daughter, to cause her to be a whore; lest the land fall to whoredom and the land become full of wickedness . . .'

Van der Merwe never set foot in church again after that Sunday.

As Salomon van der Merwe's business deteriorated, Jamie McGregor's prospered. The expense of mining for diamonds increased as the digging got deeper, and miners with working claims found they were unable to afford the elaborate equipment needed. The word quickly spread that Jamie McGregor would provide financing in exchange for a share in the mines, and in time Jamie bought out his partners. He invested in real estate and businesses and gold. He was meticulously honest in his dealings, and as his reputation spread, more people came to him to do business.

There were two banks in town, and when one of them failed because of inept management, Jamie bought it, putting in his own people and keeping his name out of the transaction.

Everything Jamie touched seemed to prosper. He was successful and wealthy beyond his boyhood dreams, but it meant little to him. He measured his successes only by Salomon van der Merwe's failures. His revenge had still only begun.

From time to time, Jamie passed Margaret on the street. He took no notice of her.

Jamie had no idea what those chance encounters did to Margaret. The sight of him took her breath away, and she had to stop until she regained control of herself. She still loved him, completely and utterly. Nothing could ever change that. He had used her body to punish her father, but Margaret knew that that could be a double-edged sword. Soon she would have Jamie's baby, and when he saw that baby, his own flesh and blood, he would marry her and give his child a name. Margaret would become Mrs Jamie McGregor, and she asked nothing more from life. At night before Margaret went to sleep, she would touch her swollen belly and whisper, 'Our son.' It was probably foolish to think she could influence its sex, but she did not want to overlook any possibility. Every man wanted a son.

As her womb swelled, Margaret became more frightened. She wished she had someone to talk to. But the women of the town did not speak to her. Their religion taught them punishment, not forgiveness. She was alone, surrounded by strangers, and she wept in the night for herself and for her unborn baby.

Jamie McGregor had bought a two-story building in the heart of Klipdrift, and he used it as headquarters for his growing enterprises. One day, Harry McMillan, Jamie's chief accountant, had a talk with him.

'We're combining your companies,' he told Jamie, 'and we need a corporate name. Do you have any suggestions?'

'I'll think about it.'

Jamie thought about it. In his mind he kept hearing the sound of long-ago echoes piercing the sea *mis* on the diamond field in the Namib Desert, and he knew there was only one name he wanted. He summoned the accountant. 'We're going to call the new company Kruger-Brent. Kruger-Brent Limited.'

Alvin Cory, Jamie's bank manager, stopped in to visit him. 'It's about Mr van der Merwe's loans,' he said. 'He's fallen very far behind. In the past he's been a good risk, but his situation has drastically changed, Mr McGregor. I think we should call in his loans.'

'No.'

Cory looked at Jamie in surprise. 'He came in this morning trying to borrow more money to –'

'Give it to him. Give him everything he wants.'

The manager got to his feet. 'Whatever you say, Mr McGregor. I'll tell him that you –'

'Tell him nothing. Just give him the money.'

Every morning Margaret arose at five o'clock to bake large loaves of wonderful-smelling bread and sourdough biscuits, and when the boarders trooped into the dining room for breakfast, she served them porridge and ham and eggs, buckwheat cakes, sweet rolls and pots of steaming coffee and *naartje*. The majority of the guests at the boardinghouse were prospectors on their way to and from their claims. They would stop off in

Klipdrift long enough to have their diamonds appraised, have a bath, get drunk and visit one of the town's brothels – usually in that order. They were for the most part rough, illiterate adventurers.

There was an unwritten law in Klipdrift that nice women were not to be molested. If a man wanted sex, he went to a whore. Margaret van der Merwe, however, was a challenge, for she fitted into neither category. Nice girls who were single did not get pregnant, and the theory went that since Margaret had fallen once, she was probably eager to bed everyone else. All they had to do was ask. They did.

Some of the prospectors were open and blatant; others were leering and furtive. Margaret handled them all with quiet dignity. But one night as Mrs Owens was preparing for bed, she heard screams coming from Margaret's room at the back of the house. The landlady flung the door open and rushed in. One of the guests, a drunken prospector, had ripped off Margaret's nightgown and had her pinned down on the bed.

Mrs Owens was on him like a tiger. She picked up a flatiron and began hitting him with it. She was half the size of the prospector, but it made no difference. Filled with an overpowering rage, she knocked the prospector unconscious and dragged him into the hallway and out to the street. Then she turned and hurried back to Margaret's room, Margaret was wiping the blood off her lips from where the man had bitten her. Her hands were trembling.

'Are you all right, Maggie?'

'Yes. I – thank you, Mrs Owens.'

Unbidden tears sprang into Margaret's eyes. In a town where few people even spoke to her, here was someone who had shown kindness.

Mrs Owens studied Margaret's swollen belly and thought, *The poor dreamer. Jamie McGregor will never marry her.*

The time of confinement was drawing close. Margaret tired easily now, and bending down and getting up again was an effort. Her only joy was when she felt her baby stir inside her. She and her son were completely alone in the world, and she talked to him hour after hour, telling him all the wonderful things that life had in store for him.

Late one evening, shortly after supper, a young black boy appeared at the boardinghouse and handed Margaret a sealed letter.

'I'm to wait for an answer,' the boy told her.

Margaret read the letter, then read it again, very slowly. 'Yes,' she said. 'The answer is yes.'

The following Friday, promptly at noon, Margaret arrived in front of Madam Agnes's bordello. A sign on the front door read Closed. Margaret rapped tentatively on the door, ignoring the startled glances of the passers-by. She wondered if she had made a mistake by coming here. It had been a difficult decision, and she had accepted only out of a terrible loneliness. The letter had read:

Dear Miss van der Merwe:

It's none of my business, but my girls and me have been discussing your unfortunate and unfair situation, and we think it's a damned shame. We would like to help you and your baby. If it would not embarrass you, we would be honoured to have you come to lunch. Would Friday at noon be convenient?

Respectfully yours,
Madam Agnes

P.S. We would be very discreet.

Margaret was debating whether to leave, when the door was opened by Madam Agnes.

She took Margaret's arm and said, 'Come in, dearie. Let's get you out of this damned heat.'

She led her into the parlour, furnished with Victorian red-plush couches and chairs and tables. The room had been decorated with ribbons and streamers and – from God knows where – brightly coloured balloons. Crudely lettered cardboard signs hanging from the ceiling read: WELCOME BABY . . . IT'S GOING TO BE A BOY . . . HAPPY BIRTHDAY.

In the parlour were eight of Madam Agnes's girls, in a variety of sizes, ages and colours. They had all dressed for the occasion under Madam

Agnes's tutelage. The wore conservative afternoon gowns and no makeup. *They look*, Margaret thought in wonder, *more respectable than most of the wives in this town.*

Margaret stared at the roomful of prostitutes, not quite knowing what to do. Some of the faces were familiar. Margaret had waited on them when she worked in her father's store. Some of the girls were young and quite beautiful. A few were older and fleshy, with obviously dyed hair. But they all had one thing in common – they *cared*. They were friendly and warm and kind, and they wanted to make her happy.

They hovered around Margaret self-consciously, afraid of saying or doing the wrong thing. No matter what the townspeople said, they knew this was a lady, and they were aware of the difference between Margaret and themselves. They were honoured that she had come to them, and they were determined not to let anything spoil this party for her.

'We fixed you a nice lunch, honey,' Madam Agnes said. 'I hope you're hungry.'

They led her into the dining-room, where a table had been festively set, with a bottle of champagne at Margaret's place. As they walked through the hallway, Margaret glanced towards the stairs that led to the bedrooms on the second floor. She knew Jamie visited here, and she wondered which of the girls he chose. All of them, perhaps. And she studied them again and wondered what it was they had for Jamie that she did not.

The luncheon turned out to be a banquet. It began with a delicious cold soup and salad, followed by fresh carp. After that came mutton and duck with potatoes and vegetables. There was a tipsy cake and cheese and fruit and coffee. Margaret found herself eating heartily and enjoying herself immensely. She was seated at the head of the table, Madam Agnes on her right, and Maggie, a lovely blonde girl who could have been no more than sixteen, on her left. In the beginning the conversation was stilted. The girls had dozens of amusing, bawdy stories to tell, but they were not the kind they felt Margaret should hear. And so they talked about the weather and about how Klipdrift was growing, and about the future of South Africa. They were knowledgeable about politics and the economy and diamonds because they got their information first-hand from experts.

Once, the pretty blonde, Maggie, said, 'Jamie's just found a new diamond field at –' And as the room went suddenly silent and she realized her gaffe, she added nervously. 'That's my *Uncle* Jamie. He's – he's married to my aunt.'

Margaret was surprised by the sudden wave of jealousy that swept through her. Madam Agnes hastily changed the subject.

When the luncheon was finished, Madam Agnes rose and said, 'This way, honey.'

Margaret and the girls followed her into a second parlour which Margaret had not seen before. It was filled with dozens of gifts, all of them beautifully wrapped. Margaret could not believe her eyes.

'I – I don't know what to say.'

'Open them,' Madam Agnes told Margaret.

There was a rocking cradle, handmade bootees, sacques, embroidered bonnets, a long, embroidered cashmere cloak. There were French-kid button shoes, a child's silver cup, gold-lined, and a comb and brush with solid sterling-silver handles. There were solid-gold baby bib pins with beaded edges, a celluloid baby rattle and rubber teething ring and a rocking horse painted dapple grey. There were toy soldiers, brightly coloured wooden blocks and the most beautiful thing of all: a long, white christening dress.

It was like Christmas. It was beyond anything Margaret had ever expected. All the bottled-up loneliness and unhappiness of the past months exploded in her, and she burst into sobs.

Madam Agnes put her arms around her and said to the other girls. 'Get out.'

They quietly left the room. Madam Agnes led Margaret to a couch and sat there holding her until the sobs subsided.

'I – I'm so sorry,' Margaret stammered. 'I – I don't know what came over me.'

'It's all right, honey. This room has seen a lot of problems come and go. And you know what I've learned? Somehow, in the end everything always gets sorted out. You and your baby are gonna be just fine.'

'Thank you,' Margaret whispered. She gestured towards the piles of presents. 'I can never thank you and your friends enough for –'

Madam Agnes squeezed Margaret's hand. 'Don't. You don't have no idea how much fun the girls and me had gettin' all this together. We don't get a chance to do this kind of thing very often. When one of *us* gets pregnant, it's a fuckin' tragedy.' Her hands flew to her mouth and she said. 'Oh! Excuse me!'

Margaret smiled. 'I just want you to know that this has been one of the nicest days of my life.'

'We're real honoured that you came to visit us, honey. As far as I'm concerned, you're worth all the women in this town put together. Those damned bitches! I could kill them for the way they're behavin' to you. And if you don't mind my sayin' so, Jamie McGregor is a damned fool.' She rose to her feet. 'Men! It would be a wonderful world if we could live without the bastards. Or maybe it wouldn't. Who knows?'

Margaret had recovered her composure. She rose to her feet and took Agnes's hand in hers. 'I'll never forget this. Not as long as I live. Someday, when my son is old enough, I'll tell him about this day.'

Madam Agnes frowned. 'You really think you should?'

Margaret smiled. 'I really think I should.'

Madam Agnes saw Margaret to the door. 'I'll have a wagon deliver all the gifts to your boardinghouse, and – good luck to you.'

'Thank you. Oh, thank you.'

And she was gone.

Madam Agnes stood there a moment watching Margaret walk clumsily down the street. Then she turned inside and called loudly. 'All right, ladies. Let's go to work.'

One hour later, Madam Agnes's was open for business as usual.

EIGHT

It was time to spring the trap. Over the previous six months, Jamie McGregor had quietly bought out Van der Merwe's partners in his various enterprises so that Jamie now had control of them. But his obsession was to own Van der Merwe's diamond fields in the Namib. He had paid for those fields a hundred times over with his blood and guts, and very nearly with his life. He had used the diamonds he and Banda had stolen there to build an empire from which to crush Salomon van der Merwe. The task had not yet been completed. Now, Jamie was ready to finish it.

Van der Merwe had gone deeper and deeper into debt. Everyone in town refused to lend him money, except the bank Jamie secretly owned. His standing instruction to his bank manager was, 'Give Salomon van der Merwe everything he wants.'

The general store was almost never open now. Van der Merwe began drinking early in the morning, and in the afternoon he would go to Madam Agnes's and sometimes spend the night there.

One morning Margaret stood at the butcher's counter waiting for the spring chickens Mrs Owens had ordered, when she glanced out the window and saw her father leaving the brothel. She could hardly recognize the unkempt old man shuffling along the street. *I did this to him. Oh, God, forgive me, I did this!*

Salomon van der Merwe had no idea what was happening to him. He knew that somehow through no fault of his own, his life was being destroyed. God had chosen him – as He had once chosen Job – to test the mettle of his faith. Van der Merwe was certain he would triumph over his unseen enemies in the end. All he needed was a little time – time and more money. He had put up his general store as security, the shares he had in six small diamond fields, even his horse and wagon. Finally, there was nothing left but the diamond field in the Namib, and the day he put that up as collateral, Jamie pounced.

'Pull in all his notes,' Jamie ordered his bank manager. 'Give him twenty-four hours to pay up in full, or foreclose.'

'Mr McGregor, he can't possibly come up with that kind of money. He –'

'Twenty-four hours.'

At exactly four o'clock the following afternoon, the assistant manager of the bank appeared at the general store with the marshal and a writ to confiscate all of Salomon van der Merwe's wordly possessions. From his office building across the street, Jamie watched Van der Merwe being evicted from his store. The old man stood outside, blinking helplessly in the sun, not knowing what to do or where to turn. He had been stripped of everything. Jamie's vengeance was complete. *Why is it,* Jamie wondered, *that I feel no sense of triumph?* He was empty inside. The man he destroyed had destroyed him first.

When Jamie walked into Madam Agnes's that night, she said, 'Have you heard the news, Jamie? Salomon van der Merwe blew his brains out an hour ago.'

The funeral was held at the dreary, windswept cemetery outside town. Besides the burying crew, there were only two people in attendance: Margaret and Jamie McGregor. Margaret wore a shapeless black dress to cover her protruding figure. She looked pale and unwell. Jamie stood tall and elegant, withdrawn and remote. The two stood at opposite sides of the grave watching the crude pine-box coffin lowered into the ground. The clods of dirt clattered against the coffin, and to Margaret they seemed to say. *Whore!* . . . *Whore!* . . .

She looked across her father's grave at Jamie, and their eyes met. Jamie's glance was cool and impersonal, as though she were a stranger.

Margaret hated him then. *You stand there feeling nothing, and you're as guilty as I am. We killed him, you and I. In God's eyes, I'm your wife. But we're partners in evil.* She looked down at the open grave and watched the last shovelful of dirt cover the pine box. 'Rest.' she whispered. 'Rest.'

When she looked up, Jamie was gone.

There were two wooden buildings in Klipdrift that served as hospitals, but they were so filthy and unsanitary that more patients died there than lived. Babies were born at home. As Margaret's time for delivery grew closer, Mrs Owens arranged for a black midwife, Hannah. Labour began at three a.m.

'Now you just bear down,' Hannah instructed. 'Nature'll do the rest.'

The first pain brought a smile to Margaret's lips. She was bringing her son into the world, and he would have a name. She would see to it that Jamie McGregor recognized his child. Her son was not going to be punished.

The labour went on, hour after hour, and when some of the boarders stepped into Margaret's bedroom to watch the proceedings, they were sent packing.

'This is personal,' Hannah told Margaret. 'Between you and God and the devil who got you into this trouble.'

'Is it going to be a boy?' Margaret gasped.

Hannah mopped Margaret's brow with a damp

cloth. 'I'll let you know as soon as I check out the plumbin'. Now press down. Real hard! Hard! Harder!'

The contractions began to come closer together and the pain tore through Margaret's body. *Oh, my God, something's wrong*, Margaret thought.

'Bear down!' Hannah said. And suddenly there was a note of alarm in her voice. 'It's twisted around,' she cried. 'I – I can't get it out!'

Through a red mist, Margaret saw Hannah bend down and twist her body, and the room began to fade out, and suddenly there was no more pain. She was floating in space and there was a bright light at the end of a tunnel and someone was beckoning to her, and it was Jamie. *I'm here, Maggie, darling. You're going to give me a fine son.* He had come back to her. She no longer hated him. She knew then she had never hated him. She heard a voice saying, 'It's almost over,' and there was a tearing inside her, and the pain made her scream aloud.

'Now!' Hannah said. 'It's coming.'

And a second later, Margaret felt a wet rush between her legs and there was a triumphant cry from Hannah. She held up a red bundle and said, 'Welcome to Klipdrift. Honey, you got yourself a son.'

She named him Jamie.

Margaret knew the news about the baby would reach Jamie quickly, and she waited for him to call on her or send for her. When several weeks had passed and Margaret had not heard anything, she sent a message to him. The messenger returned thirty minutes later.

Margaret was in a fever of impatience. 'Did you see Mr McGregor?'

'Yes, ma'am.'

'And you gave him the message?'

'Yes, ma'am.'

'What did he *say*?' she demanded.

The boy was embarrassed. 'He – he said he has no son, Miss van der Merwe.'

She locked herself and her baby in her room all that day and all that night and refused to come out. 'Your father's upset just now, Jamie. He thinks your mother did something bad to him. But you're his son, and when he sees you, he's going to take us to live in his house and he's going to love both of us very much. You'll see, darling. Everything is going to be fine.'

In the morning when Mrs Owen knocked on the door, Margaret opened it. She seemed strangely calm.

'Are you all right, Maggie?'

'I'm fine, thank you.' She was dressing Jamie in one of his new outfits. 'I'm going to take Jamie out in his carriage this morning.'

The carriage, from Madam Agnes and her girls, was a thing of beauty. It was made of the finest grade of reed, with a strong cane bottom and solid, bentwood handles. It was upholstered in imported brocade, with piped rolls of silk plush, and it had a parasol hooked on at the back, with a deep ruffle.

Margaret pushed the baby carriage down the narrow sidewalks of Loop Street. An occasional stranger stopped to smile at the baby, but the women of the town averted their eyes or crossed to the other side of the street to avoid Margaret.

Margaret did not even notice. She was looking for one person. Every day that the weather was fine, Margart dressed the baby in one of his beautiful outfits and took him out in the baby carriage. At the end of a week, when Margaret had not once encountered Jamie on the streets, she realized he was deliberately avoiding her. *Well, if he won't come to see his son, his son will go to see him*, Margaret decided.

The following morning, Margaret found Mrs Owens in the parlour. 'I'm taking a little trip, Mrs Owens. I'll be back in a week.'

'The baby's too young to travel, Maggie. He –'

'The baby will be staying in town.'

Mrs Owens frowned. 'You mean *here?*'

'No, Mrs Owens. Not here.'

Jamie McGregor had built his house on a kopje, one of the hills overlooking Klipdrift. It was a low, steep-roofed bungalow with two large wings attached to the main building by wide verandas. The house was surrounded by green lawns studded with trees and a lush rose garden. In the back was the carriage house and separate quarters for the servants. The domestic arrangements were in the charge of Eugenia Talley, a formidable middle-aged widow with six grown children in England.

Margaret arrived at the house with her infant son in her arms at ten in the morning, when she knew Jamie would be at his office. Mrs Talley opened the door and stared in surprise at Margaret and the baby. As did everyone else within a radius of a hundred miles, Mrs Talley knew who they were.

'I'm sorry, but Mr McGregor is not at home,' the housekeeper said, and started to close the door.

Margaret stopped her. 'I didn't come to see Mr McGregor. I brought him his son.'

'I'm afraid I don't know anything about that. You –'

'I'll be gone for one week. I'll return for him then.' She held the baby out. 'His name is Jamie.'

A horrified look came over Mrs Talley's face. 'You can't leave him here! Why, Mr McGregor would –'

'You have a choice,' Margaret informed her. 'You can either take him in the house or have me leave him here on your doorstep. Mr McGregor wouldn't like *that* either.'

Without another word, she thrust the baby into the arms of the housekeeper and walked away.

'Wait! You can't –! Come back here! Miss –!'

Margaret never turned around. Mrs Talley stood there, holding the tiny bundle and thinking. *Oh, my God! Mr McGregor is going to be furious!*

*   *   *

She had never seen him in such a state. 'How could you have been so *stupid?*' he yelled. 'All you had to do was slam the door in her face!'

'She didn't give me a chance, Mr McGregor. She –'

'I will not have her child in my house!'

In his agitation he paced up and down, pausing to stop in front of the hapless housekeeper from time to time. 'I should fire you for this.'

'She's coming back to pick him up in a week. I –'

'I don't care when she's coming back,' Jamie shouted. 'Get that child out of here. Now! Get rid of it!'

'How do you suggest I do that, Mr McGregor?' she asked stiffly.

'Drop it off in town. There must be someplace you can leave it.'

'Where?'

'How the devil do I know!'

Mrs Talley looked at the tiny bundle she was holding in her arms. The shouting had started the baby crying. 'There are no orphanages in Klipdrift.' She began to rock the baby in her arms, but the screams grew louder. 'Someone has to take care of him.'

Jamie ran his hands through his hair in frustration. 'Damn! All right.' he decided. 'You're the one who so generously took the baby. *You* take care of him.'

'Yes, sir.'

'And stop that unbearable wailing. Understand something, Mrs Talley. I want it kept out of my sight. I don't want to know it's in this house. And when its mother picks it up next week, I don't want to see her. Is that clear?'

The baby started up with renewed vigour.

'Perfectly, Mr McGregor.' And Mrs Talley hurried from the room.

Jamie McGregor sat alone in his den sipping a brandy and smoking a cigar. *That stupid woman. The sight of her baby is supposed to melt my heart, make me go rushing to her and say, 'I love you. I love the baby. I want to marry you.'* Well, he had not even bothered looking at the infant. It had nothing to do with him. He had not sired it out of love, or even lust. It had been sired out of vengeance. He would forever remember the look on Salomon van der Merwe's face when he had told him Margaret was pregnant. That was the beginning. The end was the dirt being thrown onto the wooden coffin. He must find Banda and let him know their mission was finished.

Jamie felt an emptiness. *I need to set new goals,* he thought. He was already wealthy beyond belief. He had acquired hundreds of acres of mineral land. He had bought it for the diamonds that might be found there, and had ended up owning gold, platinum and half a dozen other rare minerals. His bank held mortgages on half the properties in Klipdrift, and his landholdings extended from

174

Namib to Cape Town. He felt a satisfaction in this, but it was not enough. He had asked his parents to come and join him, but they did not want to leave Scotland. His brothers and sister had married. Jamie sent large sums of money back to his parents, and that gave him pleasure, but his life was at a plateau. A few years earlier it had consisted of exciting highs and lows. He had felt alive. He was alive when he and Banda sailed their raft through the reefs of the *Sperrgebiet*. He was alive crawling over the land mines through the desert sand. It seemed to Jamie that he had not been alive in a long time. He did not admit to himself that he was lonely.

He reached again for the decanter of brandy and saw that it was empty. He had either drunk more than he realized or Mrs Talley was getting careless. Jamie rose from his chair, picked up the brandy snifter and wandered out to the butler's pantry where the liquor was kept. He was opening the bottle when he heard the cooing of an infant. *It! Mrs Talley must have the baby in her quarters, off the kitchen.* She had obeyed his orders to the letter. He had neither seen nor heard the infant in the two days it had been trespassing in his home. Jamie could hear Mrs Talley talking to it in the singsong tone that women used to talk to infants.

'You're a handsome little fellow, aren't you?' She was saying. 'You're just an angel. Yes, you are. An angel.'

175

The baby cooed again. Jamie walked over to Mrs Talley's open bedroom door and looked inside. From somewhere the housekeeper had obtained a crib and the baby was lying in it. Mrs Talley was leaning over him, and the infant's fist was tightly wrapped around her finger.

'You're a strong little devil, Jamie. You're going to grow up to be a big –' She broke off in surprise as she became aware of her employer standing in the doorway.

'Oh,' she said. 'I – is there something I can get for you, Mr McGregor?'

'No.' He walked over to the crib. 'I was disturbed by the noise in here.' And Jamie took his first look at his son. The baby was bigger than he had expected, and well formed. He seemed to be smiling up at Jamie.

'Oh, I'm sorry, Mr McGregor. He's really such a good baby. And healthy. Just give him your finger and feel how strong he is.'

Without a word, Jamie turned and walked out of the room.

Jamie McGregor had a staff of over fifty employees working on his various enterprises. There was not an employee from the mail boy to the highest executive who did not know how Kruger-Brent, Ltd., got its name, and they all took fierce pride in working for Jamie McGregor. He had recently hired David Blackwell, the sixteen-year-old son of one of his foremen, an American from Oregon who had come to South Africa looking for diamonds. When Blackwell's money ran out, Jamie had hired him to supervise one of the mines. The son went to work for the company one summer, and Jamie found him such a good worker that he offered him a permanent job. Young David Blackwell was intelligent and attractive and had initiative. Jamie knew he could also keep his mouth shut, which is why he chose him to run this particular errand.

'David, I want you to go to Mrs Owen's board-inghouse. There's a woman living there named Margaret van der Merwe.'

If David Blackwell was familiar with the name or her circumstances, he gave no indication of it. 'Yes, sir.'

'You're to speak only to her. She left her baby with my housekeeper. Tell her I want her to pick it up today and get it out of my house.'

'Yes, Mr McGregor.'

Half an hour later, David Blackwell returned. Jamie looked up from his desk.

'Sir. I'm afraid I couldn't do what you asked.'

Jamie rose to his feet. 'Why not?' he demanded. 'It was a simple enough job.'

'Miss van der Merwe wasn't there, sir.'

'Then find her.'

'She left Klipdrift two days ago. She's expected back in five days. If you'd like me to make further inquiries –'

'No.' That was the last thing Jamie wanted. 'Never mind. That's all, David.'

'Yes, sir.' The boy left the office.

Damn that woman! When she returned, she was going to have a surprise coming. She was going to get her baby back!

That evening, Jamie dined at home alone. He was having his brandy in the study when Mrs Talley came in to discuss a household problem. In the middle of a sentence, she suddenly stopped to listen and said, 'Excuse me, Mr McGregor. I hear Jamie crying.' And she hurried out of the room.

Jamie slammed down his brandy snifter, spilling the brandy. *That goddamned baby! And she had the nerve to name him Jamie. He didn't look like a Jamie. He didn't look like anything.*

Ten minutes later, Mrs Talley returned to the study. She saw the spilled drink. 'Shall I get you another brandy?'

'That won't be necessary,' Jamie said coldly. 'What *is* necessary is that you remember who you're working for. I will not be interrupted because of that bastard. Is that quite clear, Mrs Talley?'

'Yes, sir.'

'The sooner that infant you brought into this house is gone, the better it will be for all of us. Do you understand?'

Her lips tightened. 'Yes, sir. Is there anything else?'

'No.'

She turned to leave.

'Mrs Talley . . .'

'Yes, Mr McGregor?'

'You said it was crying. It's not ill, is it?'

'No, sir. Just wet. He needed a change.'

Jamie found the idea revolting. 'That will be all.'

Jamie would have been furious had he been aware that the servants in the house spent hour upon hour discussing him and his son. They all agreed that the master was behaving unreasonably, but they also knew that even to mention the subject would mean instant dismissal. Jamie McGregor was not a man who took kindly to advice from anyone.

The following evening Jamie had a late business meeting. He had made an investment in a new railroad. It was a small one, to be sure, running from his mines in the Namib Desert to De Aar, linking up with the Cape Town-Kimberley line, but it would now be much cheaper to transport his diamonds and gold to the port. The first South Africa Railway had been opened in 1860, running from Dunbar to the Point, and since then new lines had been run from Cape Town to Wellington. Railroads were going to be the steel veins that allowed goods and people to flow freely through the heart of South Africa, and Jamie intended to be a part of them. That was only the beginning of his plan. *After that*, Jamie thought, *ships. My own ships to carry the minerals across the ocean.*

He arrived home after midnight, undressed and

got into bed. He had had a decorator from London design a large, masculine bedroom with a huge bed that had been carved in Cape Town. There was an old Spanish chest in one corner of the room and two enormous wardrobes which held more than fifty suits and thirty pairs of shoes. Jamie cared nothing about clothes, but it was important to him that they be there. He had spent too many days and nights wearing rags.

He was just dozing off when he thought he heard a cry. He sat up and listened. Nothing. Was it the baby? It might have fallen out of its crib. Jamie knew that Mrs Talley was a sound sleeper. It would be dreadful if something happened to the infant while it was in Jamie's house. Then it could become his responsibility. *Damn that woman!* Jamie thought.

He put on a robe and slippers and went through the house to Mrs Talley's room. He listened at her closed door and could hear nothing. Quietly, Jamie pushed open the door. Mrs Talley was sound asleep, huddled under the covers, snoring. Jamie walked over to the crib. The baby lay on its back, its eyes wide open. Jamie moved closer and looked down. There *was* a resemblance, by God! It definitely had Jamie's mouth and chin. Its eyes were blue now, but all babies were born with blue eyes. Jamie could tell by looking at it that it was going to have grey eyes. It moved its little hands in the air and made a cooing sound and smiled up at Jamie. *Now, that's a brave lad*, Jamie thought, *lying there, not making any noise, not screaming like other babies would do.* He peered closer. *Yes, he's a McGregor, all right.*

Tentatively, Jamie reached down and held out a finger. The infant grabbed it with both hands and squeezed tightly. *He's as strong as a bull*, Jamie thought. At that moment, a strained look came over the infant's face, and Jamie could smell a sour odour.

'Mrs Talley!'

She leaped up in bed, filled with alarm. 'What – what is it?'

'The baby needs attention. Do I have to do everything around here?'

And Jamie McGregor stalked out of the room.

'David, do you know anything about babies?'

'In what respect, sir?' David Blackwell asked.

'Well, you know. What they like to play with, things like that.'

The young American said,. 'I think when they're very young they enjoy rattles, Mr McGregor.'

'Pick up a dozen,' Jamie ordered.

'Yes, sir.'

No unnecessary questions. Jamie liked that. David Blackwell was going to go far.

That evening when Jamie arrived home with a small brown package, Mrs Talley said, 'I want to apologize for last night, Mr McGregor. I don't know how I could have slept through it. The baby must have been screaming something terrible for you to have heard it all the way in your room.'

'Don't worry about it,' Jamie said generously. 'As long as one of us heard it.' He handed her the package. 'Give this to it. Some rattles for him to play with. Can't be much fun for him to be a prisoner in that crib all day.'

'Oh, he's not a prisoner, sir. I take him out.'

'Where do you take him?'

'Just in the garden, where I can keep an eye on him.'

Jamie frowned. 'He didn't look well to me last night.'

'He didn't?'

'No. His colour's not good. It wouldn't do for him to get sick before his mother picks him up.'

'Oh, no, sir.'

'Perhaps I'd better have another look at him.'

'Yes, sir. Shall I bring him in here?'

'Do that, Mrs Talley.'

'Right away, Mr McGregor.'

She was back in a few minutes with little Jamie in her arms. The baby was clutching a blue rattle. 'His colour looks fine to me.'

'Well, I could have been wrong. Give him to me.'

Carefully, she held the baby out and Jamie took his son in his arms for the first time. The feeling that swept over him took him completely by surprise. It was as though he had been longing for this moment, living for this moment, without ever knowing it. This was his flesh and blood he was

182

holding in his arms – his son, Jamie McGregor, Jr. What was the point of building an empire, a dynasty, of having diamonds and gold and railroads if you had no one to pass them on to? *What a bloody fool I've been!* Jamie thought. It had never occurred to him until now what was missing. He had been too blinded by his hatred. Looking down into the tiny face, a hardness somewhere deep in the core of him vanished.

'Move Jamie's crib into my bedroom, Mrs Talley.'

Three days later when Margaret appeared at the front door of Jamie's house, Mrs Talley said, 'Mr McGregor is away at his office, Miss van der Merwe, but he asked me to send for him when you came for the baby. He wishes to speak with you.'

Margaret waited in the living room, holding little Jamie in her arms. She had missed him terribly. Several times during the week she had almost lost her resolve and rushed back to Klipdrift, afraid that something might have happened to the baby, that he might have become ill or had an accident. But she had forced herself to stay away, and her plan had worked. Jamie wanted to talk to her! Everything was going to be wonderful. The three of them would be together now.

The moment Jamie walked into the living room, Margaret felt again the familiar rush of emotion. *Oh, God*, she thought, *I love him so much*.

'Hello, Maggie.'

She smiled, a warm, happy smile. 'Hello, Jamie.'

183

'I want my son.'

Margaret's heart sang. 'Of course you want your son, Jamie. I never doubted it.'

'I'll see to it that he's brought up properly. He'll have every advantage I can give him and, naturally, I'll see that you're taken care of.'

Margaret looked at him in confusion. 'I – I don't understand.'

'I said I want my son.'

'I thought – I mean – you and I –'

'No. It's only the boy I want.'

Margaret was filled with a sudden outrage. 'I see. Well, I'll not let you take him away from me.'

Jamie studied her a moment. 'Very well. We'll work out a compromise. You can stay on here with Jamie. You can be his – his governess.' He saw the look on her face. 'What *do* you want?'

'I want my son to have a name,' she said fiercely. 'His father's name.'

'All right. I'll adopt him.'

Margaret looked at him scornfully. 'Adopt my baby? Oh, no. You will not have my son. I feel sorry for you. The great Jamie McGregor. With all your money and power, you have nothing. You're a thing of pity.'

And Jamie stood there watching as Margaret turned and walked out of the house, carrying her son in her arms.

The following morning, Margaret made preparations to leave for America.

*   *   *

'Running away won't solve anything,' Mrs Owens argued.

'I'm not running away. I'm going someplace where my baby and I can have a new life.'

She could no longer subject herself and her baby to the humiliation Jamie McGregor offered them.

'When will you leave?'

'As soon as possible. We'll take a coach to Worcester and the train from there to Cape Town. I've saved enough to get us to New York.'

'That's a long way to go.'

'It will be worth it. They call America the land of opportunity, don't they? That's all we need.'

Jamie had always prided himself on being a man who remained calm under pressure. Now he went around yelling at everyone in sight. His office was in a constant uproar. Nothing anyone did pleased him. He roared and complained about everything, unable to control himself. He had not slept in three nights. He kept thinking about the conversation with Margaret. *Damn her!* He should have known she would try to push him into marriage. Tricky, just like her father. He had mishandled the negotiations. He had told her he would take care of her, but he had not been specific. Of course. *Money!* He should have offered her money. A thousand pounds – ten thousand pounds – more.

'I have a delicate task for you,' he told David Blackwell.

'Yes, sir.'

'I want you to talk to Miss van der Merwe. Tell her I'm offering her twenty thousand pounds. She'll know what I want in exchange.' Jamie wrote out a cheque. He had long ago learned the lure of money in hand. 'Give this to her.'

'Right, sir.' And David Blackwell was gone.

He returned fifteen minutes later and handed the cheque back to his employer. It had been torn in half. Jamie could feel his face getting red. 'Thank you, David. That will be all.'

So Margaret was holding out for more money. Very well. He would give it to her. But this time he would handle it himself.

Late that afternoon, Jamie McGregor went to Mrs Owen's boardinghouse. 'I want to see Miss van der Merwe,' Jamie said.

'I'm afraid that's not possible,' Mrs Owens informed him. 'She's on her way to America.'

Jamie felt as though he had been hit in the stomach. 'She can't be! When did she leave?'

'She and her son took the noon coach to Worcester.'

The train sitting at the station in Worcester was filled to capacity, the seats and aisles crowded with noisy travellers on their way to Cape Town. There were merchants and their wives, salesmen, prospectors, kaffirs and soldiers and sailors reporting back for duty. Most of them were riding a train for the first time and there was a festive atmosphere among the passengers. Margaret had been able to get a seat near a window, where Jamie would not be crushed by the crowd. She sat there holding her baby close to her, oblivious to those around her, thinking about the new life that lay ahead of them. It would not be easy. Wherever she went, she would be an unmarried woman with a child, an offence to society. But she would find a way to make sure her son had his chance at a decent life. She heard the conductor call, 'All aboard!'

She looked up, and Jamie was standing there. 'Collect your things,' he ordered. 'You're getting off the train.'

He still thinks he can buy me, Margaret thought. 'How much are you offering this time?'

Jamie looked down at his son, peacefully asleep in Margaret's arms. 'I'm offering you marriage.'

NINE

They were married three days later in a brief, private ceremony. The only witness was David Blackwell.

During the wedding ceremony, Jamie McGregor was filled with mixed emotions. He was a man who had grown used to controlling and manipulating others, and this time it was he who had been manipulated. He glanced at Margaret. Standing next to him, she looked almost beautiful. He remembered her passion and abandon, but it was only a memory, nothing more, without heat or emotion. He had used Margaret as an instrument of vengeance, and she had produced his heir.

The minister was saying, 'I now pronounce you man and wife. You may kiss the bride.'

Jamie leaned forwards and briefly touched his lips to Margaret's cheek.

'Let's go home,' Jamie said. His son was waiting for him.

When they returned to the house, Jamie showed Margaret to a bedroom in one of the wings.

'This is your bedroom,' Jamie informed her.

'I see.'

'I'll hire another housekeeper and put Mrs Talley in charge of Jamie. If there's anything you require, tell David Blackwell.'

Margaret felt as though he had struck her. He was treating her like a servant. But that was not important. *My son has a name. That is enough for me.*

Jamie did not return home for dinner. Margaret waited for him, then finally dined alone. That night she lay awake in her bed, aware of every sound in the house. At four o'clock in the morning, she finally fell asleep. Her last thought was to wonder which of the women at Madam Agnes's he had chosen. If Margaret's relationship with Jamie was unchanged since their marriage, her relationship with the townspeople of Klipdrift underwent a miraculous transformation. Overnight, Margaret went from being an outcast to becoming Klipdrift's social arbiter. Most of the people in town depended for their living in one way or another on Jamie McGregor and Kruger-Brent, Ltd. They decided that if Margaret van der Merwe was good enough for Jamie McGregor, she was good enough for them. Now when Margaret took little Jamie for an outing, she was met with smiles and cheery greetings. Invitations poured in. She was invited to teas, charity luncheons and dinners and urged to head civic committees. When she dressed her hair in a different way, dozens of women in town instantly followed suit. She bought a new yellow dress, and yellow dresses were suddenly popular. Margaret handled their fawning in the same manner she had handled their hostility – with quiet dignity.

Jamie came home only to spend time with his son. His attitude towards Margaret remained distant and polite. Each morning at breakfast she played the role of happy wife for the servants' benefit, despite the cool indifference of the man sitting across the table from her. But when Jamie had gone and she could escape to her room, she would be drenched in perspiration. She hated herself. Where was her pride? Because Margaret knew she still loved Jamie. *I'll always love him*, she thought. *God help me.*

Jamie was in Cape Town on a three-day business trip. As he came out of the Royal Hotel, a liveried black driver said, 'Carriage, sir?'

'No,' Jamie said. 'I'll walk.'

'Banda thought you might like to ride.'

Jamie stopped and looked sharply at the man. 'Banda?'

'Yes, Mr McGregor.'

Jamie got into the carriage. The driver flicked his whip and they started off. Jamie sat back in his seat, thinking of Banda, his courage, his friendship. He had tried many times to find him in the last two years, with no success. Now he was on his way to meet his friend.

The driver turned the carriage towards the waterfront, and Jamie knew instantly where they were going. Fifteen minutes later the carriage stopped in front of the deserted warehouse where Jamie and Banda had once planned their adventure into the Namib. *What reckless young fools we were*, Jamie thought. He stepped out of the carriage and approached the warehouse. Banda was waiting for him. He looked exactly the same, except that now he was neatly dressed in a suit and shirt and tie.

They stood there, silently grinning at each other, then they embraced.

'You look prosperous,' Jamie smiled.

Banda nodded. 'I've not done badly. I bought that farm we talked about. I have a wife and two sons, and I raise wheat and ostriches.'

'Ostriches?'

'Their feathers bring in lots of money.'

'Ah. I want to meet your family, Banda.'

Jamie thought of his own family in Scotland, and of how much he missed them. He had been away from home for four years.

'I've been trying to find you.'

'I've been busy, Jamie.' Banda moved closer. 'I had to see you to give you a warning. There's going to be trouble for you.'

Jamie studied him. 'What kind of trouble?'

'The man in charge of the Namib field – Hans Zimmerman – he's bad. The workers hate him. They're talking about walking out. If they do, your guards will try to stop them and there will be a riot.'

Jamie never took his eyes from Banda's face.

'Do you remember I once mentioned a man to you – John Tengo Javabu?'

'Yes. He's a political leader. I've been reading about him. He's been stirring up a *donderstorm*.'

'I'm one of his followers.'

Jamie nodded. 'I see. I'll do what has to be done,' Jamie promised.

'Good. You've become a powerful man, Jamie. I'm glad.'

'Thank you, Banda.'

'And you have a fine-looking son.'

Jamie could not conceal his surprise. 'How do you know that?'

'I like to keep track of my friends.' Banda rose to his feet. 'I have a meeting to go to, Jamie. I'll tell them things will be straightened out at the Namib.'

'Yes. I'll attend to it.' He followed the large black man to the door. 'When will I see you again?'

Banda smiled. 'I'll be around. You can't get rid of me that easily.'

And Banda was gone.

*   *   *

When Jamie returned to Klipdrift, he sent for young David Blackwell. 'Has there been any trouble at the Namib field, David?'

'No, Mr McGregor.' He hesitated. 'But I have heard rumours that there might be.'

'The supervisor there is Hans Zimmerman. Find out if he's mistreating the workers. If he is, put a stop to it. I want you to go up there yourself.'

'I'll leave in the morning.'

When David arrived at the diamond field at the Namib, he spent two hours quietly talking to the guards and the workers. What he heard filled him with a cold fury. When he had learned what he wanted to know, he went to see Hans Zimmerman.

Hans Zimmerman was a goliath of a man. He weighed three hundred pounds and was six feet, six inches tall. He had a sweaty, porcine face and red-veined eyes, and was one of the most unattractive men David Blackwell had ever seen. He was also one of the most efficient supervisors employed by Kruger-Brent, Ltd. He was seated at a desk in his small office, dwarfing the room, when David walked in.

Zimmerman rose and shook David's hand. 'Pleasure to see you, Mr Blackwell. You should have told me you was comin'.'

David was sure that word of his arrival had already reached Zimmerman.

'Whiskey?'

'No, thank you.'

Zimmerman leaned back in his chair and grinned. 'What can I do for you? Ain't we diggin' up enough diamonds to suit the boss?'

Both men knew that the diamond production at the Namib was excellent. 'I get more work out of my kaffirs than anyone else in the company,' was Zimmerman's boast.

'We've been getting some complaints about conditions here, David said.

The smile faded from Zimmerman's face. 'What kind of complaints?'

'That the men here are being treated badly and –'

Zimmerman leapt to his feet, moving with surprising agility. His face was flushed with anger. 'These ain't men. These are kaffirs. You people sit on your asses at headquarters and –'

'Listen to me,' David said. 'There's no –'

'You listen to *me!* I produce more fuckin' diamonds than anybody else in the company, and you know why? Because I put the fear of God into these bastards.'

'At our other mines,' David said, 'we're paying fifty-nine shillings a month and keep. You're paying your workers only fifty shillings a month.'

'You complainin' 'cause I made a better deal for you? The only thing that counts is profit.'

'Jamie McGregor doesn't agree,' David replied. 'Raise their wages.'

Zimmerman said sullenly, 'Right. It's the boss's money.'

'I hear there's a lot of whipping going on.'

Zimmerman snorted. 'Christ, you can't hurt a native, mister. Their hides are so thick they don't even feel the goddamned whip. It just scares them.'

'Then you've scared three workers to death, Mr Zimmerman.'

Zimmerman shrugged. 'There's plenty more where they came from.'

He's a bloody animal, David thought. *And a dangerous one.* He looked up at the huge supervisor. 'If there's any more trouble here, you're going to be replaced.' He rose to his feet. 'You'll start treating your men like human beings. The punishments are to stop immediately. I've inspected their living quarters. They're pigsties. Clean them up.'

Hans Zimmerman was glaring at him, fighting to control his temper. 'Anything else?' he finally managed to say.

'Yes. I'll be back here in three months. If I don't like what I see, you can find yourself a job with another company. Good day.' David turned and walked out.

Hans Zimmerman stood there for a long time, filled with a simmering rage. *The fools*, he thought. *Uitlanders*. Zimmerman was a Boer, and his father had been a Boer. The land belonged to them and God had put the blacks there to serve them. If God had meant them to be treated like human beings, he would not have made their skins black. Jamie McGregor did not understand that. But what could you expect from an *uitlander*, a native-lover? Hans Zimmerman knew he would have to be a little more careful in the future. But he would show them who was in charge at the Namib.

Kruger-Brent, Ltd., was expanding, and Jamie McGregor was away a good deal of the time. He bought a paper mill in Canada and a shipyard in Australia. When he was home, Jamie spent all his time with his son, who looked more like his father each day. Jamie felt an inordinate pride in the boy. He wanted to take the child with him on his long trips, but Margaret refused to let him.

'He's much too young to travel. When he's older, he can go with you. If you want to be with him, you'll see him here.'

Before Jamie had realized it, his son had had his first birthday, and then his second, and Jamie marvelled at how the time raced by. It was 1887.

To Margaret, the last two years had dragged by. Once a week Jamie would invite guests to dinner and Margaret was his gracious hostess. The other men found her witty and intelligent and enjoyed talking to her. She knew that several of the men found her very attractive indeed, but of course they never made an overt move, for she was the wife of Jamie McGregor.

When the last of the guests had gone, Margaret would ask, 'Did the evening go well for you?'

Jamie would invariably answer, 'Fine. Good night,' and be off to look in on little Jamie. A few minutes later Margaret would hear the front door close as Jamie left the house.

Night after night, Margaret McGregor lay in her bed thinking about her life. She knew how much she was envied by the women in town, and it made her ache, knowing how little there was to envy. She was living out a charade with a husband who treated her worse than a stranger. If only he would notice her! She wondered what he would do if one morning at breakfast she took up the bowl that contained his oatmeal especially imported from Scotland and poured it over his stupid head. She could visualize the expression on his face, and the fantasy tickled her so much that she began to giggle, and the laughter turned into deep, wrenching sobs. *I don't want to love him any more. I won't. I'll stop, somehow, before I'm destroyed . . .*

By 1890, Klipdrift had more than lived up to Jamie's expectations. In the seven years he had been there, it had become a full-fledged boomtown, with prospectors pouring in from every part of the world. It was the same old story. They came by coach and in wagons and on foot. They came with nothing but the rags they wore. They needed food and equipment and shelter and grubstake money, and

Jamie McGregor was there to supply it all. He had shares in dozens of producing diamond and gold mines, and his name and reputation grew. One morning Jamie received a visit from an attorney for De Beers, the giant conglomerate that controlled the huge diamond mines at Kimberley.

'What can I do for you?' Jamie asked.

'I've been sent to make you an offer, Mr McGregor. De Beers would like to buy you out. Name your price.'

It was a heady moment. Jamie grinned and said, 'Name *yours*.'

David Blackwell was becoming more and more important to Jamie. In the young American Jamie McGregor saw himself as he once had been. The boy was honest, intelligent and loyal. Jamie made David his secretary, then his personal assistant and, finally, when the boy was twenty-one, his general manager.

To David Blackwell, Jamie McGregor was a surrogate father. When David's own father suffered a heart attack, it was Jamie who arranged for a hospital and paid for the doctors, and when David's father died, Jamie McGregor took care of the funeral arrangements. In the five years David had worked for Kruger-Brent, Ltd., he had come to admire Jamie more than any man he had ever known. He was aware of the problem between Jamie and Margaret, and deeply regretted it, because he liked them both. *But it's none of my business*, David told himself. *My job is to help Jamie in any way I can.*

Jamie spent more and more time with his son. The boy was five now, and the first time Jamie took him down in the mines, young Jamie talked of nothing else for a week. They went on camping trips, and they slept in a tent under the stars. Jamie was used to the skies of Scotland, where the stars knew their rightful places in the firmament. Here in South Africa, the constellations were confusing. In January Canopus shone brilliantly overhead, while in May it was the Southern Cross that was near the zenith. In June, which was South Africa's winter, Scorpio was the glory of the heavens. It was puzzling. Still, it was a very special feeling for Jamie to lie on the warm earth and look up at the timeless sky with his son at his side and know they were part of the same eternity.

They rose at dawn and shot game for the pot: partridge, guinea fowl, reedbuck and oribi. Little Jamie had his own pony, and father and son rode along the veld carefully avoiding the six-foot holes dug by the ant bear, deep enough to engulf a horse and rider, and the smaller holes dug by the merecat.

There was danger on the veld. On one trip Jamie and his son were camped at a riverbed where they were almost killed by a band of migrating springbok. The first sign of trouble was a faint cloud of dust on the horizon. Hares and jackals and mere-cats raced past and large snakes came out of the brush looking for rocks under which to hide. Jamie looked at the horizon again. The dust cloud was coming closer.

'Let's get out of here,' he said.

'Our tent –'

'Leave it!'

The two of them quickly mounted and headed for the top of a high hill. They heard the drumming of hooves and then they could see the front rank of the springbok, racing in a line at least three miles long. There were more than half a million of them, sweeping away everything in their path. Trees were torn down and shrubs were pulverized, and in the wake of the relentless tide were the bodies of hundreds of small animals. Hares, snakes, jackals and guinea fowl were crushed beneath the deadly hooves. The air was filled with dust and thunder, and when it was finally over, Jamie estimated that it had lasted more than three hours.

On Jamie's sixth birthday, his father said, 'I'm going to take you to Cape Town next week and show you what a real city looks like.'

'Can Mother go with us?' Jamie asked. 'She doesn't like shooting, but she likes cities.'

His father ruffled the boy's hair and said, 'She's busy here, Son. Just the two of us men, eh?'

The child was disturbed by the fact that his

mother and father seemed so distant with each other, but then he did not understand it.

They made the journey in Jamie's private railway car. By the year 1891, railways were becoming the pre-eminent means of travel in South Africa, for trains were inexpensive, convenient and fast. The private railway car Jamie ordered built for himself was seventy-one feet long and had four panelled staterooms that could accommodate twelve persons, a salon that could be used as an office, a dining compartment, a barroom and a fully equipped kitchen. The staterooms had brass beds, Pintsch gas lamps and wide picture windows.

'Where are all the passengers?' the young boy asked.

Jamie laughed. 'We're all the passengers. It's your train, Son.'

Young Jamie spent most of the trip staring out the window, marvelling at the endless expanse of land speeding past.

'This is God's land,' his father told him. 'He filled it with precious minerals for us. They're all in the ground, waiting to be discovered. What's been found so far is only the beginning, Jamie.'

When they arrived at Cape Town, young Jamie was awed by the crowds and the huge buildings. Jamie took his son down to the McGregor Shipping Line, and pointed out half a dozen ships loading and unloading in the harbour. 'You see those? They belong to us.'

When they returned to Klipdrift, young Jamie was bursting with the news of all he had seen. 'Papa owns the whole city!' the boy exclaimed. 'You'd love it, Mama. You'll see it next time.'

Margaret hugged her son to her. 'Yes, darling.'

Jamie spent many nights away from home, and Margaret knew he was at Madam Agnes's. She had heard he had bought a house for one of the women so that he could visit her privately. She had no way of knowing whether it was true. Margaret only knew that whoever she was, she wanted to kill her.

To retain her sanity, Margaret forced herself to take an interest in the town. She raised funds to build a new church and started a mission to help the families of prospectors who were in dire need. She demanded that Jamie use one of his railroad cars to transport prospectors free of charge back to Cape Town when they had run out of money and hope.

'You're asking me to throw away good money, woman,' he growled. 'Let 'em walk back the same way they came.'

'They're in no condition to walk,' Margaret argued. 'And if they stay, the town will have to bear the cost of clothing and feeding them.'

'All right,' Jamie finally grumbled. 'But it's a damn fool idea.'

'Thank you, Jamie.'

He watched Margaret march out of his office, and, in spite of himself, he could not help feeling a certain pride in her. *She'd make a fine wife for someone*, Jamie thought.

The name of the woman Jamie set up in a private house was Maggie, the pretty prostitute who had sat next to Margaret at the baby shower. It was ironic, Jamie thought, that she should bear his wife's name. They were nothing alike. This Maggie was a twenty-one-year-old blonde with a pert face and a lush body – a tigress in bed. Jamie had paid Madam Agnes well for letting him take the girl, and he gave Maggie a generous allowance. Jamie was very discreet when he visited the small house. It was almost always at night, and he was certain he was unobserved. In fact, he was observed by many people, but not one of them cared to comment about it. It was Jamie McGregor's town, and he had the right to do anything he pleased.

On this particular evening, Jamie was finding no joy. He had gone to the house anticipating pleasure, but Maggie was in a foul mood. She lay sprawled across the large bed, her rose-coloured dressing gown not quite concealing her ripe breasts or the silky, golden triangle between her thighs. 'I'm sick of stayin' locked up in this damned house,' she said. 'It's like I'm a slave or somethin'! At least at Madam Agnes's there was somethin' goin' on all the time. Why don't you ever take me with you when you travel?'

'I've explained that, Maggie. I can't –'

She leaped out of bed and stood defiantly before him, her dressing gown wide open. 'Horseshit! You take your *son* everywhere. Ain't I as good as your son?'

'No,' Jamie said. His voice was dangerously quiet. 'You're not.' He walked over to the bar and poured himself a brandy. It was his fourth – much more than he usually drank.

'I don't mean a damned thing to you,' Maggie screamed. 'I'm just a piece of arse.' She threw back her head and laughed derisively. 'Big, moral Scotchman!'

'Scot – not Scotchman.'

'For Christ's sake, will you stop criticizin' me? Everythin' I do ain't good enough. Who the hell do you think you are, my bloody father?'

Jamie had had enough. 'You can go back to Madam Agnes's tomorrow. I'll tell her you're coming.' He picked up his hat and headed for the door.

'You can't get rid of me like this, you bastard!' She followed him, wild with anger.

Jamie stopped at the door. 'I just did.' And he disappeared into the night.

To his surprise, he found he was walking unsteadily. His mind seemed fuzzy. Perhaps he had had more than four brandies. He was not sure. He thought about Maggie's naked body in bed that evening, and how she had flaunted it, teasing him, then withdrawing. She had played with him, stroking him and running her soft tongue over his body until he was hard and eager for her. And then she had begun the fight, leaving him inflamed and unsatisfied.

When Jamie reached home, he entered the front hall, and as he started towards his room, he passed the closed door of Margaret's bedroom. There was a light from under the door. She was still awake. Jamie suddenly began to picture Margaret in bed, wearing a thin nightgown. Or perhaps nothing. He remembered how her rich, full body had writhed beneath him under the trees by the Orange River. With the liquor guiding him, he opened Margaret's bedroom door and entered.

She was in bed reading by the light of a kerosene lamp. She looked up in surprise. 'Jamie . . . is something wrong?'

'Cause I decide to pay my wife a l'il visit?' His words were slurred.

She was wearing a sheer nightgown, and Jamie could see her ripe breasts straining against the fabric. *God, she has a lovely body!* He began to take off his clothes.

Margaret leaped out of bed, her eyes very wide. 'What are you doing?'

Jamie kicked the door shut behind him and walked over to her. In a moment, he had thrown her onto the bed and he was next to her, naked. 'God, I want you, Maggie.'

In his drunken confusion, he was not sure which Maggie he wanted. How she fought him! Yes, this was his little wildcat. He laughed as he finally managed to subdue her flailing arms and legs, and she was suddenly open to him and pulling him close and saying, 'Oh, my darling, my darling Jamie. I need you so much,' and he thought, *I shouldn't have been so mean to you. In the morning I'm gonna tell you you don't have to go back to Madam Agnes's . . .*

When Margaret awoke the next morning, she was alone in bed. She could still feel Jamie's strong male body inside hers and she heard him saying, *God, I want you, Maggie,* and she was filled with a wild, complete joy. She had been right all along. He did love her. It had been worth the wait, worth the years of pain and loneliness and humiliation.

Margaret spent the rest of the day in a state of rapture. She bathed and washed her hair and changed her mind a dozen times about which dress would please Jamie most. She sent the cook away so that she herself could prepare Jamie's favourite dishes. She set the dining-room table again and again before she was satisfied with the candles and flowers. She wanted this to be a perfect evening.

Jamie did not come home for dinner. Nor did he come home all night. Margaret sat in the library waiting for him until three o'clock in the morning, and then she went to her bed, alone.

When Jamie returned home the following evening, he nodded politely to Margaret and walked on to his son's room. Margaret stood staring after him in stunned bewilderment, and then slowly turned to look at herself in the mirror. The mirror told her that she had never looked as beautiful, but when she looked closer she could not recognize the eyes. They were the eyes of a stranger.

TEN

'Well, I have some wonderful news for you, Mrs McGregor,' Dr Teeger beamed. 'You're going to have a baby.'

Margaret felt the shock of his words and did not know whether to laugh or cry. *Wonderful news?* To bring another child into a loveless marriage was impossible. Margaret could no longer bear the humiliation. She would have to find a way out, and even as she was thinking it, she felt a sudden wave of nausea that left her drenched in perspiration.

Dr Teeger was saying, 'Morning sickness?'

'A bit.'

He handed her some pills. 'Take these. They'll help. You're in excellent condition, Mrs McGregor. Not a thing to worry about. You run along home and tell the good news to your husband.'

'Yes,' she said dully. 'I'll do that.'

*   *   *

They were at the dinner table when she said, 'I saw the doctor today. I'm going to have a baby.'

Without a word, Jamie threw down his napkin, arose from his chair and stormed out of the room. That was the moment when Margaret learned she could hate Jamie McGregor as deeply as she could love him.

It was a difficult pregnancy, and Margaret spent much of the time in bed, weak and tired. She lay there hour after hour, fantasizing, visualizing Jamie at her feet, begging forgiveness, making wild love to her again. But they were only fantasies. The reality was that she was trapped. She had nowhere to go, and even if she could leave, he would never allow her to take her son with her.

Jamie was seven now, a healthy, handsome boy with a quick mind and a sense of humour. He had drawn closer, to his mother, as though somehow sensing the unhappiness in her. He made little gifts for her in school and brought them home, and Margaret would smile and thank him and try to lift herself out of her depression. When young Jamie asked why his father stayed away nights and never took her out, Margaret would reply, 'Your father is a very important man, Jamie, doing important things, and he's very busy.'

What's between his father and me is my problem, Margaret thought, *and I'll not have Jamie hating his father because of it.*

* * *

Margaret's pregnancy became more and more apparent. When she went out on the street, acquaintances would stop her and say, 'It won't be long now, will it, Mrs McGregor? I'll bet it's going to be a fine boy like little Jamie. Your husband must be a happy man.'

Behind her back, they said, 'Poor thing. She's lookin' peaked – she must have found out about the whore he's taken as his mistress . . .'

Margaret tried to prepare young Jamie for the new arrival. 'You're going to have a new brother or sister, darling. Then you'll have someone to play with all the time. Won't that be nice?'

Jamie hugged her and said, 'It will be more company for you, Mother.'

And Margaret fought to keep back the tears.

The labour pains began at four o'clock in the morning. Mrs Talley sent for Hannah, and the baby was delivered at noon. It was a healthy baby girl, with her mother's mouth and her father's chin, and black hair curling around her little red face. Margaret named her Kate. *It's a good, strong name*, Margaret thought. *And she's going to need her strength. We all are. I've got to take the children away from here. I don't know how yet, but I must find a way.*

David Blackwell burst into Jamie McGregor's office without knocking, and Jamie looked up in surprise. 'What the hell –?'

'They're rioting at the Namib!'

Jamie stood up. '*What?* What happened?'

'One of the black boys was caught trying to steal a diamond. He cut a hole under his armpit and hid the stone inside it. As a lesson, Hans Zimmerman flogged him in front of the other workers. The boy died. He was twelve years old.'

Jamie's face filled with rage. 'Sweet Jesus! I ordered a stop to flogging at all the mines.'

'I warned Zimmerman.'

'Get rid of the bastard.'

'We can't find him.'

'Why not?'

'The blacks have him. The situation's out of control.'

Jamie grabbed his hat. 'Stay here and take care of things until I get back.'

'I don't think it's safe for you to go up there, Mr McGregor. The native that Zimmerman killed was from the Barolong tribe. They don't forgive, and they don't forget. I could –'

But Jamie was gone.

When Jamie McGregor was ten miles away from the diamond field, he could see the smoke. All the huts at the Namib had been set to the torch. *The damned fools!* Jamie thought. *They're burning their own houses.* As his carriage drew closer, he heard the sounds of gunshots and screams. Amid the mass confusion, uniformed constables were shooting at blacks and coloured who were

desperately trying to flee. The whites were outnum-
bered ten to one, but they had the weapons.

When the chief constable, Bernard Sothey, saw
Jamie McGregor, he hurried up to him and said,
'Don't worry, Mr McGregor. We'll get every last
one of the bastards.'

'The hell you will,' Jamie cried. 'Order your men
to stop shooting.'

'*What?* If we –'

'Do as I say!' Jamie watched, sick with rage, as
a black woman fell under a hail of bullets. 'Call
your men off.'

'As you say, sir.' The chief constable gave orders
to an aide, and three minutes later all shooting had
stopped.

There were bodies on the ground everywhere.
'If you want my advice,' Sothey said, 'I'd –'

'I don't want your advice. Bring me their leader.'

Two policemen brought a young black up to
where Jamie was standing. He was handcuffed and
covered with blood, but there was no fear in him.
He stood tall and straight, his eyes blazing, and Jamie
remembered Banda's word for Bantu pride: *isiko*.

'I'm Jamie McGregor.'

The man spat.

'What happened here was not my doing. I want
to make it up to your men.'

'Tell that to their widows.'

Jamie turned to Sothey. 'Where's Hans
Zimmerman?'

'We're still looking for him, sir.'

Jamie saw the gleam in the black man's eyes, and he knew that Hans Zimmerman was not going to be found.

He said to the man, 'I'm closing the diamond field down for three days. I want you to talk to your people. Make a list of your complaints, and I'll look at it. I promise you I'll be fair. I'll change everything here that's not right.'

The man studied him, a look of scepticism on his face.

'There will be a new foreman in charge here, and decent working conditions. But I'll expect your men back at work in three days.'

The chief constable said, incredulously, 'You mean you're gonna let him go? He killed some of my men.'

'There will be a full investigation, and –'

There was the sound of a horse galloping towards them, and Jamie turned. It was David Blackwell, and the unexpected sight of him sounded an alarm in Jamie's mind.

David leaped off his horse. 'Mr McGregor, your son has disappeared.'

The world suddenly grew cold.

Half the population of Klipdrift turned out to join in the search. They covered the countryside, looking through gulleys, ravines and klops. There was no trace of the boy.

Jamie was like a man possessed. *He's wandered away somewhere, that's all. He'll be back.*

213

He went into Margaret's bedroom. She was lying in bed, nursing the baby.

'Is there any news?' she demanded.

'Not yet, but I'll find him.' He looked at his baby daughter for an instant, then turned and walked out without another word.

Mrs Talley came into the room, twisting her hands in her apron. 'Don't you worry, Mrs McGregor. Jamie is a big boy. He knows how to take care of himself.'

Margaret's eyes were blinded by tears. *No one would harm little Jamie, would they? Of course not.*

Mrs Talley reached down and took Kate from Margaret's arms.

'Try to sleep.'

She took the baby into the nursery and laid her down in her crib. Kate was looking up at her, smiling.

'You'd better get some sleep too, little one. You've got a busy life ahead of you.'

Mrs Talley walked out of the room, closing the door behind her.

At midnight, the bedroom window silently slid open and a man climbed into the room. He walked over to the crib, threw a blanket over the infant's head and scooped her up in his arms.

Banda was gone as quickly as he had come.

It was Mrs Talley who discovered that Kate was missing. Her first thought was that Mrs McGregor had come in the night and taken her. She walked into Margaret's bedroom and asked, 'Where's the baby?'

And from the look on Margaret's face, she knew instantly what had happened.

As another day went by with no trace of his son, Jamie was on the verge of collapsing. He approached David Blackwell. 'You don't think anything bad has happened to him?' His voice was barely under control.

David tried to sound convincing. 'I'm sure not, Mr McGregor.'

But he *was* sure. He had warned Jamie McGregor that the Bantus neither forgave nor forgot, and it was a Bantu who had been cruelly murdered. David was certain of one thing: if the Bantus had taken little Jamie, he had died a horrible death, for they would exact their vengeance in kind.

Jamie returned home at dawn, drained. He had led a search party of townspeople, diggers and constables, and they had spent the night looking without success in every conceivable place for the young boy.

David was waiting when Jamie walked into the study. David rose to his feet. 'Mr McGregor, your daughter has been kidnapped.'

Jamie stared at him in silence, his face pale. Then he turned and walked into his bedroom.

Jamie had not been to bed for forty-eight hours, and he fell into bed, utterly exhausted, and slept.

He was under the shade of a large baobab tree and in the distance across the trackless veld a lion was moving towards him. Young Jamie was shaking him. *Wake up, Papa, a lion is coming.* The animal was moving towards them faster now. His son was shaking him harder. *Wake up!* Jamie opened his eyes. Banda was standing over him. Jamie started to speak, but Banda put a hand over Jamie's mouth.

'Quiet!' He allowed Jamie to sit up.

'Where's my son?' Jamie demanded.

'He's dead.'

The room began to spin.

'I'm sorry. I was too late to stop them. Your people spilled Bantu blood. My people demanded vengeance.'

Jamie buried his face in his hands. 'Oh, my God! What did they do to him?'

There was a bottomless sorrow in Banda's voice. 'They left him out in the desert. I – I found his body and buried him.'

'Oh, no! Oh, please, no!'

'I tried to save him, Jamie.'

Jamie slowly nodded, accepting it. Then dully, 'What about my daughter?'

'I took her away before they could get her. She's back in her bedroom, asleep. She'll be all right if you do what you promised.'

Jamie looked up, and his face was a mask of hatred. 'I'll keep my promise. But I want the men who killed my son. They're going to pay.'

Banda said quietly, 'Then you will have to kill my whole tribe, Jamie.'

Banda was gone.

It was only a nightmare, but she kept her eyes tightly closed, because she knew if she opened them the nightmare would become real and her children would be dead. So she played a game. She would keep her eyes squeezed shut until she felt little Jamie's hand on hers saying, 'It's all right, Mother. We're here. We're safe.'

She had been in bed for three days, refusing to talk to anyone or see anyone. Dr Teeger came and went, and Margaret was not even aware of it. In the middle of the night Margaret was lying in bed with her eyes shut when she heard a loud crash from her son's room. She opened her eyes and listened. There was another sound. Little Jamie was back!

Margaret hurriedly got out of bed and ran down the corridor towards the closed door of her son's room. Through the door, she could hear strange animal sounds. Her heart pounding wildly, she pushed the door open.

Her husband lay on the floor, his face and body contorted. One eye was closed and the other stared up at her grotesquely. He was trying to speak, and the words came out as slobbering animal sounds.

Margaret whispered, 'Oh, Jamie – Jamie!'

*   *   *

Dr Teeger said, 'I'm afraid the news is bad, Mrs McGregor. Your husband has had a severe stroke. There's a fifty-fifty chance he'll live – but if he does, he'll be a vegetable. I'll make arrangements to get him into a private sanitarium where he can get the proper care.'

'No.'

He looked at Margaret in surprise. 'No . . . what?'

'No hospital. I want him here with me.'

The doctor considered for a moment. 'All right. You'll need a nurse. I'll arrange –'

'I don't want a nurse. I'll take care of Jamie myself.'

Dr Teeger shook his head. 'That won't be possible, Mrs McGregor. You don't know what's involved. Your husband is no longer a functioning human being. He's completely paralysed and will be for as long as he lives.'

Margaret said, 'I'll take care of him.'

Now Jamie finally, truly, belonged to her.

ELEVEN

Jamie McGregor lived for exactly one year from the day he was taken ill, and it was the happiest time of Margaret's life. Jamie was totally helpless. He could neither talk nor move. Margaret cared for her husband, tended to all his needs, and kept him at her side day and night. During the day, she propped him up in a wheelchair in the sewing room, and while she knitted sweaters and throwrobes for him, she talked to him. She discussed all the little household problems he had never had time to listen to before, and she told him how well little Kate was getting along. At night she carried Jamie's skeletal body to her bedroom and gently lay him in bed next to her. Margaret tucked him in and they had their one-sided chat until Margaret was ready to go to sleep.

David Blackwell was running Kruger-Brent, Ltd. From time to time, David came to the house with papers for Margaret to sign, and it was painful for

David to see the helpless condition Jamie was in. *I owe this man everything*, David thought.

'You chose well, Jamie,' Margaret told her husband. 'David is a fine man.' She put down her knitting and smiled. 'He reminds me of you a bit. Of course, there was never anyone as clever as you, my darling, and there never will be again. You were so fair to look at, Jamie, and so kind and strong. And you weren't afraid to dream. Now all your dreams have come true. The company is getting bigger every day.' She picked up her knitting again. 'Little Kate is beginning to talk. I'll swear she said "mama" this morning . . .'

Jamie sat there, propped up in his chair, one eye staring ahead.'

'She has your eyes and your mouth. She's going to grow up to be a beauty . . .'

The following morning when Margaret awakened, Jamie McGregor was dead. She took him in her arms and held him close to her.

'Rest, my darling, rest. I've always loved you so much, Jamie. I hope you know that. Good-bye, my own dear love.'

She was alone now. Her husband and her son had left her. There was only herself and her daughter. Margaret walked into the baby's room and looked down at Kate, sleeping in her crib. *Katherine. Kate.* The name came from the Greek, and it meant clear or pure. It was a name given to saints and nuns and queens.

Margaret said aloud, 'Which are you going to be, Kate?'

It was a time of great expansion in South Africa, but was also a time of great strife. There was a long-standing Transvaal dispute between the Boers and the British, and it finally came to a head. On Thursday, October 12, 1899, on Kate' seventh birthday, the British declared war on the Boers, and three days later the Orange Free State was under attack. David tried to persuade Margaret to take Kate and leave South Africa, but Margaret refused to go.

'My husband is here,' she said.

There was nothing David could do to dissuade her. 'I'm going to join with the Boers,' David told her. 'Will you be all right?'

'Yes, of course,' Margaret said. 'I'll try to keep the company going.'

The next morning David was gone.

The British had expected a quick and easy war, no more than a mopping-up operation, and they began with a confident, light-hearted holiday spirit. At the Hyde Park Barracks in London, a send-off supper was given, with a special menu showing a British soldier holding up the head of a boar on a tray. The menu read:

SEND-OFF SUPPER
To the CAPE SQUADRON,
November 27, 1899

221

MENU
Oysters – Blue Points
Compo Soup
Toady in the Hole
Sandy Sole
Mafeking Mutton
Transvaal Turnips. Cape Sauce
Pretoria Pheasants
White Sauce
Tinker Taters
Peace Pudding. Massa Ices
Dutch Cheese
Dessert

*(You are requested not to throw shells
under the tables)*

Boer Whines – Long Tom
Hollands-in-Skin
Orange Wine

The British were in for a surprise. The Boers were on their own home territory, and they were tough and determined. The first battle of the war took place in Mafeking, hardly more than a village, and for the first time, the British began to realize what they were up against. More troops were quickly sent over from England. They laid siege to Kimberley, and it was only after a fierce and bloody fight that they went on to take Ladysmith. The cannons of the Boers had a longer range than those of the British, so long-range guns were removed from British warships, moved inland and manned by sailors hundreds of miles from their ships.

In Klipdrift, Margaret listened eagerly for news of each battle, and she and those around her lived on rumours, their moods varying from elation to despair, depending on the news. And then one morning one of Margaret's employees came running into her office and said, 'I just heard a report that the British are advancing on Klipdrift. They're going to kill us all!'

'Nonsense. They wouldn't dare touch us.'

Five hours later, Margaret McGregor was a prisoner of war.

Margaret and Kate were taken to Paardeberg, one of the hundreds of prison camps that had sprung up all over South Africa. The prisoners were kept inside an enormous open field, ringed by barbed wire and guarded by armed British soldiers. The conditions were deplorable.

Margaret took Kate in her arms and said, 'Don't worry, darling, nothing's going to happen to you.'

But neither of them believed it. Each day became a calendar of horrors. They watched those around them die by the tens and the hundreds and then by the thousands as fever swept through the camp. There were no doctors or medication for the wounded, and food was scarce. It was a constant nightmare that went on for almost three harrowing years. The worst of it was the feeling of utter helplessness. Margaret and Kate were at the complete mercy of their captors. They were dependent upon them for meals and shelter, for their very lives. Kate lived in terror. She watched the children around her die, and she was afraid that she would be next. She was powerless to protect her mother or herself, and it was a lesson she was never to forget. *Power.* If you had power, you had food. You had medicine. You had freedom. She saw those around her fall ill and die, and she equated power with life. *One day*, Kate thought, *I'll have power. No one will be able to do this to me again.*

The violent battles went on – Belmont and Graspan and Stormberg and Spioenkop – but in the end, the brave Boers were no match for the might of the British Empire. In 1902, after nearly three years of bloody war, the Boers surrendered. Fifty-five thousand Boers fought, and thirty-four thousand of their soldiers, women and children died. But what filled the survivors with a deep savage bitterness was the knowledge that twenty-eight thousand of those died in British concentration camps.

On the day the gates of the camp were flung open, Margaret and Kate returned to Klipdrift. A few weeks later, on a quiet Sunday, David Blackwell arrived. The war had matured him, but he was still the same grave, thoughtful David Margaret had learned to rely upon. David had spent these hellish years fighting and worrying about whether Margaret and Kate were dead or alive. When he found them safe at home, he was filled with joy.

'I wish I could have protected you both,' David told Margaret.

'That's all past, David. We must think only of the future.'

And the future was Kruger-Brent, Ltd.

For the world, the year 1900 was a clean slate on which history was going to be written, a new era that promised peace and limitless hope for everyone. A new century had begun, and it brought with it a series of astonishing inventions that reshaped life around the globe. Steam and electric automobiles were replaced by the combustion engine. There were submarines and airplanes. The world population exploded to a billion and a half people. It was a time to grow and expand, and during the next six years, Margaret and David took full advantage of every opportunity.

During those years, Kate grew up with almost no supervision. Her mother was too busy running the company with David to pay much attention to her. She was a wild child, stubborn and opinionated and intractable. One afternoon when Margaret came home from a business meeting, she saw her fourteen-year-old daughter in the muddy yard in a fistfight with two boys. Margaret stared in horrified disbelief.

'Bloody hell!' she said under her breath. 'That's the girl who one day is going to run Kruger-Brent, Limited! God help us all!'

BOOK TWO

Kate and David

1906–1914

TWELVE

On a hot summer night in 1914, Kate McGregor was working alone in her office at the new Kruger-Brent, Ltd., headquarters building in Johannesburg when she heard the sound of approaching automobiles. She put down the papers she had been studying, walked over to the window and looked out. Two police cars and a paddy wagon had come to a stop in front of the building. Kate watched frowning, as half a dozen uniformed policemen leaped from the cars and hurried to cover the two entrances and exits to the building. It was late, and the streets were deserted. Kate caught a wavy reflection of herself in the window. She was a beautiful woman, with her father's light-grey eyes and her mother's full figure.

There was a knock at the office door and Kate called, 'Come in.'

The door opened and two uniformed men entered. One wore the bars of a superintendent of police.

'What on earth is going on?' Kate demanded.

'I apologise for disturbing you at this late hour, Miss McGregor. I'm Superintendent Cominsky.'

'What's the problem, Superintendent?'

'We've had a report that an escaped killer was seen entering this building a short time ago.'

There was a shocked look on Kate's face. 'Entering *this* building?'

'Yes, ma'am. He's armed and dangerous.'

Kate said nervously, 'Then I would very much appreciate it, Superintendent, if you would find him and get him out of here.'

'That's exactly what we intend to do, Miss McGregor. You haven't seen or heard anything suspicious, have you?'

'No. But I'm alone here, and there are a lot of places a person could hide. I'd like you to have your men search this place thoroughly.

'We'll get started immediately, ma'am.'

The superintendent turned and called to the men in the hallway, 'Spread out. Start at the basement and work your way up to the roof.' He turned to Kate. 'Are any of the offices locked?'

'I don't believe so,' Kate said, 'but if they are, I'll open them for you.'

Superintendent Cominsky could see how nervous she was, and he did not blame her. She would be even more nervous if she knew how desperate the man was for whom they were looking. 'We'll find him,' the superintendent assured Kate.

Kate picked up the report she had been working

on, but she was unable to concentrate. She could hear the police moving through the building, going from office to office. *Would they find him?* She shivered.

The policemen moved slowly, methodically searching every possible hiding place from the basement to the roof. Forty-five minutes later, Superintendent Cominsky returned to Kate's office.

'Not yet, ma'am, but don't worry –'

'I *am* worried, Superintendent. If there is an escaped killer in this building, I want you to find him.'

'We will, Miss McGregor. We have tracking dogs.'

From the corridor came the sound of barking and a moment later a handler came into the office with two large German shepherds on leashes.

'The dogs have been all over the building, sir. They've searched everyplace but this office.'

The superintendent turned to Kate. 'Have you been out of this office anytime in the past hour or so?'

'Yes. I went to look up some records in the file room. Do you think he could have –?' She shuddered. 'I'd like you to check this office, please.'

The superintendent gave a signal and the handler slipped the leashes off the dogs and gave the command. 'Track.'

The dogs went crazy. They raced to a closed door and began barking wildly.

'Oh, my God!' Kate cried. 'He's in there!'

231

The superintendent pulled out his gun. 'Open it,' he ordered.

The two policemen moved to the closet door with drawn guns and pulled the door open. The closet was empty. One of the dogs raced to another door and pawed excitedly at it.

'Where does that door lead?' Superintendent Cominsky asked.

'To a washroom.'

The two policemen took up places on either side of the door and yanked it open. There was no one inside.

The handler was baffled. 'They've never behaved this way before.' The dogs were racing around the room frantically. 'They've got the scent,' the handler said. 'But where is he?'

Both dogs ran to the drawer of Kate's desk and continued their barking.

'There's your answer,' Kate tried to laugh. 'He's in the drawer.'

Superintendent Cominsky was embarrassed. 'I'm sorry to have troubled you, Miss McGregor.' He turned to the handler and snapped. 'Take these dogs out of here.'

'You're not leaving?' There was concern in Kate's voice.

'Miss McGregor, I can assure you you're perfectly safe. My men have covered every inch of this building. You have my personal guarantee that he's not here. I'm afraid it was a false alarm. My apologies.'

Kate swallowed. 'You certainly know how to bring excitement to a woman's evening.'

Kate stood looking out of the window, watching the last of the police vehicles drive away. When they were out of sight, she opened her desk drawer and pulled out a blood-stained pair of canvas shoes. She carried them down the corridor to a door marked *Private, Authorized Personnel Only*, and entered. The room was bare except for a large, locked, walk-in safe built into the wall, the vault where Kruger-Brent, Ltd. stored its diamonds before shipping. Quickly Kate dialled the combination on the safe and pulled open the giant door. Dozens of metal safe-deposit boxes were built into the sides of the vault, all crammed with diamonds. In the centre of the room, lying on the floor half-conscious, was Banda.

Kate knelt beside him. 'They've gone.'

Banda slowly opened his eyes and managed a weak grin. 'If I had a way out of this vault, do you know how rich I'd be, Kate?'

Kate carefully helped him to his feet. He winced with pain as she touched his arm. She had wrapped a bandage around it, but blood was seeping through.

'Can you put your shoes on?' She had taken them from him earlier, and, to confuse the tracking dogs she knew would be brought in, she had walked around her office in them and then hidden them in her drawer.

Now Kate said, 'Come on. We have to get you out of here.'

Banda shook his head. 'I'll make it on my own. If they catch you helping me, you'll be in more trouble than you can handle.'

'Let me worry about that.'

Banda took a last look around the vault.

'Do you want any samples?' Kate asked. 'You can help yourself.'

Banda looked at her and saw that she was serious. 'Your daddy made me that offer once, a long time ago.'

Kate smiled wryly. 'I know.'

'I don't need money. I just have to leave town for a while.'

'How do you think you're going to get out of Johannesburg?'

'I'll find a way.'

'Listen to me. The police have roadblocks out by now. Every exit from the city will be watched. You won't have a chance by yourself.'

He said stubbornly, 'You've done enough.' He had managed to put his shoes on. He was a forlorn-looking figure, standing there in a torn, bloodied shirt and jacket. His face was seamed and his hair was grey, but when Kate looked at him she saw the tall, handsome figure she had first met as a child.

'Banda, if they catch you, they'll kill you,' Kate said quietly. 'You're coming with me.'

She knew she was right about the roadblocks.

Every exit from Johannesburg would be guarded by police patrols. Banda's capture was a top priority and the authorities had orders to bring him in dead or alive. The railroad stations and roads would be watched.

'I hope you have a better plan than your daddy had,' Banda said. His voice was weak. Kate wondered how much blood he had lost.

'Don't talk. Save your strength. Just leave everything to me.' Kate sounded more confident than she felt. Banda's life was in her hands, and she could not bear it if anything happened to him. She wished again, for the hundredth time, that David was not away. Well, she would simply have to manage without him.

'I'm going to bring my automobile around to the alley,' Kate said. 'Give me ten minutes, then come outside. I'll have the back door of the car open. Get in and lie on the floor. There will be a blanket to cover yourself with.'

'Kate, they're going to search every automobile leaving the city. If –'

'We're not going by automobile. There's a train leaving for Cape Town at eight a.m. I ordered my private car connected to it.'

'You're getting me out of here in your private railroad car?'

'That's right.'

Banda managed a grin. 'You McGregors really like excitement.'

* * *

235

Thirty minutes later, Kate drove into the railroad yards. Banda was on the floor of the backseat, concealed by a blanket. They had had no trouble passing the roadblocks in the city, but now as Kate's car turned into the train yards, a light suddenly flashed on, and Kate saw that her way was blocked by several policemen. A familiar figure walked towards Kate's car.

'Superintendent Cominsky!'

He registered surprise. 'Miss McGregor, what are you doing here?'

Kate gave him a quick, apprehensive smile. 'You'll think I'm just a silly, weak female, Superintendent, but to tell you the truth, what happened back at the office scared the wits out of me. I decided to leave town until you catch this killer you're looking for. Or have you found him?'

'Not yet, ma'am, but we will. I have a feeling he'll make for these railroad yards. Wherever he runs, we'll catch him.'

'I certainly hope so!'

'Where are you headed?'

'My railway car is on a siding up ahead. I'm taking it to Cape Town.'

'Would you like one of my men to escort you?'

'Oh, thank you, Superintendent, but that won't be necessary. Now that I know where you and your men are, I'll breathe a lot easier, believe me.'

Five minutes later, Kate and Banda were safely inside the private railway car. It was pitch black.

'Sorry about the dark,' Kate said. 'I don't want to light any lamps.'

She helped Banda onto a bed. 'You'll be fine here until morning. When we start to pull out, you'll hide out in the washroom.'

Banda nodded. 'Thank you.'

Kate drew the shades. 'Have you a doctor who will take care of you when we get to Cape Town?'

He looked up into her eyes. '*We?*'

'You didn't think I was going to let you travel alone while I missed all the fun?'

Banda threw back his head and laughed. *She's her father's daughter, all right.*

As dawn was breaking, an engine pulled up to the private railroad car and shunted it onto the main track in back of the train that was leaving for Cape Town. The car rocked back and forth as the connection was made.

At exactly eight o'clock, the train pulled out of the station. Kate had left word that she did not wish to be disturbed. Banda's wound was bleeding again, and Kate attended to it. She had not had a chance to talk to Banda since earlier that evening, when he had stumbled half-dead into her office. Now she said, 'Tell me what happened, Banda.'

Banda looked at her and thought, *Where can I begin?* How could he explain to her the *trekboers* who pushed the Bantus from their ancestral land?

Had it started with them? Or had it started with the giant Oom Paul Kruger, President of the Transvaal, who said in a speech to the South African Parliament, 'We must be the lords over the blacks and let them be a subject race . . .' Or had it begun with the great empire-builder Cecil Rhodes, whose motto was, 'Africa for the whites'? How could he sum up the history of his people in a sentence? He thought of a way. 'The police murdered my son,' Banda said.

The story came pouring out. Banda's older son, Ntombenthle, was attending a political rally when the police charged in to break it up. Some shots were fired, and a riot began. Ntombenthle was arrested, and the next morning he was found hanged in his cell. 'They said it was suicide,' Banda told Kate. 'But I know my son. It was murder.'

'My God, he was so young,' Kate breathed. She thought of all the times they had played together, laughed together. Ntombenthle had been such a handsome boy. 'I'm sorry, Banda. I'm so sorry. But why are they after you?'

'After they killed him I began to rally the blacks. I had to fight back, Kate. I couldn't just sit and do nothing. The police called me an enemy of the state. They arrested me for a robbery I did not commit and sentenced me to prison for twenty years. Four of us made a break. A guard was shot and killed, and they're blaming me. I've never carried a gun in my life.'

'I believe you,' Kate said. 'The first thing we

have to do is get you somewhere where you'll be safe.'

'I'm sorry to involve you in all this.'

'You didn't involve me in anything. You're my friend.'

He smiled. 'You know the first white man I ever heard call me friend? Your daddy.' He sighed. 'How do you think you're going to sneak me off the train at Cape Town?'

'We're not going to Cape Town.'

'But you said –'

'I'm a woman. I have a right to change my mind.'

In the middle of the night when the train stopped at the station at Worcester, Kate arranged to have her private railroad car disconnected and shunted to a siding. When Kate woke up in the morning, she went over to Banda's cot. It was empty. Banda was gone. He had refused to compromise her any further. Kate was sorry, but she was sure he would be safe. He had many friends to take care of him. *David will be proud of me*, Kate thought.

'I can't believe you could be so stupid!' David roared, when Kate returned to Johannesburg and told him the news. 'You not only jeopardized your own safety, but you put the company in danger. If the police had found Banda here, do you know what they would have done?'

Kate said defiantly, 'Yes. They would have killed him.'

David rubbed his forehead in frustration. 'Don't you understand anything?'

'You're bloody right, I do! I understand that you're cold and unfeeling.' Her eyes were ablaze with fury.

'You're still a child.'

She raised her hand to strike him, and David grabbed her arms. 'Kate, you've got to control your temper.'

The words reverberated in Kate's head. *Kate, you've got to learn to control your temper . . .*

It was so long ago. She was four years old, in the middle of a fistfight with a boy who had dared tease her. When David appeared, the boy ran away. Kate started to chase him, and David grabbed her. 'Hold it, Kate. You've got to learn to control your temper. Young ladies don't get into fistfights.'

'I'm not a young lady,' Kate snapped. 'Let go of me.' David released her.

The pink frock she was wearing was muddied and torn, and her cheek was bruised.

'We'd better get you cleaned up before your mother sees you,' David told her.

Kate looked after the retreating boy with regret. 'I could have licked him if you had left me alone.'

David looked down into the passionate little face and laughed. 'You probably could have.'

Mollified, Kate allowed him to pick her up and carry her into her house. She liked being in David's arms. She liked everything about David. He was the only grown-up who understood her. Whenever he was in town, he spent time with her. In relaxed moments, Jamie had told young David about his adventures with Banda, and now David told the stories to Kate. She could not get enough of them.

'Tell me again about the raft they built.'

And David would tell her.

'Tell me about the sharks . . . Tell me about the sea *mis* . . . Tell me about the day . . .'

Kate did not see very much of her mother. Margaret was too involved in running the affairs of Kruger-Brent, Ltd. She did it for Jamie.

Margaret talked to Jamie every night, just as she had during the year before he died. 'David is such a great help, Jamie, and he'll be around when Kate's running the company. I don't want to worry you, but I don't know what to do with that child . . .'

Kate was stubborn and wilful and impossible. She refused to obey her mother or Mrs Talley. If they chose a dress for her to wear, Kate would discard it for another. She would not eat properly. She ate what she wanted to, when she wanted to, and no threat or bribe could sway her. When Kate was forced to go to a birthday party, she found ways to disrupt it. She had no girl friends. She refused to go to dancing class and instead spent her time playing rugby with teenage boys. When Kate finally started school, she set a record for mischief. Margaret found herself going to see the headmistress at least once a month to persuade her to forgive Kate and let her remain in school.

'I don't understand her, Mrs McGregor,' the

headmistress sighed. 'She's extremely bright, but she rebels against simply everything. I don't know what to do with her.'

Neither did Margaret.

The only one who could handle Kate was David. 'I understand you're invited to a birthday party this afternoon,' David said.

'I hate birthday parties.'

David stooped down until he was at her eye level. 'I know you do, Kate. But the father of the little girl who's having the birthday party is a friend of mine. It will make me look bad if you don't attend and behave like a lady.'

Kate stared at him. 'Is he a *good* friend of yours?'

'Yes.'

'I'll go.'

Her manners that afternoon were impeccable.

'I don't know how you do it,' Margaret told David. 'It's magic.'

'She's just high-spirited,' David laughed. 'She'll grow out of it. The important thing is to be careful not to break that spirit.'

'I'll tell you a secret,' Margaret said grimly, 'half the time I'd like to break her neck.'

When Kate was ten, she said to David, 'I want to meet Banda.'

David looked at her in surprise. 'I'm afraid that's not possible, Kate. Banda's farm is a long way from here.'

'Are you going to take me there, David, or do you want me to go by myself?'

The following week David took Kate to Banda's farm. It was a good-sized piece of land, two morgens, and on it Banda raised wheat, sheep and ostriches. The living accommodations were circular huts with walls made of dried mud. Poles supported a cone-shaped roof covered with thatches. Banda stood in front, watching as Kate and David drove up and got out of the carriage. Banda looked at the gangling, serious-faced girl at David's side and said, 'I'd have known you were Jamie McGregor's daughter.'

'And I'd have known you were Banda,' Kate said gravely. 'I came to thank you for saving my father's life.'

Banda laughed. 'Someone's been telling you stories. Come in and meet my family.'

Banda's wife was a beautiful Bantu woman named Ntame. Banda had two sons, Ntombenthle, seven years older than Kate, and Magena, six years older. Ntombenthle was a miniature of his father. He had the same handsome features and proud bearing and an inner dignity.

Kate spent the entire afteroon playing with the two boys. They had dinner in the kitchen of the small, neat farmhouse. David felt uncomfortable eating with a black family. He respected Banda, but it was traditional that there was no socializing between the two races. In addition to that, David was concerned about Banda's political activities. There were reports that he was a disciple of John Tengo Javabu, who was fighting for drastic social changes. Because mine owners could not get enough natives to work for them, the government had imposed a tax of ten shillings on all natives who did not work as mine labourers, and there were riots all over South Africa.

In the late afternoon, David said, 'We'd better get started home, Kate. We have a long ride.'

'Not yet.' Kate turned to Banda. 'Tell me about the sharks . . .'

From that time on, whenever David was in town, Kate made him take her to visit Banda and his family.

David's assurance that Kate would grow out of her high-spiritedness showed no signs of coming to pass. If anything, she grew more wilful every day. She flatly refused to take part in any of the activities that other girls her age participated in. She insisted on going into the mines with David, and he took her hunting and fishing and camping. Kate adored it. One day when Kate and David were fishing the Vaal, and Kate gleefully pulled in a trout larger than anything David had caught, he said, 'You should have been born a boy.'

She turned to him in annoyance. 'Don't be silly, David. Then I couldn't marry you.'

David laughed.

'We *are* going to be married, you know.'

'I'm afraid not, Kate. I'm twenty-two years older

than you. Old enough to be your father. You'll meet a boy one day, a nice young man –'

'I don't want a nice young man,' she said wickedly. 'I want you.'

'If you're really serious,' David said, 'then I'll tell you the secret to a man's heart.'

'Tell me!' Kate said eagerly.

'Through his stomach. Clean that trout and let's have lunch.'

There was not the slightest doubt in Kate's mind that she was going to marry David Blackwell. He was the only man in the world for her.

Once a week Margaret invited David to dinner at the big house. As a rule, Kate preferred to eat dinner in the kitchen with the servants, where she did not have to mind her manners. But on Friday nights when David came, Kate sat in the big dining room. David usually came alone, but occasionally he would bring a female guest and Kate would hate her instantly.

Kate would get David alone for a moment and say, with sweet innocence, 'I've never seen hair that shade of blonde,' or, 'She certainly has peculiar taste in dresses, hasn't she?' or, 'Did she used to be one of Madam Agnes's girls?'

When Kate was fourteen, her headmistress sent for Margaret. 'I run a respectable school, Mrs McGregor. I'm afraid your Kate is a bad influence.'

Margaret sighed. 'What's she done now?'

'She's teaching the other children words they've never heard before.' Her face was grim. 'I might add, Mrs McGregor, that *I've* never heard some of the words before. I can't imagine where the child picked them up.'

Margaret could. Kate picked them up from her street friends. *Well*, Margaret decided, *it is time to end all that.*

The headmistress was saying, 'I do wish you would speak to her. We'll give her another chance, but –'

'No. I have a better idea. I'm going to send Kate away to school.'

When Margaret told David her idea, he grinned. 'She's not going to like that.'

'I can't help it. Now the headmistress is complaining about the language Kate uses. She gets it from those prospectors she's always following around. My daughter's starting to sound like them, look like them and smell like them. Frankly, David, I don't understand her at all. I don't know why she behaves as she does. She's pretty, she's bright, she's –'

'Maybe she's too bright.'

'Well, too bright or not, she's going away to school.'

When Kate arrived home that afternoon, Margaret broke the news to her.

Kate was furious. 'You're trying to get rid of me!'

'Of course I'm not, darling. I just think you'd be better off –'

'I'm better off *here*. All my friends are here. You're trying to separate me from my friends.'

'If you're talking about that riffraff you –'

'They're *not* riffraff. They're as good as anybody.'

'Kate, I'm not going to argue with you. You're going away to a boarding school for young ladies, and that's that.'

'I'll kill myself,' Kate promised.

'All right, darling. There's a razor upstairs, and if you look around, I'm sure you'll find various poisons in the house.'

Kate burst into tears. 'Please don't do this to me, Mother.'

Margaret took her in her arms. 'It's for your own good, Kate. You'll be a young woman soon. You'll be ready for marriage. No man is going to marry a girl who talks and dresses and behaves the way you do.'

'That's not true,' Kate sniffled. 'David doesn't mind.'

'What does David have to do with this?'

'We're going to be married.'

Margaret sighed. 'I'll have Mrs Talley pack your things.'

There were half a dozen good English boarding schools for young girls. Margaret decided that Cheltenham, in Gloucestershire, was best suited for

Kate. It was a school noted for its rigid discipline. It was set on acres of land surrounded by high battlements and, according to its charter, was founded for the daughters of noblemen and gentlemen. David did business with the husband of the headmistress, Mrs Keaton, and he had no trouble arranging for Kate to be enrolled there.

When Kate heard where she was going, she exploded anew. 'I've heard about that school! It's awful. I'll come back like one of those stuffed English dolls. Is that what you'd like?'

'What I would like is for you to learn some manners,' Margaret told her.

'I don't need manners. I've got brains.'

'That's not the first thing a man looks for in a woman,' Margaret said dryly, 'and you're becoming a woman.'

'I don't want to become a woman,' Kate screamed. 'Why the bloody hell can't you just leave me alone?'

'I will not have you using that language.'

And so it went on until the morning arrived when Kate was to leave. Since David was going to London on a business trip, Margaret asked, 'Would you mind seeing that Kate gets to school safely? The Lord only knows where she'll end up if she goes on her own.'

'I'll be happy to,' David said.

'You! You're as bad as my mother! You can't wait to get rid of me.'

David grinned. 'You're wrong. I can wait.'

*　　*　　*

They travelled by private railway car from Klipdrift to Cape Town and from there by ship to Southampton. The journey took four weeks. Kate's pride would not let her admit it, but she was thrilled to be travelling with David. *It's like a honeymoon*, she thought, *except that we're not married. Not yet.*

Aboard ship, David spent a great deal of time working in his stateroom. Kate curled up on the couch, silently watching him, content to be near him.

Once she asked, 'Don't you get bored working on all those figures, David?'

He put down his pen and looked at her. 'They're not just figures, Kate. They're stories.'

'What kind of stories?'

'If you know how to read them, they're stories about companies we're buying or selling, people who work for us. Thousands of people all over the world earn a living because of the company your father founded.'

'Am I anything like my father?'

'In many ways, yes. He was a stubborn, independent man.'

'Am I a stubborn, independent woman?'

'You're a spoiled brat. The man who marries you is going to have one hell of a life.'

Kate smiled dreamily. *Poor David.*

In the dining room, on their last night at sea, David asked, 'Why are you so difficult, Kate?'

'Am I?'

'You know you are. You drive your poor mother crazy.'

Kate put her hand over his. 'Do I drive you crazy?'

David's face reddened. 'Stop that. I don't understand you.'

'Yes, you do.'

'Why can't you be like other girls your age?'

'I'd rather die first. I don't want to be like anybody else.'

'God knows you're not!'

'You won't marry anyone else until I'm grown up enough for you, will you, David? I'll get older as fast as I can. I promise. Just don't meet anybody you love, please.'

He was touched by her earnestness. He took her hand in his and said, 'Kate, when I get married, I'd like my daughter to be exactly like you.'

Kate rose to her feet and said in a voice that rang through the dining salon, 'You can bloody well go to hell, David Blackwell!' And she stormed out of the room, as everyone stared.

They had three days together in London, and Kate loved every minute of it.

'I have a treat for you,' David told her. 'I got two tickets for *Mrs Wiggs of the Cabbage Patch*.'

'Thank you, David. I want to go to the Gaiety.'

'You can't. That's a – a music-hall revue. That's not for you.'

'I won't know until I see it, will I?' she said stubbornly.

They went to the Gaiety.

Kate loved the look of London. The mixture of motorcars and carriages, the ladies beautifully dressed in lace and tulle and light satins and glittering jewellery, and the men in dinner clothes with piqué waistcoats and white shirtfronts. They had dinner at the Ritz, and a late supper at the Savoy. And when it was time to leave, Kate thought, *We'll come back here. David and I will come back here.*

When they arrived at Cheltenham, they were ushered into the office of Mrs Keaton.

'I want to thank you for enrolling Kate,' David said.

'I'm sure we'll enjoy having her. And it's a pleasure to accommodate a friend of my husband.'

At that moment, Kate knew she had been deceived. It was *David* who had wanted her sent away and had arranged for her to come here.

She was so furious and hurt she refused to say good-bye to him.

THIRTEEN

Cheltenham School was unbearable. There were rules and regulations for everything. The girls had to wear identical uniforms, down to their knickers. The school day was ten hours long, and every minute was rigidly structured. Mrs Keaton ruled the pupils and her staff with a rod of iron. The girls were there to learn manners and discipline, etiquette and decorum, so that they could one day attract desirable husbands.

Kate wrote her mother, 'It's a bloody prison. The girls here are awful. All they ever talk about are bloody clothes and bloody boys. The bloody teachers are monsters. They'll never keep me here. I'm going to escape.'

Kate managed to run away from the school three times, and each time she was caught and brought back, unrepentant.

At a weekly staff meeting, when Kate's name was brought up, one of the teachers said, 'The child is uncontrollable. I think we should send her back to South Africa.'

Mrs Keaton replied, 'I'm inclined to agree with you, but let's look upon it as a challenge. If we can succeed in disciplining Kate McGregor, we can succeed in disciplining anyone.'

Kate remained in school.

To the amazement of her teachers, Kate became interested in the farm that the school maintained. The farm had vegetable gardens, chickens, cows, pigs and horses. Kate spent as much time as possible there, and when Mrs Keaton learned of this, she was immensely pleased.

'You see,' the headmistress told her staff, 'it was simply a question of patience. Kate has finally found her interest in life. One day she will marry a landowner and be of enormous assistance to him.'

The following morning, Oscar Denker, the man in charge of running the farm, came to see the headmistress. 'One of your students,' he said, 'that Kate McGregor – I wish you'd keep her away from my farm.'

'Whatever are you talking about?' Mrs Keaton asked. 'I happen to know she's very interested.'

'Sure she is, but do you know what she's interested in? The animals fornicating, if you'll excuse my language.'

'*What?*'

'That's right. She stands around all day, just watching the animals do it to each other.'

'Bloody hell!' Mrs Keaton said.

Kate still had not forgiven David for sending her into exile, but she missed him terribly. *It's my fate*, she thought gloomily, *to be in love with a man I hate.* She counted the days she was away from him, like a prisoner marking time until the day of release. Kate was afraid he would do something dreadful, like marry another woman while she was trapped in the bloody school. *If he does*, Kate thought, *I'll kill them both. No. I'll just kill her. They'll arrest me and hang me, and when I'm on the gallows, he'll realize that he loves me. But it will be too late. He'll beg me to forgive him. 'Yes, David, my darling, I forgive you. You were too foolish to know when you held a great love in the palm of your hand. You let it fly away like a little bird. Now that little bird is about to be hanged. Good-bye, David.'* But at the last minute she would be reprieved and David would take her in his arms and carry her off to some exotic country where the food was better than the bloody slop they served at bloody Cheltenham.

Kate received a note from David saying he was going to be in London and would come to visit her. Kate's imagination was inflamed. She found a dozen hidden meanings in his note. *Why was he going to be in England? To be near her, of course.*

Why was he coming to visit her? Because he finally knew he loved her and could not bear to be away from her any longer. He was going to sweep her off her feet and take her out of this terrible place. She could scarcely contain her happiness. Kate's fantasy was so real that the day David arrived, Kate went around saying good-bye to her class-mates. 'My lover is coming to take me out of here,' she told them.

The girls looked at her in silent disbelief. All except Georgina Christy, who scoffed, 'You're lying again, Kate McGregor.'

'Just wait and see. He's tall and handsome, and he's mad about me.'

When David arrived, he was puzzled by the fact that all the girls in the school seemed to be star-ing at him. They looked at him and whispered and giggled, and the minute they caught his eye, they blushed and turned away.

'They act as though they've never seen a man before,' David told Kate. He looked at her suspi-ciously. 'Have you been saying anything about me?'

'Of course not,' Kate said haughtily. 'Why would I do that?'

They ate in the school's large dining room, and David brought Kate up to date on everything that was happening at home. 'Your mother sends her love. She's expecting you home for the summer holiday.'

'How is mother?'

'She's fine. She's working hard.'

'Is the company doing well, David?'

He was surprised by her sudden interest. 'It's doing very well. Why?'

Because, Kate thought, *someday it will belong to me, and you and I will share it.* 'I was just curious.'

He looked at her untouched plate. 'You're not eating.'

Kate was not interested in food. She was waiting for the magic moment, the moment when David would say, '*Come away with me, Kate. You're a woman now, and I want you. We're going to be married.*'

The dessert came and went. Coffee came and went, and still no magic words from David.

It was not until he looked at his watch and said, 'Well, I'd better be going or I'll miss my train,' that Kate realized with a feeling of horror that he had not come to take her away at all. The bastard was going to leave her there to rot!

David had enjoyed his visit with Kate. She was a bright and amusing child, and the waywardness she had once shown was now under control. David patted Kate's hand fondly and asked, 'Is there anything I can do for you before I leave, Kate?'

She looked him in the eye and said sweetly, 'Yes, David, there is. You can do me an enormous favour. *Get out of my bloody life!*' And she walked out of the room with great dignity, her head held high, leaving him sitting there, mouth agape.

* * *

Margaret found that she missed Kate. The girl was unruly and contrary, but Margaret realized that she was the only living person she loved. *She's going to be a great woman*, Margaret thought with pride. *But I want her to have the manners of a lady*.

Kate came home for summer vacation. 'How are you getting along in school?' Margaret asked.

'I hate it! It's like being surrounded by a hundred nannies.'

Margaret studied her daughter. 'Do the other girls feel the same way, Kate?'

'What do *they* know?' she said contemptuously. 'You should *see* the girls at that school! They've been sheltered all their lives. They don't know a damn thing about life.'

'Oh, dear,' Margaret said. 'That must be awful for you.'

'Don't laugh at me, please. They've never even been to South Africa. The only animals they've seen have been in zoos. None of them has ever seen a diamond mine or a gold mine.'

'Underprivileged.'

Kate said, 'All right. But when I turn out like them, you're going to be bloody sorry.'

'Do you think you'll turn out like them?'

Kate grinned wickedly. 'Of course not! Are you mad?'

An hour after Kate arrived home, she was outside playing rugby with the children of the servants.

Margaret watched her through the window and thought, *I'm wasting my money. She's never going to change.*

That evening, at dinner, Kate asked casually, 'Is David in town?'

'He's been in Australia. He'll be back tomorrow, I think.'

'Is he coming to dinner Friday night?'

'Probably.' She studied Kate and said, 'You like David, don't you?'

She shrugged. 'He's all right, I suppose.'

'I see,' Margaret said. She smiled to herself as she remembered Kate's vow to marry David.

'I don't *dislike* him, Mother. I mean, I like him as a human being. I just can't stand him as a *man*.'

When David arrived for dinner Friday night, Kate flew to the door to greet him. She hugged him and whispered in his ear, 'I forgive you. Oh, I've missed you so much, David! Have you missed me?'

Automatically he said, 'Yes.' And then he thought with astonishment, *By God, I have missed her.* He had never known anyone like this child. He had watched her grow up, and each time he encountered her she was a revelation to him. She was almost sixteen years old and she had started to fill out. She had let her black hair grow long, and it fell softly over her shoulders. Her features had matured, and there was a sensuality about her that he had not noticed before. She was a beauty, with a quick intelligence and a strong will. *She's going to be a handful for some man*, David thought.

At dinner David asked, 'How are you getting along in school, Kate?'

'Oh, I just love it,' she gushed. 'I'm really learning a lot. The teachers are wonderful, and I've made a lot of great friends.'

Margaret sat in stunned silence.

'David, will you take me to the mines with you?'

'Is that how you want to waste your vacation?'

'Yes, please.'

A trip down into the mines took a full day, and that meant she would be with David all that time.

'If your mother says it's all right –'

'Please, mother!'

'All right, darling. As long as you're with David, I know you'll be safe.' Margaret hoped David would be safe.

The Kruger-Brent Diamond Mine near Bloemfontein was a gigantic operation, with hundreds of workers engaged in digging, engineering, washing or sorting.

'This is one of the company's most profitable mines,' David told Kate. They were above ground in the manager's office, waiting for an escort to take them down into the mine. Against one wall was a showcase filled with diamonds of all colours and sizes.

'Each diamond has a distinct characteristic,' David explained. 'The original diamonds from the banks of the Vaal are alluvial, and their sides are worn down from the abrasion of centuries.'

He's more handsome than ever, Kate thought. *I love his eyebrows.*

'These stones all come from different mines, but they can be easily identified by their appearance. See this one? You can tell by the size and yellow cast that it comes from Paardspan. De Beer's diamonds have an oily-looking surface and are dodecahedral in shape.'

He's brilliant. He knows everything.

'You can tell this one is from the mine at Kimberley because it's an octahedron. Their diamonds range from smoky-glassy to pure white.'

I wonder if the manager thinks David is my lover. I hope so.

'The colour of a diamond helps determine its value. The colours are named on a scale of one to ten. At the top is the tone blue-white, and at the bottom is the draw, which is a brown colour.'

He smells so wonderful. It's such a – such a male smell. I love his arms and shoulders. I wish –

'Kate!'

She said guiltily, 'Yes, David?'

'Are you listening to me?'

'Of course I am.' There was indignation in her voice. 'I've heard every word.'

They spent the next two hours in the bowels of the mine, and then had lunch. It was Kate's idea of a heavenly day.

* * *

When Kate returned home late in the afternoon, Margaret said, 'Did you enjoy yourself?'

'It was wonderful. Mining is really fascinating.'

Half an hour later, Margaret happened to glance out of the window. Kate was on the ground wrestling with the son of one of the gardeners.

The following year, Kate's letters from school were cautiously optimistic. She had been made captain of the hockey and lacrosse teams, and was at the head of her class scholastically. The school was not really all *that* bad, she wrote, and there were even a few girls in her classes who were reasonably nice. She asked permission to bring two of her friends home for the summer vacation, and Margaret was delighted. The house would be alive again with the sound of youthful laughter. She could not wait for her daughter to come home. Her dreams were all for Kate now. *Jamie and I are the past*, Maggie thought. *Kate is the future. And what a wonderful, bright future it will be!'*

When Kate was home during her vacation, all the eligible young men of Klipdrift flocked around besieging her for dates, but Kate was not interested in any of them. David was in America, and she impatiently awaited his return. When he came to the house, Kate greeted him at the door. She wore a white dress circled in by a black velvet belt that accentuated her lovely bosom. When David embraced her, he was astonished by the warmth of her response. He drew back and looked at her. There was something different about her, something knowing. There was an expression in her eyes he could not define, and it made him vaguely uneasy.

The few times David saw Kate during that vacation she was surrounded by boys, and he found himself wondering which would be the lucky one. David was called back to Australia on business, and when he returned to Klipdrift, Kate was on her way to England.

In Kate's last year of school, David appeared unexpectedly one evening. Usually his visits were preceded by a letter or a telephone call. This time there had been no warning.

'David! What a wonderful surprise!' Kate hugged him. 'You should have told me you were coming. I would have –'

'Kate, I've come to take you home.'

She pulled back and looked up at him. 'Is something wrong?'

'I'm afraid your mother is very ill.'

Kate stood stark still for a moment. 'I'll get ready.'

Kate was shocked by her mother's appearance. She had seen her only a few months earlier, and Margaret had seemed to be in robust health. Now she was pale and emaciated, and the bright spirit had gone out of her eyes. It was as though the cancer that was eating at her flesh had also eaten at her soul.

Kate sat at the side of the bed and held her mother's hand in hers. 'Oh, Mother,' she said. 'I'm so bloody sorry.'

Margaret squeezed her daughter's hand. 'I'm ready, darling. I suppose I've been ready ever since your father died.' She looked up at Kate. 'Do you want to hear something silly? I've never told this to a living soul before.' She hesitated, then went on. 'I've always been worried that there was no one to take proper care of your father. Now I can do it.'

Margaret was buried three days later. Her mother's death shook Kate deeply. She had lost her father and a brother, but she had never known them; they were only storied figments of the past. Her mother's death was real and painful. Kate was eighteen years old and suddenly alone in the world, and the thought of that was frightening.

David watched her standing at her mother's graveside, bravely trying not to cry. But when they returned to the house, Kate broke down, unable to stop sobbing. 'She was always so w-wonderful to me, David, and I was such a r-rotten daughter.'

David tried to console her. 'You've been a wonderful daughter, Kate.'

'I was n-nothing b-but trouble. I'd give anything if I could m-make it up to her. I didn't want her to die, David! Why did God do this to her?'

He waited, letting Kate cry herself out. When she was calmer, David said, 'I know it's hard to believe now, but one day this pain will go away. And you know what you'll be left with, Kate? Happy memories. You'll remember all the good things you and your mother had.'

'I suppose so. Only right now it hurts so b-bloody much.'

The following morning they discussed Kate's future.

'You have family in Scotland,' David reminded her.

'No!' Kate replied sharply. 'They're not family. They're relatives.' Her voice was bitter. 'When Father wanted to come to this country, they laughed at him. No one would help him except his mother, and she's dead. No. I won't have anything to do with them.'

David sat there thinking. 'Do you plan to finish out the school term?' Before Kate could answer, David went on. 'I think your mother would have wanted you to.'

'Then I'll do it.' She looked down at the floor, her eyes unseeing. 'Bloody hell,' Kate said.

'I know,' David said gently. 'I know.'

* * *

Kate finished the school term as class valedictorian, and David was there for the graduation.

Riding from Johannesburg to Klipdrift in the private railway car, David said, 'You know, all this will belong to you in a few years. This car, the mines, the company – it's yours. You're a very rich young woman. You can sell the company for many millions of pounds.' He looked at her and added, 'Or you can keep it. You'll have to think about it.'

'I have thought about it,' Kate told him. She looked at him and smiled. 'My father was a pirate, David. A wonderful old pirate. I wish I could have known him. I'm not going to sell this company. Do you know why? Because the pirate named it after two guards who were trying to kill him. Wasn't that a lovely thing to do? Sometimes at night when I can't sleep, I think about my father and Banda crawling through the sea *mis*, and I can hear the voices of the guards: *Kruger . . . Brent . . .*' She looked up at David. 'No, I'll never sell my father's company. Not as long as you'll stay on and run it.'

David said quietly, 'I'll stay as long as you need me.'

'I've decided to enroll in business school.'

'A business school?' There was surprise in his voice.

'This is 1910,' Kate reminded him. 'They have

business schools in Johannesburg where women are allowed to attend.'

'But –'

'You asked me what I wanted to do with my money.' She looked him in the eye and said, 'I want to earn it.'

FOURTEEN

Business school was an exciting new adventure. When Kate had gone to Cheltenham, it had been a chore, a necessary evil. This was different. Every class taught her something useful, something that would help her when she ran the company. The course included accounting, management, international trade and business administration. Once a week David telephoned to see how she was getting along.

'I love it,' Kate told him. 'It's really exciting, David.'

One day she and David would be working together, side by side, late at night, all by themselves. *And one of those nights, David would turn to her and say, 'Kate, darling, I've been such a blind fool. Will you marry me?' And an instant later, she would be in his arms . . .*

But that would have to wait. In the meantime, she had a lot to learn. Resolutely, Kate turned to her homework.

The business course lasted two years, and Kate returned to Klipdrift in time to celebrate her twentieth birthday. David met her at the station. Impulsively, Kate flung her arms around him and hugged him. 'Oh, David, I'm so happy to see you.'

He pulled away and said awkwardly, 'It's nice to see you, Kate.' There was an uncomfortable stiffness in his manner.

'Is something wrong?'

'No. It's – it's just that young ladies don't go around hugging men in public.'

She looked at him a moment. 'I see. I promise not to embarrass you again.'

As they drove to the house, David covertly studied Kate. She was a hauntingly beautiful girl, innocent and vulnerable, and David was determined that he would never take advantage of that.

On Monday morning Kate moved into her new office at Kruger-Brent, Ltd. It was like suddenly being plunged into some exotic and bizarre universe that had its own customs and its own language. There was a bewildering array of divisions, subsidiaries, regional departments, franchises and foreign branches. The products that the company manufactured or owned seemed endless. There were steel mills, cattle ranches, a railroad, a shipping line and, of course, the foundation of the family fortune: diamonds and gold, zinc and platinum and magnesium, mined each hour around the clock, pouring into the coffers of the company.

Power.

It was almost too much to take in. Kate sat in David's office listening to him make decisions that affected thousands of people around the world. The general managers of the various divisions made recommendations, but as often as not, David over-ruled them.

'Why do you do that? Don't they know their jobs?' Kate asked.

'Of course they do, but that's not the point,' David explained. 'Each manager sees his own division as the centre of the world, and that's as it should be. But someone has to have an overall view and decide what's best for the company. Come on. We're having lunch with someone I want you to meet.'

David took Kate into the large, private dining room adjoining Kate's office. A young, raw-boned man with a lean face and inquisitive brown eyes was waiting for them.

'This is Brad Rogers,' David said. 'Brad, meet your new boss, Kate McGregor.'

Brad Rogers held out his hand. 'I'm pleased to meet you, Miss McGregor.'

'Brad is our secret weapon,' David said. 'He knows as much about Kruger-Brent, Limited, as I do. If I ever leave, you don't have to worry. Brad will be here.'

If I ever leave. The thought of it sent a wave of panic through Kate. *Of course, David would never leave the company.* Kate could think of nothing else through lunch, and when it was over she had no idea what she had eaten.

After lunch, they discussed South Africa.

'We're going to run into trouble soon,' David warned. 'The government has just imposed poll taxes.'

'Exactly what does that mean?' Kate asked.

'It means that blacks, coloureds and Indians have to pay two pounds each for every member of their family. That's more than a month's wages for them.'

Kate thought about Banda and was filled with a sense of apprehension. The discussion moved on to other topics.

Kate enjoyed her new life tremendously. Every decision involved a gamble of millions of pounds. Big business was a matching of wits, the courage to gamble and the instinct to know when to quit and when to press ahead.

'Business is a game,' David told Kate, 'played for fantastic stakes, and you're in competition with experts. If you want to win, you have to learn to be a master of the game.'

And that was what Kate was determined to do. Learn.

Kate lived alone in the big house, except for the servants. She and David continued their ritual Friday-night dinners, but when Kate invited him over on any other night, he invariably found an excuse not to come. During business hours they were together constantly, but even then David seemed to have erected a barrier between them, a wall that Kate was unable to penetrate.

On her twenty-first birthday, all the shares in Kruger-Brent, Ltd., were turned over to Kate. She now officially had control of the company. 'Let's have dinner tonight to celebrate,' she suggested to David.

'I'm sorry, Kate, I have a lot of work to catch up on.'

Kate dined alone that night, wondering why. *Was it she, or was it David?* He would have to be deaf, dumb and blind not to know how she felt about him, how she had always felt about him. She would have to do something about it.

The company was negotiating for a shipping line in the United States.

'Why don't you and Brad go to New York and close the deal?' David suggested to Kate. 'It will be good experience for you.'

Kate would have liked for David to have gone with her, but she was too proud to say so. She would handle this without him. Besides, she had never been to America. She looked forward to the experience.

The closing of the shipping-line deal went smoothly. 'While you're over there,' David had told her, 'you should see something of the country.'

Kate and Brad visited company subsidiaries in Detroit, Chicago, Pittsburgh and New York, and Kate was amazed by the size and energy of the United States. The highlight of Kate's trip was a visit to Dark Harbor, Maine, on an enchanting little island called Islesboro, in Penobscot Bay. She had been invited to dinner at the home of Charles Dana Gibson, the artist. There were twelve people at dinner and, except for Kate, they all had homes on the island.

'This place has an interesting history,' Gibson told Kate. 'Years ago, residents used to get here by small coasting vessels from Boston. When the boat landed, they'd be met by a buggy and taken to their houses.'

'How many people live on this island?' Kate asked.

'About fifty families. Did you see the lighthouse when the ferry docked?'

'Yes.'

'It's run by a lighthouse keeper and his dog. When a boat goes by the dog goes out and rings the bell.'

Kate laughed. 'You're joking.'

'No, ma'am. The funny thing is the dog is deaf as a stone. He puts his ear against the bell to feel if there's any vibration.'

Kate smiled. 'It sounds as if you have a fascinating island here.'

'It might be worth your while staying over and taking a look around in the morning.'

On an impulse, Kate said, 'Why not?'

She spent the night at the island's only hotel, the Islesboro Inn. In the morning she hired a horse and carriage, driven by one of the islanders. They left the centre of Dark Harbor, which consisted of a general store, a hardware store and a small restaurant, and a few minutes later they were driving through a beautiful wooded area. Kate noticed that none of the little winding roads had names, nor were there any names on the mailboxes. She turned to her guide. 'Don't people get lost here without any signs?'

'Nope. The islanders know where everythin' is.'

Kate gave him a sidelong look. 'I see.'

At the lower end of the island, they passed a burial ground.

'Would you stop, please?' Kate asked.

She stepped out of the carriage and walked over to the old cemetery and wandered around looking at the tombstones.

JOB PENDLETON, DIED JANUARY 25, 1794, AGE 47. The epitaph read: *Beneath this stone, I rest my head in slumber sweet; Christ blessed the bed.*

JANE, WIFE OF THOMAS PENDLETON, DIED FEBRUARY 25, 1802, AGE 47.

There were spirits here from another century, from an era long gone. CAPTAIN WILLIAM HATCH, DROWNED IN LONG ISLAND SOUND, OCTOBER 1866, AGE 30 YEARS. The epitaph on his stone read: *Storms all weathered and life's seas crossed.*

Kate stayed there a long time, enjoying the quiet and peace. Finally, she returned to the carriage and they drove on.

'What is it like here in the winter?' Kate asked.

'Cold. The bay used to freeze solid, and they'd come from the mainland by sleigh. Now a' course, we got the ferry.'

They rounded a curve, and there, next to the water below, was a beautiful white-shingled, two-storey house surrounded by delphinium, wild roses and poppies. The shutters on the eight front windows were painted green, and next to the double doors were white benches and six pots of red geraniums. It looked like something out of a fairly tale.

'Who owns that house?'

'That's the old Dreben house. Mrs Dreben died a few months back.'

'Who lives there now?'

'Nobody, I reckon.'

'Do you know if it's for sale?'

The guide looked at Kate and said, 'If it is, it'll probably be bought by the son of one of the families already livin' here. The islanders don't take kindly to strangers.'

It was the wrong thing to say to Kate.

One hour later, she was speaking to a lawyer for the estate. 'It's about the Dreben house,' Kate said. 'Is it for sale?'

The lawyer pursed his lips, 'Well, yes, and no.'

'What does that mean?'

'It's for sale, but a few people are already interested in buying it.'

The old families on the island, Kate thought. 'Have they made an offer?'

'Not yet, but –'

'I'm making one,' Kate said.

He said condescendingly, 'That's an expensive house.'

'Name your price.'

'Fifty thousand dollars.'

'Let's go look at it.'

The inside of the house was even more enchanting than Kate had anticipated. The large, lovely hall faced the sea through a wall of glass. On one side of the hall was a large ballroom, and on the other side, a living room with fruitwood panelling stained by time, and an enormous fireplace. There was a library, and a huge kitchen with an iron stove and a large pine worktable, and off of that was a butler's pantry and laundry room. Downstairs, the house had six bedrooms for the servants and one bathroom. Upstairs was a master bedroom suite and four smaller bedrooms. It was a much larger house than Kate had expected. *But when David and I have our children*, she thought, *we'll need all these rooms*. The grounds ran all the way down to the bay, where there was a private dock.

Kate turned to the lawyer. 'I'll take it.'

She decided to name it Cedar Hill House.

She could not wait to get back to Klipdrift to break the news to David.

On the way back to South Africa, Kate was filled with a wild excitement. The house in Dark Harbor was a sign, a symbol that she and David would be married. She knew he would love the house as much as she did.

On the afternoon Kate and Brad arrived back in Klipdrift, Kate hurried to David's office. He was seated at his desk, working, and the sight of him set Kate's heart pounding. She had not realized how much she had missed him.

David rose to his feet. 'Kate! Welcome home!' And before she could speak, he said, 'I wanted you to be the first to know. I'm getting married.'

FIFTEEN

It had begun casually six weeks earlier. In the middle of a hectic day, David received a message that Tim O'Neil, the friend of an important American diamond buyer, was in Klipdrift and asking if David would be good enough to welcome him and perhaps take him to dinner. David had no time to waste on tourists, but he did not want to offend his customer. He would have asked Kate to entertain the visitor, but she was on a tour of the company's plants in North America with Brad Rogers. *I'm stuck*, David decided. He called the hotel where O'Neil was staying and invited him to dinner that evening.

'My daughter is with me,' O'Neil told him. 'I hope you don't mind if I bring her along?'

David was in no mood to spend the evening with a child. 'Not at all,' he said politely. He would make sure the evening was a short one.

They met at the Grand Hotel, in the dining room. When David arrived, O'Neil and his daughter were already seated at the table. O'Neil was a handsome, grey-haired Irish-American in his early fifties. His daughter, Josephine, was the most beautiful woman David had ever seen. She was in her early thirties, with a stunning figure, soft blond hair and clear blue eyes. The breath went out of David at the sight of her.

'I – I'm sorry I'm late,' he said. 'Some last-minute business.'

Josephine watched his reaction to her with amusement. 'Sometimes that's the most exciting kind,' she said innocently. 'My father tells me you're a very important man, Mr Blackwell.'

'Not really – and it's David.'

She nodded. 'That's a good name. It suggests great strength.'

Before the dinner was over, David decided that Josephine O'Neil was much more than just a beautiful woman. She was intelligent, had a sense of humour and was skilful at making him feel at ease. David felt she was genuinely interested in him. She asked him questions about himself that no one had ever asked before. By the time the evening ended, he was already half in love with her.

'Where's your home?' David asked Tim O'Neil.

'San Francisco.'

'Will you be going back soon?' He made it sound as casual as he could.

'Next week.'

Josephine smiled at David. 'If Klipdrift is as

interesting as it promises to be, I might persuade Father to stay a little longer.'

'I intend to make it as interesting as possible,' David assured her. 'How would you like to go down into a diamond mine?'

'We'd love it,' Josephine answered. 'Thank you.'

At one time David had personally escorted important visitors down into the mines, but he had long since delegated that task to subordinates. Now he heard himself saying, 'Would tomorrow morning be convenient?' He had half a dozen meetings scheduled for the morning, but they suddenly seemed unimportant.

He took the O'Neils down a rockshaft, twelve hundred feet below ground. The shaft was six feet wide and twenty feet long, divided into four compartments, one for pumping, two for hoisting the blue diamondiferous earth and one with a double-decked cage to carry the miners to and from work.

'I've always been curious about something,' Josephine said. 'Why are diamonds measured in carats?'

'The carat was named for the carob seed,' David explained, 'because of its consistency in weight. One carat equals two hundred milligrams, or one one-hundred-forty-second of an ounce.'

Josephine said, 'I'm absolutely fascinated, David.'

And he wondered if she was referring only to

the diamonds. Her nearness was intoxicating. Every time he looked at Josephine, David felt a fresh sense of excitement.

'You really should see something of the countryside,' David told the O'Neils. 'If you're free tomorrow, I'd be happy to take you around.'

Before her father could say anything, Josephine replied, 'That would be lovely.'

David was with Josephine and her father every day after that, and each day David fell more deeply in love. He had never known anyone as bewitching.

When David arrived to pick up the O'Neils for dinner one evening and Tim O'Neil said, 'I'm a bit tired tonight, David. Would you mind if I didn't go along?' David tried to hide his pleasure.

'No, sir. I understand.'

Josephine gave David a mischievous smile. 'I'll try to keep you entertained,' she promised.

David took her to a restaurant in a hotel that had just opened. The room was crowded, but David was recognized and given a table immediately. A three-piece ensemble was playing American music.

David asked, 'Would you like to dance?'

'I'd love to.'

A moment later, Josephine was in his arms on the dance floor, and it was magic. David held her lovely body close to his, and he could feel her respond.

'Josephine, I'm in love with you.'

She put a finger to his lips. 'Please, David . . . don't . . .'

'Why?'

'Because I couldn't marry you.'

'Do you love me?'

She smiled up at him, her blue eyes sparkling. 'I'm crazy about you, my darling. Can't you tell?'

'Then why?'

'Because I could never live in Klipdrift. I'd go mad.'

'You could give it a try.'

'David, I'm tempted, but I know what would happen. If I married you and had to live here, I'd turn into a screaming shrew and we'd end up hating each other. I'd rather we said good-bye this way.'

'I don't want to say good-bye.'

She looked up into his face, and David felt her body melt into his. 'David, is there any chance that you could live in San Francisco?'

It was an impossible idea. 'What would I do there?'

'Let's have breakfast in the morning. I want you to talk to Father.'

Tim O'Neil said, 'Josephine has told me about your conversation last night. Looks like you two have a problem. But I might have a solution, if you're interested.'

'I'm very interested, sir.'

O'Neil picked up a brown-leather briefcase and removed some blueprints. 'Do you know anything about frozen foods?'

'I'm afraid I don't.'

'They first started freezing food in the United States in 1865. The problem was transporting it long distances without the food thawing out. We've got refrigerated railway cars, but no one's been able to come up with a way to refrigerate trucks.' O'Neil tapped the blueprints. 'Until now. I just received a patent on it. This is going to revolutionize the entire food industry, David.'

David glanced at the blueprints. 'I'm afraid these don't mean much to me, Mr O'Neil.'

'That doesn't matter. I'm not looking for a technical expert. I have plenty of those. What I'm looking for is financing and someone to run the business. This isn't some wild pipe dream. I've talked to the top food processors in the business. This is going to be big – bigger than you can imagine. I need someone like you.'

'The company headquarters will be in San Francisco,' Josephine added.

David sat there silent, digesting what he had just heard. 'You say you've been given a patent on this?'

'That's right. I'm all set to move.'

'Would you mind if I borrowed these blueprints and showed them to someone?'

'I have no objection at all.'

*　　*　　*

The first thing David did was to check on Tim O'Neil. He learned that O'Neil had a solid reputation in San Francisco. He had been head of the science department at Berkeley College there and was highly regarded. David knew nothing about the freezing of food, but he intended to find out.

'I'll be back in five days, darling. I want you and your father to wait for me.'

'As long as you like. I'll miss you,' Josephine said.

'I'll miss you, too.' And he meant it more than she knew.

David took the train to Johannesburg and made an appointment to see Edward Broderick, the owner of the largest meat-packing plant in South Africa.

'I want your opinion on something.' David handed him the blueprints. 'I need to know if this can work.'

'I don't know a damned thing about frozen foods or trucks, but I know people who do. If you come back this afternoon, I'll have a couple of experts here for you, David.'

At four o'clock that afternoon David returned to the packing plant. He found that he was nervous, in a state of uncertainty, because he was not sure how he wanted the meeting to go. Two weeks earlier, he would have laughed if anyone had even suggested he would ever leave Kruger-Brent, Ltd. It was a part of him. He would have laughed even harder if they had told him he would have considered heading a little food company in San Francisco. It was insane, except for one thing: Josephine O'Neil.

There were two men in the room with Edward Broderick. 'This is Dr Crawford and Mr Kaufman. David Blackwell.'

They exchanged greetings. David asked, 'Have you gentlemen had a chance to look at the blueprints?'

Dr Crawford replied, 'We certainly have, Mr Blackwell. We've been over them thoroughly.'

David took a deep breath. 'And?'

'I understand that the United States Patent Office has granted a patent on this?'

'That's right.'

'Well, Mr Blackwell, whoever got that patent is going to be one very rich man.'

David nodded slowly, filled with conflicting emotions.

'It's like all great inventions – it's so simple you wonder why someone didn't think of it sooner. This one can't miss.'

David did not know how to react. He had half-hoped that the decision would be taken out of his hands. If Tim O'Neil's invention was useless, there was a chance of persuading Josephine to stay in South Africa. But what O'Neil had told him was true. It *did* work. Now David had to make his decision.

284

He thought of nothing else on the journey back to Klipdrift. If he accepted, it would mean leaving the company, starting up a new, untried business. He was an American, but America was a foreign country to him. He held an important position in one of the most powerful companies in the world. He loved his job. Jamie and Margaret McGregor had been very good to him. And then there was Kate. He had cared for her since she was a baby. He had watched her grow up from a stubborn, dirty-faced tomboy to a lovely young woman. Her life was a photo album in his mind. He turned the pages and there was Kate at four, eight, ten, fourteen, twenty-one – vulnerable, unpredictable . . .

By the time the train arrived at Klipdrift, David had made up his mind. He was going to leave Kruger-Brent, Ltd.

He drove directly to the Grand Hotel and went up to the O'Neils' suite. Josephine opened the door for him.

'David!'

He took her in his arms and kissed her hungrily, feeling her warm body pressing against his.

'Oh, David, I've missed you so much. I don't ever want to be away from you again.'

'You won't have to,' David said slowly. 'I'm going to San Francisco . . .'

David had waited with growing anxiety for Kate to return from the United States. Now that he had made his decision, he was eager to get started on his new life, impatient to marry Josephine.

And now Kate was back, and he was standing in front of her saying, 'I'm getting married.'

Kate heard the words through a roaring in her ears. She felt suddenly faint, and she gripped the edge of the desk for support. *I want to die*, she thought. *Please let me die.*

Somehow, from some deep wellspring of will, she managed a smile. 'Tell me about her, David.' She was proud of how calm her voice sounded. 'Who is she?'

'Her name is Josephine O'Neil. She's been visiting here with her father. I know you two will be good friends, Kate. She's a fine woman.'

'She must be, if you love her, David.'

He hesitated. 'There's one more thing, Kate. I'm going to be leaving the company.'

The world was falling in on her. 'Just because you're getting married, doesn't mean you have to –'

'It isn't that. Josephine's father is starting a new business in San Francisco. They need me.'

'So – so you'll be living in San Francisco.'

'Yes. Brad Rogers can handle my job easily, and we'll pick a top management team to back him up. Kate, I – I can't tell you what a difficult decision this was for me.'

'Of course, David. You – you must love her very much. When do I get to meet the bride?'

David smiled, pleased at how well Kate was

taking the news. 'Tonight, if you're free for dinner.'

'Yes, I'm free.'

She would not let the tears come until she was alone.

The four of them had dinner at the McGregor mansion. The moment Kate saw Josephine, she blanched, *Oh God! No wonder he's in love with her!* She was dazzling. Just being in her presence made Kate feel awkward and ugly. And to make matters worse, Josephine was gracious and charming. And obviously very much in love with David. *Bloody hell!*

During dinner Tim O'Neil told Kate about the new company.

'It sounds very interesting,' Kate said.

'I'm afraid it's no Kruger-Brent, Limited, Miss McGregor. We'll have to start small, but with David running it, we'll do all right.'

'With David running it, you can't miss,' Kate assured him.

The evening was an agony. In the same cataclysmic moment, she had lost the man she loved and the one person who was indispensable to Kruger-Brent, Ltd. She carried on a conversation and managed to get through the evening, but afterwards she had no recollection of what she said or did. She only knew that every time David and Josephine looked at each other or touched, she wanted to kill herself.

On the way back to the hotel, Josephine said, 'She's in love with you, David.'

He smiled. 'Kate? No. We're friends. We have been since she was a baby. She liked you a lot.'

Josephine smiled. *Men are so naïve.*

In David's office the following morning, Tim O'Neil and David sat facing each other. 'I'll need about two months to get my affairs in order here,' David said. 'I've been thinking about the financing we'll need to begin with. If we go to one of the big companies they'll swallow us up and give us a small share. It won't belong to us anymore. I think we should finance it ourselves. I figure it will cost eighty thousand dollars to get started. I've saved the equivalent of about forty thousand dollars. We'll need forty thousand more.'

'I have ten thousand dollars,' Tim O'Neil said. 'And I have a brother who will loan me another five thousand.'

'So, we're twenty-five thousand dollars short,' David said. 'We'll try to borrow that from a bank.'

'We'll leave for San Francisco right away,' O'Neil told David, 'and get everything set up for you.'

Josephine and her father left for the United States two days later. 'Send them to Cape Town in the private railway car, David.' Kate offered.

'That's very generous of you, Kate.'

The morning Josephine left, David felt as though

a piece of his life had been taken away. He could not wait to join her in San Francisco.

The next few weeks were taken up with a search for a management team to back up Brad Rogers. A list of possible candidates was carefully drawn up, and Kate and David and Brad spent hours discussing each one.

'. . . Taylor is a good technician, but he's weak on management.'

'What about Simmons?'

'He's good, but he's not ready yet,' Brad decided. 'Give him another five years.'

'Babcock?'

'Not a bad choice. Let's discuss him.'

'What about Peterson?'

'Not enough of a company man,' David said. 'He's too concerned with himself.' And even as he said it, he felt a pang of guilt because he was deserting Kate.

They continued on with the list of names. By the end of the month, they had narrowed the choice to four men to work with Brad Rogers. All of them were working abroad, and they were sent for so that they could be interviewed. The first two interviews went well. 'I'd be satisfied with either one of them,' Kate assured David and Brad.

On the morning the third interview was to take place, David walked into Kate's office, his face pale. 'Is my job still open?'

Kate looked at his expression and stood up in alarm. 'What is it, David?'

'I – I –' He sank into a chair. 'Something has happened.'

Kate was out from behind the desk and by his side in an instant. 'Tell me!'

'I just got a letter from Tim O'Neil. He's sold the business.'

'What do you mean?'

'Exactly what I said. He accepted an offer of two hundred thousand dollars and a royalty for his patent from the Three Star Meat Packing Company in Chicago.' David's voice was filled with bitterness. 'The company would like to hire me to manage it for them. He regrets any inconvenience to me, but he couldn't turn down that kind of money.'

Kate looked at him intently. 'And Josephine? What does she say? She must be furious with her father.'

'There was a letter from her, too. We'll marry as soon as I come to San Francisco.'

'And you're not going?'

'Of course I'm not going!' David exploded. 'Before, I had something to offer. I could have built it into a great company. But they were in too much of a damned hurry for the money.'

'David, you're not being fair when you say "they". Just be –'

'O'Neil would never have made that deal without Josephine's approval.'

'I – I don't know what to say, David.'

'There is nothing to say. Except that I almost made the biggest mistake of my life.'

Kate walked over to the desk and picked up the list of candidates. Slowly, she began to tear it up.

In the weeks that followed, David plunged himself deeply into his work, trying to forget his bitterness and hurt. He received several letters from Josephine O'Neil, and he threw them all away, unread. But he could not get her out of his mind. Kate, deeply aware of David's pain, let him know she was there if he needed her.

Six months had passed since David received the letter from Tim O'Neil. During that time, Kate and David continued to work closely together, travel together and be alone together much of the time. Kate tried to please him in every way she could. She dressed for him, planned things he would enjoy and went out of her way to make his life as happy as possible. As far as she could tell, it was having no effect at all. And finally she lost her patience.

She and David were in Rio de Janeiro, checking on a new mineral find. They had had dinner at their hotel and were in Kate's room going over some figures late at night. Kate had changed to a comfortable kimono and slippers. When they finished, David stretched and said, 'Well, that's it for tonight. I guess I'll go on to bed.'

Kate said quietly, 'Isn't it time you came out of mourning, David?'

He looked at her in surprise. 'Mourning?'

'For Josephine O'Neil.'

'She's out of my life.'

'Then act like it.'

'Just what would you like me to do, Kate,' he asked curtly.

Kate was angry now. Angry at David's blindness, angry about all the wasted time. 'I'll tell you what I'd like you to do – kiss me.'

'What?'

'Bloody hell, David! I'm your boss, damn it!' She moved close to him. 'Kiss me.' And she pressed her lips against his and put her arms around him. She felt him resist and start to draw back. And then slowly his arms circled her body, and he kissed her.

'Kate . . .'

She whispered against his lips. 'I thought you'd never ask . . .'

They were married six weeks later. It was the biggest wedding Klipdrift had ever seen or would see again. It was held in the town's largest church and afterwards there was a reception in the town hall and everyone was invited. There were mountains of food and uncounted cases of beer and whiskey and champagne, and musicians played and the festivities lasted until dawn. When the sun came up, Kate and David slipped away.

'I'll go home and finish packing,' Kate said. 'Pick me up in an hour.'

* * *

In the pale dawn light, Kate entered the huge house alone and went upstairs to her bedroom. She walked over to a painting on the wall and pressed against the frame. The painting flew back, revealing a wall safe. She opened it and brought out a contract. It was for the purchase of the Three Star Meat Packing Company of Chicago by Kate McGregor. Next to it was a contract from the Three Star Meat Packing Company purchasing the rights to Tim O'Neil's freezing process for two hundred thousand dollars. Kate hesitated a moment, then returned the papers to the safe and locked it. David belonged to her now. He had always belonged to her. And to Kruger-Brent, Ltd. Together, they would build it into the biggest, most powerful company in the world.

Just as Jamie and Margaret McGregor would have wanted it.

BOOK THREE

Kruger-Brent, Ltd

1914–1945

SIXTEEN

They were in the library, where Jamie had once liked to sit with his brandy glass in front of him. David was arguing that there was no time for a real honeymoon. 'Someone has to mind the store, Kate.'

'Yes, Mr Blackwell. But who's going to mind me?' She curled up in David's lap, and he felt the warmth of her through her thin dress. The documents he had been reading fell to the floor. Her arms were around him, and he felt her hands sliding down his body. She pressed her hips against him, making slow, small circles, and the papers on the floor were forgotten. She felt him respond and she rose and slipped out of her dress. David watched her, marvelling at her loveliness. How could he have been so blind for so long? She was undressing him now, and there was a sudden urgency in him. They were both naked, and their bodies were pressed together. He stroked her, his fingers lightly touching her face and her neck, down to the swell of her breasts. She was moaning, and his hands moved down until he felt the velvety softness between her legs. His fingers stroked her and she whispered, 'Take me, David,' and they were on the deep, soft rug and she felt the strength of his body on top of her. There was a long sweet thrust and he was inside her, filling her, and she moved to his rhythm. It became a great tidal wave, sweeping her up higher and higher until she thought she could not bear the ecstasy of it. There was a sudden, glorious explosion deep inside her and another and another, and she thought, *I've died and gone to heaven.*

They travelled all over the world, to Paris and Zurich and Sydney and New York, taking care of company business, but wherever they went they carved out moments of time for themselves. They talked late into the night and made love and explored each other's minds and bodies. Kate was an inexhaustible delight to David. She would awaken him in the morning to make wild and pagan love to him, and a few hours later she would be at his side at a business conference, making more sense than anyone else there. She had a natural flair for business that was as rare as it was unexpected. Women were few in the top echelons of the business world. In the beginning Kate was treated with a tolerant condescension, but the attitude quickly changed to a wary respect. Kate took a delight in the manoeuvring and machinations of the game. David watched her outwit men with much greater experience. She had the instincts of a winner. She knew what she wanted and how to get it. *Power.*

They ended their honeymoon with a glorious week in Cedar Hill House at Dark Harbor.

It was on June 28, 1914, that the first talk of war was heard. Kate and David were guests at a country estate in Sussex. It was the age of country-house living and weekend guests were expected to conform to a ritual. Men dressed for breakfast, changed for midmorning lounging, changed for lunch, changed for tea – to a velvet jacket with satin piping – and changed to a formal jacket for dinner.

'For God's sake,' David protested to Kate. 'I feel like a damned peacock.'

'You're a very handsome peacock, my darling,' Kate assured him. 'When you get home, you can walk around naked.'

He took her in his arms. 'I can't wait.'

At dinner, the news came that Francis Ferdinand, heir to the Austrian-Hungarian throne, and his wife, Sophie, had been slain by an assassin.

Their host, Lord Maney, said, 'Nasty business, shooting a woman, what? But no one is going to war over some little Balkan country.'

And the conversation moved on to cricket.

Later in bed, Kate said, 'Do you think there's going to be a war, David?'

'Over some minor archduke being assassinated? No.'

It proved to be a bad guess. Austria-Hungary, suspecting that its neighbour, Serbia, had instigated the plot to assassinate Ferdinand, declared war on Serbia, and by October, most of the world's major powers were at war. It was a new kind of warfare. For the first time, mechanized vehicles were used – airplanes, airships and submarines.

The day Germany declared war, Kate said, 'This can be a wonderful opportunity for us, David.'

David frowned. 'What are you talking about?'

'Nations are going to need guns and ammunition and –'

'They're not getting them from us,' David interrupted firmly. 'We have enough business, Kate. We don't have to make profits from anyone's blood.'

'Aren't you being a bit dramatic? Someone has to make guns.'

'As long as I'm with this company, it won't be us. We won't discuss it again, Kate. The subject is closed.'

And Kate thought, *The bloody hell it is*. For the first time in their marriage, they slept apart. Kate thought, *How can David be such an idealistic ninny?*

And David thought, *How can she be so cold-blooded? The business has changed her*. The days that followed were miserable for both of them. David regretted the emotional chasm between them, but he did not know how to bridge it. Kate was too proud and headstrong to give in to him because she knew she was right.

President Woodrow Wilson had promised to keep the United States out of the war, but as German submarines began torpedoing unarmed passenger ships, and stories of German atrocities spread, pressure began to build up for America to help the Allies. 'Make the world safe for democracy,' was the slogan.

David had learned to fly in the bush country of South Africa, and when the Lafayette Escadrille was formed in France with American pilots, David went to Kate. 'I've got to enlist.'

She was appalled. 'No! It's not your war!'

'It's going to be,' David said quietly. 'The United States can't stay out. I'm an American. I want to help now.'

'You're forty-six years old!'

'I can still fly a plane, Kate. And they need all the help they can get.'

There was no way Kate could dissuade him. They spent the last few days together quietly, their differences forgotten. They loved each other, and that was all that mattered.

The night before David was to leave for France, he said, 'You and Brad Rogers can run the business as well as I can, maybe better.'

'What if something happens to you? I couldn't bear it.'

He held her close. 'Nothing will happen to me, Kate. I'll come back to you with all kinds of medals.'

He left the following morning.

David's absence was death for Kate. It had taken her so long to win him, and now every second of her day there was the ugly, creeping fear of losing him. He was always with her. She found him in the cadence of a stranger's voice, the sudden laughter on a quiet street, a phrase, a scent, a song. He was everywhere. She wrote him long letters every day. Whenever she received a letter from him, she reread it until it was in tatters. He was well, he wrote. The Germans had air superiority, but that would change. There were rumours that America would be helping soon. He would write again when he could. He loved her.

Don't let anything happen to you, my darling. I'll hate you forever if you do.

She tried to forget her loneliness and misery by plunging into work. At the beginning of the war, France and Germany had the best-equipped fighting forces in Europe, but the Allies had far greater manpower, resources and materials. Russia, with the largest army, was badly equipped and poorly commanded.

'They all need help,' Kate told Brad Roger. 'They need tanks and guns and ammunition.'

Brad Rogers was uncomfortable. 'Kate, David doesn't think –'

'David isn't here, Brad. It's up to you and me.'

But Brad Rogers knew that what Kate meant was, *It's up to me.*

Kate could not understand David's attitude about manufacturing armaments. The Allies needed weapons, and Kate felt it was her patriotic duty to supply them. She conferred with the heads of half a dozen friendly nations, and within a year Kruger-Brent, Ltd., was manufacturing guns and tanks, bombs and ammunition. The company supplied trains and tanks and uniforms and guns. Kruger-Brent was rapidly becoming one of the fastest-growing conglomerates in the world. When Kate saw the most recent revenue figures, she said to Brad Rogers, 'Have you seen these? David will have to admit he was mistaken.'

South Africa, meanwhile, was in turmoil. The party leaders had pledged their support to the Allies and accepted responsibility for defending South Africa against Germany, but the majority of Afrikaaners opposed the country's support of Great Britain. They could not forget the past so quickly.

In Europe the war was going badly for the Allies. Fighting on the western front reached a standstill. Both sides dug in, protected by trenches that stretched across France and Belgium, and the soldiers were miserable. Rain filled the dugouts with water and mud, and rats swarmed through the vermin-infested trenches. Kate was grateful that David was fighting his war in the air.

On April 6, 1917, President Wilson declared

war, and David's prediction came true. America began to mobilize.

The first American Expeditionary Force under General John J. Pershing began landing in France on June 26, 1917. New place names became a part of everyone's vocabulary: Saint-Mihiel . . . Château-Thierry . . . the Meuse-Argonne . . . Belleau Wood . . . Verdun . . . The Allies had become an irresistible force, and on November 11, 1918, the war was finally over. The world was safe for democracy.

David was on his way home.

When David disembarked from the troop ship in New York, Kate was there to meet him. They stood staring at each other for one eternal moment, ignoring the noise and the crowds around them, then Kate was in David's arms. He was thinner and tired-looking, and Kate thought, *Oh, God. I've missed him so.* She had a thousand questions to ask him, but they could wait. 'I'm taking you to Cedar Hill House,' Kate told him. 'It's a perfect place for you to rest.'

Kate had done a great deal with the house in anticipation of David's arrival home. The large, airy living room had been furnished with twin sofas covered in old rose-and-green floral chintz. Matching down-filled armchairs were grouped around the fireplace. Over the fireplace was a Vlaminck floral canvas, and, on each side of it, doré sconces. Two sets of French doors opened out onto the veranda, which ran the entire length of the house on three sides, covered with a striped awning. The rooms were bright and airy, and the view of the harbour spectacular.

Kate led David through the house, chattering away happily. He seemed strangely quiet. When they had completed the tour, Kate asked, 'Do you like what I've done with it, darling?'

'It's beautiful, Kate. Now, sit down. I want to talk to you.'

She had a sudden sinking feeling. 'Is anything wrong?'

'We seem to have become a munitions supplier for half the world.'

'Wait until you look at the books,' Kate began. 'Our profit has –'

'I'm talking about something else. As I recall, our profit was pretty good before I left. I thought we agreed we wouldn't get involved in manufacturing war supplies.'

Kate felt an anger rising in her. 'You agreed. I didn't.' She fought to control it. 'Times change, David. We have to change with them.'

He looked at her and asked quietly, 'Have you changed?'

Lying in bed that night, Kate asked herself whether it was she who had changed, or David. Had she become stronger, or had David become weaker? She thought about his argument against manufacturing armaments. It was a weak argument. After all, *someone* was going to supply the merchandise to the Allies, and there was an enormous profit in it. What had happened to David's business sense? She had always looked up to him as one of the cleverest men she knew. But now, she felt that she was more capable of running the business than David. She spent a sleepless night.

In the morning Kate and David had breakfast and walked around the grounds.

'It's really lovely,' David told her. 'I'm glad to be here.'

Kate said, 'About our conversation last night –'

'It's done. I was away, and you did what you thought was right.'

Would I have done the same thing if you had been here? Kate wondered. But she did not say the words aloud. She had done what she had for the sake of the company. *Does the company mean more to me than my marriage?* She was afraid to answer the question.

SEVENTEEN

The next five years witnessed a period of incredible world-wide growth. Kruger-Brent, Ltd., had been founded on diamonds and gold, but it had diversified and expanded all over the world, so that its centre was no longer South Africa. The company recently had acquired a publishing empire, an insurance company and half a million acres of timberland.

One night Kate nudged David awake. 'Darling, let's move the company headquarters.'

David sat up groggily. 'W-what?'

'The business centre of the world today is New York. That's where our headquarters should be. South Africa's too far away from everything. Besides, now that we have the telephone and cable, we can communicate with any of our offices in minutes.'

'Now why didn't I think of that?' David mumbled. And he went back to sleep.

* * *

New York was an exciting new world. On her previous visits there, Kate had felt the quick pulse of the city, but living there was like being caught up at the centre of a matrix. The earth seemed to spin faster, everything moved at a more rapid pace.

Kate and David selected a site for the new company headquarters on Wall Street, and the architects went to work. Kate chose another architect to design a sixteenth-century French Renaissance mansion on Fifth Avenue.

'This city is so damned *noisy*,' David complained.

And it was true. The chatter of riveters filled the air in every part of the city as skyscrapers began to soar into the heavens. New York had become the mecca for trade from all over the world, the headquarters for shipping, insurance, communications and transportation. It was a city bursting with a unique vitality. Kate loved it, but she sensed David's unhappiness.

'David, this is the future. This place is growing, and we'll grow with it.'

'My God, Kate, how much more do you want?'

And without thinking, she replied, 'All there is.'

She could not understand why David had even asked the question. The name of the game was to win, and you won by beating everyone else. It seemed so obvious to her. Why couldn't David see it? David was a good businessman, but there was something missing in him, a hunter, a compulsion to conquer, to be the biggest and the best. Her father had had that spirit, and she had it. Kate was not sure exactly when it had happened, but at some point in her life, the company had become the master, and she the slave. It owned her more than she owned it.

When she tried to explain her feelings to David, he laughed and said, 'You're working too hard.' *She's so much like her father*, David thought. And he was not sure why he found that vaguely disturbing.

How could one work too hard? Kate wondered. There was no greater joy in life. It was when she felt most alive. Each day brought a new set of problems, and each problem was a challenge, a puzzle to be solved, a new game to be won. And she was wonderful at it. She was caught up in something beyond imagination. It had nothing to do with money or achievement; it had to do with *power*. A power that controlled the lives of thousands of people in every corner of the earth. Just as her life had once been controlled. As long as she had power, she would never truly need anyone. It was a weapon that was awesome beyond belief.

Kate was invited to dine with kings and queens and presidents, all seeking her favour, her goodwill. A new Kruger-Brent factory could mean the difference between poverty and riches. *Power*. The company was alive, a growing giant that had to be fed, and sometimes sacrifices were necessary, for the giant could not be shackled. Kate understood that now. It had a rhythm, a pulse, and it had become her own.

* * *

In March, a year after they had moved to New York, Kate felt unwell. David persuaded her to see a doctor.

'His name is John Harley. He's a young doctor with a good reputation.'

Reluctantly, Kate went to see him. John Harley was a thin serious-looking young Bostonian about twenty-six, five years younger than Kate.

'I warn you,' Kate informed him, 'I don't have time to be sick.'

'I'll bear that in mind, Mrs Blackwell. Meanwhile, let's have a look at you.'

Dr Harley examined her, made some tests and said, 'I'm sure it's nothing serious. I'll have the results in a day or two. Give me a call on Wednesday.'

Early Wednesday morning Kate telephoned Dr Harley. 'I have good news for you, Mrs Blackwell,' he said cheerfully. 'You're going to have a baby.'

It was one of the most exciting moments of Kate's life. She could not wait to tell David.

She had never seen David so thrilled. He scooped her up in his strong arms and said, 'It's going to be a girl, and she'll look exactly like you.' He was thinking, *This is exactly what Kate needs. Now she'll stay home more. She'll be more of a wife.*

And Kate was thinking, *It will be a boy. One day he'll take over Kruger-Brent.*

* * *

As the time for the birth of the baby drew nearer, Kate worked shorter hours, but she still went to the office every day.

'Forget about the business and relax,' David advised her.

What he did not understand was that the business *was* Kate's relaxation.

The baby was due in December. 'I'll try for the twenty-fifth,' Kate promised David. 'He'll be our Christmas present.'

It's going to be a perfect Christmas. Kate thought. She was head of a great conglomerate, she was married to the man she loved and she was going to have his baby. If there was irony in the order of her priorities, Kate was not aware of it.

Her body had grown large and clumsy, and it was getting more and more difficult for Kate to go to the office, but whenever David or Brad Rogers suggested she stay home, her answer was, 'My brain is still working.' Two months before the baby was due, David was in South Africa on an inspection tour of the mine at Pniel. He was scheduled to return to New York the following week.

Kate was at her desk when Brad Rogers walked in unannounced. She looked at the grim expression on his face and said, 'We lost the Shannon deal!'

'No. I – Kate, I just got word. There's been an accident. A mine explosion.'

She felt a sharp pang, 'Where? Was it bad? Was anyone killed?'

Brad took a deep breath. 'Half a dozen. Kate – David was with them.'

The words seemed to fill the room and reverberate against the panelled walls, growing louder and louder, until it was a screaming in her ears, a Niagara of sound that was drowning her, and she felt herself being sucked into its centre, deeper and deeper, until she could no longer breathe.

And everything became dark and silent.

The baby was born one hour later, two months premature. Kate named him Anthony James Blackwell, after David's father. *I'll love you, my son, for me, and I'll love you for your father.*

One month later the new Fifth Avenue mansion was ready, and Kate and the baby and a staff of servants moved into it. Two castles in Italy had been stripped to furnish the house. It was a showplace, with elaborately carved sixteenth-century Italian walnut furniture and rose-marble f0loors bordered with sienna-red marble. The panelled library boasted a magnificent eighteenth-century fireplace over which hung a rare Holbein. There was a trophy room with David's gun collection, and an art gallery that Kate filled with Rembrandts and Vermeers and Velázquezes and Bellinis. There was a ballroom and a sun room and a formal dining room and a nursery next to Kate's room, and uncounted bedrooms. In the large formal gardens were statues by Rodin, Augustus Saint-Gaudens and Maillol. It was a palace fit for a king. *And the king is growing up in it*, Kate thought happily.

In 1928, when Tony was four, Kate sent him to nursery school. He was a handsome, solemn little boy, with his mother's grey eyes and stubborn chin. He was given music lessons, and when he was five he attended dancing school. Some of the best times the two of them spent together were at Cedar Hill House in Dark Harbor. Kate bought a yacht, an eighty-foot motor sailer she named the *Corsair*, and she and Tony cruised the waters along the coast of Maine. Tony adored it. But it was the work that gave Kate her greatest pleasure.

There was something mystic about the company Jamie McGregor had founded. It was alive, consuming. It was her lover, and it would never die on a winter day and leave her alone. It would live forever. She would see to it. And one day she would give it to her son.

The only disturbing factor in Kate's life was her homeland. She cared deeply about South Africa. The racial problems there were growing, and Kate was troubled. There were two political camps: the *verkramptes* – the narrow ones, the prosegregationists – and the *verligtes* – the enlightened ones, who wanted to improve the position of blacks. Prime Minister James Hertzog and Jan Smuts had formed a coalition and combined their power to have the New Land Act passed. Blacks were removed from the rolls and were no longer able to vote or own land. Millions of people belonging to different minority groups were disrupted by the new law. The areas that had no minerals, industrial centres or ports were assigned to coloureds, black and Indians.

Kate arranged a meeting in South Africa with several high government officials. 'This is a time bomb,' Kate told them. 'What you're doing is trying to keep eight million people in slavery.'

'It's not slavery, Mrs Blackwell. We're doing this for their own good.'

'Really? How would you explain that?'

'Each race has something to contribute. If the blacks mingle with the whites, they'll lose their individuality. We're trying to protect them.'

'That's bloody nonsense,' Kate retorted. 'South Africa has become a racist hell.'

'That's not true. Blacks from other countries come thousands of miles in order to enter this country. They pay as much as fifty-six pounds for a forged pass. The black is better off here than anywhere else on earth.'

'Then I pity them,' Kate retorted.

'They're primitive children, Mrs Blackwell. It's for their own good.'

Kate left the meeting frustrated and deeply fearful for her country.

Kate was also concerned about Banda. He was in the news a good deal. The South African newspapers were calling him the *scarlet pimpernel*, and there was a grudging admiration in their stories. He escaped the police by disguising himself as a labourer, a chauffeur, a janitor. He had organized a guerrilla army and he headed the police's most-wanted list. One article in the *Cape Times* told of his being carried triumphantly through the streets of a black village on the shoulders of demonstrators. He went from village to village addressing crowds of students, but every time the police got wind of his presence, Banda disappeared. He was said to have a personal bodyguard at a different house every night. Kate knew that nothing would stop him but death.

She had to get in touch with him. She summoned one of her veteran black foremen, a man she trusted. 'William, do you think you can find Banda?'

'Only if he wishes to be found.'

'Try. I want to meet with him.'

'I'll see what I can do.'

The following morning the foreman said, 'If you are free this evening, a car will be waiting to take you out to the country.'

Kate was driven to a small village seventy miles north of Johannesburg. The driver stopped in front of a small frame house, and Kate went inside. Banda was waiting for her. He looked exactly the same as when Kate had last seen him. *And he must be sixty years old*, Kate thought. He had been on the run from the police for years, and yet he appeared serene and calm.

He hugged Kate and said, 'You look more beautiful every time I see you.'

She laughed. 'I'm getting old. I'm going to be forty in a few years.'

'The years sit lightly on you, Kate.'

They went into the kitchen, and while Banda fixed coffee, Kate said, 'I don't like what's happening, Banda. Where is it going to lead?'

'It will get worse,' Banda said simply. 'The government will not allow us to speak with them. The whites have destroyed the bridges between us and them, and one day they will find they need those bridges to reach us. We have our heroes now, Kate. Nehemiah Tile, Mokone, Richard Msimang. The whites goad us and move us around like cattle to pasture.'

'Not all whites think like that,' Kate assured him. 'You have friends who are fighting to change things. It will happen one day, Banda, but it will take time.'

'Time is like sand in an hourglass. It runs out.'

'Banda, what's happened to Ntame and to Magena?'

'My wife and son are in hiding,' Banda said sadly. 'The police are still very busy looking for me.'

'What can I do to help? I can't just sit by and do nothing. Will money help?'

'Money always helps.'

'I will arrange it. What else?'

'Pray. Pray for all of us.'

The following morning, Kate returned to New York.

When Tony was old enough to travel, Kate took him on business trips during his school holidays. He was fond of museums, and he could stand for hours looking at the paintings and statues of the great masters. At home, Tony sketched copies of the paintings on the wall, but he was too self-conscious to let his mother see his work.

He was sweet and bright and fun to be with, and there was a shyness about him that people found appealing. Kate was proud of her son. He was always first in his class. 'You beat all of them, didn't you, darling?' And she would laugh and hold him fiercely in her arms.

And young Tony would try even harder to live up to his mother's expectations.

In 1936, on Tony's twelfth birthday, Kate returned from a trip to the Middle East. She had missed Tony and was eager to see him. He was at home waiting for her. She took him in her arms and hugged him. 'Happy birthday, darling! Has it been a good day?'

'Y-yes, m-ma'am. It's b-b-been wonderful.'

Kate pulled back and looked at him. She had never noticed him stutter before. 'Are you all right, Tony?'

'F-fine, thank you, Mother.'

'You mustn't stammer,' she told him. 'Speak more slowly.'

'Yes, M-mother.'

Over the next few weeks, it got worse. Kate decided to talk to Dr Harley. When he finished the examination, John Harley said, 'Physically, there's nothing wrong with the boy, Kate. Is he under any kind of pressure?'

'My son? Of course not. How can you ask that?'

'Tony's a sensitive boy. Stuttering is very often a physical manifestation of frustration, an inability to cope.'

'You're wrong, John. Tony is at the very top of all the achievement tests in school. Last term he won three awards. Best all-round athlete, best all-round scholar and best student in the arts. I'd hardly call that unable to cope.'

'I see.' He studied her. 'What do you do when Tony stammers, Kate?'

'I correct him, of course.'

'I would suggest that you don't. That will only make him more tense.'

Kate was stung to anger. 'If Tony has any psychological problems, as you seem to think, I can assure you it's not because of his mother. I adore him. And he's aware that I think he's the most fantastic child on earth.'

And that was the core of the problem. No child could live up to that. Dr Harley glanced down at his chart. 'Let's see now. Tony is twelve.'

'Yes.'

'Perhaps it might be good for him if he went away for a while. Maybe a private school somewhere.'

Kate just stared at him.

'Let him be on his own a bit. Just until he finishes high school. They have some excellent schools in Switzerland.'

Switzerland! The idea of Tony being so far away from her was appalling. He was too young, he was not ready yet, he – Dr Harley was watching her. 'I'll think about it,' Kate told him.

That afternoon she cancelled a board meeting and went home early. Tony was in his room, doing homework.

Tony said, 'I g-g-got all A's t-today, M-mother.'

'What would you think of going to school in Switzerland, darling?'

And his eyes lit up and he said, 'M-m-may I?'

Six weeks later, Kate put Tony aboard a ship. He was on his way to the Institute Le Rosey in Rolle, a small town on the shore of Lake Geneva. Kate stood at the New York pier and watched until the huge liner cut loose from the tugboats. *Bloody hell! I'm going to miss him.* Then she turned and walked back to the limousine waiting to take her to the office.

Kate enjoyed working with Brad Rogers. He was forty-six, two years older than Kate. They had become good friends through the years, and she loved him for his devotion to Kruger-Brent. Brad was unmarried and had a variety of attractive girl friends, but gradually Kate became aware that he was half in love with her. More than once he made studiously ambiguous remarks, but she chose to keep their relationship on an impersonal, business level. She broke that pattern only once.

Brad had started seeing someone regularly. He stayed out late every night and came into morning meetings tired and distracted, his mind elsewhere. It was bad for the company. When a month went by and his behaviour was becoming more flagrant, Kate decided that something had to be done. She remembered how close David had come to quitting the company because of a woman. She would not let that happen with Brad.

Kate had planned to travel to Paris alone to acquire an import-export company, but at the last minute she asked Brad to accompany her. They spent the day of their arrival in meetings and that evening had dinner at the Grand Véfour. Afterwards, Kate suggested that Brad join her in her suite at the George V to go over the reports on the new company. When he arrived, Kate was waiting for him in a filmy negligee.

'I brought the revised offer with me,' Brad began, 'so we –'

'That can wait,' Kate said softly. There was an invitation in her voice that made him look at her again. 'I wanted us to be alone Brad.'

'Kate –'

She moved into his arms and held him close.

'My God!' he said, 'I've wanted you for so long.'

'And I you, Brad.'

And they moved into the bedroom.

Kate was a sensual woman, but all of her sexual energy had long since been harnessed into other channels. She was completely fulfilled by her work. She needed Brad for other reasons.

He was on top of her, and she moved her legs apart and felt his hardness in her, and it was neither pleasant nor unpleasant.

'Kate, I've loved you for so long . . .'

He was pressing into her, moving in and out in an ancient, timeless rhythm, and she thought, *They're asking too bloody much for the company. They're going to hold out because they know I really want it.*

Brad was whispering words of endearment in her ear.

I could call off the negotiations and wait for them to come back to me. But what if they don't? Do I dare risk losing the deal?

His rhythm was faster now, and Kate moved her hips, thrusting against his body.

No. They could easily find another buyer. Better to pay them what they want. I'll make up for it by selling off one of their subsidiaries.

Brad was moaning, in a frenzy of delight, and Kate moved faster, bringing him to a climax.

I'll tell them I've decided to meet their terms.

There was a long, shuddering gasp, and Brad

said, 'Oh God, Kate, it was wonderful. Was it good for you, darling?'

'It was heaven.'

She lay in Brad's arms all night, thinking and planning, while he slept. In the morning when he woke up, she said, 'Brad, that woman you've been seeing –'

'My God! You're jealous!' He laughed happily. 'Forget about her. I'll never see her again, I promise.'

Kate never went to bed with Brad again. When he could not understand why she refused him, all she said was, 'You don't know how much I want to, Brad, but I'm afraid we wouldn't be able to work together any longer. We must both make a sacrifice.'

And he was forced to live with that.

As the company kept expanding, Kate set up charitable foundations that contributed to colleges, churches and schools. She kept adding to her art collection. She acquired the great Renaissance and post-Renaissance artists Raphael and Titian, Tintoretto and El Greco; and the baroque painters Rubens, Caravaggio and Van Dyck.

The Blackwell collection was reputed to be the most valuable private collection in the world. *Reputed*, because no one outside the invited guests was permitted to see it. Kate would not allow it to be photographed, nor would she discuss it with the press. She had strict, inflexible rules about the press. The personal life of the Blackwell family was off limits. Neither servants nor employees of the company were permitted to discuss the Blackwell family. It was impossible, of course, to stop rumours and speculation, for Kate Blackwell was an intriguing enigma – one of the richest, most powerful women in the world. There were a thousand questions about her, but few answers.

Kate telephoned the headmistress at Le Rosey. 'I'm calling to find out how Tony is.'

'Ah, he is doing very well, Mrs Blackwsell. Your son is a superb student. He –'

'I wasn't referring to that. I meant –' She hesitated, as though reluctant to admit there could be a weakness in the Blackwell family. 'I meant his stammering.'

'Madame, there is no sign of any stammering. He is perfectly fine.'

Kate heaved an inward sigh of relief. She had known all along that it was only temporary, a passing phase of some kind. So much for doctors!

Tony arrived home four weeks later, and Kate was at the airport to meet him. He looked fit and handsome, and Kate felt a surge of pride. 'Hello, my love, how are you?'

'I'm f-f-fine, M-m-mother. How are y-y-you?'

On his vacations at home. Tony eagerly looked forward to examining the new paintings his mother had acquired while he was away. He was awed by the masters, and enchanted by the French Impressionists: Monet, Renoir, Manet and Morisot. They evoked a magic world for Tony. He bought a set of paints and an easel and went to work. He thought his paintings were terrible, and he still refused to show them to anyone. How could they compare with the exquisite masterpieces?

Kate told him, 'One day all these paintings will belong to you, darling.'

The thought of it filled the thirteen-year-old boy with a sense of unease. His mother did not understand. They could never be truly his, because he had done nothing to earn them. He had a fierce determination somehow to earn his own way. He had ambivalent feelings about being away from his mother, for everything around her was always exciting. She was at the centre of a whirlwind, giving orders, making incredible deals, taking him to exotic places, introducing him to interesting people. She was an awesome figure, and Tony was inordinately proud of her. He thought she was the most fascinating woman in the world. He felt guilty because it was only in her presence that he stuttered.

Kate had no idea how deeply her son was in awe of her until one day when he was home on vacation he asked, 'M-m-mother, do you r-r-run the world?'

And she had laughed and said, 'Of course not. What made you ask such a silly question?'

'All my f-friends at school talk about you. Boy, you're really s-something.'

'I am something,' Kate said. 'I'm your mother.'

Tony wanted more than anything in the world to please Kate. He knew how much the company meant to her, how much she planned on his running it one day, and he was filled with regret, because he knew he could not. That was not what he intended to do with his life.

When he tried to explain this to his mother, she would laugh, 'Nonsense, Tony. You're much too young to know what you want to do with your future.'

And he would begin to stammer.

The idea of being a painter excited Tony. To be able to capture beauty and freeze it for all eternity; that was something worthwhile, he wanted to go abroad and study in Paris, but he knew he would have to broach the subject to his mother very carefully.

They had wonderful times together. Kate was the chatelaine of vast estates. She had acquired homes in Palm Beach and South Carolina, and a stud farm in Kentucky, and she and Tony visited all of them during his vacations. They watched the America's Cup races in Newport, and when they were in New York, they had lunch at Delmonico's and tea at the Plaza and Sunday dinner at Lüchow's. Kate was interested in horse racing, and her stable became one of the finest in the world. When one of Kate's horses was running and Tony was home from school, Kate would take him to the track with her. They would sit in her box and

Tony would watch in wonder as his mother cheered until she was hoarse. He knew her excitement had nothing to do with money.

'It's winning, Tony. Remember that. Winning is what's important.'

They had quiet, lazy times at Dark Harbor. They shopped at Pendleton and Coffin, and had ice-cream sodas at the Dark Harbor Shop. In summer they went sailing and hiking and visited art galleries. In the winter there was skiing and skating and sleigh riding. They would sit in front of a fire in the large fireplace in the library, and Kate would tell her son all the old family stories about his grandfather and Banda, and about the baby shower Madam Agnes and her girls gave for Tony's grandmother. It was a colourful family, a family to be proud of, to cherish.

'Kruger-Brent, Limited, will be yours one day, Tony. You'll run it and –'

'I d-don't want to r-run it, Mother. I'm not inter-ested in big business or p-power.'

And Kate exploded. 'You bloody fool! What do you know about big business or power? Do you think I go around the world spreading evil? Hurting people? Do you think Kruger-Brent is some kind of ruthless money machine crushing anything that gets in its way? Well, let me tell you something, Son. It's the next best thing to Jesus Christ. We're the resurrection, Tony. We save lives by the hundreds of thousands. When we open a factory in a depressed community or country, those people can afford to build schools and libraries and churches, and give their children decent food and clothing and recreation facilities.' She was breathing hard, carried away by her anger. 'We build factories where people are hungry and out of work, and because of us they're able to live decent lives and hold up their heads. We become their saviours. Don't ever again let me hear you sneer at big business and power.'

All Tony could say was, 'I'm s-s-sorry, M-m-mother.'

And he thought stubbornly: *I'm going to be an artist.*

When Tony was fifteen, Kate suggested he spend his summer vacation in South Africa. He had never been there. 'I can't get away just now, Tony, but you'll find it a fascinating place. I'll make all the arrangements for you.'

'I was s-sort of h-hoping to spend my vacation in Dark Harbor, M-mother.'

'Next summer,' Kate said firmly. 'This summer I would like you to go to Johannesburg.'

Kate carefully briefed the company super-intendent in Johannesburg, and together they laid out an itinerary for Tony. Each day was planned with one objective in view: to make this trip as exciting as possible for Tony, to make him realize his future lay with the company.

Kate received a daily report about her son. He had been taken into one of the gold mines. He had spent two days in the diamond fields. He had been on a guided tour of the Kruger-Brent plants and had gone on a safari in Kenya.

A few days before Tony's vacation ended, Kate telephoned the company manager in Johannesburg. 'How is Tony getting along?'

'Oh, he's having a great time, Mrs Blackwell. In fact, this morning he asked if he couldn't stay on a little longer.'

Kate felt a surge of pleasure. 'That's wonderful! Thank you.'

When Tony's vacation was over, he went to Southampton, England, where he boarded a Pan American Airways Systems plane for the United States. Kate flew Pan American whenever possible. It spoiled her for other airlines.

Kate left an important meeting to greet her son when he arrived at the Pan American terminal at the newly built La Guardia Airport in New York. His handsome face was filled with enthusiasm.

'Did you have a good time, darling?'

'South Africa's a f-fantastic country, M-mother. Did you know they f-flew me to the Namib Desert where grandfather s-stole those diamonds from Great-grandfather v-van der Merwe?'

'He didn't steal them, Tony,' Kate corrected him. 'He merely took what was his.'

'Sure,' Tony scoffed. 'Anyway, I was th-there. There was no sea *mis*, but they s-still have the guards and dogs and everything.' He grinned. 'They wouldn't give me any s-samples.'

Kate laughed happily. 'They don't have to give you any samples, darling. One day they will all be yours.'

'*You* t-tell them. They wouldn't l-listen to me.'

She hugged him. 'You *did* enjoy it, didn't you?' She was enormously pleased that at last Tony was excited about his heritage.

'You know what I loved m-most?'

Kate smiled lovingly. 'What?'

'The colours. I p-painted a lot of landscapes th-there. I hated to leave. I want to go back there and p-paint.'

'Paint?' Kate tried to sound enthusiastic. 'That sounds like a wonderful hobby, Tony.'

'No. I don't m-mean as a hobby, Mother. I want to be a p-painter. I've been thinking a lot about it. I'm going to P-Paris to study. I really think I might have some talent.'

Kate felt herself tensing. 'You don't want to spend the rest of your life painting.'

'Yes, I do, M-mother. It's the only thing I really c-care about.'

And Kate knew she had lost.

He has a right to live his own life, Kate thought. *But how can I let him make such a terrible mistake?*

In September, the decision was taken out of both their hands. Europe went to war.

'I want you to enrol in the Wharton School of Finance and Commerce,' Kate informed Tony. 'In two years if you still want to be an artist, you'll have my blessing.' Kate was certain that by then Tony would change his mind. It was inconceivable that her son would choose to spend his life slapping daubs of colour on bits of canvas when he could head the most exciting conglomerate in the world. He was, after all, her son.

To Kate Blackwell, World War II was another great opportunity. There were worldwide shortages of military supplies and materials and Kruger-Brent was able to furnish them. One division of the company provided equipment for the armed forces, while another division took care of civilian needs. The company factories were working twenty-four hours a day.

Kate was certain the United States was not going to be able to remain neutral. President Franklin D. Roosevelt called upon the country to be the great arsenal of democracy, and on March 11, 1941, the Lend-Lease Bill was pushed through Congress. Allied shipping across the Atlantic was menaced by the German blockade. U-boats, the German submarines, attacked and sank scores of Allied ships, fighting in wolf packs of eight.

Germany was a juggernaut that seemingly could not be stopped. In defiance of the Versailles Treaty, Adolf Hitler had built up one of the greatest war machines in history. In a new *Blitzkrieg* technique, Germany attacked Poland, Belgium and the Netherlands, and in rapid succession, the German machine crushed Denmark, Norway, Luxembourg and France.

Kate went into action when she received word that Jews working in the Nazi-confiscated Kruger-Brent, Ltd., factories were being arrested and deported to concentration camps. She made two telephone calls, and the following week she was on her way to Switzerland. When she arrived at the Baur au Lac Hotel in Zurich, there was a message that Colonel Brinkmann wished to see her. Brinkmann had been a manager of the Berlin branch of Kruger-Brent, Ltd. When the factory had been taken over by the Nazi government, Brinkmann was given the rank of colonel and kept in charge.

He came to see Kate at the hotel. He was a thin, precise man with blond hair combed carefully over his balding skull. 'I am delighted to see you, Frau Blackwell. I have a message for you from my government. I am authorized to assure you that as soon as we have won the war, your factories will be returned to you. Germany is going to be the greatest industrial power the world has ever known, and we welcome the collaboration of people such as yourself.'

'What if Germany loses?'

Colonel Brinkmann allowed a small smile to play on his lips. 'We both know that cannot happen, Frau Blackwell. The United States is wise to stay out of Europe's business. I hope it continues to do so.'

'I'm sure you do, Colonel.' She leaned forwards. 'I've heard rumours about Jews being sent to concentration camps and being exterminated. Is that true?'

'British propaganda, I assure you. It is true that *die Juden* are sent to work camps, but I give you my word as an officer that they are being treated as they should be.'

Kate wondered exactly what those words meant. She intended to find out.

The following day Kate made an appointment with a prominent German merchant named Otto Bueller. Bueller was in his fifties, a distinguished-looking man with a compassionate face and eyes that had known deep suffering. They met at a small café near the *Bahnhof*. Herr Bueller selected a table in a deserted corner.

'I've been told,' Kate said softly, 'that you've started an underground to help smuggle Jews into neutral countries. Is that true?'

'It's not true, Mrs Blackwell. Such an act would be treason against the Third Reich.'

'I have also heard that you're in need of funds to run it.'

Herr Bueller shrugged. 'Since there is no underground, I have no need of funds to run it, is that not so?'

His eyes kept nervously darting around the café. This was a man who breathed and slept with danger each day of his life.

'I was hoping I might be of some help,' Kate said carefully. 'Kruger-Brent, Limited, has factories in many neutral and Allied countries. If someone could get the refugees there, I would arrange for them to have employment.'

Herr Bueller sat there sipping a bitter coffee. Finally, he said, 'I know nothing about these things. Politics are dangerous these days. But if you are interested in helping someone in distress, I have an uncle in England who suffers from a terrible, debilitating disease. His doctors bills are very high.'

'How high?'

'Fifty thousand dollars a month. Arrangements would have to be made to deposit the money for his medical expenses in London and transfer the deposits to a Swiss bank.'

'That can be arranged.'

'My uncle would be very pleased.'

Some eight weeks later, a small but steady stream of Jewish refugees began to arrive in Allied countries to go to work in Kruger-Brent factories.

Tony quit school at the end of two years. He went up to Kate's office to tell her the news. 'I t-tried, M-mother. I really d-did. But I've m-made up m-my mind. I want to s-study p-painting. When the w-war is over, I'm g-going to P-paris.'

Each word was like a hammerblow.

'I kn-know you're d-disappointed, but I have to l-live my own life. I think I can be good – *really* good.' He saw the look on Kate's face. 'I've done what you've asked me to do. Now you've got to g-give me my chance. They've accepted me at the Art I-institute in Chicago.'

Kate's mind was in a turmoil. What Tony wanted to do was such a bloody *waste*. All she could say was, 'When do you plan to leave?'

'Enrolment starts on the fifteenth.'

What's the date today?'

'D-december sixth.'

On Sunday, December 7, 1941, squadrons of Nakajima bombers and Zero fighter planes from the Imperial Japanese Navy attacked Pearl Harbor, and the following day, the United States was at war. That afternoon Tony enlisted in the United States Marine Corps. He was sent to Quantico, Virginia, where he was graduated from Officer's Training School, and from there to the South Pacific.

Kate felt as though she were living on the edge of an abyss. Her working day was filled with the pressures of running the company, but every moment at the back of her mind was the fear that she would receive some dreaded news about Tony – that he had been wounded or killed.

The war with Japan was going badly. Japanese bombers struck at American bases on Guam, Midway and Wake islands. They took Singapore in February 1942, and quickly overran New Britain, New Ireland and the Admiralty and Solomon Islands. General Douglas MacArthur was forced to withdraw from the Philippines. The powerful forces of the Axis were slowly conquering the world, and the shadows were darkening everywhere. Kate was afraid that Tony might be taken prisoner of war and tortured. With all her power and influence, there was nothing she could do except pray. Every letter from Tony was a beacon of hope, a sign that, a few short weeks before, he had been alive. 'They keep us in the dark here,' Tony wrote. 'Are the Russians still holding on? The Japanese soldier is brutal, but you have to respect him. He's not afraid to die . . .'

'What's happening in the States? Are factory workers really striking for more money? . . .'

'The PT boats are doing a wonderful job here. Those boys are all heroes . . .'

'You have great connections, Mother. Send us a few hundred F4U's, the new Navy fighters. Miss you . . .'

On August 7, 1942, the Allies began their first offensive action in the Pacific. United States Marines landed on Guadalcanal in the Solomon Islands, and from then on they kept moving to take back the islands the Japanese had conquered.

In Europe, the Allies were enjoying an almost unbroken string of victories. On June 6, 1944, the Allied invasion of Western Europe was launched with landings by American, British and Canadian troops on the Normandy beaches, and a year later, on May 7, 1945, Germany surrendered unconditionally.

In Japan, on August 6, 1945, an atomic bomb

with a destructive force of more than twenty thousand tons of TNT was dropped on Hiroshima. Three days later, another atomic bomb destroyed the city of Nagasaki. On August 14, the Japanese surrendered. The long and bloody war was finally over.

Three months later, Tony returned home. He and Kate were at Dark Harbor, sitting on the terrace looking over the bay dotted with graceful white sails.

The war has changed him, Kate thought. There was a new maturity about Tony. He had grown a small moustache, and looked tanned and fit and handsome. There were lines about his eyes that had not been there before. Kate was sure the years overseas had given him time to reconsider his decision about not going into the company.

'What are your plans now, Son?' Kate asked.

Tony smiled. 'As I was saying before we were so rudely interrupted, Mother – I'm going to P-paris.'

BOOK FOUR

Tony

1946–1950

EIGHTEEN

Tony had been to Paris before, but this time the circumstances were different. The City of Light had been dimmed by the German occupation, but had been saved from destruction when it was declared an open city. The people had suffered a great deal, and though the Nazis had looted the Louvre, Tony found Paris relatively untouched. Besides, this time he was going to live there, to be a part of the city, rather than be a tourist. He could have stayed at Kate's penthouse on Avenue du Maréchal Foch, which had not been damaged during the occupation. Instead, he rented an unfurnished flat in an old converted house behind Grand Montparnasse. The apartment consisted of a living room with a fireplace, a small bedroom and a tiny kitchen that had no refrigerator. Between the bedroom and the kitchen crouched a bathroom with a claw-footed tub and small stained bidet and a temperamental toilet with a broken seat.

When the landlady started to make apologies, Tony stopped her. 'It's perfect.'

He spent all day Saturday at the flea market. Monday and Tuesday he toured the secondhand shops along the Left Bank, and by Wednesday he had the basic furniture he needed. A sofa bed, a scarred table, two overstuffed chairs, an old, ornately carved wardrobe, lamps and a rickety kitchen table and two straight chairs. *Mother would be horrified*, Tony thought. He could have had his apartment crammed with priceless antiques, but that would have been *playing* the part of a young American artist in Paris. He intended to *live* it.

The next step was getting into a good art school. The most prestigious art school in all of France was the Ecole des Beaux-Arts of Paris. Its standards were high, and few Americans were admitted. Tony applied for a place there. *They'll never accept me*, he thought. *But if they do!* Somehow, he had to show his mother he had made the right decision. He submitted three of his paintings and waited four weeks to hear whether he had been accepted. At the end of the fourth week, his concierge handed him a letter from the school. He was to report the following Monday.

The Ecole des Beaux-Arts was a large stone building, two storeys high, with a dozen classrooms filled with students. Tony reported to the head of the school, Maître Gessand, a towering, bitter-looking man with no neck and the thinnest lips Tony had ever seen.

'Your paintings are amateurish,' he told Tony. 'But they show promise. Our committee selected you more for what was *not* in the paintings than for what *was* in them. Do you understand?'

'Not exactly, maître.'

'You will, in time. I am assigning you to Maître Cantal. He will be your teacher for the next five years – if you last that long.'

I'll last that long, Tony promised himself.

Maître Cantal was a very short man, with a totally bald head which he covered with a purple beret. He had dark-brown eyes, a large, bulbous nose and lips like sausages. He greeted Tony with, 'Americans are dilettantes, barbarians. Why are you here?'

'To learn, maître.'

Maître Cantal grunted.

There were twenty-five pupils in the class, most of them French. Easels had been set up around the room, and Tony selected one near the window that overlooked a workingman's bistro. Scattered around the room were plaster casts of various parts of the human anatomy taken from Greek statues. Tony looked around for the model. He could see no one.

'You will begin,' Maître Cantal told the class.

'Excuse me,' Tony said. 'I – I didn't bring my paints with me.'

'You will not need paints. You will spend the first year learning to draw properly.'

The maître pointed to the Greek statuary. 'You

will draw those. If it seems too simple for you, let me warn you: before the year is over, more than half of you will be eliminated.' He warmed to his speech. 'You will spend the first year learning anatomy. The second year – for those of you who pass the course – you will draw from live models, working with oils. The third year – and I assure there will be fewer of you – you will paint with me, in my style, greatly improving on it, naturally. In the fourth and fifth years, you will find your own style, your own voice. Now let us get to work.'

The class went to work.

The maître went around the room, stopping at each easel to make criticisms or comments. When he came to the drawing Tony was working on, he said curtly, 'No! That will not do. What I see is the *outside* of an arm. I want to see the *inside*. Muscles, bones, ligaments. I want to know there is *blood* flowing underneath. Do you know how to do that?'

'Yes, maître. You think it, see it, feel it, and then you draw it.'

When Tony was not in class, he was usually in his apartment sketching. He could have painted from dawn to dawn. Painting gave him a sense of freedom he had never known before. The simple act of sitting in front of an easel with a paintbrush in his hand made him feel godlike. He could create whole worlds with one hand. He could make a tree, a flower, a human, a universe. It was a heady experience. He had been born for this. When he was not painting, he was out on the streets of Paris exploring the fabulous city. Now it was *his* city, the place where his art was being born. There were two Parises, divided by the Seine into the Left Bank and the Right Bank, and they were worlds apart. The Right Bank was for the wealthy, the established. The Left Bank belonged to the students, the artists, the struggling. It was Montparnasse and the Boulevard Raspail and Saint-Germain-de-Prés. It was the Café Flore and Henry Miller and Elliot Paul. For Tony, it was home. He would sit for hours at the Boule Blanche or La Coupole with fellow students, discussing their arcane world.

'I understand the art director of the Guggenheim Museum is in Paris, buying up everything in sight.'

'Tell him to wait for me!'

They all read the same magazines and shared them because they were expensive: *Studio* and *Cahiers d'Art, Formes et Couleurs* and *Gazette des Beaux-Arts*.

Tony had learned French at Le Rosey, and he found it easy to make friends with the other students in his class, for they all shared a common passion. They had no idea who Tony's family was, and they accepted him as one of them. Poor and struggling artists gathered at Café Flore and Les Deux Magots on Boulevard Saint-Germain, and ate at Le Pot d'Etain on the Rue des Canettes or at the Rue de l'Université. None of the others had ever seen the inside of Lasserre or Maxim's.

In 1946, giants were practicing their art in Paris. From time to time, Tony caught glimpses of Pablo Picasso, and one day Tony and a friend saw Marc Chagall, a large, flamboyant man in his fifties, with a wild mop of hair just beginning to turn grey. Chagall was seated at a table across the café, in earnest conversation with a group of people.

'We're lucky to see him,' Tony's friend whispered. 'He comes to Paris very seldom. His home is at Vence, near the Mediterranean coast.'

There was Max Ernst sipping an aperitif at a sidewalk café, and the great Alberto Giacometti walking down the Rue de Rivoli, looking like one of his own sculptures, tall and thin and gnarled. Tony was surprised to note he was clubfooted. Tony met Hans Belmer, who was making a name for himself with erotic paintings of young girls turning into dismembered dolls. But perhaps Tony's most exciting moment came when he was introduced to Braque. The artist was cordial, but Tony was tongue-tied.

The future geniuses haunted the new art galleries, studying their competition. The Drouant-David Gallery was exhibiting an unknown young artist named Bernard Buffet, who had studied at the Ecole des Beaux Arts, and Soutine, Utrillo and Dufy. The students congregated at the Salon d'Automne and the Charpentier

Gallery and Mlle Roussa's Gallery on the Rue de Seine, and spent their spare time gossiping about their successful rivals.

The first time Kate saw Tony's apartment, she was stunned. She wisely made no comment, but she thought, *Bloody hell! How can a son of mine live in this dreary closet?* Aloud she said, 'It has great charm, Tony. I don't see a refrigerator. Where do you keep your food?'

'Out on the w-windowsill.'

Kate walked over to the window, opened it and selected an apple from the sill outside. 'I'm not eating one of your subjects, am I?'

Tony laughed. 'N-no, Mother.'

Kate took a bite. 'Now,' she demanded, 'tell me about your painting.'

'There's n-not much to t-tell yet,' Tony confessed. 'We're just doing d-drawings this year.

'Do you like this Maître Cantal?'

'He's m-marvellous. The important question is whether he l-likes *me*. Only about one-third of the class is going to m-make it to next year.'

Not once did Kate mention Tony's joining the company.

Maître Cantal was not a man to lavish praise. The biggest compliment Tony would get would be a grudging, 'I suppose I've seen worse,' or 'I'm almost beginning to see *underneath*.'

At the end of the school term, Tony was among

the eight advanced to the second-year class. To celebrate, Tony and the other relieved students went to a nightclub in Montmartre, got drunk and spent the night with some young English women who were on a tour of France.

When school started again, Tony began to work with oils and live models. It was like being released from kindergarten. After one year of sketching parts of anatomy, Tony felt he knew every muscle, nerve and gland in the human body. That wasn't drawing – it was *copying*. Now, with a paintbrush in his hand and a live model in front of him, Tony began to create. Even Maître Cantal was impressed.

'You have the *feel*,' he said grudgingly. 'Now we must work on the technique.'

There were about a dozen models who sat for classes at the school. The ones Maître Cantal used most frequently were Carlos, a young man working his way through medical school; Annette, a short, buxom brunette with a clump of red pubic hair and an acne-scarred back; and Dominique Masson, a beautiful young, willowy blonde with delicate cheekbones and deep-green eyes. Dominique also posed for several well-known painters. She was everyone's favourite. Every day after class the male students would gather around her, trying to make a date.

'I never mix pleasure with business,' she told

them. 'Anyway,' she teased, 'it would not be fair. You have all seen what I have to offer. How do I know what you have to offer?'

And the ribald conversation would go on. But Dominique never went out with anyone at the school.

Late one afternoon when all the other students had left and Tony was finishing a painting of Dominique, she came up behind him unexpectedly. 'My nose is too long.'

Tony was flustered. 'Oh. I'm sorry, I'll change it.'

'No, no. The nose in the painting is fine. It is *my* nose that is too long.'

Tony smiled. 'I'm afraid I can't do much about that.'

'A Frenchman would have said, "Your nose is perfect, *chérie*."'

'I like your nose, and I'm not French.'

'Obviously. You have never asked me out. I wonder why.'

Tony was taken aback. 'I – I don't know. I guess it's because everyone else has, and you never go out with anybody.'

Dominique smiled. '*Everybody* goes out with somebody. Good night.'

And she was gone.

Tony noticed that whenever he stayed late, Dominique dressed and then returned to stand behind him and watched him paint.

'You are very good,' she announced one afternoon. 'You are going to be an important painter.'

'Thank you, Dominique. I hope you're right.'

'Painting is very serious to you, *oui*?'

'*Oui.*'

'Would a man who is going to be an important painter like to buy me dinner?' She saw the look of surprise on his face. 'I do not eat much. I must keep my figure.'

Tony laughed. 'Certainly. It would be a pleasure.'

They ate at a bistro near Sacré-Coeur, and they discussed painters and painting. Tony was fascinated with her stories of the well-known artists for whom she posed. As they were having *café au lait*, Dominique said, 'I must tell you, you are as good as any of them.'

Tony was inordinately pleased, but all he said was, 'I have a long way to go.'

Outside the café, Dominique asked, 'Are you going to invite me to see your apartment?'

'If you'd like to. I'm afraid it isn't much.'

When they arrived, Dominique looked around the tiny, messy apartment and shook her head. 'You were right. It is not much. Who takes care of you?'

'A cleaning lady comes in once a week.'

'Fire her. This place is filthy. Don't you have a girl friend?'

'No.'

She studied him a moment. 'You're not a queer?'

'No.'

348

'Good. It would be a terrible waste. Find me a pail of water and some soap.'

Dominique went to work on the apartment, cleaning and scrubbing and finally tidying up. When she had finished, she said, 'That will have to do for now. My God, I need a bath.'

She went into the tiny bathroom and ran water in the tub. 'How do you fit yourself in this?' she called out.

'I pull up my legs.'

She laughed. 'I would like to see that.'

Fifteen minutes later, she came out of the bathroom with only a towel around her waist, her blonde hair damp and curling. She had a beautiful figure, full breasts, a narrow waist and long, tapering legs. Tony had been unaware of her as a woman before. She had been merely a nude figure to be portrayed on canvas. Oddly enough, the towel changed everything. He felt a sudden rush of blood to his loins.

Dominique was watching him. 'Would you like to make love to me?'

'Very much.'

She slowly removed the towel. 'Show me.'

Tony had never known a woman like Dominique. She gave him everything and asked for nothing. She came over almost every evening to cook for Tony. When they went out to dinner, Dominique insisted on going to inexpensive bistros or sandwich bars. 'You must save your money,' she scolded him. 'It is very difficult even for a good artist to get started. And you are good, *chéri*.'

They went to Les Halles in the small hours of the morning and had onion soup at Pied de Cochon. They went to the Musée Carnavalet and out-of-the-way places where tourists did not go, like Cimetière Père-Lachaise – the final resting place of Oscar Wilde, Frédéric Chopin, Honoré de Balzac and Marcel Proust. They visited the catacombs and spent a lazy holiday week going down the Seine on a barge owned by a friend of Dominique's.

Dominique was a delight to be with. She had a quixotic sense of humour, and whenever Tony was depressed, she would laugh him out of it. She seemed to know everyone in Paris, and she took Tony to interesting parties where he met some of the most prominent figures of the day, like the poet Paul Eluard, and André Breton, in charge of the prestigious Galerie Maeght.

Dominique was a source of constant encouragement. 'You are going to be better than all of them, *chéri*. Believe me. I know.'

If Tony was in the mood to paint at night, Dominique would cheerfully pose for him, even though she had been working all day. *God, I'm lucky*, Tony thought. This was the first time he had been sure someone loved him for what he was, not who he was, and it was a feeling he cherished. Tony was afraid to tell Dominique he was the heir to one of the world's largest fortunes, afraid she would change, afraid they would lose what they had. But for her birthday Tony could not resist buying her a Russian lynx coat.

'It's the most beautiful thing I've ever seen in my life!' Dominique swirled the coat around her and danced around the room. She stopped in the middle of a spin. 'Where did it come from? Tony, where did you get the money to buy this coat?'

He was ready for her. 'It's hot – stolen. I bought it from a little man outside the Rodin Museum. He was anxious to get rid of it. It didn't cost me much more than a good cloth coat would cost at Au Printemps.'

Dominique stared at him a moment, then burst out laughing. 'I'll wear it even if we both go to prison!'

Then she threw her arms around Tony and started to cry. 'Oh, Tony, you idiot. You darling, fantastic idiot.'

It was well worth the lie, Tony decided.

One night Dominique suggested to Tony that he move in with her. Between working at the Ecole des Beaux-Arts and modelling for some of the better-known artists in Paris, Dominique was able to rent a large, modern apartment on Rue Prêtres-Saint Severin. 'You should not be living in a place like this, Tony. It is dreadful. Live with me, and you will not have to pay any rent. I can do your laundry, cook for you and –'

'No, Dominique. Thank you.'

'But why?'

How could he explain? In the beginning he might have told her he was rich, but now it was too late. She would feel he had been making a fool of her. So he said, 'It would be like living off you. You've already given me too much.'

'Then I'm giving up my apartment and moving in here. I want to be with you.'

She moved in the following day.

There was a wonderful, easy intimacy between them. They spent weekends in the country and stopped at little hostels where Tony would set up his easel and paint landscapes, and when they got hungry Dominique would spread out a picnic lunch she had prepared and they would eat in a meadow. Afterwards, they made long, sweet love. Tony had never been so completely happy.

His work was progressing beautifully. One morning Maître Cantal held up one of Tony's paintings and said to the class. 'Look at that body. You can see it *breathing*.'

Tony could hardly wait to tell Dominique that night. 'You know how I got the breathing just right? I hold the model in my arms every night.'

Dominique laughed in excitement and then grew serious. 'Tony, I do not think you need three more years of school. You are ready now. Everyone at the school sees that, even Cantal.'

Tony's fear was that he was not good enough, that he was just another painter, that his work would be lost in the flood of pictures turned out by thousands of artists all over the world every day. He could not bear the thought of it. *Winning is what's important, Tony. Remember that.*

Sometimes when Tony finished a painting he would be filled with a sense of elation and think, *I have talent. I really have talent.* At other times he would look at his work and think, *I'm a bloody amateur.*

With Dominique's encouragement, Tony was gaining more and more confidence in his work. He had finished almost two dozen paintings on his own. Landscapes, still lifes. There was a painting of Dominique lying nude under a tree, the sun dappling her body. A man's jacket and shirt were in the foreground, and the viewer knew the woman awaited her lover.

When Dominique saw the painting, she cried, 'You must have an exhibition!'

'You're mad, Dominique! I'm not ready.'

'You're wrong, *mon cher.*'

Tony arrived home late the next afternoon to find that Dominique was not alone. Anton Goerg, a thin man with an enormous potbelly and protuberant hazel eyes, was with her. He was the owner and proprietor of the Goerg Gallery, a modest gallery on the Rue Dauphine. Tony's paintings were spread around the room.

'What's going on?' Tony asked.

'What's going on, monsieur,' Anton Goerg exclaimed, 'is that I think your work is brilliant.' He clapped Tony on the back. 'I would be honoured to give you a showing in my gallery.'

Tony looked over at Dominique, and she was beaming at him.

'I – I don't know what to say.'

'You have already said it,' Goerg replied. 'On these canvases.'

Tony and Dominique stayed up half the night discussing it.

'I don't feel I'm ready. The critics will crucify me.'

'You're wrong, *chéri*. This is perfect for you. It is a small gallery. Only the local people will come and judge you. There is no way you can get hurt. Monsieur Goerg would never offer to give you an exhibition if he did not believe in you. He agrees with me that you are going to be a very important artist.'

'All right,' Tony finally said. 'Who knows? I might even sell a painting.'

The cable read: ARRIVING PARIS SATURDAY. PLEASE JOIN ME FOR DINNER. LOVE. MOTHER.

Tony's first thought as he watched his mother walk into the studio was, *What a handsome woman she is*. She was in her mid-fifties, hair untinted, with white strands laced through the black. There was a charged vitality about her. Tony had once asked her why she had not remarried. She had answered quietly. 'Only two men were ever important in my life. Your father and you.'

Now, standing in the little apartment in Paris,

facing his mother, Tony said, 'It's g-good to see you, M-mother.'

'Tony, you look absolutely wonderful! The beard is new.' She laughed and ran her fingers through it. 'You look like a young Abe Lincoln.' Her eyes swept the small apartment. 'Thank God you've gotten a good cleaning woman. It looks like a different place.'

Kate walked over to the easel, where Tony had been working on a painting, and she stopped and stared at it for a long time. He stood there, nervously awaiting his mother's reaction.

When Kate spoke, her voice was very soft. 'It's brilliant, Tony. Really brilliant.' There was no effort to conceal the pride she felt. She could not be deceived about art, and there was a fierce exultation in her that her son was so talented.

She turned to face him. 'Let me see more!'

They spent the next two hours going through his stack of paintings. Kate discussed each one in great detail. There was no condescension in her voice. She had failed in her attempt to control his life, and Tony admired her for taking her defeat so gracefully.

Kate said, 'I'll arrange for a showing. I know a few dealers who –'

'Thanks, M-mother, but you d-don't have to. I'm having a showing next F-friday. A g-gallery is giving me an exhibition.'

Kate threw her arms around Tony. 'That's wonderful! Which gallery?'

355

'The G-goerg Gallery.'

'I don't believe I know it.'

'It's s-small, but I'm not ready for Hammer or W-wildenstein yet.'

She pointed to the painting of Dominique under the tree. 'You're wrong, Tony. I think this –'

There was the sound of the front door opening. 'I'm horny, *chéri*. Take off your –' Dominique saw Kate. 'Oh, *merde!* I'm sorry. I – I didn't know you had company, Tony.'

There was a moment of frozen silence.

'Dominique, this is my m-mother. M-mother, may I present D-dominique Masson.'

The two women stood there, studying each other.

'How do you do, Mrs Blackwell.'

Kate said, 'I've been admiring my son's portrait of you.' The rest was left unspoken.

There was another awkward silence.

'Did Tony tell you he's going to have an exhibition, Mrs Blackwell?'

'Yes, he did. It's wonderful news.'

'Can you s-stay for it, Mother?'

'I'd give anything to be able to be there, but I have a board meeting the day after tomorrow in Johannesburg and there's no way I can miss it. I wish I'd known about it sooner, I'd have rearranged my schedule.'

'It's all r-right,' Tony said. 'I understand.' Tony was nervous that his mother might say more about the company in front of Dominique, but Kate's mind was on the paintings.

'It's important for the right people to see your exhibition.'

'Who are the right people, Mrs Blackwell?'

Kate turned to Dominique. 'Opinion-makers, critics. Someone like Andre d'Usseau – he should be there.'

Andre d'Usseau was the most respected art critic in France. He was a ferocious lion guarding the temple of art, and a single review from him could make or break an artist overnight. D'Usseau was invited to the opening of every exhibition, but he attended only the major ones. Gallery owners and artists trembled, waiting for his reviews to appear. He was a master of the *bon mot*, and his quips flew around Paris on poisoned wings. Andre d'Usseau was the most hated man in Parisian art circles, and the most respected. His mordant wit and savage criticism were tolerated because of his expertise.

Tony turned to Dominique. 'That's a m-mother for you.' Then to Kate, 'Andre d'Usseau doesn't g-go to little galleries.'

'Oh, Tony, he *must* come. He can make you famous overnight.'

'Or b-break me.'

'Don't you believe in yourself?' Kate was watching her son.

'Of course he does,' Dominique said. 'But we couldn't dare hope that Monsier d'Usseau would come.'

'I could probably find some friends who know him.'

Dominique's face lighted up. 'That would be fantastic!' She turned to Tony. '*Chéri*, do you know what it would mean if he came to your opening?'

'Oblivion?'

'Be serious. I know his taste, Tony. I know what he likes. He will adore your paintings.'

Kate said, 'I won't try to arrange for him to come unless you want me to, Tony.'

'Of course he wants it, Mrs Blackwell.'

Tony took a deep breath. 'I'm s-scared, but what the hell! L-let's try.'

'I'll see what I can do.' Kate looked at the painting on the easel for a long, long time, then turned back to Tony. There was a sadness in her eyes. 'Son, I must leave Paris tomorrow. Can we have dinner tonight?'

Tony replied, 'Yes, of course, Mother. *We're* f-free.'

Kate turned to Dominique and said graciously, 'Would you like to have dinner at Maxim's or –'

Tony said quickly, 'Dominique and I know a w-wonderful little café not f-far from here.'

They went to a bistro at the Place Victoire. The food was good and the wine was excellent. The two women seemed to get along well, and Tony was terribly proud of both of them. *It's one of the best nights of my life*, he thought. *I'm with my mother and the woman I'm going to marry.*

The next morning Kate telephoned from the airport. 'I've made a half a dozen phone calls,' she told Tony. 'No one could give me a definite answer

358

about Andrew d'Usseau. But whichever way it goes, darling, I'm proud of you. The paintings are wonderful. Tony, I love you.'

'I l-love you too, M-mother.'

The Goerg Gallery was just large enough to escape being called *intime*. Two dozen of Tony's paintings were being hung on the walls in frantic, last-minute preparation for the opening. On a marble side-board were slabs of cheese and biscuits and bottles of Chablis. The gallery was empty except for Anton Goerg, Tony, Dominique and a young female assistant who was hanging the last of the paintings.

Anton Goerg looked at his watch. 'The invitations said "seven o'clock." People should start to arrive at any moment now.'

Tony had not expected to be nervous. *And I'm not nervous*, he told himself. *I'm panicky!*

'What if no one shows up?' he asked. 'I mean, what if not one single, bloody person shows up?'

Dominique smiled and stroked his cheek. 'Then we'll have all this cheese and wine for ourselves.'

People began to arrive. Slowly at first, and then in larger numbers. Monsieur Goerg was at the door, effusively greeting them. *They don't look like art buyers to me*, Tony thought grimly. His discerning eye divided them into three categories. There were the artists and art students who attended each exhibition to evaluate the competition; the art dealers who came to every exhibition so they could spread derogatory news about aspiring painters;

and the *arty* crowd, consisting to a large extent of homosexuals and lesbians who seemed to spend their lives around the fringes of the art world. *I'm not going to sell a single, goddamned picture*, Tony decided.

Monsieur Goerg was beckoning to Tony from across the room.

'I don't think I want to meet any of these people,' Tony whispered to Dominique. 'They're here to rip me apart.'

'Nonsense. They came here to meet you. Now be charming, Tony.'

And so, he was charming. He met everybody, smiled a lot and uttered all the appropriate phrases in response to the compliments that were paid him. *But were they really compliments?* Tony wondered. Over the years a vocabulary had developed in art circles to cover exhibitions of unknown painters. Phrases that said everything and nothing.

'You really feel you're there . . .'

'I've never seen a style quite like yours . . .'

'Now, that's a painting!'

'It speaks to me . . .'

'You couldn't have done it any better . . .'

People kept arriving, and Tony wondered whether the attraction was curiosity about his paintings or the free wine and cheese. So far, not one of his paintings had sold, but the wine and cheese were being consumed rapaciously.

'Be patient,' Monsieur Goerg whispered to Tony. 'They are interested. First they must get a smell of the paintings. They see one they like, they keep wandering back to it. Pretty soon they ask the price, and when they nibble, *voilà!* The hook is set!'

'Jesus! I feel like I'm on a fishing cruise,' Tony told Dominique.

Monsieur Goerg bustled up to Tony. 'We've sold one!' he exclaimed. 'The Normandy landscape. Five hundred francs.'

It was a moment that Tony would remember as long as he lived. Someone had bought a painting of his! Someone had thought enough of his work to pay money for it, to hang it in his home or office, to look at it, live with it, show it to friends. It was a small piece of immortality. It was a way of living more than one life, of being in more than one place at the same time. A successful artist was in hundreds of homes and offices and museums all over the world, bringing pleasure to thousands – sometimes millions of people. Tony felt as though he had stepped into the pantheon of Da Vinci and Michelangelo and Rembrandt. He was no longer an amateur painter, he was a professional. Someone had paid money for his work.

Dominique hurried up to him, her eyes bright with excitement. 'You've just sold another one, Tony.'

'Which one?' he asked eagerly.

'The floral.'

The small gallery was filled now with people and loud chatter and the clink of glasses; and suddenly a stillness came over the room. There was an undercurrent of whispers and all eyes turned to the door.

Andre d'Usseau was entering the gallery. He was in his middle fifties, taller than the average Frenchman, with a strong, leonine face and a mane of white hair. He wore a flowing inverness cape and Borsalino hat, and behind him came an entourage of hangers-on. Automatically, everyone in the room began to make way for d'Usseau. There was not one person present who did not know who he was.

Dominique squeezed Tony's hand. 'He's come!' she said. 'He's here!'

Such an honour had never befallen Monsieur Goerg before, and he was beside himself, bowing and scraping before the great man, doing every-thing but tugging at his forelock.

'Monsieur d'Usseau,' he babbled. 'What a great pleasure this is! What an honour! May I offer you some wine, some cheese?' He cursed himself for not having bought a decent wine.

'Thank you,' the great man replied. 'I have come to feast only my eyes. I would like to meet the artist.'

Tony was too stunned to move. Dominique pushed him forwards.

'Here he is,' Monsieur Goerg said. 'M. Andre d'Usseau, this is Tony Blackwell.'

Tony found his voice. 'How do you do, sir? I – thank you for coming.'

Andre d'Usseau bowed slightly and moved towards the paintings on the walls. Everyone pushed back to give him room. He made his way slowly, looking at each painting long and carefully, then moving on to the next one. Tony tried to read his face, but he could tell nothing. D'Usseau neither frowned nor smiled. He stopped for a long time at one particular painting, a nude of Dominique, then moved on. He made a complete circle of the room, missing nothing. Tony was perspiring profusely.

When Andre d'Usseau had finished, he walked over to Tony. 'I am glad I came,' was all he said.

Within minutes after the famous critic had left, every painting in the gallery was sold. A great new artist was being born, and everyone wanted to be in at the birth.

'I have never seen anything like it,' Monsieur Goerg exclaimed. 'Andre d'Usseau came to my gallery. *My* gallery! All Paris will read about it tomorrow. 'I am glad I came.' Andre d'Usseau is not a man to waste words. This calls for champagne. Let us celebrate.'

Later that night, Tony and Dominique had their own private celebration. Dominique snuggled in his arms. 'I've slept with painters before,' she said, 'but never anyone as famous as you're going to be. Tomorrow everyone in Paris will know who you are.'

And Dominique was right.

*   *   *

At five o'clock the following morning, Tony and Dominique hurriedly got dressed and went out to get the first edition of the morning paper. It had just arrived at the kiosk. Tony snatched up the paper and turned to the art section. His review was the headline article under the by-line of Andre d'Usseau. Tony read it aloud:

'An exhibition by a young American painter, Anthony Blackwell, opened last night at the Goerg Gallery. It was a great learning experience for this critic. I have attended so many exhibitions of talented painters that I had forgotten what truly bad paintings looked like. I was forcibly reminded last night . . .'

Tony's face turned ashen.

'Please don't read any more,' Dominique begged. She tried to take the paper from Tony.

'Let go!' he commanded.

He read on.

'At first I thought a joke was being perpetrated. I could not seriously believe that anyone would have the nerve to hang such amateurish paintings and dare to call them art. I searched for the tiniest glimmer of talent. Alas, there was none. They should have hung the painter instead of his paintings. I could earnestly advise that the confused Mr Blackwell return to his real profession,

364

which I can only assume is that of house painter.'

'I can't believe it,' Dominique whispered. 'I can't believe he couldn't see it. Oh, that bastard!' Dominique began to cry helplessly.

Tony felt as though his chest were filled with lead. He had difficulty breathing. 'He saw it,' he said. 'And he does know, Dominique. He does know.' His voice was filled with pain. 'That's what hurts so much. Christ! What a fool I was!' He started to move away.

'Where are you going. Tony?'

'I don't know.'

He wandered around the cold, dawn streets, unaware of the tears running down his face. Within a few hours, everyone in Paris would have read that review. He would be an object of ridicule. But what hurt more was that he had deluded himself. He had really believed he had a career ahead of him as a painter. At least Andre d'Usseau had saved him from that mistake. *Pieces of posterity*, Tony thought grimly. *Pieces of shit!* He walked into the first open bar and proceeded to get mindlessly drunk.

When Tony finally returned to his apartment, it was five o'clock the following morning.

Dominique was waiting for him, frantic. 'Where have you been, Tony? Your mother has been trying to get in touch with you. She's sick with worry.'

'Did you read it to her?'

'Yes, she insisted. I –'

The telephone rang. Dominique looked at Tony, and picked up the receiver. 'Hello? Yes, Mrs Blackwell. He just walked in.' She held the receiver out to Tony. He hesitated, then took it.'

'Hello, M-mother.'

Kate's voice was filled with distress. 'Tony, darling, listen to me. I can make him print a retraction. I –'

'Mother,' Tony said wearily, 'this isn't a b-business transaction. This is a c-critic expressing an opinion. His opinion is that I should be h-hanged.'

'Darling, I hate to have you hurt like this. I don't think I can stand –' she broke off, unable to continue.

'It's all right, M-mother. I've had my little f-fling. I tried it and it didn't w-work. I don't have what it t-takes. It's as simple as that. I h-hate d'Usseau's guts, but he's the best g-goddamned art critic in the world, I have to g-give him that. He saved me from making a t-terrible mistake.'

'Tony, I wish there was something I could say . . .'

'D'Usseau s-said it all. It's b-better that I f-found it out now instead of t-ten years from now, isn't it? I've got to g-get out of this town.'

'Wait there for me, darling. I'll leave Johannesburg tomorrow and we'll go back to New York together.'

'All right,' Tony said. He replaced the receiver and turned towards Dominique. 'I'm sorry, Dominique. You picked the wrong fellow.'

Dominique said nothing. She just looked at him with eyes filled with an unspeakable sorrow.

The following afternoon at Kruger-Brent's office on Rue Matignon, Kate Blackwell was writing out a cheque. The man seated across the desk from her sighed. 'It is a pity. Your son has talent, Mrs Blackwell. He could have become an important painter.'

Kate stared at him coldly. 'Mr d'Usseau, there are tens of thousands of painters in the world. My son was not meant to be one of the crowd.' She passed the cheque across the desk. 'You fulfiled your part of the bargain, I'm prepared to fulfil mine. Kruger-Brent, Limited, will sponsor art museums in Johannesburg, London and New York. You will be in charge of selecting the paintings – with a handsome commission, of course.'

But long after d'Usseau had gone, Kate sat at her desk, filled with a deep sadness. She loved her son so much. If he ever found out . . . She knew the risk she had taken. But she could not stand by and let Tony throw away his inheritance. No matter what it might cost her, he had to be protected. The company had to be protected. Kate rose, feelng suddenly very tired. It was time to pick up Tony and take him home. She would help him get over this, so he could get on with what he had been born to do.

Run the company.

NINETEEN

For the next two years, Tony Blackwell felt he was on a giant treadmill that was taking him nowhere. He was the heir apparent to an awesome conglomerate. Kruger-Brent's empire had expanded to include paper mills, an airline, banks and a chain of hospitals. Tony learned that a name is a key that opens all doors. There are clubs and organizations and social cliques where the coin of the realm is not money or influence, but the proper name. Tony was accepted for membership in the Union Club, The Brook and The Links Club. He was catered to everywhere he went, but he felt like an imposter. He had done nothing to deserve any of it. He was in the giant shadow of his grandfather, and he felt he was constantly being measured against him. It was unfair, for there were no more mine fields to crawl over, no guards shooting at him, no sharks threatening him. They belonged to a past century, another time, another place, heroic acts committed by a stranger.

Tony worked twice as hard as anyone else at Kruger-Brent, Ltd. He drove himself mercilessly, trying to rid himself of memories too searing to bear. He wrote to Dominique, but his letters were returned unopened. He telephoned Maître Cantal, but Dominique no longer modelled at the school. She had disappeared.

Tony handled his job expertly and methodically, with neither passion nor love, and if he felt a deep emptiness inside himself, no one suspected it. Not even Kate. She received weekly reports on Tony, and she was pleased with them.

'He has a natural aptitude for business,' she told Brad Rogers.

To Kate, the long hours her son worked were proof of how much he loved what he was doing. When Kate thought of how Tony had almost thrown his future away, she shuddered and was grateful she had saved him.

In 1948 the Nationalist Party was in full power in South Africa, with segregation in all public places. Migration was strictly controlled, and families were split up to suit the convenience of the government. Every black man had to carry a *bewyshoek*, and it was more than a pass, it was a lifeline, his birth certificate, his work permit, his tax receipt. It regulated his movements and his life. There were increasing riots in South Africa, and they were ruthlessly put down by the police. From time to time, Kate read newspaper stories about sabotage

and unrest, and Banda's name was always promi-
nently mentioned. He was still a leader in the
underground, despite his age. *Of course he would
fight for his people*, Kate thought. *He's Banda.*

Kate celebrated her fifty-sixth birthday alone with
Tony at the house on Fifth Avenue. She thought,
*This handsome twenty-four-year-old man across
the table can't be my son. I'm too young.* And he
was toasting her, 'To m-my f-fantastic m-mother.
Happy b-birthday!'

'You should make that to my fantastic *old*
mother,' *Soon I'll be retiring*, Kate thought, *but
my son will take my place. My son!*

At Kate's insistence, Tony had moved into the
mansion on Fifth Avenue.

'The place is too bloody large for me to rattle
around in alone,' Kate told him. 'You'll have the
whole east wing to yourself and all the privacy you
need.' It was easier for Tony to give in than to
argue.

Tony and Kate had breakfast together every
morning, and the topic of conversation was always
Kruger-Brent, Ltd. Tony marvelled that his mother
could care so passionately for a faceless, soulless
entity, an amorphous collection of buildings and
machines and bookkeeping figures. *Where did the
magic lie?* With all the myriad mysteries of the
world to explore, why would anyone want to waste
a lifetime accumulating wealth to pile on more
wealth, gathering power that was beyond power?

371

Tony did not understand his mother. But he loved her. And he tried to live up to what she expected of him.

The Pan American flight from Rome to New York had been uneventful. Tony liked the airline. It was pleasant and efficient. He worked on his overseas acquisitions reports from the time the plane took off, skipping dinner and ignoring the stewardess who kept offering him drinks, pillows or whatever else might appeal to their attractive passenger.

'Thank you, miss. I'm fine.'

'If there's *anything* at all, Mr Blackwell . . .'

'Thank you.'

A middle-aged woman in the seat next to Tony was reading a fashion magazine. As she turned a page, Tony happened to glance over, and he froze. There was a picture of a model wearing a ball gown. It was Dominique. There was no question about it. There were the high, delicate cheekbones and the deep-green eyes, the luxuriant blonde hair. Tony's pulse began to race.

'Excuse me,' Tony said to his seat companion. 'May I borrow that page?'

Early the following morning, Tony called the dress shop and got the name of their advertising agency. He telephoned them. 'I'm trying to locate one of your models,' he told the switchboard operator. 'Could you —'

'One moment, please.'

A man's voice came on. 'May I help you?'

'I saw a photograph in this month's issue of *Vogue*. A model advertising a ball gown for the Rothman stores. Is that your account?'

'Yes.'

'Can you give me the name of your model agency?'

'That would be the Carleton Blessing Agency.' He gave Tony the telephone number.

A minute later, Tony was talking to a woman at the Blessing Agency. 'I'm trying to locate one of your models,' he said. 'Dominique Masson.'

'I'm sorry. It is our policy not to give out personal information.' And the line went dead.

Tony sat there, staring at the receiver. There *had* to be a way to get in touch with Dominique. He went into Brad Roger's office.

'Morning, Tony. Coffee?'

'No, thanks. Brad, have you heard of the Carleton Blessing Model Agency?'

'I should think so. We own it.'

'*What?*'

'It's under the umbrella of one of our subsidiaries.'

'When did we acquire it?'

A couple of years ago. Just about the time you joined the company. What's your interest in it?'

'I'm trying to locate one of their models. She's an old friend.'

'No problem. I'll call and –'

'Never mind. I'll do it. Thanks, Brad.'

A feeling of warm anticipation was building up inside Tony.

* * *

373

Late that afternoon, Tony went uptown to the offices of the Carleton Blessing Agency and gave his name. Sixty seconds later, he was seated in the office of the president, a Mr Tilton.

'This is certainly an honour, Mr Blackwell. I hope there's no problem. Our profits for the last quarter –'

'No problem. I'm interested in one of your models. Dominique Masson.'

Tilton's face lighted up. 'She's turned out to be one of our very best. Your mother has a good eye.'

Tony thought he had misunderstood him. 'I beg your pardon?'

'Your mother personally requested that we engage Dominique. It was part of our deal when Kruger-Brent, Limited, took us over. It's all in our file, if you'd care to –'

'No.' Tony could make no sense of what he was hearing. *Why would his mother –?* 'May I have Dominique's address, please?'

'Certainly, Mr Blackwell. She's doing a layout in Vermont today, but she should be back' – he glanced at a schedule on his desk – 'tomorrow afternoon.'

Tony was waiting outside Dominique's apartment building when a black sedan pulled up and Dominique stepped out. With her was a large, athletic-looking man carrying Dominique's suit-case. Dominique stopped dead when she saw Tony.

'Tony! My God! What – what are you doing here?'

'I need to talk to you.'

'Some other time, buddy,' the athlete said. 'We have a busy afternoon.'

Tony did not even look at him. 'Tell your friend to go away.'

'Hey! Who the hell do you think –?'

Dominique turned to the man. 'Please go, Ben. I'll call you this evening.'

He hesitated a moment, then shrugged. 'Okay.' He glared at Tony, got back in the car and roared off.

Dominique turned to Tony. 'You'd better come inside.'

The apartment was a large duplex with white rugs and drapes and modern furniture. It must have cost a fortune.

'You're doing well,' Tony said.

'Yes. I've been lucky.' Dominique's fingers were picking nervously at her blouse. 'Would you like a drink?'

'No, thanks. I tried to get in touch with you after I left Paris.'

'I moved.'

'To America?'

'Yes.'

'How did you get a job with the Carleton Blessing Agency?'

'I – I answered a newspaper advertisement,' she said lamely.

'When did you first meet my mother, Dominique?'

'I – at your apartment in Paris. Remember? We –'

'No more games,' Tony said. He felt a wild rage building in him. 'It's over. I've never hit a woman in my life, but if you tell me one more lie, I promise you your face won't be fit to photograph.'

Dominique started to speak, but the fury in Tony's eyes stopped her.

'I'll ask you once more. When did you first meet my mother?'

This time there was no hesitation. 'When you were accepted at Ecole des Beaux-Arts. Your mother arranged for me to model there.'

He felt sick to his stomach. He forced himself to go on. 'So I could meet you?'

'Yes, I –'

'And she paid you to become my mistress, to pretend to love me?'

'Yes. It was just after the war – it was terrible. I had no money. Don't you see? But Tony, believe me, I cared. I really cared –'

'Just answer my questions.' The savagery in his voice frightened her. This was a stranger before her, a man capable of untold violence.

'What was the point of it?'

'Your mother wanted me to keep an eye on you.'

He thought of Dominique's tenderness and her love-making – bought and paid for, courtesy of his mother – and he was sick with shame. All along, he had been his mother's puppet, controlled, manipulated. His mother had never given a damn about him. He was not her son. He was her crown prince, her heir apparent. All that mattered to her was the company. He took one last look at Dominique, then turned and stumbled out. She looked after him, her eyes blinded by tears, and she thought, *I didn't lie about loving you, Tony. I didn't lie about that.*

Kate was in the library when Tony walked in, very drunk.

'I t-talked to D-dominique,' he said. 'You t-two m-must have had a w-wonderful time l-laughing at me behind my back.'

Kate felt a quick sense of alarm. 'Tony –'

'From now on I want you to s-stay out of my p-personal l-life. Do you hear me?' And he turned and staggered out of the room.

Kate watched him go, and she was suddenly filled with a terrible sense of foreboding.

TWENTY

The following day, Tony took an apartment in Greenwich Village. There were no more sociable dinners with his mother. He kept his relationship with Kate on an impersonal, business-like basis. From time to time Kate made conciliatory overtures, which Tony ignored.

Kate's heart ached. But she had done what was right for Tony. Just as she had once done what was right for David. She could not have let either of them leave the company. Tony was the one human being in the world Kate loved, and she watched as he became more and more insular, drawing deep within himself, rejecting everyone. He had no friends. Where once he had been warm and outgoing, he was now cool and reserved. He had built a wall around himself that no one was able to breach. *He needs a wife to care for him,* Kate thought. *And a son to carry on. I must help him. I must.*

Brad Rogers came into Kate's office and said,

'I'm afraid we're in for some more trouble, Kate.'

'What's happened?'

He put a cable on her desk. 'The South African Parliament has outlawed the Natives' Representative Council and passed the Communist Act.'

Kate said, 'My God!' The act had nothing to do with communism. It stated that anyone who disagreed with any government policy and tried to change it in any way was guilty under the Communist Act and could be imprisoned.

'It's their way of breaking the black resistance movement,' she said. 'If –' She was interrupted by her secretary.

'There's an overseas call for you. It's Mr Pierce in Johannesburg.'

Jonathan Pierce was the manager of the Johannesburg branch office. Kate picked up the phone. 'Hello, Johnny. How are you?'

'Fine, Kate. I have some news I thought you'd better be aware of.'

'What's that?'

'I've just received a report that the police have captured Banda.'

Kate was on the next flight to Johannesburg. She had alerted the company lawyers to see what could be done for Banda. Even the power and prestige of Kruger-Brent, Ltd., might not be able to help him. He had been designated an enemy of the state, and she dreaded to think what his punishment would be. At least she must see him and talk to him and offer what support she could.

When the plane landed in Johannesburg, Kate went to her office and telephoned the director of prisons.

'He's in an isolation block, Mrs Blackwell, and he's allowed no visitors. However, in your case, I will see what can be done . . .'

The following morning, Kate was at the Johannesburg prison, face to face with Banda. He was manacled and shackled, and there was a glass partition between them. His hair was completely white. Kate had not known what to expect – despair, defiance – but Banda grinned when he saw her and said, 'I knew you'd come. You're just like your daddy. You can't stay away from trouble, can you?'

'Look who's talking,' Kate retorted. 'Bloody hell! How do we get you out of here?'

'In a box. That's the only way they're going to let me go.'

'I have a lot of fancy lawyers who –'

'Forget it, Kate. They caught me fair and square. Now I've got to get away fair and square.'

'What are you talking about?'

'I don't like cages, I never did. And they haven't built one yet that can keep me.'

Kate said, 'Banda, don't try it. Please. They'll kill you.'

'Nothing can kill me,' Banda said. 'You're talking to a man who lived through sharks and land mines and guard dogs.' A soft gleam came into his eyes. 'You know something, Kate? I think maybe that was the best time of my life.'

When Kate went to visit Banda the next day, the superintendent said, 'I'm sorry, Mrs Blackwell. We've had to move him for security reasons.'

'Where is he?'

'I'm not at liberty to say.'

When Kate woke up the following morning, she saw the headline in the newspaper carried in with her breakfast tray. It read: REBEL LEADER KILLED WHILE TRYING TO ESCAPE PRISON. She was at the prison an hour later, in the superintendent's office.

'He was shot during an attempted prison break, Mrs Blackwell. That's all there is to it.'

You're wrong, thought Kate, *there's more. Much more.* Banda was dead, but was his dream of freedom for his people dead?

Two days later, after making the funeral arrangements, Kate was on the plane to New York. She looked out the window to take one last look at her beloved land. The soil was red and rich and fertile, and in the bowels of its earth were treasures beyond man's dreams. This was God's chosen land, and He had been lavish in his generosity. But there was a curse upon the country. *I'll never come back here again*, Kate thought sadly. *Never*.

* * *

One of Brad Rogers's responsibilities was to oversee the Long-Range Planning Department of Kruger-Brent, Ltd. He was brilliant at finding businesses that would make profitable acquisitions.

One day in early May, he walked into Kate Blackwell's office. 'I've come across something interesting, Kate.' He placed two folders on her desk. 'Two companies. If we could pick up either one of them, it would be a coup.'

'Thanks, Brad. I'll look them over tonight.'

That evening, Kate dined alone and studied Brad Rogers's confidential reports on the two companies – Wyatt Oil & Tool and International Technology. The reports were long and detailed, and both ended with the letters NIS, the company code for *Not Interested in Selling*, which meant that if the companies were to be acquired, it would take more than a straightforward business transaction to accomplish it. *And*, Kate thought, *they're well worth taking over*. Each company was privately controlled by a wealthy and strong-minded individual, which eliminated any possibility of a takeover attempt. It was a challenge, and it had been a long time since Kate had faced a challenge. The more she thought about it, the more the possibilities began to excite her. She studied again the confidential balance sheets. Wyatt Oil & Tool was owned by a Texan, Charlie Wyatt, and the company's assets included producing oil wells, a utility company and dozens of potentially profitable oil leases. There was no question about it, Wyatt Oil & Tool would make a handsome acquisition for Kruger-Brent, Ltd.

Kate turned her attention to the second company. International Technology was owned by a German, Count Frederick Hoffman. The company started with a small steel mill in Essen, and over the years had expanded into a huge conglomerate, with shipyards, petrochemical plants, a fleet of oil tankers and a computer division.

As large as Kruger-Brent, Ltd., was, it could digest only one of these giants. She knew which company she was going after. NIS, the sheet read.

We'll see about that, Kate thought.

Early the following morning, she sent for Brad Rogers. 'I'd love to know how you got hold of those confidential balance sheets,' Kate grinned. 'Tell me about Charlie Wyatt and Frederick Hoffman.'

Brad had done his homework. 'Charlie Wyatt was born in Dallas. Flamboyant, loud, runs his own empire, smart as hell. He started with nothing, got lucky in oil wildcatting, kept expanding and now he owns about half of Texas.'

'How old is he?'

'Forty-seven.'

'Children?'

'One daughter, twenty-five. From what I hear, she's a raving beauty.'

'Is she married?'

'Divorced.'

'Frederick Hoffman.'

'Hoffman's a couple of years younger than Charlie Wyatt. He's a count, comes from a distinguished German family going back to the Middle Ages. He's a widower. His grandfather started with a small steel mill. Frederick Hoffman inherited it from his father and built it into a conglomerate. He was one of the first to get into the computer field. He holds a lot of patents on microprocessors. Every time we use a computer, Count Hoffman gets a royalty.'

'Children?'

'A daughter, twenty-three.'

'What is she like?'

'I couldn't find out,' Brad Rogers apologized. 'It's a very buttoned-up family. They travel in their own little circles.' He hesitated. 'We're probably wasting our time on this, Kate. I had a few drinks with a couple of top executives in both companies. Neither Wyatt nor Hoffman has the slightest interest in a sale, merger or joint venture. As you can see from their financials, they'd be crazy even to think about it.'

That feeling of challenge was there in Kate again, tugging at her.

Ten days later Kate was invited by the President of the United States to a Washington conference of leading international industrialists to discuss assistance to underdeveloped countries. Kate made a telephone call, and shortly afterwards Charlie Wyatt and Count Frederick Hoffman received invitations to attend the conference.

Kate had formed a mental impression of both the Texan and the German, and they fitted her preconceived notions almost precisely. She had never met a shy Texan, and Charlie Wyatt was no exception. He was a huge man – almost six feet four inches – with enormous shoulders and a football player's body that had gone to fat. His face was large and ruddy, and his voice loud and booming. He came off as a good ol' boy – or would have if Kate had not known better. Charlie Wyatt had not built his empire by luck. He was a business genius. Kate had talked to him for less than ten minutes when she knew that there was no way this man could be persuaded to do anything he did not want to do. He was opinionated, and he had a deep stubborn streak. No one was going to cajole him, threaten him or con him out of his company. But Kate had found his Achilles' heel, and that was enough.

Frederick Hoffman was Charlie Wyatt's opposite. He was a handsome man, with an aristocratic face and soft brown hair tinged with grey at the temples. He was punctiliously correct and filled with a sense of old-fashioned courtesy. On the surface, Frederick Hoffman was pleasant and debonair; on the inside Kate sensed a core of steel.

* * *

The conference in Washington lasted three days, and it went well. The meetings were chaired by the Vice-President, and the President made a brief appearance. Everyone there was impressed with Kate Blackwell. She was an attractive, charismatic woman, head of a corporate empire she had helped build, and they were fascinated, as Kate meant them to be.

When Kate got Charlie Wyatt alone for a moment, she asked innocently, 'Is your family with you, Mr Wyatt?'

'I brought my daughter along. She has a little shoppin' to do.'

'Oh, really? How nice.' No one would have suspected that Kate not only knew his daughter was with him, but what kind of dress she had bought at Garfinckel's that morning. 'I'm giving a little dinner party at Dark Harbor, Friday. I'd be pleased if you and your daughter would join us for the weekend.'

Wyatt did not hesitate. 'I've heard a lot about your spread, Mrs Blackwell. I'd sure like to see it.'

Kate smiled. 'Good. I'll make arrangements for you to be flown up there tomorrow night.'

Ten minutes later, Kate was speaking to Frederick Hoffman.

'Are you alone in Washington, Mr Hoffman?' she asked. 'Or is your wife with you?'

'My wife died a few years ago,' Frederick Hoffman told her. 'I'm here with my daughter.'

Kate knew they were staying at the Hay-Adams

Hotel in Suite 418. 'I'm giving a little dinner party at Dark Harbor. I would be delighted if you and your daughter could join us tomorrow for the weekend.'

'I should be getting back to Germany,' Hoffman replied. He studied her a moment, and smiled. 'I suppose another day day or two won't make much difference.'

'Wonderful. I'll arrange transportation for you.'

It was Kate's custom to give a party at the Dark Harbor estate once every two months. Some of the most interesting and powerful people in the world came to these gatherings, and the get-togethers were always fruitful. Kate intended to see to it that this one was a very special party. Her problem was to make sure Tony attended. During the past year, he had seldom bothered to show up, and when he did he had made a perfunctory appearance and left. This time it was imperative that he come and that he stay.

When Kate mentioned the weekend to Tony, he said curtly, 'I c-can't make it. I'm leaving for C-canada Monday and I have a lot of w-work to clean up before I go.'

'This is important,' Kate told him. 'Charlie Wyatt and Count Hoffman are going to be there and they're –'

'I know who they are,' he interrupted. 'I t-talked to Brad Rogers. We haven't got a p-prayer of acquiring either one of those companies.

387

'I want to give it a try.'

He looked at her and asked, 'W-which one are you after?'

'Wyatt Oil and Tool. It could increase our profits as much as fifteen percent, perhaps more. When the Arab countries realize they have the world by the throat, they're going to form a cartel, and oil prices will skyrocket. Oil is going to turn into liquid gold.'

'What about International T-t-technology?'

Kate shrugged. 'It's a good company, but the plum is Wyatt Oil and Tool. It's a perfect acquisition for us. I need you there, Tony. Canada can wait a few days.'

Tony loathed parties. He hated the endless, boring conversations, the boastful men and the predatory women. But this was business. 'All right.'

All the pieces were in place.

The Wyatts were flown to Maine in a company Cessna, and from the ferry were driven to Cedar Hill House in a limousine. Kate was at the door to greet them. Brad Rogers had been right about Charlie Wyatt's daughter, Lucy. She was strikingly beautiful. She was tall, with black hair and gold-flecked brown eyes, set in almost perfect features. Her sleek Galanos dress outlined a firm, stunning figure. She had, Brad informed Kate, been divorced from a wealthy Italian playboy two years earlier. Kate introduced Lucy to Tony and watched for her son's reaction. There was none. He greeted both the Wyatts with equal courtesy and led them into the bar, where a bartender was waiting to mix drinks.

'What a lovely room,' Lucy exclaimed. Her voice was unexpectedly soft and mellow, with no trace of a Texas accent. 'Do you spend much time here?' she asked Tony.

'No.'

She waited for him to go on. Then, 'Did you grow up here?'

'Partly.'

Kate picked up the conversation, adroitly smoothing over Tony's silence. 'Some of Tony's happiest memories are of this house. The poor man is so busy he doesn't get much chance to come back here and enjoy it, do you, Tony?'

He gave his mother a cool look and said, 'No. As a matter of fact, I should be in C-canada –'

'But he postponed it so he could meet both of you,' Kate finished for him.

'Well, I'm mighty pleased,' Charlie Wyatt said. 'I've heard a lot about you, son.' He grinned. 'You wouldn't want to come to work for me, would you?'

'I don't think that's q-quite what my mother had in mind, Mr Wyatt.'

Charlie Wyatt grinned again. 'I know.' He turned to look at Kate. 'Your mother's quite a lady. You should have seen her rope and hog-tie everybody at that White House meetin'. She –' He stopped as Frederick Hoffman and his daughter,

Marianne, entered the room. Marianne Hoffman was a pale version of her father. She had the same aristocratic features and she had long, blonde hair. She wore an off-white chiffon dress. Next to Lucy Wyatt she looked washed out.

'May I present my daughter, Marianne?' Count Hoffman said. 'I'm sorry we're late,' he apologized. 'The plane was delayed at La Guardia.'

'Oh, what a shame,' Kate said. Tony was aware that Kate had arranged the delay. She had had the Wyatts and the Hoffmans flown up to Maine in separate planes, so that the Wyatts would arrive early and the Hoffman's late. 'We were just having a drink. What would you like?'

'A Scotch, please,' Count Hoffman said.

Kate turned to Marianne. 'And you, my dear?'

'Nothing, thank you.'

A few minutes later, the other guests began to arrive, and Tony circulated among them, playing the part of the gracious host. No one except Kate could have guessed how little the festivities meant to him. It was not, Kate knew, that Tony was bored. It was simply that he was completely removed from what was happening around him. He had lost his pleasure in people. It worried Kate.

Two tables had been set in the large dining room. Kate seated Marianne Hoffman between a Supreme Court justice and a senator at one table, and she seated Lucy Wyatt on Tony's right at the other table. All the men in the room – married and unmarried – were eyeing Lucy. Kate listened to

Lucy trying to draw Tony into conversation. It was obvious that she liked him. Kate smiled to herself. It was a good beginning.

The following morning, Saturday, at breakfast, Charlie Wyatt said to Kate. 'That's a mighty pretty yacht you've got sittin' out there, Mrs Blackwell. How big is it?'

'I'm really not quite sure.' Kate turned to her son. 'Tony, how large is the *Corsair*?'

His mother knew exactly how large it was, but Tony said politely, 'Eighty f-feet.'

'We don't go in much for boats in Texas. We're in too much of a hurry. We do most of our travellin' in planes.' Wyatt gave a booming laugh. 'Guess maybe I'll try it and get my feet wet.'

Kate smiled. 'I was hoping you would let me show you around the island. We could go out on the boat tomorrow.'

Charlie Wyatt looked at her thoughtfully and said, 'That's mighty kind of you, Mrs Blackwell.'

Tony quietly watched the two of them and said nothing. The first move had just been made, and he wondered whether Charlie Wyatt was aware of it. Probably not. He was a clever businessman, but he had never come up against anyone like Kate Blackwell.

Kate turned to Tony and Lucy. 'It's such a beautiful day. Why don't you two go for a sail in the catboat?'

Before Tony could refuse, Lucy said, 'Oh, I'd love that.'

'I'm s-sorry,' Tony said curtly. 'I'm expecting s-some overseas calls.' Tony could feel his mother's disapproving eyes on him.

Kate turned to Marianne Hoffman. 'I haven't seen your father this morning.'

'He's out exploring the island. He's an early riser.'

'I understand you like to ride. We have a fine stable here.'

'Thank you, Mrs Blackwell. I'll just wander around, if you don't mind.'

'Of course not,' Kate turned back to Tony. 'Are you sure you won't change your mind about taking Miss Wyatt for a sail?' There was steel in her voice.

'I'm s-sure.'

It was a small victory, but it was a victory none-theless. The battle was joined, and Tony had no intention of losing it. Not this time. His mother no longer had the power to deceive him. She had used him as a pawn once, and he was fully aware she was planning to try it again; but this time she would fail. She wanted the Wyatt Oil & Tool Company. Charlie Wyatt had no intention of merging or selling his company. But every man has a weakness, and Kate had found his: his daughter. If Lucy were to marry into the Blackwell family, a merger of some kind would become inevitable. Tony looked across the breakfast table at his mother, despising her. She had baited the trap well. Lucy was not only beautiful, she was intelligent and charming. But she was as much of a pawn in this sick game as Tony was, and nothing in the world could induce him to touch her. This was a battle between his mother and himself.

When breakfast was over, Kate rose. 'Tony, before your phone call comes in, why don't you show Miss Wyatt the gardens?'

There was no way Tony could refuse graciously. 'All right.' He would make it short.

Kate turned to Charlie Wyatt. 'Are you interested in rare books? We have quite a collection in the library.'

'I'm interested in anything you want to show me,' the Texan said.

Almost as an afterthought, Kate turned back to Marianne Hoffman. 'Will you be all right, dear?'

'I'll be fine, thank you, Mrs Blackwell. Please don't worry about me.'

'I won't,' Kate said.

And Tony knew she meant it. Miss Hoffman was of no use to Kate, and so she dismissed her. It was done with a light charm and a smile, but beneath it was a single-minded ruthlessness that Tony detested.

Lucy was watching him. 'Are you ready, Tony?'

'Yes.'

Tony and Lucy moved towards the door. They were not quite out of earshot when Tony heard his mother say, 'Don't they make a lovely couple?'

The two of them walked through the large, formal gardens towards the dock where the *Corsair* was tied up. There were acres and acres of wildly coloured flowers staining the summer air with their scent.

'This is a heavenly place,' Lucy said.

'Yes.'

'We don't have flowers like these in Texas.'

'No?'

'It's so quiet and peaceful here.'

'Yes.'

Lucy stopped abruptly and turned to face Tony.

He saw the anger in her face. 'Have I said something to offend you?' he asked.

'You haven't said anything. That's what I find offensive. All I can get out of you is a yes or a no. You make me feel as though I'm – I'm chasing you.'

'Are you?'

She laughed. 'Yes. If I could only teach you to talk, I think we might have something.'

Tony grinned.

'What are you thinking?' Lucy asked.

'Nothing.'

He was thinking of his mother, and how much she hated losing.

Kate was showing Charlie Wyatt the large, oak-panelled library. On the shelves were first editions of Oliver Goldsmith, Laurence Sterne, Tobias Smollett and John Donne, along with a Ben Johnson first folio. There was a Samuel Butler and John Bunyan, and the rare 1813 privately printed edition of *Queen Mab*. Wyatt walked along the shelves of treasures, his eyes gleaming. He paused in front of a beautifully bound edition of John Keats's *Endymion*.

'This is a Roseberg copy,' Charlie Wyatt said.

Kate looked at him in surprise. 'Yes. There are only two known copies.'

'I have the other one,' Wyatt told her.

'I should have known,' Kate laughed. 'That "good ol' Texas boy" act you put on had me fooled.'

Wyatt grinned. 'Did it? It's good camouflage.'

'Where did you go to school?'

'Colorado School of Mining, then Oxford on a Rhodes Scholarship.' He studied Kate a moment. 'I'm told it was you who got me invited to that White House conference.'

She shrugged. 'I merely mentioned your name. They were delighted to have you.'

'That was mighty kind of you, Kate. Now, as long as you and I are alone, why don't you tell me exactly what's on your mind?'

Tony was at work in his private study, a small room off the main downstairs hallway. He was seated in a deep armchair when he heard the door open and someone come in. He turned to look. It was Marianne Hoffman. Before Tony could open his mouth to make his presence known, he heard her gasp.

She was looking at the paintings on the wall. They were Tony's paintings – the few he had brought back from his apartment in Paris, and this was the only room in the house where he would allow them to be hung. He watched her walk around the room, going from painting to painting, and it was too late to say anything.

'I don't believe it,' she murmured.

And Tony felt a sudden anger within him. He knew they were not *that* bad. As he moved, the leather of his chair creaked, and Marianne turned and saw him.

'Oh! I'm sorry,' she apologized. 'I didn't know anyone was in here.'

Tony rose. 'That's quite all right.' His tone was rude. He disliked having his sanctuary invaded. 'Were you looking for something?'

'No. I – I was just wandering around. Your collection of paintings belongs in a museum.'

'Except for these,' Tony heard himself saying.

She was puzzled by the hostility in his voice. She turned to look at the paintings again. She saw the signature. '*You* painted these?'

'I'm sorry if they don't appeal to you.'

'They're fantastic!' She moved towards him. 'I don't understand. If you can do this, why would you ever want to do anything else? You're wonderful. I don't mean you're good. I mean you're *wonderful.*'

Tony stood there, not listening, just wanting her to get out.

'I wanted to be a painter,' Marianne said. 'I studied with Oskar Kokoschka for a year. I finally quit

396

because I knew I never could be as good as I wanted to be. But you!' She turned to the paintings again. 'Did you study in Paris?'

He wished she would leave him alone. 'Yes.'

'And you quit – just like that?'

'Yes.'

'What a pity. You –'

'*There* you are!'

They both turned. Kate was standing in the doorway. She eyed the two of them a moment, then walked over to Marianne. 'I've been looking everywhere for you, Marianne. Your father mentioned that you like orchids. You must see our greenhouse.'

'Thank you,' Marianne murmured. 'I'm really –'

Kate turned to Tony. 'Tony, perhaps you should see to your other guests.' There was a note of sharp displeasure in her voice.

She took Marianne's arm, and they were gone.

There was a fascination to watching his mother manoeuvre people. It was done so smoothly. Not a move was wasted. It had started with the Wyatts arriving early and the Hoffmans arriving late. Lucy being placed next to him at every meal. The private conferences with Charlie Wyatt. It was so damned obvious, and yet Tony had to admit to himself that it was obvious only because he had the key. He knew his mother and the way her mind worked. Lucy Wyatt was a lovely girl. She would make a wonderful wife for someone, but not for him. Not with Kate Blackwell as her sponsor. His mother was a ruthless, calculating bitch, and as long as Tony remembered that, he was safe from her machinations. He wondered what her next move would be.

He did not have to wait long to find out.

They were on the terrace having cocktails. 'Mr Wyatt has been kind enough to invite us to his ranch next weekend,' Kate told Tony. 'Isn't that lovely?' Her face radiated her pleasure. 'I've never seen a Texas ranch.'

Kruger-Brent *owned* a ranch in Texas, and it was probably twice as big as the Wyatt spread.

'You will come, won't you, Tony?' Charlie Wyatt asked.

Lucy said, 'Please do.'

They were ganging up on him. It was a challenge. He decided to accept it. 'I'd be d-delighted.'

'Good.' There was real pleasure on Lucy's face. And on Kate's.

If Lucy is planning to seduce me, Tony thought, *she is wasting her time*. The hurt done to Tony by his mother and Dominique had implanted in him such a deep distrust of females that his only association with them now was with high-priced call girls. Of all the female species, they were the most honest. All they wanted was money and told you how much up front. You paid for what you got, and you got what you paid for. No complications, no tears, no deceit.

Lucy Wyatt was in for a surprise.

*   *   *

Early Sunday morning. Tony went down to the pool for a swim. Marianne Hoffman was already in the water, wearing a white maillot. She had a lovely figure, tall and slender and graceful. Tony stood there watching her cutting cleanly through the water, her arms flashing up and down in a regular, graceful rhythm. She saw Tony and swam over to him.

'Good morning.'

'Morning. You're good,' Tony said.

Marianne smiled. 'I love sports. I get that from my father.' She pulled herself up to the edge of the pool, and Tony handed her a towel. He watched as she unselfconsciously dried her hair.

'Have you had breakfast?' Tony asked.

'No. I wasn't sure the cook would be up this early.'

'This is a hotel. There's twenty-four-hour service.'

She smiled up at him. 'Nice.'

'Where is your home?'

'Mostly in Munich. We live in an old *Schloss* – a castle – outside the city.'

'Where were you brought up?'

Marianne sighed. 'That's a long story. During the war, I was sent away to school in Switzerland. After that, I went to Oxford, studied at the Sorbonne and lived in London for a few years.' She looked directly into his eyes. 'That's where I've been. Where have you been?'

'Oh, New York, Maine, Switzerland, South Africa, a few years in the South Pacific during the war, Paris . . .' He broke off abruptly, as though he were saying too much.

'Forgive me if I seem to pry, but I can't imagine why you stopped painting.'

'It's not important,' Tony said curtly. 'Let's have breakfast.'

They ate alone on the terrace overlooking the sparkling sweep of the bay. She was easy to talk to. There was a dignity about her, a gentleness that Tony found appealing. She did not flirt, she did not chatter. She seemed genuinely interested in him. Tony found himself attracted to this quiet, sensitive woman. He could not help wondering how much of that attraction was due to the thought that it would spite his mother.

'When do you go back to Germany?'

'Next week,' Marianne replied. 'I'm getting married.'

Her words caught him off guard. 'Oh,' Tony said lamely. 'That's great. Who is he?'

'He's a doctor. I've known him all my life.' *Why had she added that? Did it have some significance?*

On an impulse, Tony asked, 'Will you have dinner with me in New York?'

She studied him, weighing her answer. 'I would enjoy that.'

Tony smiled, pleased. 'It's a date.'

They had dinner at a little seashore restaurant on Long Island. Tony wanted Marianne to himself,

400

away from the eyes of his mother. It was an innocent evening, but Tony knew that if his mother
learned about it, she would find some way to
poison it. This was a private thing between him
and Marianne, and for the brief time it existed,
Tony wanted nothing to spoil it. Tony enjoyed
Marianne's company even more than he had anticipated. She had a quick, sly sense of humour, and
Tony found himself laughing more than he had
laughed since he left Paris. She made him feel light-
hearted and carefree.

When do you go back to Germany?
Next week . . . I'm getting married.

During the next five days, Tony saw a great deal
of Marianne. He cancelled his trip to Canada, and
he was not certain why. He had thought it might
be a form of rebellion against his mother's plan, a
petty vengeance, but if that had been true in the
beginning, it was no longer true. He found himself
drawn to Marianne more and more strongly. He
loved her honesty. It was a quality he had despaired
of ever finding.

Since Marianne was a tourist in New York, Tony
took her everywhere. They climbed the Statue of
Liberty and rode the ferry to Staten Island, went
to the top of the Empire State Building, and ate in
Chinatown. They spent an entire day at the
Metropolitan Museum of Art, and an afternoon at
the Frick Collection. They shared the same tastes.
They carefully avoided speaking of any personal

things, and yet both were conscious of the powerful sexual undercurrent between them. The days
spilled into one another, and it was Friday, the day
Tony was to leave for the Wyatt Ranch.

'When do you fly back to Germany?'

'Monday morning.' There was no joy in her
voice.

Tony left for Houston that afternoon. He could
have gone with his mother in one of the company
planes, but he preferred to avoid any situation
where he and Kate would be alone together. As far
as he was concerned, his mother was solely a business partner; brilliant and powerful, devious and
dangerous.

There was a Rolls-Royce to pick up Tony at the
William P. Hobby Airport in Houston, and he was
driven to the ranch by a chauffeur dressed in Levi's
and a colourful sport shirt.

'Most folks like to fly direct to the ranch,' the
driver told Tony. 'Mr Wyatt's got a big landin'
strip there. From here, it's 'bout an hour's drive
to the gate, then another half hour before we git to
the main house.'

Tony thought he was exaggerating, but he was
wrong. The Wyatt Ranch turned out to be more
of a town than a ranch. They drove through the
main gate onto a private road, and after thirty
minutes they began to pass generator buildings and
barns and corrals and guest houses and servants'
bungalows. The main house was an enormous

one-storey ranch house that seemed to go on forever. Tony thought it was depressingly ugly.

Kate had already arrived. She and Charlie Wyatt were seated on the terrace overlooking a swimming pool the size of a small lake. They were in the midst of an intense conversation when Tony appeared. When Wyatt saw him, he broke off abruptly in the middle of a sentence. Tony sensed that he had been the subject of their discussion.

'Here's our boy! Have a good trip, Tony?'

'Yes, th-thank you.'

'Lucy was hoping you'd be able to catch an earlier plane,' Kate said.

Tony turned to look at his mother. 'Was sh-she?'

Charlie Wyatt clapped Tony on the shoulder. 'We're puttin' on a whoppin' barbecue in honour of you and Kate. *Everybody's* flying in for it.'

'That's very k-kind of you,' Tony said. *If they're planning to serve fatted calf*, he thought, *they're going to go hungry.*'

Lucy appeared, wearing a white shirt and tight-fitting, well-worn jeans, and Tony had to admit she was breath-takingly lovely.

She went up to him and took his arm. 'Tony! I was wondering if you were coming.'

'S-sorry I'm late,' Tony said. 'I had some b-business to finish up.'

Lucy gave him a warm smile. 'It doesn't matter, as long as you're here. What would you like to do this afternoon?'

'What do you have to offer?'

403

Lucy looked him in the eye. 'Anything you want,' she said softly.

Kate Blackwell and Charlie Wyatt beamed.

The barbecue was spectacular, even by Texas standards. Approximately two hundred guests had arrived by private plane, Mercedes or Rolls-Royce. Two bands were playing simultaneously in different areas of the grounds. Half a dozen bartenders dispensed champagne, whiskey, soft drinks and beer, while four chefs busily prepared food over outdoor fires. There was barbecued beef, lamb, steaks, chicken and duck. There were bubbling earthen pots of chili, and whole lobsters; crabs and corn on the cob were cooking in the ground. There were baked potatoes and yams and fresh peas in the pod, six kinds of salads, homemade hot biscuits, and corn bread with honey and jam. Four dessert tables were laden with freshly baked pies, cakes and puddings, and a dozen flavours of homemade ice cream. It was the most conspicuous waste Tony had ever seen. It was, he supposed, the difference between new money and old money. Old money's motto was, *If you have it, hide it*. New money's motto was, *If you have it, flaunt it*.

This was flaunting on a scale that was unbelievable. The women were dressed in daring gowns, and the display of jewellery was blinding. Tony stood to one side watching the guests gorging themselves, calling out noisily to old friends. He felt as though he were attending some mindless, decadent rite. Every time he turned around, Tony found himself confronted with a waiter carrying a tray containing large crocks of beluga caviar or pâté or champagne. It seemed to Tony that there were almost as many servants as guests. He listened to conversations around him.

'He came out here from New York to sell me a bill of goods, and I said, "You're wastin' your time, mister. No good oil deal gets east of Houston . . ."'

'You gotta watch out for the smooth talkers. They're all hat and no cattle . . .'

Lucy appeared at Tony's side. 'You're not eating.' She was watching him intently. 'Is anything wrong, Tony?'

'No, everything's fine. It's quite a party.'

She grinned. 'You ain't seen nothin' yet, pardner. Wait until you see the fireworks display.'

'The fireworks display?'

'Uh-huh.' She touched Tony's arm. 'Sorry about the mob scene. It's not always like this. Daddy wanted to impress your mother.' She smiled. 'Tomorrow they'll all be gone.'

So will I, Tony thought grimly. It had been a mistake for him to come here. If his mother wanted the Wyatt Oil & Tool Company so badly, she would have to figure out some other way to get it. His eyes searched the crowd for his mother, and he saw her in the middle of an admiring group. She was beautiful. She was almost sixty years old, but she looked ten years younger. Her face was unlined, and her body was firm and trim, thanks to exercise and daily massage. She was as disciplined with herself as with everyone around her, and in a perverse way, Tony admired her. To a casual onlooker, Kate Blackwell seemed to be having a marvellous time. She was chatting with the guests, beaming, laughing. *She's loathing every moment of this*, Tony thought. *There isn't anything she won't suffer to get what she wants*. He thought of Marianne and of how much she would have hated this kind of senseless orgy. The thought of her was a sudden ache in him.

I'm marrying a doctor. I've known him all my life.

Half an hour later when Lucy came looking for Tony, he was on his way back to New York.

He called Marianne from a telephone booth at the airport. 'I want to see you.'

There was no hesitation. 'Yes.'

Tony had not been able to get Marianne Hoffman out of his thoughts. He had been alone for a long time, but he had not felt lonely. Being away from Marianne was a loneliness, a feeling that a part of him was missing. Being with her was a warmth, a celebration of life, a chasing away of the ugly dark shadows that had been haunting him. He had the terrifying feeling that if he let Marianne go, he would be lost. He needed her as he had never needed anyone in his life.

Marianne met him at his apartment, and as she

walked in the door, there was a hunger in Tony that he had thought forever dead. And he knew the hunger was hers, too, and there were no words for the miracle of it.

She went into his arms, and their emotion was an irresistible riptide that caught them both up and swept them away in a glorious explosion, an eruption, and a contentment beyond words. They were floating together in a velvety softness that knew no time or place, lost in the wondrous glory and magic of each other. Later they lay spent, holding each other, her hair soft against his face.

'I'm going to marry you, Marianne.'

She took his face in her hands and looked searchingly into his eyes. 'Are you sure, Tony?' Her voice was gentle. 'There's a problem, darling.'

'Your engagement?'

'No. I'll break it off. I'm concerned about your mother.'

'She has nothing to do with –'

'No. Let me finish, Tony. She's planning for you to marry Lucy Wyatt.'

'That's *her* plan.' He took her in his arms again. '*My* plans are right here.'

'She'll hate me, Tony. I don't want that.'

'Do you know what I want?' Tony whispered.

And the miracle started all over again.

It was another forty-eight hours before Kate Blackwell heard from Tony. He had disappeared from the Wyatt Ranch without an explanation or good-bye and had flown back to New York. Charlie Wyatt was baffled, and Lucy Wyatt was furious. Kate had made awkward apologies and had taken the company plane back to New York that night. When she reached home, she telephoned Tony at his apartment. There was no answer. Nor was there any answer the following day.

Kate was in her office when the private phone on her desk rang. She knew who it was before she picked it up.

'Tony, are you all right?'

'I'm f-fine, Mother.'

'Where are you?'

'On my h-honeymoon. Marianne Hoffman and I were m-married yesterday.' There was a long, long silence. 'Are you there, M-mother?'

'Yes. I'm here.'

'You might s-say congratulations, or m-much happiness or one of those c-customary phrases.' There was a mocking bitterness in his voice.

Kate said, 'Yes. Yes, of course, I wish you much happiness, Son.'

'Thank you, M-mother.' And the line went dead.

Kate replaced the receiver and pressed down an intercom button. 'Would you please come in, Brad?'

When Brad Rogers walked into the office, Kate said, 'Tony just called.'

Brad took one look at Kate's face and said, 'Jesus! Don't tell me you did it!'

'Tony did it,' Kate smiled. 'We've got the Hoffman empire in our lap.'

Brad Rogers sank into a chair. 'I can't believe it! I know how stubborn Tony can be. How did you ever get him to marry Marianne Hoffman?'

'It was really very simple,' Kate sighed. 'I pushed him in the wrong direction.'

But she knew it was really the right direction. Marianne would be a wonderful wife for Tony. She would dispel the darkness in him.

Lucy had had a hysterectomy.

Marianne would give him a son.

TWENTY-ONE

Six months from the day Tony and Marianne were married, the Hoffman company was absorbed into Kruger-Brent, Ltd. The formal signing of the contracts took place in Munich as a gesture to Frederick Hoffman, who would run the subsidiary from Germany. Tony had been surprised by the meekness with which his mother accepted his marriage. It was not like her to lose gracefully, yet she had been cordial to Marianne when Tony and his bride returned from their honeymoon in the Bahamas, and had told Tony how pleased she was with the marriage. What puzzled Tony was that her sentiments seemed genuine. It was too quick a turn-around, out of character for her. Perhaps, Tony decided, he did not understand his mother as well as he thought he did.

The marriage was a brilliant success from the beginning. Marianne filled a long-felt need in Tony, and everyone around him noticed the change in him – especially Kate.

When Tony took business trips, Marianne accompanied him. They played together, they laughed together, they truly enjoyed each other. Watching them, Kate thought happily, *I have done well for my son.*

It was Marianne who succeeded in healing the breach between Tony and his mother. When they returned from their honeymoon, Marianne said, 'I want to invite your mother to dinner.'

'No. You don't know her, Marianne. She –'

'I want to get to know her. Please, Tony.'

He hated the idea, but in the end he gave in. Tony had been prepared for a grim evening, but he had been surprised. Kate had been touchingly happy to be with them. The following week Kate invited them to the house for dinner, and after that it became a weekly ritual.

Kate and Marianne became friends. They spoke to each other over the telephone several times a week, and lunched together at least once a week.

They were meeting for lunch at Lutèce, and the moment Marianne walked in, Kate knew something was wrong.

'I'd like a double whiskey, please,' Marianne told the captain. 'Over ice.'

As a rule, Marianne drank only wine.

'What's happened, Marianne?'

'I've been to see Dr Harley.'

Kate felt a sudden stab of alarm. 'You're not ill, are you?'

411

'No. I'm just fine. Only . . .' The whole story came tumbling out.

It had begun a few days earlier. Marianne had not been feeling well, and she had made an appointment with John Harley . . .

'You look healthy enough,' Dr Harley smiled. 'How old are you, Mrs Blackwell?'

'Twenty-three.'

'Any history of heart disease in your family?'

'No.'

He was making notes. 'Cancer?'

'No.'

'Are your parents alive?'

'My father is. My mother died in an accident.'

'Have you ever had mumps?'

'No.'

'Measles?'

'Yes. When I was ten.'

'Whooping cough?'

'No.'

'Any surgery?'

'Tonsils. I was nine.'

'Other than that, you've never been hospitalized for anything?'

'No. Well, yes – that is, once. Briefly.'

'What was that for?'

'I was on the girls' hockey team at school and during a game I blacked out. I woke up in a hospital. I was only there two days. It was really nothing.'

'Did you suffer an injury during the game?'

'No. I – I just blacked out.'

'How old were you then?'

'Sixteen. The doctor said it was probably some kind of adolescent glandular upset.'

John Harley sat forwards in his chair. 'When you woke up, do you remember if you felt any weakness on either side of your body?'

Marianne thought a moment. 'As a matter of fact, yes. My right side. But it went away in a few days. I haven't had anything like it since.'

'Did you have headaches? Blurred vision?'

'Yes. But they went away, too.' She was beginning to be alarmed. 'Do you think there's something wrong with me, Dr Harley?'

'I'm not sure. I'd like to make a few tests – just to be on the safe side.'

'What kind of tests?'

'I'd like to do a cerebral angiogram. Nothing to be concerned about. We can have it done right away.'

Three days later, Marianne received a call from Dr Harley's nurse asking her to come in. John Harley was waiting for her in his office. 'Well, we've solved the mystery.'

'Is it something bad?'

'Not really. The angiogram showed that what you had, Mrs Blackwell, was a small stroke. Medically, it's called a berry aneurysm, and it's very common in women – particularly in teenage girls. A small blood vessel in the brain broke and leaked small amounts of blood. The pressure is what caused the headaches and blurred vision. Fortunately, those things are self-healing.'

Marianne sat there listening, her mind fighting panic. 'What – what does all this mean, exactly? Could it happen again?'

'It's very unlikely.' He smiled. 'Unless you're planning to go out for the hockey team again, you can live an absolutely normal life.'

'Tony and I like to ride and play tennis. Is that –?'

'As long as you don't overdo, everything goes. From tennis to sex. No problem.'

She smiled in relief. 'Thank God.'

As Marianne rose, John Harley said, 'There is one thing, Mrs Blackwell. If you and Tony are planning to have children, I would advise adopting them.'

Marianne froze. 'You said I was perfectly normal.'

'You are. Unfortunately, pregnancy increases the vascular volume enormously. And during the last six to eight weeks of pregnancy, there's an additional increase in the blood pressure. With the history of that aneurysm, the risk factor would be unacceptably high. It would not only be dangerous – it could be fatal. Adoptions are really quite easy these days. I can arrange –'

But Marianne was no longer listening. She was hearing Tony's voice: *I want us to have a baby. A little girl who looks exactly like you.*

'. . . I couldn't bear to hear any more,' Marianne told Kate. 'I ran out of his office and came straight here.'

Kate made a tremendous effort not to let her feelings show. It was a stunning blow. But there had to be a way. There was always a way.

She managed to smile and said, 'Well! I was afraid it was going to be something much worse.'

'But, Kate, Tony and I want so much to have a baby.'

'Marianne, Dr Harley is an alarmist. You had a minor problem years ago, and Harley's trying to turn it into something important. You know how doctors are.' She took Marianne's hand. 'You feel well, don't you, darling?'

'I felt wonderful until –'

'Well, there you are. You aren't going around having any fainting spells?'

'No.'

'Because it's all over. He said himself that those things are self-healing.'

'He said the risks –'

Kate sighed. 'Marianne, every time a woman gets pregnant, there's always a risk. Life is full of risks. The important thing in life is to decide which risks are the ones worth taking, don't you agree?'

'Yes.' Marianne sat there thinking. She made her decision. 'You're right. Let's not say anything to Tony. It would only worry him. We'll keep it our secret.'

Kate thought, *I could bloody well kill John*

Harley for scaring her to death. 'It will be our secret,' Kate agreed.

Three months later, Marianne became pregnant. Tony was thrilled. Kate was quietly triumphant. Dr John Harley was horrified.

'I'll arrange for an immediate abortion,' he told Marianne.

'No, Dr Harley. I feel fine. I'm going to have the baby.'

When Marianne told Kate about her visit, Kate stormed into John Harley's office. 'How dare you suggest my daughter-in-law have an abortion?'

'Kate, I told her that if she carried that baby to term, there's a chance it might kill her.'

'You don't *know* that. She's going to be fine. Stop alarming her.'

Eight months later, at four a.m. in early February, Marianne's labour pains began prematurely. Her moans awakened Tony.

He began hurriedly dressing. 'Don't worry, darling. I'll have you at the hospital in no time.'

The pains were agonizing. 'Please hurry.'

She wondered whether she should have told Tony about her conversations with Dr Harley. No, Kate had been right. It was her decision to make. Life was so wonderful that God would not let anything bad happen to her.

When Marianne and Tony arrived at the hospital, everything was in readiness. Tony was escorted to a waiting room. Marianne was taken into an examining room. The obstetrician, Dr Mattson took Marianne's blood pressure. He frowned and took it again. He looked up and said to his nurse, 'Get her into the operating room – fast!'

Tony was at the cigarette machine in the hospital corridor when a voice behind him said, 'Well, well, if it isn't Rembrandt.' Tony turned. He recognized the man who had been with Dominique in front of her apartment building. What had she called him? Ben. The man was staring at Tony, an antagonistic expression on his face. Jealousy? What had Dominique told him? At that moment. Dominique appeared. She said to Ben, 'The nurse said Michelline is in intensive care. We'll come –' She saw Tony and stopped.

'Tony!' What are you doing here?'

'My wife is having a baby.'

'Did your mother arrange it?' Ben asked.

'What's that supposed to mean?'

'Dominique told me your mother arranges everything for you, sonny.'

'Ben! Stop it!'

'Why? It's the truth, isn't it, baby? Isn't that what you said?'

Tony turned to Dominique. 'What is he talking about?'

'Nothing,' she said quickly. 'Ben, let's get out of here.'

But Ben was enjoying himself. 'I wish I had a

417

mother like yours, buddy boy. You want a beautiful model to sleep with, she buys you one. You want to have an art exhibition in Paris, she arranges it for you. You –'

'You're crazy.'

'Am I?' Ben turned to Dominique. 'Doesn't he know?'

'Don't I know what?' Tony demanded.

'Nothing, Tony.'

'He said my mother arranged the exhibition in Paris. That's a lie, isn't it?' He saw the expression on Dominique's face. *'Isn't it?'*

'No,' Dominique said reluctantly.

'You mean she had to pay Goerg to – to show my paintings?'

'Tony, he really liked your paintings.'

'Tell him about the art critic,' Ben urged.

'That's enough, Ben!' Dominique turned to go. Tony grabbed her arm. 'Wait! What about him? Did my mother arrange for him to be at the exhibition?'

'Yes.' Dominique's voice had dropped to a whisper.

'But he *hated* my paintings.'

She could hear the pain in his voice. 'No, Tony. He didn't. Andre d'Usseau told your mother you could have become a great artist.'

And he was face to face with the unbelievable. 'My mother paid d'Usseau to destroy me?'

'Not to destroy you. She believed she was doing it for your own good.'

The enormity of what his mother had done was staggering. *Everything she had told him was a lie. She had never intended to let him live his own life.* And Andre d'Usseau! How could a man like that be bought? But of course Kate would know the price of any man. Wilde could have been referring to Kate when he talked of someone who knew the price of everything, the value of nothing. Everything had always been for the company. And the company was Kate Blackwell. Tony turned and walked blindly down the corridor.

In the operating room, the doctors were fighting desperately to save Marianne's life. Her blood pressure was alarmingly low, and her heartbeat was erratic. She was given oxygen and a blood transfusion, but it was useless. Marianne was unconscious from a cerebral haemorrhage when the first baby was delivered, and dead three minutes later when the second twin was taken.

Tony heard a voice calling, 'Mr Blackwell.' He turned. Dr Mattson was at his side.

'You have two beautiful, healthy twin daughters, Mr Blackwell.'

Tony saw the look in his eyes. 'Marianne – she's all right, isn't she?'

Dr Mattson took a deep breath. 'I'm so sorry. We did everything we could. She died on the –'

'She *what*?' It was a scream. Tony grabbed Dr

Mattson's lapels and shook him. 'You're lying! She's *not* dead.'

'Mr Blackwell –'

'Where is she? I want to see her.'

'You can't go in just now. They're preparing her –'

Tony cried out, 'You killed her, you bastard! You killed her.' He began attacking the doctor. Two interns hurried in and grabbed Tony's arms.

'Now take it easy, Mr Blackwell.'

Tony fought like a madman. 'I want to see my wife!'

Dr John Harley hurried up to the group. 'Let him go,' he commanded. 'Leave us alone.'

Dr Mattson and the interns left. Tony was weeping brokenly 'John, they k-killed Marianne. They m-murdered her.'

'She's dead, Tony, and I'm sorry. But no one murdered her. I told her months ago if she went ahead with this pregnancy it could kill her.'

It took a long moment for the words to sink in. 'What are you talking about?'

'Marianne didn't tell you? Your mother didn't say anything?'

Tony was staring at him, his eyes uncomprehending. 'My mother?'

'She thought I was being an alarmist. She advised Marianne to go ahead with it. I'm so sorry, Tony. I've seen the twins. They're beautiful. Wouldn't you like to –?'

Tony was gone.

* * *

Kate's butler opened the door for Tony.

'Good morning, Mr Blackwell.'

'Good morning, Lester.'

The butler took in Tony's dishevelled appearance. 'Is everything all right, sir?'

'Everything is fine. Would you make me a cup of coffee, Lester?'

'Certainly sir.'

Tony watched the butler move towards the kitchen. *Now, Tony*, the voice in his head commanded.

Yes. Now. Tony turned and walked into the trophy room. He went to the cabinet that held the gun collection, and he stared at the gleaming array of instruments of death.

Open the cabinet, Tony.

He opened it. He selected a revolver from the gun rack and checked the barrel to make sure it was loaded.

She'll be upstairs, Tony.

Tony turned and started up the stairs. He knew now that it was not his mother's fault that she was evil. She was possessed, and he was going to cure her. The company had taken her soul, and Kate was not responsible for what she did. His mother and the company had become one, and when he killed her, the company would die.

He was outside Kate's bedroom door.

Open the door, the voice commanded.

Tony opened the door. Kate was dressing in front of a mirror when she heard the door open.

'Tony! What on earth –'

He carefully aimed the gun at her and began squeezing the trigger.

TWENTY-TWO

The right of primogeniture – the claim of the first-born to a family title or estate – is deeply rooted in history. Among royal families in Europe a high official is present at every birth of a possible heir to a queen or princess so that should twins be born, the right of succession will not be in dispute. Dr Mattson was careful to note which twin had been delivered first.

Everyone agreed that the Blackwell twins were the most beautiful babies they had ever seen. They were healthy and unusually lively, and the nurses at the hospital kept finding excuses to go in and look at them. Part of the fascination, although none of the nurses would have admitted it, was the mysterious stories that were circulating about the twins' family. Their mother had died during childbirth. The twins' father had disappeared, and there were rumours he had murdered his mother, but no one was able to substantiate the reports. There was nothing about it in the newspapers, save for a brief item that Tony Blackwell had suffered a nervous breakdown over the death of his wife and was in seclusion. When the press tried to question Dr Harley, he gave them a brusque, 'No comment.'

The past few days had been hell for John Harley. As long as he lived, he would remember the scene when he reached Kate Blackwell's bedroom after a frantic phone call from the butler. Kate was lying on the floor in a coma, bullet wounds in her neck and chest, her blood spilling onto the white rug. Tony was going through her closets, slashing his mother's clothes to shreds with a pair of scissors.

Dr Harley took one quick look at Kate and hurriedly telephoned for an ambulance. He knelt at Kate's side and felt her pulse. It was weak and thready, and her face was turning blue. She was going into shock. He swiftly gave her an injection of adrenaline and sodium bicarbonate.

'What happened?' Dr Harley asked.

The butler was soaked in perspiration. 'I – I don't know. Mr Blackwell asked me to make him some coffee. I was in the kitchen when I heard the sound of gunfire. I ran upstairs and found Mrs Blackwell on the floor, like this. Mr Blackwell was standing over her, saying. 'It can't hurt you anymore, Mother. I killed it.' And he went into the closet and started cutting her dresses.'

Dr Harley turned to Tony. 'What are you doing, Tony?'

A savage slash. 'I'm helping Mother. I'm destroying the company. It killed Marianne, you know.'

He continued slashing at the dresses in Kate's closet.

Kate was rushed to the emergency ward of a midtown private hospital owned by Kruger-Brent, Ltd. She was given four blood transfusions during the operation to remove the bullets.

It took three male nurses to force Tony into an ambulance, and it was only after Dr Harley gave him an injection that Tony was quiet. A police unit had responded to the ambulance call, and Dr Harley summoned Brad Rogers to deal with them. Through means that Dr Harley did not understand, there was no mention in the media of the shooting.

Dr Harley went to the hospital to visit Kate in intensive care. Her first words were a whispered, 'Where's my son?'

'He's being taken care of, Kate. He's all right.'

Tony had been taken to a private sanatorium in Connecticut.

'John, why did he try to kill me? Why?' The anguish in her voice was unbearable.

'He blames you for Marianne's death.'

'That's insane!'

John Harley made no comment.

He blames you for Marianne's death.

Long after Dr Harley had left, Kate lay there, refusing to accept those words. She had loved Marianne because she made Tony happy. *Everything I have done has been for you, my son. All my dreams were for you. How could you not know that?* And he hated her so much he had tried to kill her. She was filled with such a deep agony that she wanted to die. But she would not let herself die. She had done what was right. They were wrong. Tony was a weakling. They had all been weaklings. Her father had been too weak to face his son's death. Her mother had been too weak to face life alone. *But I am not weak,* Kate thought. *I can face this. I can face anything. I'm going to live. I'll survive. The company will survive.*

BOOK FIVE

Eve and Alexandra

1950–1975

TWENTY-THREE

Kate recuperated at Dark Harbor, letting the sun and the sea heal her.

Tony was in a private asylum, where he could get the best care possible. Kate had psychiatrists flown in from Paris, Vienna and Berlin, but when all the examinations and tests had been completed, the diagnosis was the same: her son was a homicidal schizophrenic and paranoiac.

'He doesn't respond to drugs or psychiatric treatment, and he's violent. We have to keep him under restraint.'

'What kind of restraint?' Kate asked.

'He's in a padded cell. Most of the time we have to keep him in a straitjacket.'

'Is that necessary?'

'Without it, Mrs Blackwell, he would kill anyone who got near him.'

She closed her eyes in pain. This was not her sweet, gentle Tony they were talking about. It was a stranger, someone possessed. She opened her eyes. 'Is there nothing that can be done?'

'Not if we can't reach his mind. We're keeping him on drugs, but the moment they wear off, he gets manic again. We can't continue this treatment indefinitely.'

Kate stood very straight. 'What do you suggest, Doctor?'

'In similar cases, we've found that removing a small portion of the brain has produced remarkable results.'

Kate swallowed. 'A lobotomy?'

'That is correct. Your son will still be able to function in every way, except that he will no longer have any strong dysfunctional emotions.'

Kate sat there, her mind and body chilled. Dr Morris, a young doctor from the Menninger Clinic, broke the silence. 'I know how difficult this must be for you, Mrs Blackwell. If you'd like to think about –'

'If that's the only thing that will stop his torment,' Kate said, 'do it.'

Frederick Hoffman wanted his granddaughters. 'I will take them back to Germany with me.'

It seemed to Kate that he had aged twenty years since Marianne's death. Kate felt sorry for him, but she had no intention of giving up Tony's children. 'They need a woman's care, Frederick. Marianne would have wanted them brought up here. You'll come and visit them often.'

And he was finally persuaded.

* * *

The twins were moved into Kate's home, and a nursery suite was set up for them. Kate interviewed governesses, and finally hired a young French woman named Solange Dunas.

Kate named the first-born Eve, and her twin, Alexandra. They were identical – impossible to tell apart. Seeing them together was like looking at an image in a mirror, and Kate marvelled at the double miracle that her son and Marianne had created. They were both bright babies, quick and responsive, but even after a few weeks, Eve seemed more mature than Alexandra. Eve was the first to crawl and talk and walk. Alexandra followed quickly, but from the beginning it was Eve who was the leader. Alexandra adored her sister and tried to imitate everything she did. Kate spent as much time with her granddaughters as possible. They made her feel young. And Kate began to dream again. *One day, when I'm old and ready to retire . . .*

On the twins' first birthday, Kate gave them a party. They each had an identical birthday cake, and there were dozens of presents from friends, company employees and the household staff. Their second birthday party seemed to follow almost immediately. Kate could not believe how rapidly the time went by and how quickly the twins were growing. She was able to discern even more clearly the differences in their personalities: Eve, the stronger, was more daring. Alexandra was softer, content to follow her sister's lead. *With no mother or father,*

Kate thought repeatedly, *it's a blessing that they have each other and love each other so much.*

The night before their fifth birthday, Eve tried to murder Alexandra.

It is written in Genesis 25:22–23:

> And the children struggled together within her . . .
>
> And the Lord said unto her, Two [nations] are in thy womb, and two manner of people shall be separated from thy bowels;
>
> and the one [people] shall be stronger than the other [people];
>
> and the elder shall serve the younger.

In the case of Eve and Alexandra, Eve had no intention of serving her younger sister.

Eve had hated her sister for as long as she could remember. She went into a silent rage when someone picked up Alexandra, or petted her or gave her a present. Eve felt she was being cheated. She wanted it all for herself – all the love and the beautiful things that surrounded the two of them. She could not have even a birthday of her own. She hated Alexandra for looking like her, dressing like her, stealing the part of her grandmother's love that belonged to her. Alexandra adored Eve, and Eve despised her for that. Alexandra was generous, eager to give up her toys and dolls, and that filled Eve with still more contempt. Eve shared nothing.

What was hers belonged to her; but it was not enough. She wanted everything Alexandra had. At night, under the watchful eye of Solange Dunas, both girls would say their prayers aloud, but Eve always added a silent prayer begging God to strike Alexandra dead. When the prayer went unanswered, Eve decided she would have to take care of it herself. Their fifth birthday was only a few days away, and Eve could not bear the thought of sharing another party with Alexandra. They were *her* friends, and *her* gifts that her sister was stealing from her. She had to kill Alexandra soon.

On the night before their birthday, Eve lay in her bed, wide awake. When she was sure the household was asleep, she went over to Alexandra's bed and awakened her. 'Alex,' she whispered, 'Let's go down to the kitchen and see our birthday cakes.'

Alexandra said sleepily. 'Everybody's sleeping.'

'We won't wake anyone up.'

'Mademoiselle Dunas won't like it. Why don't we look at the cakes in the morning?'

'Because I want to look at them now. Are you coming or not?'

Alexandra rubbed the sleep out of her eyes. She had no interest in seeing the birthday cakes, but she did not want to hurt her sister's feelings. 'I'm coming,' she said.

Alexandra got out of bed and put on a pair of slippers. Both girls wore pink nylon nightgowns.

'Come on,' Eve said. 'And don't make any noise.'

'I won't,' Alexandra promised.

They tiptoed out of their bedroom, into the long corridor, past the closed door of Mademoiselle Dunas's bedroom, down the steep back stairs that led to the kitchen. It was an enormous kitchen, with two large gas stoves, six ovens, three refrigerators and a walk-in freezer.

In the refrigerator Eve found the birthday cakes that the cook, Mrs Tyler, had made. One of them said Happy Birthday, Alexandra. The other said Happy Birthday, Eve.

Next year, Eve thought happily, *there will only be one.*

Eve took Alexandra's cake out of the refrigerator and placed it on the wooden chopping block in the middle of the kitchen. She opened a drawer and took out a package of brightly coloured candles.

'What are you doing?' Alexandra asked.

'I want to see how it looks with candles all lighted.' Eve began pressing the candles into the icing of the cake.

'I don't think you should do that, Eve. You'll ruin the cake. Mrs Tyler is going to be angry.'

'She won't mind.' Eve opened another drawer and took out two large boxes of kitchen matches. 'Come on, help me.'

'I want to go back to bed.'

Eve turned on her angrily. 'All right. Go back to bed, scaredy cat. I'll do it alone.'

434

Alexandra hesitated. 'What do you want me to do?'

Eve handed her one of the boxes of matches. 'Start lighting the candles.'

Alexandra was afraid of fire. Both girls had been warned again and again about the danger of playing with matches. They knew the horror stories about children who had disobeyed that rule. But Alexandra did not want to disappoint Eve, and so she obediently began lighting the candles.

Eve watched her a moment. 'You're leaving out the ones on the other side, silly,' she said.

Alexandra leaned over to reach the candles at the far side of the cake, her back to Eve. Quickly, Eve struck a match and touched it to the matches in the box she was holding. As they burst into flames, Eve dropped the box at Alexandra's feet, so that the bottom of Alexandra's nightgown caught fire. It was an instant before Alexandra was aware of what was happening. When she felt the first agonizing pain against her legs, she looked down and screamed, 'Help! Help me!'

Eve stared at the flaming nightgown a moment, awed by the extent of her success. Alexandra was standing there, petrified, frozen with fear.

'Don't move!' Eve said. 'I'll get a bucket of water.' She hurried off to the butler's pantry, her heart pounding with a fearful joy.

It was a horror movie that saved Alexandra's life. Mrs Tyler, the Blackwell's cook, had been escorted to the cinema by a police sergeant whose bed she shared from time to time. On this particular evening, the motion-picture screen was so filled with dead and mutilated bodies that finally Mrs Tyler could bear it no longer. In the middle of a beheading, she said, 'This may all be in a day's work for you, Richard, but I've had enough.'

Sergeant Richard Dougherty reluctantly followed her out of the theatre.

They arrived back at the Blackwell mansion an hour earlier than they had expected to, and as Mrs Tyler opened the back door, she heard Alexandra's screams coming from the kitchen. Mrs Tyler and Sergeant Dougherty rushed in, took one horrified look at the scene before them and went into action. The sergeant leaped at Alexandra and ripped off her flaming nightgown. Her legs and hips were blistered, but the flames had not reached her hair or the front of her body. Alexandra fell to the floor, unconscious. Mrs Tyler filled a large pot with water and poured it over the flames licking at the floor.

'Call an ambulance,' Sergeant Dougherty ordered. 'Is Mrs Blackwell home?'

'She should be upstairs asleep.'

'Wake her up.'

As Mrs Tyler finished phoning for an ambulance, there was a cry from the butler's pantry, and Eve ran in carrying a pan of water, sobbing hysterically.

'Is Alexandra dead?' Eve screamed. 'Is she dead?'

Mrs Tyler took Eve in her arms to soothe her. 'No, darling, she's all right. She's going to be just fine.'

'It was my fault,' Eve sobbed. 'She wanted to light the candles on her birthday cake. I shouldn't have let her do it.'

Mrs Tyler stroked Eve's back. 'It's all right. You mustn't blame yourself.'

'The m-matches fell out of my hand, and Alex caught on fire. It was t-terrible.'

Sergeant Dougherty looked at Eve and said sympathetically, 'Poor child.'

'Alexandra has second-degree burns on her legs and back,' Dr Harley told Kate, 'but she's going to be fine. We can do amazing things with burns these days. Believe me, this could have been a terrible tragedy.'

'I know,' Kate said. She had seen Alexandra's burns, and they had filled her with horror. She hesitated a moment. 'John, I think I'm even more concerned about Eve.'

'Was Eve hurt?'

'Not physically, but the poor child blames herself for the accident. She's having terrible nightmares. The last three nights I've had to go in and hold her in my arms before she could go back to sleep. I don't want this to become more traumatic. Eve is very sensitive.'

'Kids get over things pretty quickly, Kate. If

there's any problem, let me know, and I'll recommend a child therapist.'

'Thank you,' Kate said gratefully.

Eve *was* terribly upset. The birthday party had been cancelled. *Alexandra cheated me out of that*, Eve thought bitterly.

Alexandra healed perfectly, with no signs of scars. Eve got over her feelings of guilt with remarkable ease. As Kate assured her, 'Accidents can happen to anybody, darling. You mustn't blame yourself.'

Eve didn't. She blamed Mrs Tyler. Why did she have to come home and spoil everything? It had been a perfect plan.

The sanitarium where Tony was confined was in a peaceful, wooded area in Connecticut. Kate was driven out to see him once a month. The lobotomy had been successful. There was no longer the slightest sign of aggression in Tony. He recognized Kate and he always politely asked about Eve and Alexandra, but he showed no interest in seeing them. He showed very little interest in anything. He seemed happy. *No, not happy*, Kate corrected herself. *Content. But content – to do what?*

Kate asked Mr Burger, the superintendent of the asylum, 'Doesn't my son *do* anything all day?'

'Oh, yes, Mrs Blackwell. He sits by the hour and paints.'

Her son, who could have owned the world, sat

and painted all day. Kate tried not to think of the waste, that brilliant mind gone forever. 'What does he paint?'

The man was embarrassed. 'No one can quite figure it out.'

TWENTY-FOUR

During the next two years, Kate became seriously concerned about Alexandra. The child was definitely accident-prone. During Eve and Alexandra's summer vacation at the Blackwell estate in the Bahamas, Alexandra almost drowned while playing with Eve in the pool, and it was only the prompt intervention of a gardener that saved her. The following year when the two girls were on a picnic in the Palisades, Alexandra somehow slipped off the edge of a cliff and saved herself by clinging to a shrub growing out of the steep mountainside.

'I wish you would keep a closer eye on your sister,' Kate told Eve. 'She can't seem to take care of herself the way you can.'

'I know,' Eve said solemnly. 'I'll watch her, Gran.'

Kate loved both her granddaughters, but in different ways. They were seven years old now, and identically beautiful, with long, soft blonde hair, exquisite features and the McGregor eyes. They looked alike, but their personalities were quite different. Alexandra's gentleness reminded Kate of Tony, while Eve was more like her, headstrong and self-sufficient.

A chauffeur drove them to school in the family Rolls-Royce. Alexandra was embarrassed to have her classmates see her with the car and chauffeur; Eve revelled in it. Kate gave each girl a weekly allowance, and ordered them to keep a record of how they spent it. Eve invariably ran short of money before the week was out and borrowed from Alexandra. Eve learned to adjust the books so that Gran would not know. But Kate knew, and she could hardly hold back her smile. Seven years old and already a creative accountant!

In the beginning, Kate had nurtured a secret dream that one day Tony would be well again, that he would leave the asylum and return to Kruger-Brent. But as time passed, the dream slowly faded. It was tacitly understood that while Tony might leave the asylum for short visits, accompanied by a male nurse, he would never again be able to participate in the outside world.

It was 1962, and as Kruger-Brent, Ltd., prospered and expanded, the demands for new leadership grew more urgent. Kate celebrated her seventieth birthday. Her hair was white now, and she was a remarkable figure of a woman, strong and erect and vital. She was aware that the attrition of time would overtake her. She had to be prepared. The company had to be safeguarded for the family. Brad Rogers was a good manager, but he was not a Blackwell. *I have to last until the twins can take over.* She thought of Cecil Rhodes's last words: 'So little done – so much to do.'

The twins were twelve years old, on the verge of becoming young ladies. Kate had spent as much time with them as she possibly could, but now she turned even more of her attention to them. It was time to make an important decision.

During Easter week, Kate and the twins flew to Dark Harbor in a company plane. The girls had visited all the family estates except the one in Johannesburg, and of them all, Dark Harbor was their favourite. They enjoyed the wild freedom and the seclusion of the island. They loved to sail and swim and water-ski, and Dark Harbor held all these things for them. Eve asked if she could bring some schoolmates along, as she had in the past, but this time her grandmother refused. Grandmother, that powerful, imposing figure who swept in and out, dropping off a present here, a kiss on the cheek there, with occasional admonitions about how young ladies behaved, wanted to be alone with them. This time the girls sensed that something different was happening. Their grandmother was with them at every meal. She took them boating and swimming and even riding. Kate handled her horse with the sureness of an expert.

The girls still looked amazingly alike, two golden beauties, but Kate was interested less in their similarities than in their differences. Sitting

442

on the veranda watching them as they finished a tennis game, Kate summed them up in her mind. Eve was the leader, Alexandra the follower. Eve had a stubborn streak. Alexandra was flexible. Eve was a natural athlete. Alexandra was still having accidents. Only a few days before, when the two girls were out alone in a small sailboat with Eve at the rudder, the wind had come behind the sail and the sail had luffed, swinging it crashing towards Alexandra's head. She had not gotten out of the way in time and had been swept overboard and nearly drowned. Another boat nearby had assisted Eve in rescuing her sister. Kate wondered whether all these things could have anything to do with Alexandra having been born three minutes later than Eve, but the reasons did not matter. Kate had made her decision. There was no longer any question in her mind. She was putting her money on Eve, and it was a ten-billion-dollar bet. She would find a perfect consort for Eve, and when Kate retired, Eve would run Kruger-Brent. As for Alexandra, she would have a life of wealth and comfort. She might be very good working on the charitable grants Kate had set up. Yes, that would be perfect for Alexandra. She was such a sweet and compassionate child.

The first step towards implementing Kate's plan was to see that Eve got into the proper school. Kate chose Briarcrest, an excellent school in South Carolina. 'Both my granddaughters are delightful,'

Kate informed Mrs Chandler, the headmistress. 'But you'll find that Eve is the clever one. She's an extraordinary girl, and I'm sure you'll see to it that she has every advantage here.'

'All our students have every advantage here, Mrs Blackwell. You spoke of Eve. What about her sister?'

'Alexandra? A lovely girl.' It was a pejorative. Kate stood up. 'I shall be checking their progress regularly.'

In some odd way, the headmistress felt the words were a warning.

Eve and Alexandra adored the new school, particularly Eve. She enjoyed the freedom of being away from home, of not having to account to her grandmother and Solange Dunas. The rules at Briarcrest were strict, but that did not bother Eve, for she was adept at getting around rules. The only thing that disturbed her was that Alexandra was there with her. When Eve first heard the news about Briarcrest, she begged, 'May I go alone? Please, Gran?'

And Kate said, 'No, darling. I think it's better if Alexandra goes with you.'

Eve concealed her resentment. 'Whatever you say, Gran.'

She was always very polite and affectionate around her grandmother. Eve knew where the power lay. Their father was a crazy man, locked up in an insane asylum. Their mother was dead.

It was their grandmother who controlled the money. Eve knew they were rich. She had no idea how much money there was, but it was a lot – enough to buy all the beautiful things she wanted. Eve loved beautiful things. There was only one problem: Alexandra.

One of the twins' favourite activities at Briarcrest School was the morning riding class. Most of the girls owned their own jumpers, and Kate had given each twin one for her twelfth birthday. Jerome Davis, the riding instructor, watched as his pupils went through their paces in the rings, jumping over a one-foot stile, then a two-foot stile and finally a four-foot stile. Davis was one of the best riding teachers in the country. Several of his former pupils had gone on to win gold medals, and he was adept at spotting a natural-born rider. The new girl, Eve Blackwell, was a natural. She did not have to think about what she was doing, how to hold the reins or post in the saddle. She and her horse were one, and as they sailed over the hurdles, Eve's golden hair flying in the wind, it was a beautiful sight to behold. *Nothing's going to stop that one*, Mr Davis thought.

Tommy, the young groom, favoured Alexandra. Mr Davis watched Alexandra saddle up her horse, preparing for her turn. Alexandra and Eve wore different-coloured ribbons on their sleeves so he could tell them apart. Eve was helping Alexandra saddle her horse while Tommy was busy with another student. Davis was summoned to the main building for a telephone call, and what happened after that was a matter of great confusion.

From what Jerome Davis was able to piece together later. Alexandra mounted her horse, circled the ring and started towards the first low jump. Her horse inexplicably began rearing and bucking and threw Alexandra into a wall. She was knocked unconscious, and it was only by inches that the wild horse's hooves missed her face. Tommy carried Alexandra to the infirmary, where the school doctor diagnosed a mild concussion.

'Nothing broken, nothing serious,' he said. 'By tomorrow morning, she'll be right as rain, ready to get up on her horse again.'

'But she could have been killed!' Eve screamed.

Eve refused to leave Alexandra's side. Mrs Chandler thought she had never seen such devotion in a sister. It was truly touching.

When Mr Davis was finally able to corral Alexandra's horse to unsaddle it, he found the saddle blanket stained with blood. He lifted it off and discovered a large piece of jagged metal from a beer can still protruding from the horse's back, where it had been pressed down by the saddle. When he reported this to Mrs Chandler, she started an immediate investigation. All the girls who had been in the vicinity of the stable were questioned.

'I'm sure,' Mrs Chandler said, 'that whoever put that piece of metal there thought she was playing a harmless prank, but it could have led to very serious consequences. I want the name of the girl who did it.'

When no one volunteered, Mrs Chandler talked to them in her office, one by one. Each girl denied any knowledge of what had happened. When it was Eve's turn to be questioned, she seemed oddly ill at ease.

'Do you have any idea who could have done this to your sister?' Mrs Chandler asked.

Eve looked down at the rug. 'I'd rather not say,' she mumbled.

'Then you *did* see something?'

'Please, Mrs Chandler . . .'

'Eve, Alexandra could have been seriously hurt. The girl who did this must be punished so that it does not happen again.'

'It wasn't one of the girls.'

'What do you mean?'

'It was Tommy.'

'The *groom*.'

'Yes, ma'am. I saw him. I thought he was just tightening the cinch. I'm sure he didn't mean any harm. Alexandra orders him around a lot, and I guess he wanted to teach her a lesson. Oh, Mrs Chandler, I wish you hadn't made me tell you. I don't want to get anyone in trouble.' The poor child was on the verge of hysteria.

Mrs Chandler walked around the desk and put her arm around her. 'It's all right, Eve. You did right to tell me. Now you just forget about every-thing. I'll take care of it.'

The following morning when the girls went out to the stables, there was a new groom.

A few months later, there was another unpleasant incident at the school. Several of the girls had been caught smoking marijuana and one of them accused Eve of supplying it and selling it. Eve angrily denied it. A search by Mrs Chandler revealed marijuana hidden in Alexandra's locker.

'I don't believe she did it,' Eve said stoutly. 'Someone put it there. I know it.'

An account of the incident was sent to Kate by the headmistress, and Kate admired Eve's loyalty in shielding her sister. She was a McGregor, all right.

On the twins' fifteenth birthday, Kate took them to the estate in South Carolina, where she gave a large party for them. It was not too early to see to it that Eve was exposed to the proper young men, and every eligible young man around was invited to the girls' party.

The boys were at the awkward age where they were not yet seriously interested in girls, but Kate made it her business to see that acquaintances were made and friendships formed. Somewhere among these young boys could be the man in Eve's future, the future of Kruger-Brent, Ltd.

Alexandra did not enjoy parties, but she always pretended she was having a good time in order not to disappoint her grandmother. Eve adored parties. She loved dressing up, being admired. Alexandra preferred reading and painting. She spent hours looking at her father's paintings at Dark Harbor, and she wished she could have known him before he became ill. He appeared at the house on holidays with his male companion, but Alexandra found it impossible to reach her father. He was a pleasant, amiable stranger who wanted to please, but had nothing to say. Their grandfather, Frederick Hoffman, lived in Germany, but was ill. The twins seldom saw him.

In her second year at school, Eve became pregnant. For several weeks she had been pale and listless and had missed some morning classes. When she began to have frequent periods of nausea, she was sent to the infirmary and examined. Mrs Chandler had been hastily summoned.

'Eve is pregnant,' the doctor told her.

'But – that's impossible! How could it have happened?'

The doctor replied mildly, 'In the usual fashion, I would presume.'

'But she's just a child.'

'Well, this child is going to be a mother.'

Eve bravely refused to talk. 'I don't want to get anyone in trouble,' she kept saying.

It was the kind of answer Mrs Chandler expected from Eve.

'Eve, dear, you must tell me what happened.'

And so at last Eve broke down. 'I was raped,' she said, and burst into tears.

Mrs Chandler was shocked. She held Eve's trembling body close to her and demanded, 'Who was it?'

'Mr Parkinson.'

Her English teacher.

If it had been anyone else but Eve, Mrs Chandler would not have believed it. Joseph Parkinson was a quiet man with a wife and three children. He had taught at Briarcrest School for eight years, and he was the last one Mrs Chandler would have ever suspected. She called him into her office, and she knew instantly that Eve had told the truth. He sat facing her, his face twitching with nervousness.

'You know why I've sent for you, Mr Parkinson?'

'I – I think so.'

'It concerns Eve.'

'Yes. I – I guessed that.'

'She says you raped her.'

Parkinson looked at her in disbelief. '*Raped* her? My God! If anyone was raped it was me.' In his excitement he lapsed into the ungrammatical.

Mrs Chandler said contemptuously, 'Do you know what you're saying? That child is –'

'She's *not* a child.' His voice was venomous. 'She's a devil.' He wiped the perspiration from his brow. 'All semester she sat in the front row of my class, with her dress hiked up. After class she would come up and ask a lot of meaningless questions while she rubbed herself against me, I didn't take her seriously. Then one afternoon about six weeks ago she came over to my house when my wife and children were away and –' His voice broke. 'Oh. Jesus! I couldn't help it.' He burst into tears.

They brought Eve into the office. Her manner was composed. She looked into Mr Parkinson's eyes, and it was he who turned away first. In the office were Mrs Chandler, the assistant principal and the chief of police of the small town where the school was located.

The chief of police said gently, 'Do you want to tell us what happened, Eve?'

'Yes, sir.' Eve's voice was calm. 'Mr Parkinson said he wanted to discuss my English work with me. He asked me to come to his house on a Sunday afternoon. He was alone in the house. He said he wanted to show me something in the bedroom, so I followed him upstairs. He forced me onto the bed, and he –'

'It's a lie!' Parkinson yelled. 'That's not the way it happened. That's not the way it happened . . .'

Kate was sent for, and the situation was explained to her. It was decided that it was in every-one's interest to keep the incident quiet. Mr Parkinson was dismissed from the school and given forty-eight hours to leave the state. An abortion was discreetly arranged for Eve.

Kate quietly bought up the school mortgage, carried by a local bank, and foreclosed.

When Eve heard the news, she sighed, 'I'm so sorry, Gran. I really liked that school.'

*   *   *

A few weeks later when Eve had recovered from her operation, she and Alexandra were registered at L'Institut Fernwood, a Swiss finishing school near Lausanne.

TWENTY-FIVE

There was a fire burning in Eve that was so fierce she could not put it out. It was not sex alone: that was only a small part of it. It was a rage to live, a need to do everything, be everything. Life was a lover, and Eve was desperate to possess it with all she had in her. She was jealous of everyone. She went to the ballet and hated the ballerina because she herself was not up there dancing and winning the cheers of the audience. She wanted to be a scientist, a singer, a surgeon, a pilot, an actress. She wanted to do everything, and do it better than anyone else had ever done it. She wanted it all, and she could not wait.

Across the valley from L'Institut Fernwood was a boys' military school. By the time Eve was seventeen, nearly every student and almost half the instructors were involved with her. She flirted outrageously and had affairs indiscriminately, but this time she took proper precautions, for she had no intention of ever getting pregnant again. She enjoyed sex, but it was not the act itself Eve loved, it was the power it gave her. She was the one in control. She gloated over the pleading looks of the boys and men who wanted to take her to bed and make love to her. She enjoyed teasing them and watching their hunger grow. She enjoyed the lying promises they made in order to possess her. But most of all, Eve enjoyed the power she had over their bodies. She could bring them to an erection with a kiss, and wither them with a word. She did not need them, they needed her. She controlled them totally, and it was a tremendous feeling. Within minutes she could measure a man's strength and weaknesses. She decided men were fools, all of them.

Eve was beautiful and intelligent and an heiress to one of the world's great fortunes, and she had had more than a dozen serious proposals of marriage. She was not interested. The only boys who attracted her were the ones Alexandra liked.

At a Saturday-night school dance, Alexandra met an attentive young French student named Rene Mallot. He was not handsome, but he was intelligent and sensitive, and Alexandra thought he was wonderful. They arranged to meet in town the following Saturday.

'Seven o'clock,' Rene said.

'I'll be waiting.'

In their room that night, Alexandra told Eve about her new friend. 'He's not like the other boys. He's rather shy and sweet. We're going to the theatre Saturday.'

'You like him a lot, don't you, little sister?' Eve teased.

Alexandra blushed. 'I just met him, but he seems – Well, you know.'

Eve lay back on her bed, hands clasped behind her head. 'No, I don't know. Tell me. Did he try to take you to bed?'

'Eve! He's not that kind of boy at all. I told you . . . he's – he's shy.'

'Well, well. My little sister's in love.'

'Of course I'm not! Now I wish I hadn't told you.'

'I'm glad you did,' Eve said sincerely.

When Alexandra arrived in front of the theatre the following Saturday, Rene was nowhere in sight. Alexandra waited on the street corner for more than an hour, ignoring the stares of passers-by, feeling like a fool. Finally she had a bad dinner alone in a small café and returned to school, miserable. Eve was not in their room. Alexandra read until curfew and then turned out the lights. It was almost two a.m. when Alexandra heard Eve sneak into the room.

'I was getting worried about you,' Alexandra whispered.

'I ran into some old friends. How was your evening – divine?'

'It was dreadful. He never even bothered to show up.'

'That's a shame,' Eve said sympathetically. 'But you must learn never to trust a man.'

'You don't think anything could have happened to him?'

'No, Alex, I think he probably found somebody he liked better.'

Of course he did, Alexandra thought. She was not really surprised. She had no idea how beautiful she was, or how admirable. She had lived all her life in the shadow of her twin sister. She adored her, and it seemed only right to Alexandra that everyone should be attracted to Eve. She felt inferior to Eve, but it never occurred to her that her sister had been carefully nourishing that feeling since they were children.

There were other broken dates. Boys Alexandra liked would seem to respond to her, and then she would never see them again. One weekend she ran into Rene unexpectedly on the streets of Lausanne. He hurried up to her and said, 'What happened? You promised you would call me.'

'Call you? What are you talking about?'

He stepped back, suddenly wary. 'Eve. . . . ?'

'No, Alexandra.'

His face flushed. 'I – I'm sorry. I have to go.' And he turned away, leaving her staring after him in confusion.

That evening when Alexandra told Eve about the incident, Eve shrugged and said, 'He's obviously *fou*. You're much better off without him, Alex.'

* * *

In spite of her feeling of expertise about men, there was one male weakness of which Eve was unaware, and it almost proved to be her undoing. From the beginning of time, men have boasted of their conquests, and the students at the military school were no different. They discussed Eve Blackwell with admiration and awe.

'When she was through with me, I couldn't move . . .'

'I never thought I'd have a piece of ass like that . . .'

'She's got a pussy that *talks* to you . . .'

'God, she's like a tigress in bed!'

Since at least two dozen boys and half a dozen teachers were praising Eve's libidinous talents, it soon became the school's worst-kept secret. One of the instructors at the military school mentioned the gossip to a teacher at L'Institut Fernwood, and she in turn reported it to Mrs Collins, the headmistress. A discreet investigation was begun, and the result was a meeting between the headmistress and Eve.

'I think it would be better for the reputation of this school if you left immediately.'

Eve stared at Mrs Collins as though the lady were demented. 'What on earth are you talking about?'

'I'm talking about the fact that you have been servicing half the military academy. The other half seems to be lined up, eagerly waiting.'

'I've never heard such terrible lies in my whole

life,' Eve's voice was quivering with indignation. 'Don't think I'm not going to report this to my grandmother. When she hears –'

'I will spare you the trouble,' the headmistress interrupted. 'I would prefer to avoid embarrassment to L'Institut Fernwood, but if you do not leave quietly, I have a list of names I intend to send to your grandmother.'

'I'd like to see that list!'

Mrs Collins handed it to Eve without a word. It was a long list. Eve studied it and noted that at least seven names were missing. She sat there, quietly thinking.

Finally she looked up and said imperiously, 'This is obviously some kind of plot against my family. Someone is trying to embarrass my grandmother through me. Rather than let that happen, I will leave.'

'A very wise decision,' Mrs Collins said dryly. 'A car will drive you to the airport in the morning. I'll cable your grandmother that you're coming home. You're dismissed.'

Eve turned and started for the door, then suddenly thought of something. 'What about my sister?'

'Alexandra may remain here.'

When Alexandra returned to the dormitory after her last class, she found Eve packing. 'What are you doing?'

'I'm going home.'

'Home? In the middle of the term?'

Eve turned to face her sister. 'Alex, don't you really have any idea what a waste this school is? We're not learning anything here. We're just killing time.'

Alexandra was listening in surprise. 'I had no idea you felt that way, Eve.'

'I've felt like this every damn day for the whole bloody year. The only reason I stuck it out was because of you. You seemed to be enjoying it so much.'

'I am, but –'

'I'm sorry, Alex. I just can't take it any longer. I want to get back to New York. I want to go home where *we* belong.'

'Have you told Mrs Collins?'

'A few minutes ago.'

'How did she take it?'

'How did you expect her to take it? She was miserable – afraid it would make her school look bad. She begged me to stay.'

Alexandra sat down on the edge of the bed. 'I don't know what to say.'

'You don't have to say anything. This has nothing to do with you.'

'Of course it has. If you're that unhappy here –' She stopped. 'You're probably right. It is a bloody waste of time. Who needs to conjugate Latin verbs?'

'Right. Or who gives a fig about Hannibal or his bloody brother, Hasdrubal?'

Alexandra walked over to the closet, took out her suitcase and put it on the bed.

Eve smiled. 'I wasn't going to ask you to leave

459

here, Alex, but I'm really glad we're going home together.'

Alexandra pressed her sister's hand. 'So am I.'

Eve said casually, 'Tell you what. While I finish packing, call Gran and tell her we'll be on the plane home tomorrow. Tell her we can't stand this place. Will you do that?'

'Yes.' Alexandra hesitated. 'I don't think she's going to like it.'

'Don't worry about the old lady,' Eve said confidently. 'I can handle her.'

And Alexandra had no reason to doubt it. Eve was able to make Gran do pretty much what she wanted. *But then*, Alexandra thought, *how could anyone refuse Eve anything?*

She went to make the phone call.

Kate Blackwell had friends and enemies and business associates in high places, and for the last few months disturbing rumours had been coming to her ears. In the beginning she had ignored them as petty jealousies. But they persisted. Eve was seeing too much of the boys at a military school in Switzerland. Eve had an abortion. Eve was being treated for a social disease.

Thus, it was with a degree of relief that Kate learned that her granddaughters were coming home. She intended to get to the bottom of the vile rumours.

The day the girls arrived, Kate was at home waiting for them. She took Eve into the sitting room off her bedroom. 'I've been hearing some distressing

460

stories,' she said. 'I want to know why you were thrown out of school.' Her eyes bored into those of her granddaughter.

'We weren't thrown out,' Eve replied. 'Alex and I decided to leave.'

'Because of some incidents with boys?'

Eve said, 'Please, Grandmother. I'd rather not talk about it.'

'I'm afraid you're going to have to. What have you been doing?'

'I haven't been doing anything. It is Alex who –' She broke off.

'Alex who what?' Kate was relentless.

'Please don't blame her,' Eve said quickly. 'I'm sure she couldn't help it. She likes to play this childish game of pretending to be me. I had no idea what she was up to until the girls started gossiping about it. It seems she was seeing a lot of – of boys –' Eve broke off in embarrassment.

'Pretending to be you?' Kate was stunned. 'Why didn't you put a stop to it?'

'I tried,' Eve said miserably. 'She threatened to kill herself. Oh, Gran, I think Alexandra is a bit' – she forced herself to say the word – 'unstable. If you even discuss any of this with her, I'm afraid of what she might do.' There was naked agony in the child's tear-filled eyes.

Kate's heart felt heavy at Eve's deep unhappiness. 'Eve, don't. Don't cry, darling. I won't say anything to Alexandra. This will be just between the two of us.'

'I – I didn't want you to know. Oh, Gran,' she sobbed, 'I knew how much it would hurt you.'

Later, over tea, Kate studied Alexandra. *She's beautiful outside and rotten inside*, Kate thought. It was bad enough that Alexandra was involved in a series of sordid affairs, but to try to put the blame on her sister! Kate was appalled.

During the next two years, while Eve and Alexandra finished school at Miss Porter's, Eve was very discreet. She had been frightened by the close call. Nothing must jeopardize the relationship with her grandmother. The old lady could not last much longer – she was seventy-nine! – and Eve intended to make sure that she was Gran's heiress.

For the girls' twenty-first birthday, Kate took her granddaughters to Paris and bought them new wardrobes at Coco Chanel.

At a small dinner party at Le Petit Bedouin, Eve and Alexandra met Count Alfred Maurier and his wife, the Countess Vivien. The count was a distinguished-looking man in his fifties, with iron-grey hair and the disciplined body of an athlete. His wife was a pleasant-looking woman with a reputation as an international hostess.

Eve would have paid no particular attention to either of them, except for a remark she overheard someone make to the countess. 'I envy you and Alfred. You're the happiest married couple I know.

462

How many years have you been married? Twenty-five?'

'It will be twenty-six next month,' Alfred replied for her. 'And I may be the only Frenchman in history who has never been unfaithful to his wife.'

Everyone laughed except Eve. During the rest of the dinner, she studied Count Maurier and his wife. Eve could not imagine what the count saw in that flabby, middle-aged woman with her creepy neck. Count Maurier had probably never known what real love-making was. That boast of his was stupid. Count Alfred Maurier was a challenge.

The following day, Eve telephone Maurier at his office. 'This is Eve Blackwell. You probably don't remember me, but –'

'How could I forget you, child? You are one of the beautiful granddaughters of my friend Kate.'

'I'm flattered that you remember, Count. Forgive me for disturbing you, but I was told you're an expert on wines. I'm planning a surprise dinner party for Grandmother.' She gave a rueful little laugh. 'I know what I want to serve, but I don't know a thing about wines. I wondered whether you'd be kind enough to advise me.'

'I would be delighted,' he said, flattered. 'It depends on what you are serving. If you are starting with a fish, a nice, light Chablis would be –'

'Oh, I'm afraid I could never remember all this. Would it be possible for me to see you so that we could discuss it? If you're free for lunch today. . . . ?'

'For an old friend, I can arrange that.'

'Oh, good.' Eve replaced the receiver slowly. It would be a lunch the count would remember the rest of his life.

They met at Lasserre. The discussion on wines was brief. Eve listened to Maurier's boring discourse impatiently, and then interrupted. 'I'm in love with you, Alfred.'

The count stopped dead in the middle of a sentence. 'I beg your pardon?'

'I said I'm in love with you.'

He took a sip of wine. 'A vintage year.' He patted Eve's hand and smiled. 'All good friends should love one another.'

'I'm not talking about that kind of love, Alfred.'

And the count looked into Eve's eyes and knew exactly what kind of love she was talking about. It made him decidedly nervous. This girl was twenty-one years old, and he was past middle age, a happily married man. He simply could not understand what got into young girls these days. He felt uneasy sitting across from her, listening to what she was saying, and he felt even uneasier because she was probably the most beautiful, desirable young woman he had ever seen. She was wearing a beige pleated skirt and a soft green sweater that revealed the outline of a full, rich bosom. She was not wearing a brassiere, and he could see the thrust of her nipples. He looked at her innocent young face, and he was at a loss for words. 'You – you don't even know me.'

'I've dreamed about you from the time I was a little girl. I imagined a man in shining armour who was tall and handsome and –'

'I'm afraid my armour's a little rusty. I –'

'Please don't make fun of me,' Eve begged. 'When I saw you at dinner last night, I couldn't take my eyes off you. I haven't been able to think of anything else. I haven't slept. I haven't been able to get you out of my mind for a moment.' Which was almost true.

'I – I don't know what to say to you, Eve. I am a happily married man. I –'

'Oh, I can't tell you how I envy your wife! She's the luckiest woman in the world. I wonder if she realizes that, Alfred.'

'Of course she does. I tell her all the time.' He smiled nervously, and wondered how to change the subject.

'Does she *really* appreciate you? Does she know how sensitive you are? Does she worry about your happiness? I would.'

The count was becoming increasingly uncomfortable. 'You're a beautiful young woman,' he said. 'And one day you're going to find your knight in shining, *unrusted* armour, and then –'

'I've found him and I want to go to bed with him.'

He looked around, afraid that someone might have overheard. 'Eve! Please!'

She leaned forwards. 'That's all I ask. The memory will last me for the rest of my life.'

The count said firmly, 'This is impossible. You are placing me in a most embarrassing position. Young women should not go around propositioning strangers.'

Slowly, Eve's eyes filled with tears. 'Is *that* what you think of me? That I go around – I've known only one man in my life. We were engaged to be married.' She did not bother to brush the tears away. 'He was kind and loving and gentle. He was killed in a mountain-climbing accident. I saw it happen. It was awful.'

Count Maurier put his hand over hers. 'I am so sorry.'

'You remind me so much of him. When I saw you, it was as though Bill had returned to me. If you would give me just one hour, I would never bother you again. You'd never even have to see me again. Please, Alfred!'

The count looked at Eve for a long time, weighing his decision.

After all, he was French.

They spent the afternoon in a small hotel on Rue Sainte-Anne. In all his experience before his marriage, Count Maurier had never bedded anyone like Eve. She was a hurricane, a nymphet, a devil. She knew too much. By the end of the afternoon, Count Maurier was completely exhausted.

As they were getting dressed, Eve said, 'When will I see you again, darling?'

'I'll telephone you,' Maurier said.

He did not plan ever to see this woman again. There was something about her that was frightening – almost evil. She was what the Americans so appropriately called *bad news*, and he had no intention of becoming involved further with her.

The matter would have ended there, had they not been seen coming out of the hotel together by Alicia Vanderlake, who had served on a charity committee with Kate Blackwell the previous year. Mrs Vanderlake was a social climber, and this was a heaven-sent ladder. She had seen newspaper photographs of Count Maurier and his wife, and she had seen photographs of the Blackwell twins. She was not sure which twin this was, but that was not important. Mrs Vanderlake knew where her duty lay. She looked in her private telephone book and found Kate Blackwell's number.

The butler answered the telephone. '*Bonjour.*'

'I would like to speak with Mrs Blackwell, please.'

'May I tell her who is calling?'

'Mrs Vanderlake. It's a personal matter.'

A minute later, Kate Blackwell was on the phone. 'Who is this?'

'This is Alicia Vanderlake, Mrs Blackwell. I'm sure you'll remember me. We served on a committee together last year and –'

'If it's for a donation, call my –'

467

'No, no,' Mrs Vanderlake said hastily. 'It's personal. It's about your granddaughter.'

Kate Blackwell would invite her over to tea, and they would discuss it, woman to woman. It would be the beginning of a warm friendship.

Kate Blackwell said, 'What about her?'

Mrs Vanderlake had had no intention of discussing the matter over the telephone, but Kate Blackwell's unfriendly tone left her no choice. 'Well, I thought it my duty to tell you that a few minutes ago I saw her sneaking out of a hotel with Count Alfred Maurier. It was an obvious assignation.'

Kate's voice was icy. 'I find this difficult to believe. Which one of my granddaughters?'

Mrs Vanderlake gave an uncertain laugh. 'I – I don't know. I can't tell them apart. But then, no one can, can they? It –'

'Thank you for the information.' And Kate hung up.

She stood there digesting the information she had just heard. Only the evening before they had dined together. Kate had known Alfred Maurier for fifteen years, and what she had just been told was entirely out of character for him, unthinkable. And yet, men were susceptible. If Alexandra had set out to lure Alfred into bed . . .

Kate picked up the telephone and said to the operator, 'I wish to place a call to Switzerland L'Institut Fernwood at Lausanne.'

* * *

When Eve returned home late that afternoon, she was flushed with satisfaction, not because she had enjoyed sex with Count Maurier, but because of her victory over him. *If I can have him so easily*, Eve thought, *I can have anyone. I can own the world*. She walked into the library and found Kate there.

'Hello, Gran. Did you have a lovely day?'

Kate stood there studying her lovely young granddaughter. 'Not a very good one, I'm afraid. What about you?'

'Oh, I did a little shopping. I didn't see anything more I really wanted. You bought me everything. You always –'

'Close the door, Eve.'

Something in Kate's voice sent out a warning signal. Eve closed the large oak door.

'Sit down.'

'Is something wrong, Gran?'

'That's what you're going to tell me. I was going to invite Alfred Maurier here, but I decided to spare us all that humiliation.'

Eve's brain began to spin. *This was impossible! There was no way anyone could have found out about her and Alfred Maurier*. She had left him only an hour earlier. 'I – I don't understand what you're talking about.'

'Then let me put it bluntly. You were in bed this afternoon with Count Maurier.'

Tears sprang to Eve's eyes. 'I – I was hoping you'd never find out what he did to me, because he's your friend.' She fought to keep her voice steady. 'It was terrible. He telephoned and invited me to lunch and got me drunk and –'

'Shut up!' Kate's voice was like a whiplash. Her eyes were filled with loathing. 'You're despicable.'

Kate had spent the most painful hour of her life, coming to a realization of the truth about her granddaughter. She could hear again the voice of the headmistress saying, *Mrs Blackwell, young women will be young women, and if one of them has a discreet affair, it is none of my business. But Eve was so blatantly promiscuous that for the good of the school . . .*

And Eve had blamed Alexandra.

Kate started to remember the accidents. The fire, when Alexandra almost burned to death. Alexandra's fall from the cliff. Alexandra being knocked out of the boat Eve was sailing, and almost drowning. Kate could hear Eve's voice recounting the details of her 'rape' by her English teacher: *Mr Parkinson said he wanted to discuss my English work with me. He asked me to come to his house on a Sunday afternoon. When I got there, he was alone in the house. He said he wanted to show me something in the bedroom. I followed him upstairs. He forced me onto the bed, and he . . .*

Kate remembered the incident at Briarcrest when Eve was accused of selling marijuana and the blame had been put on Alexandra. Eve had not *blamed* Alexandra, she had *defended* her. That was Eve's technique – to be the villain and play the heroine. Oh, she was clever.

Now Kate studied the beautiful, angel-faced monster in front of her. *I built all my future plans around you. It was you who was going to take control of Kruger-Brent one day. It was you I loved and cherished.* Kate said, 'I want you to leave this house. I never want to see you again.'

Eve had gone very pale.

'You're a whore. I think I could live with that. But you're also deceitful and cunning and a psychopathic liar. I cannot live with that.'

It was all happening too fast. Eve said desperately, 'Gran, if Alexandra has been telling you lies about me –'

'Alexandra doesn't know anything about this. I just had a long talk with Mrs Collins.'

'Is *that* all?' Eve forced a note of relief in her voice. 'Mrs Collins hates me because –'

Kate was filled with a sudden weariness. 'It won't work, Eve. Not anymore. It's over. I've sent for my lawyer. I'm disinheriting you.'

Eve felt her world crumbling around her. 'You can't. How – how will I live?'

'You will be given a small allowance. From now on, you will live your own life. Do anything you please,' Kate's voice hardened. 'But if I ever hear or read one word of scandal about you, if you ever disgrace the Blackwell name in any way, your allowance will stop forever. Is that clear?'

Eve looked into her grandmother's eyes and

knew this time there would be no reprieve. A dozen excuses sprang to her lips, but they died there.

Kate rose to her feet and said in an unsteady voice, 'I don't suppose this will mean anything to you, but this is – this is the most difficult thing I've ever had to do in my life.'

And Kate turned and walked out of the room, her back stiff and straight.

Kate sat in her darkened bedroom alone, wondering why everything had gone wrong.

If David had not been killed, and Tony could have known his father . . .

If Tony had not wanted to be an artist . . .

If Marianne had lived . . .

If. A two-letter word for futility.

The future was clay, to be moulded day by day, but the past was bedrock, immutable. *Everyone I've loved has betrayed me*, Kate thought. *Tony. Marianne. Eve. Sartre said it well: 'Hell is other people.'* She wondered when the pain would go away.

If Kate was filled with pain, Eve was filled with fury. All she had done was to enjoy herself in bed for an hour or two, and her grandmother acted as though Eve had committed some unspeakable crime. *The old-fashioned bitch!* No, not old-fashioned: *senile*. That was it. She was senile. Eve would find a good attorney and have the new will laughed out of court. Her father and grandmother were both insane. No one was going to disinherit her. Kruger-Brent was *her* company. How many times had her grandmother told her that one day it would belong to her. And Alexandra! All this time Alexandra had been undermining her, whispering God-knows-what poison into their grandmother's ears. Alexandra wanted the company for herself. The terrible part was that now she would probably get it. What had happened this afternoon was bad enough, but the thought of Alexandra gaining control was unbearable. *I can't let that happen*, Eve thought. *I'll find a way to stop her.* She closed the snaps on her suitcase and went to find her sister.

Alexandra was in the garden reading. She looked up as Eve approached.

'Alex, I've decided to go back to New York.'

Alexandra looked at her sister in surprise. *'Now?* Gran's planning a cruise to the Dalmatian coast next week. You –'

'Who cares about the Dalmatian coast? I've been thinking a lot about this. It's time I had my own apartment.' She smiled. 'I'm a big girl now. So I'm going to find the most divine little apartment, and if you're good, I'll let you spend the night once in a while.' *That's just the right note*, Eve thought. *Friendly, but not gushy. Don't let her know you're on to her.*

Alexandra was studying her sister with concern. 'Does Gran know?'

'I told her this afternoon. She hates the idea, of course, but she understands. I wanted to get a job, but she insisted on giving me an allowance.'

Alexandra asked, 'Would you like me to come with you?'

The goddamned, two-faced bitch! First she forced her out of the house, and now she was pretending she wanted to go with her. *Well, they're not going to dispose of little Eve so easily. I'll show them all.* She would have her own apartment – she would find some fabulous decorator to do it – and she would have complete freedom to come and go as she pleased. She could invite men up to her place and have them spend the night. She would be truly free for the first time in her life. It was an exhilarating thought.

Now she said, 'You're sweet, Alex, but I'd like to be on my own for a while.'

Alexandra looked at her sister and felt a deep sense of loss. It would be the first time they had ever been parted. 'We'll see each other often, won't we?'

'Of course we will,' Eve promised. 'More than you imagine.'

TWENTY-SIX

When Eve returned to New York, she checked into a midtown hotel, as she had been instructed. An hour later, Brad Rogers telephoned.

'Your grandmother called from Paris, Eve. Apparently there's some problem between you two.'

'Not really,' Eve laughed. 'It's just a little family –' She was about to launch into an elaborate defence when she suddenly realized the danger that lay in that direction. From now on, she would have to be very careful. She had never had to think about money. It had always been there. Now it loomed large in her thoughts. She had no idea how large her allowance was going to be and for the first time in her life Eve felt fear.

'She told you she's having a new will drawn up?' Brad asked.

'Yes, she mentioned something about it.' She was determined to play it cool.

'I think we had better discuss this in person. How's Monday at three?'

'That will be fine, Brad.'
'My office. All right?'
'I'll be there.'

At five minutes before three, Eve entered the Kruger-Brent, Ltd., building. She was greeted deferentially by the security guard, the elevator starter and even the elevator operator. *Everyone knows me*, Eve thought. *I'm a Blackwell*. The elevator took her to the executive floor, and a few moments later Eve was seated in Brad Roger's office.

Brad had been surprised when Kate telephoned him to say she was going to disinherit Eve, for he knew how much Kate cared about this particular granddaughter and what plans she had for her. Brad could not imagine what had happened. Well, it was none of his business. If Kate wanted to discuss it with him, she would. His job was to carry out her orders. He felt a momentary flash of pity for the lovely young woman before him. Kate had not been much older when he had first met her. Neither had he. And now he was a grey-haired old fool, still hoping that one day Kate Blackwell would realize there was someone who loved her very deeply.

He said to Eve, 'I have some papers for you to sign. If you'll just read them over and –'

'That won't be necessary.'

'Eve, it's important that you understand.' He began to explain. 'Under your grandmother's will, you're the beneficiary of an irrevocable trust fund currently in excess of five million dollars. Your grandmother is the executor. At her discretion, the money can be paid to you at any time from the age of twenty-one to thirty-five.' He cleared his throat. 'She has elected to give it to you when you reach age thirty-five.'

It was a slap in the face.

'Beginning today, you will receive a weekly allowance of two hundred fifty dollars.'

It was impossible! One decent dress cost more than that. There was no way she could live on $250 a week. This was being done to humiliate her. This bastard was probably in on it with her grandmother. He was sitting behind his big desk, enjoying himself, laughing. She wanted to pick up the large bronze paperweight in front of him and smash his head in. She could almost feel the crunch of bone under her hand.

Brad droned on. 'You are not to have any charge accounts, private or otherwise, and you are not to use the Blackwell name at any stores. Anything you purchase must be paid for in cash.'

The nightmare was getting worse and worse.

'Next. If there is any gossip connected with your name in any newspaper or magazine – local or foreign – your weekly income will be stopped. Is that clear?'

'Yes!' Her voice was a whisper.

'You and your sister Alexandra were issued insurance policies on your grandmother's life for five million dollars apiece. The policy you hold was cancelled as of this morning. At the end of one year,' Brad went on, 'if your grandmother is satisfied with your behaviour, your weekly allowance will be doubled.' He hesitated. 'There is one final stipulation.'

She wants to hang me in public by my thumbs. 'Yes?'

Brad Rogers looked uncomfortable. 'Your grandmother does not wish ever to see you again, Eve.'

Well, I want to see you one more time, old woman. I want to see you dying in agony.

Brad's voice trickled through to the cauldron of Eve's mind. 'If you have any problems, you are to telephone me. She does not want you to come to this building again, or to visit any of the family estates.'

He had tried to argue with Kate about that. 'My God, Kate, she's your granddaughter, your flesh and blood. You're treating her like a leper.'

'She *is* a leper.'

And the discussion had ended.

Now Brad said awkwardly, 'Well, I think that covers everything. Are there any questions, Eve?'

'No.' She was in shock.

'Then if you'll just sign these papers . . .'

Ten minutes later, Eve was on the street again. There was a cheque for $250 in her purse.

The following morning Eve called on a real-estate agent and began looking for an apartment. In her fantasies, she had envisioned a beautiful penthouse overlooking Central Park, the rooms done in white with modern furniture, and a terrace where she could entertain guests. Reality came as a stunning blow. It seemed there were no Park Avenue penthouses available for someone with an income of $250 a week. What *was* available was a one-room studio apartment in Little Italy with a couch that became a bed, a nook that the real-estate agent euphemistically referred to as the 'library,' a small kitchenette and a tiny bathroom with stained tile.

'Is – is this the best you have?' Eve asked.

'No,' the agent informed her. 'I've got a twenty-room townhouse on Sutton Place for a half a million dollars, plus maintenance.'

You bastard! Eve thought.

Real despair did not hit Eve until the following afternoon when she moved in. It was a prison. Her dressing room at home had been as large as this entire apartment. She thought of Alexandra enjoying herself in the huge house on Fifth Avenue. *My God, why couldn't Alexandra have burned to death? It had been so close!* If she had died and Eve had been the only heiress, things would have been different. Her grandmother would not have dared disinherit her.

But if Kate Blackwell thought that Eve intended to give up her heritage that easily, she did not know her granddaughter. Eve had no intention of trying to live on $250 a week. There was five million dollars that belonged to her, sitting in a bank, and that vicious old woman was keeping it from her. *There has to be a way to get my hands on that money. I will find it.*

The solution came the following day.

'And what can I do for you, Miss Blackwell?' Alvin Seagram asked deferentially. He was vice-president of the National Union Bank, and he was, in fact, prepared to do almost anything. What kind Fates had brought this young woman to him? If he could secure the Kruger-Brent account, or any part of it, his career would rise like a rocket.

'There's some money in trust for me,' Eve explained. 'Five million dollars. Because of the rules of the trust, it won't come to me until I'm thirty-five years old.' She smiled ingenuously. 'That seems so long from now.'

'At your age, I'm sure it does,' the banker smiled. 'You're – nineteen?'

'Twenty-one.'

'And beautiful, if you'll permit me to say so, Miss Blackwell.'

Eve smiled demurely. 'Thank you, Mr Seagram.' It was going to be simpler than she thought. *The man's an idiot.*

He could feel the rapport between them. *She likes me.* 'How exactly may we help you?'

'Well, I was wondering if it would be possible to borrow an advance on my trust fund. You see, I need the money now more than I'll need it later.

I'm engaged to be married. My fiancé is a construction engineer working in Israel, and he won't be back in this country for another three years.'

Alvin Seagram was all sympathy. 'I understand perfectly.' His heart was pounding wildly. *Of course, he could grant her request.* Money was advanced against trust funds all the time. And when he had satisfied her, she would send him other members of the Blackwell family, and he would satisfy them. Oh, how he would satisfy them! After that, there would be no stopping him. He would be made a member of the executive board of National Union. Perhaps one day its chairman. And he owed all this to the delicious little blonde seated across the desk.

'No problem at all,' Alvin Seagram assured Eve. 'It's a very simple transaction. You understand that we could not loan you the entire amount, but we could certainly let you have, say, a million immediately. Would that be satisfactory?'

'Perfectly,' Eve said, trying not to show her exhilaration.

'Fine. If you'll just give me the details of the trust . . .' He picked up a pen.

'You can get in touch with Brad Rogers at Kruger-Brent. He'll give you all the information you need.'

'I'll give him a call right away.'

Eve rose. 'How long will it take?'

'No more than a day or two. I'll rush it through personally.'

She held out a lovely, delicate hand. 'You're very kind.'

The moment Eve was out of the office, Alvin Seagram picked up the telephone. 'Get me Mr Brad Rogers at Kruger-Brent, Limited.' The very name sent a delicious shiver up his spine.

Two days later Eve returned to the bank and was ushered into Alvin Seagram's office. His first words were, 'I'm afraid I can't help you, Miss Blackwell.'

Eve could not believe what she was hearing. 'I don't understand. You said it was simple. You said –'

'I'm sorry. I was not in possession of all the facts.'

How vividly he recalled the conversation with Brad Rogers. 'Yes, there is a five-million-dollar trust fund in Eve Blackwell's name. Your bank is perfectly free to advance any amount of money you wish against it. However, I think it only fair to caution you that Kate Blackwell would consider it an unfriendly act.'

There was no need for Brad Rogers to spell out what the consequences could be. Kruger-Brent had powerful friends everywhere. And if those friends started pulling money out of National Union, Alvin Seagram did not have to guess what it would do to his career.

'I'm sorry,' he repeated to Eve. 'There's nothing I can do.'

Eve looked at him, frustrated. But she would not let this man know what a blow he had dealt her. 'Thank you for your trouble. There are other banks in New York. Good day.'

'Miss Blackwell,' Alvin Seagram told her, 'there isn't a bank in the world that will loan you one penny against that trust.'

Alexandra was puzzled. In the past, her grandmother had made it obvious in a hundred ways that she favoured Eve. Now, overnight everything had changed. She knew something terrible had happened between Kate and Eve, but she had no idea what it could have been.

Whenever Alexandra tried to bring up the subject, her grandmother would say, 'There is nothing to discuss. Eve chose her own life.'

Nor could Alexandra get anything out of Eve.

Kate Blackwell began spending a great deal of time with Alexandra. Alexandra was intrigued. She was not merely in her grandmother's presence, she was becoming an actual part of her life. It was as though her grandmother were seeing her for the first time. Alexandra had an odd feeling she was being evaluated.

Kate *was* seeing her granddaughter for the first time, and because she had been bitterly deceived once, she was double careful in forming an opinion about Eve's twin. She spent every possible moment with Alexandra, and she probed and questioned and listened. And in the end she was satisfied.

It was not easy to know Alexandra. She was a private person, more reserved than Eve. Alexandra had a quick, lively intelligence, and her innocence, combined with her beauty, made her all the more endearing. She had always received countless invitations to parties and dinners and the theatre, but now it was Kate who decided which invitations Alexandra should accept and which ones she should refuse. The fact that a suitor was eligible was not enough – not nearly enough. What Kate was looking for was a man capable of helping Alexandra run Kate's dynasty. She said nothing of this to Alexandra. There would be time enough for that when Kate found the right man for her granddaughter. Sometimes, in the lonely early-morning hours when Kate had trouble sleeping, she thought about Eve.

Eve was doing beautifully. The episode with her grandmother had bruised her ego so badly that for a short time she had forgotten something very important: she had forgotten how attractive she was to men. At the first party she was invited to after she moved into her own apartment, she gave her telephone number to six men – four of them married – and within twenty-four hours she had heard from all six of them. From that day on, Eve knew she would no longer have to worry about money. She was showered with gifts: expensive jewellery, paints and, more often, cash.

'I've just ordered a new credenza, and my

allowance cheque hasn't come. Would you mind, darling?'

And they never minded.

When Eve went out in public, she made sure she was escorted by men who were single. Married men she saw afternoons at her apartment. Eve was very discreet. She was careful to see that her name was kept out of gossip columns, not because she was any longer concerned about her allowance being stopped, but because she was determined that one day her grandmother was going to come crawling to her. Kate Blackwell needed an heir to take over Kruger-Brent. *Alexandra is not equipped to be anything but a stupid housewife*, Eve gloated.

One afternoon, leafing through a new issue of *Town and Country*, Eve came across a photograph of Alexandra dancing with an attractive man. Eve was not looking at Alexandra, she was looking at the man. And realizing that if Alexandra married and had a son, it would be a disaster for Eve and her plans.

She stared at the picture a long time.

Over a period of a year, Alexandra had called Eve regularly, for lunch or dinner, and Eve had always put her off with excuses. Now Eve decided it was time to have a talk with her sister. She invited Alexandra to her apartment.

Alexandra had not seen the apartment before, and Eve braced herself for pity. But all Alexandra said was, 'It's charming, Eve. It's very cosy, isn't it?'

Eve smiled. 'It suits me. I wanted something *intime*.' She had pawned enough jewellery and paintings so that she could have moved into a beautiful apartment, but Kate would have learned of it and would have demanded to know where the money had come from. For the moment, the watchword was *discretion*.

'How is Gran?' Eve asked.

'She's fine.' Alexandra hesitated. 'Eve, I don't know what happened between you two, but you know if there's anything I can do to help, I'll –'

Eve sighed. 'She didn't tell you?'

'No. She won't discuss it.'

'I don't blame her. The poor dear probably feels as guilty as hell. I met a wonderful young doctor. We were going to be married. We went to bed together. Gran found out about it. She told me to get out of the house, that she never wanted to see me again. I'm afraid our grandmother is very old-fashioned, Alex.'

She watched the look of dismay on Alexandra's face. 'That's terrible! The two of you must go to Gran. I'm sure she would –'

'He was killed in an airplane accident.'

'Oh, Eve! Why didn't you tell me this before?'

'I was too ashamed to tell anyone, even you.' She squeezed her sister's hand. 'And you know I tell you everything.'

'Let me talk to Gran. I'll explain –'

'No! I have too much pride. Promise me you'll never discuss this with her. Ever!'

'But I'm sure she would –'

'Promise!'

Alexandra sighed. 'All right.'

'Believe me, I'm very happy here. I come and go as I please. It's great!'

Alexandra looked at her sister and thought how much she had missed Eve.

Eve put her arm around Alexandra and began to tease. 'Now, enough about me. Tell me what's going on in your life. Have you met Prince Charming yet? I'll bet you have!'

'No.'

Eve studied her sister. It was a mirror image of herself, and she was determined to destroy it. 'You will, darling.'

'I'm in no hurry. I decided it's time I started earning a living. I talked to Gran about it. Next week I'm going to meet with the head of an advertising agency about a job.'

They had lunch at a little bistro near Eve's apartment, and Eve insisted on paying. She wanted nothing from her sister.

When they were bidding each other good-bye, Alexandra said, 'Eve, if you need any money –'

'Don't be silly, darling. I have more than enough.'

Alexandra persisted. 'Still, if you run short, you can have anything I've got.'

Eve looked into Alexandra's eyes and said, 'I'm counting on that.' She smiled. 'But I really don't need a thing, Alex.' She did not need crumbs. She intended to have the whole cake. The question was: How was she going to get it?

There was a weekend party in Nassau.

'It wouldn't be the same without you, Eve. All your friends will be here.'

The caller was Nita Ludwig, a girl whom Eve had known at school in Switzerland.

She would meet some new men. The present crop was tiresome.

'It sounds like fun,' Eve said. 'I'll be there.'

That afternoon she pawned an emerald bracelet she had been given a week earlier by an infatuated insurance executive with a wife and three children, and bought some new summer outfits at Lord & Taylor and a round-trip ticket to Nassau. She was on the plane the following morning.

The Ludwig estate was a large, sprawling mansion on the beach. The main house had thirty rooms, and the smallest was larger than Eve's entire apartment. Eve was escorted to her room by a uniformed maid, who unpacked for her while Eve freshened up. Then she went down to meet her fellow guests.

There were sixteen people in the drawing room, and they had one thing in common: they were wealthy. Nita Ludwig was a firm believer in the 'birds of a feather' philosophy. These people felt the same way about the same things; they were comfortable with one another because they spoke the same language. They shared the commonality of the best boarding schools and colleges, luxurious estates, yachts, private jets and tax problems. A columnist had dubbed them the 'jet set', an appellation they derided publicly and enjoyed privately. They were the privileged, the chosen few, set apart from all others by a discriminating god. Let the rest of the world believe that money could not buy everything. These people knew better. Money bought them beauty and love and luxury and a place in heaven. And it was from all this that Eve had been excluded by the whim of a narrow-minded old lady. *But not for long*, Eve thought.

She entered the drawing room and the conversation dropped as Eve walked in. In a room full of beautiful women, she was the most beautiful of all. Nita took Eve around to greet her friends, and to introduce her to the people she did not know. Eve was charming and pleasant, and she studied each man with a knowing eye, expertly selecting her targets. Most of the older men were married, but that only made it easier.

A bald-headed man dressed in plaid slacks and Hawaiian sport shirt came up to her. 'I'll bet you get tired of people telling you you're beautiful, honey.'

Eve rewarded him with a warm smile. 'I never get tired of that, Mr –?'

'Peterson. Call me Dan. You should be a Hollywood star.'

'I'm afraid I have no talent for acting.'

'I'll bet you've got a lot of other talents, though.'

Eve smiled enigmatically. 'You never know until you try, do you, Dan?'

He wet his lips. 'You down here alone?'

'Yes.'

'I've got my yacht anchored in the bay. Maybe you and I could take a little cruise tomorrow?'

'That sounds lovely,' Eve said.

He grinned. 'I don't know why we've never met before. I've known your grandmother, Kate, for years.'

The smile stayed on Eve's face, but it took a great effort. 'Gran's a darling,' Eve said. 'I think we'd better join the others.'

'Sure, honey.' He winked. 'Remember tomorrow.'

From that moment on, he was unable to get Eve alone again. She avoided him at lunch, and after lunch she borrowed one of the automobiles kept in the garage for guests and drove into town. She drove past Blackbeard's Tower and the lovely Ardastra Gardens where the colourful flamingos were on parade. She stopped at the waterfront to watch the fishing boats unload their catch of giant turtles, enormous lobsters, tropical fish and a brilliantly coloured variety of conch shells, which would be polished and sold to the tourists.

The bay was smooth, and the sea sparkled like diamonds. Across the water Eve could see the crescent curve of Paradise Island Beach. A motorboat was leaving the dock at the beach, and as it picked up speed, the figure of a man suddenly rose into the sky, trailing behind the boat. It was a startling sight. He appeared to be hanging on to a metal bar fastened to a blue sail, his long, lean body stretched against the wind. *Para-sailing.* Eve watched, fascinated, as the motorboat roared towards the harbour, and the airborne figure swept closer. The boat approached the dock and made a sharp turn, and for an instant Eve caught a glimpse of the dark, handsome face of the man in the air, and then he was gone.

He walked into Nita Ludwig's drawing room five hours later, and Eve felt as though she had willed him there. She had known he would appear. Up close he was even more handsome. He was six foot three, with perfectly sculptured, tanned features, black eyes and a trim, athletic body. When he smiled, he revealed white, even teeth. He smiled down at Eve as Nita introduced him.

'This is George Mellis. Eve Blackwell.'

'My God, you belong in the Louvre,' George Mellis said. His voice was deep and husky, with the trace of an indefinable accent.

'Come along, darling,' Nita commanded. 'I'll introduce you to the other guests.'

He waved her away. 'Don't bother. I just met everybody.'

Nita looked at the two of them thoughtfully. 'I see. Well, if I can do anything, call me.' She walked away.

'Weren't you a little rude to her?' Eve asked.

He grinned. 'I'm not responsible for what I say or do. I'm in love.'

Eve laughed.

'I mean it. You're the most beautiful thing I've ever seen in my life.'

'I was thinking the same about you.'

Eve did not care whether this man had money or not. She was fascinated by him. It was more than his looks. There was a magnetism, a sense of power that excited her. No man had ever affected her this way before. 'Who are you?' Eve asked.

'Nita told you. George Mellis.'

'Who are you?' she repeated.

'Ah, you mean in the philosophical sense. The *real* me. Nothing colourful to tell, I'm afraid. I'm Greek. My family grows olives and other things.'

That Mellis! The Mellis food brands could be found in every corner grocery store and super-market in America.

'Are you married?' Eve asked.

He grinned. 'Are you always this direct?'

'No.'

'I'm not married.'

The answer gave her an unexpected feeling of pleasure. Just looking at him made Eve want to possess him, to be possessed.

'Why did you miss dinner?'

'The truth?'

'Yes.'

'It's very personal.'

She waited.

'I was busy persuading a young lady not to commit suicide.' He said it matter-of-factly, as though it were a common occurrence.

'I hope you succeeded.'

'For now. I hope you're not the suicidal type.'

'No. I hope *you're* not.'

George Mellis laughed aloud. 'I love you,' he said. 'I really love you.' He took Eve's arm, and his touch made her shiver.

He stayed at Eve's side all evening, and he was totally attentive to her, oblivious to everyone else. He had long, delicate hands, and they were constantly doing things for Eve: bringing her a drink, lighting her cigarette, touching her discreetly. His nearness set her body afire, and she could not wait to be alone with him.

Just after midnight when the guests began to retire to their rooms, George Mellis asked, 'Which is your bedroom?'

'At the end of the north hall.'

He nodded, his long-lashed eyes boring into hers.

Eve undressed and bathed and put on a new sheer, black negligee that clung to her figure. At one a.m. there was a discreet tap on the door. She hurried to open it, and George Mellis stepped in.

He stood there, his eyes filled with admiration. '*Matia mou*, you make the *Venus de Milo* look like a hag.'

'I have an advantage over her,' Eve whispered. 'I have two arms.'

And she put both arms around George Mellis and drew him to her. His kiss made something explode inside her. His lips pressed hard against hers, and she felt his tonque exploring her mouth.

'Oh, my God!' Eve moaned.

He started to strip off his jacket, and she helped him. In a moment he was free of his trousers and French shorts, and he was naked before her. He had the most glorious physique Eve had ever seen. He was hard and erect.

'Quick,' Eve said. 'Make love to me.' She moved onto the bed, her body on fire.

He commanded, 'Turn over. Give me your ass.'

She looked up at him. 'I – I don't –'

And he hit her on the mouth. She stared up at him in shock.

'Turn over.'

'No.'

He hit her again, harder, and the room began to swim in front of her.

'Please, no.'

He hit her again, savagely. She felt his powerful hands turning her over, pulling her up on her knees.

'For God's sake,' she gasped, 'stop it! I'll scream.'

He smashed his arm across the back of her neck, and Eve started to lose consciousness. Dimly, she felt him raise her hips higher into the air. He pulled her cheeks apart, and his body pressed against hers.

There was a sudden, excruciating pain as he plunged deep inside her. She opened her mouth to scream, but she stopped in terror of what he might do to her.

She begged, 'Oh, please, you're hurting me . . .'

She tried to pull away from him, but he was holding her hips tightly, plunging into her again and again, tearing her apart with his enormous penis. The pain was unbearable.

'Oh, God, no!' she whispered. 'Stop it! Please stop it!'

He kept moving in, deeper and faster, and the last thing Eve remembered was a wild groan that came from deep inside him and seemed to explode in her ears.

When she regained consciousness and opened her eyes, George Mellis was sitting in a chair, fully dressed, smoking a cigarette. He moved over to the bed and stroked her forehead. She cringed from his touch.

'How do you feel, darling?'

Eve tried to sit up, but the pain was too great. She felt as though she had been ripped apart. 'You goddamned animal . . .' Her voice was a ragged whisper.

He laughed. 'I was gentle with you.'

She looked at him in disbelief.

He smiled. 'I can sometimes be very rough.' He stroked her hair again. 'But I love you, so I was kind. You'll get used to it, *Hree-se'e-moo*. I promise you.'

If she had had a weapon at that moment, Eve would have killed him. 'You're insane!'

She saw the gleam that came into his eyes, and she saw his hand clench into a fist, and in that instant she knew stark terror. He *was* insane.

She said quickly, 'I didn't mean it. It's just that I – I've never experienced anything like that before. Please, I'd like to go to sleep now. Please.'

George Mellis stared at her for a long moment, and then relaxed. He rose and walked over to the dressing table where Eve had put her jewellery. There was a platinum bracelet and an expensive diamond necklace lying there. He scooped up the necklace, examined it and slipped it into his pocket. 'I'll keep this as a little souvenir.'

She was afraid to open her mouth to protest.

'Good night, darling.' And he walked back to the bed, leaned over and gently kissed Eve's lips.

She waited until he had gone, and then crawled out of bed, her body burning with pain. Every step was an agony. It was not until she had locked the bedroom door that she felt safe again. She was not sure she would be able to make it to the bathroom, and she fell back onto the bed, waiting for the pain to recede. She couldn't believe the enormity of the rage she felt. He had sodomized her – horribly and brutally. She wondered what he had done to that other girl who had wanted to commit suicide.

When Eve finally dragged herself into the bathroom and looked in the mirror, she was aghast.

Her face was bruised and discoloured where he had hit her, and one eye was almost swollen shut. She ran a hot bath and crawled into it like a wounded animal, letting the soothing water wash away the pain. Eve lay there for a long time, and, finally, when the water was starting to cool, she got out of the tub and took a few tentative steps. The pain had lessened, but it was still agonizing. She lay awake for the rest of the night, terrified that he might return.

When Eve arose at dawn, she saw that the sheets were stained with her blood. She was going to make him pay for that. She walked into the bathroom, moving carefully, and ran another hot bath. Her face was even more swollen and the bruises were livid. She dipped a washcloth into cold water and applied it to her cheek and eye. Then she lay in the tub, thinking about George Mellis. There was something puzzling about his behaviour that had nothing to do with his sadism. And she suddenly realized what it was. The necklace. Why had he taken it?

Two hours later, Eve went downstairs to join the other guests for breakfast, even though she had no appetite. She badly needed to talk to Nita Ludwig.

'My God! What happened to your face?' Nita asked.

Eve smiled ruefully. 'The silliest thing. I got up in the middle of the night to go to the loo, and I didn't bother turning on the light. I walked right into one of your fancy doors.'

'Would you like to have a doctor look at that?'

'It's nothing,' Eve assured her. 'It's just a little bruise.' Eve looked around. 'Where's George Mellis?'

'He's out playing tennis. He's one of the top-seeded players. He said to tell you he'll see you at lunch. I think he really likes you, darling.'

'Tell me about him,' Eve said casually. 'What's his background?'

'George? He comes from a long line of wealthy Greeks. He's the oldest son, and he's filthy rich. He works at a New York brokerage firm, Hanson and Hanson.'

'He's not in the family business?'

'No. He probably hates olives. Anyway, with the Mellis fortune, he doesn't have to work. I suppose he does it just to occupy his days.' She grinned and said, 'His nights are full enough.'

'Are they?'

'Darling, George Mellis is the most eligible bachelor around. The girls can't wait to pull their little panties down for him. They all see themselves as the future Mrs Mellis. Frankly, if my husband weren't so damned jealous, I'd go for George myself. Isn't he a gorgeous hunk of animal?'

'Gorgeous,' Eve said.

George Mellis walked onto the terrace where Eve was seated alone, and in spite of herself, she felt a stab of fear.

498

He walked up to her and said, 'Good morning, Eve. Are you all right?' His face was filled with genuine concern. He touched her bruised cheek gently. 'My darling, you are so beautiful.' He pulled up a chair and straddled it, sitting across from her, and gestured towards the sparkling sea. 'Have you ever seen anything so lovely?'

It was as though the previous night had never happened. She listened to George Mellis as he went on talking, and she felt once again the powerful magnetism of the man. Even after the nightmare she had experienced, she could still feel that. It was incredible. *He looks like a Greek god. He belongs in a museum. He belongs in an insane asylum.*

'I have to return to New York tonight,' George Mellis was saying. 'Where can I call you?'

'I just moved,' Eve said quickly. 'I don't have a telephone yet. Let me call you.'

'All right, my darling.' He grinned. 'You really enjoyed last night, didn't you?'

Eve could not believe her ears.

'I have many things to teach you, Eve,' he whispered.

And I have something to teach you, Mr Mellis, Eve promised herself.

The moment she returned home, Eve telephoned Dorothy Hollister. In New York, where an insatiable segment of the media covered the comings and goings of the so-called beautiful people, Dorothy was the fountainhead of information. She had been married to a socialite, and when he divorced her for his twenty-one-year-old secretary, Dorothy Hollister was forced to go to work. She took a job that suited her talents well: she became a gossip columnist. Because she knew everyone in the milieu she was writing about, and because they believed she could be trusted, few people kept any secrets from her.

If anyone could tell Eve about George Mellis, it would be Dorothy Hollister. Eve invited her to lunch at La Pyramide. Hollister was a heavyset woman with a fleshy face, dyed red hair, a loud, raucous voice and a braying laugh. She was loaded down with jewellery – all fake.

When they had ordered, Eve said casually, 'I was in the Bahamas last week. It was lovely there.'

'I know you were,' Dorothy Hollister said. 'I have Nita Ludwig's guest list. Was it a fun party?'

Eve shrugged. 'I saw a lot of old friends. I met an interesting man named' – she paused, her brow wrinkled in thought – 'George somebody. Miller, I think. A Greek.'

Dorothy Hollister laughed, a loud, booming laugh that could be heard across the room. 'Mellis, dear. George Mellis.'

'That's right. Mellis. Do you know him?'

'I've seen him. I thought I was going to turn into a pillar of salt. My God, he's fantastic looking.'

'What's his background, Dorothy?'

Dorothy Hollister looked around, then leaned forwards confidentially. 'No one know this, but you'll keep it to yourself, won't you? George is the black sheep of the family. His family is in the wholesale food business, and they're too rich for words, my dear. George was supposed to take over the business, but he got in so many scrapes over there with girls and boys and goats, for all I know, that his father and his brothers finally got fed up and shipped him out of the country.'

Eve was absorbing every word.

'They cut the poor boy off without a drachma, so he had to go to work to support himself.'

So that explained the necklace!

'Of course, he doesn't have to worry. One of these days George will marry rich.' She looked over at Eve and asked, 'Are you interested, sweetie?'

'Not really.'

Eve was more than interested. George Mellis might be the key she had been looking for. The key to her fortune.

Early the next morning, she telephoned him at the brokerage firm where he worked. He recognized her voice immediately.

'I've been going mad waiting for your call, Eve. We'll have dinner tonight and –'

'No. Lunch, tomorrow.'

He hesitated, surprised. 'All right. I was supposed to have lunch with a customer, but I'll put him off.'

Eve did not believe it was a *him*. 'Come to my apartment,' Eve said. She gave him the address. 'I'll see you at twelve-thirty.'

'I'll be there.' She could hear the smug satisfaction in his voice.

George Mellis was due for a surprise.

He arrived thirty minutes late, and Eve realized it was a pattern with him. It was not a deliberate rudeness, it was an indifference, the knowledge that people would always wait for him. His pleasures would be there for him whenever he bothered to reach out and take them. With his incredible looks and charm, the world belonged to him. Except for one thing: he was poor. That was his vulnerable point.

George looked around the little apartment, expertly appraising the value of its contents. 'Very pleasant.'

He moved towards Eve, his arms outstretched. 'I've thought about you every minute.'

She evaded his embrace. 'Wait. I have something to tell you, George.'

His black eyes bored into hers. 'We'll talk later.'

'We'll talk now.' She spoke slowly and distinctly. 'If you ever touch me like that again, I'm going to kill you.'

He looked at her, his lips curved in a half smile. 'What kind of joke is that?'

'It's not a joke. I mean it. I have a business proposition for you.'

There was a puzzled expression on his face. 'You called me here to discuss business?'

'Yes. I don't know how much you make conning

502

silly old ladies into buying stocks and bonds, but I'm sure it's not enough.'

His face went dark with anger. 'Are you crazy? My family –'

'Your family is rich – you're not. My family is rich – *I'm* not. We're both in the same leaky rowboat, darling. I know a way we can turn it into a yacht.' She stood there, watching his curiosity get the better of his anger.

'You'd better tell me what you're talking about.'

'It's quite simple. I've been disinherited from a very large fortune. My sister Alexandra hasn't.'

'What does that have to do with me?'

'If you married Alexandra, that fortune would be yours – ours.'

'Sorry. I could never stand the idea of being tied down to anyone.'

'As it happens,' Eve assured him, 'that's no problem. My sister has always been accident-prone.'

TWENTY-SEVEN

Berkley and Matthews Advertising Agency was the diadem in Madison Avenue's roster of agencies. Its annual billings exceeded the combined billing of its two nearest competitors, chiefly because its major account was Kruger-Brent, Ltd., and its dozens of worldwide subsidiaries. More than seventy-five account executives, copywriters, creative directors, photographers, engravers, artists and media experts were employed on the Kruger-Brent account alone. It came as no surprise, therefore, that when Kate Blackwell telephoned Aaron Berkley to ask him if he could find a position in his agency for Alexandra, a place was found for her instantly. If Kate Blackwell had desired it, they would probably have made Alexandra president of the agency.

'I believe my granddaughter is interested in being a copywriter,' Kate informed Aaron Berkley.

Berkley assured Kate that there just happened

to be a copywriter vacancy, and that Alexandra could start any time she wished.

She went to work the following Monday.

Few Madison Avenue advertising agencies are actually located on Madison Avenue, but Berkley and Matthews was an exception. The agency owned a large, modern building at the corner of Madison and Fifty-seventh Street. The agency occupied eight floors of the building and leased the other floors. In order to save a salary, Aaron Berkley and his partner, Norman Matthews, decided Alexandra Blackwell would replace a young copywriter hired six months earlier. The word spread rapidly. When the staff learned the young woman who was fired was being replaced by the granddaughter of the agency's biggest client, there was general indignation. Without even having met Alexandra, the consensus was that she was a spoiled bitch who had probably been sent there to spy on them.

When Alexandra reported for work, she was escorted to the huge, modern office of Aaron Berkley, where both Berkley and Matthews waited to greet her. The two partners looked nothing alike. Berkley was tall and thin, with a full head of white hair, and Matthews was short, tubby and completely bald. They had two things in common: they were brilliant advertising men who had created some of the most famous slogans of the past decade; and they were absolute tyrants. They treated their employees like chattels, and the only reason the employees stood for such treatment was that anyone who had worked for Berkley and Matthews could work at any advertising agency in the world. It was *the* training ground.

Also present in the office when Alexandra arrived was Lucas Pinkerton, a vice-president of the firm, a smiling man with an obsequious manner and cold eyes. Pinkerton was younger than the senior partners, but what he lacked in age, he made up for in vindictiveness towards the men and women who worked under him.

Aaron Berkley ushered Alexandra to a comfortable armchair. 'What can I get you, Miss Blackwell? Would you like some coffee, tea?'

'Nothing, thank you.'

'So. You're going to work with us here as a copywriter.'

'I really appreciate your giving me this opportunity, Mr Berkley. I know I have a great deal to learn, but I'll work very hard.'

'No need for that,' Norman Matthews said quickly. He caught himself. 'I mean – you can't rush a learning experience like this. You take all the time you want.'

'I'm sure you'll be very happy here,' Aaron Berkley added. 'You'll be working with the best people in the business.'

One hour later, Alexandra was thinking. *They may be the best, but they're certainly not the friendliest.* Lucas Pinkerton had taken Alexandra around to introduce her to the staff, and the reception everywhere had been icy. They acknowledged her presence and then quickly found other things to do. Alexandra sensed their resentment, but she had no idea what had caused it. Pinkerton led her into a smoke-filled conference room. Against one wall was a cabinet filled with Clios and Art Directors' awards. Seated around a table were a woman and two men, all of them chain-smoking. The woman was short and dumpy, with rust-coloured hair. The men were in their middle thirties, pale and harassed-looking.

Pinkerton said, 'This is the creative team you'll be working with. Alice Koppel, Vince Barnes and Marty Bergheimer. This is Miss Blackwell.'

The three of them stared at Alexandra.

'Well, I'll leave you to get acquainted with one another,' Pinkerton said. He turned to Vince Barnes. 'I'll expect the new perfume copy on my desk by tomorrow morning. See that Miss Blackwell has everything she needs.' And he left.

'What do you need?' Vince Barnes asked.

The question caught Alexandra off guard. 'I – I guess I just need to learn the advertising business.'

Alice Koppel said sweetly, 'You've come to the right place, Miss Blackwell. We're dying to play teacher.'

'Lay off,' Marty Bergheimer told her.

Alexandra was puzzled. 'Have I done something to offend any of you?'

Marty Bergheimer replied, 'No, Miss Blackwell. We're just under a lot of pressure here. We're working on a perfume campaign, and so far Mr Berkley and Mr Matthews are underwhelmed by what we've delivered.

'I'll try not to be a bother,' Alexandra promised.

'That would be peachy,' Alice Koppel said.

The rest of the day went no better. There was not a smile in the place. One of their co-workers had been summarily fired because of this rich bitch, and they were going to make her pay.

At the end of Alexandra's first day, Aaron Berkley and Norman Mathews came into the little office Alexandra had been assigned, to make sure she was comfortable. The gesture was not lost on Alexandra's fellow workers.

Everyone in the agency was on a first-name basis – except for Alexandra. She was Miss Blackwell to everyone.

'Alexandra,' she said.

'Right.'

And the next time they addressed her, it was 'Miss Blackwell.'

Alexandra was eager to learn and to make a contribution. She attended think-tank meetings where the copywriters brainstormed ideas. She watched art editors draw up their designs. She listened to

Lucas Pinkerton tear apart the copy that was brought to him for approval. He was a nasty, mean-spirited man, and Alexandra felt sorry for the copy-writers who suffered under him. Alexandra found herself shuttling from floor to floor for meetings with department heads, meetings with clients, photographic sessions, strategy discussion meetings. She kept her mouth shut, listened and learned. At the end of her first week, she felt as though she had been there a month. She came home exhausted, not from the work but from the tension that her presence seemed to create.

When Kate asked how the job was going, Alexandra replied, 'Fine, Gran. It's very interesting.'

'I'm sure you'll do well, Alex. If you have any problems, just see Mr Berkley or Mr Matthews.'

That was the last thing Alexandra intended to do.

On the following Monday Alexandra went to work determined to find a way to solve her problem. There were daily morning and afternoon coffee breaks, and the conversation was easy and casual.

'Did you hear what happened over at National Media? Some genius there wanted to call attention to the great year they had, so he printed their financial report in *The New York Times* in red ink!'

'Remember that airline promotion: *Fly Your Wife Free?* It was a smash until the airline sent letters of appreciation to the wives and got back a flood of mail demanding to know who their husbands had flown with. They –'

Alexandra walked in, and the conversation stopped dead.

'Can I get you some coffee, Miss Blackwell?'

'Thank you, I can get it.'

There was silence while Alexandra fed a quarter into the coffee machine. When she left, the conversation started again.

'Did you hear about the Pure Soap foul-up? The angelic-looking model they used turned out to be a porno star . . .'

At noon Alexandra said to Alice Koppel, 'If you're free for lunch, I thought we might –'

'Sorry. I have a date.'

Alexandra looked at Vince Barnes. 'Me, too,' he said.

She looked at Marty Bergheimer. 'I'm all booked up.'

Alexandra was too upset to eat lunch. They were making her feel as though she were a pariah, and she found herself getting angry. She did not intend to give up. She was going to find a way to reach them, to let them know that deep down under the Blackwell name she was one of *them*. She sat at meetings and listened to Aaron Berkley and Norman Matthews and Lucas Pinkerton tongue-lash the creators who were merely trying to do their jobs as well as they could. Alexandra sympathized, but they did not want her sympathy. Or her.

Alexandra waited three days before trying again. She said to Alice Koppel, 'I heard of a wonderful little Italian restaurant near here –'

'I don't eat Italian food.'

She turned to Vince Barnes. 'I'm on a diet.'

Alexandra looked at Marty Bergheimer. 'I'm going to eat Chinese.'

Alexandra's face was flushed. They did not want to be seen with her. *Well, to hell with them. To hell with all of them.* She had had enough. She had gone out of her way to try to make friends, and each time she had been slapped down. Working there was a mistake. She would find another job somewhere with a company that her grandmother had nothing to do with. She would quit at the end of the week. *But I'm going to make you all remember I was here*, Alexandra thought grimly.

At one p.m. on Thursday, everyone except the receptionist at the switchboard was out to lunch. Alexandra stayed behind. She had observed that in the executive offices there were intercoms connecting the various departments, so that if an executive wanted to talk to an underling, all he had to do was press a button on the talk box where the employee's name was written on a card. Alexandra slipped into the deserted offices of Aaron Berkley and Norman Matthews and Lucas Pinkerton and spent the next hour changing all the cards around. Thus it was that early that afternoon Lucas Pinkerton pressed down the key that connected him to his chief copywriter and said, 'Get your ass in here. Now!'

There was a moment of stunned silence, then Norman Matthews's voice bellowed, 'What did you say?'

Pinkerton stared at the machine, transfixed. 'Mr Matthews, is that you?'

'You're damned right it is. Get *your* fucking ass in *here*. Now!' A minute later, a copywriter pressed down a button on the machine on his desk and said, 'I've got some copy for you to run downstairs.'

Aaron Berkley's voice roared back him. 'You *what*?'

It was the beginning of pandemonium. It took four hours to straighten out the mess that Alexandra had created, and it was the best four hours that the employees of Berkley and Matthews had ever known. Each time a fresh incident occurred, they whooped with joy. The executives were being buzzed to run errands, fetch cigarettes and repair a broken toilet. Aaron Berkley and Norman Matthews and Lucas Pinkerton turned the place upside down trying to find out who the culprit was, but no one knew anything.

The only one who had seen Alexandra go into the various offices was Fran, the woman on the switchboard, but she hated her bosses more than she hated Alexandra, so all she would say was, 'I didn't see a soul.'

That night when Fran was in bed with Vince Barnes, she related what had happened.

He sat up in bed. 'The *Blackwell* girl did it? I'll be a sonofabitch!'

The following morning when Alexandra walked into her office, Vince Barnes, Alice Koppel and Marty Bergheimer were there, waiting. They stared at her in silence. 'Is something wrong?' Alexandra asked.

'Not a thing, Alex,' Alice Koppel said. 'The boys and I were just wondering if you'd like to join us for lunch. We know this great little Italian joint near here . . .'

TWENTY-EIGHT

From the time she was a little girl, Eve Blackwell had been aware of her ability to manipulate people. Before, it had always been a game with her, but now it was deadly serious. She had been treated shabbily, deprived of a vast fortune that was rightfully hers, by her scheming sister and her vindictive old grandmother. They were going to pay in full for what they had done to her, and the thought of it gave Eve such intense pleasure that it almost brought her to orgasm. Their lives were now in her hands.

Eve worked out her plan carefully and meticulously, orchestrating every move. In the beginning, George Mellis had been a reluctant conspirator.

'Christ, it's too dangerous. I don't need to get involved in anything like this,' he argued. 'I can get all the money I need.'

'How?' Eve asked contemptuously. 'By laying a lot of fat women with blue hair? Is that how you want to spend the rest of your life? What happens when you put on a little weight and start to get a few wrinkles around your eyes? No, George, you'll never have another opportunity like this. If you listen to me, you and I can own one of the largest conglomerates in the world. You hear me? *Own* it.'

'How do you know this plan will work?'

'Because I'm the greatest living expert on my grandmother and my sister. Believe me, it will work.'

Eve sounded confident, but she had reservations and they concerned George Mellis. Eve knew she could do her part, but she was not sure George would be able to do his. He was unstable, and there was no room for error. One mistake, and the whole plan would fall apart.

She said to him now, 'Make up your mind. Are you in or out?'

He studied her for a long time. 'I'm in.' He moved close to her and stroked her shoulders. His voice was husky. 'I want to be all the way in.'

Eve felt a sexual thrill go through her. 'All right,' she whispered, 'but we do it my way.'

They were in bed. Naked, he was the most magnificent animal Eve had ever seen. And the most dangerous, but that only added to her excitement. She had the weapon now to control him. She nibbled at his body, slowly moving down towards his groin, tiny, teasing bites that made his penis grow stiff and hard.

515

'Fuck me, George,' Eve said.

'Turn over.'

'No. My way.'

'I don't enjoy that.'

'I know. You'd like me to be a tight-assed little boy, wouldn't you, darling? I'm not. I'm a woman. Get on top of me.'

He mounted her and put his tumescent penis inside her. 'I can't be satisfied this way, Eve.'

She laughed. 'I don't care, sweetheart. *I* can.'

She began to move her hips, thrusting against him, feeling him going deeper and deeper inside her. She had orgasm after orgasm, and watched his frustration grow. He wanted to hurt her, to make her scream with pain, but he dared not.

'Again!' Eve commanded. And he pounded his body into her until she moaned aloud with pleasure. 'Ahh-h-h . . . that's enough for now.'

He withdrew and lay at her side. He reached for her breasts, 'Now it's my –'

And she said curtly, 'Get dressed.'

He rose from the bed, trembling with frustration and rage. Eve lay in bed watching him put on his clothes, a tight smile on her face. 'You've been a good boy, George. It's time you got your reward. I'm going to turn Alexandra over to you.'

Overnight, everything had changed for Alexandra. What was to have been her last day at Berkley and Matthews had turned into a triumph for her. She had gone from outcast to heroine. News of her caper spread all over Madison Avenue.

'You're a legend in your own time,' Vince Barnes grinned.

Now she was one of them.

Alexandra enjoyed her work, particularly the creative sessions that went on every morning. She knew this was not what she wanted to do for the rest of her life, but she was not sure what she wanted. She had had at least a dozen proposals of marriage, and she had been tempted by one or two of them, but something had been lacking. She simply had not found the right man.

On Friday morning, Eve telephoned to invite Alexandra to lunch. 'There's a new French restaurant that just opened. I hear the food is marvellous.'

Alexandra was delighted to hear from her sister. She was concerned about Eve. Alexandra telephoned her two or three times a week, but Eve was either out or too busy to see her. So now, even though Alexandra had an engagement, she said, 'I'd love to have lunch with you.'

The restaurant was chic and expensive, and the bar was filled with patrons waiting for tables. Eve had had to use her grandmother's name in order to get a reservation. It galled her, and she thought, *Just wait. One day you'll be begging me to eat at your crummy restaurant.* Eve was already seated when Alexandra arrived. She watched Alexandra as the maître d' escorted her to the table, and she had the odd sensation she was watching herself approach the table.

Eve greeted her sister with a kiss on the cheek. 'You look absolutely marvellous, Alex. Work must agree with you.'

They ordered, and then caught up with each other's lives.

'How's the job going?' Eve asked.

Alexandra told Eve everything that was happening to her, and Eve gave Alexandra a carefully edited version of her own life. In the midst of their conversation, Eve glanced up. George Mellis was standing there. He was looking at the two of them, momentarily confused. *My God*, Eve realized, *he doesn't know which one I am!*

'George!' she said.

He turned to her in relief. 'Eve!'

Eve said, 'What a pleasant surprise.' She nodded towards Alexandra. 'I don't believe you've met my sister. Alex, may I present George Mellis.'

George took Alexandra's hand and said, 'Enchanted.' Eve had mentioned that her sister was a twin, but it had not occurred to him that they would be identical twins.

Alexandra was staring at George, fascinated.

Eve said, 'Won't you join us?'

'I wish I could. I'm afraid I'm late for an appointment. Another time, perhaps.' He looked at Alexandra. 'And soon, I hope.'

They watched him leave. 'Good heavens!' Alexandra said. 'Who was *that*?'

'Oh, he's a friend of Nita Ludwig. I met him at her house party.'

'Am I crazy, or is he as stunning as I think he is?'

Eve laughed. 'He's not my type, but women seem to find him attractive.'

'I would think so! Is he married?'

'No. But it's not because they aren't out there trying, darling. George is very rich. You might say he has everything: looks, money, social background.' And Eve skillfully changed the subject.

When Eve asked for the check, the captain told her it had been taken care of by Mr Mellis.

Alexandra was unable to stop thinking about George Mellis.

On Monday afternoon, Eve called Alexandra and said, 'Well, it looks like you made a hit, darling. George Mellis called me and asked for your telephone number. Is it all right to give it to him?'

Alexandra was surprised to find that she was smiling. 'If you're sure *you're* not interested in –'

'I told you, Alex, he's not my type.'

'Then I don't mind if you give him my number.'

They chatted a few minutes more, and Eve hung up. She replaced the receiver and looked up at George, who was lying next to her on the bed, naked. 'The lady said yes.'

'How soon?'

'When I tell you.'

Alexandra tried to forget that George Mellis was
going to telephone her, but the more she tried to
put him out of her mind, the more she thought
about him. She had never been particularly
attracted to handsome men, for she had found that
most of them were self-centred. But George Mellis,
Alexandra thought, seemed different. There was
an overpowering quality about him. The mere
touch of his hand had stirred her. *You're crazy*,
she told herself. *You've only seen the man for two
minutes.*

He did not call all that week, and Alexandra's
emotions went from impatience to frustration to
anger. *To hell with him*, she thought. *He's found
someone else. Good!*

When the phone rang at the end of the following week and Alexandra heard his deep, husky
voice, her anger dissipated as if by magic.

'This is George Mellis,' he said. 'We met briefly
when you and your sister were having lunch. Eve
said you wouldn't mind if I telephoned you.'

'She did mention that you might call,' Alexandra
said casually. 'By the way, thank you for the lunch.'

'You deserve a feast. You deserve a monument.'

Alexandra laughed, enjoying his extravagance.

'I wonder if you would care to have dinner with
me one evening?'

'Why – I – yes. That would be nice.'

'Wonderful. If you had said no, I should have killed myself.'

'Please don't,' Alexandra said. 'I hate eating alone.'

'So do I. I know a little restaurant on Mulberry Street: Matoon's. It's very obscure, but the food is –'

'*Matoon's!* I love it!' Alexandra exclaimed. 'It's my favourite.'

'You know it?' There was surprise in his voice.

'Oh, yes.'

George looked over at Eve and grinned. He had to admire her ingenuity. She had briefed him on all of Alexandra's likes and dislikes. George Mellis knew everything there was to know about Eve's sister.

When George finally replaced the receiver, Eve thought, *It's started.*

It was the most enchanting evening of Alexandra's life. One hour before George Mellis was due, a dozen pink balloons arrived, with an orchid attached. Alexandra had been filled with a fear that her imagination might have led her to expect too much, but the moment she saw George Mellis again, all her doubts were swept away. She felt once again his overpowering magnetism.

They had a drink at the house and then went on to the restaurant.

'Would you like to look at the menu?' George asked. 'Or shall I order for you?'

Alexandra had her favourite dishes here, but she wanted to please George. 'Why don't you order?'

He chose every one of Alexandra's favourites, and she had the heady feeling he was reading her mind. They dined on stuffed artichokes, veal Matoon, a speciality of the house, and angel hair, a delicate pasta. They had a salad that George mixed at the table with a deft skill.

'Do you cook?' Alexandra asked.

'Ah, it's one of the passions of my life. My mother taught me. She was a brilliant cook.'

'Are you close to your family, George?'

He smiled, and Alexandra thought it was the most attractive smile she had ever seen.

'I'm Greek,' he said simply. 'I'm the oldest of three brothers and two sisters, and we are like one.' A look of sadness came into his eyes. 'Leaving them was the most difficult thing I ever had to do. My father and my brothers begged me to stay. We have a large business, and they felt I was needed there.'

'Why didn't you stay?'

'I will probably seem a fool to you, but I prefer to make my own way. It has always been difficult for me to accept gifts from anyone, and the business was a gift handed down from my grandfather to my father. No, I will take nothing from my father. Let my brothers have my share.'

How Alexandra admired him.

'Besides,' George added softly, 'if I had stayed in Greece, I never would have met you.'

Alexandra felt herself blushing. 'You've never been married?'

'No. I used to get engaged once a day,' he teased, 'but at the last moment I always felt there was something wrong.' He leaned forwards, and his voice was earnest. 'Beautiful Alexandra, you are going to think me very old-fashioned, but when I get married, it will be forever. One woman is enough for me, but it must be the right woman.'

'I think that's lovely,' she murmured.

'And you?' George Mellis asked. 'Have you ever been in love?'

'No.'

'How unlucky for someone,' he said. 'But how lucky for –'

At that moment, the waiter appeared with dessert. Alexandra was dying to ask George to finish the sentence, but she was afraid to.

Alexandra had never felt so completely at ease with anyone. George Mellis seemed so genuinely interested in her that she found herself telling him about her childhood, her life, the experiences she had stored up and treasured.

George Mellis prided himself on being an expert on women. He knew that beautiful women were usually the most insecure, for men concentrated on that beauty, leaving the women feeling like objects rather than human beings. When George was with a beautiful woman, he never mentioned her looks. He made the woman feel that he was interested in her mind, her feelings, that he was a soul mate sharing her dreams. It was an extra-ordinary experience for Alexandra. She told George about Kate, and about Eve.

'Your sister does not live with you and your grandmother?'

'No. She – Eve wanted an apartment of her own.'

Alexandra could not imagine why George Mellis had not been attracted to her sister. Whatever the reason, Alexandra was grateful. During the course of the dinner, Alexandra noted that every woman in the place was aware of George, but not once did he look around or take his eyes from her.

Over coffee, George said, 'I don't know if you like jazz, but there's a club on St Mark's Place called the Five Spot . . .'

'Where Cecil Taylor plays!'

He looked at Alexandra in astonishment. 'You've been there?'

'Often!' Alexandra laughed. 'I love him! It's incredible how we share the same tastes.'

George replied quietly, 'It's like some kind of miracle.'

They listened to Cecil Taylor's spellbinding piano playing, long solos that rocked the room with arpeggios and rippling glissandi. From there they went to a bar on Bleecker Street, where the customers drank, ate popcorn, threw darts and listened to good piano music. Alexandra watched as George got into a darts contest with one of the regular patrons. The man was good, but he never had a chance. George played with a grim intensity that was almost frightening. It was only a game, but he played it as though it meant life or death. *He's a man who has to win*, Alexandra thought.

It was two a.m. when they left the bar, and Alexandra hated for the evening to end.

George sat beside Alexandra in the chauffeur-driven Rolls-Royce he had rented. He did not speak. He just looked at her. The resemblance between the two sisters was startling. *I wonder if their bodies are alike*. He visualized Alexandra in bed with him, writhing and screaming with pain.

'What are you thinking?' Alexandra asked.

He looked away from her so she could not read his eyes. 'You'll laugh at me.'

'I won't. I promise.'

'I wouldn't blame you if you did. I suppose I'm considered something of a playboy. You know the life – yachting trips and parties, and all the rest of it.'

'Yes . . .'

He fixed his dark eyes on Alexandra. 'I think you are the one woman who could change all that. Forever.'

Alexandra felt her pulse quicken. 'I – I don't know what to say.'

'Please. Don't say anything.' His lips were very close to hers, and Alexandra was ready. But he made no move. *Don't make any advances*, Eve had warned. *Not on the first night. If you do, you become one of a long line of Romeos dying to get*

525

their hands on her and her fortune. She has to make the first move.

And so, George Mellis merely held Alexandra's hand in his until the car glided to a smooth stop in front of the Blackwell mansion. George escorted Alexandra to her front door. She turned to him and said, 'I can't tell you how much I've enjoyed this evening.'

'It was magic for me.'

Alexandra's smile was bright enough to light up the street.

'Good night, George,' she whispered. And she disappeared inside.

Fifteen minutes later, Alexandra's phone rang. 'Do you know what I just did? I telephoned my family. I told them about the wonderful woman I was with tonight. Sleep well, lovely Alexandra.'

When he hung up, George Mellis thought, *After we're married, I will call my family. And I'll tell them all to go fuck themselves.*

TWENTY-NINE

Alexandra did not hear from George Mellis again. Not that day, or the next, or the rest of that week. Every time the phone rang, she rushed to pick it up, but she was always disappointed. She could not imagine what had gone wrong. She kept replaying the evening in her mind: *I think you are the one woman who could change all that forever*, and *I telephoned my mother and father and brothers and told them about the wonderful woman I was with tonight*. Alexandra went through a litany of reasons why he had not telephoned her.

She had offended him in some way without realizing it.

He liked her too much, was afraid of falling in love with her and had made up his mind never to see her again.

He had decided she was not his type.

He had been in a terrible accident and was lying helpless in a hospital somewhere.

He was dead.

When Alexandra could stand it no longer, she telephoned Eve. Alexandra forced herself to make small talk for a full minute before she blurted out, 'Eve, you haven't heard from George Mellis lately, by any chance, have you?'

'Why, no. I thought he was going to call you about dinner.'

'We did have dinner – last week.'

'And you haven't heard from him since?'

'No.'

'He's probably busy.'

No one is that busy, Alexandra thought. Aloud she said, 'Probably.'

'Forget about George Mellis, darling. There's a very attractive Canadian I'd like you to meet. He owns an airline and . . .'

When Eve had hung up, she sat back, smiling. She wished her grandmother could have known how beautifully she had planned everything.

'Hey, what's eating you?' Alice Koppel asked.

'I'm sorry,' Alexandra replied.

She had been snapping at everyone all morning. It had been two full weeks since she had heard from George Mellis, and Alexandra was angry – not with him, but with herself for not being able to forget him. He owed her nothing. They were strangers who had shared an evening together, and she was acting as though she expected him to marry her, for God's sake. George Mellis could have any woman in the world. Why on earth would he want her?

Even her grandmother had noticed how irritable she had become. 'What's the matter with you, child? Are they working you too hard at that agency?'

'No, Gran. It's just that I – I haven't been sleeping well lately.'

When she did sleep, she had erotic dreams about George Mellis. *Damn him!* She wished Eve had never introduced him to her.

The call came at the office the following afternoon. 'Alex? George Mellis.' As though she didn't hear that deep voice in her dreams.

'Alex?' Are you there?'

'Yes, I'm here.' She was filled with mixed emotions. She did not know whether to laugh or cry. He was a thoughless, selfish, egotist, and she did not care whether she ever saw him again.

'I wanted to call you sooner,' George apologized, 'but I just returned from Athens a few minutes ago.'

Alexandra's heart melted. 'You've been in Athens?'

'Yes. Remember the evening we had dinner together?'

Alexandra remembered.

'The next morning Steve, my brother, telephoned me – My father had a heart attack.'

'Oh, George!' She felt so guilty for having thought such terrible things about him. 'How is he?'

'He's going to be all right, thank God. But I felt as though I was being torn in pieces. He begged me to come back to Greece and take over the family business.'

'Are you going to?' She was holding her breath.

'No.'

She exhaled.

'I know now that my place is here. There isn't one day or one hour that's gone by that I haven't thought about you. When can I see you?'

Now! 'I'm free for dinner this evening.'

He was almost tempted to name another of Alexandra's favourite restaurants. Instead he said, 'Wonderful. Where would you like to dine?'

'Anywhere. I don't care. Would you like to have dinner at the house?'

'No.' He was not ready to meet Kate yet. *Whatever you do, stay away from Kate Blackwell for now. She's your biggest obstacle.* 'I'll pick you up at eight o'clock,' George told her.

Alexandra hung up, kissed Alice Koppel, Vince Barnes and Marty Bergheimer and said, 'I'm off to the hairdresser. I'll see you all tomorrow.'

They watched her race out of the office.

'It's a man,' Alice Koppel said.

They had dinner at Maxwell's Plum. A captain led them past the crowded horseshoe bar near the front door and up the stairs to the dining room. They ordered.

'Did you think about me while I was away?' George asked.

'Yes.' She felt she had to be completely honest with this man – this man who was so open, so vulnerable. 'When I didn't hear from you, I thought something terrible might have happened. I – I got panicky. I don't think I could have stood it another day.'

Full marks for Eve, George thought. *Sit tight*, Eve had said. *I'll tell you when to call her.* For the first time George had the feeling the plan really was going to work. Until now he had let it nibble at the edges of his mind, toying with the idea of controlling the incredible Blackwell fortune, but he had not really dared believe it. It had been merely a game that he and Eve had been playing. Looking at Alexandra now, seated across from him, her eyes filled with naked adoration, George Mellis knew it was no longer just a game. Alexandra was his. That was the first step in the plan. The other steps might be dangerous, but with Eve's help, he would handle them.

We're in this together all the way, George, and we'll share everything right down the middle.

George Mellis did not believe in partners. When he had what he wanted, when he had disposed of Alexandra, then he would take care of Eve. That thought gave him enormous pleasure.

'You're smiling,' Alexandra said.

He put his hand over hers, and his touch warmed her. 'I was thinking how nice it was our being here

531

together. About our being *anywhere* together.' He reached into his pocket and pulled out a jewel box. 'I brought something for you from Greece.'

'Oh, George . . .'

'Open it, Alex.'

Inside the box was an exquisite diamond necklace.

'It's beautiful.'

It was the one he had taken from Eve. *It's safe to give it to her*. Eve had told him. *She's never seen it*.

'It's too much. Really.'

'It's not nearly enough. I'll enjoy watching you wear it.'

'I –' Alexandra was trembling. 'Thank you.'

He looked at her plate. 'You haven't eaten anything.'

'I'm not hungry.'

He saw the look in her eyes again and felt the familiar soaring sense of power. He had seen that look in the eyes of so many women: beautiful women, ugly women, rich women, poor women. He had used them. In one way or another, they had all given him something. But this one was going to give him more than all of them put together.

'What would you like to do?' His husky voice was an invitation.

She accepted it, simply and openly. 'I want to be with you.'

* * *

George Mellis had every right to be proud of his apartment. It was a tasteful jewel of a place, furnished by grateful lovers – men and women – who had tried to buy his affection with expensive gifts, and had succeeded, always temporarily.

'It's a lovely apartment,' Alexandra exclaimed.

He went over to her and slowly turned her around so that the diamond necklace twinkled in the subdued lighting of the room 'It becomes you, darling.'

And he kissed her gently, and then more urgently, and Alexandra was hardly aware when he led her into the bedroom. The room was done in tones of blue, with tasteful, masculine furniture. In the centre of the room stood a large, king-size bed. George took Alexandra in his arms again and found that she was shaking. 'Are you all right, *kale' mou?*'

'I – I'm a little nervous.' She was terrified that she would disappoint this man. She took a deep breath and started to unbutton her dress.

George whispered, 'Let me.' He began to undress the exquisite blonde standing before him, and he remembered Eve's words: *Control yourself. If you hurt Alexandra, if she finds out what a pig you really are, you'll never see her again. Do you understand that? Save your fists for your whores and your pretty little boys.*

And so George tenderly undressed Alexandra and studied her nakedness. Her body was exactly the same as Eve's: beautiful and ripe and full. He

533

had an overwhelming desire to bruise the white, delicate skin; to hit her, choke her, make her scream. *If you hurt her, you'll never see her again.*

He undressed and drew Alexandra close to his body. They stood there together, looking into each other's eyes, and then George gently led Alexandra to the bed and began to kiss her, slowly and lovingly, his tongue and fingers expertly exploring every crevice of her body until she was unable to wait another moment.

'Oh, please,' she said. 'Now. Now!'

He mounted her then, and she was plunged into an ecstasy that was almost unbearable. When finally Alexandra lay still in his arms and sighed. 'Oh, my darling. I hope it was as wonderful for you,' he lied and said, 'It was.'

She held him close and wept, and she did not know why she was weeping, only that she was grateful for the glory and the joy of it.

'There, there,' George said soothingly. 'Everything is marvellous.'

And it was.

Eve would have been so proud of him.

In every love affair, there are misunderstandings, jealousies, small hurts, but not in the romance between George and Alexandra. With Eve's careful coaching, George was able to play skilfully on Alexandra's every emotion. George knew Alexandra's fears, her fantasies, her passions and aversions, and he was always there, ready to give her exactly what she needed. He knew what made her laugh, and what made her cry. Alexandra was thrilled by his lovemaking, but George found it frustrating. When he was in bed with Alexandra, listening to her animal cries, her excitement aroused him to a fever pitch. He wanted to savage her, make her scream for mercy so he could have his own relief. But he knew if he did that he would destroy everything. His frustration kept growing. The more they made love, the more he grew to despise Alexandra.

There were certain places where George Mellis could find satisfaction, but he knew he had to be cautious. Late at night he haunted anonymous singles' bars and gay discos, and he picked up lonely widows looking for an evening's comfort, gay boys hungry for love, prostitutes hungry for money. George took them to a series of seedy hotels on the West Side, in the Bowery and in Greenwich Village. He never returned to the same hotel twice, nor would he have been welcomed back. His sexual partners usually were found either unconscious or semiconscious, their bodies battered and sometimes covered with cigarette burns.

George avoided masochists. They enjoyed the pain he inflicted, and that took away his pleasure. No, he had to hear them scream and beg for mercy, as his father had made him scream and beg for mercy when George was a small boy. His punishments for the smallest infractions were beatings that often left him unconscious. When George was eight years old and his father caught him and a neighbour's son naked together, George's father beat him until the blood ran from his ears and nose, and to make sure the boy never sinned again, his father pressed a lighted cigar to George's penis. The scar healed, but the deeper scar inside festered.

George Mellis had the wild, passionate nature of his Hellenic ancestors. He could not bear the thought of being controlled by anyone. He put up with the taunting humiliation Eve Blackwell inflicted upon him only because he needed her. When he had the Blackwell fortune in his hands, he intended to punish her until she begged him to kill her. Meeting Eve was the luckiest thing that had ever happened to him. *Lucky for me*, George mused. *Unlucky for her*.

Alexandra continually marvelled at how George always knew just what flowers to send her, what records to buy, what books would please her. When he took her to a museum, he was excited about the same paintings she loved. It was incredible to Alexandra how identical their tastes were. She looked for a single flaw in George Mellis, and she could find none. He was perfect. She grew more and more eager for Kate to meet him.

But George always found an excuse to avoid meeting Kate Blackwell.

'Why, darling? You'll love her. Besides, I want to show you off.'

'I'm sure she's wonderful,' George said boyishly.

'I'm terrified she'll think I'm not good enough for you.'

'That's ridiculous!' His modesty touched her. 'Gran will adore you.'

'Soon,' he told Alexandra. 'As soon as I get up my courage.'

He discussed it with Eve one night.

She thought about it. 'All right. You'll have to get it over with sooner or later. But you'll have to watch yourself every second. She's a bitch, but she's a smart bitch. Don't underestimate her for a second. If she suspects you're after anything, she'll cut your heart out and feed it to her dogs.'

'Why do we need her?' George asked.

'Because if you do anything to make Alexandra antagonize her, we'll all be out in the cold.'

Alexandra had never been so nervous. They were going to dine together for the first time, George and Kate and Alexandra, and Alexandra prayed that nothing would go wrong. She wanted more than anything in the world for her grandmother and George to like each other, for her grandmother to see what a wonderful person George was and for George to appreciate Kate Blackwell.

Kate had never seen her granddaughter so happy. Alexandra had met some of the most eligible young men in the world, and none of them had interested her, Kate intended to take a very close look at the man who had captivated her granddaughter. Kate had long years of experience with fortune hunters, and she had no intention of allowing Alexandra to be taken in by one.

She was eagerly looking forward to meeting Mr George Mellis. She had a feeling he had been reluctant to meet her, and she wondered why.

Kate heard the front doorbell ring, and a minute later Alexandra came into the drawing room leading a tall, classically handsome stranger by the hand.

'Gran, this is George Mellis.'

'At last,' Kate said. 'I was beginning to think you were avoiding me, Mr Mellis.'

'On the contrary, Mrs Blackwell, you have no idea how much I've been looking forward to this moment.' He was about to say, 'You're even more beautiful than Alex told me,' but he stopped himself.

Be careful. No flattery, George. It's like a red flag to the old lady.

A butler came in, fixed drinks and discreetly withdrew.

'Please sit down, Mr Mellis.'

'Thank you.'

Alexandra sat beside him on the couch, facing her grandmother.

'I understand you've been seeing quite a bit of my granddaughter.'

'That's been my pleasure, yes.'

Kate was studying him with her pale-grey eyes. 'Alexandra tells me you're employed by a brokerage firm.'

'Yes.'

'Frankly, I find it strange, Mr Mellis, that you should choose to work as a salaried employee when you could be heading a very profitable family business.'

'Gran, I explained that –'

'I would like to hear it from Mr Mellis, Alexandra.'

Be polite, but for Christ's sake, don't kowtow to her. If you show the slightest sign of weakness, she'll tear you apart.

'Mrs Blackwell, I'm not in the habit of discussing my personal life.' He hesitated, as though making a decision. 'However, under the circumstances, I suppose . . .' He looked Kate Blackwell in the eye and said, 'I'm a very independent man. I don't accept charity. If I had founded Mellis and Company, I would be running it today. But it was founded by my grandfather and built into a very profitable business by my father. It does not need me. I have three brothers who are perfectly capable of running it. I prefer being a salaried employee, as you call it, until I find something that I can build up myself and take pride in.'

Kate nodded slowly. This man was not what she had expected at all. She had been prepared for a playboy, a fortune hunter, the kind who had been pursuing her granddaughters ever since Kate could remember. This one appeared to be different. And yet, there was something disturbing about him that Kate could not define. He seemed almost *too* perfect.

'I understand your family is wealthy.'

All she has to believe is that you're filthy rich, and madly in love with Alex. Be charming. Keep your temper under control, and you've got it made.

'Money is a necessity, of course, Mrs Blackwell. But there are a hundred things that interest me more.'

Kate had checked on the net worth of Mellis and Company. According to the Dun & Bradstreet report, it was in excess of thirty million dollars.

'Are you close to your family, Mr Mellis?'

George's face lighted up. 'Perhaps too close.' He allowed a smile to play on his lips. 'We have a saying in our family, Mrs Blackwell. When one of us cuts his finger, the rest of us bleed. We are in touch with each other constantly.' He had not spoken to any member of his family for more than three years.

Kate nodded approvingly. 'I believe in closely knit families.'

Kate glanced at her granddaughter. There was a look of adoration on Alexandra's face. For one fleeting instant, it reminded Kate of herself and David in those long ago days when they were so much in love. The years had not dimmed the memory of how she had felt.

Lester came into the room. 'Dinner is served, madame.'

The conversation at dinner seemed more casual, but Kate's questions were pointed. George was prepared for the most important question when it came.

'Do you like children, Mr Mellis?'

She's desperate for a great-grandson . . . She wants that more than anything in the world.

George turned towards Kate in surprise. 'Like children? What is a man without sons and daughters? I am afraid that when I marry, my poor wife will be kept very busy. In Greece, a man's worth is measured by the number of children he has sired.'

He seems genuine, Kate thought. *But one can't be too careful. Tomorrow I'll have Brad Rogers run a check on his personal finances.*

Before Alexandra went to bed, she telephoned Eve. She had told Eve that George Mellis was coming to dinner.

'I can't wait to hear all about it, darling,' Eve had said. 'You must call me the moment he leaves. I want a full report.'

And now Alexandra was reporting. 'I think Gran liked him a lot.'

Eve felt a small *frisson* of satisfaction. 'What did she say?'

'She asked George a hundred personal questions. He handled himself beautifully.'

So he had behaved.

'Ah! Are you two lovebirds going to get married?'

'I – He hasn't asked me yet, Eve, but I think he's going to.'

She could hear the happiness in Alexandra's voice. 'And Gran will approve?'

'Oh, I'm sure she will. She's going to check on George's personal finances, but of course that will be no problem.'

Eve felt her heart lurch.

Alexandra was saying, 'You know how cautious Gran is.'

'Yes,' Eve said slowly. 'I know.'

They were finished. Unless she could think of something quickly.

'Keep me posted,' Eve said.

'I will. Good night.'

The moment Eve replaced the receiver, she dialled George Mellis's number. He had not reached home yet. She called him every ten minutes, and when he finally answered Eve said, 'Can you get your hands on a million dollars in a hurry?'

'What the hell are you talking about?'

'Kate is checking out your finances.'

'She knows what my family is worth. She –'

'I'm not talking about your family. I'm talking about you. I told you she's no fool.'

There was a silence. 'Where would I get hold of a million dollars?'

'I have an idea,' Eve told him.

When Kate arrived at her office the following morning, she said to her assistant, 'Ask Brad Rogers to run a personal financial check on George Mellis. He's employed by Hanson and Hanson.'

'Mr Rogers is out of town until tomorrow, Mrs Blackwell. Can it wait until then or –?'

'Tomorrow will be fine.'

At the lower end of Manhattan on Wall Street, George Mellis was seated at his desk at the brokerage firm of Hanson and Hanson. The stock exchanges were open, and the huge office was a bedlam of noise and activity. There were 225 employees working at the firm's headquarters: brokers, analysts, accountants, operators and customer representatives, and everyone was working at a feverish speed. Except for George Mellis. He was frozen at his desk, in a panic. What he was about to do would put him in prison if he failed. If he succeeded, he would own the world.

'Aren't you going to answer your phone?'

One of the partners was standing over him, and George realized that his phone had been ringing for – how long? He must act normally and not do anything that might arouse suspicion. He scooped up the phone. 'George Mellis,' and smiled reassuringly at the partner.

George spent the morning taking buy and sell orders, but his mind was on Eve's plan to steal a million dollars. *It's simple, George. All you have to do is borrow some stock certificates for one night. You can return them in the morning, and no one will be the wiser.*

Every stock brokerage firm has millions of dollars in stocks and bonds stored in its vaults as

543

a convenience to customers. Some of the stock certificates bear the name of the owner, but the vast majority are street-name stocks with a coded CUSIP number – the Committee of Uniform Security Identification Procedures – that identifies the owner. The stock certificates are not negotiable, but George Mellis did not plan to cash them in. He had something else in mind. At Hanson and Hanson the stocks were kept in a huge vault on the seventh floor in a security area guarded by an armed policeman in front of a gate that could only be opened by a coded plastic access card. George Mellis had no such card. But he knew someone who did.

Helen Thatcher was a lonely widow in her forties. She had a pleasant face and a reasonably good figure, and she was a remarkable cook. She had been married for twenty-three years, and the death of her husband had left a void in her life. She needed a man to take care of her. Her problem was that most of the women who worked at Hanson and Hanson were younger than she, and more attractive to the brokers at the office. No one asked Helen out.

She worked in the accounting department on the floor above George Mellis. From the first time Helen had seen George, she had decided he would make a perfect husband for her. Half a dozen times she had invited him to a home-cooked evening, as she phrased it, and had hinted that he would be served more than dinner, but George had always found an excuse. On this particular morning, when her telephone rang and she said, 'Accounting, Mrs Thatcher,' George Mellis's voice came over the line. 'Helen? This is George.' His voice was warm, and she thrilled to it. 'What can I do for you, George?'

'I have a little surprise for you. Can you come down to my office?'

'Now?'

'Yes.'

'I'm afraid I'm in the middle of –'

'Oh, if you're too busy, never mind. It will keep.'

'No, no. I – I'll be right down.'

George's phone was ringing again. He ignored it. He picked up a handful of papers and walked towards the bank of elevators. Looking around to make sure no one was observing him, he walked past the elevators and took the backstairs. When he reached the floor above, he checked to make sure Helen had left her office, then casually walked in as though he had business there. If he was caught – But he could not think of that. He opened the middle drawer where he knew Helen kept her access card to the vault. There it was. He picked it up, slipped it in his pocket, left the office and hurried downstairs. When he reached his desk, Helen was there, looking around for him.

'Sorry,' George said. 'I was called away for a minute.'

'Oh, that's all right. Tell me what the surprise is.'

'Well, a little bird told me it's your birthday,'

George said, 'and I want to take you to lunch today.' He watched the expression on her face. She was torn between telling him the truth and missing the chance of a lunch date with him.

'That's – very nice of you,' she said. 'I'd love to have lunch with you.'

'All right,' he told her. 'I'll meet you at Tony's at one o'clock.' It was a date he could have made with her over the telephone, but Helen Thatcher was too thrilled to even question it. He watched as she left.

The minute she was gone, George went into action. He had a lot to accomplish before he returned the plastic card. He took the elevator to the seventh floor and walked over to the security area where the guard stood in front of the closed grilled gate. George inserted the plastic card and the gate opened. As he started inside, the guard said, 'I don't think I've seen you here before.'

George's heart began to beat faster. He smiled. 'No. This isn't my usual territory. One of my customers suddenly decided he wanted to see his stock certificates, so I've got to dig them out. I hope it doesn't take me the whole blasted afternoon.'

The guard smiled sympathetically. 'Good luck.' He watched as George walked into the vault.

The room was concrete, thirty feet by fifteen feet. George walked back to the fireproof file cabinets that contained the stocks and opened the steel drawers. Inside were hundreds of stock certificates that represented shares of every company on the New York and American stock exchanges. The number of shares represented by each certificate was printed on the face of the certificate and ranged from one share to one hundred thousand shares. George went through them swiftly and expertly. He selected certificates of various blue-chip companies, representing a value of one million dollars. He slipped the pieces of paper into his inside jacket pocket, closed the drawer and walked back to the guard.

'That was fast,' the guard said.

George shook his head. 'The computers came up with the wrong numbers. I'll have to straighten it out in the morning.'

'Those damned computers,' the guard commiserated. 'They'll be the ruination of us all yet.'

When George returned to his desk, he found he was soaked with perspiration. *But so far so good.* He picked up the telephone and called Alexandra.

'Darling,' he said, 'I want to see you and your grandmother tonight.'

'I thought you had a business engagement tonight, George.'

'I did, but I cancelled it. I have something very important to tell you.'

At exactly one p.m. George was in Helen Thatcher's office returning the access card to her desk drawer, while she waited for him at the restaurant. He desperately wanted to hang on to the card,

547

for he would need it again, but he knew that every card that was not turned in each night was invalidated by the computer the next morning. At ten minutes past one, George was lunching with Helen Thatcher.

He took her hand in his. 'I want us to do this more often,' George said, looking at her searchingly. 'Are you free for lunch tomorrow?'

She beamed. 'Oh, yes, George.'

When George Mellis walked out of his office that afternoon, he was carrying with him one-million-dollars' worth of stock certificates.

He arrived at the Blackwell house promptly at seven o'clock and was ushered into the library, where Kate and Alexandra were waiting for him.

'Good evening,' George said. 'I hope this is not an intrusion, but I had to speak to you both.' He turned to Kate. 'I know this is very old-fashioned of me, Mrs Blackwell, but I would like your permission for your granddaughter's hand in marriage. I love Alexandra, and I believe she loves me. But it would make both of us happy if you would give us your blessing.' He reached into his jacket pocket, brought out the stock certificates and tossed them on the table in front of Kate. 'I'm giving her a million dollars as a wedding present. She won't need any of your money. But we both need your blessing.'

Kate glanced down at the stock certificates

George had carelessly scattered on the table. She recognized the names of every one of the companies. Alexandra had moved to George, her eyes shining. 'Oh, darling!' She turned to her grandmother, her eyes imploring, 'Gran?'

Kate looked at the two of them standing together, and there was no way she could deny them. For a brief instant, she envied them. 'You have my blessing,' she said.

George grinned and walked over to Kate. 'May I?' He kissed her on the cheek.

For the next two hours they talked excitedly about wedding plans. 'I don't want a large wedding, Gran,' Alexandra said. 'We don't have to do that, do we?'

'I agree,' George replied. 'Love is a private matter.'

In the end, they decided on a small ceremony, with a judge marrying them.

'Will your father be coming over for the wedding?' Kate inquired.

George laughed. 'You couldn't keep him away. My father, my three brothers and my two sisters will all be here.'

'I'll be looking forward to meeting them.'

'You'll like them, I know.' Then his eyes turned back to Alexandra.

Kate was very touched by the whole evening. She was thrilled for her granddaughter – pleased that she was getting a man who loved her so much. *I must remember*, Kate thought, *to tell*

Brad not to bother about that financial rundown on George.

Before George left, and he was alone with Alexandra, he said casually, 'I don't think it's a good idea to have a million dollars in securities lying around the house. I'll put them in my safe-deposit box for now.'

'Would you?' Alexandra asked.

George picked up the certificates and put them back into his jacket pocket.

The following morning George repeated the procedure with Helen Thatcher. While she was on her way downstairs to see him ('I have a little something for you'), he was in her office getting the access card. He gave her a Gucci scarf – 'a belated birthday present' – and confirmed his luncheon date with her. This time getting into the vault seemed easier. He replaced the stock certificates, returned the access card and met Helen Thatcher at a nearby restaurant.

She held his hand and said, 'George, why don't I fix a nice dinner for the two of us tonight?'

And George replied, 'I'm afraid that's impossible, Helen. I'm getting married.'

Three days before the wedding ceremony was to take place, George arrived at the Blackwell house, his face filled with distress. 'I've just had terrible news,' he said. 'My father suffered another heart attack.'

'Oh, I'm so sorry,' Kate said. 'Is he going to be all right?'

'I've been on the phone with the family all night. They think he'll pull through, but of course they won't be able to attend the wedding.'

'We could go to Athens on our honeymoon and see them,' Alexandra suggested.

George stroked her cheek. 'I have other plans for our honeymoon, *matia mou*. No family, just us.'

The marriage ceremony was held in the drawing room of the Blackwell mansion. There were fewer than a dozen guests in attendance, among them Vince Barnes, Alice Koppel and Marty Bergheimer, Alexandra had pleaded with her grandmother to let Eve attend the wedding, but Kate was adamant. 'Your sister will never be welcome in this house again.'

Alexandra's eyes filled with tears. 'Gran, you're being cruel. I love you both. Can't you forgive her?'

For an instant, Kate was tempted to blurt out the whole story of Eve's disloyalty, but she stopped herself. 'I'm doing what I think is best for everyone.'

A photographer took pictures of the ceremony, and Kate heard George ask him to make up some extra prints to send to his family. *What a considerate man he is*, Kate thought.

After the cake-cutting ceremony, George whispered to Alexandra, 'Darling, I'm going to have to disappear for an hour or so.'

551

'Is anything wrong?'

'Of course not. But the only way I could persuade the office to let me take time off for our honeymoon was to promise to finish up some business for an important client. I won't be long. Our plane doesn't leave until five o'clock.'

She smiled. 'Hurry back. I don't want to go on our honeymoon without you.'

When George arrived at Eve's apartment, she was waiting for him, wearing a filmy negligee. 'Did you enjoy your wedding, darling?'

'Yes, thank you. It was small but elegant. It went off without a hitch.'

'Do you know why, George? Because of me. Never forget that.'

He looked at her and said slowly, 'I won't.'

'We're partners all the way.'

'Of course.'

Eve smiled. 'Well, well. So you're married to my little sister.'

George looked at his watch. 'Yes. And I must get back.'

'Not yet,' Eve told him.

'Why not?'

'Because you're going to make love to me first, darling. I want to fuck my sister's husband.'

THIRTY

Eve had planned the honeymoon. It was expensive, but she told George, 'You mustn't stint on anything.'

She sold three pieces of jewellery she had acquired from an ardent admirer and gave the money to George.

'I appreciate this, Eve,' he said. 'I –'

'I'll get it back.'

The honeymoon was perfection. George and Alexandra stayed at Round Hill on Montego Bay, in the northern part of Jamaica. The lobby of the hotel was a small, white building set in the centre of approximately two dozen beautiful, privately owned bungalows that sprawled down a hill towards the clear, blue sea. The Mellises had the Noel Coward bungalow, with its own swimming pool and a maid to prepare their breakfast, which they ate in the open-air dining room. George rented a small boat and they went sailing and fishing.

They swam and read and played backgammon and made love. Alexandra did everything she could think of to please George in bed, and when she heard him moaning at the climax of their love-making, she was thrilled that she was able to bring him such pleasure.

On the fifth day, George said, 'Alex, I have to drive into Kingston on business. The firm has a branch office there and they asked me to look in on it.'

'Fine,' Alexandra said. 'I'll go with you.'

He frowned. 'I'd love you to, darling, but I'm expecting an overseas call. You'll have to stay and take the message.'

Alexandra was disappointed. 'Can't the desk take it?'

'It's too important. I can't trust them.'

'All right, then. Of course I'll stay.'

George rented a car and drove to Kingston. It was late afternoon when he arrived. The streets of the capital city were swarming with colourfully dressed tourists from the cruise ships, shopping at the straw market and in the small bazaars. Kingston is a city of commerce, with refineries, warehouses and fisheries, but with its landlocked harbour it is also a city of beautiful old buildings and museums and libraries.

George was interested in none of these things. He was filled with a desperate need that had been building up in him for weeks and had to be satisfied. He walked into the first bar he saw and spoke to the bartender. Five minutes later George was accompanying a fifteen-year-old black prostitute up the stairs of a cheap hotel. He was with her for two hours. When George left the room, he left alone, got into the car and drove back to Montego Bay, where Alexandra told him the urgent telephone call he was expecting had not come through.

The following morning the Kingston newspapers reported that a tourist had beaten up and mutilated a prostitute, and that she was near death.

At Hanson and Hanson, the senior partners were discussing George Mellis. There had been complaints from a number of clients about the way he handled their securities accounts. A decision had been reached to fire him. Now, however, there were second thoughts.

'He's married to one of Kate Blackwell's grand-daughters,' a senior partner said. 'That puts things in a new light.'

A second partner added, 'It certainly does. If we could acquire the Blackwell account . . .'

The greed in the air was almost palpable. They decided George Mellis deserved another chance.

When Alexandra and George returned from their honeymoon, Kate told them, 'I'd like you to move in here with me. This is an enormous house, and we wouldn't be in one another's way. You –'

George interrupted. 'That's very kind of you,'

he said. 'But I think it would be best if Alex and I had our own place.'

He had no intention of living under the same roof with the old woman hovering over him, spying on his every move.

'I understand,' Kate replied. 'In that case, please let me buy a house for you. That will be my wedding present.'

George put his arms around Kate and hugged her. 'That's very generous of you.' His voice was hoarse with emotion. 'Alex and I accept with gratitude.'

'Thank you, Gran,' Alexandra said. 'We'll look for a place not too far away.'

'Right,' George agreed. 'We want to be close enough to keep an eye on you. You're a damned attractive woman, you know!'

Within a week they found a beautiful old brownstone near the park, a dozen blocks away from the Blackwell mansion. It was a charming three-storey house, with a master bedroom, two guest bedrooms, servants' quarters, a huge old kitchen, a panelled dining room, an elegant living room and a library.

'You're going to have to do the decorating by yourself, darling,' George told Alexandra. 'I'm all tied up with clients.'

The truth was that he spent almost no time at the office, and very little time with clients. His days were occupied with more interesting matters. The police were receiving a string of assault reports from male and female prostitutes and lonely women who visited singles' bars. The victims described their attacker as handsome and cultured, and coming from a foreign background, possibly Latin. Those who were willing to look at police mug shots were unable to come up with an identification.

Eve and George were having lunch in a small downtown restaurant where there was no chance of their being recognized.

'You've got to get Alex to make a new will without Kate knowing about it.'

'How the hell do I do that?'

'I'm going to tell you, darling . . .'

The following evening George met Alexandra for dinner at Le Plaisir, one of New York's finest French restaurants. He was almost thirty minutes late.

Pierre Jourdan, the owner, escorted him to the table where Alexandra was waiting. 'Forgive me, angel,' George said breathlessly. 'I was at my attorney's, and you know how they are. They make everything so complicated.'

Alexandra asked, 'Is anything wrong, George?'

'No. I just changed my will.' He took her hands in his. 'If anything should happen to me now, everything I have will belong to you.'

'Darling, I don't want –'

'Oh, it's not much compared to the Blackwell fortune, but it would keep you very comfortably.'

'Nothing's going to happen to you. Not ever.'

'Of course not, Alex. But sometimes life plays funny tricks. These things aren't pleasant to face, but it's better to plan ahead and be prepared, don't you think?'

She sat there thoughtfully for a moment. 'I should change my will, too, shouldn't I?'

'What for?' He sounded surprised.

'You're my husband. Everything I have is yours.'

He withdrew his hand. 'Alex, I don't give a damn about your money.'

'I know that, George, but you're right. It *is* better to look ahead and be prepared.' Her eyes filled with tears. 'I know I'm an idiot, but I'm so happy that I can't bear to think of anything happening to either of us. I want us to go on forever.'

'We will,' George murmured.

'I'll talk to Brad Rogers tomorrow about changing my will.'

He shrugged. 'If that's what you wish, darling.' Then, as an afterthought, 'Come to think of it, it might be better if my lawyer made the change. He's familiar with my estate. He can coordinate everything.'

'Whatever you like. Gran thinks –'

He caressed her cheek. 'Let's keep your grandmother out of this. I adore her, but don't you think we should keep our personal affairs personal?'

'You're right, darling. I won't say anything to

Gran. Could you make an appointment for me to see your attorney tomorrow?'

'Remind me to call him. Now, I'm starved. Why don't we start with the crab. . . . ?'

One week later George met Eve at her apartment.

'Did Alex sign the new will?' Eve asked.

'This morning. She inherits her share of the company next week on her birthday.'

The following week, 49 percent of the shares of Kruger-Brent, Ltd., were transferred to Alexandra. George called to tell Eve the news. She said, 'Wonderful! Come over tonight. We'll celebrate.'

'I can't. Kate's giving a birthday party for Alex.'

There was a silence. 'What are they serving?'

'How the hell do I know?'

'Find out.' The line went dead.

Forty-five minutes later George called Eve back. 'I don't know why you're so interested in the menu,' he said nastily, 'since you aren't invited to the party, but it's *coquille Saint-Jacques, Chateaubriand*, a bibb lettuce salad, *Brie, cappuccino* and a birthday cake with Alex's favourite ice cream, Neapolitan. Satisfied?'

'Yes, George. I'll see you tonight.'

'No, Eve. There's no way I can walk out in the middle of Alex's –'

'You'll think of something.'

God damn the bitch! George hung up the phone

and looked at his watch. *God damn everything!* He had an appointment with an important client he had stood up twice already. Now he was late. He knew the partners were keeping him on only because he had married into the Blackwell family. He could not afford to do anything to jeopardize his position. He had created an image for Alexandra and Kate, and it was imperative that nothing destroy that. Soon he would not need any of them.

He had sent his father a wedding invitation, and the old man had not even bothered to reply. Not one word of congratulations. *I never want to see you again*, his father had told him. *You're dead, you understand? Dead.* Well, his father was in for a surprise. The prodigal son was going to come to life again.

Alexandra's twenty-third birthday party was a great success. There were forty guests. She had asked George to invite some of his friends, but he had demurred. 'It's your party, Alex,' he said. 'Let's just have your friends.'

The truth was that George had no friends. He was a loner, he told himself proudly. People who were dependent on other people were weaklings. He watched as Alexandra blew out the candles on her cake and make a silent wish. He knew the wish involved him, and he thought, *You should have wished for a longer life, darling.* He had to admit that Alexandra was exquisite looking. She was wearing a long white chiffon dress with delicate silver slippers and a diamond necklace, a present from Kate. The large, pear-shaped stones were strung together on a platinum chain, and they sparkled in the candlelight.

Kate looked at them and thought, *I remember our first anniversary, when David put that necklace on me and told me how much he loved me.*

And George thought, *That necklace must be worth a hundred and fifty thousand dollars.*

George had been aware all evening that several of Alexandra's female guests were eyeing him, smiling at him invitingly, touching him as they talked to him. *Horny bitches*, he thought contemptuously. Under other circumstances, he might have been tempted to risk it, but not with Alexandra's friends. They might not dare complain to Alexandra, but there was a chance they could go to the police. No, things were moving along too smoothly to take any unnecessary chances.

At one minute before ten o'clock, George positioned himself near the telephone. When it rang a minute later, he picked it up. 'Hello.'

'Mr Mellis?'

'Yes.'

'This is your answering service. You asked me to call you at ten o'clock.'

Alexandra was standing near him. He looked over at her and frowned. 'What time did he call?'

'Is this Mr Mellis?'

'Yes.'

'You left a ten o'clock call, sir.'

Alexandra was at his side.

'Very well,' he said into the phone. 'Tell him I'm on my way. I'll meet him at the Pan Am Clipper Club.'

George slammed the phone down.

'What's the matter, darling?'

He turned to Alexandra. 'One of the idiot partners is on his way to Singapore and he left some contracts at the office that he needs to take with him. I've got to pick them up and get them to him before his plane leaves.'

'*Now?*' Alexandra's voice was filled with dismay. 'Can't someone else do it?'

'I'm the only one they trust,' George sighed. 'You'd think I was the only capable one in the whole office.' He put his arms around her. 'I'm sorry, darling. Don't let me spoil your party. You go on and I'll get back as soon as I can.'

She managed a smile. 'I'll miss you.'

Alexandra watched him go, then looked around the room to make sure all her guests were enjoying themselves.

She wondered what Eve was doing on their birthday.

Eve opened the door to let George in. 'You managed,' she said. 'You're such a clever man.'

'I can't stay, Eve. Alex is –'

She took his hand. 'Come, darling. I have a surprise for you.' She led him into the small dining room. The table was set for two, with beautiful

562

silver and white napery and lighted candles in the centre of the table.

'What's this for?'

'It's my birthday, George.'

'Of course,' he said lamely. 'I – I'm afraid I didn't bring you a present.'

She stroked his cheek. 'Yes you did, love. You'll give it to me later. Sit down.'

'Thanks,' George said. 'I couldn't eat anything. I just had a big dinner.'

'Sit down.' There was no inflection to her voice.

George looked into her eyes, and sat down.

Dinner consisted of *Coquille Saint-Jacques*, *Chateaubriand*, a bibb lettuce salad, *Brie, cappuccino* and birthday cake with Neapolitan ice cream.

Eve sat across from him, watching George force the food down. 'Alex and I have always shared everything,' Eve told him. 'Tonight I'm sharing her birthday dinner. But next year there will be just one of us having a birthday party. The time has come, darling, for my sister to have an accident. And after that, poor old Gran is going to die of grief. It's going to be all ours, George. Now, come into the bedroom and give me my birthday present.'

He had been dreading this moment. He was a man, strong and vigorous, and Eve dominated him and made him feel impotent. She had him undress her slowly, and then she undressed him and skilfully excited him to an erection.

'There you are, darling,' She got astride him and

began slowly moving her hips. 'Ah, that feels so good . . . You can't have an orgasm, can you, poor baby? Do you know why? Because you're a freak. You don't like women, do you, George? You only enjoy hurting them. You'd like to hurt me, wouldn't you? Tell me you'd like to hurt me.'

'I'd like to kill you.'

Eve laughed. 'But you won't, because you want to own the company as much as I do . . . You'll never hurt me, George, because if anything ever happens to me, a friend of mine is holding a letter that will be delivered to the police.'

He did not believe her. 'You're bluffing.'

Eve raked a long, sharp nail down his naked chest. 'There's only one way you can find out, isn't there?' she taunted.

And he suddenly knew she was telling the truth. He was never going to be able to get rid of her! She was always going to be there to taunt him, to enslave him. He could not bear the idea of being at this bitch's mercy for the rest of his life. And something inside him exploded. A red film descended over his eyes, and from that moment on he had no idea what he was doing. It was as though someone outside himself was controlling him. Everything happened in slow motion. He remembered shoving Eve off him, pulling her legs apart and her cries of pain. He was battering at something over and over, and it was indescribably wonderful. The whole centre of his being was racked with a long spasm of unbearable bliss, and then another, and another, and he thought *Oh, God! I've waited so long for this*. From somewhere in the far distance, someone was screaming. The red film slowly started to clear, and he looked down. Eve was lying on the bed, covered with blood. Her nose was smashed in, her body was covered with bruises and cigarette burns and her eyes were swollen shut. Her jaw was broken, and she was whimpering out of the side of her mouth. 'Stop it, stop it, stop it . . .'

George shook his head to clear it. As the reality of the situation hit him, he was filled with sudden panic. There was no way he could ever explain what he had done. He had thrown everything away. Everything!

He leaned over her. 'Eve?'

She opened one swollen eye. 'Doctor . . . Get . . . a . . . doctor . . .' Each word was a drop of pain. 'Harley . . . John Harley.'

All George Mellis said on the phone was, 'Can you come right away? Eve Blackwell has had an accident.'

When Dr John Harley walked into the room, he took one look at Eve and the blood-spattered bed and walls and said, 'Oh, my God!' He felt Eve's fluttering pulse, and turned to George. 'Call the police. Tell them we need an ambulance.'

Through the mist of pain, Eve whispered, 'John . . .'

John Harley leaned over the bed. 'You're going to be all right. We'll get you to the hospital.'

She reached out and found his hand. 'No police . . .'

'I have to report this. I –'

Her grip tightened. 'No . . . police . . .'

He looked at her shattered cheekbone, her broken jaw and the cigarette burns on her body. 'Don't try to talk.'

The pain was excruciating, but Eve was fighting for her life. 'Please . . .' It took a long time to get the words out. 'Private . . . Gran would never . . . forgive me . . . No . . . police . . . Hit . . . run . . . accident . . .'

There was no time to argue. Dr Harley walked over to the telephone and dialled. 'This is Dr Harley.' He gave Eve's address. 'I want an ambulance sent here immediately. Find Dr Keith Webster and ask him to meet me at the hospital. Tell him it's an emergency. Have a room prepared for surgery.' He listened a moment, then said, 'A hit-and-run accident.' He slammed down the receiver.

'Thank you, Doctor,' George breathed.

Dr Harley turned to look at Alexandra's husband, his eyes filled with loathing. George's clothes had been hastily donned, but his knuckles were raw, and his hands and face were still spattered with blood. 'Don't thank me. I'm doing this for the Blackwells. But on one condition. That you agree to see a psychiatrist.'

'I don't need a –'

'Then I'm calling the police, you sonofabitch.

You're not fit to be running around loose.' Dr Harley reached for the telephone again.

'Wait a minute!' George stood there, thinking. He had almost thrown everything away, but now, miraculously, he was being given a second chance. 'All right. I'll see a psychiatrist.'

In the far distance they heard the wail of a siren.

She was being rushed down a long tunnel, and coloured lights were flashing on and off. Her body felt light and airy, and she thought, *I can fly if I want to*, and she tried to move her arms, but something was holding them down. She opened her eyes, and she was speeding down a white corridor on a gurney being wheeled by two men in green gowns and caps. *I'm starring in a play*, Eve thought. *I can't remember my lines. What are my lines?* When she opened her eyes again, she was in a large white room on an operating table.

A small, thin man in a green surgical gown was leaning over her. 'My name is Keith Webster. I'm going to operate on you.'

'I don't want to be ugly,' Eve whispered. It was difficult to talk. 'Don't let me be . . . ugly.'

'Not a chance,' Dr Webster promised. 'I'm going to put you to sleep now. Just relax.'

He gave a signal to the anaesthetist.

George managed to wash the blood off himself and clean up in Eve's bathroom, but he cursed as he glanced at his wristwatch. It was three o'clock in the morning. He hoped Alexandra was asleep, but when he walked into their living room, she was waiting for him.

'Darling! I've been frantic! Are you all right?'

'I'm fine, Alex.'

She went up to him and hugged him. 'I was getting ready to call the police. I thought something terrible had happened.'

How right you are, George thought.

'Did you bring him the contracts?'

'Contracts?' He suddenly remembered. 'Oh, those. Yes. I did.' That seemed like years ago, a lie from the distant past.

'What on earth kept you so late?'

'His plane was delayed,' George said glibly. 'He wanted me to stay with him. I kept thinking he'd take off at any minute, and then finally it got too late for me to telephone you. I'm sorry.'

'It's all right, now that you're here.'

George thought of Eve as she was being carried out on the stretcher. Out of her broken, twisted mouth, she had gasped, 'Go . . . home . . . nothing . . . happened . . .' But what if Eve died? He would be arrested for murder. If Eve lived, everything would be all right; it would be just as it was before. Eve would forgive him because she needed him.

George lay awake the rest of the night. He was thinking about Eve and the way she had screamed and begged for mercy. He felt her bones crunch again beneath his fists, and he smelled her burning flesh, and at that moment he was very close to loving her.

It was a stroke of great luck that John Harley was able to obtain the services of Keith Webster for Eve. Dr Webster was one of the foremost plastic surgeons in the world. He had a private practice on Park Avenue and his own clinic in lower Manhattan, where he specialized in taking care of those who had been born with disfigurements. The people who came to the clinic paid only what they could afford. Dr Webster was used to treating accident cases, but his first sight of Eve Blackwell's battered face had shocked him. He had seen photographs of her in magazines, and to see that much beauty deliberately disfigured filled him with a deep anger.

'Who's responsible for this, John?'

'It was a hit-and-run accident, Keith.'

Keith Webster snorted. 'And then the driver stopped to strip her and snuff out his cigarette on her behind? What's the real story?'

'I'm afraid I can't discuss it. Can you put her back together again?'

'That's what I do, John, put them back together again.'

It was almost noon when Dr Webster finally said to his assistants, 'We're finished. Get her into intensive care. Call me at the slightest sign of anything going wrong.'

The operation had taken nine hours.

Eve was moved out of intensive care forty-eight hours later. George went to the hospital. He had to see Eve, to talk to her, to make sure she was not plotting some terrible vengeance against him.

'I'm Miss Blackwell's attorney,' George told the duty nurse. 'She asked to see me. I'll only stay a moment.'

The nurse took one look at this handsome man and said, 'She's not supposed to have visitors, but I'm sure it's all right if you go in.'

Eve was in a private room, lying in bed, flat on her back, swathed in bandages, tubes connected to her body like obscene appendages. The only parts of her face visible were her eyes and her lips.

'Hello, Eve . . .'

'George . . .' Her voice was a scratchy whisper. He had to lean close to hear what she said.

'You didn't . . . tell Alex?'

'No, of course not.' He sat down on the edge of the bed. 'I came because –'

'I know why you came . . . We're . . . going ahead with it . . .'

He had a feeling of indescribably relief. 'I'm sorry about this, Eve. I really am. I –'

'Have someone call Alex . . . and tell her I've gone away . . . on a trip . . . back in a few . . . weeks . . .'

'All right.'

Two bloodshot eyes looked up at him. 'George . . . do me a favour.'

'Yes?'

'Die painfully . . .'

She slept. When she awakened, Dr Keith Webster was at her bedside.

'How are you feeling?' His voice was gentle and soothing.

'Very tired . . . What was the . . . matter with me?'

Dr Webster hesitated. The X rays had shown a fractured zygoma and a blowout fracture. There was a depressed zygomatic arch impinging on the temporal muscle, so that she was unable to open or close her mouth without pain. Her nose was broken. There were two broken ribs and deep cigarette burns on her posterior and on the soles of her feet.

'What?' Eve repeated.

Dr Webster said, as gently as possible, 'You had a fractured cheekbone. Your nose was broken. The bony floor where your eye sits had been shifted. There was pressure on the muscle that opens and closes your mouth. There were cigarette burns. Everything has been taken care of.'

'I want to see a mirror,' Eve whispered.

That was the last thing he would allow. 'I'm sorry,' he smiled. 'We're fresh out.'

She was afraid to ask the next question. 'How am I – how am I going to look when these bandages come off?'

'You're going to look terrific. Exactly the way you did before your accident.'

'I don't believe you.'

'You'll see. Now, do you want to tell me what happened? I have to write up a police report.'

There was a long silence. 'I was hit by a truck.'

Dr Keith Webster wondered again how anyone could have tried to destroy this fragile beauty, but he had long since given up pondering the vagaries of the human race and its capacity for cruelty. 'I'll need a name,' he said gently. 'Who did it?'

'Mack.'

'And the last name?'

'Truck.'

Dr Webster was puzzled by the conspiracy of silence. First John Harley, now Eve Blackwell.

'In cases of criminal assault,' Keith Webster told Eve, 'I'm required by law to file a police report.'

Eve reached out for his hand and grasped it and held it tightly. 'Please, if my grandmother or sister knew, it would kill them. If you tell the police . . . the newspapers will know. You mustn't . . . please . . .'

'I can't report it as a hit-and-run accident. Ladies don't usually run out in the street without any clothes on.'

'Please!'

He looked down at her, and was filled with pity. 'I suppose you could have tripped and fallen down the stairs of your home.'

She squeezed his hand tighter. 'That's exactly what happened . . .'

Dr Webster sighed. 'That's what I thought.'

Dr Keith Webster visited Eve every day after that, sometimes stopping by two or three times a day. He brought her flowers and small presents from the hospital gift shop. Each day Eve would ask him anxiously, 'I just lie here all day. Why isn't anyone doing anything?'

'My partner's working on you,' Dr Webster told her.

'Your partner?'

'Mother Nature. Under all those frightening-looking bandages, you're healing beautifully.'

Every few days he would remove the bandages and examine her.

'Let me have a mirror,' Eve pleaded.

But his answer was always the same: 'Not yet.'

He was the only company Eve had, and she began to look forward to his visits. He was an unprepossessing man, small and thin, with sandy, sparse hair and myopic brown eyes that constantly blinked. He was shy in Eve's presence, and it amused her.

'Have you ever been married?' she asked.

'No.'

'Why not?'

'I – I don't know. I guess I wouldn't make a very good husband. I'm on emergency call a lot.'

'But you must have a girl friend.'

He was actually blushing. 'Well, you know . . .'

'Tell me,' Eve teased him.

'I don't have a regular girl friend.'

'I'll bet all the nurses are crazy about you.'

'No. I'm afraid I'm not a very romantic kind of person.'

To say the least, Eve thought. And yet, when she discussed Keith Webster with the nurses and interns who came in to perform various indignities on her body, they spoke of him as though he were some kind of god.

'The man is a miracle worker,' one intern said. 'There's nothing he can't do with a human face.'

They told her about his work with deformed children and criminals, but when Eve asked Keith Webster about it, he dismissed the subject with, 'Unfortunately, the world judges people by their looks. I try to help those who were born with physical deficiencies. It can make a big difference in their lives.'

Eve was puzzled by him. He was not doing it for the money or the glory. He was totally selfless. She had never met anyone like him, and she wondered what motivated him. But it was an idle curiosity. She had no interest in Keith Webster, except for what he could do for her.

Fifteen days after Eve checked into the hospital, she was moved to a private clinic in upstate New York.

'You'll be more comfortable here,' Dr Webster assured her.

Eve knew it was much farther for him to travel to see her, and yet he still appeared every day.

'Don't you have any other patients?' Eve asked.

'Not like you.'

Five weeks after Eve entered the clinic, Keith Webster removed the bandages. He turned her head from side to side. 'Do you feel any pain?' he asked.

'No.'

'Any tightness?'

'No.'

Dr Webster looked up at the nurse. 'Bring Miss Blackwell a mirror.'

Eve was filled with a sudden fear. For weeks she had been longing to look at herself in a mirror. Now that the moment was here, she was terrified. She wanted her own face, not the face of some stranger.

When Dr Webster handed her the mirror, she said faintly, 'I'm afraid –'

'Look at yourself,' he said gently.

She raised the mirrow slowly. It was a miracle! There was no change at all; it was her face. She searched for the signs of scars. There were none. Her eyes filled with tears.

She looked up and said, 'Thank you,' and reached out to give Keith Webster a kiss. It was meant to be a brief thank-you kiss, but she could feel his lips hungry on hers.

He pulled away, suddenly embarrassed. 'I'm – I'm glad you're pleased,' he said.

Pleased! 'Everyone was right. You *are* a miracle worker.'

He said shyly, 'Look what I had to work with.'

THIRTY-ONE

George Mellis had been badly shaken by what had happened. He had come perilously close to destroying everything he wanted. George had not been fully aware before of how much the control of Kruger-Brent, Ltd., meant to him. He had been satisfied to live on gifts from lonely ladies, but he was married to a Blackwell now, and within his reach was a company larger than anything his father had ever conceived of. *Look at me, Papa. I'm alive again. I own a company bigger than yours.* It was no longer a game. He knew he would kill to get what he wanted.

George devoted himself to creating the image of the perfect husband. He spent every possible moment with Alexandra. They breakfasted together, he took her out to lunch and he made it a point to be home early every evening. On weekends they went to the beach house Kate Blackwell owned in East Hampton, on Long Island, or flew to Dark Harbor in the company Cessna 620. Dark

Harbor was George's favourite. He loved the rambling old house, with its beautiful antiques and priceless paintings. He wandered through the vast rooms. *Soon all this will be mine*, he thought. It was a heady feeling.

George was also the perfect grandson-in-law. He paid a great deal of attention to Kate. She was eighty-one, chairman of the board of Kruger-Brent, Ltd., and a remarkably strong, vital woman. George saw to it that he and Alexandra dined with her once a week, and he telephoned the old woman every few days to chat with her. He was carefully building up the picture of a loving husband and caring grandson-in-law.

No one would ever suspect him of murdering two people he loved so much.

George Mellis's sense of satisfaction was abruptly shattered by a telephone call from Dr John Harley.

'I've made arrangements for you to see a psychiatrist. Dr Peter Templeton.'

George made his voice warm and ingratiating. 'That's really not necessary any more, Dr Harley. I think –'

'I don't give a damn what you think. We have an agreement – I don't report you to the police, and you consult a psychiatrist. If you wish to break that agree –'

'No, no,' George said hastily. 'If that's what you want, fine.'

'Dr Templeton's telephone number is five-five-

five-three-one-six-one. He's expecting your call. Today.' And Dr Harley slammed down the receiver.

The damned busybody, George thought angrily. The last thing in the world he needed was to waste time with a shrink, but he could not risk Dr Harley's talking. He would call this Dr Templeton, see him once or twice and that would be the end of it.

Eve telephoned George at the office. 'I'm home.'

'Are you –?' He was afraid to ask. 'All right?'

'Come and see for yourself. Tonight.'

'It's difficult for me to get away just now. Alex and I –'

'Eight o'clock.'

He could hardly believe it. Eve stood in front of him, looking just as beautiful as ever. He studied her face closely and could find no sign of the terrible damage he had inflicted upon her.

'It's incredible! You – you look exactly the same.'

'Yes. I'm still beautiful, aren't I, George?' She smiled, a cat smile, thinking of what she planned to do to him. He was a sick animal, not fit to live. He would pay in full for what he had done to her, but not yet. She still needed him. They stood there, smiling at each other.

'Eve, I can't tell you how sorry I –'

She held up a hand. 'Let's not discuss it. It's over. Nothing has changed.'

But George remembered that something had

changed. 'I got a call from Harley,' he said. 'He's arranged for me to see some damned psychiatrist.'

Eve shook her head. 'No. Tell him you haven't time.'

'I tried. If I don't go, he'll turn in a report of the – the accident to the police.'

'Damn!'

She stood there, deep in thought. 'Who is he?'

'The psychiatrist? Someone named Templeton. Peter Templeton.'

'I've heard of him. He has a good reputation.'

'Don't worry. I can just lie on his couch for fifty minutes and say nothing. If –'

Eve was not listening. An idea had come to her, and she was exploring it.

She turned to George. 'This may be the best thing that could have happened.'

Peter Templeton was in his middle thirties, just over six feet, with broad shoulders, clean-cut features and inquisitive blue eyes, and he looked more like a quarterback than a doctor. At the moment, he was frowning at a notation on his schedule: *George Mellis – grandson-in-law of Kate Blackwell.*

The problems of the rich held no interest for Peter Templeton. Most of his colleagues were delighted to get socially prominent patients. When Peter Templeton had first begun his practice, he had had his share, but he had quickly found he was unable to sympathize with their problems. He had dowagers in his office literally screaming because they had not been invited to some social event, financiers threatening to commit suicide because they had lost money in the stock market, overweight matrons who alternated between feasting and fat farms. The world was full of problems, and Peter Templeton had long since decided that these were not the problems he was interested in helping to solve.

George Mellis. Peter had reluctantly agreed to see him only because of his respect for Dr John Harley. 'I wish you'd send him somewhere else, John,' Peter Templeton had said. 'I really have a full schedule.'

'Consider this a favour, Peter.'

'What's his problem?'

'That's your department. I'm just an old country doctor.'

'All right,' Peter had agreed. 'Have him call me.'

Now he was here. Dr Templeton pressed down the button on the intercom on his desk. 'Send Mr Mellis in.'

Peter Templeton had seen photographs of George Mellis in newspapers and magazines, but he was still unprepared for the overpowering vitality of the man. He gave new meaning to the word *charisma.*

They shook hands. Peter said, 'Sit down, Mr Mellis.'

George looked at the couch. 'Over there?'

'Wherever you're comfortable.'

George took the chair opposite the desk. George looked at Peter Templeton and smiled. He had thought he would dread this moment, but after his talk with Eve, he had changed his mind. Dr Templeton was going to be his ally, his witness.

Peter studied the man opposite him. When patients came to see him for the first time, they were invariably nervous. Some covered it up with bravado, others were silent or talkative or defensive. Peter could detect no signs of nervousness in this man. On the contrary, he seemed to be enjoying himself. *Curious*, Peter thought.

'Dr Harley tells me you have a problem.'

George sighed. 'I'm afraid I have two.'

'Why don't you tell me about them?'

'I feel so ashamed. That's why I – I insisted on coming to see you.' He leaned forwards in his chair and said earnestly, 'I did something I've never done before in my life, Doctor. I struck a woman.'

Peter waited.

'We were having an argument and I blacked out, and when I came to, I had . . . hit her.' He let his voice break slightly. 'It was terrible.'

Peter Templeton's inner voice told him he already knew what George Mellis's problem was. He enjoyed beating up women.

'Was it your wife you struck?'

'My sister-in-law.'

Peter had occasionally come across items about the Blackwell twins in newspapers or magazines when they appeared at charity events or society

582

affairs. They were identical, Peter recalled, and strikingly beautiful. So this man had hit his sister-in-law. Peter found that mildly interesting. He also found it interesting that George Mellis made it sound as though he had merely slapped her once or twice. If that had been true, John Harley would not have insisted that Peter see Mellis.

'You say you hit her. Did you hurt her?'

'As a matter of fact, I hurt her pretty badly. As I told you, Doctor, I blacked out. When I came to, I – I couldn't believe it.'

When I came to. The classic defence. I didn't do it, my subconscious did it.

'Do you have any idea what caused that reaction?'

'I've been under a terrible strain lately. My father has been seriously ill. He's had several heart attacks. I've been deeply concerned about him. We're a close family.'

'Is your father here?'

'He's in Greece.'

That Mellis. 'You said you had two problems.'

'Yes. My wife, Alexandra . . .' He stopped.

'You're having marital problems?'

'Not in the sense you mean. We love each other very much. It's just that –' He hesitated. 'Alexandra hasn't been well lately.'

'Physically?'

'Emotionally. She's constantly depressed. She keeps talking about suicide.'

'Has she sought professional help?'

George smiled sadly. 'She refuses.'

Too bad, Peter thought. *Some Park Avenue doctor is being cheated out of a fortune.* 'Have you discussed this with Dr Harley?'

'No.'

'Since he's the family doctor, I would suggest you speak with him. If he feels it's necessary, he'll recommend a psychiatrist.'

George Mellis said nervously, 'No. I don't want Alexandra to feel I'm discussing her behind her back. I'm afraid Dr Harley would –'

'That's all right, Mr Mellis. I'll give him a call.'

'Eve, we're in trouble,' George snapped. 'Big trouble.'

'What happened?'

'I did exactly as you told me. I said I was concerned about Alexandra, that she was suicidal.'

'And?'

'The sonofabitch is going to call John Harley and discuss it with him!'

'Oh, Christ! We can't let him.'

Eve began to pace. She stopped suddenly. 'All right. I'll handle Harley. Do you have another appointment with Templeton?'

'Yes.'

'Keep it.'

The following morning Eve went to see Dr Harley at his office. John Harley liked the Blackwell family. He had watched the children grow up. He had gone through the tragedy of Marianne's death and the attack on Kate, and putting Tony away in a sanatorium. Kate had suffered so much. And then the rift between Kate and Eve. He could not imagine what had caused it, but it was none of his business. His business was to keep the family physically healthy.

When Eve walked into his office, Dr Harley looked at her and said, 'Keith Webster did a fantastic job!' The only telltale mark was a very thin, barely visible red scar across her forehead. Eve said, 'Dr Webster is going to remove the scar in a month or so.'

Dr Harley patted Eve's arm. 'It only makes you more beautiful, Eve. I'm very pleased.' He motioned her to a chair. 'What can I do for you?'

'This isn't about me, John. It's about Alex.'

Dr Harley frowned. 'Is she having a problem? Something to do with George?'

'Oh, no,' Eve said quickly. 'George is behaving perfectly. In fact, it's George who's concerned about her. Alex has been acting strangely lately. She's been very depressed. Suicidal, even.'

Dr Harley looked at Eve and said flatly, 'I don't believe it. That doesn't sound like Alexandra.'

'I know. I didn't believe it either, so I went to see her. I was shocked by the change in her. She's in a state of deep depression. I'm really worried, John. I can't go to Gran about it – that's why I came to you. You've got to do something.' Her eyes misted. 'I've lost my grandmother. I couldn't bear to lose my sister.'

'How long has this been going on?'

'I'm not sure. I pleaded with her to talk to you about it. At first she refused, but I finally persuaded her. You've got to help her.'

'Of course I will. Have her come in tomorrow morning. And try not to worry, Eve. There are new medicines that work miracles.'

Dr Harley walked her to the door of his office. He wished Kate were not so unforgiving. Eve was such a caring person.

When Eve returned to her apartment, she carefully cold-creamed away the red scar on her forehead.

The following morning at ten o'clock, Dr Harley's receptionist announced, 'Mrs George Mellis is here to see you, Doctor.'

'Send her in.'

She walked in slowly, unsure of herself. She was pale, and there were dark circles under her eyes.

John Harley took her hand and said, 'It's good to see you, Alexandra. Now what's this I hear about your having problems?'

Her voice was low. 'I feel foolish bothering you, John. I'm sure there's nothing wrong with me. If Eve hadn't insisted, I never would have come. I feel fine, physically.'

'What about emotionally?'

She hesitated. 'I don't sleep very well.'

'What else?'

'You'll think I'm a hypochondriac . . .'

'I know you better than that, Alexandra.'

She lowered her eyes. 'I feel depressed all the time. Sort of anxious and . . . tired. George goes out of his way to make me happy and to think up things for us to do together and places for us to go. The problem is that I don't feel like doing anything or going anywhere. Everything seems so – hopeless.'

He was listening to every word, studying her. 'Anything else?'

'I – I think about killing myself.' Her voice was so soft he could barely hear her. She looked up at him and said, 'Am I going crazy?'

He shook his head. 'No. I don't think you're going crazy. Have you ever heard of anhedonia?'

She shook her head.

'It's a biological disturbance that causes the symptoms you've described. It's a fairly common condition, and there are some new drugs that make it easy to treat. These drugs have no side effects, and they're effective. I'm going to examine you, but I'm sure we won't find anything really wrong.'

When the examination was completed and she had gotten dressed again, Dr Harley said, 'I'm going to give you a prescription for Wellbutrin. It's part of a new generation of anti-depressants – one of the new wonder drugs.'

She watched listlessly as he wrote out a prescription.

'I want you to come back and see me a week from today. In the meantime, if you have any problems, call me, day or. night.' He handed her the prescription.

'Thank you, John,' she said. 'I just hope these will stop the dream.'

'What dream?'

'Oh, I thought I told you. It's the same one very night. I'm on a boat and it's windy, and I hear the sea calling. I walk to the rail and look down and I see myself in the water, drowning . . .'

She walked out of Dr Harley's office and onto the street. She leaned against the building, taking deep breaths. *I did it*, Eve thought exultantly. *I got away with it*. She threw the prescription away.

THIRTY-TWO

Kate Blackwell was tired. The meeting had gone on too long. She looked around the conference table at the three men and three women on the executive board. They all seemed fresh and vital. *So it's not the meeting that has been going on too long*, Kate thought. *I've gone on too long. I'll be eighty-two. I'm getting old.* The thought depressed her, not because she had any fear of dying, but because she was not ready yet. She refused to die until Kruger-Brent, Ltd., had a member of the Blackwell family running it. After the bitter disappointment with Eve, Kate had tried to build her future plans around Alexandra.

'You know I would do anything for you, Gran, but I'm simply not interested in becoming involved with the company. George would be an excellent executive . . .'

'Do you agree, Kate?' Brad Rogers was addressing her.

The question shook Kate out of her reverie. She

looked towards Brad guiltily. 'I'm sorry. What was the question?'

'We were discussing the Deleco merger.' His voice was patient. Brad Rogers was concerned about Kate Blackwell. In recent months she had started daydreaming during board meetings, and then just when Brad Rogers decided Kate was becoming senile and should retire from the board, she would come up with some stunning insight that would make everyone wonder why *he* had not thought of it. She was an amazing woman. He thought of their brief, long-ago affair and wondered again why it had ended so abruptly.

It was George Mellis's second visit to Peter Templeton. 'Has there been much violence in your past, Mr Mellis?'

George shook his head. 'No. I abhor violence.' *Make a note of that, you smug sonofabitch. The coroner is going to ask you about that.*

'You told me your mother and father never physically punished you.'

'That is correct.'

'Would you say you were an obedient child?'

Careful. There are traps here. 'About average, I suppose.'

'The average child usually gets punished at some time or another for breaking the rules of the grown-up world.'

George gave him a deprecating smile. 'I guess I didn't break any rules.'

He's lying, Peter Templeton thought. *The question is why? What is he concealing?* He recalled the conversation he had had with Dr Harley after the first session with George Mellis.

'He said he hit his sister-in-law, John and –'

'*Hit* her!' John Harley's voice was filled with indignation. 'It was butchery, Peter. He smashed her cheekbone, broke her nose and three ribs, and burned her buttocks and the soles of her feet with cigarettes.'

Paul Templeton felt a wave of disgust wash over him. 'He didn't mention that to me.'

'I'll bet he didn't,' Dr Harley snapped. 'I told him if he didn't go to you, I was going to report him to the police.'

Peter remembered George's words: *I feel ashamed. That's why I insisted on coming to see you.* So he had lied about that, too.

'Mellis told me his wife is suffering from depression, that she's talking about suicide.'

'Yes, I can vouch for that. Alexandra came to see me a few days ago. I prescribed Wellbutrin. I'm quite concerned about her. What's your impression of George Mellis?'

Peter said slowly, 'I don't know yet. I have a feeling he's dangerous.'

Dr Keith Webster was unable to get Eve Blackwell out of his mind. She was like a beautiful goddess, unreal and untouchable. She was outgoing and vivacious and stimulating, while he was shy and dull and drab. Keith Webster had never married, because he had never found a woman he felt was unworthy enough to be his wife. Apart from his work, his self-esteem was negligible. He had grown up with a fiercely domineering mother and a weak, bullied father. Keith Webster's sexual drive was low, and what little there was of it was sublimated in his work. But now he began to dream about Eve Blackwell, and when he recalled the dreams in the morning, he was embarrassed. She was completely healed and there was no reason for him to see her anymore, yet he knew he had to see her.

He telephoned her at her apartment. 'Eve? This is Keith Webster. I hope I'm not disturbing you. I – er – I was thinking about you the other day, and I – I was just wondering how you were getting along?'

'Fine, thank you, Keith. How are *you* getting along?' There was that teasing note in her voice again.

'Jus – just fine,' he said. There was a silence. He summoned up his nerve. 'I guess you're probably too busy to have lunch with me.'

Eve smiled to herself. He was such a deliciously timid little man. It would be amusing. 'I'd love to, Keith.'

'Would you really?' She could hear the note of surprise in his voice. 'When?'

'What about tomorrow?'

'It's a date.' He spoke quickly, before she could change her mind.

* * *

Eve enjoyed the luncheon. Dr Keith Webster acted like a young schoolboy in love. He dropped his napkin, spilled his wine and knocked over a vase of flowers. Watching him, Eve thought with amusement, *No one would ever guess what a brilliant surgeon he is.*

When the luncheon was over, Keith Webster asked shyly, 'Could we – could we do this again sometime?'

She replied with a straight face, 'We'd better not, Keith. I'm afraid I might fall in love with you.'

He blushed wildly, not knowing what to say.

Eve patted his hand. 'I'll never forget you.'

He knocked over the vase of flowers again.

John Harley was having lunch at the hospital cafeteria when Keith Webster joined him.

Keith said, 'John, I promise to keep it confidential; but I'd feel a lot better if you told me the truth about what happened to Eve Blackwell.'

Harley hesitated, then shrugged. 'All right. It was her brother-in-law, George Mellis.'

And Keith Webster felt that now he was sharing a part of Eve's secret world.

George Mellis was impatient. 'The money is there, the will has been changed – What the hell are we waiting for?'

Eve sat on the couch, her long legs curled up under her, watching him as he paced.

'I want to get this thing over with, Eve.'

He's losing his nerve, Eve thought. He was like a deadly coiled snake. Dangerous. She had made a mistake with him once by goading him too far, and it had almost cost her her life. She would not make that mistake again.

'I agree with you,' she said slowly. 'I think it's time.'

He stopped pacing. 'When?'

'Next week.'

The session was almost over and George Mellis had not once mentioned his wife. Now, suddenly he said, 'I'm worried about Alexandra, Dr Templeton. Her depression seems to be worse. Last night she kept talking about drowning. I don't know what to do.'

'I spoke to John Harley. He's given her some medication he thinks will help her.'

'I hope so, Doctor,' George said earnestly. 'I couldn't stand it if anything happened to her.'

And Peter Templeton, his ear attuned to the unspoken words, had the uneasy feeling he was witnessing a charade. There was a deadly violence in this man. 'Mr Mellis, how would you describe your past relationships with women?'

'Normal.'

'Did you ever get angry with any of them, lose your temper?'

George Mellis saw where the questions were leading. 'Never.' *I'm too damned smart for you, Doc.* 'I told you, I don't believe in violence.'

It was butchery, Peter. He smashed her cheekbone, broke her nose and three ribs, and burned her buttocks and the soles of her feet with cigarettes.

'Sometimes,' Peter said, 'to some people violence provides a necessary outlet, an emotional release.'

'I know what you mean. I have a friend who beats up whores.'

I have a friend. An alarm signal. 'Tell me about your friend.'

'He hates prostitutes. They're always trying to rip him off. So when he finishes with them, he roughs them up a little – just to teach them a lesson.' He looked at Peter's face, but saw no disapproval there. Emboldened, George went on. 'I remember once he and I were in Jamaica together. This little black hooker took him up to a hotel room, and after she got his pants off, she told him she wanted more money.' George smiled. 'He beat the shit out of her. I'll bet she won't try that on anyone again.'

He's psychotic, Peter Templeton decided. There was no friend, of course. He was boasting about himself, hiding behind an *alter ego*. The man was a megalomaniac, and a dangerous one.

Peter decided he had better have another talk with John Harley as quickly as possible.

The two men met for lunch at the Harvard Club. Peter Templeton was in a difficult position. He needed to get all the information he could about

George Mellis without breaching the confidentiality of the doctor-patient relationship.

'What can you tell me about George Mellis's wife?' he asked Harley.

'Alexandra? She's lovely. I've taken care of her and her sister, Eve, since they were babies.' He chuckled. 'You hear about identical twins, but you never really appreciate what that means until you see those two together.'

Peter asked slowly, 'They're identical twins?'

'Nobody could ever tell them apart. They used to play all kinds of pranks when they were little tykes. I remember once when Eve was sick and supposed to get a shot, I somehow wound up giving it to Alexandra.' He took a sip of his drink. 'It's amazing. Now they're grown up, and I still can't tell one from the other.'

Peter thought about that. 'You said Alexandra came to see you because she was feeling suicidal.'

'That's right.'

'John, how do you know it was Alexandra?'

'That's easy,' Dr Harley said. 'Eve still has a little scar on her forehead from the surgery after the beating George Mellis gave her.'

So that was a blind alley. 'I see.'

'How are you getting along with Mellis?'

Peter hesitated, wondering how much he could say. 'I haven't reached him. He's hiding behind a façade. I'm trying to break it down.'

'Be careful, Peter. If you want my opinion, the

man's insane.' He was remembering Eve lying in bed, in a pool of blood.

'Both sisters are heir to a large fortune, aren't they?' Peter asked.

Now it was John Harley's turn to hesitate. 'Well, it's private family business,' he said, 'but the answer is no. Their grandmother cut off Eve without a dime. Alexandra inherits everything.'

I'm worried about Alexandra, Dr Templeton. Her depression seems to be worse. She keeps talking about drowning. I couldn't stand it if anything happened to her.

It had sounded to Peter Templeton like a classic setup for murder – except that George Mellis was the heir to a large fortune of his own. There would be no reason for him to kill anyone for money. *You're imagining things*, Peter chided himself.

A woman was drowning in the cold sea, and he was trying to swim to her side, but the waves were too high, and she kept sinking under them and rising again. *Hold on*, he shouted. *I'm coming.* He tried to swim faster, but his arms and legs seemed leaden, and he watched as she went down again. When he reached the place where she had disappeared, he looked around and saw an enormous white shark bearing down on him. Peter Templeton woke up. He turned on the lights and sat up in bed, thinking about his dream.

Early the following morning, he telephoned Detective Lieutenant Nick Pappas.

Nick Pappas was a huge man, six feet four inches and weighing almost three hundred pounds. As any number of criminals could testify, not an ounce of it was fat. Lieutenant Pappas was with the homicide task force in the 'silk stocking' district in Manhattan. Peter had met him several years earlier while testifying as a psychiatric expert in a murder trial, and he and Pappas had become friends. Pappas's passion was chess, and the two met once a month to play.

Nick answered the phone. 'Homicide. Pappas.'

'It's Peter, Nick.'

'My friend! How go the mysteries of the mind?'

'Still trying to unravel them, Nick. How's Tina?'

'Fantastic. What can I do for you?'

'I need some information. Do you still have connections in Greece?'

'Do I!' Pappas moaned. 'I got a hundred relatives over there, and they all need money. The stupid part is I send it to them. Maybe you oughta analyse me.'

'Too late,' Peter told him. 'You're a hopeless case.'

'That's what Tina keeps telling me. What information do you need?'

'Have you ever heard of George Mellis?'

'The food family?'

'Yes.'

'He's not exactly on my beat, but I know who he is. What about him?'

'I'd like to know if he has any money.'

'You must be kiddin'. His family –'

'I mean money of his own.'

'I'll check it out, Peter, but it'll be a waste of time. The Mellises are rich-rich.'

'By the way, if you have anyone question George Mellis's father, tell him to handle it gently. The old man's had several heart attacks.'

'Okay. I'll put it out on the wire.'

Peter remembered the dream. 'Nick, would you mind making a telephone call instead? Today?'

There was a different note in Pappas's voice. 'Is there anything you'd like to tell me, Peter?'

'There's nothing to tell. I just want to satisfy my curiosity. Charge the phone call to me.'

'Damn right I will – and the dinner you're gonna buy me when you tell me what the fuck this is all about.'

'Deal.' Peter Templeton hung up. He felt a little better.

Kate Blackwell was not feeling well. She was at her desk talking on the telephone when she felt the sudden attack. The room started to spin, and she gripped her desk tightly until everything righted itself again.

Brad came into the office. He took one look at her pale face and asked, 'Are you all right, Kate?'

She let go of the desk. 'Just a little dizzy spell. Nothing important.'

'How long since you've had a medical checkup?'

'I don't have time for that nonsense, Brad.'

'Find time. I'm going to have Annette call and make an appointment for you with John Harley.'

'Bloody hell, Brad. Stop fussing, will you please?'

'Will you go see him?'

'If it will get you off my back.'

The following morning Peter Templeton's secretary said, 'Detective Pappas is calling on line one.'

Peter picked up the phone. 'Hello, Nick.'

'I think you and I better have a little talk, my friend.'

Peter felt a sudden anxiety stirring in him. 'Did you talk to someone about Mellis?'

'I talked to Old Man Mellis himself. First of all, he's never had a heart attack in his life, and second, he said as far as he's concerned, his son George is dead. He cut him off without a dime a few years ago. When I asked why, the old man hung up on me. Then I called one of my old buddies at headquarters in Athens. Your George Mellis is a real beauty. The police know him well. He gets his kicks beating up girls and boys. His last victim before he left Greece was a fifteen-year-old male prostitute. They found his body in a hotel, and tied him in with Mellis. The old man bought somebody off, and Georgie boy got his ass kicked out of Greece. For good. Does that satisfy you?'

It did more than satisfy Peter; it terrified him. 'Thanks, Nick. I owe you one.'

'Oh, no, pal. I think I'd like to collect on *this* one. If your boy's on the loose again, you'd better tell me.'

'I will as soon as I can, Nick. Give my love to Tina.' And Peter hung up. He had a lot to think about. George Mellis was coming in at noon.

Dr John Harley was in the middle of an examination when his receptionist said, 'Mrs George Mellis is here to see you, Doctor. She has no appointment, and I told her your schedule is –'

John Harley said, 'Bring her in the side door and put her in my office.'

Her face was paler than the last time, and the shadows under her eyes were darker. 'I'm sorry to barge in on you like this, John, but –'

'That's all right, Alexandra. What's the problem?'

'Everything. I – I feel awful.'

'Have you been taking the Wellbutrin regularly?'

'Yes.'

'And you still feel depressed?'

Her hands were clenched. 'It's worse than depression. It's – I feel desperate. I feel as though I have no control over anything anymore. I can't stand myself. I'm afraid I'm – I'm going to do something terrible.'

Dr Harley said reassuringly, 'There's nothing physically wrong with you. I'll stake my reputation on that. It's all emotional. I'm going to switch you to another drug, Nomifensine. It's very effective. You should notice a change within a few days.' He wrote out a prescription and handed it to her. 'If you don't feel better by Friday. I want you to call me. I may want to send you to a psychiatrist.'

Thirty minutes later, back in her apartment, Eve removed the pale foundation cream from her face and wiped away the smudges under her eyes.

The pace was quickening.

George Mellis sat opposite Peter Templeton, smiling and confident.

'How are you feeling today?'

'Much better, Doctor. These few sessions we've had have helped more than you know.'

'Have they? In what way?'

'Oh, just having someone to talk to. That's the principle the Catholic Church is built on, isn't it? Confession?'

'I'm glad you feel the sessions have been helpful. Is your wife feeling better?'

George frowned. 'I'm afraid not. She saw Dr Harley again, but she's talking about suicide more and more. I may take her away somewhere. I think she needs a change.'

It seemed to Peter that there was an ominous foreboding in those words. Could it be his imagination?

'Greece is a very relaxing place,' Peter said casually. 'Have you taken her there to meet your family?'

'Not yet. They're dying to meet Alex.' He grinned. 'The only problem is that every time Pop and I get together, he keeps trying to talk me into coming back and taking over the family business.'

And at that moment, Peter knew that Alexandra Mellis was in real danger.

Long after George Mellis had left Peter Templeton sat in his office going over his notes. Finally, he reached for the telephone and dialled a number.

'I want you to do me a favour, John. Can you find out where George Mellis took his wife on their honeymoon?'

'I can tell you right now. I gave them some shots before they left. They went to Jamaica.'

I have a friend who beats up whores . . . I remember once we were in Jamaica together. This little black whore took him up to a hotel room, and after she got his pants off, she told him she wanted more money . . . He beat the shit out of her. I'll bet she won't try that on anyone again.

Still, there was no proof that George Mellis was planning to kill his wife. John Harley had verified that Alexandra Mellis was suicidal. *It's not my problem*, Peter tried to tell himself. But he knew it *was* his problem.

Peter Templeton had had to work his way through school. His father had been the caretaker of a college in a small town in Nebraska, and even with a scholarship, Peter had not been able to afford to go to one of the Ivy League medical schools. He had been graduated from the University of Nebraska with honours and had gone on to study psychiatry. He had been successful from the start. His secret was that he genuinely liked people; he cared what happened to them. Alexandra Mellis was not a patient, yet he was involved with her. She was a missing part of the puzzle, and meeting her face-to-face might help him solve it. He took out George Mellis's file, found his home number and telephoned Alexandra Mellis. A maid summoned her to the phone.

'Mrs Mellis, my name is Peter Templeton. I'm –'

'Oh, I know who you are, Doctor. George has told me about you.'

Peter was surprised. He would have bet that George Mellis would not have mentioned him to his wife. 'I wondered if we could meet. Perhaps lunch?'

'Is it about George? Is something wrong?'

'No, nothing. I just thought we might have a talk.'

'Yes, certainly, Dr Templeton.'

They made an appointment for the following day.

They were seated at a corner table at La Grenouille. From the moment Alexandra had walked into the restaurant, Peter had been unable to take his eyes off her. She was dressed simply in a white skirt and blouse that showed off her figure, and she wore a single strand of pearls around her neck. Peter looked for signs of the tiredness and depression Dr Harley had mentioned. There were none. If Alexandra was aware of Peter's stare, she gave no sign of it.

'My husband is all right, isn't he, Dr Templeton?'

'Yes.' This was going to be much more difficult than Peter had anticipated. He was walking a very fine line. He had no right to violate the sanctity of the doctor-patient relationship, yet at the same time he felt that Alexandra Mellis must be warned.

After they had ordered, Peter said, 'Did your husband tell you why he's seeing me, Mrs Mellis?'

'Yes. He's been under a great strain lately. His partners at the brokerage firm where he works put most of the responsibility on his shoulders. George is very conscientious, as you probably know, Doctor.'

It was incredible. She was completely unaware of the attack on her sister. *Why had no one told her?*

'George told me how much better he felt having someone he could discuss his problems with.' She gave Peter a grateful smile. 'I'm very pleased that you're helping him.'

She was so innocent! She obviously idolized her husband. What Peter had to say could destroy her. How could he inform her that her husband was a psychopath who had murdered a young male prostitute, who had been banished by his family and who had brutally assaulted her sister? Yet, how could he *not?*

'It must be very satisfying being a psychiatrist,' Alexandra went on. 'You're able to help so many people.'

'Sometimes we can,' Peter said carefully. 'Sometimes we can't.'

The food arrived. They talked as they ate, and there was an easy rapport between them. Peter found himself enchanted by her. He suddenly became uncomfortably aware that he was envious of George Mellis.

'I'm enjoying this luncheon very much,' Alexandra finally said, 'but you wanted to see me for a reason, didn't you, Dr Templeton?'

The moment of truth had arrived.

'As a matter of fact, yes. I –'

Peter stopped. His next words could shatter her life. He had come to this luncheon determined to tell her of his suspicions and suggest that her husband be put in an institution. Now that he had met Alexandra, he found it was not so simple. He thought again of George Mellis's words: *She's not any better. It's the suicidal thing that worries me.* Peter thought he had never seen a happier, more normal person. Was that a result of the medication she was taking? At least he could ask her about that. He said, 'John Harley told me that you're taking –'

And George Mellis's voice boomed out. 'There

you are, darling! I called the house and they told me you'd be here.' He turned to Peter. 'Nice to see you, Dr Templeton. May I join you?'

And the opportunity vanished.

'*Why* did he want to meet Alex?' Eve demanded.

'I haven't the slightest idea,' George said. 'Thank God she left a message where she would be in case I wanted her. With Peter Templeton, for Christ's sake! I got over there fast!'

'I don't like it.'

'Believe me, there was no harm done. I questioned her afterwards, and she told me they didn't discuss anything in particular.'

'I think we'd better move up our plan.'

George Mellis felt an almost sexual thrill at her words. He had been waiting so long for this moment. 'When?'

'Now.'

THIRTY-THREE

The dizzy spells were getting worse, and things were beginning to blur in Kate's mind. She would sit at her desk considering a proposed merger and suddenly realize the merger had taken place ten years earlier. It frightened her. She finally decided to take Brad Roger's advice to see John Harley.

It had been a long time since Dr Harley had been able to persuade Kate Blackwell to have a checkup, and he took full advantage of her visit. He examined her thoroughly, and when he finished he asked her to wait for him in his office. John Harley was disturbed. Kate Blackwell was remarkably alert for her age, but there were disquieting signs. There was a definite hardening of the arteries, which would account for her occasional dizziness and weakened memory. She should have retired years ago, and yet she hung on tenaciously, unwilling to give the reins to anyone else. *Who am I to talk?* he thought. *I should have retired ages ago.*

Now, with the results of the examination in front of him, John Harley said, 'I wish I were in your condition, Kate.'

'Cut the soft-soap, John. What's my problem?'

'Age, mostly. There's a little hardening of the arteries, and –'

'Arteriosclerosis?'

'Oh. Is that the medical term for it?' Dr Harley asked. 'Whatever it is, you've got it.'

'How bad is it?'

'For your age, I'd say it was pretty normal. These things are all relative.'

'Can you give me something to stop these bloody dizzy spells? I hate fainting in front of a roomful of men. It looks bad for my sex.'

He nodded. 'I don't think that will be any problem. When are you going to retire, Kate?'

'When I have a great-grandson to take over the business.'

The two old friends who had known each other for so many years sized each other up across the desk. John Harley had not always agreed with Kate, but he had always admired her courage.

As though reading his mind, Kate sighed, 'Do you know one of the great disappointments of my life, John? Eve. I really cared for that child. I wanted to give her the world, but she never gave a damn about anyone but herself.'

'You're wrong, Kate. Eve cares a great deal about you.'

'Like bloody hell she does.'

'I'm in a position to know. Recently she' – he had to choose his words carefully – 'suffered a terrible accident. She almost died.'

Kate felt her heart lurch. 'Why – why didn't you tell me?'

'She wouldn't let me. She was so concerned you would be worried that she made me swear not to say a word.'

'Oh, my God.' It was an agonized whisper. 'Is – is she all right?' Kate's voice was hoarse.

'She's fine now.'

Kate sat, staring into space. 'Thank you for telling me, John. Thank you.'

'I'll write out a prescription for those pills.' When he finished writing the prescription, he looked up. Kate Blackwell had left.

Eve opened the door and stared unbelievingly. Her grandmother was standing there, stiff and straight as always, allowing no sign of frailty to show.

'May I come in?' Kate asked.

Eve stepped aside, unable to take in what was happening. 'Of course.'

Kate walked in and looked around the small apartment but she made no comment. 'May I sit down?'

'I'm sorry. Please do. Forgive me – this is so – Can I get you something? Tea, coffee, anything?'

'No, thank you. Are you well, Eve?'

'Yes, thank you. I'm fine.'

'I just came from Dr Harley. He told me you had been in a terrible accident.'

Eve watched her grandmother cautiously, not sure what was coming. 'Yes . . .'

'He said you were . . . near death. And that you would not allow him to tell me because you didn't want to worry me.'

So *that was it*. Eve was on surer ground now. 'Yes, Gran.'

'That would indicate to me.' Kate's voice was suddenly choked, 'that – that you cared.'

Eve started to cry from relief. 'Of course I care. I've always cared.'

And an instant later, Eve was in her grandmother's arms. Kate held Eve very close and pressed her lips to the blonde head in her lap. Then she whispered, 'I've been such a damned old fool. Can you ever forgive me?' Kate pulled out a linen handkerchief and blew her nose. 'I was too hard on you,' she declared. 'I couldn't bear it if anything happened to you.'

Eve stroked her grandmother's blue-veined hand soothingly and said, 'I'm all right, Gran. Everything's fine.'

Kate was on her feet, blinking back tears. 'We'll have a fresh start, all right?' She pulled Eve up to face her. 'I've been stubborn and unbending, like my father, I'm going to make amends for that. The first thing I'm going to do is put you back in my will, where you belong.'

What was happening was too good to be true! 'I – I don't care about the money. I only care about you.'

'You're my heiress – you and Alexandra. You two are all the family I have.'

'I'm getting along fine,' Eve said, 'but if it will make you happy –'

'It will make me very happy, darling. Very happy, indeed. When can you move back into the house?'

Eve hesitated for a moment. 'I think it would be better if I stayed here, but I'll see you as often as you want to see me. Oh, Gran, you don't know how lonely I've been.'

Kate took her granddaughter's hand and said, 'Can you forgive me?'

Eve looked her in the eye and said solemnly, 'Of course, I can forgive you.'

The moment Kate left, Eve mixed herself a stiff Scotch and water and sank down onto the couch to relive the incredible scene that had just occurred. She could have shouted aloud with joy. She and Alexandra were now the sole heirs to the Blackwell fortune. It would be easy enough to get rid of Alexandra. It was George Mellis Eve was concerned about. He had suddenly become a hindrance.

'There's been a change of plans,' Eve told George. 'Kate has put me back in her will.'

George paused in the middle of lighting a cigarette. 'Really? Congratulations.'

'If anything happened to Alexandra now, it

would look suspicious. So we'll take care of her later when –'

'I'm afraid later doesn't suit me.'

'What do you mean?'

'I'm not stupid, darling. If anything happens to Alexandra, *I'll* inherit her stock. You want me out of the picture, don't you?'

Eve shrugged. 'Let's say you're an unnecessary complication. I'm willing to make a deal with you. Get a divorce, and as soon as I come into the money, I'll give you –'

He laughed. 'You're funny. It's no good, baby. Nothing has changed. Alex and I have a date in Dark Harbor, Friday night. I intend to keep it.'

Alexandra was overjoyed when she heard the news about Eve and her grandmother. 'Now we're a family again,' she said.

The telephone.

'Hello. I hope I'm not disturbing you, Eve. It's Keith Webster.'

He had started telephoning her two or three times a week. At first his clumsy ardour had amused Eve, but lately he had become a nuisance.

'I can't talk to you now,' Eve said, 'I was just going out the door.'

'Oh.' His voice was apologetic. 'Then I won't keep you. I have two tickets for the horse show next week. I know you love horses, and I thought –'

'Sorry. I will probably be out of town next week.'

'I see.' She could hear the disappointment in his voice. 'Perhaps the following week, then. I'll get tickets to a play. What would you like to see?'

'I've seen them all,' Eve said curtly. 'I have to run.' She replaced the receiver. It was time to get dressed. She was meeting Rory McKenna, a young actor she had seen in an off-Broadway play. He was five years younger than she, and he was like an insatiable wild stallion. Eve visualized his making love to her, and she felt a moisture between her legs. She looked forwards to an exciting evening.

On his way home, George Mellis stopped to buy flowers for Alexandra. He was in an exuberant mood. It was a delicious irony that the old lady had put Eve back in her will, but it changed nothing. After Alexandra's accident, he would take care of Eve. The arrangements were all made. On Friday Alexandra would be waiting for him at Dark Harbor. 'Just the two of us,' he had pleaded as he kissed her. 'Get rid of all the servants, darling.'

Peter Templeton was unable to get Alexandra Mellis out of his mind. He heard the echo of George Mellis's words: *I may take her away somewhere. I think she needs a change.* Every instinct told Peter that Alexandra was in danger, yet he was powerless to act. He could not go to Nick Pappas with his suspicions. He had no proof.

* * *

Across town, in the executive offices of Kruger-Brent Ltd, Kate Blackwell was signing a new will, leaving the bulk of her estate to her two grand-daughters.

In upstate New York, Tony Blackwell was standing before his easel in the garden of the sanatorium. The painting on the easel was a jumble of colours, the kind of painting an untalented child might do. Tony stepped back to look at it and smiled with pleasure.

Friday. 10:57 a.m.

At La Guardia Airport, a taxi pulled up in front of the Eastern Airlines shuttle terminal and Eve Blackwell got out. She handed the driver a hundred-dollar bill.

'Hey, I can't change this, lady,' he said. 'Have you got anything smaller?'

'No.'

'Then you'll have to get change inside.'

'I haven't time. I have to catch the next shuttle to Washington.' She looked at the Baume & Mercier watch on her wrist and made a decision. 'Keep the hundred dollars,' she told the startled driver.

Eve hurried into the terminal. She half-walked and half-ran to the departure gate marked Washington Shuttle. 'One round trip to Washington,' Eve said breathlessly.

The man looked at the clock above his head.

'You missed this one by two minutes. It's just taking off.'

'I've got to be on that plane. I'm meeting – Isn't there anything you can do?' She was near panic.

'Take it easy, miss. There's another shuttle leaving in an hour.'

'That's too – Damn it!'

He watched her regain control of herself.

'Very well. I'll wait. Is there a coffee shop around here?'

'No ma'am. But there's a coffee machine down the corridor.'

'Thank you.'

He looked after her and thought, *What a beauty. I sure envy the guy she's in such a hurry to meet.*

Friday. 2:00 p.m.

It will be a second honeymoon, Alexandra thought. The idea excited her. *Get rid of all the servants. I want it to be just the two of us, angel. We'll have a lovely weekend.* And now Alexandra was leaving the brownstone, on her way to Dark Harbor to meet George. She was running behind schedule. She had had a luncheon engagement, and it had taken longer than Alexandra had planned. She said to the maid, 'I'm going now. I'll be back Monday morning.'

As Alexandra reached the front door, the telephone rang. *I'm late. Let it ring*, she thought, and hurried out the door.

* * *

Friday. 7:00 p.m.

George Mellis had examined Eve's plan over and over. There was not a single flaw in it. *There will be a motor launch waiting for you at Philbrook Cove. Take it to Dark Harbor and make sure you're not seen. Tie it to the stern of the* Corsair. *You'll take Alexandra for a moonlight sail. When you're out at sea, do whatever turns you on, George – just don't leave any traces of blood. Dump the body overboard, get into the launch and leave the Corsair adrift. You'll take the launch back to Philbrook Cove, then catch the Lincolnville ferry to Dark Harbor. Take a taxi to the house. Use some excuse to get the driver to go in so that you'll both notice the* Corsair *is missing from the dock. They'll never find Alexandra's body. The tide will wash it out to sea. Two eminent doctors will testify it was a probable suicide.*

He found the motorboat moored at Philbrook Cove, waiting for him, according to plan.

George crossed the bay without running lights, using the lights of the moon to steer by. He passed a number of moored boats without being detected, and arrived at the dock at the Blackwell estate. He cut the motor and made the line fast to the *Corsair*, the large motor sailer.

She was talking on the telephone, waiting for him in the living room when George walked in. She waved to him, covered the receiver with her hand and mouthed, 'It's Eve.' She listened a moment, then, 'I have to go now, Eve. My darling

617

just arrived. I'll see you at lunch next week.' She replaced the receiver and hurried over to hug George. 'You're early. I'm so pleased.'

'I got lonely for you, so I just dropped everything and came.'

She kissed him. 'I love you.'

'I love you, *matia mou*. Did you get rid of the servants?'

She smiled. 'It's just the two of us. Guess what? I made mousaka for you.'

He traced a finger lightly across the nipples straining against her silk blouse. 'Do you know what I've been thinking about all afternoon at that dreary office? Going for a sail with you. There's a brisk wind. Why don't we go out for an hour or two?'

'If you like. But my mousaka is –'

He cupped his hand over her breast. 'Dinner can wait. I can't.'

She laughed. 'All right. I'll go change. It won't take me a minute.'

'I'll race you.'

He went upstairs to his clothes closet, changed into a pair of slacks, a sweater and boat shoes. Now that the moment was here, he was filled with a sense of wild anticipation, a feeling of excitement that was almost an explosion.

He heard her voice. 'I'm ready, darling.'

He turned. She stood in the doorway, dressed in a sweater, a pair of black slacks and canvas shoes. Her long, blonde hair was tied back with a little blue ribbon. *My God, she's beautiful!* he thought. It seemed almost a shame to waste that beauty.

'So am I,' George told her.

She noticed the motor launch secured to the stern of the yacht. 'What's that for, darling?'

'There's a little island at the end of the bay that I've always wanted to explore,' George explained. 'We'll take the launch over to it so we won't have to worry about rocks.'

He cast off the lines and powered slowly out of the slip. He nosed into the wind to raise the mainsail and jib, and the boat fell off on a starboard tack. The wind caught the large sails and the *Corsair* surged forwards. George headed out to sea. As they cleared the breakwater, they were met with a stiff force-five wind, and the boat started heeling, its lee rail running under.

'It's wild and lovely,' she called out. 'I'm so happy, darling.'

He smiled. 'So am I.'

In an odd way, it gave George Mellis pleasure that Alexandra was happy, that she was going to die happy. He scanned the horizon to make certain no other boats were close by. There were only faint lights from afar. It was time.

He put the boat on automatic pilot, took one last look around the empty horizon and walked over to the lee railing, his heart beginning to pound with excitement.

'Alex,' he called. 'Come and look at this.'

She made her way over to him and looked down at the cold, dark water racing below them.

'Come to me.' His voice was a harsh command.

She moved into his arms, and he kissed her hard on the lips. His arms closed around her, hugging her, and he felt her body relax. He flexed his muscles and began to lift her in the air towards the railing.

She was fighting him suddenly. 'George!'

He lifted her higher, and he felt her try to pull away, but he was too strong for her. She was almost on top of the railing now, her feet kicking wildly, and he braced himself to shove her over the side. At that instant, he felt a sudden white-hot pain in his chest. His first thought was, *I'm having a heart attack*. He opened his mouth to speak and blood came spurting out. He dropped his arms and looked down at his chest in disbelief. Blood was pouring from a gaping wound in it. He looked up, and she was standing there with a bloody knife in her hand, smiling at him.

George Mellis's last thought was, *Eve* . . .

THIRTY-FOUR

It was ten o'clock in the evening when Alexandra arrived at the house at Dark Harbor. She had tried telephoning George there several times, but there had been no answer. She hoped he would not be angry because she had been detained. It had been a stupid mix-up. Early that afternoon, as Alexandra was leaving for Dark Harbor, the phone had rung. She had thought, *I'm late. Let it ring*, and had gone out to the car. The maid had come hurrying after her.

'Mrs Mellis! It's your sister. She says it is urgent.'

When Alexandra picked up the telephone, Eve said, 'Darling, I'm in Washington, DC. I'm having a terrible problem. I have to see you.'

'Of course,' Alexandra said instantly. 'I'm leaving for Dark Harbor now to meet George, but I'll be back Monday morning and –'

'This can't wait.' Eve sounded desperate. 'Will you meet me at La Guardia Airport? I'll be on the five o'clock plane.'

'I'd like to, Eve, but I told George –'

'This is an emergency, Alex. But, of course, if you're too busy.'

'Wait! All right. I'll be there.'

'Thanks, darling. I knew I could count on you.'

It was so seldom that Eve asked her for a favour, she could not refuse her. She would catch a later plane to the island. She telephoned George at the office to tell him she would be detained, but he was not in. She left a message with his secretary. An hour later she took a taxi to La Guardia in time to meet the five o'clock plane from Washington. Eve was not on it. Alexandra waited for two hours, and there was still no sign of Eve. Alexandra had no idea where to reach Eve in Washington. Finally, because there was nothing else she could do, Alexandra took a plane to the island. Now as she approached Cedar Hill House, she found it dark. Surely George should have arrived by now. Alexandra went from room to room, turning on the lights.

'George?'

There was no sign of him. She telephoned her home in Manhattan. The maid answered.

'Is Mr Mellis there?' Alexandra asked.

'Why, no, Mrs Mellis. He said you would both be away for the weekend.'

'Thank you, Marie. He must have been detained somewhere.'

There had to be a logical reason for his absence. Obviously some business had come up at the last minute and, as usual, the partners had asked George to handle it. He would be along at any moment. She dialled Eve's number.

'Eve!' Alexandra exclaimed. 'What on earth happened to you?'

'What happened to *you*? I waited at Kennedy, and when you didn't show up –'

'*Kennedy!* You said *La Guardia*.'

'No, darling, Kennedy.'

'But –' It did not matter any longer. 'I'm sorry,' Alexandra said. 'I must have misunderstood. Are you all right?'

Eve said, 'I am now. I've had a hellish time. I got involved with a man who's a big political figure in Washington. He's insanely jealous and –' She laughed. 'I can't go into the details over the telephone. The phone company will take out both our phones. I'll tell you all about it Monday.'

'All right,' Alexandra said. She was enormously relieved.

'Have a nice weekend,' Eve told her. 'How's George?'

'He's not here.' Alexandra tried to keep the note of concern out of her voice. 'I suppose he got tied up on business and hasn't had a chance to call me.'

'I'm sure you'll hear from him soon. Good-night, darling.'

'Good-night, Eve.'

Alexandra replaced the receiver and thought, *It would be nice if Eve found someone really wonderful. Someone as good and kind as George.* She looked at her watch. It was almost eleven o'clock. Surely he would have had a chance to call by now. She picked up the telephone and dialled the number of the brokerage firm. There was no answer. She telephoned his club. No, they had not seen Mr Mellis. By midnight, Alexandra was alarmed, and by one a.m. she was in a state of panic. She was not sure what to do. It was possible that George was out with a client and could not get to a telephone, or perhaps he had had to fly somewhere and had not been able to reach her before he left. There was some simple explanation. If she called the police and George walked in, she would feel like a fool.

At two a.m. she telephoned the police. There was no police force on the island of Isleboro itself, and the closest station was in Waldo County.

A sleepy voice said, 'Waldo County Sheriff's Department. Sergeant Lambert.'

'This is Mrs George Mellis at Cedar Hill House.'

'Yes, Mrs Mellis.' The voice was instantly alert. 'What can I do for you?'

'To tell you the truth, I'm not sure,' Alexandra said hesitantly. 'My husband was supposed to have met me at the house earlier this evening, and he – he hasn't shown up.'

'I see.' There were all kinds of implications in that phrase. The sergeant knew at least three reasons why a husband could be away from home at two a.m. in the morning: blondes, brunettes and redheads.

He said tactfully, 'Is it possible he was detained on business somewhere?'

'He – he usually calls.'

'Well, you know how it is, Mrs Mellis. Sometimes you get in a situation where you can't call. I'm sure you'll be hearing from him.'

Now she *did* feel like a fool. Of course there was nothing the police could do. She had read somewhere that a person had to be missing for twenty-four hours before the police would even start looking for him, and George was not *missing*, for heaven's sake. He was just late.

'I'm sure you're right,' Alexandra said into the telephone. 'I'm sorry to have troubled you.'

'Not at all, Mrs Mellis. I'll bet he'll be on the seven o'clock ferry first thing in the morning.'

He was not on the seven o'clock ferry, or the one after that. Alexandra telephoned the Manhattan house again. George was not there.

A feeling of disaster began to grip Alexandra. George had been in an accident; he was in a hospital somewhere, ill or dead. If only there had not been the mix-up with Eve at the airport. Perhaps George had arrived at the house, and when he found she was not there, he had gone. But that left too many things unexplained. He would have left a note. He could have surprised burglars and been attacked or kidnapped. Alexandra went through the house, room by room, looking for any possible clue. Everything was intact. She went down to the rock. The *Corsair* was there, safely moored.

She telephoned the Waldo County Sheriff's Department again. Lieutenant Philip Ingram, a twenty-year veteran of the force, was on morning duty. He was already aware that George Mellis had not been home all night. It had been the chief topic of conversation around the station all morning, most of it ribald.

Now he said to Alexandra, 'There's no trace of him at all, Mrs Mellis? All right. I'll come out there myself.' He knew it would be a waste of time. Her old man was probably tomcatting around in some alley. *But when the Blackwells call, the peasants come running*, he thought wryly. Anyway, this was a nice lady. He had met her a few times over the years.

'Back in an hour or so,' he told the desk sergeant.

Lieutenant Ingram listened to Alexandra's story, checked the house and the dock and reached the conclusion that Alexandra Mellis had a problem on her hands. George Mellis was to have met his wife the evening before at Dark Harbor, but he had not shown up. While it was not Lieutenant Ingram's problem, he knew it would do him no harm to be helpful to a member of the Blackwell family. Ingram telephoned the island airport and the ferry terminal at Lincolnville. George Mellis had used neither facility within the past twenty-four hours. 'He didn't come to Dark Harbor,' the lieutenant told Alexandra. *And where the hell did that leave things? Why would the man have dropped out of sight?* In the lieutenant's considered opinion, no man in his right mind would voluntarily leave a woman like Alexandra.

'We'll check the hospitals and mor –' He caught himself. 'And other places, and I'll put out an APB on him.'

Alexandra was trying to control her emotions, but he could see what an effort it was. 'Thank you, Lieutenant. I don't have to tell you how much I'll appreciate anything you can do.'

'That's my job,' Lieutenant Ingram replied.

When Lieutenant Ingram returned to the station, he began calling hospitals and morgues. The responses were negative. There was no accident report on George Mellis. Lieutenant Ingram's next move was to call a reporter friend on the *Maine Courier*. After that, the lieutenant sent out a missing person all-points-bulletin.

The afternoon newspapers carried the story in headlines: HUSBAND OF BLACKWELL HEIRESS MISSING.

Peter Templeton first heard the news from Detective Nick Pappas.

'Peter, remember askin' me a while ago to do some checkin' on George Mellis?'

'Yes . . .'

'He's done a vanishing act.'

'He's *what*?'

627

'Disappeared, vamoosed, gone.' He waited while Peter digested the news.

'Did he take anything with him? Money, clothes, passport?'

'Nope. According to the report we got from Maine, Mr Mellis just melted into thin air. You're his shrink. I thought you might have some idea why our boy would do a thing like that.'

Peter said truthfully, 'I haven't any idea, Nick.'

'If you think of anything, let me know. There's gonna be a lot of heat on this.'

'Yes,' Peter promised. 'I will.'

Thirty minutes later, Alexandra Mellis telephoned Peter Templeton, and he could hear the shrill edge of pain in her voice. 'I – George is missing. No one seems to know what happened to him. I was hoping he might have told you something that might have given you a clue or –' She broke off.

'I'm sorry, Mrs Mellis. He didn't. I have no idea what could have happened.'

'Oh.'

Peter wished there was some way he could comfort her. 'If I think of anything, I'll call you back. Where can I reach you?'

'I'm at Dark Harbor now, but I'm going to return to New York this evening. I'll be at my grandmother's.'

Alexandra could not bear the thought of being alone. She had talked to Kate several times that morning. 'Oh, darling, I'm sure there's nothing to worry about,' Kate said. 'He probably went off on some business deal and forgot to tell you.'

Neither of them believed it.

Eve saw the story of George's disappearance on television. There were photographs of the exterior of Cedar Hill House, and pictures of Alexandra and George after their wedding ceremony. There was a close-up of George, looking upward, with his eyes wide. Somehow it reminded Eve of the look of surprise on his face just before he died.

The television commentator was saying, 'There has been no evidence of foul play and no ransom demands have been made. The police speculate that George Mellis was possibly the victim of an accident and may be suffering from amnesia.' Eve smiled in satisfaction.

They would never find the body. It had been swept out to sea with the tide. Poor George. He had followed her plan perfectly. But she had changed it. She had flown up to Maine and rented a motor boat at Philbrook Cove, to be held for 'a friend.' She had then rented a second boat from a nearby dock and taken it to Dark Harbor, where she had waited for George. He had been totally unsuspecting. She had been careful to wipe the deck clean before she returned the yacht to the dock. After that, it had been a simple matter to tow George's rented motorboat back to its pier, return her boat and fly back to New York to await the telephone call she knew Alexandra would make.

It was a perfect crime. The police would list it as a mysterious disappearance.

The announcer was saying, 'In other news . . .' Eve switched the television set off.

She did not want to be late for her date with Rory McKenna.

At six o'clock the following morning, a fishing boat found George Mellis's body pinned against the breakwater at the mouth of Penobscot Bay. The early news reports called it a drowning and accidental death, but as more information came in, the tenor of the stories began to change. From the coroner's office came reports that what at first had been thought to have been shark bites were actually stab wounds. The evening newspaper editions screamed: MURDER SUSPECTED IN GEORGE MELLIS MYSTERY DEATH . . . MILLIONAIRE FOUND STABBED TO DEATH.

Lieutenant Ingram was studying the tide charts for the previous evening. When he was finished, he leaned back in his chair, a perplexed expression on his face. George Mellis's body would have been swept out to sea had it not been caught against the breakwater. What puzzled the lieutenant was that the body had to have been carried by the tide from the direction of Dark Harbor. Where George Mellis was not supposed to have been.

* * *

630

Detective Nick Pappas flew up to Maine to have a talk with Lieutenant Ingram.

'I think my department might be of some help to you in this case,' Nick said. 'We have some interesting background information on George Mellis. I know this is out of our jurisdiction, but if you were to ask for our cooperation, we'd be happy to give it to you, Lieutenant.'

In the twenty years Lieutenant Ingram had been with the Waldo County Sheriff's Department, the only real excitement he had seen was when a drunken tourist shot a moose head off the wall of a local curio shop. The George Mellis murder was front-page news, and Lieutenant Ingram sensed a chance to make a name for himself. With a little luck, it could lead to a job as a detective in the New York City Police Department, where the action was. And so now he looked at Nick Pappas and murmured, 'I don't know . . .'

As though reading his mind, Nick Pappas said, 'We're not looking for credit. There's gonna be a hell of a lot of pressure on this one, and it would make life easier for us if we could wrap it up fast. I could start by filling you in on George Mellis's background.'

Lieutenant Ingram decided he had nothing to lose. 'OK, you've got a deal.'

Alexandra was in bed, heavily sedated. Her mind stubbornly refused to accept the fact that George had been murdered. How could he have been?

631

There was no reason in the world for anyone to kill him. The police had talked of a knife wound, but they were wrong about that. It had to be some kind of accident. *No one would want to kill him . . . No one would want to kill him . . .* The opiate Dr Harley gave her finally took hold. She slept.

Eve had been stunned at the news that George's body had been found. *But perhaps it's a good thing*, Eve thought. *Alexandra will be the one under suspicion. She was there, on the island.*

Kate was seated next to Eve on the couch in the drawing room. The news had been a tremendous shock to Kate.

'Why would anyone want to murder George?' she asked.

Eve sighed. 'I don't know, Gran. I just don't know. My heart breaks for poor Alex.'

Lieutenant Philip Ingram was questioning the attendant on the Lincolnville-Isleboro ferry. 'Are you positive neither Mr not Mrs Mellis came over on the ferry Friday afternoon?'

'They didn't come over on my shift, Phil, and I checked with the morning man, and he didn't see 'em neither. They had to have come in by plane.'

'One more question, Lew. Did *any* strangers take the ferry across on Friday?'

'Hell,' the attendant said, 'you know we don't get no strangers goin' to the island this time of year. There might be a few tourists in the summer – but in *November*? She-e-e-it!'

Lieutenant Ingram went to talk to the manager of the Isleboro airport. 'George Mellis sure didn't fly in that evening, Phil. He musta come over to the island by ferry.'

'Lew said he didn't see him.'

'Well, hell, he couldn't a *swum* over, now could he?'

'What about Mrs Mellis?'

'Yep. She come in here in her Beechcraft about ten o'clock. I had my son, Charley, run her over to Cedar Hill from the airport.'

'What kind of mood did Mrs Mellis seem to be in?'

'Funny you should ask. She was as nervous as spit on a hot kettle. Even my boy noticed it. Usually she's calm, always has a pleasant word for everybody. But that night she was in a tearin' hurry.'

'One more question. Did any strangers fly in that afternoon or evening? Any unfamiliar faces?'

He shook his head. 'Nope. Just the regulars.'

An hour later, Lieutenant Ingram was on the phone talking to Nick Pappas. 'What I've got so far,' he told the New York detective, 'is damned confusing. Friday night Mrs Mellis arrived by private plane at the Isleboro airport around ten o'clock, but her husband wasn't with her, and he didn't come in by plane or ferry. In fact, there's nothin' to show he was on the island at all that night.'

'Except the tide.'

'Yeah.'

'Whoever killed him probably threw him over-board from a boat, figuring the tide would carry him out to sea. Did you check the *Corsair*?'

'I looked it over. No sign of violence, no blood-stains.'

'I'd like to bring a forensics expert up there. Would you mind?'

'Not as long as you remember our little deal.'

'I'll remember. See you tomorrow.'

Nick Pappas and a team of experts arrived the following morning. Lieutenant Ingram escorted them to the Blackwell dock, where the *Corsair* was tied up. Two hours later, the forensics expert said, 'Looks like we hit the jackpot, Nick. There are some bloodstains on the underside of the lee rail.'

That afternoon, the police laboratory verified that the stains matched George Mellis's blood type.

Manhattan's 'silk stocking' police precinct was busier than usual. A series of all-night drug busts had filled the prisoners' cage to capacity, and the holding cells were crowded with prostitutes, drunks and sex offenders. The noise and the stench competed for Peter Templeton's attention, as he was escorted through the din to Lieutenant Detective Pappas's office.

'Hey, Peter. Nice of you to drop by.'

On the phone Pappas had said, 'You're holdin''

out on me, chum. Be at my office before six o'clock, or I'll send a fuckin' SWAT team to bring you in.'

When his escort left the office, Peter asked, 'What's this all about, Nick? What's bothering you?'

'I'll tell you what's botherin' me. Someone's being clever. Do you know what we've got? A dead man who vanished from an island he never went to.'

'That doesn't make sense.'

'Tell me about it, pal. The ferryboat operator and the guy who runs the airport swear they never saw George Mellis on the night he disappeared. The only other way he could have gotten to Dark Harbor was by motorboat. We checked all the boat operators in the area. Zilch.'

'Perhaps he wasn't at Dark Harbor that night.'

'The forensic lab says different. They found evidence that Mellis was at the house and changed from a business suit into the sailing clothes he was wearin' when his body was found.'

'Was he killed at the house?'

'On the Blackwell yacht. His body was dumped overboard. Whoever did it figured the current would carry the body to China.'

'How did –?'

Nick Pappas raised a beefy hand. 'My turn. Mellis was your patient. He must have talked to you about his wife.'

'What does she have to do with this?'

'Everything. She's my first, second and third choice.'

'You're crazy.'

'Hey, I thought shrinks never used words like *crazy*.'

'Nick, what makes you think Alexandra Mellis killed her husband?'

'She was there, and she had a motive. She arrived at the island late that night with some cockamamy excuse about being delayed because she was waitin' at the wrong airport to meet her sister.'

'What does her sister say?'

'Give me a break. What the hell would you expect her to say? They're *twins*. We know George Mellis was at the house that night, but his wife swears she never saw him. It's a big house, Peter, but it's not *that* big. Next, Mrs M gave all the servants the weekend off. When I asked her why, she said it was George's idea. George's lips, of course, are sealed.'

Peter sat there, deep in thought. 'You said she had a motive. What?'

'You have a short memory span. You're the one who put me on the track. The lady was married to a psycho who got his kicks sexually abusing everything he could lay his fists on. He was probably slapping her around pretty good. Let's say she decided she didn't want to play anymore. She asked for a divorce. He wouldn't give it to her. Why should he? He had it made. She wouldn't dare take him to court – it would touch off too juicy a scandal. She had no choice. She had to kill him.' He leaned back in his chair.

'What do you want from me?' Peter asked.

'Information. You had lunch with Mellis's wife ten days ago.' He pressed the button on a tape recorder on the desk. 'We're going on the record now, Peter. Tell me about that lunch. How did Alexandra Mellis behave? Was she tense? Angry? Hysterical?'

'Nick, I've never seen a more relaxed, happily married lady.'

Nick Pappas glared at him and snapped off the tape recorder.

'Don't shaft me, my friend. I went to see Dr John Harley this morning. He's been giving Alexandra Mellis medication to stop her from committing suicide, for Christ's sake!'

Dr John Harley had been greatly disturbed by his meeting with Lieutenant Pappas. The detective had gotten right to the point. 'Has Mrs Mellis consulted you professionally recently?'

'I'm sorry,' Dr Harley said. 'I'm not at liberty to discuss my patients. I'm afraid I can't help you.'

'All right, Doc I understand. You're old friends. You'd like to keep the whole thing quiet. That's okay with me.' He rose to his feet. 'This is a homicide case. I'll be back in an hour with a warrant for your appointment records. When I find out what I want to know, I'm going to feed it to the newspapers.'

Dr Harley was studying him.

'We can handle it that way, or you can tell me

now what I want to know, and I'll do what I can to keep it quiet. Well?'

'Sit down,' Dr Harley said. Nick Pappas sat. 'Alexandra has been having some emotional problems lately.'

'What kind of emotional problems?'

'She's been in a severe depression. She was talking about committing suicide.'

'Did she mention using a knife?'

'No. She said she had a recurrent dream about drowning. I gave her Wellbutrin. She came back and told me it didn't seem to be helping, and I prescribed Nomifensine. I – I don't know whether it helped or not.'

Nick Pappas sat there, putting things together in his mind. Finally he looked up. 'Anything else?'

'That's everything, Lieutenant.'

But there was more, and John Harley's conscience was bothering him. He had deliberately refrained from mentioning the brutal attack George Mellis had made on Eve Blackwell. Part of his concern was that he should have reported it to the police at the time it happened, but mainly Dr Harley wanted to protect the Blackwell family. He had no way of knowing whether there was a connection between the attack on Eve and George Mellis's murder, but his instincts told him that it was better not to bring up the subject. He intended to do everything possible to protect Kate Blackwell.

* * *

Fifteen minutes after he had made that decision, his nurse said, 'Dr Keith Webster is on line two, Doctor.'

It was as if his conscience was prodding him.

Keith Webster said, 'John, I'd like to stop by this afternoon and see you. Are you free?'

'I'll make myself free. What time?'

'How's five o'clock?'

'Fine, Keith. I'll see you then.'

So, the matter was not going to be laid to rest so easily.

At five o'clock, Dr Harley ushered Keith Webster into his office. 'Would you like a drink?'

'No, thank you, John. Forgive me for barging in on you like this.'

It seemed to John Harley that every time he saw him, Keith Webster was apologizing about something. He was such a mild little man, so inoffensive and eager to please – a puppy waiting to be patted on the head. It was incredible to John Harley that within that pale, colourless person there lurked such a brilliant surgeon.

'What can I do for you, Keith?'

Keith Webster drew a deep breath. 'It's about that – you know – that beating George Mellis gave Eve Blackwell.'

'What about it?'

'You're aware she almost died?'

'Yes.'

'Well, it was never reported to the police. In view of what's happened – Mellis's murder and everything – I was wondering if maybe I shouldn't tell the police about it.'

So there it was. There seemed no way to escape the problem.

'You have to do whatever you think best, Keith.'

Keith Webster said gloomily, 'I know. It's just that I'd hate to do anything that might hurt Eve Blackwell. She's a very special person.'

Dr Harley was watching him cautiously. 'Yes, she is.'

Keith Webster sighed. 'The only thing is, John, if I do keep quiet about it now and the police find out later, it's going to look bad for me.'

For both of us, John Harley thought. He saw a possible way out. He said casually, 'It's not very likely the police would find out, is it? Eve certainly would never mention it, and you fixed her up perfectly. Except for that little scar you'd never know she'd been disfigured.'

Keith Webster blinked. 'What little scar?'

'The red scar on her forehead. She told me you said you were going to remove it in a month or two.'

Dr Webster was blinking faster now. It was some kind of nervous tic, Dr Harley decided.

'I don't re – When did you last see Eve?'

'She came in about ten days ago to talk about a problem involving her sister. As a matter of fact, the scar was the only way I could tell it was Eve instead of Alexandra. They're identical twins, you know.'

640

Keith Webster nodded slowly. 'Yes. I've seen photographs of Eve's sister in the newspapers. There's an amazing likeness. And you say the only way you could tell them apart was by the scar on Eve's forehead from the operation I performed?'

'That's right.'

Dr Webster sat there, silent, chewing on his lower lip. Finally he said, 'Perhaps I shouldn't go to the police just yet. I'd like to think about this a little more.'

'Frankly, I think that's wise, Keith. They're both lovely young women. The newspapers are hinting that the police think Alexandra killed George. That's impossible. I remember when they were little girls . . .'

Dr Webster was no longer listening.

When he left Dr Harley, Keith Webster was lost in thought. He had certainly not left even the trace of a scar on that beautiful face. Yet, John Harley had seen it. It was possible that Eve could have gotten a scar afterwards in another accident, but then why had she lied? It made no sense.

He examined it from every angle, going over all the different possibilities, and when he had come to a conclusion, he thought, *If I'm right, this is going to change my whole life . . .*

Early the following morning, Keith Webster called Dr Harley. 'John,' he began, 'excuse me for disturbing you. You said that Eve Blackwell came in to talk to you about her sister, Alexandra?'

'That's right.'

'After Eve's visit, did Alexandra happen to come in to see you?'

'Yes. As a matter of fact, she came to my office the following day. Why?'

'Just curious. Can you tell me what Eve's sister came to see you about?'

'Alexandra was in a deep depression. Eve was trying to help her.'

Eve had been beaten and almost killed by Alexandra's husband. And now the man had been murdered and it was Alexandra who was being blamed.

Keith Webster had always known he was not brilliant. In school he had to work very hard in order to achieve barely passing grades. He was the perennial butt of his classmates' jokes. He was neither an athlete nor a scholar, and he was socially inept. He was as close as one could come to being a nonentity. No one was more surprised than his own family when Keith Webster was admitted to medical school. When he elected to become a surgeon, neither his peers nor his teachers expected him to become a competent one, let alone a great one. But he had surprised them all. There was a talent deep inside him that was nothing short of genius. He was like some exquisite sculptor working his magic with living flesh instead of clay, and in a short time Keith Webster's reputation spread. In spite of his success, however, he was never able to overcome the trauma of his childhood. Inside he was still the boy who bored everyone, the one at whom the girls laughed.

When he finally reached Eve, Keith's hands were slippery with sweat. She answered the phone on the first ring. 'Rory?' Her voice was low and sultry.

'No. This is Keith Webster.'

'Oh. Hello.'

He heard the change in her voice. 'How've you been?' he asked.

'Fine.'

He could sense her impatience. 'I – I'd like to see you.'

'I'm not seeing anyone. If you read the papers, you'll know my brother-in-law was murdered. I'm in mourning.'

He wiped his hands on his trousers. 'That's what I want to see you about, Eve. I have some information you should know about.'

'What kind of information?'

'I would prefer not to discuss it on the telephone.' He could almost hear Eve's mind working.

'Very well. When?'

'Now, if it's convenient.'

When he arrived at Eve's apartment thirty minutes later, Eve opened the door for him. 'I'm very busy. What did you want to see me about?'

'About this,' Keith Webster said apologetically. He opened a manila envelope he was clutching, took out a photograph and diffidently handed it to Eve. It was a photograph of herself.

She looked at it, puzzled. 'Well?'

'It's a picture of you.'

'I can see that,' she said curtly. 'What about it?'

'It was taken after your operation.'

'So?'

'There's no scar on your forehead, Eve.'

He watched the change that came over her face.

'Sit down, Keith.'

He sat opposite her, on the edge of the couch, and he could not keep from staring at her. He had seen many beautiful women in his practice, but Eve Blackwell totally bewitched him. He had never known anyone like her.

'I think you'd better tell me what this is all about.'

He started at the beginning. He told her about his visit to Dr Harley and about the mysterious scar, and as Keith Webster talked, he watched Eve's eyes. They were expressionless.

When Keith Webster finished, Eve said, 'I don't know what you're thinking, but whatever it is, you're wasting my time. As for the scar, I was playing a little joke on my sister. It's as simple as that. Now, if you've quite finished, I have a great deal to do.'

He remained seated. 'I'm sorry to have bothered you. I just thought I should talk to you before I went to the police.' He could see that he really had her attention now.

'Why on earth would you go to the police?'

'I'm obliged to report the attack George Mellis made on you. Then there's that business about you and the scar. I don't understand it, but I'm sure you can explain it to them.'

Eve felt the first stab of fear. This stupid, dreary little man in front of her had no idea what had really happened, but he knew enough to start the police asking questions.

George Mellis had been a frequent visitor to the apartment. The police could probably find witnesses who had seen him. She had lied about being in Washington the night of George's murder. She had no real alibi. She had never thought she would need one. If the police learned that George had almost killed her, it would give them a motive. The whole scheme would begin to unravel. She had to silence this man.

'What is it you want? Money?'

'No!'

She saw the indignation on his face. 'What, then?'

Dr Webster looked down at the rug, his face red with embarrassment. 'I – I like you so much, Eve. I would hate it if anything bad happened to you.'

She forced a smile. 'Nothing bad is going to happen to me, Keith. I haven't done anything wrong. Believe me, none of this has anything to do with George Mellis's murder.' She reached out and took his hand. 'I would really appreciate it very much if you would forget about this. All right?'

He covered her hand and squeezed it. 'I'd like to, Eve. I really would. But they're holding the coroner's inquest Saturday. I'm a doctor. I'm afraid it's my duty to testify at that inquest and tell them everything I know.'

He saw the alarm that appeared in her eyes.

'You don't have to do that!'

He stroked her hand. 'Yes, I do, Eve. It's my sworn obligation. There's only one thing that could prevent me from doing it.' He watched her leap to the bait of his words.

'What is that?'

His voice was very gentle. 'A husband can't be forced to testify against his wife.'

THIRTY-FIVE

The wedding took place two days before the coroner's inquest. They were married by a judge in his private chambers. The mere idea of being married to Keith Webster made Eve's skin crawl, but she had no choice. *The fool thinks I'm going to stay married to him.* As soon as the inquest was over, she would get an annulment and that would be the end of it.

Detective Lieutenant Nick Pappas had a problem. He was sure he knew who the murderer of George Mellis was, but he could not prove it. He was confronted by a conspiracy of silence around the Blackwell family that he could not break through. He discussed the problem with his superior, Captain Harold Cohn, a street-wise cop who had worked his way up from the ranks.

Cohn quietly listened to Pappas and said, 'It's all smoke, Nick. You haven't got a fucking bit of evidence. They'd laugh us out of court.'

'I know,' Lieutenant Pappas sighed. 'But I'm right.' He sat there a moment, thinking. 'Would you mind if I talked to Kate Blackwell?'

'Jesus! What for?'

'It'll be a little fishing expedition. She runs that family. She might have some information she doesn't even know she has.'

'You'll have to watch your step.'

'I will.'

'And go easy with her, Nick. Remember, she's an old lady.'

'That's what I'm counting on,' Detective Pappas said.

The meeting took place that afternoon in Kate Blackwell's office. Nick Pappas guessed that Kate was somewhere in her eighties, but she carried her age remarkably well. She showed little of the strain the detective knew she must be feeling. She was a very private person, and she had been forced to watch the Blackwell name become a source of public speculation and scandal.

'My secretary said you wished to see me about a matter of some urgency, Lieutenant.'

'Yes, ma'am. There's a coroner's inquest tomorrow on the death of George Mellis. I have reason to think your granddaughter is involved in his murder.'

Kate went absolutely rigid. 'I don't believe it.'

'Please hear me out, Mrs Blackwell. Every police investigation begins with the question of motive. George Mellis was a fortune hunter and a vicious sadist.' He saw the reaction on her face, but he pressed on. 'He married your granddaughter and suddenly found himself with his hands on a large fortune. I figured he beat up Alexandra once too often and when she asked for a divorce, he refused. Her only way to get rid of him was to kill him.'

Kate was staring at him, her face pale.

'I began looking around for evidence to back up my theory. We knew George Mellis was at Cedar Hill House before he disappeared. There are only two ways to get to Dark Harbor from the mainland – plane or ferryboat. According to the local sheriff's office, George Mellis didn't use either. I don't believe in miracles, and I figured Mellis wasn't the kind of man who could walk on water. The only possibility left was that he took a boat from somewhere else along the coast. I started checking out boat-rental places, and I struck pay dirt at Gilkey Harbour. At four p.m. on the afternoon of the day George Mellis was murdered, a woman rented a motor launch there and said a friend would be picking it up later. She paid cash, but she had to sign the rental slip. She used the name Solange Dunas. Does that ring a bell?'

'Yes. She – she was the governess who took care of the twins when they were children. She returned to France years ago.'

Pappas nodded, a look of satisfaction on his face. 'A little further up the coast, the same woman rented a second boat. She took it out and returned it three hours later. She signed her name Solange

Dunas again. I showed both attendants a photograph of Alexandra. They were pretty sure it was her, but they couldn't be positive, because the woman who rented the boats was a brunette.'

'Then what makes you think –?'

'She wore a wig.'

Kate said stiffly, 'I don't believe Alexandra killed her husband.'

'I don't either, Mrs Blackwell,' Lieutenant Pappas told her. 'It was her sister, Eve.'

Kate Blackwell was still as stone.

'Alexandra couldn't have done it. I checked on her movements the day of the murder. She spent the early part of the day in New York with a friend, then she flew directly from New York up to the island. There's no way she could have rented those two motorboats.' He leaned forwards. 'So I was left with Alexandra's look-alike, who signed the name Solange Dunas. It had to be Eve. I started looking around for her motive. I showed a photograph of George Mellis to the tenants of the apartment house Eve lives in and it turned out that Mellis was a frequent visitor there. The superintendent of the building told me that one night when Mellis was there, Eve was almost beaten to death. Did you know that?'

'No.' Kate's voice was a whisper.

'Mellis did it. It fits his pattern. And that was Eve's motive – vengeance. She lured him out to Dark Harbor and murdered him.' He looked at Kate, and felt a pang of guilt at taking advantage of this old woman. 'Eve's alibi is that she was in Washington, DC, that day. She gave the cab driver who took her to the airport a hundred-dollar bill so he would be sure to remember her, and she made a big fuss about missing the Washington shuttle. But I don't think she went to Washington. I believe she put on a dark wig and took a commercial plane to Maine, where she rented those boats. She killed Mellis, dumped his body overboard, then docked the yacht and towed the extra motorboat back to the rental dock, which was closed by then.'

Kate looked at him a long moment. Then she said, slowly, 'All the evidence you have is circumstantial, isn't it?'

'Yes.' He was ready to move in for the kill. 'I need concrete evidence for the coroner's inquest. You know your granddaughter better than anyone in the world, Mrs Blackwell. I want you to tell me anything you can that might be helpful.'

She sat there quietly, making up her mind. Finally she said, 'I think I can give you some information for the inquest.'

And Nick Pappas's heart began to beat faster. He had taken a long shot, and it had paid off. The old lady had come through. He unconsciously leaned forwards. 'Yes, Mrs Blackwell?'

Kate spoke slowly and distinctly. 'On the day George Mellis was murdered, Lieutenant, my granddaughter Eve and I were in Washington, DC, together.'

She saw the surprised expression on his face.

You fool, Kate Blackwell thought. *Did you really think I would offer up a Blackwell as a sacrifice to you? That I would let the press have a Roman holiday with the Blackwell name? No. I will punish Eve in my own way.*

The verdict from the coroner's jury was death at the hands of an unknown assailant or assailants.

To Alexandra's surprise and gratitude, Peter Templeton was at the inquest at the county court-house.

'Just here to lend moral support,' he told her. Peter thought Alexandra was holding up remark-ably well, but the strain showed in her face and in her eyes. During a recess, he took her to lunch at the Lobster Pound, a little restaurant facing the bay in Lincolnville.

'When this is over,' Peter said, 'I think it would be good for you to take a trip, get away for a while.'

'Yes. Eve has asked me to go away with her.' Alexandra's eyes were filled with pain. 'I still can't believe George is dead. I know it has happened, but it – it still seems unreal.'

'It's nature's way of cushioning the shock until the pain becomes bearable.'

'It's so senseless. He was such a fine man.' She looked up at Peter. 'You spent time with him. He talked to you. Wasn't he a wonderful person?'

'Yes,' Peter said slowly. 'Yes, he was.'

* * *

Eve said, 'I want an annulment, Keith.'

Keith Webster blinked at his wife in surprise. 'Why on earth would you want an annulment?'

'Oh, come on, Keith. You didn't really think I was going to stay married to you, did you?'

'Of course. You're my wife, Eve.'

'What are you after? The Blackwell money?'

'I don't need money, darling. I make an excellent living. I can give you anything you want.'

'I told you what I want. An annulment.'

He shook his head regretfully. 'I'm afraid I can't give you that.'

'Then I'm going to file for divorce.'

'I don't think that would be advisable. You see, nothing has really changed, Eve. The police haven't found out who killed your brother-in-law, so the case is still open. There's no statute of limitations on murder. If you divorced me, I'd be forced to . . .' He raised his hands helplessly.

'You're talking as though *I* killed him.'

'You did, Eve.'

Her voice was scornful. 'How the hell do *you* know?'

'It's the only reason you would have married me.'

She looked at him, filled with loathing. 'You bastard! How can you do this to me?'

'It's very simple. I love you.'

'I hate you. Do you understand that? I despise you!'

He smiled sadly. 'I love you so much.'

The trip with Alexandra was called off. 'I'm going to Barbados on my honeymoon,' Eve told her.

Barbados was Keith's idea.

'I won't go,' Eve told him flatly. The idea of a honeymoon with him was disgusting.

'It will look strange if we don't have a honeymoon,' he said shyly. 'And we don't want people asking a lot of awkward questions, do we, dear?'

Alexandra began to see Peter Templeton for lunch once a week. In the beginning, it was because she wanted to talk about George, and there was no one else she could discuss him with. But after several months, Alexandra admitted to herself that she enjoyed Peter Templeton's company immensely. There was a dependability about him that she desperately needed. He was sensitive to her moods, and he was intelligent and entertaining.

'When I was an intern,' he told Alexandra, 'I went out on my first house call in the dead of winter. The patient was a frail old man in bed with a terrible cough. I was going to examine his chest with my stethoscope, but I didn't want to shock him, so I decided to warm it first. I put it on the radiator while I examined his throat and his eyes. Then I got my stethoscope and put it to his chest. The old man leaped out of bed like a scalded cat. His cough went away, but it took weeks for the burn to heal.'

Alexandra laughed. It was the first time she had laughed in a long time.

'Can we do this again next week?' Peter asked.
'Yes, please.'

Eve's honeymoon turned out much better than she had anticipated. Because of Keith's pale, sensitive skin, he was afraid to go out in the sun, so Eve went down to the beach alone every day. She was never alone for long. She was surrounded by amorous lifeguards, beach bums, tycoons and playboys. It was like feasting at a wonderful smorgasbord, and Eve chose a different dish each day. She enjoyed her sexual escapades twice as much because she knew her husband was upstairs in their suite waiting for her. He could not do enough for her. He fetched and carried for her like a little lapdog, and waited on her hand and foot. If Eve expressed a wish, it was instantly gratified. She did everything she could think of to insult him, anger him, to turn him against her so that he would let her go, but his love was unshakable. The idea of letting Keith make love to her sickened Eve, and she was grateful that he had a weak libido.

The years are beginning to catch up with me, Kate Blackwell thought. There were so many of them, and they had been so full and rich.

Kruger-Brent, Ltd., needed a strong hand at the helm. It needed someone with Blackwell blood. *There's no one to carry on after I'm gone*, Kate thought. *All the working and planning and fighting for the company. And for what? For strangers to take over one day. Bloody hell! I can't let that happen.*

A week after they returned from their honeymoon, Keith said apologetically, 'I'm afraid I'm going to have to go back to work dear. I have a lot of operations scheduled. Will you be all right during the day without me?'

Eve barely managed to keep a straight face. 'I'll try.'

Keith was up and out early every morning long before Eve awakened, and when she went into the kitchen she found he had made coffee and laid out all the breakfast things for her. He opened a generous bank account in Eve's name and kept it replenished. She spent his money recklessly. As long as she was enjoying herself, Keith was happy. Eve bought expensive jewellery for Rory, with whom she spent almost every afternoon. He worked very little.

'I can't take just any part,' he complained to Eve. 'It would hurt my image.'

'I understand, darling.'

'Do you? What the fuck do you know about show business? You were born with a silver spoon up your ass.'

And Eve would buy him an extra-nice present to placate him. She paid Rory's rent and bought him clothes for interviews, and paid for his dinners at expensive restaurants so that he could be seen by important producers. She wanted to be with him twenty-four hours a day, but there was her husband. Eve would arrive home at seven o'clock at night, and Keith would be in the kitchen preparing dinner for her in his 'Kiss the Cook' apron. He never questioned her about where she had been.

During the following year, Alexandra and Peter Templeton saw each other more and more often. Each had become an important part of the other's life. Peter accompanied Alexandra when she went to visit her father at the asylum, and somehow the sharing made the pain easier to bear.

Peter met Kate one evening when he arrived to pick up Alexandra. 'So you're a doctor, eh? I've buried a dozen doctors, and I'm still around. Do you know anything about business?'

'Not a great deal, Mrs Blackwell.'

'Are you a corporation?' Kate asked.

'No.'

She snorted. 'Bloody hell. You don't know anything. You need a good tax man. I'll set up an appointment for you with mine. The first thing he'll do is incorporate you and –'

'Thank you, Mrs Blackwell. I'm getting along just fine.'

'My husband was a stubborn man, too,' Kate said. She turned to Alexandra. 'Invite him to dinner. Maybe I can talk some sense into him.'

Outside, Peter said, 'Your grandmother hates me.'

Alexandra laughed. 'She likes you. You should *hear* how Gran behaves with people she hates.'

'I wonder how she would feel if I told her that I want to marry you, Alex. . . . ?'

And she looked up at him and beamed. 'We'd both feel wonderful, Peter!'

Kate had watched the progress of Alexandra's romance with Peter Templeton with a great deal of interest. She liked the young doctor, and she decided he would be a good husband for Alexandra. But she was a trader at heart. Now she sat in front of the fireplace facing the two of them.

'I must tell you,' Kate lied, 'that this comes as a complete surprise. I always expected Alexandra to marry an executive who would take over Kruger-Brent.'

'This isn't a business proposition, Mrs Blackwell. Alexandra and I want to get married.'

'On the other hand,' Kate continued, as if there had been no interruption, 'you're a psychiatrist. You understand the way people's minds and emotions work. You would probably be a great negotiator. I would like you to become involved with the company. You can –'

'No,' Peter said firmly. 'I'm a doctor. I'm not interested in going into a business.'

'This isn't "going into a business",' Kate snapped. 'We're not talking about some corner grocery store. You'll be part of the family, and I need someone to run –'

'I'm sorry.' There was a finality in Peter's tone. 'I'll have nothing to do with Kruger-Brent. You'll have to find someone else for that . . .'

Kate turned to Alexandra. 'What do you have to say to that?'

'I want whatever makes Peter happy, Gran.'

'Damned ingratitude,' Kate glowered. 'Selfish, the both of you.' She sighed, 'Ah, well. Who knows? You might change your mind one day.' And she added innocently, 'Are you planning to have children?'

Peter laughed. 'That's a private matter. I have a feeling you're a great manipulator, Mrs Blackwell, but Alex and I are going to live our own lives, and our children – if we have children – will live *their* lives.'

Kate smiled sweetly. 'I wouldn't have it any other way, Peter. I've made it a lifelong rule never to interfere in other people's lives.'

Two months later when Alexandra and Peter returned from their honeymoon, Alexandra was pregnant. When Kate heard the news, she thought, *Good. It will be a boy.*

Eve lay in bed watching Rory walk out of the bathroom naked. He had a beautiful body, lean and trim. Eve adored the way he made love to her. She could not get enough of him. She suspected he might have other bedmates, but she was afraid to ask, afraid to say anything that might upset him. Now, as he reached the bed, he ran his finger along her skin, just below the eyes, and said, 'Hey, baby, you're gettin' a few wrinkles. They're cute.'

Each word was a stab, a reminder of the age difference between them and the fact that she was twenty-five years old. They made love again, but for the first time Eve's mind was elsewhere.

It was almost nine o'clock when Eve arrived home. Keith was basting a roast in the oven.

He kissed her on the cheek. 'Hello, dear. I've made some of your favourite dishes. We're having –'

'Keith, I want you to remove these wrinkles.'

He blinked. 'What wrinkles?'

She pointed to the area around her eyes. 'These.'

'Those are laugh lines, darling. I love them.'

'*I* don't! I hate them!' she yelled.

'Believe me, Eve, they're not –'

'For Christ's sake, just get rid of them. That *is* what you do for a living, isn't it?'

'Yes, but – All right,' he said placatingly, 'if it will make you happy, dear.'

'When?'

'In about six weeks. My schedule is full right –'

'I'm not one of your goddamned patients,' Eve snapped. 'I'm your wife. I want you to do it now – tomorrow.'

'The clinic is closed on Saturdays.'

'Then open it!' *He was so stupid.* God, she could not wait to get rid of him. And she would. One way or another. And soon.

'Come into the other room for a moment.' He took her into the dressing room

She sat in a chair under a strong light while he carefully examined her face. In an instant he was transformed from a bumbling little milquetoast to a brilliant surgeon, and Eve could sense the transformation. She remembered the miraculous job he had done on her face. This operation might seem unnecessary to Keith, but he was wrong. It was vital. Eve could not bear the thought of losing Rory.

Keith turned off the light. 'No problem,' he assured her. 'I'll do it in the morning.'

The following morning, the two of them went to the clinic. 'I usually have a nurse to assist me,' Keith told her, 'but with something as minor as this, it won't be necessary.'

'You might as well do something with this while you're at it.' Eve tugged at a bit of skin at her throat.

'If you wish, dear. I'll give you something to put you to sleep so you won't feel any discomfort. I don't want my darling to have any pain.'

Eve watched as he filled a hypodermic and skilfully gave her an injection. She would not have minded if there had been pain. She was doing this for Rory. Darling Rory. She thought of his rock-hard body and the look in his eyes when he was hungry for her. . . . She drifted off to sleep.

She woke up in a bed in the back room of the clinic. Keith was seated in a chair next to the bed.

'How did it go?' Her voice was thick with sleep.

'Beautifully,' Keith smiled.

Eve nodded, and was asleep again.

Keith was there when she woke up later. 'We'll leave the bandages on for a few days. I'll keep you here where you can be properly cared for.'

'All right.'

He checked her each day, examined her face, nodded. 'Perfect.'

'When can I look?'

'It should be all healed by Friday,' he assured her.

She ordered the head nurse to have a private telephone installed by the bedside. The first call she made was to Rory.

'Hey, baby, where the hell are you?' he asked. 'I'm horny.'

'So am I, darling. I'm still tied up with his damned medical convention in Florida, but I'll be back next week.'

'You'd better be.'

'Have you missed me?'

'Like crazy.'

Eve heard whispering in the background. 'Is there someone there with you?'

'Yeah. We're having' a little orgy.' Rory loved to make jokes. 'Gotta go.' The line went dead.

Eve telephoned Alexandra and listened, bored,

to Alexandra's excited talk about her pregnancy. 'I can't wait,' Eve told her. 'I've always wanted to be an aunt.'

Eve seldom saw her grandmother. A coolness had developed that Eve did not understand. *She'll come around*, Eve thought.

Kate never asked about Keith, and Eve did not blame her, for he was a nothing. Perhaps one day Eve would talk to Rory about helping her get rid of Keith. That would tie Rory to her forever. It was incredible to Eve that she could cuckold her husband every day and that he neither suspected nor cared. Well, thank God he had a talent for *something*. The bandages were coming off on Friday.

Eve awakened early on Friday and waited impatiently for Keith.

'It's almost noon,' she complained. 'Where the hell have you been?'

'I'm sorry, darling,' he apologized. 'I've been in surgery all morning and –'

'I don't give a damn about that. Take these bandages off. I want to see.'

'Very well.'

Eve sat up and was still, as he deftly cut the bandages away from her face. He stood back to study her, and she saw the satisfaction in his eyes. 'Perfect.'

'Give me a mirror.'

He hurried out of the room and returned a

moment later with a hand mirror. With a proud smile, he presented it to her.

Eve raised the mirror slowly and looked at her reflection.

And screamed.

EPILOGUE

Kate

1982

THIRTY-SIX

It seemed to Kate that the wheel of time was spinning faster, hurrying the days along, blending winter into spring and summer into autumn, until all the seasons and years blurred into one. She was in her late eighties now. Eighty what? Sometimes she forgot her exact age. She could face growing old, but she could not face the idea of growing old and slovenly, and she took great pains with her appearance. When she looked in the mirror, she saw a neat erect figure of a woman, proud and indomitable.

She still went to her office every day, but it was a gesture, a ruse to ward off death. She attended every board meeting, but things were no longer as clear as they once had been. Everyone around her seemed to be speaking too rapidly. The most disturbing thing to Kate was that her mind played tricks on her. The past and present were constantly intermingling. Her world was closing in, becoming smaller and smaller.

If there was a lifeline that Kate clutched, a driving force that kept her alive, it was her passionate conviction that someone in the family must one day take charge of Kruger-Brent. Kate had no intention of letting outsiders take over what Jamie McGregor and Margaret and she and David had suffered and toiled so long and so hard for. Eve, on whom Kate had twice pinned such high hopes, was a murderer. And a *grotesque*. Kate had not had to punish her. She had seen Eve once. What had been done to her was punishment enough.

On the day Eve had seen her face in the mirror, she had tried to commit suicide. She had swallowed a bottle of sleeping pills, but Keith had pumped out her stomach and brought her home, where he hovered over her constantly. When he had to be at the hospital, day and night nurses guarded her.

'Please let me die,' Eve begged her husband. 'Please, Keith! I don't want to live like this.'

'You belong to me now,' Keith told her, 'and I'll always love you.'

The image of what her face looked like was etched in Eve's brain. She persuaded Keith to dismiss the nurses. She did not want anyone around her looking at her, staring at her.

Alexandra called again and again, but Eve refused to see her. All deliveries were left outside the front door so no one could see her face. The only person who saw her was Keith. He was, finally, the only one she had left. He was her only link with the world, and she became terrified that he would leave her, that she would be left alone with nothing but her ugliness – her unbearable ugliness.

Every morning at five o'clock, Keith arose to go to the hospital or clinic, and Eve was always up before him to fix his breakfast. She cooked dinner for him every night, and when he was late, she was filled with apprehension. What if he had found some other woman? What if he did not return to her?

When she heard his key in the door, she would rush to open it and go into his arms, holding him tightly. She never suggested they make love because she was afraid he might refuse, but when he did make love to her, Eve felt as though he was bestowing upon her a wonderful kindness.

Once she asked, timidly, 'Darling, haven't you punished me enough? Won't you repair my face?'

He looked at her and said proudly, 'It can never be repaired.'

As time went on, Keith became more demanding, more peremptory, until Eve was finally and completely a slave to him, catering to his every whim. Her ugliness bound her to him more strongly than iron chains.

Alexandra and Peter had had a son, Robert, a bright, handsome boy. He reminded Kate of Tony when he was a child. Robert was almost eight now, and precocious for his age. *Very precocious indeed*, Kate thought. *A really remarkable boy.*

All the members of the family received their invitations on the same day. The invitation read: MRS KATE BLACKWELL REQUESTS THE HONOUR OF YOUR PRESENCE TO CELEBRATE HER NINETIETH BIRTH-DAY AT CEDAR HILL HOUSE, DARK HARBOR, MAINE, ON SEPTEMBER 24, 1982, AT EIGHT O'CLOCK. BLACK TIE.

When Keith read the invitation, he looked at Eve and said, 'We're going.'

'Oh, no! I can't! You go. I'll –'

He said, 'We're both going.'

Tony Blackwell was in the garden of the sanatorium, painting, when his companion approached. 'A letter for you, Tony.'

Tony opened the envelope, and a vague smile lighted his face. 'That's nice,' he said. 'I like birth-day parties.'

Peter Templeton studied the invitation. 'I can't believe the old girl's ninety years old. She's really amazing.'

'Yes, isn't she?' Alexandra agreed. And she added thoughtfully. 'Do you know something sweet? Robert received his own invitation, addressed to him.'

670

THIRTY-SEVEN

The overnight guests had long since departed by ferry and plane, and the family was gathered in the library at Cedar Hill. Kate looked at those in the room, one by one, and she saw each with remarkable clarity. Tony, the smiling, vaguely amiable vegetable who had tried to kill her, the son who had been so full of promise and hope. Eve, the murderer, who could have owned the world if she had not had the seed of evil in her. How ironic it was, Kate thought, that her terrible punishment had come from the meek little nonentity she married. And then there was Alexandra. Beautiful, affectionate and kind – the bitterest disappointment of all. She had put her own happiness before the welfare of the company. She was not interested in Kruger-Brent and had chosen a husband who refused to have anything to do with the company. Traitors, both of them. Had all the pain of the past gone for nothing? *No*, Kate thought. *I won't let it end like this. It's not all been wasted. I've built a proud dynasty. A hospital in Cape Town is named after me. I've built schools and libraries and helped Banda's people.* Her head was beginning to hurt. The room was slowly filling with ghosts. Jamie McGregor and Margaret – looking so beautiful – and Banda smiling at her. And dear, wonderful David, holding out his arms. Kate shook her head to clear it. She was not ready for any of them yet. *Soon*, she thought. *Soon.*

There was one more member of the family in the room. She turned to her handsome great-grandson and said, 'Come here, darling.'

Robert walked up to her and took her hand.

'It sure was a great birthday party, Gran.'

'Thank you, Robert. I'm glad you enjoyed it. How are you getting along in school?'

'All A's, like you told me to get. I'm at the head of my class.'

Kate looked at Peter. 'You should send Robert to the Wharton School when he's old enough. It's the best –'

Peter laughed. 'For God's sake, Kate, my darling, don't you ever give up? Robert's going to do exactly what he likes. He has a remarkable musical talent, and he wants to be a classical musician. He's going to choose his own life.'

'You're right,' Kate sighed. 'I'm an old woman, and I have no right to interfere. If he wants to be a musician, that's what he should be.' She turned to the boy, and her eyes shone with love. 'Mind you, Robert, I can't promise anything, but I'm going to try to help you. I know someone who's a dear friend of Zubin Mehta.'

If Tomorrow Comes

*For Barry
with love*

BOOK ONE

ONE

She undressed slowly, dreamily, and when she was naked, she selected a bright red negligee to wear so that the blood would not show. Doris Whitney looked around the bedroom for the last time to make certain that the pleasant room, grown dear over the past thirty years, was neat and tidy. She opened the drawer of the bedside table and carefully removed the gun. It was shiny black, and terrifyingly cold. She placed it next to the telephone and dialled her daughter's number in Philadelphia. She listened to the echo of the distant ringing. And then there was a soft 'Hello?'

'Tracy . . . I just felt like hearing the sound of your voice, darling.'

'What a nice surprise, Mother.'

'I hope I didn't wake you up.'

'No. I was reading. Just getting ready to sleep.

3

Charles and I were going out for dinner, but the weather's too nasty. It's snowing hard here. What's it doing there?'

Dear God, we're talking about the weather, Doris Whitney thought, *when there's so much I want to tell her. And can't.*

'Mother? Are you there?'

Doris Whitney stared out the window. 'It's raining.' And she thought, *How melodramatically appropriate. Like an Alfred Hitchcock movie.*

'What's that noise?' Tracy asked.

Thunder. Too deeply wrapped in her thoughts, Doris had not been aware of it. New Orleans was having a storm. *Continued rain*, the weatherman had said. *Sixty-six degrees in New Orleans. By evening the rain will be turning to thundershowers. Be sure to carry your umbrellas.* She would not need an umbrella.

'That's thunder, Tracy.' She forced a note of cheerfulness into her voice. 'Tell me what's happening in Philadelphia.'

'I feel like a princess in a fairy tale, Mother,' Tracy said. 'I never believed anyone could be so happy. Tomorrow night I'm meeting Charles's parents.' She deepened her voice as though making a pronouncement. 'The Stanhopes, of Chestnut Hill,' she sighed. 'They're an institution. I have butterflies the size of dinosaurs.'

'Don't worry. They'll love you, darling.'

'Charles says it doesn't matter. *He* loves me. And

I adore him. I can't wait for you to meet him. He's fantastic.'

'I'm sure he is.' She would never meet Charles. She would never hold a grandchild in her lap. *No. I must not think about that.* 'Does he know how lucky he is to have you, baby?'

'I keep telling him.' Tracy laughed. 'Enough about me. Tell me what's going on there. How are you feeling?'

You're in perfect health, Doris, were Dr Rush's words. *You'll live to be a hundred.* One of life's little ironies. 'I feel wonderful.' *Talking to you.*

'Got a boyfriend yet?' Tracy teased.

Since Tracy's father had died five years earlier, Doris Whitney had not even considered going out with another man, despite Tracy's encouragement.

'No boyfriends.' She changed the subject. 'How is your job? Still enjoying it?'

'I love it. Charles doesn't mind if I keep working after we're married.'

'That's wonderful, baby. He sounds like a very understanding man.'

'He is. You'll see for yourself.'

There was a loud clap of thunder, like an off-stage cue. It was time. There was nothing more to say except a final farewell. 'Good-bye, my darling.' She kept her voice carefully steady.

'I'll see you at the wedding, Mother. I'll call you as soon as Charles and I set a date.'

'Yes.' There was one final thing to say, after all. 'I love you very, very much, Tracy.' And Doris

Whitney carefully replaced the receiver. She picked up the gun. There was only one way to do it. Quickly. She raised the gun to her temple and squeezed the trigger.

TWO

Tracy Whitney stepped out of the lobby of her block of flats into a grey, sleety rain that fell impartially on sleek limousines driven down Market Street by uniformed chauffeurs, and on the abandoned and boarded-up houses huddled together in the slums of North Philadelphia. The rain washed the limousines clean and made sodden messes of the rubbish piled high in front of the neglected row of houses. Tracy Whitney was on her way to work. Her pace was brisk as she walked east on Chestnut Street towards the bank, and it was all she could do to keep from singing aloud. She wore a bright-yellow raincoat, boots, and a yellow rain hat that barely contained a mass of shining chestnut hair. She was in her mid-twenties, with a lively, intelligent face, a full, sensuous mouth, sparkling eyes that could change from a soft moss green to a dark jade in moments, and a trim, athletic figure. Her skin ran the gamut from a translucent white to a deep rose, depending on whether she was angry, tired, or excited. Her mother had once told her, 'Honestly, child, sometimes I don't recognize you. You've got all the colours of the wind in you.'

Now, as Tracy walked down the street, people turned to smile, envying the happiness that shone on her face. She smiled back at them.

It's indecent for anyone to be this happy, Tracy Whitney thought. *I'm marrying the man I love, and I'm going to have his baby. What more could anyone ask?*

As Tracy approached the bank, she glanced at her watch. Eight-twenty. The doors of the Philadelphia Trust and Fidelity Bank would not be open to employees for another ten minutes, but Clarence Desmond, the bank's senior vice-president in charge of the international department, was already turning off the outside alarm and opening the door. Tracy enjoyed watching the morning ritual. She stood in the rain, waiting, as Desmond entered the bank and locked the door behind him.

Banks the world over have arcane safety procedures, and the Philadelphia Trust and Fidelity Bank was no exception. The routine never varied, except for the security signal, which was changed every week. The signal that week was a half-lowered venetian blind, indicating to the employees waiting outside that a search was in progress to make certain that no intruders were

8

concealed on the premises, waiting to hold the employees hostage. Clarence Desmond was checking the lavatories, storeroom, vault and safe-deposit area. Only when he was fully satisfied that he was alone would the venetian blind be raised as a sign that all was well.

The senior bookkeeper was always the first of the employees to be admitted. He would take his place next to the emergency alarm until the other employees were inside, then lock the door behind them.

Promptly at 8:30, Tracy Whitney entered the ornate lobby with her fellow workers, took off her raincoat, hat and boots, and listened with secret amusement to the others complaining about the rainy weather.

'The damned wind carried away my umbrella,' a teller complained. 'I'm soaked.'

'I passed two ducks swimming down Market Street,' the head cashier joked.

'The weatherman says we can expect another week of this. I wish I was in Florida.'

Tracy smiled and went to work. She was in charge of the cable-transfer department. Until recently, the transfer of money from one bank to another and from one country to another had been a slow, laborious process, requiring multiple forms to be filled out and dependent on national and international postal services. With the advent of computers, the situation had changed dramatically, and enormous amounts of money could be transferred instantaneously. It was Tracy's job to extract overnight transfers from the computer and to make computer transfers to other banks. All transactions were in code, changed regularly to prevent unauthorized access. Each day, millions of electronic dollars passed through Tracy's hands. It was fascinating work, the life-blood that fed the arteries of business all over the globe, and until Charles Stanhope III had come into Tracy's life, banking had been the most exciting thing in the world for her. The Philadelphia Trust and Fidelity Bank had a large international division, and at lunch Tracy and her fellow workers would discuss each morning's activities. It was heady conversation.

Deborah, the head bookkeeper, announced, 'We just closed the hundred-million-dollar syndicated loan to Turkey . . .'

Mae Trenton, secretary to the vice-president of the bank, said in a confidential tone, 'At the board meeting this morning they decided to join the new money facility to Peru. The up-front fee is over five million dollars . . .'

Jon Creighton, the bank bigot, added, 'I understand we're going in on the Mexican rescue package for fifty million. Those wetbacks don't deserve a damned cent . . .'

'It's interesting,' Tracy said thoughtfully, 'that the countries that attack America for being too money-oriented are always the first to beg us for loans.'

It was the subject on which she and Charles had had their first argument.

* * *

10

Tracy had met Charles Stanhope III at a financial symposium where Charles was the guest speaker. He ran the investment house founded by his great-grandfather, and his company did a good deal of business with the bank Tracy worked for. After Charles's lecture, Tracy had gone up to disagree with his analysis of the ability of third-world nations to repay the staggering sums of money they had borrowed from commercial banks worldwide and western governments. Charles at first had been amused, then intrigued by the impassioned arguments of the beautiful young woman before him. Their discussion had continued through dinner at the old Bookbinder's restaurant.

In the beginning, Tracy had not been impressed with Charles Stanhope III, even though she was aware that he was considered Philadelphia's prize catch. Charles was thirty-five and a rich and successful member of one of the oldest families in Philadelphia. Five feet ten inches, with thinning sandy hair, brown eyes, and an earnest, pedantic manner, he was, Tracy thought, one of the boring rich.

As though reading her mind, Charles had leaned across the table and said, 'My father is convinced they gave him the wrong baby at the hospital.'

'What?'

'I'm a throwback. I don't happen to think money is the end-all and be-all of life. But please don't ever tell my father I said so.'

There was such a charming unpretentiousness

11

about him that Tracy found herself warming to him. *I wonder what it would be like to be married to someone like him – one of the establishment.*

It had taken Tracy's father most of his life to build up a business that the Stanhopes would have sneered at as insignificant. *The Stanhopes and the Whitneys would never mix*, Tracy thought. *Oil and water. And the Stanhopes are the oil. And what am I going on about like an idiot? Talk about ego. A man asks me out to dinner and I'm deciding whether I want to marry him. We'll probably never even see each other again.*

Charles was saying, 'I hope you're free for dinner tomorrow . . . ?'

Philadelphia was a dazzling cornucopia of things to see and do. On Saturday nights Tracy and Charles went to the ballet or watched Riccardo Muti conduct the Philadelphia Orchestra. During the week they explored New Market and the unique collection of shops in Society Hill. They ate cheese steaks at a pavement table at Geno's and dined at the Café Royal, one of the most exclusive restaurants in Philadelphia. They shopped at Head House Square and wandered through the Philadelphia Museum of Art and the Rodin Museum.

Tracy paused in front of the statue of *The Thinker*. She glanced at Charles and grinned. 'It's *you*!'

Charles was not interested in exercise, but Tracy enjoyed it, so on Sunday mornings she jogged along the West River Drive or on the promenade skirting the Schuylkill River. She joined a Saturday afternoon t'ai chi ch'uan class, and after an hour's workout, exhausted but exhilarated, she would meet Charles at his apartment. He was a gourmet cook, and he liked preparing esoteric dishes such as Moroccan *bistilla* and *guo bu li*, the dumplings of northern China, and *tahine de poulet au citron* for Tracy and himself.

Charles was the most punctilious person Tracy had ever known. She had once been fifteen minutes late for a dinner appointment with him, and his displeasure had spoiled the evening for her. After that, she had vowed to be on time for him.

Tracy had had little sexual experience, but it seemed to her that Charles made love the same way he lived his life: meticulously and very properly. Once, Tracy had decided to be daring and unconventional in bed, and had so shocked Charles that she began secretly to wonder if she were some kind of sex maniac.

The pregnancy had been unexpected, and when it happened, Tracy was filled with uncertainty. Charles had not brought up the subject of marriage, and she did not want him to feel he had to marry her because of the baby. She was not certain whether she could go through with an abortion, but the alternative was an equally painful choice. Could she raise a child without the help of its father, and would it be fair to the baby?

She decided to break the news to Charles after

dinner one evening. She had prepared a *cassoulet* for him in her apartment, and in her nervousness she had burned it. As she set the scorched meat and beans in front of him, she forgot her carefully rehearsed speech and wildly blurted out, 'I'm so sorry, Charles. I'm – pregnant.'

There was an unbearably long silence, and as Tracy was about to break it, Charles said, 'We'll get married, of course.'

Tracy was filled with a sense of enormous relief. 'I don't want you to think I – You don't *have* to marry me, you know.'

He raised a hand to stop her. 'I want to marry you, Tracy. You'll make a wonderful wife.' He added, slowly, 'Of course, my mother and father will be a bit surprised.' And he smiled and kissed her.

Tracy quietly asked, 'Why will they be surprised?'

Charles sighed. 'Darling, I'm afraid you don't quite realize what you're letting yourself in for. The Stanhopes always marry – mind you, I'm using quotation marks – "their own kind". Mainline Philadelphia.'

'And they've already selected your wife,' Tracy guessed.

Charles took her in his arms. 'That doesn't matter a damn. It's whom *I've* selected that counts. We'll have dinner with Mother and Father next Friday. It's time you met them.'

At five minutes to 9:00 Tracy became aware of a difference in the noise level in the bank. The employees were beginning to speak a little faster, move a little quicker. The bank doors would open in five minutes and everything had to be in readiness. Through the front window, Tracy could see customers lined up on the pavement outside, waiting in the cold rain.

Tracy watched as the bank guard finished distributing fresh blank deposit and withdrawal slips into the metal trays on the six tables lined up along the centre aisle of the bank. Regular customers were issued deposit slips with a personal magnetized code at the bottom so that each time a deposit was made, the computer automatically credited it to the proper account. But often customers came in without their deposit slips and would fill out blank ones.

The guard glanced up at the clock on the wall, and as the hour hand moved to 9:00, he walked over to the door and ceremoniously unlocked it.

The banking day had begun.

For the next few hours Tracy was too busy at the computer to think about anything else. Every wire transfer had to be double-checked to make sure it had the correct code. When an account was to be debited, she entered the account number, the amount, and the bank to which the money was to be transferred. Each bank had its own code number, the numbers listed in a confidential directory that contained the codes for every major bank in the world.

The morning flew by swiftly. Tracy was planning to use her lunchtime to have her hair done and had made an appointment with Larry Stella Botte. He was expensive, but it would be worth it, for she wanted Charles's parents to see her at her best. *I've got to make them like me. I don't care whom they chose for him*, Tracy thought. *No one can make Charles as happy as I will.*

At 1:00, as Tracy was getting into her raincoat, Clarence Desmond summoned her to his office. Desmond was the image of an important executive. If the bank had used television commercials, he would have been the perfect spokesman. Dressed conservatively, with an air of solid, old-fashioned authority about him, he looked like a person one could trust.

'Sit down, Tracy,' he said. He prided himself on knowing every employee's first name. 'Nasty outside, isn't it?'

'Yes.'

'Ah, well. People still have to do their banking.' Desmond had used up his small talk. He leaned across his desk. 'I understand that you and Charles Stanhope are engaged to be married.'

Tracy was surprised. 'We haven't even announced it yet. How –?'

Desmond smiled. 'Anything the Stanhopes do is news. I'm very happy for you. I assume you'll be returning here to work with us. After the honeymoon, of course. We wouldn't want to lose you. You're one of our most valuable employees.'

'Charles and I talked it over, and we agreed I'd be happier if I worked.'

Desmond smiled, satisfied. Stanhope and Sons was one of the most important investment houses in the financial community, and it would be a nice plum if he could get their exclusive account for his branch. He leaned back in his chair. 'When you return from your honeymoon, Tracy, there's going to be a nice promotion for you, along with a substantial rise.'

'Oh, thank you! That's wonderful.' She knew she had earned it, she felt a thrill of pride. She could hardly wait to tell Charles. It seemed to Tracy that the gods were conspiring to do everything they could to overwhelm her with happiness.

The Charles Stanhope Seniors lived in an impressive old mansion in Rittenhouse Square. It was a city landmark that Tracy had passed often. *And now*, she thought, *it's going to be a part of my life.*

She was nervous. Her beautiful hairdo had succumbed to the dampness of the air. She had changed dresses four times. Should she dress simply? Formally? She had one Yves Saint Laurent she had scrimped to buy at Wanamaker's. *If I wear it, they'll think I'm extravagant. On the other hand, if I dress in one of my sale things from Post Horn, they'll think their son is marrying beneath him. Oh, hell, they're going to think that anyway,* Tracy decided. She finally settled on a simple grey wool skirt and a white silk blouse and fastened around her neck the slender gold chain her mother had sent her for Christmas.

The door to the mansion was opened by a liveried butler. 'Good evening, Miss Whitney.' *The butler knows my name. Is that a good sign? A bad sign?* 'May I take your coat?' She was dripping on their expensive Persian rug.

He led her through a marble hallway that seemed twice as large as the bank. Tracy thought, panicky, *Oh, my God. I'm dressed all wrong! I should have worn the Yves Saint Laurent.* As she turned into the library, she felt a ladder start at the ankle of her pantyhose, and she was face-to-face with Charles's parents.

Charles Stanhope, Sr., was a stern-looking man in his middle sixties. He *looked* a successful man; he was the projection of what his son would be like in thirty years. He had brown eyes, like Charles's, a firm chin, a fringe of white hair, and Tracy loved him instantly. He was the perfect grandfather for their child.

Charles's mother was impressive looking. She was rather short and heavy-set, but despite that, there was a regal air about her. *She looks solid and dependable*, Tracy thought. *She'll make a wonderful grandmother.*

Mrs Stanhope held out her hand. 'My dear, so good of you to join us. We've asked Charles to give us a few minutes alone with you. You don't mind?'

'Of course she doesn't mind,' Charles's father declared. 'Sit down . . . Tracy, isn't it?'

'Yes, sir.'

The two of them seated themselves on a couch facing her. *Why do I feel as though I'm about to undergo an inquisition?* Tracy could hear her mother's voice: *Baby, God will never throw anything at you that you can't handle. Just take it one step at a time.*

Tracy's first step was a weak smile that came out all wrong, because at that instant she could feel the ladder in her hose slither up to her knee. She tried to conceal it with her hands.

'So!' Mr Stanhope's voice was hearty. 'You and Charles want to get married.'

The word *want* disturbed Tracy. Surely Charles had told them they were *going* to be married.

'Yes,' Tracy said.

'You and Charles really haven't known each other long, have you?' Mrs Stanhope asked.

Tracy fought back her resentment. *I was right. It is going to be an inquisition.*

'Long enough to know that we love each other, Mrs Stanhope.'

'*Love?*' Mr Stanhope murmured.

Mrs Stanhope said, 'To be quite blunt, Miss Whitney, Charles's news came as something of a shock to his father and me.' She smiled forbearingly. 'Of course, Charles has told you about Charlotte?' She saw the expression on Tracy's face. 'I see. Well, he and Charlotte grew up together.

19

They were always very close, and – well, frankly, everyone expected them to announce their engagement this year.'

It was not necessary for her to describe Charlotte. Tracy could have drawn a picture of her. Lived next door. Rich, with the same social background as Charles. All the best schools. Loved horses and won cups.

'Tell us about your family,' Mr Stanhope suggested.

My God, this is a scene from a late-night movie, Tracy thought wildly. *I'm the Rita Hayworth character, meeting Cary Grant's parents for the first time. I need a drink. In the old movies the butler always came to the rescue with a tray of drinks.*

'Where were you born, my dear?' Mrs Stanhope asked.

'In Louisiana. My father was a mechanic.' There had been no need to add that, but Tracy was unable to resist. To hell with them. She was proud of her father.

'A *mechanic*?'

'Yes. He started a small manufacturing plant in New Orleans and built it up into a fairly large company in its field. When father died five years ago, my mother took over the business.'

'What does this – er – company manufacture?'

'Exhaust pipes and other automotive parts.'

Mr and Mrs Stanhope exchanged a look and said in unison, 'I see.'

Their tone made Tracy tense up. *I wonder how long it's going to take me to love them?* she asked herself. She looked into the two unsympathetic faces across from her, and to her horror began babbling inanely. 'You'll really like my mother. She's beautiful, and intelligent, and charming. She's from the South. She's very small, of course, about your height, Mrs Stanhope –' Tracy's words trailed off, weighed down by the oppressive silence. She gave a silly little laugh that died away under Mrs Stanhope's stare.

It was Mr Stanhope who said without expression, 'Charles informs us you're pregnant.'

Oh, how Tracy wished he had not! Their attitude was so nakedly disapproving. It was as though their son had had nothing to do with what had happened. They made her feel it was a stigma. *Now I know what I should have worn*, Tracy thought. *A scarlet letter.*

'I don't understand how in this day and –' Mrs Stanhope began, but she never finished the sentence, because at that moment Charles came into the room. Tracy had never been so glad to see anyone in her entire life.

'Well,' Charles beamed. 'How are you all getting along?'

Tracy rose and hurried into his arms. 'Fine, darling.' She held him close to her, thinking, *Thank goodness Charles isn't like his parents. He could never be like them. They're narrowminded and snobbish and cold.*

There was a discreet cough behind them, and the butler stood there with a tray of drinks. *It's going to be all right*, Tracy told herself. *This movie's going to have a happy ending.*

The dinner was excellent, but Tracy was too nervous to eat. They discussed banking and politics and the distressing state of the world, and it was all very impersonal and polite. No one actually said aloud, 'You trapped our son into marriage.' *In all fairness*, Tracy thought, *they have every right to be concerned about the woman their son marries. One day Charles will own the firm, and it's important that he have the right wife.* And Tracy promised herself, *He will have.*

Charles gently took her hand which had been twisting the napkin under the table and smiled and gave a small wink. Tracy's heart soared.

'Tracy and I prefer a small wedding,' Charles said, 'and afterwards –'

'Nonsense,' Mrs Stanhope interrupted. 'Our family does not have small weddings, Charles. There will be dozens of friends who will want to see you married.' She looked over at Tracy, evaluating her figure. 'Perhaps we should see that the wedding invitations are sent at once.' And as an afterthought, 'That is, if that's acceptable to you?'

'Yes. Yes, of course.' There *was* going to be a wedding. *Why did I even doubt it?*

Mrs Stanhope said, 'Some of the guests will be

coming from abroad. I'll make arrangements for them to stay here at the house.'

Mr Stanhope asked, 'Have you decided where you're going on your honeymoon?'

Charles smiled. 'That's privileged information, Father.' He gave Tracy's hand a squeeze.

'How long a honeymoon are you planning?' Mrs Stanhope enquired.

'About fifty years,' Charles replied. And Tracy adored him for it.

After dinner they moved into the library for brandy, and Tracy looked around at the lovely old oak-panelled room with its shelves of leather-bound volumes, the two Corots, a small Copley, and a Reynolds. It would not have mattered to her if Charles had no money at all, but she admitted to herself that this was going to be a very pleasant way to live.

It was almost midnight when Charles drove her back to her small flat off Fairmount Park.

'I hope the evening wasn't too difficult for you, Tracy. Mother and Father can be a bit stiff sometimes.'

'Oh, no, they were lovely,' Tracy lied.

She was exhausted from the tension of the evening, but when they reached the door of her flat, she asked, 'Are you going to come in, Charles?' She needed to have him hold her in his arms. She wanted him to say, 'I love you, darling. No one in this world will ever keep us apart.'

He said, 'Afraid not tonight. I've got a heavy morning.'

Tracy concealed her disappointment. 'Of course. I understand, darling.'

'I'll talk to you tomorrow.' He gave her a brief kiss, and she watched him disappear down the hallway.

The flat was ablaze and the insistent sound of loud fire bells crashed abruptly through the silence. Tracy jerked upright in her bed, groggy with sleep, sniffing for smoke in the darkened room The ringing continued, and she slowly became aware that it was the telephone. The bedside clock read 2:30 A.M. Her first panicky thought was that something had happened to Charles. She snatched up the phone. 'Hello?'

A distant male voice asked, 'Tracy Whitney?'

She hesitated. If this was an obscene phone call . . . 'Who is this?'

'This is Lieutenant Miller of the New Orleans Police Department. Is this Tracy Whitney?'

'Yes.' Her heart began to pound.

'I'm afraid I have bad news for you.'

Her hand clenched around the phone.

'It's about your mother.'

'Has – has Mother been in some kind of accident?'

'She's dead, Miss Whitney.'

'No!' It was a scream. This *was* an obscene phone call. Some crank trying to frighten her. There was nothing wrong with her mother. Her mother was alive. *I love you very, very much, Tracy.*

24

'I hate to break it to you this way,' the voice said.

It was real. It was a nightmare, but it was happening. She could not speak. Her mind and her tongue were frozen.

The lieutenant's voice was saying, 'Hello . . . ? Miss Whitney? Hello . . . ?'

'I'll be on the first plane.'

She sat in the tiny kitchen of her flat thinking about her mother. It was impossible that she was dead. She had always been so vibrant, so alive. They had had such a close and loving relationship. From the time Tracy was a small girl, she had been able to go to her mother with her problems, to discuss school and boys and, later, men. When Tracy's father had died, many overtures had been made by people who wanted to buy the business. They had offered Doris Whitney enough money so that she could have lived well for the rest of her life, but she had stubbornly refused to sell. 'Your father built up this business. I can't throw away all his hard work.' And she had kept the business flourishing.

Oh, Mother, Tracy thought. *I love you so much. You'll never meet Charles, and you'll never see your grandchildren*, and she began to weep.

She made a cup of coffee and let it grow cold while she sat in the dark. Tracy wanted desperately to call Charles and tell him what had happened, to have him at her side. She looked at the kitchen clock. It was 3:30 A.M. She did not want to awaken him; she would telephone him from New Orleans. She wondered whether this would affect their wedding plans, and instantly felt guilty at the thought. How could she even think of herself at a time like this? Lieutenant Miller had said, 'When you get here, grab a taxi and come to police headquarters.' *Why police headquarters? Why? What had happened?*

Standing in the crowded New Orleans airport waiting for her suitcase, surrounded by pushing, impatient travellers, Tracy felt suffocated. She tried to move close to the baggage carousel, but no one would let her through. She was becoming increasingly nervous, dreading what she would have to face in a little while. She kept trying to tell herself that it was all some kind of mistake, but the words kept reverberating in her head: *I'm afraid I have bad news for you . . . She's dead, Miss Whitney . . . I hate to break it to you this way . . .*

When Tracy finally retrieved her suitcase, she got into a taxi and repeated the address the lieutenant had given her: 'Seven fifteen South Broad Street, please.'

The driver grinned at her in the rearview mirror. 'Fuzzville, huh?'

No conversation. Not now. Tracy's mind was too filled with turmoil.

The taxi headed east towards the Lake Ponchartrain Causeway. The driver chattered on. 'Come here for the big show, miss?'

She had no idea what he was talking about, but she thought, *No. I came here for death*. She was aware of the drone of the driver's voice, but she did not hear the words. She sat stiffly in her seat, oblivious to the familiar surroundings that sped past. It was only as they approached the French Quarter that Tracy became conscious of the growing noise. It was the sound of a mob gone mad, rioters yelling some ancient berserk litany.

'Far as I can take you,' the driver informed her.

And then Tracy looked up and saw it. It was an incredible sight. There were hundreds of thousands of shouting people, wearing masks, disguised as dragons and giant alligators and pagan gods, filling the streets and pavements ahead with a wild cacophony of sound. It was an insane explosion of bodies and music and floats and dancing.

'Better get out before they turn my cab over,' the driver said. 'Damned Mardi Gras.'

Of course. It was February, the time when the whole city celebrated the beginning of Lent. Tracy got out of the cab and stood at the curb, suitcase in hand, and the next moment she was swept up in the screaming, dancing crowd. It was obscene, a black witches' sabbath, a million Furies celebrating the death of her mother. Tracy's suitcase was torn from her hand and disappeared. She was grabbed by a fat man in a devil's mask and kissed. A deer squeezed her breasts, and a giant panda grabbed her from behind and lifted her up. She struggled free and tried to run, but it

27

was impossible. She was hemmed in, trapped, a part of the singing, dancing celebration. She moved with the chanting mob, tears streaming down her face. There was no escape. When she was finally able to break away and flee to a quiet street, she was near hysteria. She stood still for a long time, leaning against a lamp-post, taking deep breaths, slowly regaining control of herself. She headed for the police station.

Lieutenant Miller was a middle-aged, harassed-looking man with a weather-beaten face, who seemed genuinely uncomfortable in his role. 'Sorry I couldn't meet you at the airport,' he told Tracy, 'but the whole town's gone nuts. We went through your mother's things, and you're the only one we could find to call.'

'Please, Lieutenant, tell me what – what happened to my mother.'

'She committed suicide.'

A cold chill went through her. 'That's – that's impossible! Why would she kill herself? She had everything to live for.' Her voice was ragged.

'She left a note addressed to you.'

The morgue was cold and indifferent and terrifying. Tracy was led down a long white corridor into a large, sterile, empty room, and suddenly she realized that the room was not empty. It was filled with the dead. Her dead.

A white-coated attendant strolled over to a wall,

reached for a handle, and pulled out an oversized drawer. 'Wanna take a look?'

No! I don't want to see the empty, lifeless body lying in that box. She wanted to get out of this place. She wanted to go back a few hours in time when the fire bell was ringing. *Let it be a real fire alarm, not the telephone, not my mother dead.* Tracy moved forward slowly, each step a screaming inside her. Then she was staring down at the lifeless remains of the body that had borne her, nourished her, laughed with her, loved her. She bent over and kissed her mother on the cheek. The cheek was cold and rubbery. 'Oh, Mother,' Tracy whispered. 'Why? Why did you do it?'

'We gotta perform an autopsy,' the attendant was saying. 'It's the state law with suicides.'

The note Doris Whitney left offered no answer.

My darling Tracy,

Please forgive me. I failed, and I couldn't stand being a burden on you. This is the best way. I love you so much.

Mother

The note was as lifeless and devoid of meaning as the body that lay in the drawer.

That afternoon Tracy made the funeral arrangements, then took a taxi to the family home. In the far distance she could hear the roar of the Mardi Gras revellers, like some alien, lurid celebration.

The Whitney residence was a Victorian house located in the Garden District in the residential section known as Uptown. Like most of the homes in New Orleans, it was built of wood and had no basement, for the area was situated below sea level.

Tracy had grown up in that house, and it was filled with warm, comfortable memories. She had not been home in the past year, and as her taxi slowed to a stop in front of the house, she was shocked to see a large sign on the lawn: FOR SALE – NEW ORLEANS REALTY COMPANY. It was impossible. *I'll never sell this old house*, her mother had often told her. *We've all been so happy together here.*

Filled with a strange, unreasoning fire, Tracy moved past a giant magnolia tree towards the front door. She had been given her own key to the house when she was in the seventh grade and had carried it with her since, as a talisman, a reminder of the haven that would always be there waiting for her.

She opened the door and stepped inside. She stood there, stunned. The rooms were completely empty, stripped of furniture. All the beautiful antique pieces were gone. The house was like a barren shell deserted by the people who had once occupied it. Tracy ran from room to room, her disbelief growing. It was as though some sudden disaster had struck. She hurried upstairs and stood in the doorway of the bedroom she had occupied most of her life. It stared back at her, cold and empty. *Oh, God, what could have happened?* Tracy heard the sound of the front doorbell and walked as if in a trance down the stairs to answer it.

Otto Schmidt stood in the doorway. The foreman of the Whitney Automotive Parts Company was an elderly man with a seamed face and a body that was rail-thin, except for a protruding beer belly. A tonsure of straggly grey hair framed his scalp.

'Tracy,' he said in a heavy German accent, 'I just heard the news. I – I can't tell you how sorry I am.'

Tracy clasped his hands. 'Oh, Otto. I'm so glad to see you. Come in.' She led him into the empty living room. 'I'm sorry there's no place to sit down,' she apologized. 'Do you mind sitting on the floor?'

'No, no.'

They sat down across from each other, their eyes dumb with misery. Otto Schmidt had been an employee of the company for as long as Tracy could remember. She knew how much her father had depended on him. When her mother had inherited the business, Schmidt had stayed on to run it for her. 'Otto, I don't understand what's happening. The police say Mother committed suicide, but you know there was no reason for her to kill herself.' A sudden thought stabbed at her. 'She wasn't ill, was she? She didn't have some terrible –'

'No. It wasn't that. Not that.' He looked away, uncomfortable, something unspoken in his words.

Tracy said slowly, 'You know what it was.'

31

He peered at her through rheumy blue eyes. 'Your mama didn't tell you what's been happening lately. She didn't want to worry you.'

Tracy frowned. 'Worry me about what? Go on . . . *please*.'

His work-worn hands opened and closed. 'Have you heard of a man called Joe Romano?'

'Joe Romano? No. Why?'

Otto Schmidt blinked. 'Six months ago Romano got in touch with your mother and said he wanted to buy the company. She told him she wasn't interested in selling, but he offered her ten times what the company was worth, and she couldn't refuse. She was so excited. She was going to invest all the money in bonds that would bring in an income that both of you could live on comfortably for the rest of your lives. She was going to surprise you. I was so glad for her. I've been ready to retire for the last three years, Tracy, but I couldn't leave Mrs Doris, could I? This Romano –' Otto almost spat out the word. 'This Romano gave her a small down payment. The big money – the balloon payment – was to have come last month.'

Tracy said impatiently, 'Go on, Otto. What happened?'

'When Romano took over, he fired everybody and brought in his own people to run things. Then he began to raid the company. He sold all the assets and ordered a lot of equipment, selling it off but not paying for it. The suppliers weren't worried about the delay in payment because they thought they were still dealing with your mother. When they finally began pressing your mother for their money, she went to Romano and demanded to know what was going on. He told her he had decided not to go ahead with the deal and was returning the company to her. By then, the company was not only worthless but your mother owed half a million dollars she couldn't pay. Tracy, it nearly killed me and the wife to watch how your mother fought to save that company. There was no way. They forced her into bankruptcy. They took everything – the business, this house, even her car.'

'Oh, my God!'

'There's more. The district attorney served your mother notice that he was going to ask for an indictment against her for fraud, that she was facing a prison sentence. That was the day she really died, I think.'

Tracy was seething with a wave of helpless anger. 'But all she had to do was tell them the truth – explain what that man did to her.'

The old foreman shook his head. 'Joe Romano works for a man named Anthony Orsatti. Orsatti runs New Orleans. I found out too late that Romano's done this before with other companies. Even if your mother had taken him to court, it would have been years before it was all untangled, and she didn't have the money to fight him.'

'Why didn't she tell me?' It was a cry of anguish, a cry for her mother's anguish.

'Your mother was a proud woman. And what could you do? There's nothing anyone can do.'

You're wrong, Tracy thought fiercely. 'I want to see Joe Romano. Where can I find him?'

Schmidt said flatly, 'Forget about him. You have no idea how powerful he is.'

'Where does he live, Otto?'

'He has an estate near Jackson Square, but it won't help to go there, Tracy, believe me.'

Tracy did not answer. She was filled with an emotion totally unfamiliar to her: hatred. *Joe Romano is going to pay for killing my mother*, Tracy swore to herself.

THREE

She needed time. Time to think, time to plan her next move. She could not bear to go back to the despoiled house, so she checked into a small hotel on Magazine Street, far from the French Quarter, where the mad parades were still going on. She had no luggage, and the suspicious clerk behind the desk said, 'You'll have to pay in advance. That'll be forty dollars for the night.'

From her room Tracy telephoned Clarence Desmond to tell him she would be unable to come to work for a few days.

He concealed his irritation at being inconvenienced. 'Don't worry about it,' he told Tracy. 'I'll find someone to fill in until you return.' He hoped she would remember to tell Charles Stanhope how understanding he had been.

Tracy's next call was to Charles. 'Charles, darling –'

'Where the devil *are* you, Tracy? Mother has

35

been trying to reach you all morning. She wanted to have lunch with you today. You two have a lot of arrangements to go over.'

'I'm sorry, darling. I'm in New Orleans.'

'You're *where*? What are you doing in New Orleans?'

'My mother – died.' The word stuck in her throat.

'Oh.' The tone of his voice changed instantly. 'I'm sorry, Tracy. It must have been very sudden. She was quite young, wasn't she?'

She was very young, Tracy thought miserably. Aloud she said, 'Yes. Yes, she was.'

'What happened? Are you all right?'

Somehow Tracy could not bring herself to tell Charles that it was suicide. She wanted desperately to cry out the whole terrible story about what they had done to her mother, but she stopped herself. *It's my problem*, she thought. *I can't throw my burden on Charles*. She said, 'Don't worry. I'm all right, darling.'

'Would you like me to come down there, Tracy?'

'No. Thank you. I can handle it. I'm burying Mama tomorrow. I'll be back in Philadelphia on Monday.'

When she hung up, she lay on the hotel bed, her thoughts unfocused. She counted stained acoustical tiles on the ceiling. One . . . two . . . three . . . Romano . . . four . . . five . . . Joe Romano . . . six . . . seven . . . he was going to pay. She had no plan. She knew only that she was not going to let Joe Romano get away with what

36

he had done, that she would find some way to avenge her mother.

Tracy left her hotel in the late afternoon and walked along Canal Street until she came to a pawn shop. A cadaverous-looking man wearing an old-fashioned green eyeshade sat in a cage behind a counter.

'Help you?'

'I – I want to buy a gun.'

'What kind of gun?'

'You know . . . a . . . revolver.'

'You want a thirty-two, a forty-five, a –'

Tracy had never even held a gun. 'A – a thirty-two will do.'

'I have a nice thirty-two calibre Smith and Wesson here for two hundred and twenty-nine dollars, or a Charter Arms thirty-two for a hundred and fifty-nine . . .'

She had not brought much cash with her. 'Have you got something cheaper?'

He shrugged. '*Cheaper* is a slingshot, lady. Tell you what. I'll let you have the thirty-two for a hundred and fifty, and I'll throw in a box of bullets.'

'All right.' Tracy watched as he moved over to an arsenal on a table behind him and selected a revolver. He brought it to the counter. 'You know how to use it?'

'You – you pull the trigger.'

He grunted. 'Do you want me to show you how to load it?'

She started to say no, that she was not going to

use it, that she just wanted to frighten someone, but she realized how foolish that would sound. 'Yes, please.'

Tracy watched as he inserted the bullets into the chamber. 'Thank you.' She reached in her purse and counted out the money.

'I'll need your name and address for the police records.'

That had not occurred to Tracy. Threatening Joe Romano with a gun was a criminal act. *But he's the criminal, not I.*

The green eyeshade made the man's eyes a pale yellow as he watched her. 'Name?'

'Smith. Joan Smith.'

He made a note on a card. 'Address?'

'Dowman Road. Thirty-twenty Dowman Road.'

Without looking up he said, 'There is no Thirty-twenty Dowman Road. That would be in the middle of the river. We'll make it Fifty-twenty.' He pushed the receipt in front of her.

She signed JOAN SMITH. 'Is that it?'

'That's it.' He carefully pushed the revolver through the cage. Tracy stared at it, then picked it up, put it in her handbag, turned and hurried out of the shop.

'Hey, lady,' he yelled after her. 'Don't forget that gun is loaded!'

Jackson Square is in the heart of the French Quarter, with the beautiful St Louis Cathedral towering over it like a benediction. Lovely old homes and estates in the square are sheltered from the bustling street traffic by tall hedges and graceful magnolia trees. Joe Romano lived in one of those houses.

Tracy waited until dark before she set out. The parades had moved on to Chartres Street, and in the distance Tracy could hear an echo of the pandemonium she had been swept up in earlier.

She stood in the shadows, studying the house, conscious of the heavy weight of the gun in her handbag. The plan she had worked out was simple. She was going to reason with Joe Romano, ask him to clear her mother's name. If he refused, she would threaten him with the gun and force him to write out a confession. She would take it to Lieutenant Miller, and he would arrest Romano, and her mother's name would be protected. She wished desperately that Charles were there with her, but it was best to do it alone. Charles had to be left out of it. She would tell him about it when it was all over and Joe Romano was behind bars, where he belonged. A pedestrian was approaching. Tracy waited until he had walked past and the street was deserted.

She walked up to the house and pressed the doorbell. There was no answer. *He's probably at one of the private krewes balls given during Mardi Gras. But I can wait*, Tracy thought. *I can wait until he gets home.* Suddenly, the porch light snapped on, the front door opened, and a man stood in the doorway. His appearance was a surprise to Tracy. She had visualized a sinister-looking mobster, evil

39

written all over his face. Instead, she found herself facing an attractive, pleasant-looking man who could easily have been mistaken for a university professor. His voice was low and friendly. 'Hello. May I help you?'

'Are you Joseph Romano?' Her voice was shaky.

'Yes. What can I do for you?' He had an easy, engaging manner. *No wonder my mother was taken in by this man*, Tracy thought.

'I – I'd like to talk to you, Mr Romano.'

He studied her figure for a moment. 'Certainly. Please come in.'

Tracy walked into a living room filled with beautiful, burnished antique furniture. Joseph Romano lived well. *On my mother's money*, Tracy thought bitterly.

'I was just about to mix myself a drink. What would you like?'

'Nothing.'

He looked at her curiously. 'What was it you wanted to see me about, Miss –?'

'Tracy Whitney. I'm Doris Whitney's daughter.'

He stared at her blankly for an instant, and then a look of recognition flashed across his face. 'Oh, yes. I heard about your mother. Too bad.'

Too bad! He had caused the death of her mother, and his only comment was: 'Too bad'.

'Mr Romano, the district attorney believes that my mother was guilty of fraud. You know that's not true. I want you to help me clear her name.'

He shrugged. 'I never talk business during Mardi

Gras. It's against my religion.' Romano walked over to the bar and began mixing drinks. 'I think you'll feel better after you've had a drink.'

He was leaving her no choice. Tracy opened her handbag and pulled out the revolver. She pointed it at him. 'I'll tell you what will make me feel better, Mr Romano. Having you confess to exactly what you did to my mother.'

Joseph Romano turned and saw the gun. 'You'd better put that away, Miss Whitney. It could go off.'

'It's *going* to go off if you don't do exactly what I tell you to. You're going to write down how you stripped the company, put it into bankruptcy, and drove my mother to suicide.'

He was watching her carefully now, his dark eyes wary. 'I see. What if I refuse?'

'Then I'm going to kill you.' She could feel the gun shaking in her hand.

'You don't look like a killer, Miss Whitney.' He was moving towards her now, a drink in his hand. His voice was soft and sincere. 'I had nothing to do with your mother's death, and believe me, I –' He threw the drink in her face.

Tracy felt the sharp sting of the alcohol in her eyes, and an instant later the gun was knocked from her hand.

'Your old lady held out on me,' Joe Romano said. 'She didn't tell me she had a horny-looking daughter.'

He was holding her, pinning her arms, and Tracy was blinded and terrified. She tried to move away

41

from him, but he backed her into a wall, pressing against her.

'You have guts, baby. I like that. It turns me on.' His voice was hoarse. Tracy could feel his body hard against hers, and she tried to twist away, but she was helpless in his grip.

'You came here for a little excitement, huh? Well, Joe's going to give it to you.'

She tried to scream, but her voice came out in a gasp. 'Let me go!'

He ripped her blouse away. 'Hey! Look at those tits,' he whispered. He began pinching her nipples. 'Fight me, baby,' he whispered. 'I love it.'

'Let go of me!'

He was squeezing harder, hurting her. She felt herself being forced down to the floor.

'I'll bet you've never been fucked by a real man,' he said. He was astride her now, his body heavy on hers, his hands moving up her thighs. Tracy pushed out blindly, and her fingers touched the gun. She grabbed for it, and there was a sudden, loud explosion.

'Oh, Jesus!' Romano cried. His grip suddenly relaxed. Through a red mist, Tracy watched in horror as he fell off her and slumped to the floor, clutching his side. 'You shot me . . . you bitch. You shot me . . .'

Tracy was transfixed, unable to move. She felt she was going to be sick, and her eyes were blinded by stabbing pain. She pulled herself to her feet, turned, and stumbled to a door at the far end of the room. She pushed it open. It was a bathroom. She staggered over to the sink, filled the basin with cold water, and bathed her eyes until the pain began to subside and her vision cleared. She looked into the cabinet mirror. Her eyes were bloodshot and wild looking. *My God, I've just killed a man.* She ran back into the living room.

Joe Romano lay on the floor, his blood seeping onto the white rug. Tracy stood over him, white-faced. 'I'm sorry,' she said inanely. 'I didn't mean to –'

'Ambulance . . .' His breathing was ragged.

Tracy hurried to the telephone on the desk and dialled the operator. When she tried to speak, her voice was choked. 'Operator, send an ambulance right away. The address is Four-twenty-one Jackson Square. A man has been shot.'

She replaced the receiver and looked down at Joe Romano. *Oh, God*, she prayed, *please don't let him die. You know I didn't mean to kill him.* She knelt beside the body on the floor to see if he was still alive. His eyes were closed, but he was breathing. 'An ambulance is on its way,' Tracy promised.

She fled.

She tried not to run, afraid of attracting attention. She pulled her jacket close around her to conceal her ripped blouse. Four blocks from the house Tracy tried to hail a taxi. Half a dozen sped past her, filled with happy, laughing passengers. In the distance Tracy heard the sound of an approaching siren, and seconds later an ambulance raced past her, headed in the direction of Joe Romano's house. *I've got to get away from here*, Tracy thought. Ahead of her, a taxi pulled to the curb and discharged its passengers. Tracy ran towards it, afraid of losing it. 'Are you free?'

'That depends. Where you goin'?'

'The airport.' She held her breath.

'Get in.'

On the way to the airport, Tracy thought about the ambulance. What if they were too late and Joe Romano was dead? She would be a murderess. She had left the gun back at the house, and her fingerprints were on it. She could tell the police that Romano had tried to rape her and that the gun had gone off accidentally, but they would never believe her. She had purchased the gun that was lying on the floor beside Joe Romano. How much time had passed? Half an hour? An hour? She had to get out of New Orleans as quickly as possible.

'Enjoy the carnival?' the driver asked.

Tracy swallowed. 'I – yes.' She pulled out her hand mirror and did what she could to make herself presentable. She had been stupid to try to make Joe Romano confess. Everything had gone wrong. *How can I tell Charles what happened?* She knew how shocked he would be, but after she explained, he would understand. Charles would know what to do.

When the taxi arrived at New Orleans International Airport, Tracy wondered, *Was it only this morning that I was here? Did all this happen in just one day?* Her mother's suicide . . . the horror of being swept up in the carnival . . . the man snarling, 'You shot me . . . you bitch . . .'

When Tracy walked into the terminal, it seemed to her that everyone was staring at her accusingly. *That's what a guilty conscience does*, she thought. She wished there were some way she could learn about Joe Romano's condition, but she had no idea what hospital he would be taken to or whom she could call. *He's going to be all right. Charles and I will come back for Mother's funeral, and Joe Romano will be fine.* She tried to push from her mind the vision of the man lying on the white rug, his blood staining it red. She had to hurry home to Charles.

Tracy approached the Delta Airlines counter. 'I'd like a one-way ticket on the next flight to Philadelphia, please. Tourist.'

The passenger representative consulted his computer. 'That will be Flight three-o-four. You're in luck. I have one seat left.'

'What time does the plane leave?'

'In twenty minutes. You just have time to board.'

As Tracy reached into her handbag, she sensed rather than saw two uniformed police officers step up on either side of her. One of them said, 'Tracy Whitney?'

Her heart stopped beating for an instant. *It would be stupid to deny my identity.* 'Yes . . .'

'You're under arrest.'

And Tracy felt the cold steel of handcuffs snapped on her wrists.

Everything was happening in slow motion to someone else. Tracy watched herself being led through the airport, manacled to one of the policemen, while passersby turned to stare. She was shoved into the back of a black-and-white squad car with steel mesh separating the front seat from the rear. The police car sped away from the curb with red lights flashing and sirens screaming. She huddled in the back seat, trying to become invisible. She was a murderess. Joseph Romano had died. But it had been an accident. She would explain how it happened. They had to believe her. They *had* to.

The police station Tracy was taken to was in the Algiers district, on the west bank of New Orleans, a grim and foreboding building with a look of hopelessness about it. The booking room was crowded with seedy-looking characters – prostitutes, pimps, muggers and their victims. Tracy was marched to the desk of the sergeant-on-watch.

One of her captors said, 'The Whitney woman, Sarge. We caught her at the airport tryin' to escape.'

'I wasn't –'

'Take the cuffs off.'

The handcuffs were removed. Tracy found her voice. 'It was an accident. I didn't mean to kill him. He tried to rape me and –' She could not control the hysteria in her voice.

The desk sergeant said curtly, 'Are you Tracy Whitney?'

'Yes. I –'

'Lock her up.'

'No! Wait a minute,' she pleaded. 'I have to call someone. I – I'm entitled to make a phone call.'

The desk sergeant grunted, 'You know the routine, huh? How many times you been in the slammer, honey?'

'None. This is –'

'You get one call. Three minutes. What number do you want?'

She was so nervous that she could not remember Charles's telephone number. She could not even recall the area code for Philadelphia. *Was it two-five-one?* No. That was not it. She was trembling.

'Come on. I haven't got all night.'

Two-one-five. That was it! 'Two-one-five-five-five-five-nine-three-zero-one.'

The desk sergeant dialled the number and handed the phone to Tracy. She could hear the phone ringing. And ringing. There was no answer. *Charles had to be home.*

The desk sergeant said, 'Time's up.' He started to take the phone from her.

'Please wait!' she cried. But she suddenly remembered that Charles shut off his phone at night so that he would not be disturbed. She listened to the hollow ringing and realized there was no way she could reach him.

The desk sergeant asked, 'You through?'

47

Tracy looked up at him and said dully, 'I'm through.'

A policeman in shirt-sleeves took Tracy into a room where she was booked and fingerprinted, then led down a corridor and locked in a holding cell, by herself.

'You'll have a hearing in the morning,' the policeman told her. He walked away, leaving her alone.

None of this is happening, Tracy thought. *This is all a terrible dream. Oh, please, God, don't let any of this be real.*

But the stinking cot in the cell was real, and the seatless toilet in the corner was real, and the bars were real.

The hours of the night dragged by endlessly. *If only I could have reached Charles.* She needed him now more than she had ever needed anyone in her life. *I should have confided in him in the first place. If I had, none of this would have happened.*

At 6:00 A.M. a bored guard brought Tracy a breakfast of tepid coffee and cold oatmeal. She could not touch it. Her stomach was in knots. At 9:00 a matron came for her.

'Time to go, sweetie.' She unlocked the cell door.

'I must make a call,' Tracy said. 'It's very –'

'Later,' the matron told her. 'You don't want to keep the judge waiting. He's a mean son of a bitch.'

She escorted Tracy down a corridor and through a door that led into a courtroom. An elderly judge was seated on the bench. His head and hands kept moving in small, quick jerks. In front of him stood the district attorney, Ed Topper, a slight man in his forties, with crinkly salt-and-pepper hair cut en brosse, and cold, black eyes.

Tracy was led to a seat, and a moment later the bailiff called out, 'People against Tracy Whitney', and Tracy found herself moving towards the bench. The judge was scanning a sheet of paper in front of him, his head bobbing up and down.

Now. Now was Tracy's moment to explain to someone in authority the truth about what had happened. She pressed her hands together to keep them from trembling. 'Your Honour, it wasn't murder. I shot him, but it was an accident. I only meant to frighten him. He tried to rape me and –'

The district attorney interrupted. 'Your Honour, I see no point in wasting the court's time. This woman broke into Mr Romano's home, armed with a thirty-two-calibre revolver, stole a Renoir painting worth half a million dollars, and when Mr Romano caught her in the act, she shot him in cold blood and left him for dead.'

Tracy felt the colour draining from her face. 'What – what are you *talking* about?'

None of this was making any sense.

The district attorney rapped out, 'We have the gun with which she wounded Mr Romano. Her fingerprints are on it.'

Wounded! Then Joseph Romano was alive! She had not killed anyone.

'She escaped with the painting, Your Honour. It's probably in the hands of a fence by now. For that reason, the state is requesting that Tracy Whitney be held for attempted murder and armed robbery and that bail be set at half a million dollars.'

The judge turned to Tracy, who stood there in shock. 'Are you represented by counsel?'

She did not even hear him.

He raised his voice. 'Do you have an attorney?'

Tracy shook her head. 'No. I – what – what this man said isn't true. I never –'

'Do you have money for an attorney?'

There was her employees' fund at the bank. There was Charles. 'I . . . no, Your Honour, but I don't understand –'

'The court will appoint one for you. You are ordered held in jail, in lieu of five hundred thousand dollars bail. Next case.'

'Wait! This is all a mistake! I'm not –'

She had no recollection of being led from the courtroom.

The name of the attorney appointed by the court was Perry Pope. He was in his late thirties, with a craggy, intelligent face and sympathetic blue eyes. Tracy liked him immediately.

He walked into her cell, sat on the cot, and said, 'Well! You've created quite a sensation for a lady who's been in town only twenty-four hours.' He grinned. 'But you're lucky. You're a lousy shot. It's only a flesh wound. Romano's going to live.' He took out a pipe. 'Mind?'

'No.'

He filled his pipe with tobacco, lit it, and studied Tracy. 'You don't *look* like the average desperate criminal, Miss Whitney.'

'I'm not. I *swear* I'm not.'

'Convince me,' he said. 'Tell me what happened. From the beginning. Take your time.'

Tracy told him. Everything. Perry Pope sat quietly listening to her story, not speaking until Tracy had finished. Then he leaned back against the wall of the cell, a grim expression on his face. 'That bastard,' Pope said softly.

'I don't understand what they were talking about.' There was confusion in Tracy's eyes. 'I don't understand anything about a painting.'

'It's really very simple. Joe Romano used you as a patsy, the same way he used your mother. You walked right into a set-up.'

'I still don't understand.'

'Then let me lay it out for you. Romano will put in an insurance claim for half a million dollars for the Renoir he's hidden away somewhere, and he'll collect. The insurance company will be after *you*, not him. When things cool down, he'll sell the painting to a private party and make another half million, thanks to your do-it-yourself approach. Didn't you realise that a confession obtained at the point of a gun is worthless?'

'I – I suppose so. I just thought that if I could

get the truth out of him, someone would start an investigation.'

His pipe had gone out. He relit it. 'How did you enter his house?'

'I rang the front doorbell, and Mr Romano let me in.'

'That's not his story. There's a smashed window at the back of the house, where he says you broke in. He told the police he caught you sneaking out with the Renoir, and when he tried to stop you, you shot him and ran.'

'That's a lie! I –'

'But it's *his* lie, and his house, and your gun. Do you have any idea with whom you're dealing?'

Tracy shook her head mutely.

'Then let me tell you the facts of life, Miss Whitney. This town is sewn up tight by the Orsatti Family. Nothing goes down here without Anthony Orsatti's okay. If you want a permit to put up a building, pave a highway, run girls, numbers, or dope, you see Orsatti. Joe Romano started out as his hit man. Now he's the top man in Orsatti's organisation.' He looked at her in wonder. 'And you walked into Romano's house and pulled a gun on him.'

Tracy sat there, numb and exhausted. Finally she asked, 'Do you believe my story?'

He smiled. 'You're damned right. It's so dumb it has to be true.'

'Can you help me?'

He said slowly, 'I'm going to try. I'd give anything

to put them all behind bars. They own this town and most of the judges in it. If you go to trial, they'll bury you so deep you'll never see daylight again.'

Tracy looked at him, puzzled. '*If* I go to trial?'

Pope stood and paced up and down in the small cell. 'I don't want to put you in front of a jury, because, believe me, it will be *his* jury. There's only one judge Orsatti has never been able to buy. His name is Henry Lawrence. If I can arrange for him to hear this case, I'm pretty sure I can make a deal for you. It's not strictly ethical, but I'm going to speak to him privately. He hates Orsatti and Romano as much as I do. Now all we've got to do is get to Judge Lawrence.'

Perry Pope arranged for Tracy to place a telephone call to Charles. Tracy heard the familiar voice of Charles's secretary. 'Mr Stanhope's office.'

'Harriet. This is Tracy Whitney. Is –?'

'Oh! He's been trying to reach you, Miss Whitney, but we didn't have a telephone number for you. Mrs Stanhope is most anxious to discuss the wedding arrangements with you. If you could call her as soon as possible –'

'Harriet, may I speak to Mr Stanhope, please?'

'I'm sorry, Miss Whitney. He's on his way to Houston for a meeting. If you'll give me your number, I'm sure he'll telephone you as soon as he can.'

'I –' There was no way she could have him telephone her at the jail. Not until she had a chance to explain things to him first.

'I – I'll have to call Mr Stanhope back.' She slowly replaced the receiver.

Tomorrow. Tracy thought wearily. *I'll explain it all to Charles tomorrow.*

That afternoon Tracy was moved to a larger cell. A delicious hot dinner appeared from Galatoire's, and a short time later fresh flowers arrived with a note attached. Tracy opened the envelope and pulled out the card. CHIN UP, WE'RE GOING TO BEAT THE BASTARDS. PERRY POPE.

He came to visit Tracy the following morning. The instant she saw the smile on his face, she knew there was good news.

'We got lucky,' he exclaimed. 'I've just left Judge Lawrence and Topper, the district attorney. Topper screamed like a banshee, but we've got a deal.'

'A deal?'

'I told Judge Lawrence your whole story. He's agreed to accept a guilty plea from you.'

Tracy stared at him in shock. 'A *guilty* plea? But I'm not –'

He raised a hand. 'Hear me out. By pleading guilty, you save the state the expense of a trial. I've per-suaded the judge that you didn't steal the painting. He knows Joe Romano, and he believes me.'

'But . . . if I plead guilty,' Tracy asked slowly, 'what will they do to me?'

'Judge Lawrence will sentence you to three months in prison with –'

'Prison!'

'Wait a minute. He'll suspend the sentence, and you can do your probation out of state.'

'But then I'll – I'll have a record.'

Perry Pope sighed. 'If they put you on trial for armed robbery and attempted murder during the commission of a felony, you could be sentenced to ten years.'

Ten years in jail!

Perry Pope was patiently watching her. 'It's your decision,' he said. 'I can only give you my best advice. It's a miracle that I got away with this. They want an answer now. You don't have to take the deal. You can get another lawyer and –'

'No.' She knew that this man was honest. Under the circumstances, considering her insane behaviour, he had done everything possible for her. If only she could talk to Charles. But they needed an answer now. She was probably lucky to get off with a three-month suspended sentence.

'I'll – I'll take the deal,' Tracy said. She had to force the words out.

He nodded. 'Smart girl.'

She was not permitted to make any phone calls before she was returned to the courtroom. Ed Topper stood on one side of her, and Perry Pope on the other. Seated on the bench was a distinguished-looking man in his fifties, with a smooth, unlined face and thick, styled hair.

Judge Henry Lawrence said to Tracy, 'The court has been informed that the defendant wishes to change her plea from not guilty to guilty. Is that correct?'

'Yes, Your Honour.'

'Are all parties in agreement?'

Perry Pope nodded. 'Yes, Your Honour.'

'The state agrees, Your Honour,' the district attorney said.

Judge Lawrence sat there in silence for a long moment. Then he leaned forward and looked into Tracy's eyes. 'One of the reasons this great country of ours is in such pitiful shape is that the streets are crawling with vermin who think they can get away with anything. People who laugh at the law. Some judicial systems in this country coddle criminals. Well, in Louisiana, we don't believe in that. When, during the commission of felony, someone tries to kill in cold blood, we believe that that person should be properly punished.'

Tracy began to feel the first stirrings of panic. She turned to look at Perry Pope. His eyes were fixed on the judge.

'The defendant has admitted that she attempted to murder one of the outstanding citizens of this community – a man noted for his philanthropy and good works. The defendant shot him while in the act of stealing an art object worth half a million dollars.' His voice grew harsher. 'Well, this court is going to see to it that you don't get to enjoy that money – not for the next fifteen years, because for the next fifteen years you're going to be incarcerated in the Southern Louisiana Penitentiary for Women.'

Tracy felt the courtroom begin to spin. Some horrible joke was being played. The judge was an actor typecast for the part, but he was reading the wrong lines. He was not supposed to say any of those things. She turned to explain that to Perry Pope, but his eyes were averted. He was juggling papers in his briefcase, and for the first time, Tracy noticed that his fingernails were bitten to the quick. Judge Lawrence had risen and was gathering up his notes. Tracy stood there, numb, unable to comprehend what was happening to her.

A bailiff stepped to Tracy's side and took her arm. 'Come along,' he said.

'No,' Tracy cried. 'No, please!' She looked up at the judge. 'There's been a terrible mistake, Your Honour. I –'

And as she felt the bailiff's grip tighten on her arm, Tracy realised there had been no mistake. She had been tricked. They were going to destroy her.

Just as they had destroyed her mother.

FOUR

The news of Tracy Whitney's crime and sentencing appeared on the front page of the *New Orleans Courier*, accompanied by a police photograph of her. The major wire services picked up the story and flashed it to correspondent newspapers around the country, and when Tracy was taken from the courtroom to await transport to the state penitentiary, she was confronted by a crew of television reporters. She hid her face in humiliation, but there was no escape from the cameras. Joe Romano was big news, and the attempt on his life by a beautiful female burglar was even bigger news. It seemed to Tracy that she was surrounded by enemies. *Charles will get me out*, she kept repeating to herself. *Oh, please, God, let Charles get me out. I can't have our baby born in prison.*

It was not until the following afternoon that the desk sergeant would permit Tracy to use the telephone. Harriet answered. 'Mr Stanhope's office.'

'Harriet, this is Tracy Whitney. I'd like to speak to Mr Stanhope.'

'Just a moment, Miss Whitney.' She heard the hesitation in the secretary's voice. 'I'll – I'll see if Mr Stanhope is in.'

After a long, harrowing wait, Tracy finally heard Charles's voice. She could have wept with relief. 'Charles –'

'Tracy? Is that you, Tracy?'

'Yes, darling. Oh, Charles, I've been trying to reach –'

'I've been going crazy, Tracy! The newspapers here are full of wild stories about you. I can't believe what they're saying.'

'None of it is true, darling. *None* of it. I –'

'Why didn't you call me?'

'I tried. I couldn't reach you. I –'

'Where are you now?'

'I'm – I'm in jail in New Orleans. Charles, they're going to send me to prison for something I didn't do.' To her horror, she was weeping.

'Hold on. Listen to me. The papers say that you shot a man. That's not true, is it?'

'I did shoot him, but –'

'Then it *is* true.'

'It's not the way it sounds, darling. It's not like that at all. I can explain everything to you. I –'

'Tracy, did you plead guilty to attempted murder and stealing a painting?'

'Yes, Charles, but only because –'

'My God, if you needed money that badly, you

should have discussed it with me . . . And trying to kill someone . . . I can't believe this. Neither can my parents. You're the headline in this morning's Philadelphia *Daily News*. This is the first time a breath of scandal has ever touched the Stanhope family.'

It was the bitter self-control of Charles's voice that made Tracy aware of the depth of his feelings. She had counted on him so desperately, and he was on *their* side. She forced herself not to scream. 'Darling, I need you. Please come down here. You can straighten all this out.'

There was a long silence. 'It doesn't sound like there's much to straighten out. Not if you've confessed to doing all those things. The family can't afford to get mixed up in a thing like this. Surely you can see that. This has been a terrible shock for us. Obviously, I never really knew you.'

Each word was a hammerblow. The world was falling in on her. She felt more alone than she had ever felt in her life. There was no one to turn to now, no one. 'What – what about the baby?'

'You'll have to do whatever you think best with your baby,' Charles said. 'I'm sorry, Tracy.' And the connection was broken.

She stood there holding the dead receiver in her hand.

A prisoner behind her said, 'If you're through with the phone, honey, I'd like to call my lawyer.'

When Tracy was returned to her cell, the matron had instructions for her. 'Be ready to leave in the morning. You'll be picked up at five o'clock.'

She had a visitor. Otto Schmidt seemed to have aged years during the few hours since Tracy had last seen him. He looked ill.

'I just came to tell you how sorry my wife and I are. We know whatever happened wasn't your fault.'

If only Charles had said that!

'The wife and I will be at Mrs Doris's funeral tomorrow.'

'Thank you, Otto.'

They're going to bury both of us tomorrow, Tracy thought miserably.

She spent the night wide awake, lying on her narrow prison bunk, staring at the ceiling. In her mind she replayed the conversation with Charles again and again. He had never even given her a chance to explain.

She had to think of the baby. She had read of women having babies in prison, but the stories had been so remote from her own life that it was as though she were reading about people from another planet. Now it was happening to her. *You'll have to do whatever you think best with your baby*, Charles had said. She wanted to have her baby. *And yet*, she thought, *they won't let me keep it. They'll take it away from me because I'm going to be in prison for the next fifteen years. It's better that it never knows about its mother.*

She wept.

At 5:00 in the morning a male guard, accompanied by a matron, entered Tracy's cell. 'Tracy Whitney?'

'Yes.' She was surprised at how odd her voice sounded.

'By order of the Criminal Court of the State of Louisiana, Orleans Parish, you are forthwith being transferred to the Southern Louisiana Penitentiary for Women. Let's move it, babe.'

She was walked down a long corridor, past cells filled with inmates. There was a series of catcalls.

'Have a good trip, honey . . .'

'You tell me where you got that paintin' hidden, Tracy, baby, and I'll split the money with you . . .'

'If you're headin' for the big house, ask for Ernestine Littlechap. She'll take real good care of you . . .'

Tracy passed the telephone where she had made her call to Charles. *Good-bye, Charles.*

She was outside in a courtyard. A yellow prison bus with barred windows stood there, its engine idling. Half a dozen women already were seated in the bus, watched over by two armed guards. Tracy looked at the faces of her fellow passengers. One was defiant, and another bored; others wore expressions of despair. The lives they had lived were about to come to an end. They were out-casts, headed for cages where they would be locked up like animals. Tracy wondered what crimes they had committed and whether any of them was as innocent as she was, and she wondered what they saw in *her* face.

The ride on the prison bus was interminable, the bus hot and smelly, but Tracy was unaware of it. She had withdrawn into herself, no longer conscious of the other passengers or of the lush green countryside the bus passed through. She was in another time, in another place.

She was a little girl at the shore with her mother and father, and her father was carrying her into the ocean on his shoulders, and when she cried out her father said *Don't be a baby, Tracy*, and he dropped her into the cold water. When the water closed over her head, she panicked and began to choke, and her father lifted her up and did it again, and from that moment on she had been terrified of the water . . .

The college auditorium was filled with students and their parents and relatives. She was class vale-dictorian. She spoke for fifteen minutes, and her speech was filled with soaring idealism, clever references to the past, and shining dreams for the future. The dean had presented her with a Phi Beta Kappa key. *I want you to keep it*, Tracy told her mother, and the pride on her mother's face was beautiful . . .

63

I'm going to Philadelphia, Mother. I have a job at a bank there.

Annie Mahler, her best friend, was calling her. *You'll love Philadelphia, Tracy. It's full of all kinds of cultural things. It has beautiful scenery and a shortage of women. I mean, the men here are really hungry! I can get you a job at the bank where I work . . .*

Charles was making love to her. She watched the moving shadows on the ceiling and thought, *How many girls would like to be in my place?* Charles was a prime catch. And she was instantly ashamed of the thought. She loved him. She could feel him inside her, beginning to thrust harder, faster and faster, on the verge of exploding, and he gasped out, *Are you ready?* And she lied and said yes. *Was it wonderful for you? Yes, Charles.* And she thought, *Is that all there is?* and the guilt again . . .

'You! I'm talkin' to you. Are you deaf for Christ's sake? Let's go.'

Tracy looked up and she was in the yellow prison bus. It had stopped in an enclosure surrounded by a gloomy pile of masonry. A series of nine fences topped with barbed wire surrounded the five hundred acres of farm pasture and woodlands that made up the prison grounds of the Southern Louisiana Penitentiary for Women.

'Get out,' the guard said. 'We're here.'

Here was hell.

FIVE

A stocky, stony-faced matron with sable-brown dyed hair was addressing the new arrivals: 'Some of you are gonna be here for a long, long time. There's only one way you're gonna make it, and that's by forgettin' all about the outside world. You can do your time the easy way or the hard way. We have rules here, and you'll follow those rules. We'll tell you when to get up, when to work, when to eat, and when to go to the toilet. You break any of our rules, and you'll wish you was dead. We like to keep things peaceful here, and we know how to handle troublemakers.' Her eyes flicked over to Tracy. 'You'll be taken for your physical examinations now. After that you'll go to the showers and be assigned your cells. In the mornin' you'll receive your work duties. That's all.' She started to turn away.

A pale young girl standing next to Tracy said, 'Excuse me, please, could –'

The matron whirled around, her face filled with

fury. 'Shut your fuckin' mouth. You speak only when you're spoken to, do you understand? That goes for all you assholes.'

The tone, as much as the words, was a shock to Tracy. The matron signalled to two women guards at the back of the room. 'Get these no-good bitches out of here.'

Tracy found herself being herded out of the room with the others, down a long corridor. The prisoners were marched into a large, white-tiled room, where a fat, middle-aged man in a soiled smock stood next to an examination table.

One of the matrons called out, 'Line up', and formed the women into one long line.

The man in the smock said, 'I'm Dr Glasco, ladies. Strip!'

The women turned to look at one another, uncertainly. One of them said, 'How far should we –?'

'Don't you know what the hell *strip* means? Get your clothes off – all of them.'

Slowly, the women began to undress. Some of them were self-conscious, some outraged, some indifferent. On Tracy's left was a woman in her late forties, shivering violently, and on Tracy's right was a pathetically thin girl who looked to be no more than seventeen years old. Her skin was covered with acne.

The doctor gestured to the first woman in line. 'Lie down on the table and put your feet in the stirrups.'

The woman hesitated.

'Come on. You're holding up the line.'

She did as she was told. The doctor inserted a speculum into her vagina. As he probed, he asked, 'Do you have a venereal disease?'

'No.'

'We'll soon find out about that.'

The next woman replaced her on the table. As the doctor started to insert the same speculum into her, Tracy cried out, 'Wait a minute!'

The doctor stopped and looked up in surprise. 'What?'

Everyone was staring at Tracy. She said, 'I . . . you didn't sterilize that instrument.'

Dr Glasco gave Tracy a slow, cold smile. 'Well! We have a gynaecologist in the house. You're worried about germs, are you? Move down to the end of the line.'

'What?'

'Don't you understand English? Move down.'

Tracy, not understanding why, took her place at the end of the line.

'Now, if you don't mind,' the doctor said, 'we'll continue.' He inserted the speculum into the woman on the table, and Tracy suddenly realized why she was the last in line. He was going to examine all of them with the same unsterilized speculum, and she would be the last one on whom he used it. She could feel an anger boiling up inside her. He could have examined them separately, instead of deliberately stripping away their dignity.

And they were letting him get away with it. *If they all protested* – It was her turn.

'On the table, *Ms Doctor*.'

Tracy hesitated, but she had no choice. She climbed up on the table and closed her eyes. She could feel him spread her legs apart, and then the cold speculum was inside her, probing and pushing and hurting. Deliberately hurting. She gritted her teeth.

'You got syphilis or gonorrhoea?' the doctor asked.

'No.' She was not going to tell him about the baby. Not this monster. She would discuss that with the warden.

She felt the speculum being roughly pulled out of her. Dr Glasco was putting on a pair of rubber gloves. 'All right,' he said. 'Line up and bend over. We're going to check your pretty little asses.'

Before she could stop herself, Tracy said, 'Why are you doing this?'

Dr Glasco stared at her. 'I'll tell you why, *Doctor*. Because assholes are great hiding places. I have a whole collection of marijuana and cocaine that I got from ladies like you. Now bend over.' And he went down the line, plunging fingers into anus after anus. Tracy was sickened. She could feel the hot bile rise in her throat and she began to gag.

'You vomit in here, and I'll rub your face in it.' He turned to the guards. 'Get them to the showers. They stink.'

Carrying their clothes, the naked prisoners were

marched down another corridor to a large concrete room with a dozen open shower stalls.

'Lay your clothes in the corner,' a matron ordered. 'And get into the showers. Use the disinfectant soap. Wash every part of your body from head to toe, and shampoo your hair.'

Tracy stepped from the rough cement floor into the shower. The spray of water was cold. She scrubbed herself hard, thinking, *I'll never be clean again. What kind of people are these? How can they treat other human beings in this way? I can't stand fifteen years of this.*

A guard called out to her, 'Hey, you! Time's up. Get out.'

Tracy stepped out of the shower, and another prisoner took her place. Tracy was handed a thin, worn towel and half dried her body.

When the last of the prisoners had showered, they were marched to a large supply room where there were shelves of clothes guarded by a Latino inmate who sized up each prisoner and handed out grey uniforms. Tracy and the others were issued two uniform dresses, two pairs of panties, two brassieres, two pairs of shoes, two nightgowns, a sanitary belt, a hairbrush, and a laundry bag. The matrons stood watching while the prisoners dressed. When they had finished, they were herded to a room where a trusty operated a large portrait camera set on a tripod.

'Stand over there against the wall.'

Tracy moved over to the wall.

'Full face.'

She stared at the camera. Click.

'Turn your head to the right.'

She obeyed. Click.

'Left.' Click. 'Over to the table.'

The table had fingerprint equipment on it. Tracy's fingers were rolled across an inky pad, then pressed onto a white card.

'Left hand. Right hand. Wipe your hands with that rag. You're finished.'

She's right, Tracy thought numbly. *I'm finished. I'm a number. Nameless, faceless.*

A guard pointed to Tracy. 'Whitney? Warden wants to see you. Follow me.'

Tracy's heart suddenly soared. Charles had done something after all! *Of course* he had not abandoned her, any more than she ever could have abandoned him. It was the sudden shock that had made him behave the way he had. He had had time to think it over now and to realize he still loved her. He had talked to the warden and explained the terrible mistake that had been made. She was going to be set free.

She was marched down a different corridor, through two sets of heavily barred doors manned by male and female guards. As Tracy was admitted through the second door, she was almost knocked down by a prisoner. She was a giant, the biggest woman Tracy had ever seen – well over six feet tall, she must have weighed over twenty stone. She had a flat, pockmarked face, with feral yellow eyes.

She grabbed Tracy's arm to steady her and pressed her arm against Tracy's breasts.

'Hey!' the woman said to the guard. 'We got a new fish. How 'bout you put her in with me?' She had a heavy Swedish accent.

'Sorry. She's already been assigned, Bertha.'

The amazon stroked Tracy's face. Tracy jerked away, and the giant woman laughed. 'It's okay, *littbarn*. Big Bertha will see you later. We got plenty of time. You ain't goin' nowhere.'

They reached the warden's office. Tracy was faint with anticipation. Would Charles be there? Or would he have sent his attorney?

The warden's secretary nodded to the guard, 'He's expecting her. Wait here.'

Warden George Brannigan was seated at a scarred desk, studying some papers in front of him. He was in his mid-forties, a thin, careworn-looking man, with a sensitive face and deep-set hazel eyes.

Warden Brannigan had been in charge of the Southern Louisiana Penitentiary for Women for five years. He had arrived with the background of a modern penologist and the zeal of an idealist, determined to make sweeping reforms in the prison. But it had defeated him, as it had defeated others before him.

The prison originally had been built to accommodate two inmates to a cell, and now each cell held as many as four to six prisoners. He knew that the same situation applied everywhere. The country's prisons were all overcrowded and understaffed. Thousands of criminals were penned up day and night with nothing to do but nurse their hatred and plot their vengeance. It was a stupid, brutal system, but it was all there was.

He buzzed his secretary. 'All right. Send her in.'

The guard opened the door to the inner office, and Tracy stepped inside.

Warden Brannigan looked up at the woman standing before him. Dressed in the drab prison uniform, her face bruised with fatigue, Tracy Whitney still looked beautiful. She had a lovely, candid face, and Warden Brannigan wondered how long it would remain that way. He was particularly interested in this prisoner because he had read about her case in the newspapers and had studied her record. She was a first offender, had not killed anyone, and fifteen years was an inordinately harsh sentence. The fact that Joseph Romano was her accuser made her conviction all the more suspect. But the warden was simply the custodian of bodies. He could not buck the system. He *was* the system.

'Please have a seat,' he said.

Tracy was glad to sit down. Her knees were weak. He was going to tell her now about Charles, and how soon she would be released.

'I've been looking over your record,' the warden began.

Charles would have asked him to do that.

'I see you're going to be with us a long time. Your sentence is fifteen years.'

It took a moment for his words to sink in. Something was dreadfully wrong. 'Didn't – didn't you speak to – to Charles?' In her nervousness she was stammering.

He looked at her blankly. 'Charles?'

And she knew. Her stomach turned to water. 'Please,' she said. 'Please listen to me. I'm innocent. I don't belong here.'

How many times had he heard that? A hundred? A thousand? *I'm innocent.*

He said, 'The courts have found you guilty. The best advice I can give you is to try to do easy time. Once you accept the terms of your imprisonment, it will be a lot easier for you. There are no clocks in prison, only calendars.'

I can't be locked up here for fifteen years, Tracy thought in despair. *I want to die. Please, God, let me die. But I can't die, can I? I would be killing my baby. It's your baby, too, Charles. Why aren't you here helping me?* That was the moment she began to hate him.

'If you have any special problems,' Warden Brannigan said, 'I mean, if I can help you in any way, I want you to come and see me.' Even as he spoke, he knew how hollow his words were. She was young and beautiful and fresh. The bull-dykes in the prison would fall on her like animals. There was not even a safe cell to which he could assign her. Nearly every cell was controlled by a stud. Warden Brannigan had heard rumours of rapes in the showers, in the toilets, and in the corridors at

73

night. But they were only rumours, because the victims were always silent afterwards. Or dead.

Warden Brannigan said gently, 'With good behaviour, you might be released in twelve or –'

'No!' It was a cry of black despair, of desperation. Tracy felt the walls of the office closing in on her. She was on her feet, screaming. The guard came hurrying in and grabbed Tracy's arms.

'Easy,' Warden Brannigan commanded him.

He sat there, helpless, and watched as Tracy was led away.

She was taken down a series of corridors past cells filled with inmates of every description. They were black and white and brown and yellow. They stared at Tracy as she passed and called out to her in a dozen accents. Their cries made no sense to Tracy.

'Fish night . . .'

'French mate . . .'

'Fresh mite . . .'

'Flesh meet . . .'

It was not until Tracy reached her cell block that she realized what the women were chanting: 'Fresh meat'.

SIX

There were sixty women in Cell Block C, four to a cell. Faces peered out from behind bars as Tracy was marched down the long, smelly corridor, and the expressions varied from indifference to lust to hatred. She was walking underwater in some strange, unknown land, an alien in a slowly unfolding dream. Her throat was raw from the screaming inside her trapped body. The summons to the warden's office had been her last faint hope. Now there was nothing. Nothing except the mind-numbing prospect of being caged in this purgatory for the next fifteen years.

The matron opened a cell door. 'Inside!'

Tracy blinked and looked around. In the cell were three women, silently watching her.

'Move,' the matron ordered.

Tracy hesitated, then stepped into the cell. She heard the door slam behind her.

She was home.

The cramped cell barely held four bunks, a little

table with a cracked mirror over it, four small lockers, and a seatless toilet in the far corner.

Her cell mates were staring at her. The Puerto Rican woman broke the silence. 'Looks like we got ourselves a new cellie.' Her voice was deep and throaty. She would have been beautiful if it had not been for a livid knife scar that ran from her temple to her throat. She appeared to be no older than fourteen, until you looked into her eyes.

A squat, middle-aged Mexican woman said, '*Que suerte verte!* Nice to see you. What they got you in for, *querida*?'

Tracy was too paralysed to answer.

The third woman was black. She was almost six feet tall, with narrow, watchful eyes and a cold, hard mask of a face.

Her head was shaved and her skull shone blue-black in the dim light. 'Tha's your bunk over in the corner.'

Tracy walked over to the bunk. The mattress was filthy, stained with the excreta of God only knew how many previous occupants. She could not bring herself to touch it. Involuntarily, she voiced her revulsion. 'I – I can't sleep on this mattress.'

The fat Mexican woman grinned. 'You don't have to, honey. *Hay tiempo*. You can sleep on mine.'

Tracy suddenly became aware of the undercurrents in the cell, and they hit her with a physical force. The three women were watching her, staring, making her feel naked. *Fresh meat.* She was suddenly terrified. *I'm wrong*, Tracy thought. *Oh, please let me be wrong.*

She found her voice. 'Who – who do I see about getting a clean mattress?'

'God,' the black woman grunted. 'But he ain't been around here lately.'

Tracy turned to look at the mattress again. Several large black roaches were crawling across it. *I can't stay in this place*, Tracy thought. *I'll go insane.*

As though reading her mind, the black woman told her, 'You go with the flow, baby.'

Tracy heard the warden's voice. *The best advice I can give you is to try to do easy time . . .*

The black woman continued. 'I'm Ernestine Littlechap.' She nodded towards the woman with the long scar. 'Tha's Lola. She's from Puerto Rico, and fatso here is Paulita, from Mexico. Who are you?'

'I'm – I'm Tracy Whitney.' She had almost said, 'I *was* Tracy Whitney.' She had the nightmarish feeling that her identity was slipping away. A spasm of nausea swept through her, and she gripped the edge of the bunk to steady herself.

'Where you come from, honey?' the fat woman asked.

'I'm sorry, I – I don't feel like talking.' She suddenly felt too weak to stand. She slumped down on the edge of the filthy bunk and wiped the beads of cold perspiration from her face with her skirt. *My baby*, she thought. *I should have told the*

*warden I'm going to have a baby. He'll move me
into a clean cell. Perhaps they'll even let me have
a cell to myself.*

She heard footsteps coming down the corridor.
A matron was walking past the cell. Tracy hurried
to the cell door. 'Excuse me,' she said, 'I have to
see the warden. I'm –'

'I'll send him right down,' the matron said over
her shoulder.

'You don't understand. I'm –'

The matron was gone.

Tracy crammed her knuckles in her mouth to
keep from screaming.

'You sick or somethin', honey?' the Puerto Rican
asked.

Tracy shook her head, unable to speak. She
walked back to the bunk, looked at it a moment,
then slowly lay down on it. It was an act of hopelessness, an act of surrender. She closed her eyes.

Her tenth birthday was the most exciting day of
her life. *We're going to Antoine's for dinner*, her
father announced.

Antoine's! It was a name that conjured up
another world, a world of beauty and glamour and
wealth. Tracy knew that her father did not have
much money: *We'll be able to afford a vacation
next year*, was the constant refrain in the house.
And now they were going to Antoine's! Tracy's
mother dressed her in a new green frock.

Just look at you two, her father boasted. *I'm*

78

with the two prettiest women in New Orleans. Everyone's going to be jealous of me.

Antoine's was everything Tracy had dreamed it would be, and more. So much more. It was a fairy-land, elegant and tastefully decorated, with white napery and gleaming silver-and-gold mono-grammed dishes. *It's a palace,* Tracy thought. *I'll bet kings and queens come here.* She was too excited to eat, too busy staring at all the beauti-fully dressed men and women. *When I'm grown up,* Tracy promised herself, *I'm going to come to Antoine's every night, and I'll bring my mother and father with me.*

You're not eating, Tracy, her mother said.

And to please her, Tracy forced herself to eat a few mouthfuls. There was a cake for her, with ten candles on it, and the waiters sang Happy Birthday and the other guests turned and applauded, and Tracy felt like a princess. Outside she could hear the clang of a street-car bell as it passed.

The clanging of the bell was loud and insistent.

'Suppertime,' Ernestine Littlechap announced.

Tracy opened her eyes. Cell doors were slam-ming open throughout the cell block. Tracy lay on her bunk, trying desperately to hang on to the past.

'Hey! Chow time,' the young Puerto Rican said.

The thought of food sickened her. 'I'm not hungry.'

Paulita, the fat Mexican woman spoke. '*Es llano.*

79

It's simple. They don' care if you're hungry or not. Everybody gotta go to mess.'

Inmates were lining up in the corridor outside.

'You better move it, or they'll have your ass,' Ernestine warned.

I can't move, Tracy thought. *I'll stay here.*

Her cell mates left the cell and lined up in a double file. A short, squat matron with peroxided-blonde hair saw Tracy lying on her bunk. 'You!' she said. 'Didn't you hear the bell! Get out here.'

Tracy said, 'I'm not hungry, thank you. I'd like to be excused.'

The matron's eyes widened in disbelief. She stormed inside the cell and strode over to where Tracy lay. 'Who the fuck do you think you are? You waitin' for room service? Get your ass in that line. I could put you on report for this. If it happens again, you go to the bing. Understand?'

She did not understand. She did not understand anything that was happening to her. She dragged herself from the bunk and walked out into the line of women. She was standing next to the black woman. 'Why do I –?'

'Shut up!' Ernestine Littlechap growled out of the corner of her mouth. 'No talkin' in line.'

The women were marched down a narrow, cheerless corridor past two sets of security doors, into an enormous mess hall filled with large wooden tables and chairs. There was a long serving counter with steam tables, where prisoners lined up for their food. The menu of the day consisted of a watery tuna casserole, limp green beans, a pale custard, and a choice of weak coffee or a synthetic fruit drink. Ladles of the unappetizing-looking food were thrown into the tin plates of the prisoners as they moved along the line, and the inmates who were serving behind the counter kept up a steady cry: 'Keep the line moving. Next . . . keep the line moving. Next . . .'

When Tracy was served, she stood there uncertainly, not sure where to go. She looked around for Ernestine Littlechap, but the black woman had disappeared. Tracy walked over to a table where Lola and Paulita, the fat Mexican woman, were seated. There were twenty women at the table, hungrily wolfing down their food. Tracy looked down at what was on her plate, then pushed it away, as the bile rose and welled in her throat.

Paulita reached over and grabbed the plate from Tracy. 'If you ain't gonna eat that, I'll take it.'

Lola said, 'Hey, you gotta eat, or you won't last here.'

I don't want to last, Tracy thought hopelessly. *I want to die. How could these women tolerate living like this? How long had they been here? Months? Years?* She thought of the foetid cell and her verminous mattress, and she wanted to scream. She clenched her jaw shut so that no sound would come out.

The Mexican woman was saying, 'If they catch you not eatin', you go to the bing.' She saw the uncomprehending look on Tracy's face. 'The hole – solitary. You wouldn't like it.' She leaned forward. 'This is your first time in the joint, huh? Well, I'm gonna give you a tip, querida. Ernestine Littlechap runs this place. Be nice to her an' you got it made.'

Thirty minutes from the time the women had entered the room, a loud bell sounded and the women stood up. Paulita snatched a lone green bean from a plate next to her. Tracy joined her in the line, and the women began the march back to their cells. Supper was over. It was four o'clock in the afternoon – five long hours to endure before lights out.

When Tracy returned to the cell, Ernestine Littlechap was already there. Tracy wondered incuriously where she had been at dinnertime. Tracy looked at the toilet in the corner. She desperately needed to use it, but she could not bring herself to do so in front of these women. She would wait until lights went out. She sat down on the edge of her bunk.

Ernestine Littlechap said, 'I understan' you didn't eat none of your supper. Tha's stupid.'

How could she have known that? And why should she care? 'How do I see the warden?'

'You put in a written request. The guards use it for toilet paper. They figure any cunt who wants to see the warden is a troublemaker.' She walked over to Tracy. 'There's lotsa things kin get you in trouble here. What you need is a friend who kin he'p keep you *outta* trouble.' She smiled, showing a gold front tooth. Her voice was soft. 'Someone who knows their way around the zoo.'

Tracy looked up into the black woman's grinning face. It seemed to be floating somewhere near the ceiling.

It was the tallest thing she had ever seen.

That's a giraffe, her father said.

They were at the zoo in Audubon Park. Tracy loved the park. On Sundays they went there to listen to the band concerts, and afterwards her mother and father took her to the aquarium or the zoo. They walked slowly, looking at the animals in their cages.

Don't they hate being locked up, Papa?

Her father laughed. *No, Tracy. They have a wonderful life. They're taken care of and fed, and their enemies can't get at them.*

They looked unhappy to Tracy. She wanted to open their cages and let them out. *I wouldn't ever want to be locked up like that*, Tracy thought.

At 8:45 the warning bells rang throughout the prison. Tracy's cell mates began to undress. Tracy did not move.

Lola said, 'You got fifteen minutes to get ready for bed.'

The women had stripped and put on night-gowns. The peroxided-blonde matron passed the cell. She stopped when she saw Tracy lying on her cot.

'Get undressed,' she ordered. She turned to Ernestine. 'Didn't you tell her?'

'Yeah. We tol' her.'

The matron turned back to Tracy. 'We got a way of takin' care of troublemakers,' she warned. 'You do what you're told here, or I'll bust your ass.' The matron moved down the hall.

Paulita cautioned, 'You better listen to her, baby. Old Iron Pants is one mean bitch.'

Slowly, Tracy rose and began to undress, keeping her back to the others. She took off all her clothes, with the exception of her panties, and slipped the coarse nightgown over her head. She felt the eyes of the other women on her.

'You got a real nice body,' Paulita commented.

'Yeah, real nice,' Lola echoed.

Tracy felt a shiver go through her.

Ernestine moved over to Tracy and looked down at her. 'We're your friends. We gonna take good care of you.' Her voice was hoarse with excitement.

Tracy wildly jerked around. 'Leave me alone! All of you. I'm – I'm not that way.'

The black woman chuckled. 'You'll be any way we want you to be, baby.'

'*Hay tiempo*. There's plenty of time.'

The lights went out.

The dark was Tracy's enemy. She sat on the edge of her bunk, her body tense. She could sense the others waiting to pounce on her. Or was it her imagination? She was so overwrought that everything seemed to be a threat. Had they threatened her? Not really. They were probably just trying to be friendly, and she had read sinister implications into their overtures. She had heard about homosexual activity in prisons, but that had to be the exception rather than the rule. A prison would not permit that sort of behaviour.

Still, there was a nagging doubt. She decided she would stay awake all night. If one of them made a move, she would call for help. It was the responsibility of the guards to see that nothing happened to the inmates. She reassured herself that there was nothing to worry about. She would just have to stay alert.

Tracy sat on the edge of her bunk in the dark, listening to every sound. One by one she heard the three women go to the toilet, use it, and return to their bunks. When Tracy could stand it no longer, she made her way to the toilet. She tried to flush it, but it did not work. The stench was almost unbearable. She hurried back to her cot and sat there. *It will be light soon*, she thought. *In the morning I'll ask to see the warden. I'll tell him about the baby. He'll have me moved to another cell.*

Tracy's body was tense and cramped. She lay back on her bunk and within seconds felt something crawling across her neck. She stifled a scream. *I've got to stand it until morning. Everything will be all right in the morning*, Tracy thought. One minute at a time.

At 3:00 she could no longer keep her eyes open. She slept.

She was awakened by a hand clamped across her mouth and two hands grabbing at her breasts. She tried to sit up and scream, and she felt her nightgown and underpants being ripped away. Hands slid between her thighs, forcing her legs apart. Tracy fought savagely, struggling to rise.

'Take it easy,' a voice in the dark whispered, 'and you won't get hurt.'

Tracy lashed out at the voice with her feet. She connected with solid flesh.

'*Carajo!* Give it to the bitch,' the voice gasped. 'Get her on the floor.'

A hard fist smashed into Tracy's face and another into her stomach. Someone was on top of her, holding her down, smothering her, while obscene hands violated her.

Tracy broke loose for an instant, but one of the women grabbed her and slammed her head against the bars. She felt the blood spurt from her nose. She was thrown to the concrete floor, and her hands and legs were pinned down. Tracy fought like a mad-woman, but she was no match for the three of them. She felt cold hands and hot tongues caressing her body. Her legs were spread apart and a hard, cold object was shoved inside her. She writhed helplessly, desperately trying to call out.

An arm moved across her mouth, and Tracy sank her teeth into it, biting down with all her strength.

There was a muffled cry. 'You cunt!'

Fists pounded her face . . . She sank into the pain, deeper and deeper, until finally she felt nothing.

It was the clanging of the bell that awakened her. She was lying on the cold cement floor of her cell, naked. Her three cell mates were in their bunks.

In the corridor, Iron Pants was calling, 'Rise and shine'. As the matron passed the cell, she saw Tracy lying on the floor in a small pool of blood, her face battered and one eye swollen shut.

'What the hell's goin' on here?' She unlocked the door and stepped inside the cell.

'She musta fell outta her bunk,' Ernestine Littlechap offered.

The matron walked over to Tracy's side and nudged her with her foot. 'You! Get up.'

Tracy heard the voice from a far distance. *Yes,* she thought, *I must get up; I must get out of here.* But she was unable to move. Her body was screaming out with pain.

The matron grabbed Tracy's elbows and pulled her to a sitting position, and Tracy almost fainted from the agony.

'What happened?'

Through one eye Tracy saw the blurred outlines of her cell mates silently waiting for her to answer.

'I – I –' Tracy tried to speak, but no words

would come out. She tried again, and some deep-seated atavistic instinct made her say, 'I fell off my bunk . . .'

The matron snapped, 'I hate smart asses. Let's put you in the bing till you learn some respect.'

It was a form of oblivion, a return to the womb. She was alone in the dark. There was no furniture in the cramped basement cell, only a thin, worn mattress thrown on the cold cement floor. A noisome hole in the floor served as a toilet. Tracy lay there in the blackness, humming folk songs to herself that her father had taught her long ago. She had no idea how close she was to the edge of insanity.

She was not sure where she was, but it did not matter. Only the suffering of her brutalized body mattered. *I must have fallen down and hurt myself, but Mama will take care of it.* She called out in a broken voice, 'Mama . . .', and when there was no answer, she fell asleep again.

She slept for forty-eight hours, and the agony finally receded to pain, and the pain gave way to soreness. Tracy opened her eyes. She was surrounded by nothingness. It was so dark that she could not even make out the outline of the cell. Memories came flooding back. They had carried her to the doctor. She could hear his voice: '. . . a broken rib and a fractured wrist. We'll tape them up . . . The cuts and bruises are bad, but they'll heal. She's lost the baby . . .'

'Oh, my baby,' Tracy whispered. 'They've murdered my baby.'

And she wept. She wept for the loss of her baby. She wept for herself. She wept for the whole sick world.

Tracy lay on the thin mattress in the cold darkness, and she was filled with such an overpowering hatred that it literally shook her body. Her thoughts burned and blazed until her mind was empty of every emotion but one: *vengeance*. It was not a vengeance directed against her three cell mates. They were victims as much as she. No; she was after the men who had done this to her, who had destroyed her life.

Joe Romano: 'Your old lady held out on me. She didn't tell me she had a horny-looking daughter . . .'

Anthony Orsatti: 'Joe Romano works for a man named Anthony Orsatti. Orsatti runs New Orleans . . .'

Perry Pope: 'By pleading guilty, you save the state the expense of a trial . . .'

Judge Henry Lawrence: 'For the next fifteen years you're going to be incarcerated in the Southern Louisiana Penitentiary for Women . . .'

Those were her enemies. And then there was Charles, who had never even listened to her: 'If you needed money that badly, you could have discussed it with me . . . Obviously I never really knew you . . . You'll have to do whatever you think best with your baby . . .'

She was going to make them pay. Every one of them. She had no idea how. But she knew she was going to get revenge. *Tomorrow*, she thought. *If tomorrow comes.*

SEVEN

Time lost all meaning. There was never light in the cell, so there was no difference between night and day, and she had no idea how long she was kept in solitary confinement. From time to time cold meals were shoved through a slot in the bottom of the door. Tracy had no appetite, but she forced herself to eat every morsel. *You gotta eat, or you won't last here.* She understood that now; she knew she would need every bit of her strength for what she planned to do. She was in a situation that anyone else would have considered hopeless: she was locked away for fifteen years, with no money, no friends, no resources of any kind. But there was a wellspring of strength deep within her. *I will survive*, Tracy thought. *I face mine enemies naked, and my courage is my shield.* She would survive as her ancestors had survived. In her was the mixed blood of the English and the Irish and the Scots, and she had inherited the best of their qualities, the intelligence and the courage and the will. *My ancestors survived famine and plagues and floods, and I'm going to survive this.* They were with her now in her stygian cell: the shepherds and trappers, the farmers and shopkeepers, the doctors and teachers. The ghosts of the past, and every one was a part of her. *I won't let you down*, Tracy whispered in the darkness.

She began to plan her escape.

Tracy knew that the first thing she had to do was regain her physical strength. The cell was too cramped for extensive exercise, but it was large enough for t'ai chi ch'uan, the centuries-old martial art that was taught warriors to prepare them for combat. The exercises required little space, and they used every muscle in the body. Tracy stood up and went through the opening moves. Each movement had a name and a significance. She started with the militant Punching the Demons, then into the softer Gathering the Light. The movements were fluid and graceful and done very slowly. Every gesture came from tan tien, the psychic centre, and all the movements were circular. Tracy could hear the voice of her teacher: *Arouse your chi, your vital energy. It starts heavy as a mountain and becomes light as a bird's feather.* Tracy could feel the chi flowing through her fingers, and she concentrated until her whole being was focused on her body moving through the timeless patterns.

Grasp the bird's tail, become the white stork, repulse the monkey, face the tiger, let your hands become clouds and circulate the water of life. Let the white snake creep down and ride the tiger. Shoot the tiger, gather your chi, and go back to tan tien, the centre.

The complete cycle took an hour, and when it was finished Tracy was exhausted. She went through the ritual each morning and afternoon until her body began to respond and grow strong.

When she was not exercising her body, Tracy exercised her mind. She lay in the dark, doing complicated mathematical equations, mentally operating the computer at the bank, reciting poetry, recalling the lines of plays she had been in at college. She was a perfectionist, and when she had got a part in a school play where she had to use different accents, she had studied accents for weeks before the play went on. A talent scout had once approached her to offer her a screen test in Hollywood. 'No, thank you. I don't want the limelight. That's not for me,' Tracy had told him.

Charles's voice: *You're the headline in this morning's* Daily News.

Tracy pushed the memory of Charles away. There were doors in her mind that had to remain closed for now.

She played the teaching game: Name three absolutely impossible things to teach.

To teach an ant the difference between Catholics and Protestants.

To make a bee understand that it is the earth that travels around the sun.

To explain to a cat the difference between communism and democracy.

But she concentrated mostly on how she was going to destroy her enemies, each of them in turn. She remembered a game she had played as a child. By holding up one hand towards the sky, it was possible to blot out the sun. That's what they had done to her. They had raised a hand and blotted out her life.

Tracy had no idea how many prisoners had been broken by their confinement in the bing, nor would it have mattered to her.

On the seventh day, when the cell door opened, Tracy was blinded by the sudden light that flooded the cell. A guard stood outside. 'On your feet. You're going back upstairs.'

He reached down to give Tracy a helping hand, and to his surprise, she rose easily to her feet and walked out of the cell unaided. The other prisoners he had moved from solitary had come out either broken or defiant, but this prisoner was neither. There was an aura of dignity about her, a self-confidence that was alien to this place. Tracy stood in the light, letting her eyes gradually get accustomed to it. *What a great-looking piece of ass*, the guard thought. *Get her cleaned up and you could take her anywhere. I'll bet she'd do anything for a few favours.*

Aloud he said, 'A pretty girl like you shouldn't have to go through this kind of thing. If you and me was friends, I'd see that it didn't happen again.'

Tracy turned to face him, and when he saw the look in her eyes, he hastily decided not to pursue it.

The guard walked Tracy upstairs and turned her over to a matron.

The matron sniffed, 'Jesus, you stink. Go in and take a shower. We'll burn those clothes.'

The cold shower felt wonderful. Tracy shampooed her hair and scrubbed herself from head to foot with the harsh lye soap.

When she had dried herself and put on a change of clothing, the matron was waiting for her. 'Warden wants to see you.'

The last time Tracy had heard those words, she had believed it meant her freedom. Never again would she be that naïve.

Warden Brannigan was standing at the window when Tracy walked into his office. He turned and said, 'Sit down, please.' Tracy took a chair. 'I've been away in Washington at a conference. I just returned this morning and saw a report on what happened. You should not have been put in solitary.'

She sat watching him, her impassive face giving nothing away.

The warden glanced at a paper on his desk. 'According to this report, you were sexually assaulted by your cell mates.'

'No, sir.'

Warden Brannigan nodded understandingly. 'I understand your fear, but I can't allow the inmates to run this prison. I want to punish whoever did this to you, but I'll need your testimony. I'll see that you're protected. Now, I want you to tell me exactly what happened and who was responsible.'

Tracy looked him in the eye. 'I was. I fell off my bunk.'

The warden studied her a long time, and she could see the disappointment cloud his face. 'Are you quite sure?'

'Yes, sir.'

'You won't change your mind?'

'No, sir.'

Warden Brannigan sighed. 'All right. If that's your decision. I'll have you transferred to another cell where –'

'I don't want to be transferred.'

He looked at her in surprise. 'You mean you want to go back to the same cell?'

'Yes, sir.'

He was puzzled. Perhaps he had been wrong about her; maybe she had invited what had happened to her. God only knew what those damned female prisoners were thinking or doing. He wished he could be transferred to some nice, sane men's prison, but his wife and Amy, his small daughter, liked it here. They all lived in a charming cottage, and there were lovely grounds around the prison farm. To them, it was like living in the country, but he had to cope with these crazy women twenty-four hours a day.

He looked at the young woman sitting before him and said awkwardly, 'Very well. Just stay out of trouble in the future.'

'Yes, sir.'

Returning to her cell was the most difficult thing Tracy had ever done. The moment she stepped inside she was assailed by the horror of what had happened there. Her cell mates were away at work. Tracy lay on her bunk, staring at the ceiling, planning. Finally, she reached down to the bottom of her bunk and prised a piece of the metal side loose. She placed it under her mattress. When the 11:00 A.M. lunch bell rang, Tracy was the first to line up in the corridor.

In the mess hall, Paulita and Lola were seated at a table near the entrance. There was no sign of Ernestine Littlechap.

Tracy chose a table filled with strangers, sat down, and finished every bite of the tasteless meal. She spent the afternoon alone in her cell. At 2:45 her three cell mates returned.

Paulita grinned with surprise when she saw Tracy. 'So you came back to us, pretty pussy. You liked what we did to you, huh?'

'Good. We got more for you,' Lola said.

Tracy gave no indication that she heard their taunting. She was concentrating on the black woman. Ernestine Littlechap was the reason Tracy had come back to this cell. Tracy did not trust her. Not for a moment. But she needed her.

I'm gonna give you a tip, querida. Ernestine Littlechap runs this place . . .

That night, when the fifteen-minute warning bell sounded for lights out, Tracy rose from her bunk and began to undress. This time there was no false modesty. She stripped, and the Mexican woman gave a long, low whistle as she looked at Tracy's full, firm breasts and her long, tapering legs and creamy thighs. Lola was breathing hard. Tracy put on a nightgown and lay back on her bunk. The lights went out. The cell was in darkness.

Thirty minutes went by. Tracy lay in the dark listening to the breathing of the others.

Across the cell, Paulita whispered, 'Mama's gonna give you some real lovin' tonight. Take off your nightgown, baby.'

'We're gonna teach you how to eat pussy, and you'll do it till you get it right,' Lola giggled.

Still not a word from the black woman. Tracy felt the rush of wind as Lola and Paulita came at her, but Tracy was ready for them. She lifted the piece of metal she had concealed in her hand and swung with all her might, hitting one of the women in the face. There was a scream of pain, and Tracy kicked out at the other figure and saw her fall to the floor.

'Come near me again and I'll kill you,' Tracy said.

'You bitch!'

Tracy could hear them start for her again, and she raised the piece of metal.

Ernestine's voice came abruptly out of the darkness. 'Tha's enough. Leave her alone.'

'Ernie, I'm bleedin'. I'm gonna fix her –'

'Do what the fuck I tell you.'

There was a long silence. Tracy heard the two women moving back to their bunks, breathing hard. Tracy lay there, tensed, ready for their next move.

Ernestine Littlechap said, 'You got guts, baby.'

Tracy was silent.

'You didn't sing to the warden.' Ernestine laughed softly in the darkness. 'If you had, you'd be dead meat.'

Tracy believed her.

'Why di'n' you let the warden move you to another cell?'

So she even knew about that. 'I wanted to come back here.'

'Yeah? What fo'?' There was a puzzled note in Ernestine Littlechap's voice.

This was the moment Tracy had been waiting for. 'You're going to help me escape.'

EIGHT

A matron came up to Tracy and announced, 'You got a visitor, Whitney.'

Tracy looked at her in surprise. 'A visitor?' Who could it be? And suddenly she knew. *Charles*. He had come after all. But he was too late. He had not been there when she so desperately needed him. *Well, I'll never need him again. Or anyone else.*

Tracy followed the matron down the corridor to the visitors' room.

Tracy stepped inside.

A total stranger was seated at a small wooden table. He was one of the most unattractive men Tracy had ever seen. He was short, with a bloated, androgynous body, a long, pinched-in nose, and a small, bitter mouth. He had a high, bulging forehead and intense brown eyes, magnified by the thick lenses of his glasses.

He did not rise. 'My name is Daniel Cooper. The warden gave me permission to speak to you.'

'About what?' Tracy asked suspiciously.

'I'm an investigator for IIPA – the International Insurance Protection Association. One of our clients insured the Renoir that was stolen from Mr Joseph Romano.'

Tracy drew a deep breath. 'I can't help you. I didn't steal it.' She started for the door.

Cooper's next words stopped her. 'I know that.'

Tracy turned and looked at him, wary, every sense alert.

'No one stole it. You were framed, Miss Whitney.'

Slowly, Tracy sank into a chair.

Daniel Cooper's involvement with the case had begun three weeks earlier when he had been summoned to the office of his superior, J. J. Reynolds, at IIPA headquarters in Manhattan.

'I've got an assignment for you, Dan,' Reynolds said.

Daniel Cooper loathed being called Dan.

'I'll make this brief.' Reynolds intended to make it brief because Cooper made him nervous. In truth, Cooper made everyone in the organization nervous. He was a strange man – *weird*, was how many described him. Daniel Cooper kept entirely to himself. No one knew where he lived, whether he was married or had children. He socialized with no one, and never attended office parties or office meetings. He was a loner, and the only reason Reynolds tolerated him was because the man was a goddamned genius. He was a bulldog, with a computer for a brain. Daniel

Cooper was single-handedly responsible for recovering more stolen merchandise, and exposing more insurance frauds, than all the other investigators put together. Reynolds just wished he knew what the hell Cooper was all about. Merely sitting across from the man with those fanatical brown eyes staring at him made him uneasy. Reynolds said, 'One of our client companies insured a painting for half a million dollars and –'

'The Renoir. New Orleans. Joe Romano. A woman named Tracy Whitney was convicted and sentenced to fifteen years. The painting hasn't been recovered.'

The son of a bitch! Reynolds thought. *If it were anyone else, I'd think he was showing off.* 'That's right,' Reynolds acknowledged grudgingly. 'The Whitney woman has stashed that painting away somewhere, and we want it back. Go to it.'

Cooper turned and left the office without a word. Watching him leave, J. J. Reynolds thought, not for the first time, *Someday I'm going to find out what makes that bastard tick.*

Cooper walked through the office, where fifty employees were working side by side, programming computers, typing reports, answering telephones. It was bedlam.

As Cooper passed a desk, a colleague said, 'I hear you got the Romano assignment. Lucky you. New Orleans is –'

Cooper walked by without replying. Why couldn't they leave him alone? That was all he asked of anybody, but they were always pestering him with their nosey overtures.

It had become a game in the office. They were determined to break through his mysterious reserve and find out who he really was.

'What are you doing for dinner Friday night, Dan . . . ?'

'If you're not married, Sarah and I know a wonderful girl, Dan . . . ?'

Couldn't they see he did not need any of them – didn't *want* any of them?

'Come on, it's only for a drink . . .'

But Daniel Cooper knew what that could lead to. An innocent drink could lead to dinner, and a dinner could start friendships, and friendships could lead to confidences. Too dangerous.

Daniel Cooper lived in mortal terror that one day someone would learn about his past. *Let the dead past bury its dead* was a lie. The dead never stayed buried. Every two or three years one of the scandal sheets would dig up the old scandal, and Daniel Cooper would disappear for several days. Those were the only times he ever got drunk.

Daniel Cooper could have kept a psychiatrist busy full-time had he been able to expose his emotions, but he could never bring himself to speak of the past to anyone. The one piece of physical evidence that he retained from that terrible day long ago was a faded, yellowed newspaper clipping, safely locked away in his room, where no one could ever find it. He looked at it from time to time as a punishment, but every word in the article was emblazoned on his mind.

He showered or bathed at least three times a day, but never felt clean. He firmly believed in hell and hell's fire, and he knew his only salvation on earth was expiation, atonement. He had tried to join the New York police force, but when he had failed the physical because he was four inches too short, he had become a private investigator. He thought of himself as a hunter, tracking down those who broke the law. He was the vengeance of God, the instrument that brought down God's wrath on the heads of wrongdoers. It was the only way he could atone for the past, and prepare himself for eternity.

He wondered if there was time to take a shower before he caught his plane.

Daniel Cooper's first stop was New Orleans. He spent five days in the city, and before he was through, he knew everything he needed to know about Joe Romano, Anthony Orsatti, Perry Pope and Judge Henry Lawrence. Cooper read the transcripts of Tracy Whitney's court hearing and sentencing. He interviewed Lieutenant Miller and learned about the suicide of Tracy Whitney's mother. He talked to Otto Schmidt and found out how Whitney's company had been stripped. During all these meetings, Daniel Cooper made not one note, yet he could have recited every conversation verbatim. He was 99 percent sure that Tracy

Whitney was an innocent victim, but to Daniel Cooper, those were unacceptable odds. He flew to Philadelphia and talked to Clarence Desmond, vice-president of the bank where Tracy Whitney had worked. Charles Stanhope III had refused to meet with him.

Now, as Cooper looked at the woman seated across from him, he was 100 percent convinced that she had had nothing to do with the theft of the painting. He was ready to write his report.

'Romano framed you, Miss Whitney. Sooner or later, he would have put in a claim for the theft of the painting. You just happened to come along at the right moment to make it easy for him.'

Tracy could feel her heartbeat accelerate. This man *knew* she was innocent. He probably had enough evidence against Joe Romano to clear her. He would speak to the warden or the governor, and get her out of this nightmare. She found it suddenly difficult to breathe. 'Then you'll help me?'

Daniel Cooper was puzzled. 'Help you?'

'Yes. Get a pardon or –'

'No.'

The word was like a slap. '*No? But why?* If you know I'm innocent –'

How could people be so stupid? 'My assignment is finished.'

When he returned to his hotel room, the first thing Cooper did was to undress and step into the shower. He scrubbed himself from head to foot, letting the steaming-hot spray wash over his body for almost half an hour. When he had dried himself and dressed, he sat down and wrote his report.

TO:
J. J. Reynolds   File No. Y-72-830-412

FROM:
Daniel Cooper

SUBJECT: *Deux Femmes dans le Café Rouge*, Renoir – Oil on Canvas

It is my conclusion that Tracy Whitney is in no way involved in the theft of above painting. I believe that Joe Romano took out the insurance policy with the intention of faking a burglary, collecting the insurance, and reselling the painting to a private party, and that by this time the painting is probably out of the country. Since the painting is well known, I would expect it to turn up in Switzerland, which has a good-faith purchase and protection law. If a purchaser says he bought a work of art in good faith, the Swiss government permits him to keep it, even though it is stolen.

Recommendation: Since there is no concrete proof of Romano's guilt, our client will have to pay him off on the policy. Further, it would be useless to look to Tracy Whitney for either the recovery of the painting or damages, since she has neither knowledge of the painting nor any assets that I have been able to uncover. In addition, she will be incarcerated in the Southern Louisiana Penitentiary for Women for the next fifteen years.

Daniel Cooper stopped a moment to think about Tracy Whitney. He supposed other men would consider her beautiful. He wondered, without any real interest, what fifteen years in prison would do to her. It had nothing to do with him.

Daniel Cooper signed the memo and debated whether he had time to take another shower.

NINE

Old Iron Pants had Tracy Whitney assigned to the laundry. Of the thirty-five work assignments available to prisoners, the laundry was the worst. The enormous, hot room was filled with rows of washing machines and ironing boards, and the loads of laundry that poured in were endless. Filling and emptying the washing machines and toting heavy baskets to the ironing section was a mindless, backbreaking job.

Work began at 6:00 A.M., and prisoners were permitted one 10-minute rest period every two hours. By the end of the nine-hour day, most of the women were ready to drop from exhaustion. Tracy went about her work mechanically, speaking to no one, cocooned in her own thoughts.

When Ernestine Littlechap heard about Tracy's assignment, she remarked, 'Old Iron Pants is out for your ass.'

Tracy said, 'She doesn't bother me.'

Ernestine Littlechap was puzzled. This was a

different woman from the terrified young girl who had been brought into prison three weeks earlier. Something had changed her, and Ernestine Littlechap was curious to know what it was.

On Tracy's eighth day working in the laundry, a guard came up to her in the early afternoon. 'I got a transfer here for you. You're assigned to the kitchen.' *The most coveted job in the prison.*

There were two standards of food in the penitentiary: the prisoners ate hash, hot dogs, beans, or inedible casseroles, while the meals for the guards and prison officials were prepared by professional chefs. Their range of meals included steaks, fresh fish, chops, chicken, fresh vegetables and fruits, and tempting desserts. The convicts who worked in the kitchen had access to those meals, and they took full advantage of it.

When Tracy reported to the kitchen, she was somehow not surprised to see Ernestine Littlechap there.

Tracy approached her. 'Thank you.' With difficulty, she forced a friendly note into her voice.

Ernestine grunted and said nothing.

'How did you get me past Old Iron Pants?'

'She ain't with us no mo'.'

'What happened to her?'

'We got a little system. If a guard is hard-ass and starts givin' us too much of a bad time, we get rid of 'em.'

'You mean the warden listens to –'

'Shee-et. What's the warden got to do with it?'

'Then how can you –?'

'It's easy. When the guard you want to get rid of is on duty, hassles begin to happen. Complaints start comin' in. A prisoner reports that Old Iron Pants grabbed her pussy. The next day 'nother prisoner accuses her of brutality. Then someone complains she took somethin' from her cell – say a radio – and sure enough, it turns up in Old Iron Pants's room. Old Iron Pants is gone. The guards don't run this prison, *we* do.'

'What are you in here for?' Tracy asked. She had no interest in the answer. The important thing was to establish a friendly relationship with this woman.

'Through no fault of Ernestine Littlechap, you'd better believe it. I had a whole bunch of girls workin' for me.'

Tracy looked at her. 'You mean as –?' She hesitated.

'Hookers?' She laughed. 'Naw. They worked as maids in big homes. I opened me a employment agency. I had at least twenty girls. Rich folks have a hell of a time findin' maids. I did a lot of fancy advertisin' in the best newspapers, and when they called me I placed my girls with 'em. The girls would size up the houses, and when their employers was at work or outta town, the girls would gather up all the silver and jewellery and furs and whatever other goodies were around and skip.' Ernestine sighed. 'If I told you how much fuckin' tax-free money we was pullin' down, you wouldn't believe me.'

'How did you get caught?'

'It was the fickle finger of fate, honey. One of my maids was servin' a luncheon at the mayor's house, and one of the guests was a old lady the maid had worked for and cleaned out. When the police used hoses on her, my girl began singin', and she sang the whole opera, and here's poor ol Ernestine.'

They were standing at a stove by themselves. 'I can't stay in this place,' Tracy whispered. 'I've got to take care of something on the outside. Will you help me escape? I –'

'Start slicin' up them onions. We're havin' Irish stew tonight.'

And she walked away.

The prison grapevine was incredible. The prisoners knew everything that was going to happen long before it occurred. Inmates known as garbage rats picked up discarded memos, eavesdropped on phone calls, and read the warden's mail, and all information was carefully digested and sent around to the inmates who were important. Ernestine Littlechap was at the head of the list. Tracy was aware of how the guards and prisoners deferred to Ernestine. Since the other inmates had decided that Ernestine had become Tracy's protector, she was left strictly alone. Tracy waited warily for Ernestine to make advances towards her, but the big black kept her distance. *Why?* Tracy wondered.

* * *

111

Rule number 7 in the official ten-page pamphlet issued to new prisoners read, 'Any form of sex is strictly forbidden. There will be no more than four inmates to a cell. Not more than one prisoner shall be permitted to be on a bunk at one time.'

The reality was so startlingly different that the prisoners referred to the pamphlet as the prison joke book. As the weeks went by, Tracy watched new prisoners – fish – enter the prison every day, and the pattern was always the same. First offenders who were sexually normal never had a chance. They came in timid and frightened, and the bull-dykes were there, waiting. The drama was enacted in planned stages. In a terrifying and hostile world, the bull-dyke was friendly and sympathetic. She would invite her victim to the recreation hall, where they would watch television together, and when the bull-dyke held her hand, the new prisoner would allow it, afraid of offending her only friend. The new prisoner quickly noticed that the other inmates left her alone, and as her dependence on the bull-dyke grew, so did the intimacies, until finally, she was willing to do anything to hold onto her only friend.

Those who refused to give in were raped. Ninety percent of the women who entered the prison were forced into homosexual activity – willingly or unwillingly – within the first thirty days. Tracy was horrified.

'How can the authorities allow it to happen?' she asked Ernestine.

'It's the system,' Ernestine explained, 'and it's the same in every prison, baby. There ain't no way you can separate twelve hundred women from their men and expect them not to fuck somebody. We don't just rape for sex. We rape for power, to show 'em right off who's boss. The new fish who come in here are targets for everybody who wants to gang-fuck 'em. The only protection they got is to become the wife of a bull-dyke. That way, nobody'll mess with 'em.'

Tracy had reason to know she was listening to an expert.

'It ain't only the inmates,' Ernestine went on. 'The guards are just as bad. Some fresh meat comes in and she's on H. She's strung out and needs a fix real bad. She's sweatin' and shakin' herself to pieces. Well, the matron can get heroin for her, but the matron wants a little favour in exchange, see? So the fish goes down on the matron and she gets her fix. The male guards are even worse. They got keys to these cells, and all they have to do is walk in at night and he'p themselves to free pussy. They might get you pregnant, but they can do a lot of favours. You want a candy bar or a visit from your boyfriend, you give the guard a piece of ass. It's called barterin', and it goes on in every prison system in the country.'

'It's horrible!'

'It's survival.' The overhead cell light shone on Ernestine's bald head. 'You know why they don't allow no chewin' gum in this place?'

'No.'

'Because the girls use it to jam up the locks on the doors so they don't close all the way, and at night they slip out and visit one another. We follow the rules we want to follow. The girls who make it out of here may be dumb, but they're *smart* dumb.'

Love affairs within the prison walls flourished, and the protocol between lovers was even more strictly enforced than on the outside. In an unnatural world, the artificial roles of studs and wives were created and played out. The studs assumed a man's role in a world where there were no men. They changed their names. Ernestine was called Ernie; Tessie was Tex; Barbara became Bob; Katherine was Kelly. The stud cut her hair short or shaved her head, and she did no chores. The Mary Femme, the wife, was expected to do the cleaning, mending, and ironing for her stud. Lola and Paulita competed fiercely for Ernestine's attentions, each fighting to outdo the other.

The jealousy was fierce and frequently led to violence, and if the wife was caught looking at another stud or talking to one in the prison yard, tempers would flare. Love letters were constantly flying around the prison, delivered by the garbage rats.

The letters were folded into small triangular shapes, known as kites, so they could easily be hidden in a bra or a shoe. Tracy saw kites being passed among women as they brushed by one another entering the dining hall or on their way to work.

Time after time, Tracy watched inmates fall in love with their guards. It was a love born of despair and helplessness and submissiveness. The prisoners were dependent on the guards for everything: their food, their well-being, and sometimes, their lives. Tracy allowed herself to feel no emotion for anyone.

Sex went on day and night. It ocurred in the shower room, in toilets, in cells, and at night there was oral sex through the bars. The Mary Femmes who belonged to guards were let out of their cells at night to go to the guards' quarters.

After lights out, Tracy would lie in her bunk and put her hands over her ears to shut out the sounds.

One night Ernestine pulled out a box of Rice Krispies from under her bunk and began scattering them in the corridor outside the cell. Tracy could hear inmates from other cells doing the same thing.

'What's going on?' Tracy asked.

Ernestine turned to her and said harshly, 'Non'a your business. Jest stay in your bunk. Jest stay in your fuckin' bunk.'

A few minutes later there was a terrified scream from a nearby cell, where a new prisoner had just arrived. 'Oh, God, no. Don't! Please leave me alone!'

Tracy knew then what was happening, and she was sick inside. The screams went on and on, until they finally diminished into helpless, racking sobs. Tracy squeezed her eyes tightly shut, filled with burning rage. How could women do this to one another? She had thought that prison had hardened her, but when she awoke in the morning, her face was stained with dried tears.

She was determined not to show her feelings to Ernestine. Tracy asked casually, 'What were the Rice Krispies for?'

'That's our early warnin' system. If the guards try sneakin' up on us, we kin hear 'em comin'.'

Tracy soon learned why inmates referred to a term in the penitentiary as 'going to college'. Prison was an educational experience, but what the prisoners learned was unorthodox.

The prison was filled with experts of every conceivable type of crime. They exchanged methods of grifting, shoplifting, and rolling drunks. They brought one another up to date on badger games and exchanged information on snitches and undercover cops.

In the recreation yard one morning, Tracy listened to an older inmate give a seminar on pickpocketing to a fascinated young group.

'The real pros come from Columbia. They got a school in Bogotá, called the school of the ten bells, where you pay twenty-five hundred bucks to learn to be a pickpocket. They hang a dummy from the ceilin', dressed in a suit with ten pockets, filled with money and jewellery.'

'What's the gimmick?'

'The gimmick is that each pocket has a bell on it. You don't graduate till you kin empty every damn pocket without ringin' the bell.'

Lola sighed, 'I used to go with a guy who walked through crowds dressed in an overcoat, with both his hands out in the open, while he picked everybody's pockets like crazy.'

'How the hell could he do that?'

'The right hand was a dummy. He slipped his real hand through a slit in the coat and picked his way through pockets and wallets and purses.'

In the recreation room the education continued.

'I like the locker-key rip-off,' a veteran said. 'You hang around a railway station till you see a little old lady tryin' to lift a suitcase or a big package into one of them lockers. You put it in for her and hand her the key. Only it's the key to an empty locker. When she leaves, you empty her locker and split.'

In the yard another afternoon, two inmates convicted of prostitution and possession of cocaine were talking to a new arrival, a pretty young girl who looked no more than seventeen.

'No wonder you got busted, honey,' one of the older women scolded. 'Before you talk price to a John, you gotta pat him down to make sure he ain't carryin' a gun, and *never* tell him what you're gonna do for him. Make *him* tell you what he wants. Then if he turns out to be a cop, it's entrapment, see?'

117

The other pro added, 'Yeah. And always look at their hands. If a trick says he's a workin' man, see if his hands are rough. That's the tip-off. A lot of plainsclothes cops wear workin' men's outfits, but when it comes to their hands, they forget, so their hands are smooth.'

Time went neither slowly nor quickly. It was simply time. Tracy thought of St Augustine's aphorism: 'What is time? If no one asks me, I know. But if I have to explain it, I do not know.'

The routine of the prison never varied:

4:40	A.M.	Warning bell
4:45	A.M.	Rise and dress
5:00	A.M.	Breakfast
5:30	A.M.	Return to cell
5:55	A.M.	Warning bell
6:00	A.M.	Work detail lineup
10:00	A.M.	Exercise yard
10:30	A.M.	Lunch
11:00	A.M.	Work detail lineup
3:30	P.M.	Supper
4:00	P.M.	Return to cell
5:00	P.M.	Recreation room
6:00	P.M.	Return to cell
8:45	P.M.	Warning bell
9:00	P.M.	Lights out

The rules were inflexible. All inmates had to go to meals, and no talking was permitted in the lines.

No more than five cosmetic items could be kept in the small cell lockers. Beds had to be made prior to breakfast and kept neat during the day.

The penitentiary had a music all its own: the clanging bells, shuffle of feet on cement, slamming iron doors, day whispers and night screams . . . the hoarse crackle of the guards' walkie-talkies, the clash of trays at mealtime. And always there was the barbed wire and the high walls and the loneliness and isolation and the pervading aura of hate.

Tracy became a model prisoner. Her body responded automatically to the sounds of prison routine: the bat sliding across her cell at count time and sliding back at wake-up time; the bell for reporting to work and the buzzer when work was finished.

Tracy's body was a prisoner in this place, but her mind was free to plan her escape.

Prisoners could make no outside telephone calls, and they were permitted to receive two five-minute calls a month. Tracy received a call from Otto Schmidt.

'I thought you'd want to know,' he said awkwardly. 'It was a real nice funeral. I took care of the bills, Tracy.'

'Thank you, Otto. I – thank you.' There was nothing more for either of them to say.

There were no more phone calls for her.

'Girl, you best forget the outside world,' Ernestine

warned her. 'There ain't nobody out there for you.'

You're wrong, Tracy thought grimly.

Joe Romano
Perry Pope
Judge Henry Lawrence
Anthony Orsatti
Charles Stanhope III

It was in the exercise yard that Tracy encountered Big Bertha again. The yard was a large outdoor rectangle bounded by the high outer prison wall on one side and the inner wall of the prison on the other. The inmates were allowed in the yard for thirty minutes each morning. It was one of the few places where talking was permitted, and clusters of prisoners gathered together exchanging the latest news and gossip before lunch. When Tracy walked into the yard for the first time, she felt a sudden sense of freedom, and she realized it was because she was in the open air. She could see the sun, high above, and cumulus clouds, and somewhere in the distant blue sky she heard the drone of a plane, soaring free.

'You! I been lookin' for you,' a voice said.

Tracy turned to see the huge Swede who had brushed into her on Tracy's first day in prison.

'I hear you got yourself a nigger bull-dyke.'

Tracy started to brush past the woman. Big Bertha grabbed Tracy's arm, with an iron grip. 'Nobody walks away from me,' she breathed. 'Be nice, *littbarn*.' She was backing Tracy towards the wall, pressing her huge body into Tracy's.

120

'Get away from me.'

'What you need is a real good lickin'. You know what I mean? An' I'm gonna give it to you. You're gonna be all mine, *alskade*.'

A familiar voice behind Tracy rasped, 'Get your fuckin' hands off her, you asshole.'

Ernestine Littlechap stood there, big fists clenched, eyes blazing, the sun reflecting off her shiny shaved skull.

'You ain't man enough for her, Ernie.'

'I'm man enough for *you*,' the black woman exploded. 'You bother her again, and I'll have your ass for breakfast. *Fried*.'

The air was suddenly charged with electricity. The two amazons were eyeing each other with naked hatred. *They're ready to kill each other over me*, Tracy thought. And then she realized it had very little to do with her. She remembered something Ernestine had told her: 'In this place, you have to fight, fuck, or hit the fence. You gotta hold your mud, or you're dead.'

It was Big Bertha who backed down. She gave Ernestine a contemptuous look. 'I ain't in no hurry.' She leered at Tracy. 'You're gonna be here a long time, baby. So am I. I'll be seein' you.'

She turned and walked away.

Ernestine watched her go. 'She's a bad mother. 'Member that nurse in Chicago who killed off all them patients? Stuck 'em full of cyanide and stayed there an' watched 'em die? Well, that angel of mercy is the one who got the hots for you, Whitney.

Sheeet! You need a fuckin' keeper. She ain't gonna let up on you.'

'Will you help me escape?'

A bell rang.

'It's chow time,' Ernestine Littlechap said.

That night, lying in her bunk, Tracy thought about Ernestine.

Even though she had never tried to touch Tracy again, Tracy still did not trust her. She could never forget what Ernestine and her other cell mates had done to her. But she needed the black woman.

Each afternoon after supper, the inmates were allowed to spend one hour in the recreation room, where they could watch television or talk or read the latest magazines and newspapers. Tracy was thumbing through a copy of a magazine when a photograph caught her eye. It was a wedding picture of Charles Stanhope III and his new bride, coming out of a chapel, arm in arm, laughing. It hit Tracy like a blow. Seeing his photograph now, the happy smile on his face, she was filled with a pain that turned to cold fury. She had once planned to share her life with this man, and he had turned his back on her, let them destroy her, let their baby die. But that was another time, another place, another world. *That was fantasy. This is reality.*

Tracy slammed the magazine shut.

On visiting days it was easy to know which inmates had friends or relatives coming to see them. The prisoners would shower and put on fresh clothes and makeup. Ernestine usually returned from the visitors' room smiling and cheerful.

'My Al, he always comes to see me,' she told Tracy. 'He'll be waitin' for me when I get out. You know why? 'Cause I give him what no other woman gives him.'

Tracy could not hide her confusion. 'You mean . . . sexually?'

'You bet your ass. What goes on behind these walls has nothin' to do with the outside. In here, sometimes we need a warm body to hold – some-body to touch us and tell us they love us. We gotta feel there's somebody who gives a damn about us. It don't matter if it ain't real or don't last. It's all we got. But when I get on the outside' – Ernestine broke into a broad grin – 'then I become a fuckin' nymphomaniac, hear?'

There was something that had been puzzling Tracy. She decided to bring it up now. 'Ernie, you keep protecting me. Why?'

Ernestine shrugged. 'Beats the shit out of me.'

'I really want to know.' Tracy chose her words carefully. 'Everyone else who's your – your *friend* belongs to you. They do whatever you tell them to do.'

'If they don't want to walk around with half an ass, yeah.'

'But not me. Why?'

'You complainin'?'

'No. I'm curious.'

Ernestine thought about it for a moment. 'Okay. You got somethin' I want.' She saw the look on Tracy's face. 'No, not that. I get all that I want, baby. You got class. I mean, real, honest-to-God class. Like those cool ladies you see in *Vogue* and *Town and Country*, all dressed up and servin' tea from silver pots. That's where you belong. This ain't your world. I don't know how you got mixed up with all that rat shit on the outside, but my guess is you got suckered by somebody.' She looked at Tracy and said, almost shyly, 'I ain't come across many decent things in my life. You're one of 'em.' She turned away so that her next words were almost inaudible. 'And I'm sorry about your kid. I really am . . .'

That night, after lights out, Tracy whispered in the dark, 'Ernie, I've got to escape. Help me. Please.'

'I'm tryin' to sleep, for Christ's sake! Shut up now, hear?'

Ernestine initiated Tracy into the arcane language of the prison. Groups of women in the yard were talking: 'This bull-dyker dropped the belt on the grey broad, and from then on you had to feed her with a long-handled spoon . . .'

'She was short, but they caught her in a snow-storm, and a stoned cop turned her over to the butcher. That ended her getup. Good-bye, Ruby-do . . .'

To Tracy, it was like listening to a group of Martians. 'What are they talking about?' she asked.

Ernestine roared with laughter. 'Don't you speak no English, girl? When the lesbian "dropped the belt", it meant she switched from bein' the guy to bein' a Mary Femme. She got involved with a "grey broad" – that's a honky, like you. She couldn't be trusted, so that meant you stayed away from her. She was "short", meanin' she was near the end of her prison sentence, but she got caught takin' heroin by a stoned cop – that's someone who lives by the rules and can't be bought – and they sent her to the "butcher", the prison doctor.'

'What's a "Ruby-do" and a "getup"?'

'Ain't you learned nothin'? A "Ruby-do" is a parole. A "getup" is the day of release.'

Tracy knew she would wait for neither.

The explosion between Ernestine Littlechap and Big Bertha happened in the yard the following day. The prisoners were playing a game of softball, supervised by the guards. Big Bertha, at bat with two strikes against her, hit a hard line drive on the third pitch and ran to first base, which Tracy was covering. Big Bertha slammed into Tracy, knocking her down, and then was on top of her. Her hands snaked up between Tracy's legs, and she whispered, 'Nobody says no to me, you cunt. I'm comin' to get you tonight, *littbarn*, and I'm gonna fuck your ass off.'

Tracy fought wildly to get loose. Suddenly she felt Big Bertha being lifted off her. Ernestine had the huge Swede by the neck and was throttling her.

125

'You goddamn bitch!' Ernestine was screaming. 'I warned you!' She lashed her fingernails across Big Bertha's face, clawing at her eyes.

'I'm blind!' Big Bertha screamed. 'I'm blind!' She grabbed Ernestine's breasts and started pulling them. The two women were punching and clawing at each other as four guards came running up. It took the guards five minutes to pull them apart. Both women were taken to the infirmary. It was late that night when Ernestine was returned to her cell. Lola and Paulita hurried to her bunk to console her.

'Are you all right?' Tracy whispered.

'Damned right,' Ernestine told her. Her voice sounded muffled, and Tracy wondered how badly she had been hurt. 'I made my Ruby-do yesterday. I'm gettin' outta this joint. You got a problem. That mother aint gonna leave you alone now. No way. And when she's finished fuckin' with you, she's gonna kill you.'

They lay there in the silent darkness. Finally, Ernestine spoke again. 'Maybe it's time you and me talked about bustin' you the hell outta here.'

TEN

'You're going to lose your governess tomorrow,' Warden Brannigan announced to his wife.

Sue Ellen Brannigan looked up in surprise. 'Why? Judy's very good with Amy.'

'I know, but her sentence is up. She's being released in the morning.'

They were having breakfast in the comfortable cottage that was one of the perquisites of Warden Brannigan's job. Other benefits included a cook, a maid, a chauffeur, and a governess for their daughter, Amy, who was almost five. All the servants were trusties. When Sue Ellen Brannigan had arrived there five years earlier, she had been nervous about living on the grounds of the penitentiary, and even more apprehensive about having a house full of servants who were all convicted criminals.

'How do you know they won't rob us and cut our throats in the middle of the night?' she had demanded.

'If they do,' Warden Brannigan had promised, 'I'll put them on report.'

He had persuaded his wife, without convincing her, but Sue Ellen's fears had proved groundless. The trusties were anxious to make a good impression and cut their time down as much as possible, so they were very conscientious.

'I was just getting comfortable with the idea of leaving Amy in Judy's care,' Mrs Brannigan complained. She wished Judy well, but she did not want her to leave. Who knew what kind of woman would be Amy's next governess? There were so many horror stories about the terrible things strangers did to children.

'Do you have anyone in particular in mind to replace Judy, George?'

The warden had given it considerable thought. There were a dozen trusties suitable for the job of taking care of their daughter. But he had not been able to get Tracy Whitney out of his mind. There was something about her case that he found deeply disturbing. He had been a professional criminologist for fifteen years, and he prided himself that one of his strengths was his ability to assess prisoners. Some of the convicts in his care were hardened criminals, others were in prison because they had committed crimes of passion or succumbed to a momentary temptation, but it seemed to Warden Brannigan that Tracy Whitney belonged to neither category. He had not been swayed by her protests of innocence, for that was standard operating procedure for all convicts. What bothered him was the people who had conspired to send Tracy Whitney to prison. The warden had been appointed by a New Orleans civil commission headed by the governor of the state, and although he steadfastly refused to become involved in politics, he was aware of all the players. Joe Romano was Mafia, a runner for Anthony Orsatti. Perry Pope, the attorney who had defended Tracy Whitney, was on their payroll, and so was Judge Henry Lawrence. Tracy Whitney's conviction had a decidedly rank odour to it.

Now Warden Brannigan made his decision. He said to his wife, 'Yes. I do have someone in mind.'

There was an alcove in the prison kitchen with a small Formica-topped dining table and four chairs, the only place where it was possible to have a reasonable amount of privacy. Ernestine Littlechap and Tracy were seated there, drinking coffee during their ten-minute break.

'I think it's about time you tol' me what your big hurry is to bust outta here,' Ernestine suggested.

Tracy hesitated. Could she trust Ernestine? She had no choice. 'There – there are some people who did things to my family and me. I've got to get out to pay them back.'

'Yeah? What'd they do?'

Tracy's words came out slowly, each one a drop of pain. 'They killed my mother.'

'Who's *they*?'

'I don't think the names would mean anything to you. Joe Romano, Perry Pope, a judge named Henry Lawrence, Anthony Orsatti –'

Ernestine was staring at her with her mouth open. 'Jesus H. Christ! You puttin' me on, girl?'

Tracy was surprised. 'You've heard of them?'

'*Heard* of 'em! Who hasn't heard of 'em? Nothin' goes down in New Or-fuckin'-leans unless Orsatti or Romano says so. You can't mess with *them*. They'll blow you away like smoke.'

Tracy said tonelessly, 'They've already blown me away.'

Ernestine looked around to make sure they could not be overheard. 'You're either crazy or you're the dumbest broad I've ever met. Talk about the *untouchables*!' She shook her head. 'Forget about 'em. Fast!'

'No. I can't. I have to break out of here. Can it be done?'

Ernestine was silent for a long time. When she finally spoke, she said, 'We'll talk in the yard.'

They were in the yard, off in a corner by themselves.

'There've been twelve bust-outs from this joint,' Ernestine said. 'Two of the prisoners were shot and killed. The other ten were caught and brought back.' Tracy made no comment. 'The tower's manned twenty-four hours by guards with machine guns, and they're mean sons of bitches. If anyone escapes, it costs the guards their jobs, so they'd just as soon kill you as look at you. There's barbed

130

wire all around the prison, and if you get through that and past the machine guns, they got hound dogs that can track a mosquito's fart. There's a National Guard station a few miles away, and when a prisoner escapes from here they send up helicopters with guns and searchlights. Nobody gives a shit if they bring you back dead or alive, girl. They figure dead is better. It discourages anyone else with plans.'

'But people still try,' Tracy said stubbornly.

'The ones who broke out had help from the out-side – friends who smuggled in guns and money and clothes. They had getaway cars waitin' for 'em.' She paused for effect. 'And they *still* got caught.'

'They won't catch me,' Tracy swore.

A matron was approaching. She called out to Tracy, 'Warden Brannigan wants you. On the double.'

'We need someone to take care of our young daughter,' Warden Brannigan said. 'It's a voluntary job. You don't have to take it if you don't wish to.'

Someone to take care of our young daughter. Tracy's mind was racing. This might make her escape easier. Working in the warden's house, she could probably learn a great deal more about the prison setup.

'Yes,' Tracy said. 'I'd like to take the job.'

George Brannigan was pleased. He had an odd, unreasonable feeling that he owed this woman something. 'Good. It pays sixty cents an hour. The money will be put in your account at the end of each month.'

Prisoners were not allowed to handle cash, and all monies accumulated were handed over upon the prisoner's release.

I won't be here at the end of the month, Tracy thought, but aloud she said, 'That will be fine.'

'You can start in the morning. The head matron will give you the details.'

'Thank you, Warden.'

He looked at Tracy and was tempted to say something more. He was not quite sure what. Instead, he said, 'That's all.'

When Tracy broke the news to Ernestine, the black woman said thoughtfully, 'That means they gonna make you a trusty. You'll get the run of the prison. That might make bustin' out a little easier.'

'How do I do it?' Tracy asked.

'You got three choices, but they're all risky. The first way is a sneak-out. You use chewin' gum one night to jam the locks on your cell door and the corridor doors. You sneak outside to the yard, throw a blanket over the barbed wire, and you're off and runnin'.'

With dogs and helicopters after her. Tracy could feel the bullets from the guns of the guards tearing into her. She shuddered. 'What are the other ways?'

'The second way's a breakout. That's where you use a gun and take a hostage with you. If they catch you, they'll give you a deuce with a nickel tail.' She saw Tracy's puzzled expression. 'That's another two to five years on your sentence.'

'And the third way?'

'A walkaway. That's for trusties who are out on a work detail. Once you're out in the open, girl, you jest keep movin'.'

Tracy thought about that. Without money and a car and a place to hide out, she would have no chance. 'They'd find out I was gone at the next head count and come looking for me.'

Ernestine sighed. 'There ain't no perfect escape plan, girl. That's why no one's ever made it outta this place.'

I will, Tracy vowed. *I will*.

The morning Tracy was taken to Warden Brannigan's home marked her fifth month as a prisoner. She was nervous about meeting the warden's wife and child, for she wanted this job desperately. It was going to be her key to freedom.

Tracy walked into the large, pleasant kitchen and sat down. She could feel the perspiration bead and roll down from her underarms. A woman clad in a muted rose-coloured housecoat appeared in the doorway.

She said, 'Good morning.'

'Good morning.'

The woman started to sit, changed her mind, and stood. Sue Ellen Brannigan was a pleasant-faced blonde in her middle thirties, with a vague, distracted manner. She was thin and hyper, never quite sure how to treat the convict servants. Should she thank them for doing their jobs, or just give them orders? Should she be friendly, or treat them like prisoners? Sue Ellen still had not got used to the idea of living in the midst of drug addicts and thieves and killers.

'I'm Mrs Brannigan,' she rattled on. 'Amy is almost five years old, and you know how active they are at that age. I'm afraid she has to be watched all the time.' She glanced at Tracy's left hand. There was no wedding ring there, but these days, of course, that meant nothing. *Particularly with the lower classes*, Sue Ellen thought. She paused and asked delicately, 'Do you have children?'

Tracy thought of her unborn baby. 'No.'

'I see.' Sue Ellen was confused by this young woman. She was not at all what she had expected. There was something almost elegant about her. 'I'll bring Amy in.' She hurried out of the room.

Tracy looked around. It was a fairly large cottage, neat and attractively furnished. It seemed to Tracy that it had been years since she had been in anyone's home. That was all part of the other world, the world outside.

Sue Ellen came back into the room holding the hand of a young girl. 'Amy, this is –' Did one call a prisoner by her first or last name? She compromised. 'This is Tracy Whitney.'

'Hi,' Amy said. She had her mother's thinness and deep-set, intelligent hazel eyes. She was not a pretty child, but there was an open friendliness about her that was touching.

I won't let her touch me.

'Are you going to be my new nanny?'

'Well, I'm going to help your mother look after you.'

'Judy went out on parole, did you know that? Are you going out on parole, too?'

No, Tracy thought. She said, 'I'm going to be here for a long while, Amy.'

'That's good,' Sue Ellen said brightly. She coloured in embarrassment and bit her lip. 'I mean –' She whirled around the kitchen and started explaining Tracy's duties to her. 'You'll have your meals with Amy. You can prepare breakfast for her and play with her in the morning. The cook will make lunch here. After lunch, Amy has a nap, and in the afternoon she likes walking around the grounds of the farm. I think it's so good for a child to see growing things, don't you?'

'Yes.'

The farm was on the other side of the main prison, and the twenty acres, planted with vegetables and fruit trees, were tended by trusties. There was a large artificial lake used for irrigation, surrounded by a stone wall that rose above it.

The next five days were almost like a new life for Tracy. Under different circumstances, she would have enjoyed getting away from the bleak prison walls, free to walk around the farm and breathe

the fresh country air, but all she could think about was escaping. When she was not on duty with Amy, she was required to report back to the prison. Each night Tracy was locked in her cell, but in the daytime she had the illusion of freedom. After breakfast in the prison kitchen, she walked over to the warden's cottage and made breakfast for Amy. Tracy had learned a good deal about cooking from Charles, and she was tempted by the varieties of foodstuffs on the warden's shelves, but Amy preferred a simple breakfast of oatmeal or cereal with fruit. Afterwards, Tracy would play games with the little girl or read to her. Without thinking, Tracy began teaching Amy the games her mother had played with her.

Amy loved puppets. Tracy tried to copy Shari Lewis's Lamb Chop for her from one of the warden's old socks, but it turned out looking like a cross between a fox and a duck. 'I think it's beautiful,' Amy said loyally.

Tracy made the puppet speak with different accents: French, Italian, German, and the one Amy adored the most, Paulita's Mexican lilt. Tracy would watch the pleasure on the child's face and think, *I won't become involved. She's just my means of getting out of this place.*

After Amy's afternoon nap, the two of them would take long walks, and Tracy saw to it that they covered areas of the prison grounds she had not seen before. She carefully observed every exit and entrance and how the guard towers were manned and noted when the shifts changed. It became obvious to her that none of the escape plans she had discussed with Ernestine would work.

'Has anyone ever tried to escape by hiding in one of the service trucks that deliver things to the prison? I've seen milk trucks and food –'

'Forget it,' Ernestine said flatly. 'Every vehicle comin' in and goin' out of the gate is searched.'

At breakfast one morning, Amy said, 'I love you, Tracy. Will you be my mother?'

The words sent a pang through Tracy. 'One mother is enough. You don't need two.'

'Yes, I do. My friend Sally Ann's father got married again, and Sally Ann has two mothers.'

'You're not Sally Ann,' Tracy said curtly. 'Finish your breakfast.'

Amy was looking at her with hurt eyes. 'I'm not hungry any more.'

'All right. I'll read to you, then.'

As Tracy started to read, she felt Amy's soft little hand on hers.

'Can I sit on your lap?'

'No.' *Get your affection from your own family*, Tracy thought. *You don't belong to me. Nothing belongs to me.*

The easy days away from the routine of the prison somehow made the nights worse. Tracy loathed returning to her cell, hated being caged in like an animal. She was still unable to get used to the screams that came from nearby cells in the uncaring darkness. She would grit her teeth until her jaws ached. *One night at a time*, she promised herself. *I can stand one night at a time.*

She slept little, for her mind was busy planning. Step one was to escape. Step two was to deal with Joe Romano, Perry Pope, Judge Henry Lawrence, and Anthony Orsatti. Step three was Charles. But that was too painful even to think about yet. *I'll handle that when the time comes*, she told herself.

It was becoming impossible to stay out of the way of Big Bertha. Tracy was sure the huge Swede was having her spied upon. If Tracy went to the recreation room, Big Bertha would show up a few minutes later, and when Tracy went out to the yard, Big Bertha would appear shortly afterwards.

One day Big Bertha walked up to Tracy and said, 'You're looking beautiful today, *littbarn*. I can't wait for us to get together.'

'Stay away from me,' Tracy warned.

The amazon grinned. 'Or what? Your black bitch is gettin' out. I'm arrangin' to have you transferred to my cell.'

Tracy stared at her.

Big Bertha nodded. 'I can do it, honey. Believe it.'

Tracy knew then her time was running out. She had to escape before Ernestine was released.

Amy's favourite walk was through the meadow, rainbowed with colourful wildflowers. The huge artificial lake was nearby, surrounded by a low concrete wall with a long drop to the deep water.

'Let's go swimming,' Amy pleaded. 'Please, let's, Tracy?'

'It's not for swimming,' Tracy said. 'They use the water for irrigation.' The sight of the cold, forbidding-looking lake made her shiver.

Her father was carrying her into the ocean on his shoulders, and when she cried out, her father said, *Don't be a baby, Tracy*, and he dropped her into the cold water, and when the water closed over her head she panicked and began to choke . . .

When the news came, it was a shock, even though Tracy had expected it.

'I'm gettin' outta here a week from Sattiday,' Ernestine said.

The words sent a cold chill through Tracy. She had not told Ernestine about her conversation with Big Bertha. Ernestine would not be here to help her. Big Bertha probably had enough influence to have Tracy transferred to her cell. The only way Tracy could avoid it would be to talk to the warden, and she knew that if she did that, she was as good as dead. Every convict in the prison would turn on her. *You gotta fight, fuck, or hit the fence.* Well, she was going to hit the fence.

She and Ernestine went over the escape possibilities again. None of them was satisfactory.

'You ain't got no car, and you ain't got no one on the outside to he'p you. You're gonna get caught, sure as hell, and then you'll be worse off.

You'd be better doin' cool time and finishin' out your gig.'

But Tracy knew there would be no cool time. Not with Big Bertha after her. The thought of what the giant bull-dyke had in mind for her made her physically ill.

It was Saturday morning, seven days before Ernestine's release. Sue Ellen Brannigan had taken Amy into New Orleans for the weekend, and Tracy was at work in the prison kitchen.

'How's the nursemaid job goin'?' Ernestine asked.

'All right.'

'I seen that little girl. She seems real sweet.'

'She's okay.' Her tone was indifferent.

'I'll sure be glad to get outta here. I'll tell you one thing, I ain't never comin' back to this joint. If there's anythin' Al or me kin do for you on the outside –'

'Coming through,' a male voice called out.

Tracy turned. A laundryman was pushing a huge cart piled to the top with soiled uniforms and linens. Tracy watched, puzzled, as he headed for the exit.

'What I was sayin' was if me and Al can do any-thin' for you – you know – send you things or –'

'Ernie, what's a laundry truck doing here? The prison has its own laundry.'

'Oh, that's for the guards,' Ernestine laughed. 'They used to send their uniforms to the prison laundry, but all the buttons managed to get ripped off, sleeves were torn, obscene notes were sewn inside, shirts were shrunk, and the material got mysteriously slashed. Ain't that a fuckin' shame, Miss Scarlett? Now the guards gotta send their stuff to an outside laundry.' Ernestine laughed her Butterfly McQueen imitation.

Tracy was no longer listening. She knew how she was going to escape.

ELEVEN

'George, I don't think we should keep Tracy on.'

Warden Brannigan looked up from his newspaper. 'What's the problem?'

'I'm not sure, exactly. I have the feeling that Tracy doesn't like Amy. Maybe she just doesn't like children.'

'She hasn't been mean to Amy, has she? Hit her, yelled at her?'

'No . . .'

'What, then?'

'Yesterday Amy ran over and put her arms around Tracy, and Tracy pushed her away. It bothered me because Amy's so crazy about her. To tell you the truth, I might be a little jealous. Could that be it?'

Warden Brannigan laughed. 'That could explain a lot, Sue Ellen. I think Tracy Whitney is just right for the job. Now, if she gives you any real problems, let me know, and I'll do something about it.'

'All right, dear.' Sue Ellen was still not satisfied.

She picked up her needlepoint and began stabbing at it. The subject was not closed yet.

'*Why* can't it work?'

'I tol' you, girl. The guards search every truck going through the gate.'

'But a truck carrying a basket of laundry – they're not going to dump out the laundry to check it.'

'They don't have to. The basket is taken to the utility room, where a guard watches it bein' filled.'

Tracy stood there thinking. 'Ernie . . . could someone distract the guard for five minutes?'

'What the hell good would –?' She broke off, a slow grin lighting her face. 'While someone pumps him full of sunshine, you get into the bottom of the hamper and get covered up with laundry!' She nodded. 'You know, I think the damned thing might work.'

'Then you'll help me?'

Ernestine was thoughtful for a moment. Then she said softly, 'Yeah. I'll he'p you. It's my last chance to give Big Bertha a kick in the ass.'

The prison grapevine buzzed with the news of Tracy Whitney's impending escape. A breakout was an event that affected all prisoners. The inmates lived vicariously through each attempt, wishing they had the courage to try it themselves. But there were the guards and the dogs and the helicopters, and, in the end, the bodies of the prisoners who had been brought back.

With Ernestine's help, the escape plan moved ahead swiftly. Ernestine took Tracy's measurements, Lola boosted the material for a dress from the millinery shop, and Paulita had a seamstress in another cell block make it. A pair of prison shoes was stolen from the wardrobe department and dyed to match the dress. A hat, gloves, and handbag appeared, as if by magic.

'Now we gotta get you some ID,' Ernestine informed Tracy. 'You'll need a couple of credit cards and a driver's licence.'

'How can I –?'

Ernestine grinned. 'You just leave it to old Ernie Littlechap.'

The following evening Ernestine handed Tracy three major credit cards in the name of Jane Smith.

'Next, you need a driver's licence.'

Sometime after midnight Tracy heard the door of her cell being opened. Someone had sneaked into the cell. Tracy sat up in her bunk, instantly on guard.

A voice whispered, 'Whitney? Let's go!'

Tracy recognized the voice of Lillian, a trusty. 'What do you want?' Tracy asked.

Ernestine's voice shot out of the darkness. 'What kind of idiot child did your mother raise? Shut up and don't ask questions.'

Lillian said softly, 'We got to do this fast. If we get caught, they'll have my ass. Come on.'

'Where are we going?' Tracy asked, as she followed Lillian down the dark corridor to a stairway. They went up to the landing above and, after making sure there were no guards about, hurried down a hallway until they came to the room where Tracy had been fingerprinted and photographed. Lillian pushed the door open. 'In here,' she whispered.

Tracy followed her into the room. Another inmate was waiting inside.

'Step up against the wall.' She sounded nervous.

Tracy moved against the wall, her stomach in knots.

'Look into the camera. Come on. Try and look relaxed.'

Very funny, Tracy thought. She had never been so nervous in her life. The camera clicked.

'The picture will be delivered in the morning,' the inmate said. 'It's for your driver's licence. Now get out of here – fast.'

Tracy and Lillian retraced their steps. On the way, Lillian said, 'I hear you're changin' cells.'

Tracy froze. 'What?'

'Didn't you know? You're moving in with Big Bertha.'

Ernestine, Lola, and Paulita were waiting up for Tracy when she returned. 'How'd it go?'

'Fine.'

Didn't you know? You're moving in with Big Bertha.

'The dress'll be ready for you Sattiday,' Paulita said.

145

The day of Ernestine's release. *That's my dead-line*, Tracy thought.

Ernestine whispered, 'Everythin' is cool. The laundry pickup Sattiday is two o'clock. You gotta be in the utility room by one-thirty. You don' have to worry about the guard. Lola will keep him busy next door. Paulita will be in the utility room waitin' for you. She'll have your clothes. Your ID will be in your handbag. You'll be drivin' out the prison gates by two-fifteen.'

Tracy found it difficult to breathe. Just talking about the escape made her tremble. *Nobody gives a shit if they bring you back dead or alive . . . They figure dead is better.*

In a few days she would be making her break for freedom. She had no illusions: the odds were against her. They would eventually find her and bring her back. But there was something she had sworn to take care of first.

The prison grapevine knew all about the contest that had been fought between Ernestine Littlechap and Big Bertha over Tracy. Now that the word was out that Tracy was being transferred to Big Bertha's cell, it was no accident that no one had mentioned anything to Big Bertha about Tracy's escape plan: Big Bertha did not like to hear bad news. She was often apt to confuse the news with the bearer and treat that person accordingly. Big Bertha did not learn about Tracy's plan until the morning the escape was to take place, and it was revealed to

146

her by the trusty who had taken Tracy's picture.

Big Bertha took the news in ominous silence. Her body seemed to grow bigger as she listened.

'What time?' was all she asked.

'This afternoon at two o'clock, Bert. They're gonna hide her in the bottom of a laundry hamper in the utility room.'

Big Bertha thought about it for a long time. Then she waddled over to a matron and said, 'I gotta see Warden Brannigan right away.'

Tracy had not slept all night. She was sick with tension. The months she had been in prison seemed like a dozen eternities. Images of the past flashed through her mind as she lay on her bunk, staring into the dark.

I feel like a princess in a fairy tale, Mother. I didn't know anyone could be this happy.

So! You and Charles want to get married.

How long a honeymoon are you planning?

You shot me, you bitch! . . .

Your mother committed suicide . . .

I never really knew you . . .

The wedding picture of Charles smiling at his bride . . .

How many eons ago? How many planets away?

The morning bell clanged through the corridor like a shock wave. Tracy sat up on her bunk, wide awake. Ernestine was watching her. 'How you feelin', girl?'

'Fine,' Tracy lied. Her mouth was dry, and her heart was beating erratically.

'Well, we're both leavin' here today.'

Tracy found it hard to swallow. 'Uh-huh.'

'You sure you kin get away from the warden's house by one-thirty?'

'No problem. Amy always takes a nap after lunch.'

Paulita said, 'You can't be late, or it won't work.'

'I'll be there.'

Ernestine reached under her mattress and took out a roll of bills. 'You're gonna need some walkin' around money. It's only two hundred bucks, but it'll get you on your way.'

'Ernie, I don't know what to –'

'Oh, jest shut up, girl, and take it.'

Tracy forced herself to swallow some breakfast. Her head was pounding, and every muscle in her body ached. *I'll never make it through the day*, she thought. *I've got to make it through the day*.

There was a strained, unnatural silence in the kitchen, and Tracy suddenly realized she was the cause of it. She was the object of knowing looks and nervous whispers. A breakout was about to happen, and she was the heroine of the drama. In a few hours she would be free. Or dead.

She rose from her unfinished breakfast and headed for Warden Brannigan's house. As Tracy waited for a guard to unlock the corridor door, she came face-to-face with Big Bertha. The huge Swede was grinning at her.

148

She's going to be in for a big surprise, Tracy thought.

She's all mine now, Big Bertha thought.

The morning passed so slowly that Tracy felt she would go out of her mind. The minutes seemed to drag on interminably. She read to Amy and had no idea what she was reading. She was aware of Mrs Brannigan watching from the window.

'Tracy, let's play hide-and-seek.'

Tracy was too nervous to play games, but she dared not do anything to arouse Mrs Brannigan's suspicions. She forced a smile. 'Sure. Why don't you hide first, Amy?'

They were in the front yard of the bungalow. In the far distance Tracy could see the building where the utility room was located. She had to be there at exactly 1:30. She would change into the street clothes that had been made for her, and by 1:45 she would be lying in the bottom of the large clothes hamper, covered over with uniforms and linens. At 2:00 the laundryman would come by for the hamper and wheel it out to his truck. By 2:15 the truck would drive through the gates on its way to the nearby town where the laundry plant was located.

The driver can't see in the back of the truck from the front seat. When the truck gets to town and stops for a red light, just open the door, step out, real cool, and catch a bus to wherever you're goin'.

'Can you see me?' Amy called. She was half-hidden behind the trunk of a magnolia tree. She held her hand over her mouth to stifle a giggle.

I'll miss her, Tracy thought. *When I leave here, the two people I'll miss will be a black, bald-headed bull-dyke and a young girl.* She wondered what Charles Stanhope would have made of that.

'I'm coming to find you,' Tracy said.

Sue Ellen watched the game from inside the house. It seemed to her that Tracy was acting strangely. All morning she had kept looking at her watch, as though expecting someone, and her mind was obviously not on Amy.

I must speak to George about it when he comes home for lunch, Sue Ellen decided. *I'm going to insist that he replace her.*

In the yard, Tracy and Amy played hopscotch for a while, then jacks, and Tracy read to Amy, and finally, blessedly, it was twelve-thirty, time for Amy's lunch. Time for Tracy to make her move. She took Amy into the cottage.

'I'll be leaving now, Mrs Brannigan.'

'What? Oh. Didn't anyone tell you, Tracy? We're having a delegation of VIP visitors today. They'll be having lunch here at the house, so Amy won't be having her nap. You may take her with you.'

Tracy stood there, willing herself not to scream. 'I – I can't do that, Mrs Brannigan.'

Sue Ellen Brannigan stiffened. 'What do you mean you can't do that?'

Tracy saw the anger in her face and thought, *I mustn't upset her. She'll call the warden, and I'll be sent back to my cell.*

Tracy forced a smile. 'I mean . . . Amy hasn't had her lunch. She'll be hungry.'

'I've had the cook prepare a picnic lunch for both of you. You can go for a nice walk in the meadow and have it there. Amy enjoys picnics, don't you darling?'

'I love picnics.' She looked at Tracy pleadingly. 'Can we, Tracy? Can we?'

No! Yes. Careful. It could still work.

Be in the utility room by one-thirty. Don't be late.

Tracy looked at Mrs Brannigan. 'What – what time do you want me to bring Amy back?'

'Oh, about three o'clock. They should be gone by then.'

So would the truck. The world was tumbling in on her. 'I –'

'Are you all right? You look pale.'

That was it. She would say she was ill. Go to the hospital. But then they would want to check her over and keep her there. She would never be able to get out in time. There had to be some other way.

Mrs Brannigan was staring at her.

'I'm fine.'

There's something wrong with her, Sue Ellen

151

Brannigan decided. *I'm definitely going to have George get someone else.*

Amy's eyes were alight with joy. 'I'll give you the biggest sandwiches, Tracy. We'll have a good time, won't we?'

Tracy had no answer.

The VIP tour was a surprise visit. Governor William Haber himself was escorting the prison reform committee through the penitentiary. It was something that Warden Brannigan had to live with once a year.

'It goes with the territory, George,' the governor had explained. 'Just clean up the place, tell your ladies to smile pretty, and we'll get our budget increased again.'

The word had gone out from the chief guard that morning: 'Get rid of all the drugs, knives, and dildos.'

Governor Haber and his party were due to arrive at 10:00 A.M. They would inspect the interior of the penitentiary first, visit the farm, and then have lunch with the warden at his cottage.

Big Bertha was impatient. When she had put in a request to see the warden, she had been told, 'The warden is very pressed for time this morning. Tomorrow would be easier. He –'

'Fuck tomorrow!' Big Bertha had exploded. 'I want to see him now. It's important.'

There were few inmates in the prison who

could have got away with it, but Big Bertha was one of them. The prison authorities were well aware of her power. They had seen her start riots, and they had seen her stop them. No prison in the world could be run without the cooperation of the inmate leaders, and Big Bertha was a leader.

She had been seated in the warden's outer office for almost an hour, her huge body overflowing the chair she sat in. *She's a disgusting-looking creature*, the warden's secretary thought. *She gives me the creeps.*

'How much longer?' Bertha demanded.

'It shouldn't be too much longer. He has a group of people in with him. The warden's very busy this morning.'

Big Bertha said, 'He's gonna be busier.' She looked at her watch. Twelve-forty-five. *Plenty of time.*

It was a perfect day, cloudless and warm, and the singing breeze carried a tantalizing mixture of scents across the green farmland. Tracy had spread out a tablecloth on a grassy area near the lake, and Amy was happily munching on an egg salad sandwich. Tracy glanced at her watch. It was already 1:00. She could not believe it. The morning had dragged and the afternoon was winging by. She had to think of something quickly, or time was going to steal away her last chance at freedom.

One-ten. In the warden's reception office Warden Brannigan's secretary put down the telephone and said to Big Bertha, 'I'm sorry. The warden says it's impossible for him to see you today. We'll make another appointment for –'

Big Bertha pushed herself to her feet. 'He's *got* to see me! It's –'

'We'll fit you in tomorrow.'

Big Bertha started to say, 'Tomorrow will be too late', but she stopped herself in time. No one but the warden himself must know what she was doing. Snitches suffered fatal accidents. But she had no intention of giving up. There was no way she was going to let Tracy Whitney get away from her. She walked into the prison library and sat down at one of the long tables at the far end of the room. She scribbled a note, and when the matron walked over to an aisle to help an inmate, Big Bertha dropped the note on her desk and left.

When the matron returned, she found the note and opened it. She read it twice:

YOU BETTER CHEK THE LAUNDREY TRUCK
TO DAY.

There was no signature. A hoax? The matron had no way of knowing. She picked up the telephone. 'Get me the superintendent of guards . . .'

One-fifteen. 'You're not eating,' Amy said. 'You want some of my sandwich?'

'No! Leave me alone.' She had not meant to speak so harshly.

Amy stopped eating. 'Are you mad at me, Tracy? Please don't be mad at me. I love you so much. I never get mad at you.' Her soft eyes were filled with hurt.

'I'm not angry.' *She was in hell.*

'I'm not hungry if you're not. Let's play ball, Tracy.' And Amy pulled her rubber ball out of her pocket.

One-sixteen. She should have been on her way. It would take her at least fifteen minutes to get to the utility room. She could just make it if she hurried. But she could not leave Amy alone. Tracy looked around, and in the far distance she saw a group of trusties picking crops. Instantly, Tracy knew what she was going to do.

'Don't you want to play ball, Tracy?'

Tracy rose to her feet. 'Yes. Let's play a new game. Let's see who can throw the ball the farthest. I'll throw the ball, and then it will be your turn.' Tracy picked up the hard rubber ball and threw it as far as she could in the direction of the workers.

'Oh, that's good,' Amy said admiringly. 'That's real far.'

'I'll go get the ball,' Tracy said. 'You wait here.'

And she was running, running for her life, her feet flying across the fields. It was 1:18. If she was late, they would wait for her. *Or would they?* She ran faster. Behind her, she heard Amy calling, but she paid no attention. The farm workers were moving in the other direction now. Tracy yelled at them, and they stopped. She was breathless when she reached them.

'Anythin' wrong?' one of them asked.

'No, n-nothing.' She was panting, fighting for breath. 'The little girl back there. One of you look after her. I have something important to do. I –'

She heard her name called from a distance and turned. Amy was standing on top of the concrete wall surrounding the lake. She waved. 'Look at me, Tracy.'

'No! Get down!' Tracy screamed.

And as Tracy watched in horror, Amy lost her balance and plunged into the lake.

'Oh, dear God!' The blood drained from Tracy's face. She had a choice to make, but there was no choice. *I can't help her. Not now. Someone will save her. I have to save myself. I've got to get out of this place or I'll die.* It was 1:20.

Tracy turned and began running as fast as she had ever run in her life. The others were calling after her, but she did not hear them. She flew through the air, unaware that her shoes had fallen off, not caring that the sharp ground was cutting into her feet. Her heart was pounding, and her lungs were bursting, and she pushed herself to run faster, faster. She reached the wall around the lake and vaulted on top of it. Far below, she could see Amy in the deep, terrifying water, struggling to stay afloat. Without a second's hesitation, Tracy jumped in after her. And as she hit the water, Tracy thought, *Oh, my God! I can't swim . . .*

BOOK TWO

TWELVE

Lester Torrance, a cashier at the First Merchants Bank of New Orleans, prided himself on two things: his sexual prowess with the ladies and his ability to size up his customers. Lester was in his late forties, a lanky, sallow-faced man with a Tom Selleck moustache and long sideburns. He had been passed over for promotion twice, and in retaliation, Lester used the bank as a personal dating service. He could spot hookers a mile away, and he enjoyed trying to persuade them to give him their favours for nothing. Lonely widows were an especially easy prey. They came in all shapes, ages and states of desperation, and sooner or later they would appear in front of Lester's cage. If they were temporarily overdrawn, Lester would lend a sympathetic ear and delay bouncing their cheques. In return, perhaps they could have a quiet little dinner together? Many of his female customers sought his help and confided delicious secrets to him: they needed a loan without their husbands' knowledge . . . They wanted to keep confidential certain cheques they had written . . . They were contemplating a divorce, and could Lester help them close out their joint account right away? . . . Lester was only too eager to please. And to be pleased.

On this particular Friday morning, Lester knew he had hit the jackpot. He saw the woman the moment she walked in the door of the bank. She was an absolute stunner. She had sleek black hair falling to her shoulders, and she wore a tight skirt and sweater that outlined a figure a Las Vegas chorine would have envied.

There were four other cashiers in the bank, and the young woman's eyes went from one cage to the other, as though seeking help. When she glanced at Lester, he nodded eagerly and gave her an encouraging smile. She walked over to his cage, just as Lester had known she would.

'Good *morning*,' Lester said warmly. 'What may I do for you?' He could see her nipples pushing against her cashmere sweater, and he thought, *Baby, what I'd like to do for you!*

'I'm afraid I have a problem,' the woman said softly. She had the most delightful southern accent Lester had ever heard.

'That's what I'm here for,' he said heartily, 'to solve problems.'

'Oh, I do hope so. I'm afraid I've done somethin' just terrible.'

Lester gave her his best paternal, you-can-lean-on-me smile. 'I can't believe a lovely lady like you could do anything terrible.'

'Oh, but I *have*.' Her soft brown eyes were wide with panic. 'I'm Joseph Romano's secretary, and he told me to order new blank cheques for his current account a week ago, and I simply forgot all about it, and now we've just about run out, and when he finds out, I don't know what he'll do to me.' It came out in a soft, velvety rush.

Lester was only too familiar with the name of Joseph Romano. He was a prized customer of the bank's, even though he kept relatively small amounts in his account. Everyone knew that his real money was laundered elsewhere.

He sure has great taste in secretaries, Lester thought. He smiled again. 'Well, now, that's not too serious, Mrs –?'

'Miss. Hartford. Lureen Hartford.'

Miss. This was his lucky day. Lester sensed that this was going to work out splendidly. 'I'll just order those new cheques for you right now. You should have them in two or three weeks and –'

She gave a little moan, a sound that seemed to Lester to hold infinite promise. 'Oh, that's too late, and Mr Romano's already so upset with me. I just can't seem to keep my mind on my work, you know?' She leaned forward so that her breasts were touching the front of the cage. She said breathlessly,

'If you could just rush those cheques out, I'd be happy to pay extra.'

Lester said ruefully, 'Gee, I'm sorry, Lureen, it would be impossible to –' He saw that she was near to tears.

'To tell you the truth, this might cost me my job. Please . . . I'll do *anything*.'

The words fell like music on Lester's ears.

'I'll tell you what I'll do,' Lester declared. 'I'll phone in a special rush on them, and you'll have them Monday. How's that?'

'Oh, you're just *wonderful*!' Her voice was filled with gratitude.

'I'll send them to the office and –'

'It would be better if I picked them up myself. I don't want Mr Romano to know how stupid I was.'

Lester smiled indulgently. 'Not stupid, Lureen. We all get a little forgetful sometimes.'

She said softly, 'I'll never forget *you*. See you Monday.'

'I'll be here.' It would take a broken back to keep him home.

She gave him a dazzling smile and walked slowly out of the bank, and her walk was a sight to behold. Lester was grinning as he went over to a file cabinet, got the number of Joseph Romano's account, and phoned in a rush order for the new cheques.

The hotel in Carmen Street was indistinguishable from a hundred other hotels in New Orleans, which was why Tracy had chosen it. She had been in the small, cheaply furnished room for a week. Compared to her cell, it was a palace.

When Tracy returned from her encounter with Lester, she took off the black wig, ran her fingers through her own luxuriant hair, removed the soft contact lenses, and creamed off her dark makeup. She sat down on the single straight chair in the room and breathed deeply. It was going well. It had been easy to learn where Joe Romano kept his bank account. Tracy had looked up the cancelled cheque from her mother's estate, issued by Romano. 'Joe Romano? You can't touch him,' Ernestine had said.

Ernestine was wrong and Joe Romano was just the first. The others would follow. Every one of them.

She closed her eyes and relived the miracle that had brought her there . . .

She felt the cold, dark waters closing over her head. She was drowning, and she was filled with terror. She dived down, and her hands found the child and grabbed her and pulled her to the surface. Amy struggled in blind panic to break free, dragging them both under again, her arms and legs flailing wildly. Tracy's lungs were bursting. She fought her way out of the watery grave, hanging on to the little girl in a death grip, and she felt her strength ebbing. *We're not going to make it*, she thought. *We're dying.* Voices were calling out, and she felt Amy's body torn from her arms and she screamed, 'Oh, God, no!'

Strong hands were around Tracy's waist and a voice said, 'Everything's fine now. Take it easy. It's over.'

Tracy looked around frantically for Amy and saw that she was safe in a man's arms. Moments later they were both hauled up from the deep, cruel water . . .

The incident would have been worth no more than a paragraph on the inside page of the morning newspapers, except for the fact that a prisoner who could not swim had risked her life to save the child of the warden. Overnight the newspapers and television commentators turned Tracy into a heroine. Governor Haber himself visited the prison hospital with Warden Brannigan to see Tracy.

'That was a very brave thing you did,' the warden said. 'Mrs Brannigan and I want you to know how grateful we are.' His voice was choked with emotion.

Tracy was still weak and shaken from her experience. 'How is Amy?'

'She's going to be fine.'

Tracy closed her eyes. *I couldn't have borne it if anything had happened to her*, she thought. She remembered her coldness, when all the child had wanted was love, and Tracy felt bitterly ashamed. The incident had cost her her chance to escape, but she knew that if she had to do it over again, she would do the same thing.

There was a brief inquiry into the accident.

'It was my fault,' Amy told her father. 'We were playing ball, and Tracy ran after the ball and told me to wait, but I climbed up on the wall so I could see her better and I fell in the water. But Tracy saved me, Daddy.'

They kept Tracy in the hospital that night for observation, and the next morning she was taken to Warden Brannigan's office. The media was waiting for her. They knew a human-interest story when they saw one, and stringers from UPI and the Associated Press were present; the local television station had sent a news team.

That evening the report of Tracy's heroism unfolded, and the account of the rescue went on national television and began to snowball. *Time*, *Newsweek*, *People*, and hundreds of newspapers all over the country carried the story. As the press coverage continued, letters and telegrams poured into the penitentiary, demanding that Tracy Whitney be pardoned.

Governor Haber discussed it with Warden Brannigan.

'Tracy Whitney is in here for some serious crimes,' Warden Brannigan observed.

The governor was thoughtful. 'But she has no previous record, right, George?'

'That's right, sir.'

'I don't mind telling you, I'm getting a hell of a lot of pressure to do something about her.'

'So am I, Governor.'

'Of course, we can't let the public tell us how to run our prisons, can we?'

'Certainly not.'

'On the other hand,' the governor said judiciously, 'the Whitney girl has certainly demonstrated a remarkable amount of courage. She's become quite a heroine.'

'No question about it,' Warden Brannigan agreed.

The governor paused to light a cigar. 'What's your opinion, George?'

George Brannigan chose his words carefully. 'You're aware, of course, Governor, that I have a very personal interest in this. It was my child she saved. But, putting that aside, I don't think Tracy Whitney is the criminal type, and I can't believe she would be a danger to society if she were out in the world. My strong recommendation is that you give her a pardon.'

The governor, who was about to announce his candidacy for a new term, recognized a good idea when he heard it. 'Let's play this close to the chest for a bit.' In politics, timing was everything.

After discussing it with her husband, Sue Ellen said to Tracy, 'Warden Brannigan and I would like it very much if you moved into the cottage. We have a spare bedroom in the back. You could take care of Amy full-time.'

'Thank you,' Tracy said gratefully. 'I would like that.'

It worked out perfectly. Not only did Tracy not have to spend each night locked away in a cell, but her relationship with Amy changed completely. Amy adored Tracy, and Tracy responded. She enjoyed being with this bright, loving little girl. They played their old games and watched Disney films on television and read together. It was almost like being part of a family.

But whenever Tracy had an errand that took her into the cell blocks, she invariably ran into Big Bertha.

'You're a lucky bitch,' Big Bertha growled. 'But you'll be back here with the common folks one day soon. I'm workin' on it, *littbarn*.'

Three weeks after Amy's rescue Tracy and Amy were playing tag in the yard when Sue Ellen Brannigan hurried out of the house. She stood there a moment watching them. 'Tracy, the warden just telephoned. He would like to see you in his office right away.'

Tracy was filled with a sudden fear. *Did it mean that she was going to be transferred back to the prison?* Had Big Bertha used her influence to arrange it? Or had Mrs Brannigan decided that Amy and Tracy were getting too close?

'Yes, Mrs Brannigan.'

The warden was standing in the doorway of his office when Tracy was escorted in. 'You'd better sit down,' he said.

Tracy tried to read the answer to her fate from the tone of his voice.

'I have some news for you.' He paused, filled with some emotion that Tracy did not understand.

'I have just received an order from the governor of Louisiana,' Warden Brannigan went on, 'giving you a full pardon, effective immediately.'

Dear God, did he say what I think he said? She was afraid to speak.

'I want you to know,' the warden continued, 'that this is not being done because it was my child you saved. You acted instinctively in the way any decent citizen would have acted. By no stretch of the imagination could I ever believe that you would be a threat to society.' He smiled and added, 'Amy is going to miss you. So are we.'

Tracy had no words. If the warden only knew the truth: that if the accident had not happened, the warden's men would have been out hunting her as a fugitive.

'You'll be released the day after tomorrow.'

Her 'getup'. And still Tracy could not absorb it. 'I – I don't know what to say.'

'You don't have to say anything. Everyone here is very proud of you. Mrs Brannigan and I expect you to do great things on the outside.'

So it was true: she was free. Tracy felt so weak that she had to steady herself against the arm of the chair. When she finally spoke, her voice was firm. 'There's a lot I want to do, Warden Brannigan.'

On Tracy's last night in prison an inmate from Tracy's old cell block walked up to her. 'So you're getting out.'

'That's right.'

The woman, Betty Franciscus, was in her early forties, still attractive, with an air of pride about her.

'If you need any help on the outside, there's a man you should see in New York. His name is Conrad Morgan.' She slipped Tracy a piece of paper. 'He's into criminal reform. He likes to give a hand to people who've been in prison.'

'Thank you, but I don't think I'll need –'

'You never know. Keep his address.'

Two hours later, Tracy was walking through the penitentiary gates, moving past the television cameras. She would not speak to the reporters, but when Amy broke away from her mother and threw herself into Tracy's arms, the cameras whirred. That was the picture that came out over the evening news.

Freedom to Tracy was no longer simply an abstract word. It was something tangible, physical, a condition to be enjoyed and savoured. Freedom meant breathing fresh air, privacy, not standing in lines for meals, not listening for bells. It meant hot baths and good-smelling soaps, soft lingerie, pretty dresses and high-heeled shoes. It meant having a name instead of a number. Freedom meant escape from Big Bertha and fear of gang rapes and the deadly monotony of prison routine.

Tracy's newfound freedom took getting used to. Walking along a street, she was careful not to jostle anyone. In the penitentiary bumping into another prisoner could be the spark that set off a conflagration. It was the absence of constant menace that Tracy found most difficult to adjust to. No one was threatening her.

She was free to carry out her plans.

In Philadelphia, Charles Stanhope III saw Tracy on television, leaving the prison. *She's still beautiful*, he thought. Watching her, it seemed impossible that she had committed any of the crimes for which she had been convicted. He looked at his exemplary wife, placidly seated across the room, knitting. *I wonder if I made a mistake.*

Daniel Cooper watched Tracy on the television news in his apartment in New York. He was totally indifferent to the fact that she had been released from prison. He clicked off the television set and returned to the file he was working on.

When Joe Romano saw the television news, he laughed aloud. The Whitney girl was a lucky bitch. *I'll bet prison was good for her. She must be really horny by now. Maybe one day we'll meet again.*

Romano was pleased with himself. He had already passed the Renoir to a fence, and it had been purchased by a private collector in Zurich. Five hundred grand from the insurance company, and another two hundred thousand from the fence. Naturally, Romano had split the money with Anthony Orsatti. Romano was very meticulous in his dealings with him, for he had seen examples of what happened to people who were *not* correct in their transactions with Orsatti.

At noon on Monday Tracy, in her Lureen Hartford persona, returned to the First Merchants Bank of New Orleans. At that hour it was crowded with customers. There were several people in front of Lester Torrance's window. Tracy joined the line, and when Lester saw her, he beamed and nodded. She was even more goddamned beautiful than he had remembered.

When Tracy finally reached his window, Lester crowed, 'Well, it wasn't easy, but I did it for you, Lureen.'

A warm, appreciative smile lit Lureen's face. 'You're just too wonderful.'

'Yes, sir, got 'em right here.' Lester opened a drawer, found the box of cheques he had carefully put away, and handed it to her. 'There you are. Four hundred blank cheques. Will that be enough?'

'Oh, more than enough, unless Mr Romano goes on a cheque-writing spree.' She looked into Lester's eyes and sighed, 'You saved my life.'

Lester felt a pleasurable stirring in his groin. 'I believe people have to be nice to people, don't you, Lureen?'

'You're so right, Lester.'

'You know, you should open your account here. I'd take real good care of you. *Real* good.'

'I just know you would,' Tracy said softly.

'Why don't you and me talk about it over a nice quiet dinner somewhere?'

'I'd surely love that.'

'Where can I call you, Lureen?'

'Oh, I'll call *you*, Lester.' She moved away.

'Wait a min –' The next customer stepped up and handed the frustrated Lester a sackful of coins.

In the centre of the bank were four tables that held containers of blank deposit and withdrawal slips, and the tables were crowded with people busily filling out forms. Tracy moved away from Lester's view. As a customer made room at a table, Tracy took her place. The box that Lester had given her contained eight packets of blank cheques. But it was not the cheques Tracy was interested in: it was the deposit slips at the back of the packets.

She carefully separated the deposit slips from the cheques and, in fewer than three minutes, she was holding eighty deposit slips in her hand. Making sure she was unobserved, Tracy put twenty slips in the metal container.

She moved on to the next table, where she placed twenty more deposit slips. Within a few minutes, all of them had been left on the various tables. The deposit slips were blank, but each one contained a magnetized code at the bottom, which the computer used to credit the various accounts. No matter who deposited money, because of the magnetic code, the computer would automatically credit Joe Romano's account with each deposit. From her experience working in a bank, Tracy knew that within two days all the magnetized deposit slips would be used up and that it would take at least five days before the mix-up was noticed. That would give her more than enough time for what she planned to do.

On the way back to her hotel, Tracy threw the blank cheques into a rubbish bin. Mr Joe Romano would not be needing them.

Tracy's next stop was at the New Orleans Holiday Travel Agency. The young woman behind the desk asked, 'May I help you?'

'I'm Joseph Romano's secretary. Mr Romano would like to make a reservation for Rio de Janeiro. He wants to leave this Friday.'

'Will that be one ticket?'

'Yes. First class. An aisle seat. Smoking, please.'

'Round trip?'

'One way.'

The travel agent turned to her desk computer. In a few seconds, she said, 'We're all set. One first-class seat on Pan American's Flight seven twenty-eight, leaving at six-thirty P.M. on Friday, with a short stopover in Miami.'

'He'll be very pleased,' Tracy assured the woman.

'That will be nineteen hundred and twenty-nine dollars. Will that be cash or charge?'

'Mr Romano always pays cash. COD. Could you have the ticket delivered to his office on Thursday, please?'

'We could have it delivered tomorrow, if you like.'

'No. Mr Romano won't be there tomorrow. Would you make it Thursday at eleven A.M.?'

'Yes. That will be fine. And the address?'

'Mr Joseph Romano, Two-seventeen Poydras Street, Suite four-zero-eight.'

The woman made a note of it. 'Very well. I'll see that it's delivered Thursday morning.'

'Eleven sharp,' Tracy said. 'Thank you.'

Half a block down the street was Acme Luggage Store. Tracy studied the display in the window before she walked inside.

A clerk approached her. 'Good morning. And what can I do for you this morning?'

'I want to buy some luggage for my husband.'

'You've come to the right place. We're having a sale. We have some nice, inexpensive –'

'No,' Tracy said. 'Nothing inexpensive.'

She stepped over to a display of Vuitton suit-cases stacked against a wall. 'That's more what I'm looking for. We're going away on a trip.'

'Well, I'm sure he'll be pleased with one of these. We have three different sizes. Which one would –?'

'I'll take one of each.'

'Oh. Fine. Will that be charge or cash?'

'COD. The name is Joseph Romano. Could you have them delivered to my husband's office on Thursday morning?'

'Why, certainly, Mrs Romano.'

'At eleven o'clock?'

'I'll see to it personally.'

As an afterthought, Tracy added, 'Oh . . . would you put his initials on them – in gold? That's J. R.'

'Of course. It will be a pleasure, Mrs Romano.'

Tracy smiled and gave him the office address.

At a nearby Western Union office, Tracy sent a paid cable to the Rio Othon Place on Copacabana Beach in Rio de Janeiro. It read: REQUEST YOUR BEST SUITE COMMENCING THIS FRIDAY FOR TWO MONTHS. PLEASE CONFIRM BY COLLECT CABLE. JOSEPH ROMANO, 217 POYDRAS STREET, SUITE 408, NEW ORLEANS, LOUISIANA, USA.

Three days later Tracy telephoned the bank and asked to speak to Lester Torrance. When she heard his voice, she said softly, 'You probably don't remember me, Lester, but this is Lureen Hartford, Mr Romano's secretary, and –'

Not remember her! His voice was eager. 'Of *course* I remember you, Lureen. I –'

'You do? Why, I'm flattered. You must meet so many people.'

'Not like you,' Lester assured her. 'You haven't forgotten about our dinner date, have you?'

'You don't know how much I'm lookin' forward to it. Would next Tuesday suit you, Lester?'

'Great!'

'Then it's a date. Oh. I'm such an idiot! You got me so excited talkin' to you I almost forgot why I called. Mr Romano asked me to check on his bank balance. Would you give me that figure?'

'You bet. No trouble at all.'

Ordinarily, Lester Torrance would have asked for a birth date or some form of identification from the caller, but in this case it was certainly not necessary. No, sir. 'Hang on, Lureen,' he said.

He walked over to the file, pulled out Joseph Romano's sheet, and studied it in surprise. There had been an extraordinary number of deposits made to Romano's acount in the past several days. Romano had never kept so much money in his account before. Lester Torrance wondered what was going on. Some big deal, obviously. When he had dinner with Lureen Hartford, he intended to pump her. A little inside information never hurt. He returned to the phone.

'Your boss has been keeping us busy,' he told Tracy. 'He has just over three hundred thousand dollars in his current account.'

'Oh, good. That's the figure I have.'

'Would he like us to transfer it to an investment account? It's not drawing any interest sitting here, and I could –'

'No. He wants it right where it is,' Tracy assured him.

'Okay.'

'Thank you so much, Lester. You're a darlin'.'

'Wait a minute! Should I call you at the office about the arrangements for Tuesday?'

'I'll call you, honey,' Tracy told him.

And the connection was broken.

* * *

The modern high-rise office building owned by Anthony Orsatti stood on Poydras Street between the riverfront and the gigantic Louisiana Superdrome, and the offices of the Pacific Import-Export Company occupied the entire fourth floor of the building. At one end of the suite were Orsatti's offices, and at the other end, Joe Romano's rooms. The space in between was occupied by four young receptionists who were available evenings to entertain Anthony Orsatti's friends and business acquaintances. In front of Orsatti's suite sat two very large men whose lives were devoted to guarding their boss. They also served as chauffeurs, masseurs and errand boys for the capo.

On this Thursday morning Orsatti was in his office checking out the previous day's receipts from running numbers, book-making, prostitution, and a dozen other lucrative activities that the Pacific Import-Export Company controlled.

Anthony Orsatti was in his late sixties. He was a strangely built man with a large, heavy torso and short, bony legs that seemed to have been designed for a smaller man. Standing up he looked like a seated frog. He had a face criss-crossed with an erratic web of scars that could have been woven by a drunken spider, an over-sized mouth and black, bulbous eyes. He had been totally bald from the age of fifteen after an attack of alopecia, and had worn a black wig ever since. It fitted him badly, but in all the years no one had dared mention it to his face. Orsatti's cold eyes were gambler's eyes, giving away nothing, and his face, except when he was with his five daughters, whom he adored, was expressionless. The only clue to Orsatti's emotions was his voice. He had a hoarse, raspy voice, the result of a wire having been tightened around his throat on his twenty-first birthday, when he had been left for dead. The two men who had made that mistake had turned up in the morgue the following week. When Orsatti got really upset, his voice lowered to a strangled whisper that could barely be heard.

Anthony Orsatti was a king who ran his fiefdom with bribes, guns and blackmail. He ruled New Orleans, and it paid him obeisance in the form of untold riches. The capos of the other Families across the country respected him and constantly sought his advice.

At the moment, Anthony Orsatti was in a benevolent mood. He had had breakfast with his mistress, whom he kept in an block of flats he owned in Lake Vista. He visited her three times a week, and this morning's visit had been particularly satisfactory. She did things to him in bed that other women never dreamed of, and Orsatti sincerely believed it was because she loved him so much. His organization was running smoothly. There were no problems, because Anthony Orsatti knew how to solve difficulties before they became problems. He had once explained his philosophy to Joe Romano: 'Never let a little problem become a big problem, Joe, or it grows like a fuckin' snowball. You got a precinct captain who thinks he oughta get a bigger cut – you *melt* him, see? No more snowball. You get some hot-shot from Chicago who asks permission to open up his own little operation here in New Orleans? You know that pretty soon that "little" operation is gonna turn into a *big* operation and start cuttin' into your profits. So you say yes, and then when he gets here, you *melt* the son of a bitch. No more snowball. Get the picture?'

Joe Romano got the picture.

Anthony Orsatti loved Romano. He was like a son to him. Orsatti had picked him up when Romano was a punk kid rolling drunks in alleys. He himself had trained Romano, and now the kid could tap-dance his way around with the best of them. He was fast, he was smart and he was honest. In ten years Romano had risen to the rank of Anthony Orsatti's chief lieutenant. He supervised all the Family's operations and reported only to Orsatti.

Lucy, Orsatti's private secretary, knocked and came into the office. She was twenty-four years old, a college graduate, with a face and figure that had won several local beauty contests. Orsatti enjoyed having beautiful young women around him.

He looked at the clock on his desk. It was

10:45. He had told Lucy he did not want any interruptions before noon. He scowled at her. 'What?'

'I'm sorry to bother you, Mr Orsatti. There's a Miss Gigi Dupres on the phone. She sounds hysterical, but she won't tell me what she wants. She insists on speaking with you personally. I thought it might be important.'

Orsatti sat there, running the name through the computer in his brain. *Gigi Dupres?* One of the broads he had up in his suite his last time in Vegas? *Gigi Dupres?* Not that he could remember, and he prided himself on a mind that forgot nothing. Out of curiosity, Orsatti picked up the phone and waved a dismissal at Lucy.

'Yeah? Who's this?'

'Is thees Mr Anthony Orsatti?' She had a French accent.

'So?'

'Oh, thank God I got hold of you, Meester Orsatti!'

Lucy was right. The dame was hysterical. Anthony Orsatti was not interested. He started to hang up, when her voice went on.

'You must stop him, please!'

'Lady, I don't know who you're talkin' about, and I'm busy –'

'My Joe. Joe Romano. He promised to take me with him, *comprenez vous?*'

'Hey, you got a beef with Joe, take it up with him. I ain't his nursemaid.'

'He lie to me! I just found out he is leave for Brazil without me. Half of that three hundred thousand dollars is mine.'

Anthony Orsatti suddenly found he was interested, after all. 'What three hundred thousand you talkin' about?'

'The money Joe is hiding in his current account. The money – how you say? – *skimmed*.'

Anthony Orsatti was *very* interested.

'Please tell Joe he must take me to Brazil with him. Please! Weel you do thees?'

'Yeah,' Anthony Orsatti promised. 'I'll take care of it.'

Joe Romano's office was modern, all white and chrome, done by one of New Orleans's most fashionable decorators. The only touches of colour were the three expensive French Impressionist paintings on the walls. Romano prided himself on his good taste. He had fought his way up from the slums of New Orleans, and on the way he had educated himself. He had an eye for paintings and an ear for music. When he dined out, he had long, knowledgeable discussions with the sommelier about wines. Yes, Joe Romano had every reason to be proud. While his contemporaries had survived by using their fists, he had succeeded by using his brains. If it was true that Anthony Orsatti owned New Orleans, it was also true that it was Joe Romano who ran it for him.

His secretary walked into his office. 'Mr Romano,

there's a messenger here with an airplane ticket for Rio de Janeiro. Shall I write out a cheque? It's COD.'

'*Rio de Janeiro?*' Romano shook his head. 'Tell him there's some mistake.'

The uniformed messenger was in the doorway. 'I was told to deliver this to Joseph Romano at this address.'

'Well, you were told wrong. What is this, some kind of a new airline promotion gimmick?'

'No, sir. I –'

'Let me see that.' Romano took the ticket from the messenger's hand and looked at it. 'Friday. Why would I be going to Rio on Friday?'

'That's a good question,' Anthony Orsatti said. He was standing behind the messenger. 'Why would you, Joe?'

'It's some kind of dumb mistake, Tony.' Romano handed the ticket back to the messenger. 'Take this back where it came from and –'

'Not so fast.' Anthony Orsatti took the ticket and examined it. 'It says here one first-class ticket, aisle seat, smoking, to Rio de Janeiro for Friday. One way.'

Joe Romano laughed. 'Someone made a mistake.' He turned to his secretary. 'Madge, call the travel agency and tell them they goofed. Some poor slob is going to be missing his plane ticket.'

Joleen, the assistant secretary, walked in. 'Excuse me, Mr Romano. The luggage has arrived. Do you want me to sign for it?'

Joe Romano stared at her. 'What luggage? I didn't order any luggage.'

'Have them bring it in,' Anthony Orsatti commanded.

'Jesus!' Joe Romano said. 'Has everyone gone nuts?'

A messenger walked in carrying three Vuitton suitcases.

'What's all this? I never ordered those.'

The messenger checked his delivery slip. 'It says Mr Joseph Romano, Two-seventeen Poydras Street, Suite four-zero-eight?'

Joe Romano was losing his temper. 'I don't care what the fuck it says. I didn't order them. Now get them out of here.'

Orsatti was examining the luggage. 'They have your initials on them, Joe.'

'What? Oh. Wait a minute! It's probably some kind of present.'

'Is it your birthday?'

'No. But you know how broads are, Tony. They're always givin' you gifts.'

'Have you got somethin' going in Brazil?' Anthony Orsatti enquired.

'*Brazil?*' Joe Romano laughed. 'This must be someone's idea of a joke, Tony.'

Orsatti smiled gently, then turned to the secretaries and the two messengers. 'Out.'

When the door was closed behind them, Anthony Orsatti spoke. 'How much money you got in your bank account, Joe?'

Joe Romano looked at him, puzzled. 'I don't know. Fifteen hundred, I guess, maybe a couple of grand. Why?'

'Just for fun, why don't you call your bank and check it out?'

'What for? I –'

'Check it out, Joe.'

'Sure. If it'll make you happy.' He buzzed his secretary. 'Get me the head bookkeeper over at First Merchants.'

A minute later she was on the line.

'Hello, honey. Joseph Romano. Would you give me the current balance in my current account? My birth date is October fourteenth.'

Anthony Orsatti picked up the extension phone. A few moments later the bookkeeper was back on the line.

'Sorry to keep you waiting, Mr Romano. As of this morning, your current account balance is three hundred and ten thousand, nine hundred and five dollars and thirty-two cents.'

Romano could feel the blood draining from his face. 'It's *what*?'

'Three hundred and ten thousand, nine hundred and five –'

'You stupid bitch!' he yelled. 'I don't have that kind of money in my account. You made a mistake. Let me talk to the –'

He felt the telephone being taken out of his hand, as Anthony Orsatti replaced the receiver. 'Where'd that money come from, Joe?'

Joe Romano's face was pale. 'I swear to God, Tony, I don't know anything about that money.'

'No?'

'Hey, you've got to believe me! You know what's happening? Someone is setting me up.'

'It must be someone who likes you a lot. He gave you a going-away present of three hundred and ten thousand dollars.' Orsatti sat down heavily on the Scalamander silk-covered armchair and looked at Joe Romano for a long moment, then spoke very quietly. 'Everything was all set, huh? A one-way ticket to Rio, new luggage . . . Like you was planning a whole new life.'

'No!' There was panic in Joe Romano's voice. 'Jesus, you know me better than that, Tony. I've always been on the level with you. You're like a father to me.'

He was sweating now. There was a knock at the door, and Madge poked her head in. She held an envelope.

'I'm sorry to interrupt, Mr Romano. There's a cable for you, but you have to sign for it yourself.'

With the instincts of a trapped animal, Joe Romano said, 'Not now. I'm busy.'

'I'll take it,' Anthony Orsatti said, and he was out of the chair before the woman could close the door. He took his time reading the cable, then he focused his eyes on Joe Romano.

In a voice so low that Romano could barely hear him, Anthony Orsatti said, 'I'll read it out to you, Joe. "Pleased to confirm your reservation for our Princess Suite for two months this Friday, first September." It's signed, "S. Montalband, manager, Rio Othon Palace, Copacabana Beach, Rio de Janeiro." It's your reservation, Joe. You won't be needin' it, will you?'

THIRTEEN

Andre Gillian was in the kitchen making preparations for *spaghetti alla carbonara*, a large Italian salad, and a pear torte when he heard a loud, ominous popping sound, and a moment later the comfortable hum of the central air conditioner trailed off into silence.

Andre stamped his foot and said, '*Merde!* Not the night of the *game*.'

He hurried to the utility cupboard where the breaker box was located and flicked the electrical switches, one by one. Nothing happened.

Oh, Mr Pope was going to be furious. Simply *furious*! Andre knew how much his employer looked forward to his weekly Friday-night poker game. It was a tradition that had been going on for years, and it was always with the same elite group of players. Without air-conditioning, the house would be unbearable. *Simply unbearable!* New Orleans in September was only for the uncivilized. Even after the sun went down, there was no relief from the heat and humidity.

Andre returned to the kitchen and consulted the kitchen clock. Four o'clock. The guests would be arriving at 8:00. Andre thought about telephoning Mr Pope and telling him the problem, but then he remembered that the lawyer had said he was going to be tied up in court all day. *The dear man was so busy. He needed his relaxation. And now this!*

Andre took a small black telephone book from a kitchen drawer, looked up a number and dialled.

After three rings, a metallic voice intoned, 'You have reached the Eskimo Air-Conditioning Service. Our technicians are not available at this time. If you will leave your name and number and a brief message, we will get back to you as soon as possible. Please wait for the beep.'

Foutre! Only in America were you forced to hold a conversation with a machine.

A shrill, annoying beep sounded in Andre's ear. He spoke into the mouthpiece: 'This is the residence of Monsieur Perry Pope, Forty-two Charles Street. Our air-conditioning has ceased to function. You must send someone here as quickly as possible. *Vite!*'

He slammed down the receiver. *Of course no one was available. Air-conditioning was probably going off all over this dreadful city. It was impossible for air conditioners to cope with the damnable heat and humidity. Well, someone had*

190

better come soon. Mr Pope had a temper. A nasty temper.

In the three years Andre Gillian had worked as a cook for the attorney, he had learned how influential his employer was. *It was amazing. All that brilliance in one so young.* Perry Pope knew simply everybody. When he snapped his fingers, people jumped.

It seemed to Andre Gillian that the house was already feeling warmer. *Ça va chier dur. If something is not done quickly, the shit's going to hit the fan.*

As Andre went back to cutting paper-thin slices of salami and provolone cheese for the salad, he could not shake the terrible feeling that the evening was fated to be a disaster.

When the doorbell rang thirty minutes later, Andre's clothes were soaked with perspiration, and the kitchen was like an oven. Gillian hurried to open the back door.

Two workmen in overalls stood in the doorway, carrying tool-boxes. One of them was a tall black man. His companion was white, several inches shorter, with a sleepy, bored look on his face. In the rear driveway stood their service truck.

'Gotta problem with your air-conditioning?' the black man asked.

'*Oui!* Thank heaven you're here. You've just got to get it working right away. There'll be guests arriving soon.'

The black man walked over to the oven, sniffed the baking torte and said, 'Smells good.'

191

'Please!' Gillian urged. '*Do* something!'

'Let's take a look in the furnace room,' the short man said. 'Where is it?'

'This way.'

Andre hurried them down a corridor to a utility room, where the air-conditioning unit stood.

'This is a good unit, Ralph,' the black man said to his companion.

'Yeah, Al. They don't make 'em like this any more.'

'Then for heaven's sake why isn't it *working*?' Gillian demanded.

They both turned to stare at him.

'We just got here,' Ralph said reprovingly. He knelt down and opened a small door at the bottom of the unit, took out a flashlight, got down on his stomach and peered inside. After a moment, he rose to his feet. 'The problem's not here.'

'Where is it, then?' Andre asked.

'Must be a short in one of the outlets. Probably shorted out the whole system. How many air-conditioning vents do you have?'

'Each room has one. Let's see. That must be at least nine.'

'That's probably the problem. Transduction overload. Let's go take a look.'

The three of them trooped back down the hall. As they passed the living room, Al said, 'This is sure a beautiful place Mr Pope has got here.'

The living room was exquisitely furnished, filled with signed antiques worth a fortune. The floors were covered with muted-coloured Persian rugs. To the left of the living room was a large, formal dining room, and to the right a den, with a large, green baize-covered gaming table in the centre. In one corner of the room was a round table, already set up for supper. The two servicemen walked into the den, and Al shone his flashlight into the air-conditioning vent high on the wall.

'Hmm,' he muttered. He looked up at the ceiling over the card table. 'What's above this room?'

'The attic.'

'Let's take a look.'

The workmen followed Andre up to the attic, a long, low-ceilinged room, dusty and spattered with cobwebs.

Al walked over to an electrical box set in the wall. He inspected the tangle of wires. 'Ha!'

'Did you find something?' Andre asked anxiously.

'Condenser problem. It's the humidity. We musta had a hundred calls this week. It's shorted out. We'll have to replace the condenser.'

'Oh, my God! Will it take long?'

'Naw. We got a new condenser out in the truck.'

'Please hurry,' Andre begged them. 'Mr Pope is going to be home soon.'

'You leave everything to us,' Al said.

Back in the kitchen, Andre confided, 'I must finish preparing my salad dressing. Can you find your way back up to the attic?'

Al raised a hand. 'No sweat, pal. You just go on about your business, and we'll go on about ours.'

'Oh, thank you. *Thank* you.'

Andre watched the men go out to the truck and return with two large canvas bags. 'If you need anything,' he told them, 'just call me.'

'You betcha!'

The workmen went up the stairs, and Andre returned to his kitchen.

When Ralph and Al reached the attic, they opened their canvas bags and removed a small folding camp chair, a drill with a steel bit, a tray of sandwiches, two cans of beer, a pair of 12 by 40 Zeiss binoculars for viewing distant objects in a dim light, and two live hamsters that had been injected with three quarters of a milligramme of acetyl promazine.

The two men went to work.

'Ol Ernestine is gonna be proud of me,' Al chortled as they started.

In the beginning, Al had stubbornly resisted the idea.

'You must be outta your mind, woman. I ain't gonna fuck around with no Perry Pope. That dude'll come down on my ass so hard I'll never see daylight again.'

'You don't gotta worry about him. He won't never be botherin' *no one* again.'

They were naked on the water bed in Ernestine's apartment.

'What you gettin' out of this deal, anyway, honey?' Al demanded.

194

'He's a prick.'

'Hey baby, the world's full of pricks, but you don't spend your life goin' round cuttin' off their balls.'

'All right. I'm doin' it for a friend.'

'Tracy?'

'That's right.'

Al liked Tracy. They had all had dinner together the day she got out of prison.

'She's a classy dame,' Al admitted. 'But why we stickin' our necks out for her?'

'Because if we don't he'p her, she's gonna have to settle for someone who ain't half as good as you, and if she gets caught, they'll cart her ass right back to the joint.'

Al sat up in bed and looked at Ernestine curiously. 'Does it mean that much to you, baby?'

'Yeah, hon.'

She would never be able to make him understand it, but the truth was simply that Ernestine could not stand the thought of Tracy back in prison at the mercy of Big Bertha. It was not only Tracy whom Ernestine was concerned about: it was herself. She had made herself Tracy's protector, and if Big Bertha got her hands on her, it would be a defeat to Ernestine.

So all she said now was, 'Yeah. It means a lot to me, honey. You gonna do it?'

'I damn sure can't do it alone,' Al grumbled.

And Ernestine knew she had won. She started nibbling her way down his long, lean body. And she murmured, 'Wasn't ol Ralph due to be released a few days ago . . . ?'

It was 6:30 before the two men returned to Andre's kitchen, grimy with sweat and dust.

'Is it fixed?' Andre asked anxiously.

'It was a real bitch,' Al informed him. 'You see, what you got here is a condenser with an AC/DC cutoff that –'

'Never mind that,' Andre interrupted impatiently. 'Did you *fix* it?'

'Yeah. It's all set. In five minutes we'll have it goin' again as good as new.'

'*Formidable!* If you'll just leave your bill on the kitchen table –'

Ralph shook his head. 'Don't worry about it. The company'll bill you.'

'Bless you both. *Au 'voir.*'

Andre watched the two men leave by the back door, carrying their canvas bags. Out of his sight, they walked around to the yard and opened the casing that housed the outside condenser of the air-conditioning unit. Ralph held the flashlight while Al reconnected the wires he had loosened a couple of hours earlier. The air-conditioning unit immediately sprang into life.

Al copied down the telephone number on the service tag attached to the condenser. When he telephoned the number a short time later and reached the recorded voice of the Eskimo Air-Conditioning Company, Al said, 'This is Perry Pope's residence at Forty-two Charles Street. Our air-conditioning is workin' fine now. Don't bother to send anyone. Have a nice day.'

The weekly Friday-night poker game at Perry Pope's house was an event to which all the players looked forward. It was always the same carefully selected group: Anthony Orsatti, Joe Romano, Judge Henry Lawrence, an alderman, a state senator, and of course their host. The stakes were high, the food was great, and the company was raw power.

Perry Pope was in his bedroom changing into white silk slacks and matching sports shirt. He hummed happily, thinking of the evening ahead. He had been on a winning streak lately. *In fact, my whole life is just one big winning streak*, he thought.

If anyone needed a legal favour in New Orleans, Perry Pope was the attorney to see. His power came from his connections with the Orsatti Family. He was known as The Arranger, and could fix anything from a traffic ticket to a drug-dealing charge to a murder rap. Life was good.

When Anthony Orsatti arrived, he brought a guest with him. 'Joe Romano won't be playin' any more,' Orsatti announced. 'You all know Inspector Newhouse.'

The men shook hands all round.

'Drinks are on the sideboard, gentlemen,' Perry Pope said. 'We'll have supper later. Why don't we start a little action going?'

The men took their accustomed chairs around the green felt table in the den. Orsatti pointed to Joe Romano's vacant chair and said to Inspector Newhouse, 'That'll be your seat from now on, Mel.'

While one of the men opened fresh packs of cards, Pope began distributing poker chips. He explained to Inspector Newhouse, 'The black chips are five dollars, red chips ten dollars, blue chips fifty dollars, white chips a hundred. Each man starts out buying five hundred dollars' worth of chips. We play table stakes, three raises, dealer's choice.'

'Sounds good to me,' the inspector said.

Anthony Orsatti was in a bad mood. 'Come on. Let's get started.' His voice was a strangled whisper. Not a good sign.

Perry Pope would have given a great deal to learn what had happened to Joe Romano, but the lawyer knew better than to bring up the subject. Orsatti would discuss it with him when he was ready.

Orsatti's thoughts were black: *I been like a father to Joe Romano. I trusted him, made him my chief lieutenant. And the son of a bitch stabbed me in the back. If that dizzy French dame hadn't telephoned, he might have got away with it, too. Well, he won't ever get away with nothin' again. Not where he is. If he's so clever, let him fuck around with the fish down there.*

'Tony, are you in or out?'

Anthony Orsatti turned his attention back to the game. Huge sums of money had been won and lost at this table. It always upset Anthony Orsatti to lose, and it had nothing to do with money. He could not bear to be on the losing end of anything. He thought of himself as a natural-born winner. Only winners rose to his position in life. For the last six weeks, Perry Pope had been on some kind of crazy winning streak, and tonight Anthony Orsatti was determined to break it.

Since they played dealer's choice, each dealer chose the game in which he felt the strongest. Hands were dealt for five-card stud, seven-card stud, low ball, draw poker – but tonight, no matter which game was chosen, Anthony Orsatti kept finding himself on the losing end. He began to increase his bets, playing recklessly, trying to recoup his losses. By midnight when they stopped to have the meal Andre had prepared, Orsatti was out $50,000, with Perry Pope the big winner.

The food was delicious. Usually Orsatti enjoyed the free midnight snack, but this evening he was impatient to get back to the table.

'You're not eating, Tony,' Perry Pope said.

'I'm not hungry.' Orsatti reached for the silver coffee urn at his side, poured coffee into a Victoria-patterned Herend-china cup, and sat down at the poker table. He watched the others eat and wished they would hurry. He was impatient to win his money back. As he started to stir his coffee, a small particle fell into his cup. Distastefully, Orsatti removed the particle with a spoon and examined it. It appeared to be a piece of plaster. He looked up at the ceiling, and something hit him on the forehead. He suddenly became aware of a scurrying noise overhead.

'What the hell's goin' on upstairs?' Anthony Orsatti asked.

Perry Pope was in the middle of telling an anecdote to Inspector Newhouse. 'I'm sorry, what did you say, Tony?'

The scurrying noise was more noticeable now. Bits of plaster began to trickle onto the green felt.

'It sounds to me like you have mice,' the senator said.

'Not in *this* house.' Perry Pope was indignant.

'Well, you sure as hell got somethin',' Orsatti growled.

A larger piece of plaster fell on the green felt table.

'I'll have Andre take care of it,' Pope said. 'If we're finished eating, why don't we get back to the game?'

Anthony Orsatti was staring up at a small hole in the ceiling directly above his head. 'Hold it. Let's go take a look up there.'

'What for, Tony? Andre can –'

Orsatti had already risen and started for the stairway. The others looked at one another, then hurried after him.

'A squirrel probably got into the attic,' Perry Pope guessed. 'This time of year they're all over the place. Probably hiding his nuts for the winter.' He laughed at his little joke.

When they reached the door to the attic, Orsatti pushed it open, and Perry Pope turned on the light. They caught a glimpse of two white hamsters frantically racing around the room.

'Jesus!' Perry Pope said. 'I've got rats!'

Anthony Orsatti was not listening. He was staring at the room. In the middle of the attic was a camp chair with a packet of sandwiches on top of it and two open cans of beer. On the floor next to the chair was a pair of binoculars.

Orsatti walked over to them, picked up the objects one by one, and examined them. Then he got down on his knees on the dusty floor and moved the tiny wooden cylinder that concealed a peephole that had been drilled into the ceiling. Orsatti put his eye to the peephole. Directly beneath him the card table was clearly visible.

Perry Pope was standing in the middle of the attic, dumb-founded. 'Who the hell put all this junk up here? I'm going to raise hell with Andre about this.'

Orsatti rose slowly to his feet and brushed the dust from his trousers.

Perry Pope glanced down at the floor. 'Look!' he exclaimed. 'They left a goddamned hole in the ceiling. Workmen today aren't worth a shit.'

He crouched down and took a look through the hole, and his face suddenly lost its colour. He stood up and looked around wildly, to find all the men staring at him.

'Hey!' Perry Pope said. 'You don't think I –?

Come on, fellas, this is *me*. I don't know anything about this. I wouldn't cheat you. My God, we're *friends*!' His hand flew to his mouth, and he began biting furiously at his cuticles.

Orsatti patted him on the arm. 'Don't worry about it.' His voice was almost inaudible.

Perry Pope kept gnawing desperately at the raw flesh of his right thumb.

FOURTEEN

'That's two down, Tracy,' Ernestine Littlechap chortled. 'The word on the street is that your lawyer friend Perry Pope ain't practisin' law no more. He had a real bad accident.'

They were having *café au lait* and *beignets* at a small pavement café off Royal Street.

Ernestine gave a high giggle. 'You got a brain, girl. You wouldn't like to go into business with me, would you?'

'Thanks, Ernestine. I have other plans.'

Ernestine asked eagerly, 'Who's next?'

'Lawrence. Judge Henry Lawrence.'

Henry Lawrence had begun his career as a small-town lawyer in Leesville, Louisiana. He had very little aptitude for the law, but he had two very important attributes: he was impressive looking, and he was morally flexible. His philosophy was that the law was a frail rod, meant to be bent to suit the needs of his clients. With that in mind, it was not surprising that shortly after he moved to New Orleans, Henry Lawrence's law practice began to flourish with a special group of clients. He went from handling misdemeanours and traffic accidents to handling felonies and capital crimes, and by the time he reached the big leagues, he was an expert at suborning juries, discrediting witnesses, and bribing anyone who could help his case. In short, he was Anthony Orsatti's kind of man, and it was inevitable that the paths of the two should cross. It was a marriage made in Mafia heaven. Lawrence became the mouthpiece for the Orsatti Family, and when the timing was right, Orsatti had him elevated to a judgeship.

'I don't know how you kin nail the judge,' Ernestine said. 'He's rich an' powerful an' untouchable.'

'He's rich and powerful,' Tracy corrected her, 'but he's not untouchable.'

Tracy had worked out her plan, but when she telephoned Judge Lawrence's chambers, she knew, immediately, that she would have to change it.

'I'd like to speak to Judge Lawrence, please.'

A secretary said, 'I'm sorry, Judge Lawrence is not in.'

'When do you expect him?' Tracy asked.

'I really couldn't say.'

'It's very important. Will he be in tomorrow morning?'

'No. Judge Lawrence is out of town.'

'Oh. Perhaps I can reach him somewhere?'

'I'm afraid that would be impossible. His Honour is out of the country.'

Tracy carefully kept the disappointment from her voice. 'I see. May I ask where?'

'His Honour is in Europe, attending an international judiciary symposium.'

'What a shame,' Tracy said.

'Who's calling, please?'

Tracy's mind was racing. 'This is Elizabeth Rowane Dastin, chairwoman of the southern division of the American Trial Lawyers' Association. We're having our annual awards dinner in New Orleans on the twentieth of this month, and we've chosen Judge Henry Lawrence to be our man of the year.'

'That's lovely,' the judge's secretary said, 'but I'm afraid His Honour won't be back by then.'

'What a pity. We were all so looking forward to hearing one of his famous speeches. Judge Lawrence was the unanimous choice of our selection committee.'

'He'll be disappointed to miss it.'

'Yes. I'm sure you know what a great honour this is. Some of our country's most prominent judges have been chosen in the past. Wait a minute! I have an idea. Do you suppose the judge might tape a brief acceptance speech for us – a few words of thanks, perhaps?'

'Well, I – I really can't say. He has a very busy schedule –'

'There'll be a great deal of national television and newspaper coverage.'

There was a silence. Judge Lawrence's secretary knew how much His Honour enjoyed media coverage. In fact, as far as she could see, the tour he was presently on seemed to be mainly for that purpose.

She said, 'Perhaps he might find time to record a few words for you. I could ask him.'

'Oh, that would be wonderful,' Tracy enthused. 'It would really make the whole evening.'

'Would you like His Honour to address his remarks towards anything specific?'

'Oh, definitely. We'd like him to talk about –' She hesitated. 'I'm afraid it's a bit complicated. It would be better if I could explain to him directly.'

There was a momentary silence. The secretary faced a dilemma. She had orders not to reveal her boss's itinerary. On the other hand, it would be just like him to blame her if he missed receiving an award as important as this.

She said, 'I'm really not supposed to give out any information, but I'm sure he would want me to make an exception for something as prestigious as this. You can reach him in Moscow, at the Rossia Hotel. He'll be there for the next five days, and after that –'

'Wonderful. I'll get in touch with him right away. Thank you so much.'

'Thank *you*, Miss Dastin.'

The cables were addressed to Judge Henry Lawrence, Rossia Hotel, Moscow. The first cable read:

NEXT JUDICIARY COUNCIL MEETING CAN
NOW BE ARRANGED. CONFIRM CONVEN-
IENT DATE AS SPACE MUST BE REQUESTED.
                                    BORIS

The second cable, which arrived the next day, read:

ADVISE PROBLEM TRAVEL PLANS. YOUR
SISTER'S PLANE ARRIVED LATE BUT LANDED
SAFELY. LOST PASSPORT AND MONEY. SHE
WILL BE PLACED IN FIRST-CLASS SWISS
HOTEL. WILL SETTLE ACCOUNT LATER.
                                    BORIS

The last cable read:

YOUR SISTER WILL TRY AMERICAN EMBASSY
TO OBTAIN TEMPORARY PASSPORT. NO
INFORMATION AVAILABLE YET ON NEW
VISA. SWISS MAKE RUSSIANS SEEM SAINTS.
WILL SHIP SISTER TO YOU SOONEST.
                                    BORIS

The NKVD sat back and waited to see if there
were any further cables. When no more were forthcoming, they arrested Judge Lawrence.

The interrogation lasted for ten days and
nights.

'To whom did you send the information?'

'*What* information? I don't know what you're
talking about.'

'We're talking about plans. Who gave you the plans?'

'What plans?'

'The plans for the Soviet atomic submarine.'

'You must be crazy. What do I know about Soviet submarines?'

'That's what we intend to find out. Who were your secret meetings with?'

'*What* secret meetings? I have no secrets.'

'Good. Then you can tell us who Boris is.'

'Boris, who?'

'The man who deposited money in your Swiss account.'

'*What* Swiss account?'

They were furious. 'You're a stubborn fool,' they told him. 'We're going to make an example of you and all the other American spies trying to undermine our great motherland.'

By the time the American ambassador was permitted to visit him, Judge Henry Lawrence had lost fifteen pounds. He could not remember the last time his captors had allowed him to sleep, and he was a trembling wreck of a man.

'Why are they doing this to me?' the judge croaked. 'I'm an American citizen. I'm a judge. For God's sake, get me out of here!'

'I'm doing everything I can,' the ambassador assured him. He was shocked by Lawrence's appearance. The ambassador had greeted Judge Lawrence and the other members of the Judiciary Committee when they had arrived two weeks earlier. The man the ambassador met then bore no resemblance to the cringing, terrified creature who grovelled before him now.

What the hell are the Russians up to this time? the ambassador wondered. *The judge is no more a spy than I am.* Then he thought wryly, *I suppose I could have chosen a better example.*

The ambassador demanded to see the president of the Politburo, and when the request was refused, he settled for one of the ministers.

'I must make a formal protest,' the ambassador angrily declared. 'Your country's behaviour in the treatment of Judge Henry Lawrence is inexcusable. To call a man of his stature a spy is ridiculous.'

'If you're quite finished,' the minister said coldly, 'you will please take a look at these.'

He handed copies of the cables to the ambassador.

The ambassador read them and looked up, bewildered. 'What's wrong with them? They're perfectly innocent.'

'Really? Perhaps you had better read them again. Decoded.' He handed the ambassador another copy of the cables. Every fourth word had been underlined.

NEXT JUDICIARY COUNCIL <u>MEETING</u> CAN NOW BE <u>ARRANGED</u>. CONFIRM CONVENIENT DATE <u>AS</u> SPACE MUST BE <u>REQUESTED</u>.
                                              BORIS

ADVISE PROBLEM TRAVEL <u>PLANS</u>. YOUR SISTER'S PLANE <u>ARRIVED</u> LATE BUT LANDED <u>SAFELY</u>. LOST PASSPORT AND <u>MONEY</u>. SHE WILL BE <u>PLACED</u> IN FIRST-CLASS <u>SWISS</u> HOTEL. WILL SETTLE <u>ACCOUNT</u> LATER.

BORIS

YOUR SISTER WILL <u>TRY</u> AMERICAN EMBASSY TO <u>OBTAIN</u> TEMPORARY PASS-PORT. NO <u>INFORMATION</u> AVAILABLE YET ON <u>NEW</u> VISA. SWISS MAKE <u>RUSSIANS</u> SEEM SAINTS. WILL <u>SHIP</u> SISTER TO YOU <u>SOONEST</u>.

BORIS

I'll be a son of a bitch, the ambassador thought.

The press and public were barred from the trial. The prisoner remained stubborn to the last, continuing to deny he was in the Soviet Union on a spying mission. The prosecution promised him leniency if he would divulge who his bosses were, and Judge Lawrence would have given his soul to have been able to do so, but alas, he could not.

The day after the trial there was a brief mention in *Pravda* that the notorious American spy Judge Henry Lawrence had been convicted of espionage and sentenced to Siberia for fourteen years of hard labour.

The American intelligence community was

baffled by the Lawrence case. Rumours buzzed among the CIA, the FBI, the Secret Service and the Treasury Department.

'He's not one of ours,' the CIA said. 'He probably belongs to Treasury.'

The Treasury Department disclaimed any knowledge of the case. 'No, sir. Lawrence isn't our baby. Probably the fucking FBI butting into our territory again.'

'Never heard of him,' the FBI said. 'He was probably run by State, or the Defence Intelligence Agency.'

The Defence Intelligence Agency, as much in the dark as the others, cannily said, 'No comment.'

Each agency was sure that Judge Henry Lawrence had been sent abroad by one of the others.

'Well, you've got to admire his guts,' the head of the CIA said. 'He's tough. He hasn't confessed and he hasn't named names. To tell you the truth, I wish we had a lot more like him.'

Things were not going well for Anthony Orsatti, and the capo was unable to figure out why. For the first time in his life, his luck was going bad. It had started with Joe Romano's defection, then Perry Pope, and now the judge was gone, mixed up in some crazy spy deal. They had all been an intrinsic part of Orsatti's machine – people he had relied on.

Joe Romano had been the linchpin in the Family organization, and Orsatti had not found anyone to take his place. The business was being run sloppily, and complaints were coming in from people who had never dared complain before. The word was out that Tony Orsatti was getting old, that he couldn't keep his men in line, that his organization was coming apart.

The final straw was a telephone call from New Jersey.

'We hear you're in a little trouble back there. Tony. We'd like to help you out.'

'I ain't in no trouble,' Orsatti bristled. 'Sure, I've had a couple of problems lately, but they're all straightened out.'

'That's not what we hear, Tony. The word's out that your town's goin' a little wild; there's no one controlling it.'

'*I'm* controlling it.'

'Maybe it's too much for you. Could be you're working too hard. Maybe you need a little rest.'

'This is *my* town. No one's takin' it away from me.'

'Hey, Tony, who said anything about taking it away from you? We just want to help. The Families back east got together and decided to send a few of our people down there to give you a little hand. There's nothing wrong with that between old friends, is there?'

Anthony Orsatti felt a deep chill go through him. There was only one thing wrong with it: the little hand was going to become a big hand, and it was going to snowball.

Ernestine had prepared shrimp gumbo for dinner, and it was simmering on the stove while she and Tracy waited for Al to arrive. The September heat wave had burned itself deeply into everyone's nerves, and when Al finally walked into the small flat, Ernestine screamed, 'Where the hell you been? The fuckin' dinner's burnin', and so am I.'

But Al's spirits were too euphoric to be affected. 'I been busy diggin' the scam, woman. An' wait'll you hear what I got.' He turned to Tracy. 'The mob's puttin' the arm on Tony Orsatti. The Family from New Jersey's comin' in to take over.' His face split into a broad grin. 'You *got* the son of a bitch!' He looked into Tracy's eyes, and his smile died. 'Ain't you happy, Tracy?'

What a strange word, Tracy thought. *Happy*. She had forgotten what it meant. She wondered whether she would ever be happy again, whether she would ever feel any normal emotions again. For so long now, her every waking thought had been to avenge what had been done to her mother and herself. And now that it was almost finished, there was only an emptiness inside her.

The following morning Tracy stopped at a florist. 'I want some flowers delivered to Anthony Orsatti. A funeral wreath of white carnations on a stand, with a wide ribbon. I want the ribbon to read: "REST IN PEACE".' She wrote out a card. It said, FROM DORIS WHITNEY'S DAUGHTER.

213

BOOK THREE

FIFTEEN

It was time to deal with Charles Stanhope III. The others had been strangers. Charles had been her lover, the father of her unborn child, and he had turned his back on both of them.

Ernestine and Al had been at the New Orleans Airport to see Tracy off.

'I'm gonna miss you,' Ernestine had said. 'You sure set this town on its ass. They oughta run you for people's mayor.'

'Whatcha gonna do in Philly?' Al had asked.

She had told them half the truth. 'Go back to my old job at the bank.'

Ernestine and Al had exchanged a glance. 'They – er – know you're comin'?'

'No. But the vice-president likes me. There won't

be a problem. Good computer operators are hard to find.'

'Well, good luck. Keep in touch, ya hear? And stay out of trouble, girl.'

Thirty minutes later Tracy had been in the air, bound for Philadelphia.

She checked into the Hilton Hotel and steamed out her one good dress over the hot tub. At 11:00 the following morning she walked into the bank and approached Clarence Desmond's secretary.

'Hello, Mae.'

The girl stared at Tracy as though she were seeing a ghost. 'Tracy!' She did not know where to look. 'I – how are you?'

'Fine. Is Mr Desmond in?'

'I – I don't know. Let me see. Excuse me.' She rose from her chair, flustered, and hurried into the vice-president's office.

She came out a few moments later. 'You may go in.' She edged away as Tracy walked towards the door.

What's the matter with her? Tracy wondered.

Clarence Desmond was standing next to his desk.

'Hello, Mr Desmond. Well, I've come back,' Tracy said brightly.

'What for?' His tone was unfriendly. Definitely unfriendly.

It caught Tracy by surprise. She pressed on. 'Well, you said I was the best computer operator you had ever seen, and I thought –'

218

'You thought I'd give you back your old job?'

'Well, yes, sir. I haven't forgotten any of my skills. I can still –'

'Miss Whitney.' It was no longer Tracy. 'I'm sorry, but what you're asking is quite out of the question. I'm sure you can understand that our customers would not wish to deal with someone who served time in the penitentiary for armed robbery and attempted murder. That would hardly fit in with our high ethical image. I think it unlikely that given your background, *any* bank would hire you. I would suggest that you try to find employment more suitable to your circumstances. I hope you understand there is nothing personal in this.'

Tracy listened to his words, first with shock and then with growing anger. He made her sound like an outcast, a leper. *We wouldn't want to lose you. You're one of our most valuable employees.*

'Was there anything else, Miss Whitney?' It was a dismissal.

There were a hundred things Tracy wanted to say, but she knew they would do no good. 'No. I think you've said it all.' Tracy turned and walked out the office door, her face burning. All the bank employees seemed to be staring at her. Mae had spread the word: the convict had come back. Tracy moved towards the exit, head held high, dying inside. *I can't let them do this to me. My pride is all I have left, and no one is going to take that away from me.*

* * *

219

Tracy stayed in her room all day, miserable. How could she have been naïve enough to believe that they would welcome her back with open arms? She was notorious now. 'You're the headline in the Philadelphia *Daily News.*' *Well, to hell with Philadelphia*, Tracy thought. She had some unfinished business there, but when that was done, she would leave. She would go to New York, where she would be anonymous. The decision made her feel better.

That evening, Tracy treated herself to dinner at the Café Royal. After the sordid meeting with Clarence Desmond that morning, she needed the reassuring atmosphere of soft lights, elegant surroundings, and soothing music. She ordered a vodka martini, and as the waiter brought it to her table, Tracy glanced up, and her heart suddenly skipped a beat. Seated in a booth across the room were Charles and his wife. They had not yet seen her. Tracy's first impulse was to get up and leave. She was not ready to face Charles, not until she had a chance to put her plan into action.

'Would you like to order now?' the head waiter was asking.

'I'll – I'll wait, thank you.' She had to decide whether she was going to stay.

She looked over at Charles again, and an astonishing phenomenon occurred: it was as though she were looking at a stranger. She was seeing a sallow, drawn-looking, middle-aged, balding

220

man, with stooped shoulders and an air of ineffable boredom on his face. It was impossible to believe that she had once thought she loved this man, that she had slept with him, planned to spend the rest of her life with him. Tracy glanced at his wife. She wore the same bored expression as Charles. They gave the impression of two people trapped together for eternity, frozen in time. They simply sat there, speaking not one word to each other. Tracy could visualize the endless, tedious years ahead of the two of them. No love. No joy. *That is Charles's punishment*, Tracy thought, and she felt a sudden surge of release, a freedom from the deep, dark, emotional chains that had bound her.

Tracy signalled to the head waiter and said, 'I'm ready to order now.'

It was over. The past was finally buried.

It was not until Tracy returned to her hotel room that evening that she remembered she was owed money from the bank's employees' fund. She sat down and calculated the amount. It came to $1,375.65.

She composed a letter to Clarence Desmond, and two days later she received a reply from Mae.

Dear Miss Whitney:
In response to your request, Mr Desmond has asked me to inform you that because of the morals policy in the employees' financial plan, your share has reverted to the general fund.

He wants to assure you that he bears no personal ill will towards you.
Sincerely,
Mae Trenton
Secretary to the Senior Vice-president

Tracy could not believe it. They were stealing her money, and doing it under the pretext of protecting the morals of the bank! She was outraged. *I'm not going to let them cheat me*, she vowed. *No one is ever going to cheat me again.*

Tracy stood outside the familiar entrance to the Philadelphia Trust and Fidelity Bank. She wore a long black wig and heavy, dark makeup, with a raw red scar on her chin. If anything went wrong, it would be the scar they remembered. Despite her disguise, Tracy felt naked, for she had worked in this bank for five years, and it was staffed with people who knew her well. She would have to be very careful not to give herself away.

She removed a bottle cap from her handbag, placed it in her shoe, and limped into the bank. The bank was crowded with customers, for Tracy had carefully chosen a time when the bank would be doing peak business. She limped over to one of the customer-service desks, and the man seated behind it finished a phone call and said, 'Yes?'

It was Jon Creighton, the bank bigot. He hated Jews, blacks, and Puerto Ricans, but not necessarily in that order. He had been an irritant to

Tracy during the years she had worked there. Now there was no sign of recognition on his face.

'*Buenas dias, señor*. I would like to open a current account, *ahora*,' Tracy said. Her accent was Mexican, the accent she had heard for all those months from her cell mate Paulita.

There was a look of disdain on Creighton's face. 'Name?'

'Rita Gonzales.'

'And how much would you like to put in your account?'

'Ten dollars.'

His voice was a sneer. 'Will that be by cheque or cash?'

'Cash, I theenk.'

She carefully took a crumpled, half-torn ten-dollar bill from her purse and handed it to him. He shoved a white form towards her.

'Fill this out –'

Tracy had no intention of putting anything in her hand-writing. She frowned. 'I'm sorry, señor. I hurt *mi mano* – my hand – in an accident. Would you min' writin' it for me, *si se puede*?'

Creighton snorted. *These illiterate wetbacks!* 'Rita Gonzales, you said?'

'*Sí.*'

'Your address?'

She gave him the address and telephone number of her hotel.

'Your mother's maiden name?'

'Gonzales. My mother, she married her uncle.'

'And your date of birth?'

'December twentieth, 1958.'

'Place of birth?'

'Ciudad de Mexico.'

'Mexico City. Sign here.'

'I will have to use my left hand,' Tracy said. She picked up a pen and clumsily scrawled out an illegible signature. Jon Creighton wrote out a deposit slip.

'I'll give you a temporary chequebook. Your printed cheques will be mailed to you in three or four weeks.'

'*Bueno. Muchas gracias, señor.*'

'Yeah.'

He watched her walk out of the bank. *Fuckin' spic.*

There are numerous illegal ways to gain entry to a computer, and Tracy was an expert. She had helped set up the security system at the Philadelphia Trust and Fidelity Bank, and now she was about to circumvent it.

Her first step was to find a computer shop, where she could use a terminal to tap into the bank's computer. The shop, some distance from the bank, was almost empty.

An eager salesman approached Tracy. 'May I help you, miss?'

'*Eso si que no, señor*. I am just looking.'

His eye was caught by a teenager playing a computer game. 'Excuse me.' He hurried away.

Tracy turned to the desk-model computer in front of her, which was connected to a telephone. Getting into the system would be easy, but without the proper access code, she was stymied, and the access code was changed daily. Tracy had been at the meeting when the original authorization code had been decided on.

'We must keep changing it,' Clarence Desmond had said, 'so no one can break in; yet we want to keep it simple enough for people who are authorized to use it.'

The code they had finally settled on used the four seasons of the year and the current day's date.

Tracy turned on the terminal and tapped out the code for the Philadelphia Trust and Fidelity Bank. She heard a high-pitched whine and placed the telephone receiver into the terminal modem. A sign flashed on the small screen: YOUR AUTHORIZATION CODE, PLEASE?

Today was the tenth.

AUTUMN 10, Tracy tapped out.

THAT IS AN IMPROPER AUTHORIZATION CODE. The computer screen went blank.

Had they changed the code? Out of the corner of her eye, Tracy saw the salesman coming towards her again. She moved over to another computer, gave it a casual glance, and ambled along the aisle. The salesman checked his stride. *A looker,* he decided. He hurried forward to greet a prosperous-looking couple coming in the door. Tracy returned to the desk-model computer.

She tried to put herself into Clarence Desmond's mind. He was a creature of habit, and Tracy was sure he would not have varied the code too much. He had probably kept the original concept of the seasons and the numbers, but how had he changed them? It would have been too complicated to reverse all the numbers, so he had probably shifted the seasons around.

Tracy tried again.

YOUR AUTHORIZATION CODE, PLEASE?
WINTER 10.

THAT IS AN IMPROPER AUTHORIZATION CODE. The blank screen again.

It's not going to work, Tracy thought despairingly. *I'll give it one more try.*

YOUR AUTHORIZATION CODE, PLEASE?
SPRING 10.

The screen went blank for a moment, and then the message appeared: PLEASE PROCEED.

So he *had* switched the seasons. She quickly typed out: DOMESTIC MONEY TRANSACTION.

Instantly, the bank menu, the category of available transactions, flashed onto the screen:

DO YOU WISH TO
A DEPOSIT MONEY
B TRANSFER MONEY
C WITHDRAW MONEY FROM SAVINGS ACCOUNT
D INTERBRANCH TRANSFER
E WITHDRAW MONEY FROM CURRENT ACCOUNT
PLEASE ENTER YOUR CHOICE

226

Tracy chose B. The screen went blank and a new menu appeared.

AMOUNT OF TRANSFER?

WHERE TO?

WHERE FROM?

She typed in: FROM GENERAL RESERVE FUND TO RITA GONZALES. When she came to the amount, she hesitated for an instant. *Tempting*, Tracy thought. Since she had access, there was no limit to the amount the now subservient computer would give her. She could have taken millions. But she was no thief. All she wanted was what was rightfully owed her.

She typed in $1,375.65, and added Rita Gonzales's account number.

The screen flashed: TRANSACTION COMPLETED. DO YOU WISH OTHER TRANSACTIONS?

NO.

SESSION COMPLETED. THANK YOU.

The money would automatically be transferred by CHIPS, the Clearing House Interbank Payment System that kept track of the $220 billion shifted from bank to bank every day.

The store clerk was approaching Tracy again, frowning. Tracy hurriedly pressed a key, and the screen went blank.

'Are you interested in purchasing this machine, miss?'

'No, *gracias*,' Tracy apologized. 'I don' understan' these computers.'

She telephoned the bank from a corner drug store and asked to speak to the head cashier.

'*Hola*. Thees is Rita Gonzales. I would like to have my current account transferred to the main branch of the First Hanover Bank of New York City, *por favor*.'

'Your account number, Miss Gonzales?'

Tracy gave it to her.

An hour later Tracy had checked out of the Hilton and was on her way to New York City.

When the first Hanover Bank of New York opened at 10:00 the following morning, Rita Gonzales was there to withdraw all the money from her account.

'How much ees in it?' she asked.

The cashier checked. 'Thirteen hundred and eighty-five dollars and sixty-five cents.'

'*Sí*, that ees correct.'

'Would you like a certified cheque for that, Miss Gonzales?'

'No, *gracias*,' Tracy said. 'I don' trust banks. I weel take the cash.'

Tracy had received the standard two hundred dollars from the state prison upon her release, plus the small amount of money she had earned taking care of Amy, but even with her money from the bank fund, she had no financial security. It was imperative she get a job as quickly as possible.

She checked into an inexpensive hotel on Lexington Avenue and began sending out applications to New York banks, applying for a job as a computer expert. But Tracy found that the computer

228

had suddenly become her enemy. Her life was no longer private. The computer banks held her life's story, and readily told it to everyone who pressed the right buttons. The moment Tracy's criminal record was revealed, her application was automatically rejected.

I think it unlikely that given your background, any bank would hire you. Clarence Desmond had been right.

Tracy sent in more job applications to insurance companies and dozens of other computer-oriented businesses. The replies were always the same: *negative*.

Very well, Tracy thought, *I can always do something else*. She bought a copy of *The New York Times* and began searching the situations vacant ads.

There was a position listed as secretary in an export firm.

The moment Tracy walked in the door, the personnel manager said, 'Hey, I seen you on television. You saved a kid in prison, didn't you?'

Tracy turned and fled.

The following day she was hired as a saleswoman in the children's department at Saks Fifth Avenue. The salary was a great deal less than she had been used to, but at least it was enough to support herself.

On her second day, an hysterical customer recognized her and informed the floor manager that she refused to be waited on by a murderess who had drowned a small child. Tracy was given no chance to explain. She was discharged immediately.

It seemed to Tracy that the men upon whom she had exacted vengeance had had the last word after all. They had turned her into a public criminal, an outcast. The unfairness of what was happening to her was corrosive. She had no idea how she was going to live, and for the first time she began to have a feeling of desperation. That night she looked through her purse to see how much money remained, and tucked away in a corner of her wallet she came across a slip of paper that Betty Franciscus had given her in prison. CONRAD MORGAN, JEWELLER, 640 FIFTH AVENUE, NEW YORK CITY. *He's into criminal reform. He likes to give a hand to people who've been in prison.*

Conrad Morgan et Cie Jewellers was an elegant establishment, with a liveried doorman on the outside and an armed guard on the inside. The shop itself was tastefully understated, but the jewels were exquisite and expensive.

Tracy told the receptionist, 'I'd like to see Mr Conrad Morgan, please.'

'Do you have an appointment?'

'No. A – a mutual friend suggested that I see him.'

'Your name?'

'Tracy Whitney.'

'Just a moment, please.'

The receptionist picked up a telephone and murmured something into it that Tracy could not hear.

She replaced the receiver. 'Mr Morgan is occupied just now. He wonders if you could come back at six o'clock.'

'Yes, thank you,' Tracy said.

She walked out of the shop and stood on the pavement, uncertainly. Coming to New York had been a mistake. There was probably nothing Conrad could do for her. And why should he? She was a complete stranger to him. *He'll give me a lecture and a handout. Well, I don't need either. Not from him or anyone else. I'm a survivor. Somehow I'm going to make it. To hell with Conrad Morgan. I won't go back to see him.*

Tracy wandered the streets aimlessly, passing the glittering salons of Fifth Avenue, the guarded apartment buildings on Park Avenue, the bustling shops on Lexington and Third. She walked the streets of New York mindlessly, seeing nothing, filled with a bitter frustration.

At 6:00 she found herself back on Fifth Avenue, in front of Conrad Morgan et Cie Jewellers. The doorman was gone, and the door was locked. Tracy pounded on the door in a gesture of defiance and then turned away, but to her surprise, the door suddenly opened.

An avuncular-looking man stood there looking at her. He was bald, with ragged tufts of grey hair above his ears, and he had a jolly, rubicund face and twinkling blue eyes. He looked like a cheery little gnome. 'You must be Miss Whitney?'

'Yes . . .'

'I'm Conrad Morgan. Please, do come in, won't you?'

Tracy entered the deserted shop.

'I've been waiting for you,' Conrad Morgan said. 'Let's go into my office where we can talk.'

He led her through the shop to a closed door, which he unlocked with a key. His office was elegantly furnished, and it looked more like a flat than a place of business, with no desk, just couches, chairs, and tables artfully placed. The walls were covered with old masters.

'Would you care for a drink?' Conrad Morgan offered. 'Whisky, cognac, or perhaps sherry?'

'No, nothing, thank you.'

Tracy was suddenly nervous. She had dismissed the idea that this man would do anything to help her, yet at the same time she found herself desperately hoping that he could.

'Betty Franciscus suggested that I look you up, Mr Morgan. She said you – you helped people who have been in . . . trouble.' She could not bring herself to say *prison*.

Conrad Morgan clasped his hands together, and Tracy noticed how beautifully manicured they were.

'Poor Betty. Such a lovely lady. She was unlucky, you know.'

'Unlucky?'

'Yes. She got caught.'

'I – I don't understand.'

'It's really quite simple, Miss Whitney. Betty used to work for me. She was well protected. Then the poor dear fell in love with a chauffeur from New Orleans and went off on her own. And, well . . . they caught her.'

Tracy was confused. 'She worked for you here as a saleslady?'

Conrad Morgan sat back and laughed until his eyes filled with tears. 'No, my dear,' he said, wiping the tears away. 'Obviously, Betty didn't explain everything to you.' He leaned back in his chair and steepled his fingers. 'I have a very profitable little sideline, Miss Whitney, and I take great pleasure in sharing those profits with my colleagues. I have been most successful employing people like yourself – if you'll forgive me – who have served time in prison.'

Tracy studied his face, more puzzled than ever.

'I'm in a unique position, you see. I have an extremely wealthy clientele. My clients become my friends. They confide in me.' He tapped his fingers together delicately. 'I know when my customers take trips. Very few people travel with jewellery in these parlous times, so their jewels are locked away at home. I recommend to them the security measures they should take to protect them. I know exactly what jewels they own because they purchased them from me. They –'

Tracy found herself on her feet. 'Thank you for your time, Mr Morgan.'

'Surely you're not leaving already?'

'If you're saying what I think you're saying –'

'Yes. Indeed, I am.'

She could feel her cheeks burning. 'I'm not a criminal. I came here looking for a job.'

'And I'm offering you one, my dear. It will take an hour or two of your time, and I can promise you twenty-five thousand dollars.' He smiled impishly. 'Tax free, of course.'

Tracy was fighting hard to control her anger. 'I'm not interested. Would you let me out, please?'

'Certainly, if that is your wish.' He rose to his feet and showed her to the door. 'You must understand, Miss Whitney, that if there were the slightest danger of anyone's being caught, I would not be involved in this. I have my reputation to protect.'

'I promise you I won't say anything about it,' Tracy said coldly.

He grinned. 'There's really nothing you could say, my dear, is there? I mean, who would believe you? *I* am Conrad Morgan.'

As they reached the front entrance of the store, Morgan said, 'You will let me know if you change your mind, won't you? The best time to telephone me is after six o'clock in the evening. I'll wait for your call.'

'Don't,' Tracy said curtly, and she walked out into the approaching night. When she reached her room, she was still trembling.

She sent the hotel's one bellboy out for a sandwich and coffee. She did not feel like facing anyone. The meeting with Conrad Morgan had made her feel unclean. He had lumped her with all the sad, confused and beaten criminals she had been surrounded by at the Southern Louisiana Penitentiary for Women. She was not one of them. She was Tracy Whitney, a computer expert, a decent, law-abiding citizen.

Whom no one would hire.

Tracy lay awake all night thinking about her future. She had no job, and very little money left. She made two resolutions: in the morning she would move to a cheaper place and she would find a job. Any kind of job.

The cheaper place turned out to be a dreary fourth-floor walk-up, one-room flat on the Lower East Side. From her room, through the paper-thin walls, Tracy could hear her neighbours screaming at one another in foreign languages. The windows and doors of the small shops that lined the streets were heavily barred, and Tracy could understand why. The neighbourhood seemed to be populated by drunks, prostitutes and bag ladies.

On her way to the market to shop, Tracy was accosted three times – twice by men and once by a woman.

I can stand it. I won't be here long, Tracy assured herself.

She went to a small employment agency a short distance from her flat. It was run by a Mrs Murphy, a matronly looking, heavy-set lady. She put down Tracy's résumé and studied her quizzically. 'I don't know what you need me for. There must be a dozen companies that'd give their eyeteeth to get someone like you.'

Tracy took a deep breath. 'I have a problem,' she said. She explained as Mrs Murphy sat listening quietly, and when Tracy was finished, Mrs Murphy said flatly, 'You can forget about looking for a computer job.'

'But you said –'

'Companies are jumpy these days about computer crimes. They're not gonna hire anybody with a record.'

'But I *need* a job. I –'

'There are other kinds of jobs. Have you thought about working as a saleslady?'

Tracy remembered her experience at the department store. She could not bear to go through that again. 'Is there anything else?'

The woman hesitated. Tracy Whitney was obviously overqualified for the job Mrs Murphy had in mind. 'Look,' she said. 'I know this isn't up your alley, but there's a waitress job open at Jackson Hole. It's a hamburger place on the Upper East Side.'

'A waitress job?'

'Yeah. If you take it, I won't charge you any commission. I just happened to hear about it.'

Tracy sat there, debating. She had waited on tables in college. Then it had been fun. Now it was a question of surviving.

'I'll try it,' she said.

* * *

Jackson Hole was bedlam, packed with noisy impatient customers, and harassed, irritable fry cooks. The food was good and the prices reasonable, and the place was always jammed. The waitresses worked at a frantic pace with no time to relax, and by the end of the first day Tracy was exhausted. But she was earning money.

At noon on the second day, as Tracy was serving a table filled with salesmen, one of the men ran his hand up her skirt, and Tracy dropped a bowl of chili on his head. That was the end of the job.

She returned to Mrs Murphy and reported what had happened.

'I may have some good news,' Mrs Murphy said. 'The Wellington Arms needs an assistant housekeeper. I'm going to send you over there.'

The Wellington Arms was a small, elegant hotel on Park Avenue that catered to the rich and famous. Tracy was interviewed by the housekeeper and hired. The work was not difficult, the staff was pleasant, and the hours reasonable.

A week after she started, Tracy was summoned to the housekeeper's office. The assistant manager was also there.

'Did you check Suite eight-twenty-seven today?' the housekeeper asked Tracy. The suite was occupied by Jennifer Marlowe, a Hollywood actress. Part of Tracy's job was to inspect each suite and see that the maids had done their work properly.

'Why, yes,' she said.

'What time?'

'At two o'clock. Is something wrong?'

The assistant manager spoke up. 'At three o'clock Miss Marlowe returned and discovered that a valuable diamond ring was missing.'

Tracy could feel her body grow tense.

'Did you go into the bedroom, Tracy?'

'Yes. I checked every room.'

'When you were in the bedroom, did you see any jewellery lying around?'

'Why . . . no. I don't think so.'

The assistant manager pounced on it. 'You don't *think* so? You're not *sure*?'

'I wasn't looking for jewellery,' Tracy said. 'I was checking the beds and towels.'

'Miss Marlowe insists that her ring was on the dressing table when she left the suite.'

'I don't know anything about it.'

'No one else has access to that room. The maids have been with us for many years.'

'I didn't take it.'

The assistant manager sighed. 'We're going to have to call in the police to investigate.'

'It *had* to be someone else,' Tracy cried. 'Or perhaps Miss Marlowe misplaced it.'

'With your record –' the assistant manager said.

And there it was, out in the open. *With your record* . . .

'I'll have to ask you to please wait in the security office until the police get here.'

Tracy felt her face flush. 'Yes, sir.'

She was accompanied to the office by one of

238

the security guards, and she felt as though she were back in prison again. She had read of convicts being hounded because they had prison records, but it had never occurred to her that this kind of thing could happen to her. They had stuck a label on her, and they expected her to live up to it. *Or down to it*, Tracy thought bitterly.

Thirty minutes later the assistant manager walked into the office, smiling. 'Well!' he said. 'Miss Marlowe found her ring. She had misplaced it, after all. It was just a little mistake.'

'Wonderful,' Tracy said.

She walked out of the office and headed for Conrad Morgan et Cie Jewellers.

'It's ridiculously simple,' Conrad Morgan was saying. 'A client of mine, Lois Bellamy, has gone to Europe. Her house is in Sea Cliff on Long Island. On weekends the servants are off, so there's no one there. A private patrol makes a check every four hours. You can be in and out of the house in a few minutes.'

They were seated in Conrad Morgan's office.

'I know the alarm system, and I have the combination to the safe. All you have to do, my dear, is walk in, pick up the jewels, and walk out again. You bring the jewels to me, I take them out of their settings, recut the larger ones, and sell them again.'

'If it's so simple, why don't you do it yourself?' Tracy asked bluntly.

His blue eyes twinkled. 'Because I'm going to be out of town on business. Whenever one of these little "incidents" occurs, I'm always out of town on business.'

'I see.'

'If you have any scruples about the robbery hurting Mrs Bellamy, you needn't have. She's really quite a horrible woman, who has houses all over the world filled with expensive goodies. Besides, she's insured for twice the amount the jewels are worth. Naturally, I did all the appraisals.'

Tracy sat there looking at Conrad Morgan, thinking, *I must be crazy. I'm sitting here calmly discussing a jewel robbery with this man.*

'I don't want to go back to prison, Mr Morgan.'

'There's no danger of that. Not one of my people has ever been caught. Not while they were working for me. Well . . . what do you say?'

That was obvious. She was going to say no. The whole idea was insane.

'You said twenty-five thousand dollars?'

'Cash on delivery.'

It was a fortune, enough to take care of her until she could figure out what to do with her life. She thought of the dreary little room she lived in, of the screaming tenants, and the customer yelling, 'I don't want a murderess waiting on me', and the assistant manager saying, 'We're going to have to call in the police to investigate.'

But Tracy still could not bring herself to say yes.

'I would suggest this Saturday night,' Conrad

Morgan said. 'The staff leaves at noon on Saturdays. I'll arrange a driver's licence and a credit card for you in a false name. You'll rent a car here in Manhattan and drive out to Long Island, arriving at eleven o'clock. You'll pick up the jewellery, drive back to New York, and return the car . . . You do drive, don't you?'

'Yes.'

'Excellent. There's a train leaving for St Louis at seven-forty-five A.M. I'll reserve a compartment for you. I'll meet you at the station in St Louis, you'll turn over the jewels, and I'll give you your twenty-five thousand.'

He made it all sound so simple.

This was the moment to say no, to get up and walk out. *Walk out to where?*

'I'll need a blonde wig,' Tracy said slowly.

When Tracy had left, Conrad Morgan sat in the dark in his office, thinking about her. A beautiful woman. Very beautiful indeed. It was a shame. Perhaps he should have warned her that he was not really that familiar with that particular burglar-alarm system.

SIXTEEN

With the thousand dollars that Conrad Morgan advanced her, Tracy purchased two wigs – one blonde and one black, with a multitude of tiny braids. She bought a dark-blue pants suit, black overalls, and an imitation Gucci valise from a street vendor on Lexington Avenue. So far everything was going smoothly. As Morgan had promised, Tracy received an envelope containing a driver's licence in the name of Ellen Branch, a diagram of the security system in the Bellamy house, the combination to the bedroom safe, and an Amtrak ticket to St Louis, in a private compartment. Tracy packed her few belongings and left. *I'll never live in a place like this again*, Tracy promised herself. She rented a car and headed for Long Island. She was on her way to commit a burglary.

What she was doing had the unreality of a dream, and she was terrified. What if she were caught? Was the risk worth what she was about to do?

It's ridiculously simple, Conrad Morgan had said.

He wouldn't be involved in anything like this if he weren't sure about it. He has his reputation to protect. I have a reputation, too, Tracy thought bitterly, *and it's all bad. Any time a piece of jewellery is missing, I'll be guilty until proven innocent.*

Tracy knew what she was doing: she was trying to work herself up into a rage, trying to psych herself up to commit a crime. It did not work. By the time she reached Sea Cliff, she was a nervous wreck. Twice, she almost ran the car off the road. *Maybe the police will pick me up for reckless driving*, she thought hopefully, *and I can tell Mr Morgan that things went wrong.*

But there was not a police car in sight. *Sure*, Tracy thought in disgust. *They're never around when you need them.*

She headed towards Long Island Sound, following Conrad Morgan's directions. *The house is right on the water. It's called the Embers. It's an old Victorian mansion.* You can't miss it.

Please let me miss it, Tracy prayed.

But there it was, looming up out of the dark like some ogre's castle in a nightmare. It looked deserted. *How dare the servants take the weekend off*, Tracy thought indignantly. *They should all be discharged.*

She drove the car behind a stand of giant willow trees, where it was hidden from view, and turned off the engine, listening to the nocturnal sounds of

243

insects. Nothing else disturbed the silence. The house was off the main road, and there was no traffic at that time of night.

The property is screened by trees, my dear, and the nearest neighbour is acres away, so you don't have to be concerned about being seen. The security patrol makes its check at ten P.M. *and again at two* A.M. *You'll be long gone by the two* A.M. *check.*

Tracy looked at her watch. It was 11:00. The first patrol had gone. She had three hours before the patrol was due to arrive for its second check. Or three seconds to turn the car around and head back to New York and forget about this insanity. But head back to *what*? The images flashed unbidden into her mind. The assistant manager at Saks: 'I'm terribly sorry, Miss Whitney, but our customers must be humoured . . .'

'You can forget about running a computer. They're not going to hire anybody with a record . . .'

'Twenty-five thousand tax-free dollars for an hour or two. If you have scruples, she's really a horrible woman.'

What am I doing? Tracy thought. *I'm not a burglar. Not a real one. I'm a dumb amateur who's about to have a nervous breakdown.*

If I had half a brain, I'd get away from here while there's still time. Before the SWAT team catches me and there's a shoot-out and they carry my riddled body to the morgue. I can see the head-line: DANGEROUS CRIMINAL KILLED DURING BUNGLED BURGLARY ATTEMPT.

Who would be there to cry at her funeral? Ernestine and Amy. Tracy looked at her watch. 'Oh, my God.' She had been sitting there, day-dreaming, for twenty minutes. *If I'm going to do it, I'd better move.*

She could not move. She was frozen with fear. *I can't sit here forever*, she told herself. *Why don't I just go take a look at the house? A quick look.*

Tracy took a deep breath and got out of the car. She was wearing black overalls; her knees were shaking. She approached the house slowly, and she could see that it was completely dark.

Be sure to wear gloves.

Tracy reached in her pocket and took out a pair of gloves, and put them on. *Oh, God, I'm doing it*, she thought. *I'm really going ahead with it.* Her heart was pounding so loudly she could no longer hear any other sounds.

The alarm is to the left of the front door. There are five buttons. The red light will be on, which means the alarm is activated. The code to turn it off is three-two-four-one-one. When the red light goes off, you'll know the alarm is deactivated. Here's the key to the front door. When you enter, be sure to close the door after you. Use this flash-light. Don't turn on any of the lights in the house in case someone happens to drive past. The master bedroom is upstairs, to your left, overlooking the bay. You'll find the safe behind a portrait of Lois Bellamy. It's a very simple safe. All you have to do is follow this combination.

Tracy stood stock-still, trembling, ready to flee at the slightest sound. Silence. Slowly, she reached out and pressed the sequence of alarm buttons, praying that it would not work. The red light went out. The next step would commit her. She remembered that airplane pilots had a phrase for it: the point of no return.

Tracy put the key in the lock, and the door swung open. She waited a full minute before she stepped inside. Every nerve in her body throbbed to a savage beat as she stood in the hallway, listening, afraid to move. The house was filled with a deserted silence. She took out a flashlight, turned it on, and saw the staircase. She moved forward and started up. All she wanted to do now was get it over with as quickly as possible and run.

The upstairs hallway looked eerie in the glow of her flash-light, and the wavering beam made the walls seem to pulse back and forth. Tracy peered into each room she passed. They were all empty.

The master bedroom was at the end of the hallway, looking out over the bay, just as Morgan had described it. The bedroom was beautiful, done in dusky pink, with a canopied bed and a commode decorated with pink roses. There were two love seats, a fireplace, and a table in front of it for dining. *I almost lived in a house like this with Charles and our baby*, Tracy thought.

She walked over to the picture window and looked out at the distant boats anchored in the bay. *Tell me, God, what made you decide that Lois*

Bellamy should live in this beautiful house and that I should be here robbing it? Come on, girl, she told herself, *don't get philosophical. This is a one-time thing. It will be over in a few minutes, but not if you stand here doing nothing.*

She turned from the window and walked over to the portrait Morgan had described. Lois Bellamy had a hard, arrogant look. *It's true. She does look like a horrible woman.* The painting swung outward, away from the wall, and behind it was a small safe. Tracy had memorized the combination. *Three turns to the right, stop at forty-two. Two turns to the left, stop at ten. One turn to the right, stop at thirty.* Her hands were trembling so much that she had to start again twice. She heard a click. The door was open.

The safe was filled with thick envelopes and papers, but Tracy ignored them. At the back, resting on a small shelf, was a chamois jewellery bag. Tracy reached for it and lifted it from the shelf. At that instant the burglar alarm went off, and it was the loudest sound Tracy had ever heard. It seemed to reverberate from every corner of the house, screaming out its warning. She stood there, paralysed, in shock.

What had gone wrong? Had Conrad Morgan not known about the alarm inside the safe that was activated when the jewels were removed?

She had to get out quickly. She scooped the chamois bag into her pocket and started running towards the stairs. And then, over the sound of the alarm, she heard another sound, the sound of an approaching siren. Tracy stood at the top of the staircase, terrified, her heart racing, her mouth dry. She hurried to a window, raised the curtain and peered out. A black-and-white patrol car was pulling up in front of the house. As Tracy watched, a uniformed policeman ran towards the back of the house, while a second one moved towards the front door. There was no escape. The alarm bells were still clanging, and suddenly they sounded like the terrible bells in the corridors of the Southern Louisiana Penitentiary for Women.

No! thought Tracy. *I won't let them send me back there.*

The front doorbell shrilled.

Lieutenant Melvin Durkin had been on the Sea Cliff police force for ten years. Sea Cliff was a quiet town, and the main activity of the police was handling vandalism, a few car thefts, and occasional Saturday-night drunken brawls. The setting-off of the Bellamy alarm was in a different category. It was the type of criminal activity for which Lieutenant Durkin had joined the force. He knew Lois Bellamy and was aware of what a valuable collection of paintings and jewellery she owned. With her away, he had made it a point to check the house from time to time, for it was a tempting target for a cat burglar. *And now*, Lieutenant Durkin thought, *it looks like I've caught one*. He had been only a short distance away when the radio call had come in from the security company. *This is going to look good on my record. Damned good.*

Lieutenant Durkin pressed the front doorbell again. He wanted to be able to state in his report that he had rung it three times before making a forcible entry. His partner was covering the back, so there was no chance of the burglar's escaping. He would probably try to conceal himself on the premises, but he was in for a surprise. No one could hide from Melvin Durkin.

As the lieutenant reached for the bell for the third time, the front door suddenly opened. The policeman stood there staring. In the doorway was a woman dressed in a filmy nightgown that left little to the imagination. Her face was covered with a mudpack, and her hair was tucked into a curler cap.

She demanded, 'What on earth is going on?'

Lieutenant Durkin swallowed. 'I . . . who are you?'

'I'm Ellen Branch. I'm a houseguest of Lois Bellamy's. She's away in Europe.'

'I know that.' The lieutenant was confused. 'She didn't tell us she was having a houseguest.'

The woman in the doorway nodded knowingly. 'Isn't that just like Lois? Excuse me, I can't stand that noise.'

As Lieutenant Durkin watched, Lois Bellamy's houseguest reached over to the alarm buttons, pressed a sequence of numbers, and the sound stopped.

'That's better,' she sighed. 'I can't tell you how glad I am to see you.' She laughed shakily. 'I was just getting ready for bed when the alarm went off. I was sure there were burglars in the house and I'm all alone here. The servants left at noon.'

'Do you mind if we look around?'

'Please, I insist!'

It took the lieutenant and his partner only a few minutes to make sure there was no one lurking on the premises.

'All clear,' Lieutenant Durkin said. 'False alarm. Something must have set it off. Can't always depend on these electronic things. I'd call the security company and have them check out the system.'

'I most certainly will.'

'Well, guess we'd better be running along,' the lieutenant said.

'Thank you so much for coming by. I feel safer now.'

She sure has a great body, Lieutenant Durkin thought. He wondered what she looked like under that mudpack and without the curler cap. 'Will you be staying here long, Miss Branch?'

'Another week or two, until Lois returns.'

'If there's anything I can do for you, just let me know.'

'Thank you, I will.'

Tracy watched as the police car drove away into the night. She felt faint with relief. When the car was out of sight, she hurried upstairs, washed off the mudpack she had found in the bathroom,

250

stripped off Lois Bellamy's curler cap and night-gown, changed into her own black overalls, and left by the front door, carefully resetting the alarm.

It was not until Tracy was halfway back to Manhattan that the audacity of what she had done struck her. She giggled, and the giggle turned into a shaking, uncontrollable laughter, until she finally had to pull the car off onto the side of the road. She laughed until the tears streamed down her face. It was the first time she had laughed in a year. It felt wonderful.

SEVENTEEN

It was not until the Amtrak train pulled out of Pennsylvania Station that Tracy began to relax. At every second she had expected a heavy hand to grip her shoulder, a voice to say, 'You're under arrest.'

She had carefully watched the other passengers as they boarded the train, and there was nothing alarming about them. Still, Tracy's shoulders were knots of tension. She kept assuring herself that it was unlikely anyone would have discovered the burglary this soon, and even if they had, there was nothing to connect her with it. Conrad Morgan would be waiting in St Louis with $25,000. Twenty-five thousand dollars to do with as she pleased! She would have had to work at the bank for a year to earn that much money. *I'll travel to Europe*, Tracy thought, *Paris*. No. Not Paris. *Charles and I were going to honeymoon there. I'll go to London. There, I won't be a jailbird.* In a curious way, the experience she had just gone through had made Tracy feel like a different person. It was as though she had been reborn.

She locked the door to the compartment and took out the chamois bag and opened it. A cascade of glittering colours spilled into her hands. There were three large diamond rings, an emerald pin, a sapphire bracelet, three pairs of earrings, and two necklaces, one of rubies, one of pearls.

There must be more than a million dollars' worth of jewellery here, Tracy marvelled. As the train rolled through the countryside, she leaned back in her seat and replayed the evening in her mind. Renting the car . . . the drive to Sea Cliff . . . the stillness of the night . . . turning off the alarm and entering the house . . . opening the safe . . . the shock of the alarm going off, and the police appearing. It had never occurred to them that the woman in the nightgown with a mudpack on her face and a curler cap on her head was the burglar they were looking for.

Now, seated in her compartment on the train to St Louis, Tracy allowed herself a smile of satisfaction. She had enjoyed outwitting the police. There was something wonderfully exhilarating about being on the edge of danger. She felt daring and clever and invincible. She felt absolutely great.

There was a knock at the door of her compartment. Tracy hastily put the jewels back into the chamois bag and placed the bag in her suitcase. She took out her train ticket and unlocked the compartment door for the conductor.

Two men in grey suits stood in the corridor. One appeared to be in his early thirties, the other one about ten years older. The younger man was attractive, with the build of an athlete. He had a strong chin, a small, neat moustache, and wore horn-rimmed glasses behind which were intelligent blue eyes. The older man had a thick head of black hair and was heavy-set. His eyes were a cold brown.

'Can I help you?' Tracy asked.

'Yes, ma'am,' the older man replied. He pulled out a wallet and held up an identification card:

FEDERAL BUREAU OF INVESTIGATION
UNITED STATES DEPARTMENT OF JUSTICE

'I'm Special Agent Dennis Trevor. This is Special Agent Thomas Bowers.'

Tracy's mouth was suddenly dry. She forced a smile. 'I – I'm afraid I don't understand. Is something wrong?'

'I'm afraid there is, ma'am,' the younger agent said. He had a soft, southern accent. 'A few minutes ago this train crossed into New Jersey. Transporting stolen merchandise across a state line is a federal offence.'

Tracy felt suddenly faint. A red film appeared in front of her eyes, blurring everything.

The older man, Dennis Trevor, was saying, 'Would

you open your luggage, please?' It was not a question but an order.

Her only hope was to try to bluff it out. 'Of course I won't! How dare you come barging into my compartment like this!' Her voice was filled with indignation. 'Is that all you have to do – go around bothering innocent citizens? I'm going to call the conductor.'

'We've already spoken to the conductor,' Trevor said.

Her bluff was not working. 'Do – do you have a search warrant?'

The younger man said gently, 'We don't need a search warrant, Miss Whitney. We're apprehending you during the commission of a crime.' They even knew her name. She was trapped. There was no way out. *None.*

Trevor was at her suitcase, opening it. It was useless to try to stop him. Tracy watched as he reached inside and pulled out the chamois bag. He opened it, looked at his partner, and nodded. Tracy sank down onto the seat, suddenly too weak to stand.

Trevor took a list from his pocket, checked the contents of the bag against the list, and put the bag in his pocket. 'It's all here, Tom.'

'How – how did you find out?' Tracy asked miserably.

'We're not permitted to give out any information,' Trevor replied. 'You're under arrest. You have the right to remain silent, and to have an attorney present before you say anything. Anything you say now may be used as evidence against you. Do you understand?'

Her answer was a whispered, 'Yes.'

Tom Bowers said, 'I'm sorry about this. I mean, I know about your background, and I'm really sorry.'

'For Christ's sake,' the older man said, 'this isn't a social visit.'

'I know, but still –'

The older man held out a pair of handcuffs to Tracy. 'Hold out your wrists, please.'

Tracy felt her heart twisting in agony. She remembered the airport in New Orleans when they had handcuffed her, the staring faces. 'Please! Do you – do you have to do that?'

'Yes, ma'am.'

The younger man said, 'Can I talk to you alone for a minute, Dennis?'

Dennis Trevor shrugged. 'Okay.'

The two men stepped outside into the corridor. Tracy sat there, dazed, filled with despair. She could hear snatches of their conversation.

'For God's sake, Dennis, it isn't necessary to put cuffs on her. She's not going to run away . . .'

'When are you going to stop being such a boy scout? When you've been with the Bureau as long as I have . . .'

'Come on. Give her a break. She's embarrassed enough, and . . .'

'That's nothing to what she's going to . . .'

She could not hear the rest of the conversation. She did not want to hear the rest of the conversation.

In a moment they returned to the compartment. The older man seemed angry. 'All right,' he said. 'We're not cuffing you. We're taking you off at the next station. We're going to radio ahead for a Bureau car. You're not to leave this compartment. Is that clear?'

Tracy nodded, too miserable to speak.

The younger man, Tom Bowers, gave her a sympathetic shrug, as though to say, 'I wish there was something more I could do.'

There was nothing anyone could do. Not now. It was too late. She had been caught red-handed. Somehow the police had traced her and informed the FBI.

The agents were outside in the corridor talking to the conductor. Bowers pointed to Tracy and said something she could not hear. The conductor nodded. Bowers closed the door of the compartment, and to Tracy, it was like a cell door slamming.

The countryside sped by, flashing vignettes briefly framed by the window, but Tracy was unaware of the scenery. She sat there, paralysed by fear. There was a roaring in her ears that had nothing to do with the sounds of the train. She would get no second chance. She was a convicted felon. They would give her the maximum sentence, and this time there would be no warden's daughter to rescue, there would be nothing but the deadly, endless years of prison facing her. And the Big Berthas. *How had they caught her?* The only person who knew about the robbery was Conrad Morgan, and he could have no possible reason to turn her and the jewellery over to the FBI. Possibly some clerk in his shop had learned of the plan and tipped off the police. But how it happened made no difference. She had been caught. At the next stop she would be on her way to prison again. There would be a preliminary hearing and then the trial, and then . . .

Tracy squeezed her eyes tightly shut, refusing to think about it any further. She felt hot tears brush her cheeks.

The train began to lose speed. Tracy started to hyperventilate. She could not get enough air. The two FBI agents would be coming for her at any moment. A station came into view, and a few seconds later the train jerked to a stop. It was time to go. Tracy closed her suitcase, put on her coat, and sat down. She stared at the closed compartment door, waiting for it to open. Minutes went by. The two men did not appear. What could they be doing? She recalled their words, 'We're taking you off at the next station. We're going to radio ahead for a Bureau car. You're not to leave this compartment.'

She heard the conductor call, 'All aboard . . .'

Tracy started to panic. Perhaps they had meant

they would wait for her on the platform. *That must be it.* If she stayed on the train, they would accuse her of trying to run away from them, and it would make things even worse. Tracy grabbed her suitcase, opened the compartment door, and hurried out into the corridor.

The conductor was approaching. 'Are you getting off here, miss?' he asked. 'You'd better hurry. Let me help you. A woman in your condition shouldn't be lifting things.'

She stared. 'In my condition?'

'You don't have to be embarrassed. Your brothers told me you're pregnant and to sort of keep an eye on you.'

'My brothers –?'

'Nice chaps. They seemed really concerned about you.'

The world was spinning around. Everything was topsy-turvy.

The conductor carried the suitcase to the end of the carriage and helped Tracy down the steps. The train began to move.

'Do you know where my brothers went?' Tracy called.

'No, ma'am. They jumped into a taxi when the train stopped.'

With a million dollars' worth of stolen jewellery.

Tracy headed for the airport. It was the only place she could think of. If the men had taken a taxi, it meant they did not have their own transportation, and they would surely want to get out of town as fast as possible. She sat back in the cab, filled with rage at what they had done to her and with shame at how easily they had conned her. Oh, they were good, both of them. Really good. They had been so convincing. She blushed to think how she had fallen for the ancient good cop-bad cop routine.

For God's sake, Dennis, it isn't necessary to put cuffs on her. She's not going to run away . . .

When are you going to stop being such a boy scout? When you've been with the Bureau as long as I have . . .

The Bureau? They were probably both fugitives from the law. Well, she was going to get those jewels back. She had gone through too much to be outwitted by two con artists. She *had* to get to the airport in time.

She leaned forward in her seat and said to the driver, 'Could you go faster, please.'

They were standing in the boarding line at the departure gate, and she did not recognize them immediately. The younger man, who had called himself Thomas Bowers, no longer wore glasses, his eyes had changed from blue to grey, and his moustache was gone. The other man, Dennis Trevor, who had had thick black hair, was now totally bald. But still, there was no mistaking them. They had not had time to change their clothes. They were almost at the boarding gate when Tracy reached them.

'You forgot something,' Tracy said.

They turned to look at her, startled. The younger man frowned. 'What are you doing here? A car from the Bureau was supposed to have been at the station to pick you up.' His southern accent was gone.

'Then why don't we go back and find it?' Tracy suggested.

'Can't. We're on another case,' Trevor explained. 'We have to catch this plane.'

'Give me back the jewellery, first,' Tracy demanded.

'I'm afraid we can't do that,' Thomas Bowers told her. 'It's evidence. We'll send you a receipt for it.'

'No. I don't want a receipt. I want the jewellery.'

'Sorry,' said Trevor. 'We can't let it out of our possession.'

They had reached the gate. Trevor handed his boarding pass to the attendant. Tracy looked around, desperate, and saw an airport policeman standing nearby. She called out, '*Officer! Officer!*'

The two men looked at each other, startled.

'What the hell do you think you're doing?' Trevor hissed. 'Do you want to get us all arrested?'

The policeman was moving towards them. 'Yes, miss? Any problem?'

'Oh, no problem,' Tracy said gaily. 'These two wonderful gentlemen found some valuable jewellery I lost, and they're returning it to me. I was afraid I was going to have to go to the FBI about it.'

The two men exchanged a frantic look.

'They suggested that perhaps you wouldn't mind escorting me to a taxi.'

'Certainly. Be happy to.'

Tracy turned towards the men. 'It's safe to give the jewels to me now. This nice officer will take care of me.'

'No, really,' Tom Bowers objected. 'It would be much better if we –'

'Oh, no, I insist,' Tracy urged. 'I know how important it is for you to catch your plane.'

The two men looked at the policeman, and then at each other, helpless. There was nothing they could do. Reluctantly, Tom Bowers pulled out the chamois bag from his pocket.

'That's it!' Tracy said. She took the bag from his hand, opened it, and looked inside. 'Thank goodness. It's all here.'

Tom Bowers made one last-ditch try. 'Why don't we keep it safe for you until –'

'That won't be necessary,' Tracy said cheerfully. She opened her handbag, put the jewellery inside, and took out two $5.00 bills. She handed one to each of the men. 'Here's a little token of my appreciation for what you've done.'

The other passengers had all departed through the gate. The airline attendant said, 'That was the last call. You'll have to board now, gentlemen.'

'Thank you again,' Tracy beamed as she walked away with the policeman at her side. 'It's so rare to find an honest person these days.'

EIGHTEEN

Thomas Bowers – née Jeff Stevens – sat at the plane window looking out as the aircraft took off. He raised his handkerchief to his eyes, and his shoulders heaved up and down.

Dennis Taylor – a.k.a. Brandon Higgins – seated next to him, looked at him in surprise. 'Hey,' he said, 'it's only money. It's nothing to cry about.'

Jeff Stevens turned to him with tears streaming down his face, and Higgins, to his astonishment, saw that Jeff was convulsed with laughter.

'What the hell's the matter with you?' Higgins demanded. 'It's nothing to *laugh* about, either.'

To Jeff, it was. The manner in which Tracy Whitney had outwitted them at the airport was the most ingenious con he had ever witnessed. A scam on top of a scam. Conrad Morgan had told them the woman was an amateur. *My God*, Jeff thought, *what would she be like if she were a professional?* Tracy Whitney was without doubt the most beautiful woman Jeff Stevens had ever seen. And clever.

Jeff prided himself on being the best confidence artist in the business, and she had outsmarted him. *Uncle Willie would have loved her*, Jeff thought.

It was Uncle Willie who had educated Jeff. Jeff's mother was the trusting heiress to a farm-equipment fortune, married to an improvident schemer filled with get-rich-quick projects that never quite worked out. Jeff's father was a charmer, darkly handsome and persuasively glib, and in the first five years of marriage he had managed to run through his wife's inheritance. Jeff's earliest memories were of his mother and father quarrelling about money and his father's extramarital affairs. It was a bitter marriage, and the young boy had resolved, *I'm never going to get married. Never.*

His father's brother, Uncle Willie, owned a small travelling carnival, and whenever he was near Marion, Ohio, where the Stevenses lived, he came to visit them. He was the most cheerful man Jeff had ever known, filled with optimism and promises of a rosy tomorrow. He always managed to bring the boy exciting gifts, and he taught Jeff wonderful magic tricks. Uncle Willie had started out as a magician at a carnival and had taken it over when it went broke.

When Jeff was fourteen, his mother died in an car accident. Two months later Jeff's father married a nineteen-year-old cocktail waitress. 'It isn't natural for a man to live by himself,' his father had explained. But the boy was filled with a deep resentment, feeling betrayed by his father's callousness.

Jeff's father had been hired as a siding salesman and was on the road three days a week. One night when Jeff was alone in the house with his step-mother, he was awakened by the sound of his bedroom door opening. Moments later he felt a soft, naked body next to his. Jeff sat up in alarm.

'Hold me, Jeffie,' his stepmother whispered. 'I'm afraid of thunder.'

'It – it isn't thundering,' Jeff stammered.

'But it *could* be. The paper said rain.' She pressed her body close to his. 'Make love to me, baby.'

The boy was in a panic. 'Sure. Can we do it in Dad's bed?'

'Okay.' She laughed. 'Kinky, huh?'

'I'll be right there,' Jeff promised.

She slid out of bed and went into the other bed-room. Jeff had never dressed faster in his life. He went out the window and headed for Cimarron, Kansas, where Uncle Willie's carnival was playing. He never looked back.

When Uncle Willie asked Jeff why he had run away from home all he would say was, 'I don't get along with my stepmother.'

Uncle Willie telephoned Jeff's father, and after a long conversation, it was decided that the boy should remain with the carnival. 'He'll get a better education here than any school could ever give him,' Uncle Willie promised.

* * *

The carnival was a world unto itself. 'We don't run a Sunday school show,' Uncle Willie explained to Jeff. 'We're flimflam artists. But remember, sonny, you can't con people unless they're greedy to begin with. W. C. Fields had it right. You can't cheat an honest man.'

The carnies became Jeff's friends. There were the 'front-end' men, who had the concessions, and the 'back-end' people, who ran shows like the fat woman and the tattooed lady, and the flatstore operators, who operated the games. The carnival had its share of nubile girls, and they were attracted to the young boy. Jeff had inherited his mother's sensitivity and his father's dark, good looks, and the ladies fought over who was going to relieve Jeff of his virginity. His first sexual experience was with a pretty contortionist, and for years she was the high-water mark that other women had to live up to.

Uncle Willie arranged for Jeff to work at various jobs around the carnival.

'Someday all this will be yours,' Uncle Willie told the boy, 'and the only way you're gonna hang on to it is to know more about it than anybody else does.'

Jeff started out with the six-cat 'hanky-pank', a scam where customers paid to throw balls to try to knock six cats made out of canvas with a wood-base bottom into a net. The operator running the joint would demonstrate how easy it was to knock them over, but when the customer tried it, a 'gunner' hiding in the back of the canvas lifted a rod to keep the wooden base on the cats steady. Not even Sandy Koufax could have downed the cats.

'Hey, you hit it too low,' the operator would say. 'All you have to do is hit it nice and easy.'

Nice and easy was the password, and the moment the operator said it, the hidden gunner would drop the rod, and the operator would knock the cat off the board. He would then say, 'See what I mean?' and that was the gunner's signal to put up the rod again. There was always another rube who wanted to show off his pitching arm to his giggling girl friend.

Jeff worked the 'count stores', where clothespins were arranged in a line. The customer would pay to throw rubber rings over the clothespins, which were numbered, and if the total added up to twenty-nine, he would win an expensive toy. What the sucker did not know was that the clothespins had different numbers at both ends, so that the man running the count store could conceal the number that would add up to twenty-nine and make sure the mark never won.

One day Uncle Willie said to Jeff, 'You're doin' real good, kid, and I'm proud of you. You're ready to move up to the skillo.'

The skillo operators were the *crème de la crème*, and all the other carnies looked up to them. They made more money than anyone else in the carnival, stayed at the best hotels, and drove flashy cars. The skillo game consisted of a flat wheel with an arrow balanced very carefully on glass with a thin piece of paper in the centre. Each section was numbered, and when the customer spun the wheel and it stopped on a number, that number would be blocked off. The customer would pay again for another spin of the wheel, and another space would be blocked off. The skillo operator explained that when all the spaces were blocked off, the customer would win a large sum of money. As the customer got closer to filling in all the spaces, the skillo operator would encourage him to increase his bets. The operator would look around nervously and whisper, 'I don't own this game, but I'd like to win. If you do, maybe you'll give me a small piece.'

The operator would slip the customer five or ten dollars and say, 'Bet this for me, will you? You can't lose now.' And the mark would feel as though he had a confederate. Jeff became an expert at milking the customers. As the open spaces on the board became smaller and the odds of winning grew greater, the excitement would intensify.

'You can't miss now!' Jeff would exclaim, and the player would eagerly put up more money. Finally, when there was only one tiny space left to fill, the excitement would peak. The mark would put up all the money he had, and often hurry home to get more. The customer never won, however, because the operator or his shill would give the table an imperceptible nudge, and the arrow would invariably land at the wrong place.

Jeff quickly learned all the carnie terms: The 'gaff' was a term for fixing the games so that the marks could not win. The men who stood in front of a sideshow making their spiel were called 'barkers' by outsiders, but the carnie people called them 'talkers'. The talker got 10 percent of the take for building the tip – the 'tip' being a crowd. 'Slum' was the prize given away. The 'postman' was a cop who had to be paid off.

Jeff became an expert at the 'blow-off'. When customers paid to see a sideshow exhibition, Jeff would make his spiel: 'Ladies and gentlemen: everything that's pictured, painted and advertised outside, you will see within the walls of this tent for the price of your general admission. *However*, immediately after the young lady in the electric chair gets finished being tortured, her poor body racked by fifty thousand watts of electricity, we have an extra added attraction that has absolutely nothing to do with the show and is not advertised outside. Behind this enclosure you are going to see something so truly remarkable, so chilling and hair-raising, that we dare not portray it outside, because it might come under the eyes of innocent children or susceptible women.'

And after the suckers had paid an extra dollar Jeff would usher them inside to see a girl with no middle, or a two-headed baby, and of course it was all done with mirrors.

One of the most profitable carnival games was the 'mouse running'. A live mouse was put in the centre of a table and a bowl was placed over it. The rim of the table had ten holes around its perimeter into any one of which the mouse could run when the bowl was lifted. Each patron bet on a numbered hole. Whoever selected the hole into which the mouse would run won the prize.

'How do you gaff a thing like that?' Jeff asked Uncle Willie. 'Do you use trained mice?'

Uncle Willie roared with laughter. 'Who the hell's got time to train mice? No, no. It's simple. The operator sees which number no one has bet on, and he puts a little vinegar on his finger and touches the edge of the hole he wants the mouse to run into. The mouse will head for that hole every time.'

Karen, an attractive belly dancer, introduced Jeff to the 'key' game.

'When you've made your spiel on Saturday night,' Karen told him, 'call some of the men customers aside, one at a time, and sell them a key to my trailer.'

The keys cost five dollars. By midnight, a dozen or more men would find themselves milling around outside her trailer. Karen, by that time, was at a hotel in town, spending the night with Jeff. When the marks came back to the carnival the following morning to get their revenge, the show was long gone.

During the next four years Jeff learned a great deal about human nature. He found out how easy it was to arouse greed, and how gullible people could be. They believed incredible tales because their greed

270

made them *want* to believe. At eighteen, Jeff was strikingly handsome. Even the most casual woman observer would instantly note and approve his grey, well-spaced eyes, tall build, and curly dark hair. Men enjoyed his wit and air of easy good humour. Even children, as if speaking to some answering child in him, gave him their confidence immediately. Customers flirted outrageously with Jeff, but Uncle Willie cautioned, 'Stay away from the townies, my boy. Their fathers are always the sheriff.'

It was the knife thrower's wife who caused Jeff to leave the carnival. The show had just arrived at Milledgeville, Georgia, and the tents were being set up. A new act had signed on, a Sicilian knife thrower called the Great Zorbini and his attractive blonde wife. While the Great Zorbini was at the carnival setting up his equipment, his wife invited Jeff to their hotel room in town.

'Zorbini will be busy all day,' she told Jeff. 'Let's have some fun.'

It sounded good.

'Give me an hour and then come up to the room,' she said.

'Why wait an hour?' Jeff asked.

She smiled and said, 'It will take me that long to get everything ready.'

Jeff waited, his curiosity increasing, and when he finally arrived at the hotel room, she greeted him at the door, half naked. He reached for her, but she took his hand and said, 'Come in here.'

He walked into the bathroom and stared in disbelief. She had filled the bath with six flavours of Jell-O, mixed with warm water.

'What's that?' Jeff asked.

'It's dessert. Get undressed baby.'

Jeff undressed.

'Now, into the bath.'

He stepped into the bath and sat down, and it was the wildest sensation he had ever experienced. The soft, slippery Jell-O seemed to fill every crevice of his body, massaging him all over. The blonde joined him in the bath.

'Now,' she said, 'lunch.'

She started down his chest towards his groin, licking the Jell-O as she went. 'Mmmm, you taste delicious. I like the strawberry best . . .'

Between her rapidly flicking tongue and the friction of the warm, viscous Jell-O, it was an erotic experience beyond description. In the middle of it, the bathroom door flew open and the Great Zorbini strode in. The Sicilian took one look at his wife and the startled Jeff, and howled, '*Tu sei una puttana! Vi ammazzo tutti e due! Dove sono i miei coltelli?*'

Jeff did not recognize any of the words, but the tone was familiar. As the Great Zorbini raced out of the room to get his knives, Jeff leaped out of the bath, his body looking like a rainbow with the multicoloured Jell-O clinging to it, and grabbed his clothes. He jumped out of the window, naked, and began running down the alley. He heard a shout behind him and felt a knife sing past his head. Zing! Another, and then he was out of range. He dressed in a culvert, pulling his shirt and pants over the sticky Jell-O, and squished his way to the depot, where he caught the first bus out of town.

Six months later, he was in Vietnam.

Every soldier fights a different war, and Jeff came out of his Vietnam experience with a deep contempt for bureaucracy and a lasting resentment of authority. He spent two years in a war that could never be won, and he was appalled by the waste of money and matériel and lives, and sickened by the treachery and deceit of the generals and politicians who performed their verbal sleight of hand. *We've been suckered into a war that nobody wants*, Jeff thought. *It's a con game. The biggest con game in the world.*

A week before Jeff's discharge, he received the news of Uncle Willie's death. The carnival had folded. The past was finished. It was time for him to enjoy the future.

The years that followed were filled with a series of adventures. To Jeff, the whole world was a carnival, and the people in it were his marks. He devised his own con games. He placed ads in newspapers offering a colour picture of the President for a dollar. When he received a dollar, he sent his victim a postage stamp with a picture of the President on it.

He put announcements in magazines warning

273

the public that there were only sixty days left to send in five dollars, that after that it would be too late. The ad did not specify what the five dollars would buy, but the money poured in.

For three months Jeff worked in a boiler room, selling phony oil stocks over the telephone.

He loved boats, and when a friend offered him a job working on a sailing schooner bound for Tahiti, Jeff signed on as a seaman.

The ship was a beauty, a 165-foot white schooner, glistening in the sun, all sails drawing well. It had teak decking, long, gleaming Oregon fir for the hull, with a main salon that sat twelve and a galley forward, with electric ovens. The crew's quarters were in the forepeak. In addition to the captain, the steward, and a cook, there were five deckhands. Jeff's job consisted of helping hoist the sails, polishing the brass port-holes, and climbing up the ratlines to the lower spreader to mast the sails. The schooner was carrying a party of eight.

'The owner is named Hollander,' Jeff's friend informed him.

Hollander turned out to be Louise Hollander, a twenty-five-year-old, golden-haired beauty, whose father owned half of Central America. The other passengers were her friends, whom Jeff's buddies sneeringly referred to as the 'jest set'.

The first day out Jeff was working in the hot sun, polishing the brass on deck. Louise Hollander stopped beside him.

'You're new on board.'

274

He looked up. 'Yes.'

'Do you have a name?'

'Jeff Stevens.'

'That's a nice name.' He made no comment. 'Do you know who I am?'

'No.'

'I'm Louise Hollander. I own this boat.'

'I see. I'm working for you.'

She gave him a slow smile. 'That's right.'

'Then if you want to get your money's worth, you'd better let me get on with my work.' Jeff moved on to the next stanchion.

In their quarters at night, the crew members disparaged the passengers and made jokes about them. But Jeff admitted to himself that he was envious of them – their backgrounds, their educations, and their easy manners. They had come from monied families and had attended the best schools. *His* school had been Uncle Willie and the carnival.

One of the carnies had been a professor of archaeology until he was thrown out of college for stealing and selling valuable relics. He and Jeff had had long talks, and the professor had imbued Jeff with an enthusiasm for archaeology. 'You can read the whole future of mankind in the past,' the professor would say. 'Think of it, son. Thousands of years ago there were people just like you and me dreaming dreams, spinning tales, living out their lives, giving birth to our ancestors.' His eyes had taken on a faraway look. 'Carthage – that's where

I'd like to go on a dig. Long before Christ was born, it was a great city, the Paris of ancient Africa. The people had their games, and baths, and chariot racing. The Circus Maximus was as large as five football fields.' He had noted the interest in the boy's eyes. 'Do you know how Cato the Elder used to end his speeches in the Roman Senate? He'd say, "*Delenda est cartaga*"; "Carthage must be destroyed". His wish finally came true. The Romans reduced the place to rubble and came back twenty-five years later to build a great city on its ashes. I wish I could take you there on a dig one day, my boy.'

A year later the professor had died of alcoholism, but Jeff had promised himself that one day he would go on a dig. Carthage, first, for the professor.

On the last night before the schooner was to dock in Tahiti, Jeff was summoned to Louise Hollander's stateroom. She was wearing a sheer silk robe.

'You wanted to see me, ma'am?'

'Are you a homosexual, Jeff?'

'I don't believe it's any of your business, Miss Hollander, but the answer is no. What I am is choosy.'

Louise Hollander's mouth tightened. 'What kind of women do you like? Whores, I suppose.'

'Sometimes,' Jeff said agreeably. 'Was there anything else Miss Hollander?'

'Yes. I'm giving a dinner party tomorrow night. Would you like to come?'

Jeff looked at the woman for a long moment before he answered. 'Why not?'

And that was the way it began.

Louise Hollander had had two husbands before she was twenty-one, and her lawyer had just made a settlement with her third husband when she met Jeff. The second night they were moored at the harbour in Papeete, and as the passengers and crew were going ashore, Jeff received another summons to Louise Hollander's quarters. When Jeff arrived, she was dressed in a colourful silk pareu slit all the way up to the thigh.

'I'm trying to get this off,' she said. 'I'm having a problem with the zipper.'

Jeff walked over and examined the costume. 'It doesn't have a zipper.'

She turned to face him, and smiled. 'I know. That's my problem.'

They made love on the deck, where the soft tropical air caressed their bodies like a blessing. Afterwards, they lay on their sides, facing each other. Jeff propped himself up on an elbow and looked down at Louise. 'Your daddy's not the sheriff, is he?' Jeff asked.

She sat up in surprise. 'What?'

'You're the first townie I ever made love to. Uncle Willie used to warn me that their daddies always turned out to be the sheriff.'

They were together every night after that. At first Louise's friends were amused. *He's another*

277

one of Louise's playthings, they thought. But when she informed them that she intended to marry Jeff, they were frantic.

'For Christ's sake, Louise, he's a *nothing*. He worked in a carnival. My God, you might as well be marrying a stable hand. He's handsome – granted. And he has a fab bod. But outside of sex, you have absolutely nothing in common, darling.'

'Louise, Jeff's for breakfast, not *dinner*.'

'You have a social position to uphold.'

'Frankly, angel, he just won't fit in, will he?'

But nothing her friends said could dissuade Louise. Jeff was the most fascinating man she had ever met. She had found that men who were out-standingly handsome were either monumentally stupid or unbearably dull. Jeff was intelligent and amusing, and the combination was irresistible.

When Louise mentioned the subject of marriage to Jeff, he was as surprised as her friends had been.

'Why marriage? You've already got my body. I can't give you anything you don't have.'

'It's very simple, Jeff. I love you. I want to share the rest of my life with you.'

Marriage had been an alien idea, and suddenly it no longer was. Beneath Louise Hollander's worldly, sophisticated veneer, there was a vulner-able, lost little girl. *She needs me*, Jeff thought. The idea of a stable homelife and children was sud-denly immensely appealing. It seemed to him that ever since he could remember, he had been running. It was time to stop.

They were married in the town hall in Tahiti three days later.

When they returned to New York, Jeff was summoned to the office of Scott Fogarty, Louise Hollander's attorney, a small, frigid man, tight-lipped and probably, Jeff thought, tight-assed.

'I have a paper here for you to sign,' the attorney announced.

'What kind of paper?'

'It's a release. It simply states that in the event of the dissolution of your marriage to Louise Hollander –'

'Louise Stevens.'

'– Louise Stevens, that you will not participate financially in any of her –'

Jeff felt the muscles of his jaw tightening. 'Where do I sign?'

'Don't you want me to finish reading?'

'No. I don't think you get the point. I didn't marry her for her fucking money.'

'Really, Mr Stevens! I just –'

'Do you want me to sign it or don't you?'

The lawyer placed the paper in front of Jeff. He scrawled his signature and stormed out of the office. Louise's limousine and driver were waiting for him downstairs. As Jeff climbed in, he had to laugh to himself. *What the hell am I so pissed off about? I've been a con artist all my life, and when*

I go straight for the first time and someone thinks I'm out to take them, I behave like a fucking Sunday school teacher.

Louise took Jeff to the best tailor in Manhattan. 'You'll look fantastic in a dinner jacket,' she coaxed. And he did. Before the second month of the marriage, five of Louise's best friends had tried to seduce the attractive newcomer in their circle, but Jeff ignored them. He was determined to make this marriage work.

Budge Hollander, Louise's brother, put Jeff up for membership in the exclusive New York Pilgrim Club, and Jeff was accepted. Budge was a beefy, middle-aged man who had obtained his sobriquet playing right tackle on the Harvard football team, where he got the reputation of being a player his opponents could not budge. He owned a shipping line, a banana plantation, cattle ranches, a meat-packing company, and more corporations than Jeff could count. Budge Hollander was not subtle in concealing his contempt for Jeff Stevens.

'You're really out of our class, aren't you, old boy? But as long as you amuse Louise in bed, that will do nicely. I'm fond of my sister.'

It took every ounce of willpower for Jeff to control himself. *I'm not married to this prick. I'm married to Louise.*

The other members of the Pilgrim Club were equally obnoxious. They found Jeff terribly amusing.

All of them dined at the club every noontime, and pleaded for Jeff to tell them stories about his 'carnie days', as they liked to call them. Perversely, Jeff made the stories more and more outrageous.

Jeff and Louise lived in a twenty-room townhouse filled with servants, on the East Side of Manhattan. Louise had estates in Long Island and the Bahamas, a villa in Sardinia, and a large apartment on Avenue Foch in Paris. Aside from the yacht, Louise owned a Maserati, a Rolls Corniche, a Lamborghini and a Daimler.

It's fantastic, Jeff thought.

It's great, Jeff thought.

It's boring, Jeff thought. *And degrading.*

One morning he got up from his eighteenth-century four-poster bed, put on a Sulka robe, and went looking for Louise. He found her in the breakfast room.

'I've got to get a job,' he told her.

'For heaven's sake, darling, why? We don't need the money.'

'It has nothing to do with money. You can't expect me to sit around on my hands and be spoon-fed. I have to work.'

Louise gave it a moment's thought. 'All right, angel. I'll speak to Budge. He owns a stockbrokerage firm. Would you like to be a stockbroker, darling?'

'I just want to get off my ass,' Jeff muttered.

* * *

He went to work for Budge. He had never had a job with regular hours before. *I'm going to love it*, Jeff thought.

He hated it. He stayed with it because he wanted to bring home a salary cheque to his wife.

'When are you and I going to have a baby?' he asked Louise, after a lazy Sunday brunch.

'Soon, darling. I'm trying.'

'Come to bed. Let's try again.'

Jeff was seated at the luncheon table reserved for his brother-in-law and half a dozen other captains of industry at the Pilgrim Club.

Budge announced, 'We just issued our annual report for the meat-packing company, fellas. Our profits are up forty percent.'

'Why shouldn't they be?' one of the men at the table laughed. 'You've got the fucking inspectors bribed.' He turned to the others at the table. 'Old clever Budge, here, buys inferior meat and has it stamped prime and sells it for a bloody fortune.'

Jeff was shocked. 'People *eat* meat, for Christ's sake. They feed it to their children. He's kidding, isn't he, Budge?'

Budge grinned and whooped, 'Look who's being moral!'

Over the next three months Jeff became very well acquainted with his table companions. Ed Zeller had paid a million in bribes in order to build a factory in Libya. Mike Quincy, the head of a conglomerate, was a raider who bought companies and illegally tipped off his friends when to buy and sell the stock. Alan Thompson, the richest man at the table, boasted of his company's policy. 'Before they changed the damn law, we used to fire the old grey hairs one year before their pensions were due. Saved a fortune.'

All the men cheated on taxes, had insurance scams, falsified expense accounts, and put their current mistresses on their payroll as secretaries or assistants.

Christ, Jeff thought. *They're just dressed-up carnies. They all run flat stores.*

The wives were no better. They grabbed everything they could get their greedy hands on and cheated on their husbands. *They're playing the key game*, Jeff marvelled.

When he tried to tell Louise how he felt, she laughed. 'Don't be naïve, Jeff. You're enjoying your life, aren't you?'

The truth was that he was not. He had married Louise because he believed she needed him. He felt that children would change everything.

'Let's have one of each. It's time. We've been married a year now.'

'Angel, be patient. I've been to the doctor, and he told me I'm fine. Maybe you should have a checkup and see if *you're* all right.'

Jeff went.

'You should have no trouble producing healthy children,' the doctor assured him.

And still nothing happened.

On Black Monday Jeff's world fell apart. It started in the morning when he went into Louise's medicine chest for an aspirin. He found a shelf full of birth control pills. One of the cases was almost empty. Lying innocently next to it was a vial of white powder and a small golden spoon. And that was only the start of the day.

At noon, Jeff was seated in a deep armchair in the Pilgrim Club, waiting for Budge to appear, when he heard two men behind him talking.

'She swears that her Italian singer's cock is over ten inches long.'

There was a snicker. 'Well, Louise always liked them big.'

They're talking about another Louise, Jeff told himself.

'That's probably why she married that carnival person in the first place. But she does tell the most amusing stories about him. You won't believe what he did the other day . . .'

Jeff rose and blindly made his way out of the club.

He was filled with a rage such as he had never known. He wanted to kill. He wanted to kill the unknown Italian. He wanted to kill Louise. How many other men had she been sleeping with during the past year? They had been laughing at him all this time. Budge and Ed Zeller and Mike Quincy and Alan Thompson and their wives had been having an enormous joke at his expense. And Louise, the woman he had wanted to protect. Jeff's immediate reaction was to pack up and leave. But that was not good enough. He had no intention of letting the bastards have the last laugh.

That afternoon when Jeff arrived home, Louise was not there. 'Madame went out this morning,' Pickens, the butler, said. 'I believe she had several appointments.'

I'll bet she did, Jeff thought. *She's out fucking that ten-inch-cock Italian. Jesus Christ!*

By the time Louise arrived home, Jeff had himself under tight control. 'Did you have a nice day?' Jeff asked.

'Oh, the usual boring things, darling. A beauty appointment, shopping . . . How was your day, angel?'

'It was interesting,' Jeff said truthfully. 'I learned a lot.'

'Budge tells me you're doing beautifully.'

'I am,' Jeff assured her. 'And very soon I'm going to be doing even better.'

Louise stroked his hand. 'My bright husband. Why don't we go to bed early?'

'Not tonight,' Jeff said. 'I have a headache.'

He spent the next week making his plans.

He began at lunch at the club. 'Do any of you know anything about computer frauds?' Jeff asked.

'Why?' Ed Zeller wanted to know. 'You planning to commit one?'

There was a sputter of laughter.

'No, I'm serious,' Jeff insisted. 'It's a big problem. People are tapping into computers and ripping off banks and insurance companies and other businesses for billions of dollars. It gets worse all the time.'

'Sounds right up your alley,' Budge murmured.

'Someone I met has come up with a computer he says can't be tampered with.'

'And you want to have him knocked off,' Mike Quincy kidded.

'As a matter of fact, I'm interested in raising money to back him. I just wondered if any of you might know something about computers.'

'No,' Budge grinned, 'but we know everything about backing inventors, don't we fellas?'

There was a burst of laughter.

Two days later at the club, Jeff passed by the usual table and explained to Budge, 'I'm sorry I won't be able to join you fellows today. I'm having a guest for lunch.'

When Jeff moved to another table, Alan Thompson grinned, 'He's probably having lunch with the bearded lady from the circus.'

A stooped, grey-haired man entered the dining room and was ushered to Jeff's table.

'Jesus!' Mike Quincy said. 'Isn't that Professor Ackerman?'

'Who's Professor Ackerman?'

'Don't you ever read anything but financial reports, Budge? Vernon Ackerman was on the cover of *Time* last month. He's chairman of the President's National Scientific Board. He's the most brilliant scientist in our country.'

'What the hell is he doing with my dear brother-in-law?'

Jeff and the professor were engrossed in a deep conversation all during lunch, and Budge and his friends grew more and more curious. When the professor left, Budge motioned Jeff over to his table.

'Hey, Jeff. Who was that?'

Jeff looked guilty. 'Oh . . . you mean Vernon?'

'Yeah. What were you two talking about?'

'We . . . ah . . .' The others could almost watch Jeff's thought processes as he tried to dodge the question. 'I . . . ah . . . might write a book about him. He's a very interesting character.'

'I didn't know you were a writer.'

'Well, I guess we all have to start sometime.'

Three days later Jeff had another luncheon guest. This time it was Budge who recognized him. 'Hey! That's Seymour Jarrett, chairman of the board of Jarrett International Computer. What the hell would he be doing with Jeff?'

Again, Jeff and his guest held a long, animated conversation. When the luncheon was over, Budge sought Jeff out.

'Jeffrey, boy, what's with you and Seymour Jarrett?'

'Nothing,' Jeff said quickly. 'Just having a chat.' He started to walk away. Budge stopped him.

'Not so fast, old buddy. Seymour Jarrett is a very busy fellow. He doesn't sit around having long chats about nothing.'

Jeff said earnestly, 'All right. The truth is, Budge, that Seymour collects stamps, and I told him about a stamp I might be able to acquire for him.'

The truth, my ass, Budge thought.

The following week, Jeff lunched at the Club with Charles Bartlett, the president of Bartlett & Bartlett, one of the largest private capital venture groups in the world. Budge, Ed Zeller, Alan Thompson, and Mike Quincy watched in fascination as the two men talked, their heads close together.

'Your brother-in-law is sure in high-flying company lately,' Zeller commented. 'What kind of deal has he got cooking, Budge?'

Budge said testily, 'I don't know, but I'm sure in hell going to find out. If Jarrett and Bartlett are interested, there must be a pot of money involved.'

They watched as Bartlett rose, enthusiastically pumped Jeff's hand, and left. As Jeff passed their table, Budge caught his arm. 'Sit down, Jeff. We want to have a little talk with you.'

'I should get back to the office,' Jeff protested. 'I –'

'You work for *me*, remember? Sit down.' Jeff sat. 'Who were you having lunch with?'

Jeff hesitated. 'No one special. An old friend.'

'Charlie Bartlett's an old friend?'

'Kind of.'

'What were you and your old friend Charlie discussing, Jeff?'

'Uh . . . cars, mostly. Old Charlie likes antique cars, and I heard about this '37 Packard, four-door convertible –'

'Cut the horseshit!' Budge snapped. 'You're not collecting stamps or selling cars, or writing any fucking book. What are you really up to?'

'Nothing. I –'

'You're raising money for something, aren't you, Jeff?' Ed Zeller asked.

'No!' But he said it a shade too quickly.

Budge put a beefy arm around Jeff. 'Hey, buddy, this is your brother-in-law. We're family, remember?' He gave Jeff a bear hug. 'It's something about that tamperproof computer you mentioned last week, right?'

They could see by Jeff's face that they had trapped him.

'Well, yes.'

It was like pulling teeth to get anything out of the son of a bitch. 'Why didn't you tell us Professor Ackerman was involved?'

'I didn't think you'd be interested.'

'You were wrong. When you need capital, you go to your friends.'

'The professor and I don't need capital,' Jeff said. 'Jarrett and Bartlett –'

'Jarrett and Bartlett are fuckin' sharks! They'll eat you alive,' Alan Thompson exclaimed.

Ed Zeller picked it up. 'Jeff, when you deal with friends, you don't get hurt.'

'Everything is already arranged,' Jeff told them. 'Charlie Bartlett –'

'Have you signed anything yet?'

'No, but I gave my word –'

'Then *nothing*'s arranged. Hell, Jeff boy, in business people change their minds every hour.'

'I shouldn't even be discussing this with you,' Jeff protested. 'Professor Ackerman's name can't be mentioned. He's under contract to a government agency.'

'We know that,' Thompson said soothingly. 'Does the professor think this thing will work?'

'Oh, he *knows* it works.'

'If it's good enough for Ackerman, it's good enough for us, right fellows?'

There was a chorus of assent.

'Hey, I'm not a scientist,' Jeff said. 'I can't guarantee anything. For all I know, this thing may have no value at all.'

'Sure. We understand. But say it *does* have a value, Jeff. How big could this thing be?'

'Budge, the market for this is worldwide. I couldn't even begin to put a value on it. Everybody will be able to use it.'

'How much initial financing are you looking for?'

'Two million dollars, but all we need is two hundred and fifty thousand dollars down. Bartlett promised –'

'Forget Bartlett. That's chicken feed, old buddy. We'll put that up ourselves. Keep it in the family. Right, fellas?'

'Right!'

Budge looked up and snapped his fingers, and a waiter came hurrying over to the table. 'Dominick, bring Mr Stevens some paper and a pen.'

It was produced almost instantly.

'We can wrap up this little deal right here,' Budge said to Jeff. 'You just make out this paper, giving us the rights, and we'll sign it, and in the morning you'll have a certified cheque for two hundred and fifty thousand dollars. How does that suit you?'

Jeff was biting his lower lip. 'Budge, I promised Mr Barlett –'

'Fuck Barlett,' Budge snarled. 'Are you married to his sister or mine? Now *write*.'

'We don't have a patent on this, and –'

'*Write*, goddamn it!' Budge shoved the pen in Jeff's hand.

Reluctantly, Jeff began to write. 'This will transfer all my rights, title and interest to a mathematical computer called SUCABA, to the buyers, Donald "Budge" Hollander, Ed Zeller, Alan Thompson and Mike Quincy, for the consideration of two million dollars, with a payment of two hundred and fifty thousand dollars on signing. SUCABA has been extensively tested, is inexpensive, trouble-free, and uses less power than any computer currently on the market. SUCABA will require no maintenance or parts for a minimum period of ten years.' They were all looking over Jeff's shoulder as he wrote.

'Jesus!' Ed Zeller said. 'Ten years! There's not a computer on the market that can claim that!'

Jeff continued. 'The buyers understand that neither Professor Vernon Ackerman nor I holds a patent on SUCABA –'

'We'll take care of all that,' Alan Thompson interrupted impatiently. 'I've got one hell of a patent attorney.'

Jeff kept writing. 'I have explained to the buyers that SUCABA may have no value of any kind, and that neither Professor Vernon Ackerman nor I makes any representations or warranties about SUCABA except as written above.' He signed it and held up the paper. 'Is that satisfactory?'

'You sure about the ten years?' Budge asked.

'Guaranteed. I'll just make a copy of this,' Jeff said. They watched as he carefully made a copy of what he had written.

Budge snatched the papers out of Jeff's hand and signed them. Zeller, Quincy and Thompson followed suit.

Budge was beaming. 'A copy for us and a copy for you. Old Seymour Jarrett and Charlie Bartlett are sure going to have egg on their faces, huh, boys? I can't wait until they hear that they got screwed out of this deal.'

The following morning Budge handed Jeff a certified cheque for $250,000.

'Where's the computer?' Budge asked.

'I arranged for it to be delivered here at the club at noon. I thought it only fitting that we should all be together when you receive it.'

Budge clapped him on the shoulder. 'You know, Jeff, you're a smart fellow. See you at lunch.'

At the stroke of noon a messenger carrying a box appeared in the dining room of the Pilgrim Club and was ushered to Budge's table, where he was seated with Zeller, Thompson, and Quincy.

'Here it is!' Budge exclaimed. 'Jesus! The damned thing's even portable.'

'Should we wait for Jeff?' Thompson asked.

'Fuck him. This belongs to us now.' Budge ripped the paper away from the box. Inside was a nest of straw. Carefully, almost reverently, he lifted out the object that lay in the nest. The men sat there, staring at it. It was a square frame about a foot in diameter, holding a series of wires across which were strung rows of beads. There was a long silence.

'What is it?' Quincy finally asked.

Alan Thompson said, 'It's an abacus. One of those things Orientals use to count –' The expression on his face changed. 'Jesus! SUCABA is *abacus* spelled backwards!' He turned to Budge. 'Is this some kind of joke?'

Zeller was sputtering. 'Low power, trouble-free, uses less power than any computer currently on the market . . . Stop the goddamned cheque!'

There was a concerted rush to the telephone.

'Your certified cheque?' the head bookkeeper said. 'There's nothing to worry about. Mr Stevens cashed it this morning.'

Pickens, the butler, was very sorry, indeed, but Mr Stevens had packed and left. 'He mentioned something about an extended journey.'

That afternoon, a frantic Budge finally managed to reach Professor Vernon Ackerman.

'Of course. Jeff Stevens. A charming man. Your brother-in-law, you say?'

'Professor, what were you and Jeff discussing?'

'I suppose it's no secret. Jeff is eager to write a book about me. He has convinced me that the world wants to know the human being behind the scientist . . .'

Seymour Jarrett was reticent. 'Why do you want to know what Mr Stevens and I discussed? Are you a rival stamp collector?'

'No, I –'

'Well, it won't do you any good to snoop around. There's only one stamp like it in existence, and Mr Stevens has agreed to sell it to me when he acquires it.'

And he slammed down the receiver.

Budge knew what Charlie Bartlett was going to say before the words were out. 'Jeff Stevens? Oh, yes.

I collect antique cars. Jeff knows where this '37 Packard four-door convertible in mint condition –'

This time it was Budge who hung up.

'Don't worry,' Budge told his partners. 'We'll get our money back and put the son of a bitch away for the rest of his life. There are laws against fraud.'

The group's next stop was at the office of Scott Fogarty.

'He took us for two hundred and fifty thousand dollars,' Budge told the attorney. 'I want him put behind bars for the rest of his life. Get a warrant out for –'

'Do you have the contract with you, Budge?'

'It's right here.' He handed Fogarty the paper Jeff had written out.

The lawyer scanned it quickly, then read it again, slowly. 'Did he forge your names to this paper?'

'Why, no,' Mike Quincy said. 'We signed it.'

'Did you read it first?'

Ed Zeller angrily said, 'Of course we read it. Do you think we're stupid?'

'I'll let you be the judge of that, gentlemen. You signed a contract stating that you were informed that what you were purchasing with a down payment of two hundred and fifty thousand dollars was an object that had not been patented and could be completely worthless. In the legal parlance of an old professor of mine, "You've been royally fucked."'

*　　*　　*

Jeff had obtained the divorce in Reno. It was while he was establishing residence there that he had run into Conrad Morgan. Morgan had once worked for Uncle Willie. 'How would you like to do me a small favour, Jeff?' Conrad Morgan had asked. 'There's a young lady travelling on a train from New York to St Louis with some jewellery . . .'

Jeff looked out of the plane window and thought about Tracy. There was a smile on his face.

When Tracy returned to New York, her first stop was at Conrad Morgan et Cie Jewellers. Conrad Morgan ushered Tracy into his office and closed the door. He rubbed his hands together and said, 'I was getting very worried, my dear. I waited for you in St Louis and –'

'You weren't in St Louis.'

'What? What do you mean?' His blue eyes seemed to twinkle.

'I mean, you didn't go to St Louis. You never intended to meet me.'

'But of course I did! You have the jewels and I –'

'You sent two men to take them away from me.'

There was a puzzled expression on Morgan's face. 'I don't understand.'

'At first I thought there might be a leak in your organization, but there wasn't, was there? It was you. You told me that you personally arranged for my train ticket, so you were the only one who knew the number of my compartment. I used a different name and a disguise, but your men knew exactly where to find me.'

There was a look of surprise on his cherubic face. 'Are you trying to tell me that some men robbed you of the jewels?'

Tracy smiled. 'I'm trying to tell you that they *didn't*.'

This time the surprise on Morgan's face was genuine. '*You* have the jewels?'

'Yes. Your friends were in such a big hurry to catch a plane that they left them behind.'

Morgan studied Tracy a moment. 'Excuse me.'

He went through a private door, and Tracy sat down on the couch, perfectly relaxed.

Conrad Morgan was gone for almost fifteen minutes, and when he returned, there was a look of dismay on his face. 'I'm afraid a mistake has been made. A *big* mistake. You're a very clever young lady, Miss Whitney. You've earned your twenty-five thousand dollars.' He smiled admiringly. 'Give me the jewels and –'

'Fifty thousand.'

'I beg your pardon?'

'I had to steal them twice. That's fifty thousand dollars, Mr Morgan.'

'No,' he said flatly. His eyes had lost their twinkle. 'I'm afraid I can't give you that much for them.'

Tracy rose. 'That's perfectly all right. I'll try to find someone in Las Vegas who thinks they're worth that.' She moved towards the door.

'Fifty thousand dollars?' Conrad Morgan asked.

Tracy nodded.

'Where are the jewels?'

'In a locker at Penn Station. As soon as you give me the money – in cash – and put me in a taxi, I'll hand you the key.'

Conrad Morgan gave a sigh of defeat. 'You've got a deal.'

'Thank you,' Tracy said cheerfully. 'It's been a pleasure doing business with you.'

NINETEEN

Daniel Cooper was already aware of what the meeting in J. J. Reynolds's office that morning was about, for all the company's investigators had been sent a memo the day before regarding the Lois Bellamy burglary that had taken place a week earlier. Daniel Cooper loathed conferences. He was too impatient to sit around listening to stupid chatter.

He arrived in J. J. Reynolds's office forty-five minutes late, while Reynolds was in the middle of a speech.

'Nice of you to drop by,' J. J. Reynolds said sarcastically. There was no response. *It's a waste of time*, Reynolds decided. Cooper did not understand sarcasm – or anything else, as far as Reynolds was concerned. Except how to catch criminals. There, he had to admit, the man was a goddamned genius.

Seated in the office were three of the agency's top investigators: David Swift, Robert Schiffer, and Jerry Davis.

'You've all read the report on the Bellamy burglary,' Reynolds said, 'but something new has been added. It turns out that Lois Bellamy is a cousin of the police commissioner. He's raising holy hell.'

'What are the police doing?' Davis asked.

'Hiding from the press. Can't blame them. The investigating officers acted like the Keystone Kops. They actually *talked* to the burglar they caught in the house and let her get away.'

'Then they should have a good description of her,' Swift suggested.

'They have a good description of her nightgown,' Reynolds retorted witheringly. 'They were so goddamned impressed with her figure that their brains melted. They don't even know the colour of her hair. She wore some kind of curler cap, and her face was covered with a mudpack. Their description is of a woman somewhere in her middle twenties, with a fantastic ass and tits. There's not one single clue. We have no information to go on. Nothing.'

Daniel Cooper spoke for the first time. 'Yes, we have.'

They all turned to look at him, with varying degrees of dislike.

'What are you talking about?' Reynolds asked.

'I know who she is.'

When Cooper had read the memo the morning before, he had decided to take a look at the Bellamy house, as a logical first step. To Daniel Cooper, logic was the orderliness of God's mind, the basic solution to every problem, and to apply logic, one always started at the beginning. Cooper drove out to the Bellamy estate in Long Island, took one look at it, and, without getting out of his car, turned around and drove back to Manhattan. He had learned all he needed to know. The house was isolated, and there was no public transportation nearby, which meant that the burglar could have reached the house only by car.

He was explaining his reasoning to the men assembled in Reynolds's office. 'Since she probably would have been reluctant to use her own car, which could have been traced, the vehicle either had to be stolen or rented. I decided to try the rental agencies first. I assumed that she would have rented the car in Manhattan, where it would be easier for her to cover her trail.'

Jerry Davis was not impressed. 'You've got to be kidding, Cooper. There must be thousands of cars a day rented in Manhattan.'

Cooper ignored the interruption. 'All car-rental operations are computerized. Relatively few cars are rented by women. I checked them all out. The lady in question went to Budget Rent a Car at Pier Sixty-one on West twenty-third Street, rented a Chevy Caprice at eight P.M. the night of the burglary, and returned it to the office at two A.M.'

'How do you know it was the getaway car?' Reynolds asked sceptically.

Cooper was getting bored with the stupid

questions. 'I checked the elapsed mileage. It's thirty-two miles to the Lois Bellamy estate and another thirty-two miles back. That checks exactly with the odometer on the Caprice. The car was rented in the name of Ellen Branch.'

'A phony,' David Swift surmised.

'Right. Her real name is Tracy Whitney.'

They were all staring at him. 'How the hell do you know that?' Schiffer demanded.

'She gave a false name and address, but she had to sign a rental agreement. I took the original down to One Police Plaza and had them run it through for fingerprints. They matched the prints of Tracy Whitney. She served time at the Southern Louisiana Penitentiary for Women. If you remember, I talked to her about a year ago about a stolen Renoir.'

'I remember,' Reynolds nodded. 'You said then that she was innocent.'

'She was – then. She's not innocent any more. She pulled the Bellamy job.'

The little bastard had done it again! And he had made it seem so simple. Reynolds tried not to sound grudging. 'That's – that's fine work, Cooper. Really fine work. Let's nail her. We'll have the police pick her up and –'

'On what charge?' Cooper asked mildly. 'Renting a car? The police can't identify her, and there's not a shred of evidence against her.'

'What are we supposed to do?' Schiffer asked. 'Let her walk away scot-free?'

'This time, yes,' Cooper said. 'But I know who

302

she is now. She'll try something again. And when she does, I'll catch her.'

The meeting was finally over. Cooper desperately wanted a shower. He took out a little black book and wrote in it very carefully: TRACY WHITNEY.

TWENTY

It's time to begin my new life, Tracy decided. *But what kind of life? I've gone from an innocent, naïve victim to a . . . what? A thief – that's what.* She thought of Joe Romano and Anthony Orsatti and Perry Pope and Judge Lawrence. *No. An avenger. That's what I've become. And an adventuress, perhaps.* She had outwitted the police, two professional con artists, and a double-crossing jeweller. She thought of Ernestine and Amy and felt a pang. On an impulse, Tracy went to F.A.O. Schwarz and bought a puppet theatre, complete with half a dozen characters, and had it mailed to Amy. The card read: SOME NEW FRIENDS FOR YOU. MISS YOU. LOVE TRACY.

Next she visited a furrier on Madison Avenue and bought a blue fox boa for Ernestine and mailed it with a money order for two hundred dollars. The card simply read: THANKS, ERNIE. TRACY.

All my debts are paid now, Tracy thought. It

was a good feeling. She was free to go anywhere she liked, do anything she pleased.

She celebrated her independence by checking into a Tower Suite in The Helmsley Palace Hotel. From her forty-seventh-floor living room, she could look down at St Patrick's Cathedral and see the George Washington Bridge in the distance. Only a few miles in another direction was the dreary place she had recently lived in. *Never again*, Tracy swore.

She opened the bottle of champagne that the management had sent up and sat sipping it, watching the sun set over the skyscrapers of Manhattan. By the time the moon had risen, Tracy had made up her mind. She was going to London. She was ready for all the wonderful things life had to offer. *I've paid my dues*, Tracy thought. *I deserve some happiness.*

She lay in bed and turned on the late television news. Two men were being interviewed. Boris Melnikov was a short, stocky Russian, dressed in an ill-fitting brown suit, and Pietr Negulesco was his opposite, tall and thin and elegant-looking. Tracy wondered what the two men could possibly have in common.

'Where is the chess match going to be held?' the news anchorman asked.

'At Sochi, on the beautiful Black Sea,' Melnikov replied.

'You are both international grand masters, and this one has created quite a stir, gentlemen. In your previous matches you have taken the title from each other, and your last one was a draw. Mr Negulesco, Mr Melnikov currently holds the title. Do you think you will be able to take it away from him again?'

'Absolutely,' the Romanian replied.

'He has no chance,' the Russian retorted.

Tracy knew nothing about chess, but there was an arrogance about both men that she found distasteful. She pressed the remote-control button that turned off the television set and went to sleep.

Early the following morning Tracy stopped at a travel agency and reserved a suite on the Signal Deck of the *Queen Elizabeth II*. She was as excited as a child about her first trip abroad, and spent the next three days buying clothes and luggage.

On the morning of the sailing Tracy hired a limousine to drive her to the pier. When she arrived at Pier 90, Berth 3, at West Fifty-fifth and Twelfth Avenue, where the *QE II* was docked, it was crowded with photographers and television reporters, and for a moment, Tracy was panic-stricken. Then she realized they were interviewing the two men posturing at the foot of the gangplank – Melnikov and Negulesco, the international grand masters. Tracy brushed past them, showed her passport to a ship's officer at the gangplank, and walked up onto the ship. On deck, a steward looked at Tracy's ticket and directed her to her stateroom. It was a lovely suite, with a private terrace. It had been ridiculously expensive, but Tracy decided it was going to be worth it.

She unpacked and then wandered along the corridor. In almost every cabin there were farewell parties going on, with laughter and champagne and conversation. She felt a sudden ache of loneliness. There was no one to see her off, no one for her to care about, no one who cared about her. *That's not true*, Tracy told herself. *Big Bertha wants me.* And she laughed aloud.

She made her way up to the Boat Deck and had no idea of the admiring glances of the men and the envious stares of the women cast her way.

Tracy heard the sound of a deep-throated boat whistle and calls of 'All ashore who's going ashore', and she was filled with a sudden excitement. She was sailing into a completely unknown future. She felt the huge ship shudder as the tugs started to pull it out of the harbour, and she stood among the passengers on the Boat Deck, watching the Statue of Liberty slide out of sight, and then she went exploring.

The *QE II* was a city, more than nine hundred feet long and thirteen storeys high. It had four restaurants, six bars, two ballrooms, two night-clubs, and a 'Golden Door Spa at Sea'. There were scores of shops, four swimming pools, a gymnasium, a golf driving range, a jogging track. *I may never want to leave the ship*, Tracy marvelled.

She had reserved a table upstairs in the Princess Grill, which was smaller and more elegant than the main dining room. She barely had been seated when a familiar voice said, 'Well, hello there!'

She looked up, and there stood Tom Bowers, the bogus FBI man. *Oh, no. I don't deserve this*, Tracy thought.

'What a pleasant surprise. Do you mind if I join you?'

'Very much.'

He slid into the chair across from her and gave her an engaging smile. 'We might as well be friends. After all, we're both here for the same reason, aren't we?'

Tracy had no idea what he was talking about. 'Look, Mr Bowers –'

'Stevens,' he said easily. 'Jeff Stevens.'

'Whatever.' Tracy started to rise.

'Wait. I'd like to explain about the last time we met.'

'There's nothing to explain,' Tracy assured him. 'An idiot child could have figured it out – and did.'

'I owed Conrad Morgan a favour.' He grinned ruefully. 'I'm afraid he wasn't too happy with me.'

There was that same easy, boyish charm that had completely taken her in before. *For God's sake, Dennis, it isn't necessary to put cuffs on her. She's not going to run away . . .*

She said hostilely, 'I'm not too happy with you, either. What are you doing aboard this ship? Shouldn't you be on a riverboat?'

He laughed. 'With Maximilian Pierpont on board, this *is* a riverboat.'

'Who?'

He looked at her in surprise. 'Come on. You mean you really don't know?'

'Know what?'

'Max Pierpont is one of the richest men in the world. His hobby is forcing competitive companies out of business. He loves slow horses and fast women, and he owns a lot of both. He's the last of the big-time spenders.'

'And you intend to relieve him of some of his excess wealth.'

'Quite a lot of it, as a matter of fact.' He was eyeing her speculatively. 'Do you know what you and I should do?'

'I certainly do, Mr Stevens. We should say goodbye.'

And he sat there watching as Tracy got up and walked out of the dining room.

She had dinner in her cabin. As she ate, she wondered what ill fate had placed Jeff Stevens in her path again. She wanted to forget the fear she had felt on that train when she thought she was under arrest. *Well, I'm not going to let him spoil this trip. I'll simply ignore him.*

After dinner Tracy went up on deck. It was a fantastic night, with a magic canopy of stars sprayed against a velvet sky. She was standing at the rail in the moonlight, watching the soft phosphorescence of the waves and listening to the sounds of the night wind, when he moved up beside her.

'You have no idea how beautiful you look

standing there. Do you believe in shipboard romances?'

'Definitely. What I don't believe in is *you*.' She started to walk away.

'Wait. I have some news for you. I just found out that Max Pierpont isn't on board, after all. He cancelled at the last minute.'

'Oh, what a shame. You wasted your fare.'

'Not necessarily.' He eyed her speculatively. 'How would you like to pick up a small fortune on this voyage?'

The man is unbelievable. 'Unless you have a submarine or a helicopter in your pocket, I don't think you'll get away with robbing anyone on this ship.'

'Who said anything about robbing anyone? Have you ever heard of Boris Melnikov or Pietr Negulesco?'

'What if I have?'

'Melnikov and Negulesco are on their way to Russia for a championship match. If I can arrange for you to play the two of them,' Jeff said earnestly, 'we can win a lot of money. It's a perfect setup.'

Tracy was looking at him incredulously. 'If you can arrange for *me* to play the two of them? *That's* your perfect setup?'

'Uh-huh. How do you like it?'

'I love it. There's just one tiny hitch.'

'What's that?'

'I don't play chess.'

He smiled benignly. 'No problem. I'll teach you.'

'You're insane,' Tracy said. 'If you want some

310

advice, you'll find yourself a good psychiatrist. Good night.'

The following morning Tracy literally bumped into Boris Melnikov. He was jogging on the Boat Deck, and as Tracy rounded a corner, he ran into her, knocking her off her feet.

'Watch where you're going,' he growled. And he kept running.

Tracy sat on the deck, looking after him. 'Of all the rude –!' She stood up and brushed herself off.

A steward approached. 'Are you hurt, miss? I saw him –'

'No, I'm fine, thank you.'

Nobody was going to spoil this trip.

When Tracy returned to her cabin, there were six messages to call Mr Jeff Stevens. She ignored them. In the afternoon she swam and read and had a massage, and by the time she went into the bar that evening to have a cocktail before dinner, she was feeling wonderful. Her euphoria was short-lived. Pietr Negulesco, the Romanian, was seated at the bar. When he saw Tracy, he stood up and said, 'May I buy you a drink, beautiful lady?'

Tracy hesitated, then smiled. 'Why, yes, thank you.'

'What would you like?'

'A vodka and tonic, please.'

Negulesco gave the order to the barman and turned back to Tracy. 'I'm Pietr Negulesco.'

'I know.'

'Of course. Everyone knows me. I am the greatest chess player in the world. In my country, I am a national hero.' He leaned close to Tracy, put a hand on her knee, and said, 'I am also a great fuck.'

Tracy thought she had misunderstood him. 'What?'

'I am a great fuck.'

Her first reaction was to throw her drink in his face, but she controlled herself. She had a better idea. 'Excuse me,' she said, 'I have to meet a friend.'

She went to look for Jeff Stevens. She found him in the Princess Grill, but as Tracy started towards his table, she saw that he was dining with a lovely looking blonde with a spectacular figure, dressed in an evening gown that looked as if it had been painted on. *I should have known better*, Tracy thought. She turned and headed down the corridor. A moment later Jeff was at her side.

'Tracy . . . did you want to see me?'

'I don't want to take you away from your . . . dinner.'

'She's dessert,' Jeff said lightly. 'What can I do for you?'

'Were you serious about Melnikov and Negulesco?'

'Absolutely. Why?'

'I think they both need a lesson in manners.'

'So do I. And we'll make money while we teach them.'

'Good. What's your plan?'

'You're going to beat them at chess.'

'I'm serious.'

'So am I.'

'I told you, I don't play chess. I don't know a pawn from a king. I –'

'Don't worry,' Jeff promised her. 'A couple of lessons from me, and you'll slaughter them both.'

'*Both?*'

'Oh, didn't I tell you? You're going to play them simultaneously.'

Jeff was seated next to Boris Melnikov in the Double Down Piano Bar.

'The woman is a fantastic chess player,' Jeff confided to Melnikov. 'She's travelling incognito.'

The Russian grunted. 'Women know nothing about chess. They cannot think.'

'This one does. She says she could beat you easily.'

Boris Melnikov laughed aloud. '*Nobody* beats me – easily or not.'

'She's willing to bet you ten thousand dollars that she can play you and Pietr Negulesco at the same time and get a draw with at least one of you.'

Boris Melnikov choked on his drink. '*What!* That's – that's ridiculous! Play *two* of us at the same time? This – this female *amateur*?'

'That's right. For ten thousand dollars each.'

'I should do it just to teach the stupid idiot a lesson.'

'If you win, the money will be deposited in any country you choose.'

A covetous expression flitted across the Russian's face. 'I've never even heard of this person. And to play the *two* of us! My God, she must be insane.'

'She has the twenty thousand dollars in cash.'

'What nationality is she?'

'American.'

'Ah, that explains it. All rich Americans are crazy, especially their women.'

Jeff started to rise. 'Well, I guess she'll just have to play Pietr Negulesco alone.'

'*Negulesco* is going to play her?'

'Yes, didn't I tell you? She wanted to play the two of you, but if you're afraid . . .'

'*Afraid!* Boris Melnikov *afraid*?' His voice was a roar. 'I will *destroy* her. When is this ridiculous match to take place?'

'She thought perhaps Friday night. The last night out.'

Boris Melnikov was thinking hard. 'The best two out of three?'

'No. Only one game.'

'For ten thousand dollars?'

'That is correct.'

The Russian sighed. 'I do not have that much cash with me.'

'No problem,' Jeff assured him. 'All Miss Whitney really wants is the glory of playing the great Boris Melnikov. If you lose, you give her a personally autographed picture. If you win, you get ten thousand dollars.'

'Who holds the stakes?' There was a sharp note of suspicion in his voice.

'The ship's purser.'

'Very well,' Melnikov decided. 'Friday night. We will start at ten o'clock, promptly.'

'She'll be so pleased,' Jeff assured him.

The following morning Jeff was talking to Pietr Negulesco in the gymnasium, where the two men were working out.

'She's an American?' Pietr Negulesco said. 'I should have known. All Americans are cuckoo.'

'She's a great chess player.'

Pietr Negulesco made a gesture of contempt. 'Great is not good enough. *Best* is what counts. And I am the best.'

'That's why she's so eager to play against you. If you lose, you give her an autographed picture. If you win, you get ten thousand dollars in cash . . .'

'Negulesco does not play amateurs.'

'. . . deposited in any country you like.'

'Out of the question.'

'Well, then, I guess she'll have to play only Boris Melnikov.'

'*What?* Are you saying Melnikov has agreed to play against this woman?'

'Of course. But she was hoping to play you both at once.'

'I've never heard of anything so – so –' Negulesco sputtered, at a loss for words. 'The

315

arrogance! Who is she that she thinks she can defeat the two top chess masters in the world? She must have escaped from some lunatic asylum.'

'She's a little erratic,' Jeff confessed, 'but her money is good. All cash.'

'You said ten thousand dollars for defeating her?'

'That's right.'

'And Boris Melnikov gets the same amount?'

'*If* he defeats her.'

Pietr Negulesco grinned. 'Oh, he will defeat her. And so will I.'

'Just between us, I wouldn't be a bit surprised.'

'Who will hold the stakes?'

'The ship's purser.'

Why should Melnikov be the only one to take money from this woman? thought Pietr Negulesco.

'My friend, you have a deal. Where and when?'

'Friday night. Ten o'clock. The Queen's Room.'

Pietr Negulesco smiled wolfishly. 'I will be there.'

'You mean they *agreed*?' Tracy cried.

'That's right.'

'I'm going to be sick.'

'I'll get you a cold towel.'

Jeff hurried into the bathroom of Tracy's suite, ran cold water on a towel, and brought it back to her. She was lying on the chaise longue. He placed the towel on her forehead. 'How does that feel?'

'Terrible. I think I have a migraine.'

'Have you ever had a migraine before?'

'No.'

'Then you don't have one now. Listen to me, Tracy, it's perfectly natural to be nervous before something like this.'

She leapt up and flung down the towel. 'Something like *this*? There's never *been* anything like this! I'm playing two international master chess players with *one* chess lesson from you and –'

'Two,' Jeff corrected her. 'You have a natural talent for chess.'

'My God, why did I ever let you talk me into this?'

'Because we're going to make a lot of money.'

'I don't want to make a lot of money,' Tracy wailed. 'I want this boat to sink. Why couldn't this be the *Titanic*?'

'Now, just stay calm,' Jeff said soothingly. 'It's going to be –'

'It's going to be a *disaster*! Everyone on this ship is going to be watching.'

'That's exactly the point, isn't it?' Jeff beamed.

Jeff had made all the arrangements with the ship's purser. He had given the purser the stakes to hold – $20,000 in traveller's cheques – and asked him to set up two chess tables for Friday evening. The word spread rapidly throughout the ship, and passengers kept approaching Jeff to ask if the matches were actually going to take place.

'Absolutely,' Jeff assured all who enquired. 'It's incredible. Poor Miss Whitney believes she can win. In fact, she's betting on it.'

'I wonder,' a passenger asked, 'if I might place a small bet?'

'Certainly. As much money as you like. Miss Whitney is asking only ten-to-one odds.'

A million-to-one odds would have made more sense. From the moment the first bet was accepted, the floodgates opened. It seemed that everyone on board, including the engine-room crew and the ship's officers, wanted to place bets on the game. The amounts varied from five dollars to five thousand dollars and every single bet was on the Russian and the Romanian.

The suspicious purser reported to the captain. 'I've never seen anything like it, sir. It's a stampede. Nearly all the passengers have placed wagers. I must be holding two hundred thousand dollars in bets.'

The captain studied him thoughtfully. 'You say Miss Whitney is going to play Melnikov and Negulesco at the same time?'

'Yes, Captain.'

'Have you verified that the two men are really Pietr Negulesco and Boris Melnikov?'

'Oh, yes, of course, sir.'

'There's no chance they would deliberately throw the chess game, is there?'

'Not with *their* egos. I think they'd rather die first. And if they lost to this woman, that's probably exactly what would happen to them when they got home.'

The captain ran his fingers through his hair, a

puzzled frown on his face. 'Do you know anything about Miss Whitney or this Mr Stevens?'

'Not a thing, sir. As far as I can determine, they're travelling separately.'

The captain made his decision. 'It smells like some kind of con game, and ordinarily I would put a stop to it. However, I happen to be a bit of an expert myself, and if there was one thing I'd stake my life on, it's the fact that there is *no* way to cheat at chess. Let the match go on.' He walked over to his desk and withdrew a black leather wallet. 'Put down fifty pounds for me. On the masters.'

By 9:00 Friday evening the Queen's Room was packed with passengers from first class, those who had sneaked in from second and third class, and the ship's officers and members of the crew who were off duty. At Jeff Stevens's request, two rooms had been set up for the tournament. One table was in the centre of the Queen's Room, and the other table was in the adjoining salon. Curtains had been drawn to separate the two rooms.

'So that the players aren't distracted by each other,' Jeff explained. 'And we would like the spectators to remain in whichever room they choose.'

Velvet ropes had been placed around the tables to keep the crowds back. The spectators were about to witness something they were sure they would never see again. They knew nothing about the beautiful young American woman, except that it would be impossible for her – or anyone else –

to play the great Negulesco and Melnikov simultaneously and obtain a draw with either of them.

Jeff introduced Tracy to the two grand masters shortly before the game was to begin. Tracy looked like a Grecian painting in a muted green chiffon Galanos gown which left one shoulder bare. Her eyes seemed tremendous in her pale face.

Pietr Negulesco looked her over carefully. 'Have you won all the national tournaments you have played in?' he asked.

'Yes,' Tracy replied truthfully.

He shrugged. 'I have never heard of you.'

Boris Melnikov was equally rude. 'You Americans do not know what to do with your money,' he said. 'I wish to thank you in advance. My winnings will make my family very happy.'

Tracy's eyes were green jade. 'You haven't won, yet, Mr Melnikov.'

Melnikov's laugh boomed out through the room. 'My dear lady, I don't know who you are, but I know who *I* am. I am the great Boris Melnikov.'

It was 10:00. Jeff looked around and saw that both salons had filled up with spectators. 'It's time for the match to start.'

Tracy sat down across the table from Melnikov and wondered for the hundredth time how she had got herself into this.

'There's nothing to it,' Jeff had assured her. 'Trust me.'

And like a fool she had trusted him. *I must have been out of my mind*, Tracy thought. She was playing the two greatest chess players in the world, and she knew nothing about the game, except what Jeff had spent four hours teaching her.

The big moment had arrived. Tracy felt her legs trembling. Melnikov turned to the expectant crowd and grinned. He made a hissing noise at a steward. 'Bring me a brandy. Napoleon.'

'In order to be fair to everyone,' Jeff said to Melnikov, 'I suggest you play the white so that you go first, and in the game with Mr Negulesco, Miss Whitney will play the white and she will go first.'

Both grand masters agreed.

While the audience stood hushed, Boris Melnikov reached across the board and played the queen's gambit decline opening, moving his queen's pawn two squares. *I'm not simply going to beat this woman. I'm going to crush her.*

He glanced up at Tracy. She studied the board, nodded, and stood up, without moving a piece. A steward cleared the way through the crowd as Tracy walked into the second salon, where Pietr Negulesco was seated at a table waiting for her. There were at least a hundred people crowding the room as Tracy took her seat opposite Negulesco.

'Ah, my little pigeon. Have you defeated Boris yet?' Pietr Negulesco laughed uproariously at his joke.

'I'm working on it, Mr Negulesco,' Tracy said quietly.

She reached forward and moved her white queen's pawn two squares. Negulesco looked up at her and grinned. He had arranged for a massage in one hour, but he planned to finish this game before then. He reached down and moved his black queen's pawn two squares. Tracy studied the board a moment, then rose. The steward escorted her back to Boris Melnikov.

Tracy sat down at the table and moved her black queen's pawn two squares. In the background she saw Jeff's almost imperceptible nod of approval.

Without hesitation, Boris Melnikov moved his white queen's bishop pawn two squares.

Two minutes later, at Negulesco's table, Tracy moved her white queen's bishop two squares.

Negulesco played his king's pawn square.

Tracy rose and returned to the room where Boris Melnikov was waiting. Tracy played her king's pawn square.

So! She is not a complete amateur, Melnikov thought in surprise. *Let us see what she does with this.* He played his queen's knight to queen's bishop 3.

Tracy watched his move, nodded, and returned to Negulesco, where she copied Melnikov's move.

Negulesco moved the queen's bishop pawn two squares, and Tracy went back to Melnikov and repeated Negulesco's move.

With growing astonishment, the two grand masters realized they were up against a brilliant opponent. No matter how clever their moves, this amateur managed to counteract them.

Because they were separated, Boris Melnikov and

Pietr Negulesco had no idea that, in effect, they were playing against each other. Every move that Melnikov made with Tracy, Tracy repeated with Negulesco. And when Negulesco countered with a move, Tracy used that move against Melnikov.

By the time the grand masters entered the middle game, they were no longer smug. They were fighting for their reputations. They paced the floor while they contemplated moves and puffed furiously on cigarettes. Tracy appeared to be the only calm one.

In the beginning, in order to end the game quickly, Melnikov had tried a knight's sacrifice to allow his white bishop to put pressure on the black king's side. Tracy had carried the move to Negulesco. Negulesco had examined the move carefully, then refuted the sacrifice by covering his exposed side, and when Negulesco had sacked a bishop to advance a rook to white's seventh rank, Melnikov had refuted it before the black rook could damage his own structure.

There was no stopping Tracy. The game had been going on for four hours, and not one person in either audience had stirred.

Every grand master carries in his head hundreds of games played by other grand masters. It was as this particular match was going into the end game that both Melnikov and Negulesco recognized the hallmark of the other.

The bitch, Melnikov thought. *She has studied with Negulesco. He has tutored her.*

And Negulesco thought, *She is Melnikov's pro-tégée. The bastard has taught her his game.*

The harder they fought Tracy, the more they came to realize there was simply no way they could beat her. The match was appearing drawish.

In the sixth hour of play, at 4:00 A.M., when the players had reached the end game, the pieces on each board had been reduced to three pawns, one rook and a king. There was no way for either side to win. Melnikov studied the board for a long time, then took a deep, choked breath and said, 'I offer a draw.'

Over the hubbub, Tracy said, 'I accept.'

The crowd went wild.

Tracy rose and made her way through the crowd into the next room. As she started to take her seat, Negulesco, in a strangled voice said, 'I offer a draw.'

And the uproar from the other room was repeated. The crowd could not believe what it had just witnessed. A woman had come out of nowhere to simultaneously stalemate the two greatest chess masters in the world.

Jeff appeared at Tracy's side. 'Come on,' he grinned. 'We both need a drink.'

When they left, Boris Melnikov and Pietr Negulesco were still slumped in their chairs, mind-lessly staring at their boards.

Tracy and Jeff sat at a table for two in the Upper Deck bar.

'You were beautiful,' Jeff laughed. 'Did you

notice the look on Melnikov's face? I thought he was going to have a heart attack.'

'I thought *I* was going to have a heart attack,' Tracy said. 'How much did we win?'

'About two hundred thousand dollars. We'll collect it from the purser in the morning when we dock at Southampton. I'll meet you for breakfast in the dining room.'

'Fine.'

'I think I'll turn in now. Let me walk you to your stateroom.'

'I'm not ready to go to bed yet, Jeff. I'm too excited. You go ahead.'

'You were a champion,' Jeff told her. He leaned over and kissed her lightly on the cheek. 'Good night, Tracy.'

'Good night, Jeff.'

She watched him leave. Go to sleep? Impossible! It had been one of the most fantastic nights of her life. The Russian and the Romanian had been so sure of themselves, so arrogant. Jeff had said, 'Trust me', and she had. She had no illusions about what he was. He was a con artist. He was bright and amusing and clever, easy to be with. But of course she could never be seriously interested in him.

Jeff was on the way to his stateroom when he encountered one of the ship's officers.

'Good show, Mr Stevens. The word about the match has already gone out over the wireless. I imagine the press will be meeting you both at

Southampton. Are you Miss Whitney's manager?'

'No, we're just shipboard acquaintances,' Jeff said easily, but his mind was racing. If he and Tracy were linked together, it would look like a setup. There could even be an investigation. He decided to collect the money before any suspicions were aroused.

Jeff wrote a note to Tracy. HAVE PICKED UP MONEY AND WILL MEET YOU FOR A CELEBRATION BREAKFAST AT THE SAVOY HOTEL. YOU WERE MAGNIFICENT. JEFF. He sealed it in an envelope and handed it to a steward. 'Please see that Miss Whitney gets this first thing in the morning.'

'Yes, sir.'

Jeff headed for the purser's office.

'Sorry to bother you,' Jeff apologized, 'but we'll be docking in a few hours, and I know how busy you're going to be, so I wondered whether you'd mind paying me off now?'

'No trouble at all,' the purser smiled. 'Your young lady is really wizard, isn't she?'

'She certainly is.'

'If you don't mind my asking, Mr Stevens, where in the world did she learn to play chess like that?'

Jeff leaned close and confided, 'I heard she studied with Bobby Fischer.'

The purser took two large manila envelopes out of the safe. 'This is a lot of cash to carry around. Would you like me to give you a cheque for this amount?'

'No, don't bother. The cash will be fine,' Jeff assured him. 'I wonder if you could do me a favour? The mail boat comes out to meet the ship before it docks, doesn't it?'

'Yes, sir. We're expecting it at six A.M.'

'I'd appreciate it if you could arrange for me to leave on the mail boat. My mother is seriously ill, and I'd like to get to her before it's' – his voice dropped – 'before it's too late.'

'Oh, I'm dreadfully sorry, Mr Stevens. Of course I can handle that for you. I'll make the arrangements with customs.'

At 6:15 A.M. Jeff Stevens, with the two envelopes carefully stashed away in his suitcase, climbed down the ship's ladder into the mail boat. He turned to take one last look at the outline of the huge ship towering above him. The passengers on the liner were sound asleep. Jeff would be on the dock long before the *QE II* landed. 'It was a beautiful voyage,' Jeff said to one of the crewmen on the mail boat.

'Yes, it was, wasn't it?' a voice agreed.

Jeff turned around. Tracy was seated on a coil of rope, her hair blowing softly around her face.

'Tracy! What are you doing here?'

'What do you think I'm doing?'

He saw the expression on her face. 'Wait a minute! You didn't think I was going to run out on you?'

'Why would I think that?' Her tone was bitter.

'Tracy, I left a note for you. I was going to meet you at the Savoy and –'

'Of course you were,' she said cuttingly. 'You never give up, do you?'

He looked at her, and there was nothing more for him to say.

In Tracy's suite at the Savoy, she watched carefully as Jeff counted out the money. 'Your share comes to one hundred and one thousand dollars.'

'Thank you.' Her tone was icy.

Jeff said, 'You know, you're wrong about me, Tracy. I wish you'd give me a chance to explain. Will you have dinner with me tonight?'

She hesitated, then added. 'All right.'

'Good. I'll pick you up at eight o'clock.'

When Jeff Stevens arrived at the hotel that evening and asked for Tracy, the room clerk said, 'I'm sorry, sir. Miss Whitney checked out early this afternoon. She left no forwarding address.'

TWENTY-ONE

It was the handwritten invitation, Tracy decided later, that changed her life.

After collecting her share of the money from Jeff Stevens, Tracy checked out of the Savoy and moved into 47 Park Street, a quiet, semi-residential hotel with large, pleasant rooms and superb service.

On her second day in London the invitation was delivered to her suite by the hall porter. It was written in a fine, copperplate handwriting: 'A mutual friend has suggested that it might be advantageous for us to become acquainted. Won't you join me for tea at the Ritz this afternoon at 4:00? If you will forgive the cliché, I will be wearing a red carnation.' It was signed 'Gunther Hartog'.

Tracy had never heard of him. Her first inclination was to ignore the note, but her curiosity got the better of her, and at 4:15 she was at the entrance of the elegant dining hall of the Ritz Hotel. She noticed him immediately. He was in his sixties, Tracy guessed, an interesting-looking man with a lean, intellectual face. His skin was smooth and clear, almost translucent. He was dressed in an expensively tailored grey suit and wore a red carnation in his lapel.

As Tracy walked towards his table, he rose and bowed slightly. 'Thank you for accepting my invitation.'

He seated her with an old-fashioned gallantry that Tracy found attractive. He seemed to belong to another world. Tracy could not imagine what on earth he wanted with her.

'I came because I was curious,' Tracy confessed, 'but are you sure you haven't confused me with some other Tracy Whitney?'

Gunther Hartog smiled. 'From what I have heard, there is only one Tracy Whitney.'

'What exactly have you heard?'

'Shall we discuss that over tea?'

Tea consisted of finger sandwiches, filled with chopped egg, salmon, cucumber, watercress and chicken. There were hot scones with clotted cream and jam, and freshly made pastries, accompanied by Twinings tea. As they ate, they talked.

'Your note mentioned a mutual friend,' Tracy began.

'Conrad Morgan. I do business with him from time to time.'

I did business with him once, Tracy thought grimly. *And he tried to cheat me.*

'He's a great admirer of yours,' Gunther Hartog was saying.

Tracy looked at her host more closely. He had the bearing of an aristocrat and the look of wealth. *What does he want with me?* Tracy wondered again. She decided to let him pursue the subject, but there was no further mention of Conrad Morgan or of what possible mutual benefit there could be between Gunther Hartog and Tracy Whitney.

Tracy found the meeting enjoyable and intriguing. Gunther told her about his background. 'I was born in Munich. My father was a banker. He was wealthy, and I'm afraid I grew up rather spoiled, surrounded by beautiful paintings and antiques. My mother was Jewish, and when Hitler came to power, my father refused to desert my mother, and so he was stripped of everything. They were both killed in the bombings. Friends smuggled me out of Germany to Switzerland, and when the war was over, I decided not to return to Germany. I moved to London and opened a small antique shop on Mount Street. I hope that you will visit it one day.'

That's what this is all about, Tracy thought in surprise. *He wants to sell me something.*

As it turned out, she was wrong.

As Gunther Hartog was paying the bill, he said, casually, 'I have a little country house in Hampshire. I'm having a few friends down for the weekend, and I'd be delighted if you would join us.'

Tracy hesitated. The man was a complete

stranger, and she still had no idea what he wanted from her. She decided she had nothing to lose.

The weekend turned out to be fascinating. Gunther Hartog's 'little country house' was a beautiful seventeenth-century manor home on a thirty-acre estate. Gunther was a widower, and except for his servants, he lived alone. He took Tracy on a tour of the grounds. There was a barn stabling half a dozen horses, and a yard where he raised chickens and pigs.

'That's so we'll never go hungry,' he said gravely. 'Now, let me show you my real hobby.'

He led Tracy to a cote full of pigeons. 'These are homing pigeons.' Gunther's voice was filled with pride. 'Look at these little beauties. See that slate-grey one over there? That's Margo.' He picked her up and held her. 'You really are a dreadful girl, do you know that? She bullies the others, but she's the brightest.' He gently smoothed the feathers over the small head and carefully set her down.

The colours of the birds were spectacular. There was a variety of blue-black, blue-grey with checked patterns, and silver.

'But no white ones,' Tracy noticed.

'Homing pigeons are never white,' Gunther explained, 'because white feathers come off too easily, and when pigeons are homing, they fly at an average of forty miles an hour.'

Tracy watched Gunther as he fed the birds a special racing feed with added vitamins.

'They are an amazing species,' Gunther said. 'Do you know they can find their way home from over five hundred miles away?'

'That's fascinating.'

The guests were equally fascinating. There was a cabinet minister, with his wife; an earl; a general and his girlfriend; and the Maharani of Morvi, a very attractive, friendly young woman. 'Please call me V. J.,' she said, in an almost unaccented voice. She wore a deep-red sari shot with golden threads, and the most beautiful jewels Tracy had ever seen.

'I keep most of my jewellery in a vault,' V. J. explained. 'There are so many robberies these days.'

On Sunday afternoon, shortly before Tracy was to return to London, Gunther invited her into his study. They sat across from each other over a tea tray. As Tracy poured the tea into the wafer-thin Belleek cups, she said, 'I don't know why you invited me here, Gunther, but whatever the reason, I've had a wonderful time.'

'I'm pleased, Tracy.' Then, after a moment, he continued. 'I've been observing you.'

'I see.'

'Do you have any plans for the future?'

She hesitated. 'No. I haven't decided what I'm going to do yet.'

'I think we could work well together.'

'You mean in your antique shop?'

He laughed. 'No, my dear. It would be a shame

to waste your talents. You see, I know about your escapade with Conrad Morgan. You handled it brilliantly.'

'Gunther . . . all that's behind me.'

'But what's ahead of you? You said you have no plans. You must think about your future. Whatever money you have is surely going to run out one day. I'm suggesting a partnership. I travel in very affluent, international circles. I attend charity balls and hunting parties and yachting parties. I know the comings and goings of the rich.'

'I don't see what that has to do with me –'

'I can introduce you into that golden circle. And I do mean golden, Tracy. I can supply you with information about fabulous jewels and paintings, and how you can safely acquire them. I can dispose of them privately. You would be balancing the ledgers of people who have become wealthy at the expense of others. Everything would be divided evenly between us. What do you say?'

'I say no.'

He studied her thoughtfully. 'I see. You will call me if you change your mind?'

'I won't change my mind, Gunther.'

Late that afternoon Tracy returned to London.

Tracy adored London. She dined at Le Gavroche and Bill Bentley's and Coin du Feu, and went to Drones after the theatre, for real American hamburgers and hot chili. She went to the National Theatre and the Royal Opera House and attended auctions at Christie's and Sotheby's. She shopped at Harrods, and Fortnum and Mason's, and browsed for books at Hatchards and Foyles, and W. H. Smith. She hired a car and driver and spent a memorable weekend at the Chewton Glen Hotel in Hampshire, on the fringe of the New Forest, where the setting was spectacular and the service impeccable.

But all these things were expensive. *Whatever money you have is sure to run out some day.* Gunther Hartog was right. Her money was not going to last forever, and Tracy realized she would have to make plans for the future.

She was invited back for more weekends at Gunther's country home, and she thoroughly enjoyed each visit and delighted in Gunther's company.

One Sunday evening at dinner a member of Parliament turned to Tracy and said, 'I've never met a real Texan, Miss Whitney. What are they like?'

Tracy went into a wicked imitation of a noveau riche Texas dowager and had the company roaring with laughter.

Later, when Tracy and Gunther were alone, he asked, 'How would you like to make a small fortune doing that imitation?'

'I'm not an actress, Gunther.'

'You underestimate yourself. There's a jewellery firm in London – Parker and Parker – that takes a delight in – as you Americans would say – ripping off their customers. You've given me an idea how to make them pay for their dishonesty.' He told Tracy his idea.

'No,' Tracy said. But the more she thought about it, the more intrigued she was. She remembered the excitement of outwitting the police in Long Island, and Boris Melnikov and Pietr Negulesco, and Jeff Stevens. It had been a thrill that was indescribable. Still, that was part of the past.

'No, Gunther,' she said again. But this time there was less certainty in her voice.

London was unseasonably warm for October, and Englishmen and tourists alike took advantage of the bright sunshine. The noon traffic was heavy with hold-ups at Trafalgar Square, Charing Cross, and Piccadilly Circus. A white Daimler turned off Oxford Street to New Bond Street and threaded its way through the traffic, passing Roland Cartier, Geigers, and the Royal Bank of Scotland. A few doors further on, it coasted to a stop in front of a jewellery shop. A discreet, polished sign at the side of the door read: PARKER & PARKER. A liveried chauffeur stepped out of the limousine and hurried around to open the rear door for his passenger. A young woman with blonde Sassooned hair, wearing far too much makeup and a tight-fitting Italian knit dress under a sable coat, totally inappropriate for the weather, jumped out of the car.

'Which way's the joint, junior?' she asked. Her voice was loud, with a grating Texas accent.

The chauffeur indicated the entrance. 'There, madame.'

'Okay, honey. Stick around. This ain't gonna take long.'

'I may have to circle the block, madame. I won't be permitted to park here.'

She clapped him on the back and said, 'You do what you gotta do, sport.'

Sport! The chauffeur winced. It was his punishment for being reduced to chauffeuring rental cars. He disliked all Americans, particularly Texans. They were savages; but savages with money. He would have been astonished to learn that his passenger had never even seen the Lone Star State.

Tracy checked her reflection in the display window, smiled broadly, and strutted towards the door, which was opened by a uniformed attendant.

'Good afternoon, madame.'

'Afternoon, sport. You sell anythin' besides costume jewellery in this joint?' She chuckled at her joke.

The doorman blanched. Tracy swept into the shop, trailing an overpowering scent of Chloé behind her.

Arthur Chilton, a salesman in a morning coat, moved towards her. 'May I help you, madame?'

'Maybe, maybe not. Old P. J. told me to buy myself a little birthday present, so here I am. Whatcha got?'

'Is there something in particular Madame is interested in?'

'Hey, pardner, you English fellows are fast workers, ain'cha?' She laughed raucously and clapped him on the shoulder. He forced himself to remain impassive. 'Mebbe somethin' in emeralds. Old P. J. loves to buy me emeralds.'

'If you'll step this way, please . . .'

Chilton led her to a vitrine where several trays of emeralds were displayed.

The bleached blonde gave them one disdainful glance. 'These're the babies. Where are the mamas and papas?'

Chilton said stiffly, 'These range in price up to thirty thousand dollars.'

'Hell, I tip my hairdresser that.' The woman guffawed. 'Old P. J. would be insulted if I came back with one of them little pebbles.'

Chilton visualized old P. J. Fat and paunchy and as loud and obnoxious as this woman. They deserved each other. *Why did money always flow to the undeserving?* he wondered.

'What price range was Madame interested in?'

'Why don't we start with somethin' around a hundred G's.'

He looked blank. 'A hundred G's?'

'Hell, I thought you people was supposed to speak the king's English. A hundred grand. A hundred thou.'

He swallowed. 'Oh. In that case, perhaps it would be better if you spoke with our managing director.'

The managing director, Gregory Halston,

insisted on personally handling all large sales, and since the employees of Parker & Parker received no commission, it made no difference to them. With a customer as distasteful as this one, Chilton was relieved to let Halston deal with her. Chilton pressed a button under the counter, and a moment later a pale, reedy-looking man bustled out of a back room. He took a look at the outrageously dressed blonde and prayed that none of his regular customers appeared until the woman had departed.

Chilton said, 'Mr Halston, this is Mrs . . . er . . . ?' He turned to the woman.

'Benecke, honey. Mary Lou Benecke. Old P. J. Benecke's wife. Betcha you all have heard of P. J. Benecke.'

'Of course.' Gregory Halston gave her a smile that barely touched his lips.

'Mrs Benecke is interested in purchasing an emerald, Mr Halston.'

Gregory Halston indicated the trays of emeralds. 'We have some fine emeralds here that –'

'She wanted something for approximately a hundred thousand dollars.'

This time the smile that lit Gregory Halston's face was genuine. What a nice way to start the day.

'You see, it's my birthday, and old P. J. wants me to buy myself somethin' pretty.'

'Indeed,' Halston said. 'Would you follow me, please?'

'You little rascal, what you got in mind?' The blonde giggled.

Halston and Chilton exchanged a pained look. *Bloody Americans!*

Halston led the woman to a locked door and opened it with a key. They entered a small, brightly lit room, and Halston carefully locked the door behind them.

'This is where we keep our merchandise for our valued customers,' he said.

In the centre of the room was a showcase filled with a stunning array of diamonds, rubies and emeralds, flashing their bright colours.

'Well, this is more like it. Old P. J.'d go crazy in here.'

'Does Madame see something she likes?'

'Well, let's jest see what we got here.' She walked over to the jewellery case containing emeralds. 'Let me look at that there bunch.'

Halston extracted another small key from his pocket, unlocked the case, lifted out a tray of emeralds, and placed it on top of the table. There were ten emeralds in the velvet case. Halston watched as the woman picked up the largest of them, an exquisite pin in a platinum setting.

'As old P. J. would say, "This here one's got my name writ on it."'

'Madame has excellent taste. This is a ten-carat grass-green Colombian. It's flawless and –'

'Emeralds ain't never flawless.'

Halston was taken aback for an instant. 'Madame

is correct, of course. What I meant was –' For the first time he noticed that the woman's eyes were as green as the stone she twisted in her hands, turning it around, studying its facets.

'We have a wider selection if –'

'No sweat, sweetie. I'll take this here one.'

The sale had taken fewer than three minutes.

'Splendid,' Halston said. Then he added delicately, 'In dollars it comes to one hundred thousand. How will Madame be paying?'

'Don't you worry, Ralston, old sport, I have a dollar account at a bank here in London. I'll write out a little ol personal cheque. Then P. J. can jest pay me back.'

'Excellent. I'll have the stone cleaned for you and delivered to your hotel.'

The stone did not need cleaning, but Halston had no intention of letting it out of his possession until her cheque had cleared, for too many jewellers he knew had been bilked by clever swindlers. Halston prided himself on the fact that he had never been cheated out of one pound.

'Where shall I have the emerald delivered?'

'We got ourselves the Oliver Messel Suite at the Dorch.'

Halston made a note. 'The Dorchester.'

'I call it the Oliver *Messy* Suite,' she laughed. 'Lots of people don't like the hotel any more because it's full of A-rabs, but old P. J. does a lot of business with them. "Oil is its own country", he always says. P. J. Benecke's one smart fella.'

'I'm sure he is,' Halston replied dutifully.

He watched as she tore out a cheque and began writing. He noted that it was a Barclays Bank cheque. Good. He had a friend there who would verify the Beneckes' account.

He picked up the cheque. 'I'll have the emerald delivered to you personally tomorrow morning.'

'Old P. J.'s gonna love it,' she beamed.

'I am sure he will,' Halston said politely.

He walked her to the front door.

'Ralston –'

He almost corrected her, then decided against it. Why bother? He was never going to lay eyes on her again, thank God! 'Yes, madame?'

'You gotta come up and have tea with us some afternoon. You'll love old P. J.'

'I am sure I would. Unfortunately, I work afternoons.'

'Too bad.'

He watched as his customer walked out to the kerb. A white Daimler slithered up, and a chauffeur got out and opened the door for her. The blonde turned to give Halston the thumbs-up sign as she drove off.

When Halston returned to his office, he immediately picked up the telephone and called his friend at Barclays. 'Peter, dear, I have a cheque here for a hundred thousand dollars drawn on the account of a Mrs Mary Lou Benecke. Is it good?'

'Hold on, old boy.'

Halston waited. He hoped the cheque was good,

for business had been slow lately. The miserable Parker brothers, who owned the store, were constantly complaining, as though it were he who was responsible for the recession. Of course, profits were not down as much as they *could* have been, for Parker & Parker had a department that specialized in cleaning jewellery, and at frequent intervals the jewellery that was returned to the customer was inferior to the original that had been brought in. Complaints had been lodged, but nothing had ever been proven.

Peter was back on the line. 'No problem, Gregory. There's more than enough money in the account to cover the cheque.'

Halston felt a little frisson of relief. 'Thank you, Peter.'

'Not at all.'

'Lunch next week – on me.'

The cheque cleared the following morning, and the Colombian emerald was delivered by bonded messenger to Mrs P. J. Benecke at the Dorchester Hotel.

That afternoon, shortly before closing time, Gregory Halston's secretary said, 'A Mrs Benecke is here to see you, Mr Halston.'

His heart sank. She had come to return the pin, and he could hardly refuse to take it back. *Damn all women, all Americans, and all Texans!* Halston put on a smile and went out to greet her.

'Good afternoon, Mrs Benecke. I assume your husband didn't like the pin.'

'You assume wrong, buster. Old P. J. was just plain crazy about it.'

Halston's heart began to sing. 'He was?'

'In fact, he liked it so much he wants me to get another one so we can have 'em made into a pair of earrings. Let me have a twin to the one I got.'

A small frown appeared on Gregory Halston's face. 'I'm afraid we might have a little problem there, Mrs Benecke.'

'What kinda problem, honey?'

'Yours is a unique stone. There's not another one like it. Now, I have a lovely set in a different style I could –'

'I don't want a different style. I want one jest like the one I bought.'

'To be perfectly candid, Mrs Benecke, there aren't very many ten-carat Colombian flawless' – he saw her look – '*nearly* flawless stones available.'

'Come on, sport. There's gotta be one somewhere.'

'In all honesty, I've seen very few stones of that quality, and to try to duplicate it exactly in shape and colour would be almost impossible.'

'We got a sayin' in Texas that the impossible jest takes a little longer. Saturday's my birthday. P. J. wants me to have those earrings, and what P. J. wants, P. J. gets.'

'I don't think I can –'

'How much did I pay for that pin – a hundred grand? I know old P. J. will go up to two hundred or three hundred thousand for another one.'

344

Gregory Halston was thinking fast. There *had* to be a duplicate of that stone somewhere, and if P. J. Benecke was willing to pay an extra $200,000 for it, that would mean a tidy profit. *In fact*, Halston thought, *I can work it out so that it means a tidy profit for me.*

Aloud he said, 'I'll enquire around, Mrs Benecke. I'm sure that no other jeweller in London has the identical emerald, but there are always estates coming up for auction. I'll do some advertising and see what results I get.'

'You got till the end of the week,' the blonde told him. 'And jest between you and me and the lamp-post, old P. J. will probably be willin' to go up to three hundred and fifty thousand for it.'

And Mrs Benecke was gone, her sable coat billowing out behind her.

Gregory Halston sat in his office in a daydream. Fate had placed in his hands a man who was so besotted with his blonde tart that he was willing to pay $350,000 for a $100,000 emerald. That was a net profit of $250,000. Gregory Halston saw no need to burden the Parker brothers with the details of the transaction. It would be a simple matter to record the sale of the second emerald at $100,000 and pocket the rest. The extra $250,000 would set him up for life.

All he had to do now was to find a twin to the emerald he had sold to Mrs P. J. Benecke.

It turned out to be even more difficult than

Halston had anticipated. None of the jewellers he telephoned had anything in stock that resembled what he required. He placed advertisements in the London *Times* and the *Financial Times*, and he called Christie's and Sotheby's, and a dozen estate agents. In the next few days Halston was inundated with a flood of inferior emeralds, good emeralds, and a few first-quality emeralds, but none of them came close to what he was looking for.

On Wednesday Mrs Benecke telephoned. 'Old P. J.'s gettin' mighty restless,' she warned. 'Did you find it yet?'

'Not yet, Mrs Benecke,' Halston assured her, 'but don't worry, we will.'

On Friday she telephoned again. 'Tomorrow's my birthday,' she reminded Halston.

'I know, Mrs Benecke. If I only had a few more days, I know I could –'

'Well, never mind sport. If you don't have that emerald by tomorrow mornin', I'll return the one I bought from you. Old P. J. – bless his heart – says he's gonna buy me a big ol country estate instead. Ever hear of a place called Sussex?'

Halston broke out in perspiration, 'Mrs Benecke,' he moaned earnestly, 'you would *hate* living in Sussex. You would loathe living in a country house. Most of them are in deplorable condition. They have no central heating and –'

'Between you and I,' she interrupted, 'I'd rather have them earrings. Old P. J. even mentioned somethin' about bein' willin' to pay four hundred

346

thousand dollars for a twin to that stone. You got no idea how stubborn old P. J. can be.'

Four hundred thousand! Halston could feel the money slipping between his fingers. 'Believe me, I'm doing everything I can,' he pleaded. 'I need a little more time.'

'It ain't up to me, honey,' she said. 'It's up to P. J.'

And the line went dead.

Halston sat there cursing fate. Where could he find an identical ten-carat emerald? He was so busy with his bitter thoughts that he did not hear his intercom until the third buzz. He pushed down the button and snapped, 'What is it?'

'There's a Contessa Marissa on the telephone, Mr Halston. She's calling about our advertisement for the emerald.'

Another one! He had had at least ten calls that morning, every one of them a waste of time. He picked up the telephone and said ungraciously, 'Yes?'

A soft female voice with an Italian accent said, '*Buon giorno, signore.* I have read you are interested possibly in buying an emerald, *sì*?'

'If it's my qualifications, yes.' He could not keep the impatience out of his voice.

'I have an emerald that has been in my family for many years. It is a *peccato* – a pity – but I am in a situation now where I am forced to sell it.'

He had heard *that* story before. *I must try*

Christie's again, Halston thought. *Or Sotheby's. Maybe something came in at the last minute, or –*

'*Signore?* You are looking for a ten-carat emerald, *sì?*'

'Yes.'

'I have a ten-carat *verde* – green – Colombian.'

When Halston started to speak, he found that his voice was choked. 'Would – would you say that again, please?'

'*Sì*. I have a ten-carat grass-green Colombian. Would you be interested in that?'

'I might be,' he said carefully. 'I wonder if you could drop by and let me have a look at it.'

'No, *scusi*, I am afraid I am very busy right now. We are preparing a party at the embassy for my husband. Perhaps next week I could –'

No! Next week would be too late. 'May I come to see you?' He tried to keep the eagerness out of his voice. 'I could come up now.'

'*Ma, no. Sono occupata stamani.* I was planning to go shopping –'

'Where are you staying, Contessa?'

'At the Savoy.'

'I can be there in fifteen minutes. *Ten.*' His voice was feverish.

'*Molto bene*. And your name is –'

'Halston. Gregory Halston.'

'Suite *ventisei* – twenty-six.'

The taxi ride was interminable. Halston transported himself from the heights to the depths of hell, and back again. If the emerald was indeed similar to the other one, he would be wealthy beyond his wildest dreams. *Four hundred thousand dollars, he'll pay.* A $300,000 profit. He would buy a place on the Riviera. Perhaps get a cruiser. With a villa and his own boat, he would be able to attract as many handsome young men as he liked . . .

Gregory Halston was an atheist, but as he walked down the corridor of the Savoy Hotel to Suite 26, he found himself praying, *Let the stone be similar enough to satisfy old P. J. Benecke.*

He stood in front of the door of the contessa's room taking slow, deep breaths, fighting to get control of himself. He knocked on the door, and there was no answer.

Oh, my God, Halston thought. *She's gone; she didn't wait for me. She went out shopping and –*

The door opened, and Halston found himself facing an elegant-looking lady in her fifties, with dark eyes, a lined face, and black hair laced with grey.

When she spoke, her voice was soft, with the familiar melodic Italian accent. '*Sì?*'

'I'm G-Gregory Halston. You t-telephoned me.' In his nervousness he was stuttering.

'Ah, *sì*. I am the Contessa Marissa. Come in, *signore, per favore.*'

'Thank you.'

He entered the suite, pressing his knees together to keep them from trembling. He almost blurted out, 'Where's the emerald?' But he knew he must control himself. He must not seem too eager. If the stone was satisfactory, he would have the advantage of bargaining. After all, he was the expert. She was an amateur.

'Please to sit yourself,' the contessa said.

He took a chair.

'*Scusi. Non parlo molto bene inglese.* I speak poor English.'

'No, no. It's charming, charming.'

'*Grazie.* Would you take perhaps coffee? Tea?'

'No, thank you, Contessa.'

He could feel his stomach quivering. Was it too soon to bring up the subject of the emerald? He could not wait another second. 'The emerald –'

She said, 'Ah, *sì*. The emerald was given to me by my grandmother. I wish to pass it on to my daughter when she is twenty-five, but my husband is going into a new business in Milano, and I –'

Halston's mind was elsewhere. He was not interested in the boring life story of the stranger sitting across from him. He was burning to see the emerald. The suspense was more than he could bear.

'*Credo che sia importante* to help my husband get started in his business.' She smiled ruefully. 'Perhaps I am making a mistake –'

'No, no,' Halston said hastily. 'Not at all, Contessa. It's a wife's duty to stand by her husband. Where is the emerald now?'

'I have it here,' the contessa said.

350

She reached into her pocket, pulled out a jewel wrapped in a tissue, and held it out to Halston. He stared at it, and his spirits soared. He was looking at the most exquisite ten-carat grass-green Colombian emerald he had ever seen. It was so close in appearance, size, and colour to the one he had sold Mrs Benecke that the difference was almost impossible to detect. *It is not exactly the same*, Halston told himself, *but only an expert would be able to tell the difference.* His hands began to tremble. He forced himself to appear calm.

He turned the stone over, letting the light catch the beautiful facets, and said casually, 'It's a rather nice little stone.'

'*Splendente, sì.* I have loved it very much all these years. I will hate to part with it.'

'You're doing the right thing,' Halston assured her. 'Once your husband's business is successful, you will be able to buy as many of these as you wish.'

'That is exactly what I feel. You are *molto simpatico.*'

'I'm doing a little favour for a friend, Contessa. We have much better stones than this in our shop, but my friend wants one to match an emerald that his wife bought. I imagine he would be willing to pay as much as sixty thousand dollars for this stone.'

The contessa sighed. 'My grandmother would haunt me from her grave if I sold it for sixty thousand dollars.'

Halston pursed his lips. He could afford to go higher. He smiled. 'I'll tell you what . . . I think I might persuade my friend to go as high as one hundred thousand. That's a great deal of money, but he's anxious to have the stone.'

'That sounds fair,' the contessa said.

Gregory Halston's heart swelled within his breast. '*Bene!* I brought my chequebook with me, so I'll just write out a cheque –'

'*Ma, no* . . . I am afraid it will not solve my problem.' The contessa's face was sad.

Halston stared at her. 'Your problem?'

'*Sì.* As I explain, my husband is going into his new business, and he needs three hundred and fifty thousand dollars. I have a hundred thousand of my money to give him, but I need two hundred and fifty thousand more. I was hope to get it for this emerald.'

He shook his head. 'My dear Contessa, no emerald in the world is worth that kind of money. Believe me, one hundred thousand dollars is more than a fair offer.'

'I am sure it is so, Mr Halston,' the contessa told him, 'but it will not help my husband, will it?' She rose to her feet. 'I will save this to give to our daughter.' She held out a slim, delicate hand. '*Grazie, signore.* Thank you for coming.'

Halston stood there in panic. 'Wait a minute,' he said. His greed was duelling with his common sense, but he knew he must not lose the emerald now. 'Please sit down, Contessa. I'm sure we can

352

come to some equitable arrangement. If I can persuade my client to pay a hundred and fifty thousand –?'

'Two hundred and fifty thousand dollars.'

'Let's say, two hundred thousand?'

'Two hundred and fifty thousand dollars.'

There was no budging her. Halston made his decision. A $150,000 profit was better than nothing. It would mean a smaller villa and a boat, but it was still a fortune. It would serve the Parker brothers right for the shabby way they treated him. He would wait a day or two and then give them his notice. By next week he would be on the Côte d'Azur.

'You have a deal,' he said.

'Meraviglioso! Sono contenta!'

You should be contented, you bitch, Halston thought. But he had nothing to complain about. He was set for life. He took one last look at the emerald and slipped it into his pocket. 'I'll give you a cheque written on the shop's account.'

'Bene, signore.'

Halston wrote out the cheque and handed it to her. He would have Mrs P. J. Benecke make out her $400,000 cheque to cash. Peter would cash the cheque for him, and he would exchange the contessa's cheque for the Parker brothers' cheque and pocket the difference. He would arrange it with Peter so that the $250,000 cheque would not appear on the Parker brothers' monthly statement. One hundred and fifty thousand dollars.

He could already feel the warm French sun on his face.

The taxi ride back to the shop seemed to take only seconds. Halston visualized Mrs Benecke's happiness when he broke the good news to her. He had not only found the jewel she wanted, he had spared her from the excruciating experience of living in a draughty, rundown country house.

When Halston floated into the shop, Chilton said, 'Sir, a customer here is interested in –'

Halston cheerfully waved him aside. 'Later.'

He had no time for customers. Not now, not ever again. From now on people would wait on *him*. He would shop at Hermes and Gucci and Lanvin.

Halston fluttered into his office, closed the door, set the emerald on the desk in front of him, and dialled a number.

An operator's voice said, 'Dorchester Hotel.'

'The Oliver Messel Suite, please.'

'To whom did you wish to speak?'

'Mrs P. J. Benecke.'

'One moment, please.'

Halston whistled softly while he waited.

The operator came back on the line. 'I'm sorry, Mrs Benecke has checked out.'

'Then ring whatever suite she's moved to.'

'Mrs Benecke has checked out of the hotel.'

'That's impossible. She –'

'I'll connect you with reception.'

A male voice said, 'Reception. May I help you?'

'Yes. What suite is Mrs P. J. Benecke in?'

'Mrs Benecke checked out of the hotel this morning.'

There had to be an explanation. Some unexpected emergency.

'May I have her forwarding address, please. This is –'

'I'm sorry. She didn't leave one.'

'*Of course* she left one.'

'I checked Mrs Benecke out myself. She left no forwarding address.'

It was a jab to the pit of his stomach. Halston slowly replaced the receiver and sat there, bewildered. He *had* to find a way to get in touch with her, to let her know that he had finally located the emerald. In the meantime, he had to get back the $250,000 cheque from the Contessa Marissa.

He hurriedly dialled the Savoy Hotel. 'Suite twenty-six.'

'Whom are you calling, please?'

'The Contessa Marissa.'

'One moment, please.'

But even before the operator came back on the line, some terrible premonition told Gregory Halston the disastrous news he was about to hear.

'I'm sorry. The Contessa Marissa has checked out.'

He hung up. His fingers were trembling so hard that he was barely able to dial the number of the bank. 'Give me the head bookkeeper . . . quickly! I wish to stop payment on a cheque.'

But, of course, he was too late. He had sold an emerald for $100,000 and had bought back the same emerald for $250,000. Gregory Halston sat there slumped in his chair, wondering how he was going to explain it to the Parker brothers.

TWENTY-TWO

It was the beginning of a new life for Tracy. She purchased a beautiful old Georgian house at 45 Eaton Square that was bright and cheerful and perfect for entertaining. It had a Queen Anne – British slang for a front garden – and a Mary Anne – a back garden – and in season the flowers were magnificent. Gunther helped Tracy furnish the house, and before the two of them were finished, it was one of the showplaces of London.

Gunther introduced Tracy as a wealthy young widow whose husband had made his fortune in the import-export business. She was an instant success; beautiful, intelligent and charming, she was soon inundated with invitations.

At intervals, Tracy made short trips to France and Switzerland and Belgium and Italy, and each time she and Gunther Hartog profited.

Under Gunther's tutelage, Tracy studied the *Almanach de Gotha* and *Debrett's Peerage and Baronetage*, the authoritative books listing detailed information on all the royalty and titles in Europe. Tracy became a chameleon, an expert in make-up and disguises and accents. She acquired half a dozen passports. In various countries, she was a British duchess, a French airline stewardess, and a South American heiress. In a year she had accumulated more money than she would ever need. She set up a fund from which she made large, anonymous contributions to organizations that helped former women prisoners, and she arranged for a generous pension to be sent to Otto Schmidt every month. She no longer entertained the thought of quitting. She loved the challenge of outwitting clever, successful people. The thrill of each daring escapade acted like a drug, and Tracy found that she constantly needed new and bigger challenges. There was one credo she lived by: she was careful never to hurt the innocent. The people who jumped at her swindles were greedy or immoral, or both. *No one will ever commit suicide because of what I've done to them*, Tracy promised herself.

The newspapers began to carry stories of the daring escapades that were occurring all over Europe, and because Tracy used different disguises, the police were convinced that a rash of ingenious swindles and burglaries was being carried out by a gang of women. Interpol began to take an interest.

At the Manhattan headquarters of the International Insurance Protection Association, J. J. Reynolds sent for Daniel Cooper.

'We have a problem,' Reynolds said. 'A large number of our European clients are being hit – apparently by a gang of women. Everybody's screaming bloody murder. They want the gang caught. Interpol has agreed to cooperate with us. It's your assignment, Dan. You leave for Paris in the morning.'

Tracy was having dinner with Gunther at Scott's on Mount Street.

'Have you ever heard of Maximilian Pierpont, Tracy?'

The name sounded familiar. Where had she heard it before? She remembered. Jeff Stevens, on board the *QE II*, had said, 'We're here for the same reason. Maximilian Pierpont.'

'Very rich, isn't he?'

'And quite ruthless. He specializes in buying up companies and stripping them.'

When Joe Romano took over the business, he fired everybody and brought in his own people to run things. Then he began to raid the company . . . They took everything – the business, this house, your mother's car . . .

Gunther was looking at her oddly. 'Tracy, are you all right?'

'Yes. I'm fine.' *Sometimes life can be unfair*, she thought, *and it's up to us to even things out.* 'Tell me more about Maximilian Pierpont.'

'His third wife just divorced him, and he's alone now. I think it might be profitable if you made the gentleman's acquaintance. He's booked on the *Orient Express* Friday, from London to Istanbul.'

Tracy smiled. 'I've never been on the *Orient Express*. I think I'd enjoy it.'

Gunther smiled back. 'Good. Maximilian Pierpont has the only important Fabergé egg collection outside of the Hermitage Museum in Leningrad. It's conservatively estimated to be worth twenty million dollars.'

'If I managed to get some of the eggs for you,' Tracy asked, curious, 'what would you do with them, Gunther? Wouldn't they be too well known to sell?'

'Private collectors, dear Tracy. You bring the little eggs to me, and I will find a nest for them.'

'I'll see what I can do.'

'Maximilian Pierpont is not an easy man to approach. However, there are two other pigeons also booked on the *Orient Express* Friday, bound for the film festival in Venice. I think they're ripe for plucking. Have you heard of Silvana Luadi?'

'The Italian movie star? Of course.'

'She's married to Alberto Fornati, who produces those terrible epic films. Fornati is infamous for hiring actors and directors for very little cash, promising them big percentages of the profits, and keeping all the profits for himself. He manages to make enough to buy his wife very expensive jewels. The more unfaithful he is to her, the more jewellery he gives her. By this time Silvana should be able to open her own jewellery shop. I'm sure you'll find all of them interesting company.'

'I'm looking forward to it,' Tracy said.

The *Venice Simplon Orient Express* departs from Victoria Station in London every Friday morning at 11:44, travelling from London to Istanbul, with intermediate stops in Boulogne, Paris, Lausanne, Milan and Venice. Thirty minutes before departure a portable check-in counter is set up at the entrance to the boarding platform in the terminal, and two burly uniformed men roll a red rug up to the counter, elbowing aside eagerly waiting passengers.

The new owners of the *Orient Express* had attempted to recreate the golden age of rail travel as it existed in the late nineteenth century, and the rebuilt train was a duplicate of the original, with a British Pullman car, wagon-lit restaurants, a bar-salon car, and sleeping cars.

An attendant in a 1920's marine-blue uniform with gold braid carried Tracy's two suitcases and her vanity case to her cabin, which was disappointingly small. There was a single seat, upholstered with a flower-patterned mohair. The rug, as well as the ladder that was used to reach the top berth, was covered in the same green plush. It was like being in a chocolate box.

Tracy read the card accompanying a small bottle of champagne in a silver bucket: OLIVER AUBERT, TRAIN MANAGER.

I'll save it until I have something to celebrate, Tracy decided. *Maximilian Pierpont*. Jeff Stevens had failed. It would be a wonderful feeling to top Mr Stevens. Tracy smiled at the thought.

She unpacked in the cramped space and hung up the clothes she would be needing. She preferred travelling on a Pan American jet rather than a train, but this journey promised to be an exciting one.

Exactly on schedule, the *Orient Express* began to move out of the station. Tracy sat back in her seat and watched the southern suburbs of London roll by.

At 1:15 that afternoon the train arrived at the port of Folkestone, where the passengers transferred to the Sealink ferry, which would take them across the channel to Boulogne, where they would board another *Orient Express* heading south.

Tracy approached one of the attendants. 'I understand Maximilian Pierpont is travelling with us. Could you point him out to me?'

The attendant shook his head. 'I wish I could, ma'am. He booked his cabin and paid for it, but he never showed up. Very unpredictable gentleman, so I'm told.'

That left Silvana Luadi and her husband, the producer of forgettable epics.

In Boulogne, the passengers were escorted onto the continental *Oriental Express*. Unfortunately, Tracy's cabin on the second train was identical to the one she had left, and the rough railway track made the journey even more uncomfortable. She remained in her cabin all day making her plans, and at 8:00 in the evening she began to dress.

The dress code of the *Orient Express* recommended evening clothes, and Tracy chose a stunning dove-grey chiffon gown with grey hose and grey satin shoes. Her only jewellery was a single strand of matched pearls. She checked herself in the mirror before she left her quarters, staring at her reflection for a long time. Her green eyes had a look of innocence, and her face looked guileless and vulnerable. *The mirror is lying*, Tracy thought. *I'm not that woman any more. I'm living a masquerade. But an exciting one.*

As Tracy left her cabin, her handbag slipped out of her hand, and as she knelt down to retrieve it, she quickly examined the outside locks on the door. There were two of them: a Yale lock and a Universal lock. *No problem.* Tracy rose and moved on towards the dining cars.

There were three dining cars aboard the train. The seats were plush-covered, the walls were veneered, and the soft lights came from brass sconces topped with Lalique shades. Tracy entered the first dining room and noted several empty tables. The maître d' greeted her. 'A table for one, mademoiselle?'

Tracy looked around the room. 'I'm joining some friends, thank you.'

She continued on to the next dining car. This one was more crowded, but there were still several unoccupied tables.

'Good evening,' the maître d' said. 'Are you dining alone?'

'No, I'm meeting someone. Thank you.'

She moved on to the third dining car. There, every table was occupied.

The maître d' stopped her at the door. 'I'm afraid there will be a wait for a table, madame. There are available tables in the other dining cars, however.'

Tracy looked around the room, and at a table in the far corner she saw what she was looking for. 'That's all right,' Tracy said. 'I see friends.'

She moved past the maître d' and walked over to the corner table. 'Excuse me,' she said apologetically. 'All the tables seem to be occupied. Would you mind if I joined you?'

The man quickly rose to his feet, took a good look at Tracy, and exclaimed, '*Prego! Con piacere!* I am Alberto Fornati and this is my wife, Silvana Luadi.'

'Tracy Whitney.' She was using her own passport.

'Ah! *È Americana!* I speak the excellent English.'

Alberto Fornati was short, bald and fat. Why Silvana Luadi had ever married him had been the most lively topic in Rome for the twelve years they had been together. Silvana Luadi was a classic beauty, with a sensational figure and a compelling, natural talent. She had won an Oscar and a Silver Palm award and was always in great demand. Tracy recognized that she was dressed in a

Valentino evening gown that sold for five thousand dollars, and the jewellery she wore must have been worth close to a million. Tracy remembered Gunther Hartog's words: *The more unfaithful he is to her, the more jewellery he gives her. By this time Silvana should be able to open her own jewellery shop.*

'This is your first time on the *Orient Express*, signorina?' Fornati opened the conversation, after Tracy was seated.

'Yes, it is.'

'Ah, it is a very romantic train, filled with legend.' His eyes were moist. 'There are many *interessante* tales about it. For instance, Sir Basil Zaharoff, the arms tycoon, used to ride the old *Orient Express* – always in the seventh compartment. One night he hears a scream and a pounding on his door. A *bellissima* young Spanish duchess throws herself upon him.' Fornati paused to butter a roll and take a bite. 'Her husband was trying to murder her. The parents had arranged the marriage, and the poor girl now realized her husband was insane. Zaharoff restrained the husband and calmed the hysterical young woman and thus began a romance that lasted forty years.'

'How exciting,' Tracy said. Her eyes were wide with interest.

'*Si*. Every year after that they meet on the *Orient Express*, he in compartment number seven, she in number eight. When her husband died, the lady and Zaharoff were married, and as a token of his love, he bought her the casino at Monte Carlo as a wedding gift.'

'What a beautiful story, Mr Fornati.'

Silvana Luadi sat in stony silence.

'*Mangia*,' Fornati urged Tracy. 'Eat.'

The menu consisted of six courses, and Tracy noted that Alberto Fornati ate each one and finished what his wife left on her plate. In between bites he kept up a constant chatter.

'You are an actress, perhaps?' he asked Tracy.

She laughed. 'Oh no. I'm just a tourist.'

He beamed at her. '*Bellissima*. You are beautiful enough to be an actress.'

'She said she is not an actress,' Silvana said sharply.

Alberto Fornati ignored her. 'I produce motion pictures,' he told Tracy. 'You have heard of them, of course: *Wild Savages*, *The Titans versus Superwoman* . . .'

'I don't see many movies,' Tracy apologized. She felt his fat leg press against hers under the table.

'Perhaps I can arrange to show you some of mine.'

Silvana turned white with anger.

'Do you ever get to Rome, my dear?' His leg was moving up and down against Tracy's.

'As a matter of fact, I'm planning to go to Rome after Venice.'

'Splendid! *Benissimo!* We will all get together for dinner. Won't we, *cara?*' He gave a quick glance towards Silvana before he continued. 'We have a lovely villa off the Appian Way. Ten acres of –'

His hand made a sweeping gesture and knocked a bowl of gravy into his wife's lap. Tracy could not be sure whether it was deliberate or not.

Silvana Luadi rose to her feet and looked at the spreading stain on her dress. '*Sei un mascalzone!*' she screamed. '*Tieni le tue puttane lontano da me.*'

She stormed out of the dining car, every eye following her.

'What a shame,' Tracy murmured. 'It's such a beautiful dress.' She could have slapped the man for degrading his wife. *She deserves every carat of jewellery she has*, Tracy thought, *and more.*

He sighed. 'Fornati will buy her another one. Pay no attention to her manners. She is very jealous of Fornati.'

'I'm sure she has good reason to be.' Tracy covered her irony with a small smile.

He peered. 'It is true. Women find Fornati very attractive.'

It was all Tracy could do to keep from bursting out laughing at the pompous little man. 'I can understand that.'

He reached across the table and took her hand. 'Fornati likes you,' he said. 'Fornati likes you very much. What do you do for a living?'

'I'm a legal secretary. I saved up all my money for this trip. I hope to get an interesting position in Europe.'

His bulging eyes roved over her body. 'You will have no problem, Fornati promises you. He is very nice to people who are very nice to him.'

'How wonderful of you,' Tracy said shyly.

He lowered his voice. 'Perhaps we could discuss this later this evening in your cabin?'

'That might be embarrassing.'

'*Perché?* Why?'

'You're so famous. Everyone on the train probably knows who you are.'

'Naturally.'

'If they see you come to my cabin – well, you know, some people might misunderstand. Of course, if your cabin is near mine . . . What number are you in?'

'*E settanta* – seventy.' He looked at her hopefully.

Tracy sighed. 'I'm in another car. Why don't we meet in Venice?'

He beamed. '*Bene!* My wife, she stays in her room most of the time. She cannot stand the sun on her face. Have you ever been to Venezia?'

'No.'

'Ah. You and I shall go to Torcello, a beautiful little island with a wonderful restaurant, the Locanda Cipriani. It is also a small hotel.' His eyes gleamed. '*Molto privato.*'

Tracy gave him a slow, understanding smile. 'It sounds exciting.' She lowered her eyes, too overcome to say more.

Fornati leaned forward, squeezed her hand, and whispered wetly, 'You do not know what excitement is yet, *cara.*'

Half an hour later Tracy was back in her cabin.

* * *

The *Orient Express* sped through the lonely night, past Paris and Dijon and Vallarbe, while the passengers slept. They had turned in their passports the evening before, and the border formalities would be handled by the conductors.

At 3:30 in the morning Tracy quietly left her compartment. The timing was critical. The train would cross the Swiss border and reach Lausanne at 5:21 A.M. and was due to arrive in Milan, Italy, at 9:15 A.M.

Clad in pyjamas and robe, and carrying a sponge bag, Tracy moved down the corridor, every sense alert, the familiar excitement making her pulse leap. There were no toilets in the cabins of the train, but there were some located at the end of each carriage. If Tracy was questioned, she was prepared to say that she was looking for the ladies' room, but she encountered no one. The conductors and porters were taking advantage of the early-morning hours to catch up on their sleep.

Tracy reached Cabin E 70 without incident. She quietly tried the doorknob. The door was locked. Tracy opened the sponge bag and took out a metallic object and a small bottle with a syringe, and went to work.

Ten minutes later she was back in her cabin, and thirty minutes after that she was asleep, with the trace of a smile on her freshly scrubbed face.

At 7:00 A.M., two hours before the *Orient Express* was due to arrive in Milan, a series of piercing screams rang out. They came from Cabin E 70, and they awakened the entire carriage. Passengers poked their heads out of their cabins to see what was happening. A conductor came hurrying along the carriage and entered E 70.

Silvana Luadi was in hysterics. '*Aiuto! Help!*' she screamed. 'All my jewellery is gone! This miserable train is full of *ladri* – thieves!'

'Please calm down, madame,' the conductor begged. 'The other –'

'*Calm down!*' Her voice went up an octave. 'How dare you tell me to calm down, *stupido maiale!* Someone has stolen more than a million dollars' worth of my jewels!'

'How could this have happened?' Alberto Fornati demanded. 'The door was locked – and Fornati is a light sleeper. If anyone had entered, I would have awakened instantly.'

The conductor sighed. He knew only too well how it had happened, because it had happened before. During the night someone had crept down the corridor and sprayed a syringe full of ether through the keyhole. The locks would have been child's play for someone who knew what he was doing. The thief would have closed the door behind him, looted the room, and, having taken what he wanted, quietly crept back to his compartment while his victims were still unconscious. But there was one thing about this burglary that was different from the others. In the past the thefts had not been discovered until *after* the train had reached its destination, so the thieves had had a chance to escape. This was a different situation. No one had disembarked since the robbery, which meant that the jewellery still had to be on board.

'Don't worry,' the conductor promised the Fornatis. 'You'll get your jewels back. The thief is still on this train.'

He hurried forward to telephone the police in Milan.

When the *Orient Express* pulled into the Milan terminal, twenty uniformed policemen and plain-clothes detectives lined the station platform, with orders not to let any passengers or baggage off the train.

Luigi Ricci, the inspector in charge, was taken directly to the Fornati compartment.

If anything, Silvana Luadi's hysteria had increased. 'Every bit of jewellery I owned was in that jewel case,' she screamed. 'And none of it was insured!'

The inspector examined the empty jewel case. 'You are sure you put your jewels in there last night, signora?'

'*Of course* I am sure. I put them there every night.' Her luminous eyes, which had thrilled millions of adoring fans, pooled over with large tears, and Inspector Ricci was ready to slay dragons for her.

He walked over to the compartment door, bent down, and sniffed the keyhole. He could detect the lingering odour of ether. There had been a robbery, and he intended to catch the unfeeling bandit.

371

Inspector Ricci straightened up and said, 'Do not worry, signora. There is no way the jewels can be removed from this train. We will catch the thief, and your gems will be returned to you.'

Inspector Ricci had every reason to be confident. The trap was tightly sealed, and there was no possibility for the culprit to get away.

One by one, the detectives escorted the passengers to a station waiting room that had been roped off, and they were expertly body searched. The passengers, many of them people of prominence, were outraged by this indignity.

'I'm sorry,' Inspector Ricci explained to each of them, 'but a million-dollar theft is a very serious business.'

As each passenger was led from the train, detectives turned their cabins upside down. Every inch of space was examined. This was a splendid opportunity for Inspector Ricci, and he intended to make the most of it. When he recovered the stolen jewels, it would mean a promotion and a rise. His imagination became inflamed. Silvana Luadi would be so grateful to him that she would probably invite him to . . . He gave orders with renewed vigour.

There was a knock at Tracy's cabin door and a detective entered. 'Excuse me, signorina. There has been a robbery. It is necessary to search all passengers. If you will come with me, please . . .'

'A robbery?' Her voice was shocked. 'On this train?'

'I fear so, signorina.'

When Tracy stepped out of her compartment, two detectives moved in, opened her suitcases, and began carefully sifting through the contents.

At the end of four hours the search had turned up several packets of marijuana, five ounces of cocaine, a knife, and an illegal gun. There was no sign of the missing jewellery.

Inspector Ricci could not believe it. 'Have you searched the entire train?' he demanded of his lieutenant.

'Inspector, we have searched every inch. We have examined the engine, the dining rooms, the bar, the toilets, the compartments. We have searched the passengers and crew and examined every piece of luggage. I can swear to you that the jewellery is not on board this train. Perhaps the lady imagined the theft.'

But Inspector Ricci knew better. He had spoken to the waiters, and they had confirmed that Silvana Luadi had indeed worn a dazzling display of jewellery at dinner the evening before.

A representative of the *Orient Express* had flown to Milan. 'You cannot detain this train any longer,' he insisted. 'We are already far behind schedule.'

Inspector Ricci was defeated. He had no excuse for holding the train any further. There was nothing more he could do. The only explanation he could think of was that somehow, during the night, the thief had tossed the jewels off the train to a waiting confederate. But could it have happened that way?

The timing would have been impossible. The thief could not have known in advance when the corridor would be clear, when a conductor or passenger might be prowling about, what time the train would be at some deserted assignation point. This was a mystery beyond the inspector's power to solve.

'Let the train go on,' he ordered.

He stood watching helplessly as the *Orient Express* slowly pulled out of the station. With it went his promotion, his rise, and a blissful orgy with Silvana Luadi.

The sole topic of conversation in the breakfast car was the robbery.

'It's the most exciting thing that's happened to me in years,' confessed a prim teacher at a girls' school. She fingered a small gold necklace with a tiny diamond chip. 'I'm lucky they didn't take this.'

'Very,' Tracy gravely agreed.

When Alberto Fornati walked into the dining car, he caught sight of Tracy and hurried over to her. 'You know what happened, of course. But did you know it was Fornati's wife who was robbed?'

'No!'

'Yes! My life was in great danger. A gang of thieves crept into my cabin and chloroformed me. Fornati could have been murdered in his sleep.'

'How terrible.'

'*È una bella fregatura!* Now I shall have to replace all of Silvana's jewellery. It's going to cost me a fortune.'

'The police didn't find the jewels?'

'No, but Fornati knows how the thieves got rid of them.'

'Really! How?'

He looked around and lowered his voice. 'An accomplice was waiting at one of the stations we passed during the night. The *ladri* threw the jewels out of the train, and – *ecco* – it was done.'

Tracy said admiringly, 'How clever of you to figure that out.'

'*Sì.*' He raised his brows meaningfully. 'You will not forget our little tryst in Venezia?'

'How could I?' Tracy smiled.

He squeezed her arm hard. 'Fornati is looking forward to it. Now I must go console Silvana. She is hysterical.'

When the *Orient Express* arrived at the Santa Lucia station in Venice, Tracy was among the first passengers to disembark. She had her luggage taken directly to the airport and was on the next plane to London with Silvana Luadi's jewellery.

Gunther Hartog was going to be pleased.

TWENTY-THREE

The seven-storey headquarters building of Interpol, the International Criminal Police Organization, is at 26 Rue Armengaud, in the hills of St Cloud, about six miles west of Paris, discreetly hidden behind a high green fence and white stone walls. The gate at the street entrance is locked twenty-four hours a day, and visitors are admitted only after being scrutinized through a closed-circuit television system. Inside the building, at the head of the stairs at each floor, are white iron gates which are locked at night, and every floor is equipped with a separate alarm system and closed-circuit television.

The extraordinary security is mandatory, for within this building are kept the world's most elaborate dossiers with files on two and a half million criminals. Interpol is a clearinghouse of information for 126 police forces in 78 countries, and coordinates the worldwide activities of police forces in dealing with swindlers, counterfeiters, narcotics smugglers, robbers, and murderers. It disseminates up-to-the-second information by an updated bulletin called a *circulation*; by radio, photo-telegraphy, and early-bird satellite. The Paris headquarters is manned by former detectives from the Sûreté Nationale or the Paris Préfecture.

On an early May morning a conference was under way in the office of Inspector Andre Trignant, in charge of Interpol headquarters. The office was comfortable and simply furnished, and the view was breathtaking. In the far distance to the east, the Eiffel Tower loomed, and in another direction the white dome of the Sacré Coeur in Montmartre was clearly visible. The inspector was in his mid-forties, an attractive, authoritative figure, with an intelligent face, dark hair, and shrewd brown eyes behind black horn-rimmed glasses. Seated in the office with him were detectives from England, Belgium, France and Italy.

'Gentlemen,' Inspector Trignant said, 'I have received urgent requests from each of your countries for information about the rash of crimes that has recently sprung up all over Europe. Half a dozen countries have been hit by an epidemic of ingenious swindles and burglaries, in which there are several similarities. The victims are of unsavoury reputation, there is never violence involved, and the perpetrator is always a female. We have reached the conclusion that we are facing an international gang of women. We have identi-kit pictures based on the descriptions by victims and random witnesses.

As you will see, none of the women in the pictures is alike. Some are blonde, some brunette. They have variously been reported as being English, French, Spanish, Italian, American – or Texan.'

Inspector Trignant pressed a switch, and a series of pictures began to appear on the wall screen. 'Here you see an identi-kit sketch of a brunette with short hair.' He pressed the button again. 'Here is a young blonde with a shag cut . . . Here is another blonde with a perm . . . a brunette with a pageboy . . . Here is an older woman with a French twist . . . a young woman with blonde streaks . . . an older woman with a *coup sauvage*.' He turned off the projector. 'We have no idea who the gang's leader is or where their headquarters is located. They never leave any clues behind, and they vanish like smoke rings. Sooner or later we will catch one of them, and when we do, we shall get them all. In the meantime, gentlemen, until one of you can furnish us with some specific information, I am afraid we are at a dead end . . .'

When Daniel Cooper's plane landed in Paris, he was met at Charles de Gaulle Airport by one of Inspector Trignant's assistants, and driven to the Prince de Galles, next door to its more illustrious sister hotel, the George V.

'It is arranged for you to meet Inspector Trignant tomorrow,' his escort told Cooper. 'I will pick you up at eight-fifteen.'

*   *   *

378

Daniel Cooper had not been looking forward to the trip to Europe. He intended to finish his assignment as quickly as possible and return home. He knew about the fleshpots of Paris, and he had no intention of becoming involved.

He checked into his room and went directly into the bathroom. To his surprise, the bath was satisfactory. In fact, he admitted to himself, it was much larger than the one at home. He ran the bath water and went into the bedroom to unpack. Near the bottom of his suitcase was the small locked box, safe between his extra suit and his underwear. He picked up the box and held it in his hands, staring at it, and it seemed to pulse with a life of its own. He carried it into the bathroom and placed it on the sink. With the tiny key dangling from his key ring, he unlocked the box and opened it, and the words screamed up at him from the yellowed newspaper clipping.

BOY TESTIFIES IN MURDER TRIAL

Twelve-year-old Daniel Cooper today testified in the trial of Fred Zimmer, accused of the rape-murder of the young boy's mother. According to his testimony, the boy returned home from school and saw Zimmer, a next-door neighbour, leaving the Cooper home with blood on his hands and face. When the boy entered his home, he discovered the body of his mother in the bath. She had been savagely stabbed to death. Zimmer confessed to being Mrs Cooper's lover, but denied that he had killed her.

The young boy has been placed in the care of an aunt.

Daniel Cooper's trembling hands dropped the clipping back into the box and locked it. He looked around wildly. The walls and ceiling of the hotel bathroom were spattered with blood. He saw his mother's naked body floating in the red water. He felt a wave of vertigo and clutched the sink. The screams inside him became guttural moans, and he frantically tore off his clothes and sank down into the blood-warm bath.

'I must inform you, Mr Cooper,' Inspector Trignant said, 'that your position here is most unusual. You are not a member of any police force, and your presence here is unofficial. However, we have been requested by the police departments of several European countries to extend our cooperation.'

Daniel Cooper said nothing.

'As I understand it, you are an investigator for the International Protective Association, a consortium of insurance companies.'

'Some of our European clients have had heavy losses lately. I was told there are no clues.'

Inspector Trignant sighed. 'I'm afraid that is the case. We know we are dealing with a gang of very clever women, but beyond that –'

'No information from informers?'

'No. Nothing.'

'Doesn't that strike you as odd?'

'What do you mean, monsieur?'

It seemed so obvious to Cooper that he did not bother to keep the impatience out of his voice. 'When a gang is involved, there's always someone who talks too much, drinks too much, spends too much. It's impossible for a large group of people to keep a secret. Would you mind giving me your files on this gang?'

The inspector started to refuse. He thought Daniel Cooper was one of the most physically unattractive men he had ever met. And certainly the most arrogant. He was going to be a *chierie*, 'a pain in the ass'; but the inspector had been asked to cooperate fully.

Reluctantly, he said, 'I will have copies made for you.' He spoke into an intercom and gave the order. To make conversation, Inspector Trignant said, 'An interesting report just crossed my desk. Some valuable jewels were stolen aboard the *Orient Express* while it –'

'I read about it. The thief made a fool of the Italian police.'

'No one has been able to figure out how the robbery was accomplished.'

'It's obvious,' Daniel Cooper said rudely. 'A matter of simple logic.'

Inspector Trignant looked over his glasses in surprise. *Mon Dieu, he has the manners of a pig.* He continued, coolly, 'In this case, logic does not help. Every inch of that train was examined, and the employees, passengers, and all the luggage searched.'

'No,' Daniel Cooper contradicted.

This man is crazy, Inspector Trignant decided. 'No – *what*?'

'They didn't search all the luggage.'

'And I tell you they did,' Inspector Trignant insisted. 'I have seen the police report.'

'The woman from whom the jewels were stolen – Silvana Luadi?'

'Yes?'

'She had placed her jewels in an overnight case from which they were taken?'

'That is correct.'

'Did the police search Miss Luadi's luggage?'

'Only her overnight case. She was the victim. Why should they search her luggage?'

'Because that's logically the only place the thief could have hidden the jewels – in the bottom of one of her other suitcases. He probably had a duplicate case, and when all the luggage was piled on the platform at the Venice station, all he had to do was exchange suitcases and disappear.' Daniel Cooper rose. 'If those reports are ready, I'll be running along.'

Thirty minutes later, Inspector Trignant was speaking to Alberto Fornati in Venice.

'Monsieur,' the inspector said, 'I was calling to enquire whether there happened to be any problem with your wife's luggage when you arrived in Venice.'

'*Sì, sì,*' Fornati complained. 'The idiot porter got her suitcases mixed up with someone else's. When my wife opened her bag at the hotel, it contained nothing but a lot of old magazines. I reported it to the office of the *Orient Express*. Have they located my wife's suitcase?' he asked hopefully.

'No, monsieur,' the inspector said. And he added silently to himself, *Nor would I expect it, if I were you.*

When he completed the telephone call, he sat back in his chair thinking, *This Daniel Cooper is très formidable.* Very formidable, indeed.

TWENTY-FOUR

Tracy's house in Eaton Square was a haven. It was in one of the most beautiful areas in London, with the old Georgian houses facing tree-filled private parks. Nannies in stiffly starched uniforms wheeled their small charges in status-named prams along the gravelled paths, and children played their games. *I miss Amy*, Tracy thought.

Tracy walked along the storied old streets and shopped at the greengrocers and the chemist on Elizabeth Street; she marvelled at the variety of brilliantly coloured flowers sold outside the little shops.

Gunther Hartog saw to it that Tracy contributed to the right charities and met the right people. She dated wealthy dukes and impoverished earls and had numerous proposals of marriage. She was young and beautiful and rich, and she seemed so vulnerable.

'Everyone thinks you're a perfect target,' Gunther laughed. 'You've really done splendidly for yourself, Tracy. You're set now. You have every-thing you'll ever need.'

It was true. She had money in safe-deposit boxes all over Europe, the house in London, and a chalet in St Moritz. Everything she would ever need. Except for someone to share it with. Tracy thought of the life she had almost had, with a husband and a baby. Would that ever be possible for her again? She could never reveal to any man who she really was, nor could she live a lie by concealing her past. She had played so many parts, she was no longer sure who she really was, but she did know that she could never return to the life she had once had. *It's all right*, Tracy thought defiantly. *A lot of people are lonely. Gunther is right. I have everything.*

She was giving a cocktail party the following evening, the first since her return from Venice.

'I'm looking forward to it,' Gunther told her. 'Your parties are the hottest ticket in London.'

Tracy said fondly, 'Look who my sponsor is.'

'Who's going to be there?'

'Everybody,' Tracy told him.

Everybody turned out to be one more guest than Tracy had anticipated. She had invited the Baroness Howarth, an attractive young heiress, and when Tracy saw the baroness arrive, she walked over to greet her. The greeting died on Tracy's lips. With the baroness was Jeff Stevens.

'Tracy, darling, I don't believe you know Mr Stevens. Jeff, this is Mrs Tracy Whitney, your hostess.'

Tracy said stiffly, 'How do you do, Mr Stevens?'

Jeff took Tracy's hand, holding it a fraction longer than necessary. 'Mrs Tracy Whitney?' he said. 'Of course! I was a friend of your husband's. We were together in India.'

'Isn't that exciting!' Baroness Howarth exclaimed.

'Strange, he never mentioned you,' Tracy said coolly.

'Didn't he, really? I'm surprised. Interesting old fella. Pity he had to go the way he did.'

'Oh, what happened?' Baroness Howarth asked.

Tracy glared at Jeff. 'It was nothing, really.'

'*Nothing!*' Jeff said reproachfully. 'If I remember correctly, he was hanged in India.'

'Pakistan,' Tracy said tightly. 'And I believe I *do* remember my husband mentioning you. How is your wife?'

Baroness Howarth looked at Jeff. 'You never mentioned that you were married, Jeff.'

'Cecily and I are divorced.'

Tracy smiled sweetly. 'I meant Rose.'

'Oh, *that* wife.'

Baroness Howarth was astonished. 'You've been married twice?'

'Once,' he said easily. 'Rose and I got an annulment. We were very young.' He started to move away.

Tracy asked, 'But weren't there twins?'

Baroness Howarth exclaimed, 'Twins?'

'They live with their mother,' Jeff told her. He looked at Tracy. 'I can't tell you how pleasant it's been talking to you, Mrs Whitney, but we mustn't monopolize you.' And he took the baroness's hand and walked away.

The following morning Tracy ran into Jeff in an elevator at Harrods. The store was crowded with shoppers. Tracy got off at the second floor. As she left the elevator, she turned to Jeff and said in a loud, clear voice, 'By the way, how did you ever come out on that morals charge?' The door closed, and Jeff was trapped in an elevator filled with indignant strangers.

Tracy lay in bed that night thinking of Jeff, and she had to laugh. He really was a charmer. A scoundrel, but an engaging one. She wondered what his relationship with Baroness Howarth was: she knew very well what his relationship with Baroness Howarth was. *Jeff and I are two of a kind*, Tracy thought. Neither of them would ever settle down. The life they led was too exciting and stimulating and rewarding.

She turned her thoughts towards her next job. It was going to take place in the South of France, and it would be a challenge. Gunther had told her that the police were looking for a gang. She fell asleep with a smile on her lips.

In his hotel room in Paris, Daniel Cooper was reading the reports Inspector Trignant had given him. It was 4:00 A.M., and Cooper had been poring over the papers for hours, analysing the imaginative mix of robberies and swindles. Some of the scams Cooper was familiar with, but others were new to him. As Inspector Trignant had mentioned, all the victims had unsavoury reputations. *This gang apparently thinks they're Robin Hoods*, Cooper reflected.

He had nearly finished. There were only three reports left. The one on top was headed BRUSSELS. Cooper opened the cover and glanced at the report. Two million dollars' worth of jewellery had been stolen from the wall safe of a Mr Van Ruysen, a Belgian stock-broker, who had been involved in some questionable financial dealings.

The owners were away on vacation, and the house was empty, and – Cooper caught something on the page that made his heart quicken. He went back to the first sentence and began rereading the report, focusing on every word. This one varied from the others in one significant respect: the burglar had set off an alarm, and when the police arrived, they were greeted at the door by a woman wearing a filmy négligée. Her hair was tucked into a curler cap, and her face was thickly covered with cold cream. She claimed to be a houseguest of the Van Ruysens'. The police accepted her story, and by the time they were able to check it out with the absent owners, the woman and the jewellery had vanished.

Cooper laid down the report. Logic, logic.

Inspector Trignant was losing his patience. 'You're wrong. I tell you it is impossible for one woman to be responsible for all these crimes.'

'There's a way to check it out,' Daniel Cooper said.

'How?'

'I'd like to see a computer run on the dates and locations of the last few burglaries and swindles that fit into this category.'

'That's simple enough, but –'

'Next, I would like to get an immigration report on every female American tourist who was in those same cities at the times the crimes were committed. It's possible that she uses false passports some of the time, but the probabilities are that she also uses her real identity.'

Inspector Trignant was thoughtful. 'I see your line of reasoning, monsieur.' He studied the little man before him and found himself half hoping that Cooper was mistaken. He was much too sure of himself. 'Very well. I will set the wheels in motion.'

The first burglary in the series had been committed in Stockholm. The report from Interpol Sektionen Rikspolis Styrelsen, the Interpol branch in Sweden, listed the American tourists in Stockholm that week, and the names of the women were fed into a computer. The next city checked was Milan. When the names of American women tourists in Milan at the time of the burglary was cross-checked with the names of women who had been in Stockholm during that burglary, there were fifty-five names on the list. That list was checked against the names of female Americans who had been in Ireland during a swindle, and the list was reduced to fifteen. Inspector Trignant handed the printout to Daniel Cooper.

'I'll start checking these names against the Berlin swindle,' Inspector Trignant said, 'and –'

Daniel Cooper looked up. 'Don't bother.'

The name at the top of the list was *Tracy Whitney.*

With something concrete finally to go on, Interpol went into action. Red *circulations*, which meant top priority, were sent to each member nation, advising them to be on the lookout for Tracy Whitney.

'We're also Teletyping green notices,' Inspector Trignant told Cooper.

'Green notices?'

'We use a colour-code system. A red *circulation* is top priority, blue is an enquiry for information about a suspect, a green notice puts police departments on warning that an individual is under suspicion and should be watched, black is an enquiry into unidentified bodies. X-D signals that a message is very urgent, while D is urgent. No matter what country Miss Whitney goes to, from the moment she checks through customs, she will be under observation.'

The following day Telephoto pictures of Tracy Whitney from the Southern Louisiana Penitentiary for Women were in the hands of Interpol.

Daniel Cooper put in a call to J. J. Reynolds's home. The phone rang a dozen times before it was answered.

'Hello . . .'

'I need some information.'

'Is that you, Cooper? For Christ's sake, it's four o'clock in the morning here. I was sound –'

'I want you to send me everything you can find on Tracy Whitney. Press clippings, videotapes – everything.'

'What's happening over –?'

Cooper had hung up.

One day I'll kill the son of a bitch, Reynolds swore.

Before, Daniel Cooper had been only casually interested in Tracy Whitney. Now she was his assignment. He taped her photographs on the walls of his small Paris hotel room and read all the newspaper accounts about her. He rented a video cassette player and ran and reran the television news shots of Tracy after her sentencing, and after her release from prison. Cooper sat in his darkened room hour after hour, looking at the film, and the first glimmering of suspicion became a certainty. 'You're the gang of women, Miss Whitney,' Daniel Cooper said aloud. Then he flicked the rewind button of the cassette player once more.

TWENTY-FIVE

Every year, on the first Saturday in June, the Count de Matigny sponsored a charity ball for the benefit of the Children's Hospital in Paris. Tickets for the white-tie affair were a thousand dollars apiece, and society's élite flew in from all over the world to attend.

The Château de Matigny, at Cap d'Antibes, was one of the showplaces of France. The carefully manicured grounds were superb, and the château itself dated back to the fifteenth century. On the evening of the fête, the grand ballroom and the petit ballroom were filled with beautifully dressed guests and smartly liveried servants offering endless glasses of champagne. Huge buffet tables were set up, displaying an astonishing array of hors d'oeuvres on Georgian silver platters.

Tracy, looking ravishing in a white lace gown, her hair dressed high and held in place by a diamond tiara, was dancing with her host, Count de Matigny, a widower in his late sixties, small and trim, with pale, delicate features. *The benefit ball the count gives each year for the Children's Hospital is a racket*, Gunther Hartog had told Tracy. *Ten percent of the money goes to the children – ninety percent goes into his pocket.*

'You are a superb dancer, Duchess,' the count said.

Tracy smiled. 'That's because of my partner.'

'How is it that you and I have not met before?'

'I've been living in South America,' Tracy explained. 'In the jungles, I'm afraid.'

'Why on earth!'

'My husband owns a few mines in Brazil.'

'Ah. And is your husband here this evening?'

'No. Unfortunately, he had to stay in Brazil and take care of business.'

'Unlucky for him. Lucky for me.' His arm tightened around her waist. 'I look forward to our becoming very good friends.'

'And I, too,' Tracy murmured.

Over the count's shoulder Tracy suddenly caught sight of Jeff Stevens, looking suntanned and ridiculously fit. He was dancing with a beautiful, willowy brunette in crimson taffeta, who was clinging to him possessively. Jeff saw Tracy at the same moment and smiled.

The bastard has every reason to smile, Tracy thought grimly. During the previous two weeks Tracy had meticulously planned two burglaries. She had broken into the first house and opened the safe, only to find it empty. Jeff Stevens had been there first. On the second occasion Tracy was moving through the grounds towards the targeted house when she heard the sudden acceleration of a car and caught a glimpse of Jeff as he sped away. He had beaten her to it again. He was infuriating. *Now he's here at the house I'm planning to burgle next*, Tracy thought.

Jeff and his partner danced nearer. Jeff smiled and said, 'Good evening, Count.'

The Count de Matigny smiled. 'Ah, Jeffrey. Good evening. I'm so pleased that you could come.'

'I wouldn't have missed it.' Jeff indicated the voluptuous-looking woman in his arms. 'This is Miss Wallace. The Count de Matigny.'

'*Enchanté!*' The count indicated Tracy. 'Duchess, may I present Miss Wallace and Mr Jeffrey Stevens? The Duchess de Larosa.'

Jeff's eyebrows raised questioningly. 'Sorry. I didn't hear the name.'

'De Larosa,' Tracy said evenly.

'De Larosa . . . De Larosa.' Jeff was studying Tracy. 'That name seems so familiar. Of *course*! I know your husband. Is the dear fellow here with you?'

'He's in Brazil.' Tracy found that she was gritting her teeth.

Jeff smiled. 'Ah, too bad. We used to go hunting together. Before he had his accident, of course.'

'Accident?' the count asked.

'Yes.' Jeff's tone was rueful. 'His gun went off and shot him in a very sensitive area. It was one

394

of those stupid things.' He turned to Tracy. 'Is there any hope that he'll be normal again?'

Tracy said tonelessly. 'I'm sure that one day he'll be as normal as you are, Mr Stevens.'

'Oh, good. You will give him my best regards when you talk to him, won't you, Duchess?'

The music stopped. The Count de Matigny apologized to Tracy. 'If you'll excuse me, my dear, I have a few hostly duties to attend to.' He squeezed her hand. 'Don't forget you're seated at my table.'

As the count moved away, Jeff said to his companion, 'Angel, you put some aspirin in your bag, didn't you? Could you get one for me? I'm afraid I'm getting a terrible headache.'

'Oh, my poor darling.' There was an adoring look in her eyes. 'I'll be right back, sweetheart.'

Tracy watched her slink across the floor. 'Aren't you afraid she'll give you diabetes?'

'She is sweet, isn't she? And how have you been lately, Duchess?'

Tracy smiled for the benefit of those around them. 'That's really none of your concern, is it?'

'Ah, but it is. In fact, I'm concerned enough to give you some friendly advice. Don't try to rob this château.'

'Why? Are you planning to do it first?'

Jeff took Tracy's arm and walked her over to a deserted spot near the piano, where a dark-eyed young man was soulfully massacring American show tunes.

Only Tracy could hear Jeff's voice over the

music. 'As a matter of fact, I *was* planning a little something, but it's too dangerous.'

'Really?' Tracy was beginning to enjoy the conversation.

It was a relief to be herself, to stop playacting. *The Greeks had the right word for it*, Tracy thought. *Hypocrite* was from the Greek word for 'actor'.

'Listen to me, Tracy.' Jeff's tone was serious. 'Don't try this. First of all, you'd never get through the grounds alive. A killer guard dog is let loose at night.'

Suddenly, Tracy was listening intently. Jeff *was* planning to rob the place.

'Every window and door is wired. The alarms connect directly to the police station. Even if you did manage to get inside the house, the whole place is crisscrossed with invisible infra-red beams.'

'I know all that.' Tracy was a little smug.

'Then you must also know that the beam doesn't sound the alarm when you step into it. It sounds the alarm when you step *out* of it. It senses the heat change. There's no way you can get through it without setting it off.'

She had not known that. *How had Jeff learned it?*

'Why are you telling me all this?'

He smiled, and she thought he had never looked more attractive. 'I really don't want you to get caught, Duchess. I like having you around. You know, Tracy, you and I could become very good friends.'

'You're wrong,' Tracy assured him. She saw Jeff's date hurrying towards them. 'Here comes Ms Diabetes. Enjoy yourself.'

As Tracy walked away, she heard Jeff's date say, 'I brought you some champagne to wash it down with, poor baby.'

The dinner was sumptuous. Each course was accompanied by the appropriate wine, impeccably served by white-gloved footmen. The first course was a native asparagus with a white truffle sauce, followed by a consommé with delicate morels. After that came a saddle of lamb with an assortment of fresh vegetables from the count's gardens. A crisp endive salad was next. For dessert there were individually moulded ice-cream servings and a silver epergne, piled high with petits fours. Coffee and brandy came last. Cigars were offered to the men, and the women were given Joy perfume in a Baccarat crystal *flacon*.

After dinner, the Count de Matigny turned to Tracy. 'You mentioned that you were interested in seeing some of my paintings. Would you like to take a look now?'

'I'd love to,' Tracy assured him.

The picture gallery was a private museum filled with Italian masters, French Impressionists, and Picassos. The long hall was ablaze with the bewitching colours and forms painted by immortals. There were Monets and Renoirs, Canalettos and Guardis and Tintorettos. There was an exquisite Tiepolo and a Guercino and a Titian, and there was almost a full wall of Cezannes. There was no calculating the value of the collection.

Tracy stared at the paintings a long time, savouring their beauty. 'I hope these are well guarded.'

The count smiled. 'On three occasions thieves have tried to get at my treasures. One was killed by my dog, the second was maimed, and the third is serving a life term in prison. The château is an invulnerable fortress, Duchess.'

'I'm so relieved to hear that, Count.'

There was a bright flash of light outside. 'The fireworks display is beginning,' the count said. 'I think you'll be amused.' He took Tracy's soft hand in his papery, dry one and led her out of the picture gallery. 'I'm leaving for Deauville in the morning, where I have a villa on the sea. I've invited a few friends down next weekend. You might enjoy it.'

'I'm sure I would,' Tracy said regretfully, 'but I'm afraid my husband is getting restless. He insists that I return.'

The fireworks display lasted for almost an hour, and Tracy took advantage of the distraction to reconnoitre the house. What Jeff had said was true: the odds against a successful burglary were formidable, but for that very reason Tracy found the challenge irresistible. She knew that upstairs in the count's bedroom were $2 million in jewels, and half a dozen masterpieces, including a Leonardo.

The château is a treasure house, Gunther Hartog

had told her, *and it's guarded like one. Don't make a move unless you have a foolproof plan.*

Well, I've worked out a plan, Tracy thought. *Whether it's foolproof or not, I'll know tomorrow.*

The following night was chilly and cloudy, and the high walls around the château appeared grim and forbidding as Tracy stood in the shadows, wearing black overalls, rubber-soled shoes, and supple black kid gloves, carrying a shoulder bag. For an unguarded moment Tracy's mind embraced the memory of the walls of the penitentiary, and she gave an involuntary shiver.

She had driven the rented van alongside the stone wall at the back of the estate. From the other side of the wall came a low, fierce growl that developed into a frenzied barking, as the dog leapt into the air, trying to attack. Tracy visualized the Doberman's powerful, heavy body and deadly teeth.

She called out softly to someone in the van, 'Now.'

A slight, middle-aged man, also dressed in black, with a rucksack on his back, came out of the van holding onto a female Doberman. The dog was in season, and the tone of barking from the other side of the stone wall suddenly changed to an excited whine.

Tracy helped lift the bitch to the top of the van, which was almost the exact height of the wall.

'One, two, three,' she whispered.

And the two of them tossed the bitch over the

wall into the grounds of the estate. There were two sharp barks, followed by a series of snuffling noises, then the sound of the dogs running. After that all was quiet.

Tracy turned to her confederate. 'Let's go.'

The man, Jean Louis, nodded. She had found him in Antibes. He was a thief who had spent most of his life in prison. Jean Louis was not bright, but he was a genius with locks and alarms, perfect for this job.

Tracy stepped from the roof of the van onto the top of the wall. She unrolled a scaling ladder and hooked it to the edge of the wall. They both moved down it onto the grass below. The estate appeared vastly different from the way it had looked the evening before, when it was brightly lit and crowded with laughing guests. Now, everything was dark and bleak.

Jean Louis trailed behind Tracy, keeping a fearful watch for the Dobermans.

The château was covered with centuries-old ivy clinging to the wall up to the rooftop. Tracy had casually tested the ivy the evening before. Now, as she put her weight on a vine, it held. She began to climb, scanning the grounds below. There was no sign of the dogs. *I hope they stay busy for a long time*, she prayed.

When Tracy reached the roof, she signalled to Jean Louis and waited until he climbed up beside her. From the pinpoint light Tracy switched on, they saw a glass skylight, securely locked from below. As Tracy watched, Jean Louis reached into the rucksack on his back and pulled out a small glass cutter. It took him less than a minute to remove the glass.

Tracy glanced down and saw that their way was blocked by a spiderweb of alarm wires. 'Can you handle that, Jean?' she whispered.

'*Je peux faire ça.* No problem.' He reached into his pack and pulled out a foot-long wire with an alligator clamp on each end. Moving slowly, he traced the beginning of the alarm wire, stripped it, and connected the alligator clamp to the end of the alarm. He pulled out a pair of pliers and carefully cut the wire. Tracy tensed herself, waiting for the sound of the alarm, but all was quiet. Jean Louis looked up and grinned. '*Voilà. Fini.*'

Wrong, Tracy thought. *This is just the beginning.*

They used a second scaling ladder to climb down through the skylight. So far so good. They had made it safely into the attic. But when Tracy thought of what lay ahead, her heart began to pound.

She pulled out two pairs of red-lens goggles and handed one of them to Jean Louis. 'Put these on.'

She had figured out a way to distract the Doberman, but the infra-red ray alarms had proved to be a more difficult problem to solve. Jeff had been correct: the house was criss-crossed with invisible beams. Tracy took several long, deep breaths. *Centre your energy, your chi. Relax.* She forced her mind into a crystal clarity: *When a person moves into a beam, the sensor detects the difference in temperature and the alarm is set off. It has been devised to go off before the burglar opens the safe, leaving him no time to do anything before the police arrive.*

And there, Tracy had decided, was the weakness in the system. She had needed to devise a way to keep the alarm silent until *after* the safe was opened. At 6:30 in the morning she had found the solution. The burglary was possible, and Tracy had felt that familiar feeling of excitement begin to build within her.

Now, she slipped on the infra-red goggles, and instantly everything in the room took on an eerie red glow. In front of the attic door Tracy saw a beam of light that would have been invisible without the glasses.

'Slip under it,' she warned Jean Louis. 'Careful.'

They crawled under the beam and found themselves in a dark hallway leading to Count de Matigny's bedroom. Tracy flicked on the flashlight and led the way. Through the infra-red goggles, Tracy saw another light beam, this one low across the threshold of the bedroom door. Gingerly, she jumped over it. Jean Louis was right behind her.

Tracy played her flashlight around the walls, and there were the paintings, impressive, awesome.

Promise to bring me the Leonardo, Gunther had said. *And of course the jewellery.*

Tracy took down the picture, turned it over, and laid it on the floor. She carefully removed it from its frame, rolled up the vellum, and stored it in her shoulder bag. All that remained now was to get into the safe, which stood in a curtained alcove at the far end of the bedroom.

Tracy opened the curtains. Four infra-red lights transversed the alcove from the floor to the ceiling, crisscrossing one another. It was impossible to reach the safe without breaking one of the beams.

Jean Louis stared at the beams with dismay. '*Bon Dieu de merde!* We can't get through those. They're too low to crawl under and too high to jump over.'

'I want you to do just as I tell you,' Tracy said. She stepped round the back of him and put her arms tightly around his waist. 'Now, walk with me. Left foot first.'

Together, they took a step towards the beams, then another.

Jean Louis breathed, '*Alors!* We're going into them!'

'Right.'

They moved directly into the centre of the beams, where they converged, and Tracy stopped.

'Now, listen carefully,' she said. 'I want you to walk over to the safe.'

'But the beams –'

'Don't worry. It will be all right.' She fervently hoped she was right.

Hesitantly, Jean Louis stepped out of the infra-red beams. All was quiet. He looked back at Tracy with large, frightened eyes. She was standing in the middle of the beams, her body heat keeping the sensors from sounding the alarm. Jean Louis hurried over to the safe. Tracy stood stock-still, aware that the instant she moved, the alarm would sound.

Out of the corner of one eye, Tracy could see Jean Louis as he removed some tools from his pack and began to work on the dial of the safe. Tracy stood motionless, taking slow, deep breaths. Time stopped. Jean Louis seemed to be taking forever. The calf of Tracy's right leg began to ache, then went into spasm. Tracy gritted her teeth. She dared not move.

'How long?' she whispered.

'Ten, fifteen minutes.'

It seemed to Tracy she had been standing there a lifetime. The leg muscles in her left leg were beginning to cramp. She felt like screaming from the pain. She was pinned in the beams, frozen. She heard a click. The safe was open.

'*Magnifique! C'est la banque!* Do you wish everything?' Jean Louis asked.

'No papers. Only the jewels. Whatever cash is there is yours.'

'*Merci.*'

Tracy heard Jean Louis rifling through the safe, and a few moments later he was walking towards her.

'*Formidable*,' he said. 'But how do we get out of here without breaking the beam?'

'We don't,' Tracy informed him.

He stared at her. '*What?*'

'Stand in front of me.'

'But –'

'Do as I say.'

Panicky, Jean Louis stepped into the beam.

Tracy held her breath. Nothing happened. 'All right. Now, very slowly, we're going to back out of the room.'

'And then?' Jean Louis's eyes looked enormous behind the goggles.

'Then, my friend, we run for it.'

Inch by inch, they backed through the beams towards the curtains, where the beams began. When they reached them, Tracy took a deep breath. 'Right. When I say *now*, we go out the same way we came in.'

Jean Louis swallowed and nodded. Tracy could feel his small body tremble.

'*Now!*'

Tracy spun around and raced towards the door, Jean Louis after her. The instant they stepped out of the beams, the alarm sounded. The noise was deafening, shattering.

Tracy streaked to the attic and scurried up the hook ladder, Jean close behind. They raced across the roof and clambered down the ivy, and the two of them sped across the grounds towards the wall where the second ladder was waiting. Moments later they reached the roof of the van and scurried down. Tracy leapt into the driver's seat, Jean Louis at her side.

As the van raced down the side road, Tracy saw a dark sedan parked under a grove of trees. For an instant the headlights of the van lit the interior of the car. Behind the wheel sat Jeff Stevens. At his side was a large Doberman. Tracy laughed aloud and blew a kiss to Jeff as the van sped away.

From the distance came the wail of approaching police sirens.

TWENTY-SIX

Biarritz, on the southwestern coast of France, has lost much of its turn-of-the-century glamour. The once-famed Casino Bellevue is closed for badly needed repairs, while the Casino Municipal on Rue Mazagran is now a run-down building housing small shops and a dancing school. The old villas on the hills have taken on a look of shabby gentility.

Still, in high season, from July to September, the wealthy and titled of Europe continue to flock to Biarritz to enjoy the gambling and the sun and their memories. Those who do not have their own châteaux stay at the luxurious Hôtel du Palais, at 1 Avenue Impératrice. The former summer residence of Napoleon III, the hotel is situated on a promontory over the Atlantic Ocean, in one of nature's most spectacular settings: a lighthouse on one side, flanked by huge jagged rocks looming out of the grey ocean like prehistoric monsters, and the boardwalk on the other side.

On an afternoon in late August the French

Baroness Marguerite de Chantilly swept into the lobby of the Hôtel du Palais. The baroness was an elegant young woman with a sleek cap of ash-blonde hair. She wore a green-and-white silk Givenchy dress that set off a figure that made the women turn and watch her enviously, and the men gape.

The baroness walked up to the concierge. '*Ma clé, s'il vous plaît,*' she said. She had a charming French accent.

'Certainly, Baroness.' He handed Tracy her key and several telephone messages.

As Tracy walked towards the lift, a bespectacled rumpled-looking man turned abruptly away from the vitrine displaying Hermes scarves and crashed into her, knocking the handbag from her hand.

'Oh, dear,' he said. 'I'm terribly sorry.' He picked up her bag and handed it to her. 'Please forgive me.' He spoke with a Middle European accent.

The Baroness Marguerite de Chantilly gave him an imperious nod and moved on.

An attendant ushered her into the lift and let her off at the third floor. Tracy had chosen Suite 312, having learned that often the selection of the hotel accommodations was as important as the hotel itself. In Capri, it was Bungalow 522 in the Quisisana. In Majorca, it was the Royal Suite of Son Vida, overlooking the mountains and the distant bay. In New York, it was Tower Suite 4717 at The Helmsley Palace Hotel, and in Amsterdam, Room 325 at the Amstel, where one was lulled to sleep by the soothing lapping of the canal waters.

Suite 312 at the Hôtel du Palais had a panoramic view of both the ocean and the city. From every window Tracy could watch the waves crashing against the timeless rocks protruding from the sea like drowning figures. Directly below her window was an enormous kidney-shaped swimming pool, its bright blue water clashing with the grey of the ocean, and next to it a large terrace with umbrellas to ward off the summer sun. The walls of the suite were upholstered in blue-and-white silk damask, with marble baseboards, and the rugs and curtains were the colour of faded sweetheart roses. The wood of the doors and shutters was stained with the soft patina of time.

When Tracy had locked the door behind her, she took off the tight-fitting blonde wig and massaged her scalp. The baroness persona was one of her best. There were hundreds of titles to choose from in *Debrett's Peerage and Baronetage* and *Almanach de Gotha*. There were ladies and duchesses and princesses and baronesses and countesses by the score from two dozen countries, and the books were invaluable to Tracy, for they gave family histories dating back centuries, with the names of fathers and mothers and children, schools and houses, and addresses of family residences. It was a simple matter to select a prominent family and become a distant cousin – particularly a *wealthy* distant cousin. People were so impressed by titles and money.

Tracy thought of the stranger who had bumped into her in the hotel lobby and smiled. It had begun.

At 8:00 that evening the Baroness Marguerite de Chantilly was seated in the hotel's bar when the man who had collided with her earlier approached her table.

'Excuse me,' he said diffidently, 'but I must apologize again for my inexcusable clumsiness this afternoon.'

Tracy gave him a gracious smile. 'That's quite all right. It was an accident.'

'You are most kind.' He hesitated. 'I would feel much better if you would permit me to buy you a drink.'

'*Oui*. If you wish.'

He slid into a chair opposite her. 'Allow me to introduce myself. I am Professor Adolf Zuckerman.'

'Marguerite de Chantilly.'

Zuckerman signalled the waiter. 'What are you drinking?' Zuckerman asked Tracy.

'Champagne. But perhaps –'

He raised a reassuring hand. 'I can afford it. In fact, I am on the verge of being able to afford anything in the world.'

'Really?' Tracy gave him a small smile. 'How nice for you.'

'Yes.'

Zuckerman ordered a bottle of Bollinger, then turned to Tracy. 'The most extraordinary thing has

410

happened to me. I really should not be discussing this with a stranger, but it is too exciting to keep to myself.' He leaned closer and lowered his voice. 'To tell you the truth, I am a simple schoolteacher – or I was, until recently. I teach history. It is most enjoyable, you understand, but not too exciting.'

She listened, a look of polite interest on her face.

'That is to say, it was not exciting until a few months ago.'

'May I ask what happened a few months ago, Professor Zuckerman?'

'I was doing research on the Spanish Armada, looking for odd bits and pieces that might make the subject more interesting for my students, and in the archives of the local museum, I came across an old document that had somehow got mixed in with other papers. It gave the details of a secret expedition that Prince Philip sent out in 1588. One of the ships, loaded with gold bullion, was supposed to have sunk in a storm and vanished without a trace.'

Tracy looked at him thoughtfully. '*Supposed* to have sunk?'

'Exactly. But according to these records, the captain and crew deliberately sank the ship in a deserted cove, planning to come back later and retrieve the treasure, but they were attacked and killed by pirates before they could return. The document survived only because none of the sailors on the pirate ship could read or write. They did not know the significance of what they had.' His voice was trembling with excitement. 'Now' – he lowered his voice and looked around to make sure it was safe to continue – '*I* have the document, with detailed instructions on how to get to the treasure.'

'What a fortunate discovery for you, Professor.' There was a note of admiration in her voice.

'That gold bullion is probably worth fifty million dollars today,' Zuckerman said. 'All I have to do is bring it up.'

'What's stopping you?'

He gave an embarrassed shrug. 'Money. I must outfit a ship to bring the treasure to the surface.'

'I see. How much would that cost?'

'A hundred thousand dollars. I must confess, I did something extremely foolish. I took twenty thousand dollars – my life's savings – and I came to Biarritz to gamble at the casino, hoping to win enough to . . .' His voice trailed off.

'And you lost it.'

He nodded. Tracy saw the glint of tears behind his spectacles.

The champagne arrived, and the waiter popped the cork and poured the golden liquid into their glasses.

'*Bonne chance*,' Tracy toasted.

'Thank you.'

They sipped their drinks in contemplative silence.

'Please forgive me for boring you with all this,' Zuckerman said. 'I should not be telling a beautiful lady my troubles.'

'But I find your story fascinating,' she assured him. 'You are sure the gold is there, *oui?*'

'Beyond a shadow of a doubt. I have the original shipping orders and a map drawn by the captain, himself. I know the exact location of the treasure.'

She was studying him with a thoughtful expression on her face. 'But you need a hundred thousand dollars?'

Zuckerman chuckled ruefully. 'Yes. For a treasure worth fifty million.' He took another sip of his drink.

'*C'est possible* . . .' She stopped.

'What?'

'Have you considered taking in a partner?'

He looked at her in surprise. 'A partner? No. I planned to do this alone. But of course now that I've lost my money . . .' His voice trailed off again.

'Professor Zuckerman, suppose I were to give you the hundred thousand dollars?'

He shook his head. 'Absolutely not, Baroness. I could not permit that. You might lose your money.'

'But if you're sure the treasure is there –?'

'Oh, of that I am positive. But a hundred things could go wrong. There are no guarantees.'

'In life, there are few guarantees. Your problem is *très intéressant*. Perhaps if I help you solve it, it could be lucrative for both of us.'

'No, I could never forgive myself if by any *remote* chance you should lose your money.'

'I can afford it,' she assured him. 'And I would

stand to make a great deal on my investment, *n'est-ce pas?*'

'Of course, there *is* that side of it,' Zuckerman admitted. He sat there weighing the matter, obviously torn with doubts. Finally, he said, 'If that is what you wish, you will be fifty-fifty partner.'

She smiled, pleased. '*D'accord.* I accept.'

The professor added quickly, 'After expenses, of course.'

'*Naturellement.* How soon can we get started?'

'Immediately.' The professor was charged with a sudden vitality. 'I have already found the boat I want to use. It has modern dredging equipment and a crew of four. Of course, we will have to give them a small percentage of whatever we bring up.'

'*Bien sûr.*'

'We should get started as quickly as possible, or we might lose the boat.'

'I can have the money for you in five days.'

'Wonderful!' Zuckerman exclaimed. 'That will give me time to make all the preparations. Ah, this was a fortuitous meeting for both of us, was it not?'

'*Oui. Sans doute.*'

'To our adventure.' The professor raised his glass.

Tracy raised hers and toasted, 'May it prove to be as profitable as I feel it will be.'

They clinked glasses. Tracy looked across the room and froze. At a table in the far corner was Jeff Stevens, watching her with an amused smile on his face. With him was an attractive woman ablaze with jewels.

Jeff nodded to Tracy, and she smiled, remembering how she had last seen him outside the de Matigny estate, with that silly dog beside him. *That was one for me*, Tracy thought happily.

'So, if you will excuse me,' Zuckerman was saying, 'I have much to do. I will be in touch with you.' Tracy graciously extended her hand, and he kissed it and departed.

'I see your friend has deserted you, and I can't imagine why. You look absolutely terrific as a blonde.'

Tracy glanced up. Jeff was standing beside her table. He sat down in the chair Adolf Zuckerman had occupied a few minutes earlier.

'Congratulations,' Jeff said. 'The de Matigny caper was ingenious. Very neat.'

'Coming from you, that's high praise, Jeff.'

'You're costing me a lot of money, Tracy.'

'You'll get used to it.'

He toyed with the glass in front of him. 'What did Professor Zuckerman want?'

'Oh, you know him?'

'You might say that.'

'He . . . er . . . just wanted to have a drink.'

'And tell you all about his sunken treasure?'

Tracy was suddenly wary. 'How do you know about that?'

Jeff looked at her in surprise. 'Don't tell me you *fell* for it? It's the oldest con game in the world.'

'Not this time.'

'You mean you *believed* him?'

Tracy said stiffly, 'I'm not at liberty to discuss it, but the professor happens to have some inside information.'

Jeff shook his head in disbelief. 'Tracy, he's trying to take you. How much did he ask you to invest in his sunken treasure?'

'Never mind,' Tracy said primly. 'It's my money and my business.'

Jeff shrugged. 'Right. Just don't say old Jeff didn't try to warn you.'

'It couldn't be that you're interested in that gold for yourself, could it?'

He threw up his hands in mock despair. 'Why are you always so suspicious of me?'

'It's simple,' Tracy replied. 'I don't trust you. Who was the woman you were with?' She instantly wished she could have withdrawn the question.

'Suzanne? A friend.'

'Rich, of course.'

Jeff gave her a lazy smile. 'As a matter of fact, I think she does have a bit of money. If you'd like to join us for luncheon tomorrow, the chef on her two-hundred-and-fifty-foot yacht in the harbour makes a –'

'Thank you. I wouldn't dream of interfering with your lunch. What are you selling her?'

'That's personal.'

'I'm sure it is.' It came out more harshly than she had intended.

Tracy studied him over the rim of her glass. He

really was too damned attractive. He had clean, regular features, beautiful grey eyes with long lashes, and the heart of a snake. A very intelligent snake.

'Have you ever thought of going into a legitimate business?' Tracy asked. 'You'd probably be very successful.'

Jeff looked shocked. 'What? And give up all this? You must be joking!'

'Have you always been a con artist?'

'Con artist? I'm an *entrepreneur*,' he said reprovingly.

'How did you become a – an – entrepreneur?'

'I ran away from home when I was fourteen and joined a carnival.'

'At fourteen?' It was the first glimpse Tracy had had into what lay beneath the sophisticated, charming veneer.

'It was good for me – I learned to cope. When that wonderful war in Vietnam came along, I joined up as a Green Beret and got an advanced education. I think the main thing I learned was that that war was the biggest con of all. Compared to that, you and I are amateurs.' He changed the subject abruptly. 'Do you like pelota?'

'If you're selling it, no thank you.'

'It's a game, a variation of jai alai. I have two tickets for tonight, and Suzanne can't make it. Would you like to go?'

Tracy found herself saying yes.

*   *   *

They dined at a little restaurant in the town square, where they had a local wine and *confit de canard l'aile* – roast duck simmered in its own juices with roasted potatoes and garlic. It was delicious.

'The speciality of the house,' Jeff informed Tracy.

They discussed politics and books and travel, and Tracy found Jeff surprisingly knowledgeable.

'When you're on your own at fourteen,' Jeff told her, 'you pick up things fast. First you learn what motivates you, then you learn what motivates other people. A con game is similar to ju jitsu. In ju jitsu you use your opponent's strength to win. In a con game, you use his greed. You make the first move, and he does the rest of your work for you.'

Tracy smiled, wondering if Jeff had any idea how much alike they were. She enjoyed being with him, but she was sure that given the opportunity, he would not hesitate to double-cross her. He was a man to be careful of, and that she intended to be.

The fronton where pelota was played was a large outdoor arena the size of a football field, high in the hills of Biarritz. There were huge green concrete backboards at either end of the court, and a playing area in the centre, with four tiers of stone benches on both sides of the field. At dusk, floodlights were turned on. When Tracy and Jeff arrived, the stands were almost full, crowded with fans, as the two teams went into action.

Members of each team took turns slamming the

ball into the concrete wall and catching it on the rebound in their cestas, the long, narrow baskets strapped to their arms. Pelota was a fast, dangerous game.

When one of the players missed the ball, the crowd screamed.

'They really take this very seriously,' Tracy commented.

'A lot of money is bet on these games. The Basques are a gambling race.'

As spectators kept filing in, the benches became more crowded, and Tracy found herself being pressed against Jeff. If he was aware of her body against his, he gave no sign of it.

The pace and ferocity of the game seemed to intensify as the minutes passed, and the screams of the fans kept echoing through the night.

'Is it as dangerous as it looks?' Tracy asked.

'Baroness, that ball travels through the air at almost a hundred miles an hour. If you get hit in the head, you're dead. But it's rare for a player to miss.' He patted her hand absently, his eyes glued to the action.

The players were experts, moving gracefully, in perfect control. But in the middle of the game, without warning, one of the players hurled the ball at the backboard at the wrong angle, and the lethal ball came hurtling straight towards the bench where Tracy and Jeff sat. The spectators scrambled for cover. Jeff grabbed Tracy and shoved her to the ground, his body covering hers. They heard

419

the sound of the ball sailing directly over their heads and smashing into the side wall. Tracy lay on the ground, feeling the hardness of Jeff's body. His face was very close to hers.

He held her a moment, then lifted himself up and pulled her to her feet. There was a sudden awkwardness between them.

'I – I think I've had enough excitement for one evening,' Tracy said. 'I'd like to go back to the hotel, please.'

They said good night in the lobby.

'I enjoyed this evening,' Tracy told Jeff. She meant it.

'Tracy, you're not really going ahead with Zuckerman's crazy sunken-treasure scheme, are you?'

'Yes, I am.'

He studied her for a long moment. 'You still think I'm after that gold, don't you?'

She looked him in the eye. 'Aren't you?'

His expression hardened. 'Good luck.'

'Good night, Jeff.'

Tracy watched him turn and walk out of the hotel. She supposed he was on his way to see Suzanne. *Poor woman.*

The concierge said, 'Ah, good evening, Baroness. There is a message for you.'

It was from Professor Zuckerman.

Adolf Zuckerman had a problem. A very large problem. He was seated in the office of Armand

420

Grangier, and Zuckerman was so terrified of what was happening that he discovered he had wet his pants. Grangier was the owner of an illegal private casino located in an elegant private villa at 123 Rue de Frias. It made no difference to Grangier whether the Casino Municipal was closed or not, for the club at Rue de Frias was always filled with wealthy patrons. Unlike the government-supervised casinos, bets there were unlimited, and that was where the high rollers came to play roulette, chemin de fer and craps. Grangier's customers included Arab princes, English nobility, Oriental businessmen, African heads of state. Scantily clad young ladies circulated around the room taking orders for complimentary champagne and whiskey, for Armand Grangier had learned long before that, more than any other class of people, the rich appreciated getting something for nothing. Grangier could afford to give drinks away. His roulette wheels and his card games were rigged.

The club was usually filled with beautiful young women escorted by older gentlemen with money, and sooner or later the women were drawn to Grangier. He was a miniature of a man, with perfect features, liquid brown eyes, and a soft, sensual mouth. He stood five feet four inches, and the combination of his looks and his small stature drew women like a magnet. Grangier treated each one with feigned admiration.

'I find you irresistible, *chérie*, but unfortunately for both of us, I am madly in love with someone.'

And it was true. Of course, that *someone* changed from week to week, for in Biarritz there was an endless supply of beautiful young men, and Armand Grangier gave each one his brief place in the sun.

Grangier's connections with the underworld and the police were powerful enough for him to maintain his casino. He had worked his way up from being a ticket runner for the mob to running drugs, and finally, to ruling his own little fiefdom in Biarritz; those who opposed him found out too late how deadly the little man could be.

Now Adolf Zuckerman was being cross-examined by Armand Grangier.

'Tell me more about this baroness you talked into the sunken-treasure scheme.'

From the furious tone of his voice, Zuckerman knew that something was wrong, terribly wrong.

He swallowed and said, 'Well, she's a widow whose husband left her a lot of money, and she said she's going to come up with a hundred thousand dollars.' The sound of his own voice gave him confidence to go on: 'Once we get the money, of course, we'll tell her that the salvage ship had an accident and that we need another fifty thousand. Then it'll be another hundred thousand, and – you know – just like always.'

He saw the look of contempt on Armand Grangier's face. 'What's – what's the problem, chief?'

'The problem,' said Grangier in a steely tone, 'is

that I just received a call from one of my boys in Paris. He forged a passport for your baroness. Her name is Tracy Whitney, and she's an American.'

Zuckerman's mouth was suddenly dry. He licked his lips. 'She – she really seemed interested, chief.'

'*Balle! Conneau!* She's a con artist. You tried to pull a swindle on a swindler!'

'Then w-why did she say yes? Why didn't she just turn it down!'

Armand Grangier's voice was icy. 'I don't know, Professor, but I intend to find out. And when I do, I'm sending the lady for a swim in the bay. Nobody can make a fool out of Armand Grangier. Now, pick up that phone. Tell her a friend of yours has offered to put up half the money, and that I'm on my way over to see her. Do you think you can handle that?'

Zuckerman said eagerly, 'Sure, chief. Not to worry.'

'I do worry,' Armand Grangier said slowly. 'I worry a lot about you, Professor.'

Armand Grangier did not like mysteries. The sunken-treasure game had been worked for centuries, but the victims had to be gullible. There was simply no way a con artist would ever fall for it. That was the mystery that bothered Grangier, and he intended to solve it; and when he had the answer, the woman would be turned over to Bruno Vicente. Vicente enjoyed playing games with his victims before disposing of them.

Armand Grangier stepped out of the limousine as it stopped in front of the Hôtel du Palais, walked into the lobby, and approached Jules Bergerac, the white-haired Basque who had worked at the hotel from the age of thirteen.

'What's the number of the Baroness Marguerite de Chantilly's suite?'

There was a strict rule that desk clerks do not divulge the room numbers of guests, but rules did not apply to Armand Grangier.

'Suite three-twelve, Monsieur Grangier.'

'*Merci.*'

'And Room three-eleven.'

Grangier stopped. 'What?'

'The countess also has a room adjoining her suite.'

'Oh? Who occupies it?'

'No one.'

'No one? Are you sure?'

'*Oui, monsieur*. She keeps it locked. The maids have been ordered to keep out.'

A puzzled frown appeared on Grangier's face. 'You have a passkey?'

'Of course.' Without an instant's hesitation, the concierge reached under the desk for a passkey and handed it to Armand Grangier. Jules watched as Armand Grangier walked towards the lift. One never argued with a man like Grangier.

When Armand Grangier reached the door of the baroness's suite, he found it ajar. He pushed it open and entered. The living room was deserted. 'Hello. Anyone here?'

A feminine voice from another room sang out, 'I'm in the bath. I'll be with you in a minute. Please help yourself to a drink.'

Grangier wandered around the suite, familiar with its furnishings, for over the years he had arranged for many of his friends to stay in the hotel. He strolled into the bedroom. Expensive jewellery was carelessly spread out on a dressing table.

'I won't be a minute,' the voice called out from the bathroom.

'No hurry, Baroness.'

Baroness mon cul! he thought angrily. *Whatever little game you're playing, chérie, is going to backfire.* He walked over to the door that connected it to the adjoining room. It was locked. Grangier took out the passkey and opened the door. The room he stepped into had a musty, unused smell. The concierge had said that no one occupied it. Then why did she need –? Grangier's eye was caught by something oddly out of place. A heavy black electrical cord attached to a wall socket snaked along the length of the floor and disappeared into a cupboard. The door was open just enough to allow the cord to pass through. Curious, Grangier walked over to the cupboard and opened it.

A row of wet hundred-dollar bills held up by clothespegs on a wire was strung across the cupboard, hanging out to dry. On a typewriter stand was an object covered by a draped cloth. Grangier flicked up the cloth. He uncovered a small printing press with a still-wet hundred-dollar bill in it. Next to the press were sheets of blank paper the size of American currency and a paper cutter. Several one-hundred-dollar bills that had been unevenly cut were scattered on the floor.

An angry voice behind Grangier demanded, 'What are you doing in here?' Grangier spun round. Tracy Whitney, her hair damp from the bath and wrapped in a towel, had come into the room.

Armand Grangier said softly, '*Counterfeit!* You were going to pay us off with counterfeit money.' He watched the expressions that played across her face. Denial, outrage, and then defiance.

'All right,' Tracy admitted. 'But it wouldn't have mattered. No one can tell these from the real thing.'

'*Con!*' It was going to be a pleasure to destroy this one.

'These bills are as good as gold.'

'Really?' There was a contempt in Grangier's voice. He pulled one of the wet bills from the wire and glanced at it. He looked at one side, then the other, and then examined them more closely. They were excellent. 'Who cut these dies?'

'What's the difference? Look, I can have the hundred thousand dollars ready by Friday.'

Grangier stared at her, puzzled. And then he realized what she was thinking, and he laughed aloud. 'Jesus,' he said. 'You're really stupid. There's no treasure.'

Tracy was bewildered. 'What do you mean, no treasure? Professor Zuckerman told me —'

'And you believed him? Shame, *Baroness*.' He studied the bill in his hand again. 'I'll take this.'

Tracy shrugged. 'Take as many as you like. It's only paper.'

Grangier grabbed a handful of the wet hundred-dollar bills. 'How do you know one of the maids won't walk in here?' he asked.

'I pay them well to keep away. And when I'm out, I lock the cupboard.'

She's cool, Armand Grangier thought. *But it's not going to keep her alive.*

'Don't leave the hotel,' he ordered. 'I have a friend I want you to meet.'

Armand Grangier had intended to turn the woman over to Bruno Vicente immediately, but some instinct held him back. He examined one of the bills again. He had handled a lot of counterfeit money, but nothing nearly as good as this. Whoever had cut the dies was a genius. The paper felt authentic, and the lines were crisp and clean. The colours remained sharp and fixed, even with the bill wet, and the picture of Benjamin Franklin was perfect. The bitch was right. It *was* hard to tell the difference between what he held in his hand and the real thing. Grangier wondered whether it would be possible to pass it off as genuine currency. It was a tempting idea.

He decided to hold off on Bruno Vicente for a while.

Early the following morning Armand Grangier

sent for Zuckerman and handed him one of the hundred-dollar bills. 'Go down to the bank and exchange this for francs.'

'Sure, chief.'

Grangier watched him hurry out of the office. This was Zuckerman's punishment for his stupidity. If he was arrested, he would never tell where he got the counterfeit bill, not if he wanted to live. But if he managed to pass the bill sucessfully . . . *I'll see*, Grangier thought.

Fifteen minutes later Zuckerman returned to the office. He counted out a hundred dollars' worth of French francs. 'Anything else, chief?'

Grangier stared at the francs. 'Did you have any trouble?'

'Trouble? No. Why?'

'I want you to go back to the same bank,' Grangier ordered. 'This is what I want you to say . . .'

Adolf Zuckerman walked into the lobby of the Banque de France and approached the desk where the bank manager sat. This time Zuckerman was aware of the danger he was in, but he preferred facing that than Grangier's wrath.

'May I help you?' the manager asked.

'Yes.' He tried to conceal his nervousness. 'You see, I got into a poker game last night with some Americans I met at a bar.' He stopped.

The bank manager nodded wisely. 'And you lost your money and perhaps wish to make a loan?'

'No,' Zuckerman said. 'As – as a matter of fact, I won. The only thing is, the men didn't look quite honest to me.' He pulled out two $100 bills. 'They paid me with these, and I'm afraid they – they might be counterfeit.'

Zuckerman held his breath as the bank manager leaned forward and took the bills in his pudgy hands. He examined them carefully, first one side and then the other, then held them up to the light.

He looked at Zuckerman and smiled. 'You were lucky, monsieur. These bills are genuine.'

Zuckerman allowed himself to exhale. *Thank God!* Everything was going to be all right.

'No problem at all, chief. He said they were genuine.'

It was almost too good to be true. Armand Grangier sat there thinking, a plan already half-formed in his mind.

'Go to the baroness.'

Tracy was seated in Armand Grangier's office, facing him across his Empire desk.

'You and I are going to be partners,' Grangier informed her.

Tracy started to rise. 'I don't need a partner and –'

'Sit down.'

She looked into Grangier's eyes and sat down.

'Biarritz is my town. You try to pass a single one of those bills and you'll get arrested so fast you won't know what hit you. *Comprenez vous?* Bad things happen to pretty ladies in our jails. You can't make a move here without me.'

She studied him. 'So what I'm buying from you is protection?'

'Wrong. What you're buying from me is your life.'

Tracy believed him.

'Now, tell me where you got your printing press.'

Tracy hesitated, and Grangier enjoyed her squirming. He watched her surrender.

She said reluctantly, 'I bought it from an American living in Switzerland. He was an engraver with the U.S. Mint for twenty-five years, and when they retired him there was some technical problem about his pension and he never received it. He felt cheated and decided to get even, so he smuggled out some hundred-dollar plates that were supposed to have been destroyed and used his contacts to get the paper that the Treasury Department prints its money on.'

That explains it, Grangier thought triumphantly. *That is why the bills look so good.* His excitement grew. 'How much money can that press turn out in a day?'

'Only one bill an hour. Each side of the paper has to be processed and –'

He interrupted. 'Isn't there a larger press?'

'Yes, he has one that will turn out fifty bills every eight hours – five thousand dollars a day – but he wants half a million dollars for it.'

'Buy it,' Grangier said.

'I don't have five hundred thousand dollars.'

'I do. How soon can you get hold of the press?'

She said reluctantly, 'Now, I suppose, but I don't –'

Grangier picked up the telephone and spoke into it. 'Louis, I want five hundred thousand dollars' worth of French francs. Take what we have from the safe and get the rest from the banks. Bring it to my office. *Vite!*'

Tracy stood up nervously. 'I'd better go and –'

'You're not going anywhere.'

'I really should –'

'Just sit there and keep quiet. I'm thinking.'

He had business associates who would expect to be cut in on this deal, *but what they don't know won't hurt them*, Grangier decided. He would buy the large press himself and replace what he borrowed from the casino's bank account with money he would print. After that, he would tell Bruno Vicente to handle the woman. She did not like partners.

Well, neither did Armand Grangier.

Two hours later the money arrived in a large sack. Grangier said to Tracy, 'You're checking out of the Palais. I have a house up in the hills that's very private. You will stay there until we set up the operation.' He pushed the phone towards her. 'Now, call your friend in Switzerland and tell him you're buying the big press.'

'I have his phone number at the hotel. I'll call from there. Give me the address of your house, and I'll tell him to ship the press there and –'

'*Non!*' Grangier snapped. 'I don't want to leave a trail. I'll have it picked up at the airport. We will talk about it at dinner tonight. I'll see you at eight o'clock.'

It was a dismissal. Tracy rose to her feet.

Grangier nodded towards the sack. 'Be careful with the money. I wouldn't want anything to happen to it – or to you.'

'Nothing will,' Tracy assured him.

He smiled lazily. 'I know. Professor Zuckerman is going to escort you back to your hotel.'

The two of them rode in the limousine in silence, the money bag between them, each busy with his own thoughts. Zuckerman was not exactly sure what was happening, but he sensed it was going to be very good for him. The woman was the key. Grangier had ordered him to keep an eye on her, and Zuckerman intended to do that.

Armand Grangier was in a euphoric mood that evening. By now, the large printing press would have been arranged for. The Whitney woman had said it would print $5,000 a day, but Grangier had a better plan. He intended to work the press on twenty-four hour shifts. That would bring it to $15,000 a day, more than $100,000 a week, $1 million every ten weeks. And that was just the beginning. Tonight he would learn who the

432

engraver was and make a deal with him for more machines. There was no limit to the fortune it would make him.

At precisely 8:00, Grangier's limousine pulled into the sweeping curve of the driveway of the Hôtel du Palais, and Grangier stepped out of the car. As he walked into the lobby, he noticed with satisfaction that Zuckerman was seated near the entrance, keeping a watchful eye on the doors.

Grangier walked over to the desk. 'Jules, tell the Baroness de Chantilly I am here. Have her come down to the lobby.'

The concierge looked up and said, 'But the baroness has checked out, Monsieur Grangier.'

'You're mistaken. Call her.'

Jules Bergerac was distressed. It was unhealthy to contradict Armand Grangier. 'I checked her out myself.'

Impossible. 'When?'

'Shortly after she returned to the hotel. She asked me to bring her bill to her suite so she could settle it in cash –'

Armand Grangier's mind was racing. 'In cash? French francs?'

'As a matter of fact, yes, monsieur.'

Grangier asked frantically, 'Did she take anything out of her suite? Any baggage or boxes?'

'No. She said she would send for her luggage later.'

So she had taken his money and gone to Switzerland to make her own deal for the large printing press.

'Take me to her suite. Quickly!'

'*Oui, Monsieur Grangier.*'

Jules Bergerac grabbed a key from a rack and raced with Armand Grangier towards the lift.

As Grangier passed Zuckerman, he hissed, 'Why are you sitting there, you idiot? She's gone.'

Zuckerman looked up at him uncomprehendingly. 'She can't be gone. She hasn't come down to the lobby. I've been watching for her.'

'*Watching for her*,' Grangier mimicked. 'Have you been watching for a nurse – a grey-haired old lady – a maid going out the service door?'

Zuckerman was bewildered. 'Why would I do that?'

'Get back to the casino,' Grangier snapped. 'I'll deal with you later.'

The suite looked exactly the same as when Grangier had seen it last. The connecting door to the adjoining room was open. Grangier stepped in and hurried over to the cupboard and yanked open the door. The printing press was still there, thank God! The Whitney woman had left in too big a hurry to take it with her. That was her mistake. *And it is not her only mistake*, Grangier thought. She had cheated him out of $500,000, and he was going to pay her back with a vengeance. He would let the police help him find her and put her in jail, where his men could get at her. They would make her tell who the engraver was and then shut her up for good.

Armand Grangier dialled the number of police

434

headquarters and asked to talk to Inspector Dumont. He spoke earnestly into the phone for three minutes and then said, 'I'll wait here.'

Fifteen minutes later his friend the inspector arrived, accompanied by a man with an epicene figure and one of the most unattractive faces Grangier had ever seen. His forehead looked ready to burst out of his face, and his brown eyes, almost hidden behind thick spectacles, had the piercing look of a fanatic.

'This is Monsieur Daniel Cooper,' Inspector Dumont said. 'Monsieur Grangier. Mr Cooper is also interested in the woman you telephoned me about.'

Cooper spoke up. 'You mentioned to Inspector Dumont that she's involved in a counterfeiting operation.'

'*Vraiment*. She is on her way to Switzerland at this moment. You can pick her up at the border. I have all the evidence you need right here.'

He led them to the cupboard, and Daniel Cooper and Inspector Dumont looked inside.

'There is the press she printed her money on.'

Daniel Cooper walked over to the machine and examined it carefully. 'She printed the money on this press?'

'I just told you so,' Grangier snapped. He took a bill from his pocket. 'Look at this. It is one of the counterfeit hundred-dollar bills she gave me.'

Cooper walked over to the window and held the bill up to the light. 'This is a genuine bill.'

'It only *looks* like one. That is because she used stolen plates she brought from an engraver who once worked at the Mint in Philadelphia. She printed these bills on this press.'

Cooper said rudely, 'You're stupid. This is an ordinary printing press. The only thing you could print on this is letterheads.'

'Letterheads?' The room was beginning to spin.

'You actually *believed* in the fable of a machine that turns paper into genuine hundred-dollar bills?'

'I tell you I saw with my own eyes –' Grangier stopped. What had he seen? Some wet hundred-dollar bills strung up to dry, some blank paper and a paper cutter. The enormity of the swindle began to dawn on him. There *was* no counterfeiting operation, no engraver waiting in Switzerland. Tracy Whitney had never fallen for the sunken-treasure story. The bitch had used his own scheme as the bait to swindle him out of half a million dollars. If the word of this got out . . .

The two men were watching him.

'Do you wish to press charges of some kind, Armand?' Inspector Dumont asked.

How could he? What could he say? That he had been cheated while trying to finance a counterfeiting operation? And what were his associates going to do to him when they learned he had stolen half a million dollars of their money and given it away? He was filled with sudden dread.

'No. I – I don't wish to press charges.' There was panic in his voice.

Africa, Armand Grangier thought. *They'll never find me in Africa.*

Daniel Cooper was thinking, *Next time. I'll get her next time.*

TWENTY-SEVEN

It was Tracy who suggested to Gunther Hartog that they meet in Majorca. Tracy loved the island. It was one of the truly picturesque places in the world. 'Besides,' she told Gunther, 'it was once the refuge of pirates. We'll feel right at home there.'

'It might be best if we are not seen together,' he suggested.

'I'll arrange it.'

It had started with Gunther's phone call from London. 'I have something for you that is quite out of the ordinary, Tracy. I think you'll find it a real challenge.'

The following morning Tracy flew to Palma, Majorca's capital. Because of Interpol's red *circulation* on Tracy, her departure from Biarritz and her arrival in Majorca were reported to the local authorities. When Tracy checked into the Royal Suite at the Son Vida Hotel, a surveillance team was set up on a twenty-four-hour basis.

Police Commandant Ernesto Marze at Palma had spoken with Inspector Trignant at Interpol.

'I am convinced,' Trignant said, 'that Tracy Whitney is a one-woman crime wave.'

'All the worse for her. If she commits a crime in Majorca, she will find that our justice is swift.'

Inspector Trignant said, 'Monsieur, there is one other thing I should mention.'

'*Si?*'

'You will be having an American visitor. His name is Daniel Cooper.'

It seemed to the detectives trailing Tracy that she was interested only in sightseeing. They followed her as she toured the island, visiting the cloister of San Francisco and the colourful Bellver Castle and the beach at Illetas. She attended a bullfight in Palma and dined on *sobrasadas* and *camaiot* in the Plaza de la Reine; and she was always alone.

She took trips to Formentor and Valldemosa and La Granja, and visited the pearl factories at Manacor.

'*Nada*,' the detectives reported to Ernesto Marze. 'She is here as a tourist, Commandant.'

The commandant's secretary came into the office. 'There is an American here to see you. Señor Daniel Cooper.'

Commandant Marze had many American friends. He liked Americans, and he had the feeling that despite what Inspector Trignant had said, he was going to like this Daniel Cooper.

439

He was wrong.

'You're idiots. All of you,' Daniel Cooper snapped. 'Of *course* she's not here as a tourist. She's after something.'

Commandant Marze barely managed to hold his temper in check. 'Señor, you yourself have said that Miss Whitney's targets are always something spectacular, that she enjoys doing the impossible. I have checked carefully, Señor Cooper. There is nothing in Majorca that is worthy of attracting Señorita Whitney's talents.'

'Has she met anyone here . . . talked to anyone?'

The insolent tone of the *ojete*! 'No. No one.'

'Then she will,' Daniel Cooper said flatly.

I finally know, Commandant Marze told himself, *what they mean by the Ugly American.*

There are two hundred known caves in Majorca, but the most exciting is the Cuevas del Drach, the 'Caves of the Dragon', near Porto Cristo, an hour's journey from Palma. The ancient caves go deep into the ground, enormous vaulted caverns carved with stalagmites and stalactites, tomb-silent except for the occasional rush of meandering, underground streams, with the water turning green or blue or white, each colour denoting the extent of the tremendous depths.

The caves are a fairyland of pale-ivory architecture, a seemingly endless series of labyrinths, dimly lit by strategically placed torches.

No one is permitted inside the caves without a guide, but from the moment the caves are opened to the public in the morning, they are filled with tourists.

Tracy chose Saturday to visit the caves, when they were most crowded, packed with hundreds of tourists from countries all over the world. She bought her ticket at the small counter and disappeared into the crowd. Daniel Cooper and two of Commandant Marze's men were close behind her. A guide led the excursionists along narrow stone paths, made slippery by the dripping water from the stalactites above, pointing downwards like accusing skeletal fingers.

There were alcoves where the visitors could step off the paths to stop and admire the calcium formations that looked like huge birds and strange animals and trees. There were pools of darkness along the dimly lit paths, and it was into one of these that Tracy disappeared.

Daniel Cooper hurried forward, but she was nowhere in sight. The press of the crowd moving down the steps made it impossible to locate her. He had no way of knowing whether she was ahead of him or behind him. *She is planning something here*, Cooper told himself. *But how? Where? What?*

In an arena-sized grotto at the lowest point in the caves, facing the Great Lake, is a Roman theatre. Tiers of stone benches have been built to accommodate the audiences that come to watch the spectacle staged every hour, and the sightseers take their seats in darkness, waiting for the show to begin.

Tracy counted her way up to the tenth tier and moved in twenty seats. The man in the twenty-first seat turned to her. 'Any problem?'

'None, Gunther.' She leaned over and kissed him on the cheek.

He said something, and she had to lean closer to hear him above the babel of voices surrounding them.

'I thought it best that we not be seen together, in case you're being followed.'

Tracy glanced around at the huge, packed black cavern. 'We're safe here.' She looked at him, curious. 'It must be important.'

'It is.' He leaned closer to her. 'A wealthy client is eager to acquire a certain painting. It's a Goya, called *Puerto*. He'll pay whoever can obtain it for him half a million dollars in cash. That's above my commission.'

Tracy was thoughtful. 'Are there others trying?'

'Frankly, yes. In my opinion, the chances of success are limited.'

'Where is the painting?'

'In the Prado Museum in Madrid.'

'*The Prado!*' The word that flashed through Tracy's mind was *impossible*.

He was leaning very close, speaking into her ear, ignoring the chattering going on around them as the arena filled up. 'This will take a great deal of ingenuity. That is why I thought of you, my dear Tracy.'

'I'm flattered,' Tracy said. 'Half a million dollars?'

'Free and clear.'

The show began, and there was a sudden hush. Slowly, invisible bulbs began to glow and music filled the enormous cavern. The centre of the stage was a large lake in front of the seated audience, and on it, from behind a stalagmite, a gondola appeared, lit by hidden spotlights. An organist was in the boat, filling the air with a melodic serenade that echoed across the water. The spectators watched, rapt, as the coloured lights rainbowed the darkness, and the boat slowly crossed the lake and finally disappeared, as the music faded.

'Fantastic,' Gunther said. 'It was worth travelling here just to see this.'

'I love travelling,' Tracy said. 'And do you know what city I've always wanted to see, Gunther? Madrid.'

Standing at the exit to the caves, Daniel Cooper watched Tracy Whitney come out.

She was alone.

TWENTY-EIGHT

The Ritz Hotel, on the Plaza de la Lealtad in Madrid, is considered the best hotel in Spain, and for more than a century it has housed and fed monarchs from a dozen European countries. Presidents, dictators, and billionaires have slept there. Tracy had heard so much about the Ritz that the reality was a disappointment. The lobby was faded and seedy-looking.

The assistant manager escorted her to the suite she had requested, 411–412, in the south wing of the hotel on Calle Felipe V.

'I trust this will be satisfactory, Miss Whitney.'

Tracy walked over to the window and looked out. Directly below, across the street, was the Prado Museum. 'This will do nicely, thank you.'

The suite was filled with blaring sounds of the heavy traffic from the streets below, but it had what she wanted: a bird's-eye view of the Prado.

Tracy ordered a light dinner in her room and retired early. When she got into the bed, she decided that trying to sleep in it had to be a modern form of medieval torture.

At midnight a detective stationed in the lobby was relieved by a colleague. 'She hasn't left her room. I think she's settled in for the night.'

In Madrid, Dirección General de Seguridad, police headquarters, is located in the Puerta del Sol and takes up an entire city block. It is a grey building with red brick, boasting a large clock tower at the top. Over the main entrance the red-and-yellow Spanish flag flies, and there is always a policeman at the door, wearing a beige uniform and a dark-brown beret, and equipped with a machine gun, a billy club, a small gun and handcuffs. It is at this headquarters that liaison with Interpol is maintained.

On the previous day an X-D Urgent cable had come in for Santiago Ramiro, the police commandant in Madrid, informing him of Tracy Whitney's impending arrival. The commandant had read the final sentence of the cable twice and then telephoned Inspector Andre Trignant at Interpol headquarters in Paris.

'I do not comprehend your message,' Ramiro had said. 'You ask me to extend my department's full cooperation to an American who is not even a policeman? For what reason?'

'Commandant, I think you will find Mr Cooper most useful. He understands Miss Whitney.'

'What is there to understand?' the commandant

445

retorted. 'She is a criminal. Ingenious, perhaps, but Spanish prisons are full of ingenious criminals. This one will not slip through our net.'

'*Bon*. And you will consult with Mr Cooper?'

The commandant said grudgingly, 'If you say he can be useful, I have no objection.'

'*Merci, monsieur.*'

'*De nada, señor.*'

Commandant Ramiro, like his counterpart in Paris, was not fond of Americans. He found them rude, materialistic and naïve. *This one*, he thought, *may be different. I will probably like him.*

He hated Daniel Cooper on sight.

'She's outsmarted half the police forces in Europe,' Daniel Cooper asserted, as he entered the commandant's office. 'And she'll probably do the same to you.'

It was all the commandant could do to control himself. 'Señor, we do not need anyone to tell us our business. Señorita Whitney has been under surveillance from the moment she arrived at Barajas Airport this morning. I assure you that if someone drops even a pin on the street and your Miss Whitney picks it up, she will be whisked to jail. She has not dealt with the Spanish police before.'

'She's not here to pick up a pin in the street.'

'Why do you think she *is* here?'

'I'm not sure. I can only tell you that it will be something big.'

446

Commandant Ramiro said smugly. 'The bigger the better. We will watch her every move.'

When Tracy awakened in the morning, groggy from a torturous night's sleep in the bed designed by Tomás de Torquemada, she ordered a light breakfast and hot, black coffee, and walked over to the window over-looking the Prado. It was an imposing fortress, built of stone and red bricks from the native soil, and was surrounded by grass and trees. Two Doric columns stood in front, and, on either side, twin staircases led up to the front entrance. At the street level were two side entrances. Schoolchildren and tourists from a dozen countries were lined up in front of the museum, and at exactly 10:00 A.M., the two large front doors were opened by guards, and the visitors began to move through the revolving door in the centre and through the two side passages at ground level.

The telephone rang, startling Tracy. No one except Gunther Hartog knew she was in Madrid. She picked up the telephone. 'Hello?'

'*Buenos días, señorita.*' It was a familiar voice. 'I'm calling for the Madrid Chamber of Commerce, and they have instructed me to do everything I can to make sure you have an exciting time in our city.'

'How did you know I was in Madrid, Jeff?'

'Señorita, the Chamber of Commerce knows everything. Is this your first time here?'

'Yes.'

'*Bueno!* Then I can show you a few places. How long do you plan to be here, Tracy?'

It was a leading question. 'I'm not sure,' she said lightly. 'Just long enough to do a little shopping and sightseeing. What are you doing in Madrid?'

'The same.' His tone matched hers. 'Shopping and sightseeing.'

Tracy did not believe in coincidence. Jeff Stevens was there for the same reason she was: to steal the *Puerto*.

He asked, 'Are you free for dinner?'

It was a dare. 'Yes.'

'Good. I'll make a reservation at the Jockey.'

Tracy certainly had no illusions about Jeff, but when she stepped out of the lift into the lobby and saw him standing there waiting for her, she was unreasonably pleased to see him.

Jeff took her hand in his. '*Fantástico, querida!* You look lovely.'

She had dressed carefully. She wore a Valentino navy-blue suit with a Russian sable flung around her neck. Maud Frizon pumps, and she carried a navy hand-bag emblazoned with the Hermes H.

Daniel Cooper, seated at a small round table in a corner of the lobby with a glass of Perrier before him, watched Tracy as she greeted her escort, and he felt a sense of enormous power: *Justice is mine, sayeth the Lord, and I am His sword and His instrument of vengeance. My life is a penance, and you shall help me pay. I'm going to punish you.*

Cooper knew that no police force in the world

was clever enough to catch Tracy Whitney. *But I am*, Cooper thought. *She belongs to me.*

Tracy had become more than an assignment to Daniel Cooper. She had become an obsession. He carried her photographs and file with him everywhere, and at night before he went to sleep, he lovingly pored over them. He had arrived in Biarritz too late to catch her, and she had eluded him in Majorca, but now that Interpol had picked up her trail again, Cooper was determined not to lose it.

He dreamed about Tracy at night. She was in a giant cage, naked, pleading with him to set her free. *I love you*, he said, *but I'll never set you free.*

The Jockey was a small, elegant restaurant on Amador de los Ríos.

'The food here is superb,' Jeff promised.

He was looking particularly handsome, Tracy thought. There was an inner excitement about him that matched Tracy's, and she knew why: they were competing with each other, matching wits in a game for high stakes. *But I'm going to win*, Tracy thought. *I'm going to find a way to steal that painting from the Prado before he does.*

'There's a strange rumour around,' Jeff was saying.

She focused her attention on him. 'What kind of rumour?'

'Have you ever heard of Daniel Cooper? He's an insurance investigator, very bright.'

'No. What about him?'

'Be careful. He's dangerous. I wouldn't want anything to happen to you.'

'Don't worry.'

'But I have been, Tracy.'

She laughed. 'About me? Why?'

He put a hand over hers and said lightly, 'You're very special. Life is more interesting with you around, my love.'

He's so damned convincing, Tracy thought. *If I didn't know better, I'd believe him.*

'Let's order,' Tracy said. 'I'm starved.'

In the days that followed, Jeff and Tracy explored Madrid. They were never alone. Two of Commandant Ramiro's men followed them everywhere, accompanied by the strange American. Ramiro had given permission for Cooper to be a part of the surveillance team simply to keep the man out of his hair. The American was *loco*, convinced that the Whitney woman was somehow going to steal some great treasure from under the noses of the police. *Que ridículo!*

Tracy and Jeff dined at Madrid's classic restaurants – Horcher, the Príncipe de Viana and Casa Botín – but Jeff also knew the places undiscovered by tourists: Casa Paco and La Chuletta and El Lacón, where he and Tracy dined on delicious native stews like *cocido Madrileño* and *olla podrida*, and then visited a small bar where they had delicious *tapas*.

Wherever they went, Daniel Cooper and the two detectives were never far behind.

Watching them from a careful distance, Daniel Cooper was puzzled by Jeff Stevens's role in the drama that was being played out. Who was he? Tracy's next victim? Or were they plotting something together?

Cooper talked to Commandant Ramiro. 'What information do you have on Jeff Stevens?' Cooper asked.

'*Nada*. He has no criminal record and is registered as a tourist. I think he is just a companion the lady picked up.'

Cooper's instincts told him differently. But it was not Jeff Stevens he was after. *Tracy*, he thought. *I want you, Tracy.*

When Tracy and Jeff returned to the Ritz at the end of a late evening, Jeff escorted Tracy to her door. 'Why don't I come in for a nightcap?' he suggested.

Tracy was almost tempted. She leaned forward and kissed him lightly on the cheek. 'Think of me as your sister, Jeff.'

'What's your position on incest?'

But she had closed the door.

A few minutes later he telephoned her from his room. 'How would you like to spend tomorrow with me in Segovia? It's a fascinating old city just a few hours' drive outside Madrid.'

'It sounds wonderful. Thanks for a lovely evening,' Tracy said. 'Good night, Jeff.'

She lay awake a long time, her mind filled with thoughts she had no right to be thinking. It had been so long since she had been emotionally involved with a man. Charles had hurt her badly, and she had no wish to be hurt again. Jeff Stevens was an amusing companion, but she knew she must never allow him to become any more than that. It would be easy to fall in love with him. And foolish.

Ruinous.

Fun.

Tracy had difficulty falling asleep.

The trip to Segovia was perfect. Jeff had rented a small car, and they drove out of the city into the beautiful wine country of Spain. An unmarked Seat trailed behind them during the entire day, but it was not an ordinary car.

The Seat is the only car manufactured in Spain, and it is the official car of the Spanish police. The regular model has only 100 horsepower, but the ones sold to the Policía Nacional and the Guardia Civil are souped up to 150 horsepower, so there was no danger that Tracy Whitney and Jeff Stevens would elude Daniel Cooper and the two detectives.

Tracy and Jeff arrived in Segovia in time for lunch and dined at a charming restaurant in the main square under the shadow of the two-thousand-year-old aqueduct built by the Romans. After lunch they wandered around the medieval city and visited the old Cathedral of Santa María and the Renaissance town hall, and then drove up to the Alcázar, the old Roman fortress perched on a rocky spur high over the city. The view was breathtaking.

'I'll bet if we stayed here long enough, we'd see Don Quixote and Sancho Panza riding along the plains below,' Jeff said.

She studied him. 'You enjoy tilting at windmills, don't you?'

'Depends on the shape of the windmill,' he said softly. He moved closer to her.

Tracy stepped away from the edge of the cliff. 'Tell me more about Segovia.'

And the spell was broken.

Jeff was an enthusiastic guide, knowledgeable about history, archaeology and architecture, and Tracy had to keep reminding herself that he was also a con artist. It was the most pleasant day Tracy could remember.

One of the Spanish detectives, José Pereira, grumbled to Cooper, 'The only thing they're stealing is our time. They're just two people in love, can't you see that? Are you sure she's planning something?'

'I'm sure,' Cooper snarled. He was puzzled by his own reactions. All he wanted was to catch Tracy Whitney, to punish her, as she deserved. She was just another criminal, an assignment. Yet, every time Tracy's companion took her arm, Cooper found himself stung with fury.

When Tracy and Jeff arrived back in Madrid, Jeff said, 'If you're not too exhausted, I know a special place for dinner.'

'Lovely.' Tracy did not want the day to end. *I'll give myself this day, this one day to be like other women.*

Madrileños dine late, and few restaurants open for dinner before 9:00 P.M. Jeff made a reservation for 10:00 at the Zalacaín, an elegant restaurant where the food was superb and perfectly served. Tracy ordered no dessert, but the waiter brought a delicate flaky pastry that was the most delicious thing she had ever tasted. She sat back in her chair, sated and happy.

'It was a wonderful dinner. Thank you.'

'I'm so glad you enjoyed it. This is the place to bring people if you want to impress them.'

She studied him. 'Are you trying to impress me, Jeff?'

He grinned. 'You bet I am. Wait until you see what's next.'

What was next was an unprepossessing *bodega*, a smoky café filled with leather-jacketed Spanish workmen drinking at the bar and at the dozen tables in the room. At one end was a *tablado*, a slightly elevated platform, where two men strummed guitars. Tracy and Jeff were seated at a small table near the platform.

'Do you know anything about flamenco?' Jeff asked. He had to raise his voice over the noise level in the bar.

'Only that it's a Spanish dance.'

'Gypsy, originally. You can go to fancy night-clubs in Madrid and see imitations of flamenco, but tonight you'll see the real thing.'

Tracy smiled at the enthusiasm in Jeff's voice.

'You're going to see a classic *cuadro flamenco*. That's a group of singers, dancers and guitarists. First they perform together, then each one takes his turn.'

Watching Tracy and Jeff from a table in the corner near the kitchen, Daniel Cooper wondered what they were discussing so intently.

'The dance is very subtle, because everything has to work together – movements, music, costumes, the building of the rhythm . . .'

'How do you know so much about it?' Tracy asked.

'I used to know a flamenco dancer.'

Naturally, Tracy thought.

The lights in the *bodega* dimmed, and the small stage was lit by spotlights. Then the magic began. It started slowly. A group of performers casually ascended to the platform. The women wore colourful skirts and blouses, and high combs with flowers banked on their beautiful Andalusian coiffures. The male dancers were dressed in the traditional tight trousers and vests and wore gleaming cordovan-leather half boots. The guitarists strummed a wistful melody, while one of the seated women sang in Spanish.

> *Yo quería dejar*
> *A mi amante,*
> *Pero antes de que pudiera,*

455

Hacerlo ella me abandonó
Y destrozó mi corazón.

'Do you understand what she's saying?' Tracy whispered.

'Yes. "I wanted to leave my lover, but before I could, he left me and he broke my heart."'

A dancer moved to the centre of the stage. She started with a simple *zapateado*, a beginning stamping step, gradually pushed faster and faster by the pulsating guitars. The rhythm grew, and the dancing became a form of sensual violence, variations on steps that had been born in gypsy caves a hundred years earlier. As the music mounted in intensity and excitement, moving through the classic figures of the dance, from *alegría* to *fandanguillo* to *zambra* to *seguiriya*, and as the frantic pace increased, there were shouts of encouragement from the performers at the side of the stage.

Cries of '*Olé tu madre*', and '*Olé tus santos*', and '*Anda, anda*', the traditional *jaleos* and *piropos*, or shouts of encouragement, goaded the dancers on to wilder, more frantic rhythms.

When the music and dancing ended abruptly, a silence roared through the bar, and then there was a loud burst of applause.

'She's marvellous!' Tracy exclaimed.

'Wait,' Jeff told her.

A second woman stepped to the centre of the stage. She had a dark, classical Castilian beauty and seemed deeply aloof, completely unaware of the audience. The guitars began to play a *bolero*, plaintive and low key, an Oriental-sounding *canto*. A male dancer joined her, and the castanets began to click in a steady, driving beat.

The seated performers joined in the *jaleo*, and the handclaps that accompany the flamenco dance, and the rhythmic beat of the palms embraced the music and dancing, lifting it, building it, until the room began to rock with the echo of the *zapateado*, the hypnotic beat of the half toe, the heel, and the full sole clacking out an endless variation of tone and rhythmic sensations.

Their bodies moved apart and came together in a growing frenzy of desire, until they were making mad, violent, animal love without ever touching, moving to a wild, passionate climax that had the audience screaming. As the lights blacked out and came on again, the crowd roared, and Tracy found herself screaming with the others. To her embarrassment, she was sexually aroused. She was afraid to meet Jeff's eyes. The air between them vibrated with tension. Tracy looked down at the table, at his strong, tanned hands, and she could feel them caressing her body, slowly, swiftly, urgently, and she quickly put her hands in her lap to hide their trembling.

They said very little during the ride back to the hotel. At the door to Tracy's room, she turned and said, 'It's been a –'

Jeff's lips were on hers, and her arms went around him, and she held him tightly to her.

'Tracy –?'

The word on her lips was *yes*, and it took the last ounce of her willpower to say, 'It's been a long day, Jeff. I'm a sleepy lady.'

'Oh.'

'I think I'll just stay in my room tomorrow and rest.'

His voice was level when he answered. 'Good idea. I'll probably do the same.'

Neither of them believed the other.

TWENTY-NINE

At 10:00 the following morning Tracy was standing in the long line at the entrance to the Prado Museum. As the doors opened, a uniformed guard operated a turnstile that admitted one visitor at a time.

Tracy purchased a ticket and moved with the crowd going into the large rotunda. Daniel Cooper and Detective Pereira stayed well behind her, and Cooper began to feel a growing excitement. He was certain that Tracy Whitney was not there as a visitor. Whatever her plan was, it was beginning.

Tracy moved from room to room, walking slowly through the salons filled with Rubens paintings and Titians, Tintorettos, Bosches, and paintings by Domenikos Theotokopoulos, who became famous as El Greco. The Goyas were exhibited in a special gallery below, on the ground floor.

Tracy noted that a uniformed guard was stationed at the entrance to each room, and at his elbow was a red alarm button. She knew that the

459

moment the alarm sounded, all entrances and exits to the museum would be sealed off, and there would be no chance to escape.

She sat on the bench in the centre of the Muses room, filled with eighteenth-century Flemish masters, and let her gaze wander towards the floor. She could see a round access fixture on each side of the doorway. That would be the infra-red beams that were turned on at night. In other museums Tracy had visited, the guards had been sleepy and bored, paying little attention to the stream of chattering tourists, but here the guards were alert. Works of art were being defaced by fanatics in museums around the world, and the Prado was taking no chance that it could happen there.

In a dozen different rooms artists had set up their easels and were assiduously at work copying paintings of the masters. The museum permitted it, but Tracy noticed that the guards kept a close eye even on the copiers.

When Tracy had finished with the rooms on the main floor, she took the stairs to the ground floor, to the Francisco de Goya exhibition.

Detective Pereira said to Cooper. 'See, she's not doing anything but looking. She –'

'You're wrong.' Cooper started down the stairs in a run.

It seemed to Tracy that the Goya exhibition was more heavily guarded than the others, and it well deserved to be. Wall after wall was filled with an incredible display of timeless beauty, and Tracy moved from canvas to canvas, caught up in the genius of the man. Goya's *Self-Portrait*, making him look like a middle-aged Pan . . . the exquisitely coloured portrait of *The Family of Charles IV* . . . *The Clothed Maja* and the famed *Nude Maja*.

And there, next to *The Witches' Sabbath*, was the *Puerto*. Tracy stopped and stared at it, her heart beginning to pound. In the foreground of the painting were a dozen beautifully dressed men and women standing in front of a stone wall, while in the background, seen through a luminous mist, were fishing boats in a harbour and a distant lighthouse. In the lower left-hand corner of the picture was Goya's signature.

This was the target. *Half a million dollars.*

Tracy glanced around. A guard stood at the entrance. Beyond him, through the long corridor leading to other rooms, Tracy could see more guards. She stood there a long time, studying the *Puerto*. As she started to move away, a group of tourists was coming down the stairs. In the middle of them was Jeff Stevens. Tracy averted her head and hurried out the side entrance before he could see her.

It's going to be a race, Mr Stevens, and I'm going to win it.

'She's planning to steal a painting from the Prado.'

Commandant Ramiro looked at Daniel Cooper

incredulously. '*Cagajón!* No one can steal a painting from the Prado.'

Cooper said stubbornly, 'She was there all morning.'

'There has never been a theft at the Prado, and there never will be. And do you know why? Because it is impossible.'

'She's not going to try any of the usual ways. You must have the museum vents protected, in case of a gas attack. If the guards drink coffee on the job, find out where they get it and if it can be drugged. Check the drinking water –'

The limits of Commandant Ramiro's patience was exhausted. It was bad enough that he had had to put up with this rude, unattractive American for the past week, and that he had wasted valuable manpower having Tracy Whitney followed around the clock, when his Policía Nacional was already working under an austerity budget; but now, confronted by this *pito*, telling him how to run *his* police department, he could stand no more.

'In my opinion, the lady is in Madrid on a holiday. I am calling off the surveillance.'

Cooper was stunned. 'No! You can't do that. Tracy Whitney is –'

Commandant Ramiro rose to his full height. 'You will kindly refrain from telling me what I can do, señor. And now, if you have nothing further to say, I am a very busy man.'

Cooper stood there, filled with frustration. 'I'd like to continue alone, then.'

The commandant smiled. 'To keep the Prado Museum safe from the terrible threat of this woman? Of course, Señor Cooper. Now I can sleep at night.'

THIRTY

The chances of success are extremely limited, Gunther Hartog had told Tracy. *It will take a great deal of ingenuity.*

That is the understatement of the century, Tracy thought.

She was staring out the window of her suite, down at the skylight roof of the Prado, mentally reviewing everything she had learned about the museum. It was open from 10:00 in the morning until 6:00 in the evening, and during that time the alarms were off, but guards were stationed at each entrance and in every room.

Even if one could manage to take a painting off the wall, Tracy thought, *there's no way to smuggle it out.* All packages had to be checked at the door.

She studied the roof of the Prado and considered a night foray. There were several drawbacks: the first one was the high visibility. Tracy had watched as the spotlights came on at night, flooding the roof, making it visible for miles around. Even if it were possible to get into the building unseen, there were still the infra-red beams inside the building and the night watchmen.

The Prado seemed to be impregnable.

What was Jeff planning? Tracy was certain he was going to make a try for the Goya. *I'd give anything to know what he has in his crafty little mind.* Of one thing Tracy was sure: she was not going to let him get there ahead of her. She had to find a way.

She returned to the Prado the next morning.

Nothing had changed except the faces of the visitors. Tracy kept a careful lookout for Jeff, but he did not appear.

Tracy thought, *He's already figured out how he's going to steal it. The bastard. All this charm he's been using was just to try to distract me, and keep me from getting the painting first.*

She suppressed her anger and replaced it with clear, cold logic.

Tracy walked over to the *Puerto* again, and her eyes wandered over the nearby canvases, the alert guards, the amateur painters sitting on stools in front of their easels, the crowds, flowing in and out of the room, and as she looked around, Tracy's heart suddenly began to beat faster.

I know how I'm going to do it!

She made a telephone call from a public booth on the Gran Vía, and Daniel Cooper, who stood in a coffee shop doorway watching, would have given a year's pay to know whom Tracy was calling. He was sure it was an overseas call and that she was phoning collect, so that there would be no record of it. He was aware of the lime-green linen dress that he had not seen before and that her legs were bare. *So that men can stare at them*, he thought. *Whore.*

He was filled with rage.

In the telephone booth, Tracy was ending her conversation. 'Just make sure he's fast, Gunther. He'll have only about two minutes. Everything will depend on speed.'

TO:
J. J. Reynolds   File No. Y-72-830-412

FROM:
Daniel Cooper   CONFIDENTIAL

SUBJECT: Tracy Whitney

It is my opinion that the subject is in Madrid to carry out a major criminal endeavour. The likely target is the Prado Museum. The Spanish police are being uncooperative, but I will personally keep the subject under surveillance and apprehend her at the appropriate time.

Two days later, at 9:00 A.M., Tracy was seated on a bench in the gardens of the Retiro, the beautiful park running through the centre of Madrid, feeding the pigeons. The Retiro, with its lake and graceful trees and well-kept grass, and miniature stages with shows for children, was a magnet for the Madrileños.

Cesar Porretta, an elderly, grey-haired man with a slight hunchback, walked along the park path, and when he reached the bench, he sat down beside Tracy, opened a paper sack, and began throwing out bread crumbs to the birds. '*Buenos días, señorita.*'

'*Buenos días.* Do you see any problems?'

'None, señorita. All I need is the time and the date.'

'I don't have it,' Tracy told him. 'Soon.'

He smiled, a toothless smile. 'The police will go crazy. No one has ever tried anything like this before.'

'That's why it's going to work,' Tracy said. 'You'll hear from me.' She tossed out a last crumb to the pigeons and rose. She walked away, her silk dress swaying provocatively around her knees.

While Tracy was in the park with Cesar Porretta, Daniel Cooper was searching her hotel room. He had watched from the lobby as Tracy left the hotel and headed for the park. She had not ordered anything from room service, and Cooper had decided that she was going out to breakfast. He had given himself thirty minutes. Entering her suite had been a simple matter of avoiding the floor maids and using a lock pick. He knew what he was looking

467

for: a copy of a painting. He had no idea how Tracy planned to substitute it, but he was sure it had to be her scheme.

He searched the suite with swift, silent efficiency, missing nothing and saving the bedroom for last. He looked through her wardrobe, examining her dresses, and then the dressing table. He opened the drawers, one by one. They were filled with panties and bras and pantyhose. He picked up a pair of pink underpants and rubbed them against his cheek and imagined her sweet-smelling flesh in them. The scent of her was suddenly everywhere. He replaced the garment and quickly looked through the other drawers. No painting.

Cooper walked into the bathroom. There were drops of water in the tub. Her body had lain there, covered with water as warm as the womb, and Cooper could visualize Tracy lying in it, naked, the water caressing her breasts as her hips undulated up and down. He felt an erection begin. He picked up the damp flannel from the bath and brought it to his lips. The odor of her body swirled around him as he unzipped his trousers. He rubbed a cake of damp soap onto the flannel and began stroking himself with it, facing the mirror, looking into his blazing eyes.

A few minutes later he left, as quietly as he had arrived, and headed directly for a nearby church.

The following morning when Tracy left the Ritz Hotel, Daniel Cooper followed her. There was an intimacy between them that had not existed before. He knew her smell; he had seen her in her bath, had watched her naked body writhing in the warm water. She belonged completely to him; she was his to destroy. He watched her as she wandered along the Gran Vía, examining the merchandise in the shops, and he followed her into a large department store, careful to remain out of sight. He saw her speak to a clerk, then head for the ladies' room. Cooper stood near the door, frustrated. It was the one place he could not follow her.

If Cooper had been able to go inside, he would have seen Tracy talking to a grossly overweight, middle-aged woman.

'*Mañana*,' Tracy said, as she applied fresh lipstick before the mirror. 'Tomorrow morning, eleven o'clock.'

The woman shook her head. 'No, señorita. He will not like that. You could not choose a worse day. Tomorrow the Prince of Luxembourg arrives on a state visit, and the newspapers say he will be taken on a tour of the Prado. There will be extra security guards and police all over the museum.'

'The more the better. Tomorrow.'

Tracy walked out the door, and the woman looked after her muttering, '*La cucha es loca . . .*'

The royal party was scheduled to appear at the Prado at exactly 11:00 A.M., and the streets around the Prado had been roped off by the Guardia Civil. Because of a delay in the ceremony at the presidential palace, the entourage did not arrive until close to noon. There were the screams of sirens as police motorcycles came into view, escorting a procession of half a dozen black limousines to the front steps of the Prado.

At the entrance, the director of the museum, Christian Machada, nervously awaited the arrival of His Highness.

Machada had made a careful morning inspection to be sure everything was in order, and the guards had been forewarned to be especially alert. The director was proud of his museum, and he wanted to make a good impression on the prince.

It never hurts to have friends in high places, Machada thought. *Quién sabe? I might even be invited to dine with His Highness this evening at the presidential palace.*

Christian Machada's only regret was that there was no way to stop the hordes of tourists that wandered about. But the prince's bodyguards and the museum's security guards would ensure that the prince was protected. Everything was in readiness for him.

The royal tour began upstairs, on the main floor. The director greeted His Highness with an effusive welcome and escorted him, followed by the armed guards, through the rotunda and into the rooms where the sixteenth-century Spanish painters were on exhibit: Juan de Juanes, Pedro Machuca, Fernando Yáñez.

The prince moved slowly, enjoying the visual

470

feast spread before him. He was a patron of the arts and genuinely loved the painters who could make the past come alive and remain eternal. Having no talent for painting himself, the prince, as he looked around the rooms, nonetheless envied the painters who stood before their easels trying to snatch sparks of genius from the masters.

When the official party had visited the upstairs salons, Christian Machada said proudly, 'And now, if Your Highness will permit me, I will take you downstairs to our Goya exhibit.'

Tracy had spent a nerve-racking morning. When the prince had not arrived at the Prado at 11:00 as scheduled, she had begun to panic. All her arrangements had been made and timed to the second, but she needed the prince in order to make them work.

She moved from room to room, mixing with the crowds, trying to avoid attracting attention. *He's not coming,* Tracy thought finally. *I'm going to have to call it off.* And at that moment, she had heard the sound of approaching sirens from the street.

Watching Tracy from a vantage point in the next room, Daniel Cooper, too, was aware of the sirens. His reason told him it was impossible for anyone to steal a painting from the museum, but his instinct told him that Tracy was going to try it, and Cooper trusted his instinct. He moved closer to her, letting the crowds conceal him from view. He intended to keep her in sight every moment.

Tracy was in the room next to the salon where the *Puerto* was being exhibited. Through the open doorway she could see the hunchback, Cesar Porretta, seated before an easel, copying Goya's *Clothed Maja*, which hung next to the *Puerto*. A guard stood three feet away. In the room with Tracy, a woman painter stood at her easel, studiously copying *The Milkmaid of Bordeaux*, trying to capture the brilliant browns and greens of Goya's canvas.

A group of Japanese tourists fluttered into the salon, chattering like a flock of exotic birds. *Now!* Tracy told herself. This was the moment she had been waiting for, and her heart was pounding so loudly she was afraid the guard could hear it. She moved out of the path of the approaching Japanese tour group, backing towards the woman painter. As a Japanese man brushed in front of Tracy, Tracy fell backwards, as if pushed, bumping the artist and sending her, the easel, canvas and paints flying to the ground.

'Oh, I'm terribly sorry!' Tracy exclaimed. 'Let me help you.'

As she moved to assist the startled artist, Tracy's heels stamped into the scattered paints, smearing them into the floor. Daniel Cooper, who had seen everything, hurried closer, every sense alert. He was sure Tracy Whitney had made her first move.

The guard rushed over, calling out, '¿Qué pasa? ¿Qué pasa?'

The accident had attracted the attention of the

tourists, and they milled around the fallen woman, smearing the paints from the crushed tubes into grotesque images on the hardwood floor. It was an unholy mess, and the prince was due to appear at any moment. The guard was in a panic. He yelled out, 'Sergio! *Ven acá! Pronto!*'

Tracy watched as the guard from the next room came running in to help. Cesar Porretta was alone in the salon with the *Puerto*.

Tracy was in the middle of the uproar. The two guards were trying vainly to push the tourists away from the area of the paint-smeared floor.

'Get the director,' Sergio yelled. *'¡En seguida!'*

The other guard hurried off towards the stairs. *¡Que birria! What a mess!*

Two minutes later Christian Machada was at the scene of the disaster. The director took one horrified look and screamed, 'Get some cleaning women down here – quickly! Mops and cloths and turpentine. *¡Pronto!*'

A young aide rushed to do his bidding.

Machada turned to Sergio. 'Get back to your post,' he snapped.

'Yes, sir.'

Tracy watched the guard push his way through the crowd to the room where Cesar Porretta was working.

Cooper had not taken his eyes off Tracy for an instant. He had waited for her next move. But it had not come. She had not gone near any of the paintings, nor had she made contact with an

473

accomplice. All she had done was knock over an easel and spill some paints on the floor, but he was certain it had been done deliberately. But to what purpose? Somehow, Cooper felt that whatever had been planned had already happened. He looked around the walls of the salon. None of the paintings were missing.

Cooper hurried into the adjoining room. There was no one there but the guard and an elderly hunchback seated at his easel, copying the *Clothed Maja*. All the paintings were in place. But something was wrong. Cooper *knew* it.

He hurried back to the harassed director, whom he had met earlier. 'I have reason to believe,' Cooper blurted out, 'that a painting has been stolen from here in the past few minutes.'

Christian Machada stared at the wild-eyed American. 'What are you talking about? If that were so, the guards would have sounded the alarm.'

'I think that somehow a fake painting was substituted for a real one.'

The director gave him a tolerant smile. 'There is one small thing wrong with your theory, señor. It is not known to the general public, but there are sensors hidden behind each painting. If anyone tried to lift a painting from the wall – which they would certainly have to do to substitute another painting – the alarm would instantly sound.'

Daniel Cooper was still not satisfied. 'Could your alarm be disconnected?'

'No. If someone cut the wire to the power, that

also would cause the alarm to go off. Señor, it is *impossible* for anyone to steal a painting from this museum. Our security is what you call proof from fools.'

Cooper stood there shaking with frustration. Everything the director said was convincing. It *did* seem impossible. But then why had Tracy Whitney deliberately spilled those paints?

Cooper would not give up. 'Humour me. Would you ask your staff to go through the museum and check to make sure nothing is missing? I'll be at my hotel.'

There was nothing more Daniel Cooper could do.

At 7:00 that evening Christian Machada telephoned Cooper. 'I have personally made an inspection, señor. Every painting is in its proper place. Nothing is missing from the museum.'

So that was that. Seemingly, it *had* been an accident. But Daniel Cooper, with the instincts of a hunter, sensed that his quarry had escaped.

Jeff had invited Tracy to dinner in the main dining room of the Ritz Hotel.

'You're looking especially radiant this evening,' Jeff complimented her.

'Thank you. I feel absolutely wonderful.'

'It's the company. Come with me to Barcelona next week, Tracy. It's a fascinating city. You'd love –'

'I'm sorry, Jeff. I can't. I'm leaving Spain.'

475

'Really?' His voice was filled with regret. 'When?'

'In a few days.'

'Ah. I'm disappointed.'

You're going to be more disappointed, Tracy thought, *when you learn I've stolen the Puerto*. She wondered how he had planned to steal the painting. Not that it mattered any longer. *I've out-witted clever Jeff Stevens*. Yet, for some inexplicable reason Tracy felt a faint trace of regret.

Christian Machada was seated in his office enjoying his morning cup of strong black coffee and congratulating himself on what a success the prince's visit had been. Except for the regrettable incident of the spilled paints, everything had gone off precisely as planned. He was grateful that the prince and his retinue had been diverted until the mess could be cleaned up. The director smiled when he thought about the idiot American investigator who had tried to convince him that someone had stolen a painting from the Prado. *Not yesterday, not today, not tomorrow*, he thought smugly.

His secretary walked into the office. 'Excuse me, sir. There is a gentleman to see you. He asked me to give you this.'

She handed the director a letter. It was on the letterhead of the Kunsthaus museum in Zürich.

My Esteemed Colleague:

This letter will serve to introduce Monsieur Henri Rendell, our senior art expert. Monsieur

Rendell is making a tour of world museums and is particularly eager to see your incomparable collection. I would greatly appreciate any courtesies you extend to him.

The letter was signed by the curator of the museum.

Sooner or later, the director thought happily, *everyone comes to me.*

'Send him in.'

Henri Rendell was a tall, distinguished-looking, balding man with a heavy Swiss accent. When they shook hands, Machada noticed that the index finger on the right hand of his visitor was missing.

Henri Rendell said, 'I appreciate this. It is the first opportunity I have had to visit Madrid, and I am looking forward to seeing your renowned works of art.'

Christian Machada said modestly, 'I do not think you will be disappointed, Monsieur Rendell. Please come with me. I shall personally escort you.'

They moved slowly, walking through the rotunda with its Flemish masters, and Rubens and his followers, and they visited the central gallery, filled with Spanish masters, and Henri Rendell studied each painting carefully. The two men spoke as one expert to another, evaluating the various artists' style and perspective and colour sense.

'*Now*,' the director declared, 'for the pride of Spain.' He led his visitor downstairs, into the gallery filled with Goyas.

'It is a feast for the eyes!' Rendell exclaimed,

overwhelmed. 'Please! Let me just stand and look.'

Christian Machada waited, enjoying the man's awe.

'Never have I seen anything so magnificent,' Rendell declared. He walked slowly through the salon, studying each painting in turn. '*The Witches' Sabbath*,' Rendell said. 'Brilliant!'

They moved on.

'Goya's *Self-Portrait* – fantastic!'

Christian Machada beamed.

Rendell paused in front of the *Puerto*. 'A nice fake.' He started to move on.

The director grabbed his arm. '*What?* What was it you said, señor?'

'I said it is a nice fake.'

'You are very much mistaken.' He was filled with indignation.

'I do not think so.'

'You most certainly are,' Machada said stiffly. 'I assure you, it is genuine. I have its provenance.'

Henri Rendell stepped up to the picture and examined it more closely. 'Then its provenance has also been faked. This was done by Goya's disciple, Eugenio Lucas y Padilla. You must be aware, of course, that Lucas painted hundreds of fake Goyas.'

'Certainly I am aware of that,' Machada snapped. 'But this is not one of them.'

Rendell shrugged. 'I bow to your judgment.' He started to move on.

'I personally purchased this painting. It has passed the spectrograph test, the pigment test –'

'I do not doubt it. Lucas painted in the same period as Goya, and used the same materials.' Henri Rendell bent down to examine the signature at the bottom of the painting. 'You can reassure yourself very simply, if you wish. Take the painting back to your restoration room and test the signature.' He chuckled with amusement. 'Lucas's ego made him sign his own paintings, but his wallet forced him to forge Goya's name over his own, increasing the price enormously.' Rendell glanced at his watch. 'You must forgive me. I'm afraid I am late for an engagement. Thank you so much for sharing your treasures with me.'

'Not at all,' the director said coldly. *The man is obviously a fool*, he thought.

'I am at the Villa Magna, if I can be of service. And thank you again, señor.' Henri Rendell departed.

Christian Machada watched him leave. How dare that Swiss idiot imply that the precious Goya was a fake!

He turned to look at the painting again. It was beautiful, a masterpiece. He leaned down to examine Goya's signature. Perfectly normal. But still, *was* it possible? The tiny seed of doubt would not go away. Everyone knew that Goya's contemporary, Eugenio Lucas y Padilla, had painted hundreds of fake Goyas, making a career out of forging the master. Machada had paid $3.5 million for the Goya *Puerto*. If he *had* been deceived, it would be a terrible black mark against him, something he could not bear to think about.

Henri Rendell had said one thing that made sense: there was, indeed, a simple way to ascertain its authenticity. He would test the signature and then telephone Rendell and suggest most politely that perhaps he should seek a more suitable vocation.

The director summoned his assistant and ordered the *Puerto* moved to the restoration room.

The testing of a masterpiece is a very delicate operation, for if it is done carelessly, it can destroy something both priceless and irreplaceable. The restorers at the Prado were experts. Most of them were unsuccessful painters who had taken up restoration work so they could remain close to their beloved art. They started as apprentices, studying under master restorers, and worked for years before they became assistants and were allowed to handle masterpieces, always under the supervision of senior craftsmen.

Juan Delgado, the man in charge of art restoration at the Prado, placed the *Puerto* on a special wooden rack, as Christian Machada watched.

'I want you to test the signature,' the director informed him.

Delgado kept his surprise to himself. '*Sí, Señor Director.*'

He poured isopropyl alcohol onto a small cotton ball and set it on the table next to the painting. On a second cotton ball he poured petroleum distillate, the neutralizing agent.

'I am ready, señor.'

480

'Go ahead then. But be careful!'

Machada found that it was suddenly difficult for him to breathe. He watched Delgado lift the first cotton ball and gently touch it to the G in Goya's signature. Instantly, Delgado picked up the second cotton ball and neutralized the area, so that the alcohol could not penetrate too deeply. The two men examined the canvas.

Delgado was frowning. 'I'm sorry, but I cannot tell yet,' he said. 'I must use a stronger solvent.'

'Do it,' the director commanded.

Delgado opened another bottle. He carefully poured dimenthyl petone onto a fresh cotton ball and with it touched the first letter of the signature again, instantly applying the second cotton ball. The room was filled with a sharp, pungent odour from the chemicals. Christian Machada stood there staring at the painting, unable to believe what he was seeing. The G in Goya's name was fading, and in its place was a clearly visible L.

Delgado turned to him, his face pale. 'Shall – shall I go on?'

'Yes,' Machada said hoarsely. 'Go on.'

Slowly, letter by letter, Goya's signature faded under the application of the solvent, and the signature of Lucas materialized. Each letter was a blow to Machada's stomach. He, the head of one of the most important museums in the world, had been deceived. The board of directors would hear of it; the King of Spain would hear of it; the world would hear of it. He was ruined.

He stumbled back to his office and telephoned Henri Rendell.

The two men were seated in Machada's office.

'You were right,' the director said heavily. 'It is a Lucas. When word of this gets out, I shall be a laughing stock.'

'Lucas has deceived many experts,' Rendell said comfortingly. 'His forgeries happen to be a hobby of mine.'

'I paid three and a half million dollars for that painting.'

Rendell shrugged. 'Can you get your money back?'

The director shook his head in despair. 'I purchased it directly from a widow who claimed it had been in her husband's family for three generations. If I sued her, the case would drag on through the courts and it would be bad publicity. Everything in this museum would become suspect.'

Henri Rendell was thinking hard. 'There is really no reason for the publicity at all. Why don't you explain to your superiors what has happened, and quietly get rid of the Lucas? You could send the painting to Sotheby's or Christie's and let them auction it off.'

Machada shook his head. 'No. Then the whole world would learn the story.'

Rendell's face brightened. 'You may be in luck. I have a client who would be willing to purchase the Lucas. He collects them. He is a man of discretion.'

482

'I would be glad to get rid of it. I never want to see it again. A *fake* among my beautiful treasures. I'd like to give it away,' he added bitterly.

'That will not be necessary. My client would probably be willing to pay you, say, fifty thousand dollars for it. Shall I make a telephone call?'

'That would be most kind of you, Señor Rendell.'

At a hastily held meeting the stunned board of directors decided that the exposure of one of the Prado's prize paintings as a forgery had to be avoided at any cost. It was agreed that the prudent course of action would be to get rid of the painting as quietly and as quickly as possible. The dark-suited men filed out of the room silently. No one spoke a word to Machada, who stood there, sweltering in his misery.

That afternoon a deal was struck. Henri Rendell went to the Bank of Spain and returned with a certified cheque for $50,000, and the Eugenio Lucas y Padilla was handed over to him, wrapped in an inconspicuous piece of burlap.

'The board of directors would be very upset if this incident were to become public,' Machada said delicately, 'but I assured them that your client is a man of discretion.'

'You can count on it,' Rendell promised.

When Henri Rendell left the museum, he took a taxi to a residential area in the northern end of Madrid, carried the canvas up some stairs to a third-floor apartment, and knocked on the door.

It was opened by Tracy. Behind her stood Cesar Porretta. Tracy looked at Rendell questioningly, and he grinned.

'They couldn't wait to get this off their hands!' Henri Rendell gloated.

Tracy hugged him. 'Come in.'

Porretta took the painting and placed it on a table.

'Now,' the hunchback said, 'you are going to see a miracle – a Goya brought back to life.'

He reached for a bottle of methylated spirits and opened it. The pungent odour instantly filled the room. As Tracy and Rendell looked on, Porretta poured some of the spirits onto a piece of cotton and very gently touched the cotton to Lucas's signature, one letter at a time. Gradually the signature of Lucas began to fade. Under it was the signature of Goya.

Rendell stared at it in awe. 'Brilliant!'

'It was Miss Whitney's idea,' the hunchback admitted. 'She asked whether it would be possible to cover up the original artist's signature with a fake signature and then cover that with the original name.'

'He figured out how it could be done,' Tracy smiled.

Porretta said modestly, 'It was ridiculously simple. Took fewer than two minutes. The trick was in the paints I used. First, I covered Goya's signature with a layer of super-refined white French polish, to protect it. Then, over that I

484

painted Lucas's name with a quick-drying acrylic-based paint. On top of that I painted in Goya's name with an oil-based paint with a light picture varnish. When the top signature was removed, Lucas's name appeared. If they had gone further, they would have discovered that Goya's original signature was hidden underneath. But of course, they didn't.'

Tracy handed each man a fat envelope and said, 'I want to thank you both.'

'Anytime you need an art expert,' Henri Rendell winked.

Porretta asked, 'How do you plan to carry the painting out of the country?'

'I'm having a messenger collect it here. Wait for him.' She shook the hands of both men and walked out.

On her way back to the Ritz, Tracy was filled with a sense of exhilaration. *Everything is a matter of psychology*, she thought.

From the beginning she had seen that it would be impossible to steal the painting from the Prado, so she had had to trick them, to put them in a frame of mind where they *wanted* to get rid of it. Tracy visualized Jeff Stevens's face when he learned how he had been outwitted, and she laughed aloud.

She waited in her hotel suite for the messenger, and when he arrived, Tracy telephoned Cesar Porretta.

'The messenger is here now,' Tracy said. 'I'm

sending him over to pick up the painting. See that
he –'

'*What?* What are you talking about?' Porretta
screamed. 'Your messenger picked up the painting
half an hour ago.'

THIRTY-ONE

Paris
Wednesday, 9 July – Noon

In a private office off the Rue Matignon, Gunther Hartog said, 'I understand how you feel about what happened in Madrid, Tracy, but Jeff Stevens got there first.'

'No,' Tracy corrected him bitterly. '*I* got there first. He got there last.'

'But Jeff delivered it. The *Puerto* is already on its way to my client.'

After all her planning and scheming, Jeff Stevens had outwitted her. He had sat back and let her do the work and take all the risks, and at the last moment he had calmly walked off with the prize. How he must have been laughing at her all the time! *You're a very special lady, Tracy.* She could not bear the waves of humiliation that washed over her when she thought of the night of the flamenco dancing. *My God, what a fool I almost made of myself.*

'I never thought I could kill anyone,' Tracy told Gunther, 'but I could happily slaughter Jeff Stevens.'

Gunther said mildly, 'Oh, dear. Not in this room, I hope. He's on his way here.'

'He's *what*?' Tracy jumped to her feet.

'I told you I have a proposition for you. It will require a partner. In my opinion, he is the only one who –'

'I'd rather *starve* first!' Tracy snapped. 'Jeff Stevens is the most contemptible –'

'Ah, did I hear my name mentioned?' He stood in the doorway, beaming. 'Tracy, darling, you look even more stunning than usual. Gunther, my friend, how are you?'

The two men shook hands. Tracy stood there, filled with a cold fury.

Jeff looked at her and sighed. 'You're probably upset with me.'

'*Upset!* I –' She could not find the words.

'Tracy, if I may say so, I thought your plan was brilliant. I mean it. Really brilliant. You made only one little mistake. Never trust a Swiss with a missing index finger.'

She took deep breaths, trying to control herself. She turned to Gunther. 'I'll talk to you later, Gunther.'

'Tracy –'

'No. Whatever it is, I want no part of it. Not if he's involved.'

Gunther said, 'Would you at least listen to it?'

'There's no point. I –'

'In three days De Beers is shipping a four-million-dollar packet of diamonds from Paris to Amsterdam on an Air France cargo plane. I have a client who's eager to acquire those stones.'

'Why don't you hijack them on the way to the airport? Your friend here is an expert on hijacking.' She could not keep the bitterness from her voice.

By God, she's magnificent when she's angry, Jeff thought.

Gunther said, 'The diamonds are too well guarded. We're going to hijack the diamonds during the flight.'

Tracy looked at him in surprise. '*During* the flight? In a cargo plane?'

'We need someone small enough to hide inside one of the containers. When the plane is in the air, all that person has to do is step out of the crate, open the De Beers container, remove the package of diamonds, replace the package with a duplicate, which will have been prepared, and get back in the other crate.'

'And I'm small enough to fit in a crate.'

Gunther said, 'It's much more than that, Tracy. We need someone who's bright and has nerve.'

Tracy stood there, thinking. 'I like the plan, Gunther. What I don't like is the idea of working with *him*. This person is a crook.'

Jeff grinned. 'Aren't we all, dear heart? Gunther is offering us a million dollars if we can pull this off.'

Tracy stared at Gunther. 'A million dollars?'

He nodded. 'Half a million for each of you.'

'The reason it can work,' Jeff explained, 'is that I have a contact at the loading dock at the airport. He'll help us set it up. He can be trusted.'

'Unlike you,' Tracy retorted. 'Goodbye, Gunther.' She sailed out of the room.

Gunther looked after her. 'She's really upset with you about Madrid, Jeff. I'm afraid she's not going to do this.'

'You're wrong,' Jeff said cheerfully. 'I know Tracy. She won't be able to resist it.'

'The pallets are sealed before they are loaded onto the plane,' Ramon Vauban was explaining. The speaker was a young Frenchman, with an old face that had nothing to do with his years and black, dead eyes. He was a dispatcher with Air France Cargo, and the key to the success of the plan.

Vauban, Tracy, Jeff, and Gunther were seated at a rail-side table on the *Bateau Mouche*, the sightseeing boat that cruises the Seine, circling Paris.

'If the pallet is sealed,' Tracy asked, her voice crisp, 'how do I get into it?'

'For last-minute shipments,' Vauban replied, 'the company uses what we call soft pallets, large wooden crates with canvas on one side, fastened down only with rope. For security reasons, valuable cargo like diamonds always arrives at the last minute so it is the last to go on and the first to come off.'

Tracy said, 'So the diamonds would be in a soft pallet?'

'That is correct, mademoiselle. As would you. I would arrange for the container with you in it to be placed next to the pallet with the diamonds. All you have to do when the plane is in flight is cut the ropes, open the pallet with the diamonds, exchange a box identical to theirs, get back in your container, and close it up again.'

Gunther added, 'When the plane lands in Amsterdam, the guards will pick up the substitute box of diamonds and deliver it to the diamond cutters. By the time they discover the substitution, we'll have you on an airplane out of the country. Believe me, nothing can go wrong.'

A sentence that chilled Tracy's heart. 'Wouldn't I freeze to death up there?' she asked.

Vauban smiled. 'Mademoiselle, these days, cargo planes are heated. They often carry livestock and pets. No, you will be quite comfortable. A little cramped, perhaps, but otherwise fine.'

Tracy had finally agreed to *listen* to their idea. A half million dollars for a few hours' discomfort. She had examined the scheme from every angle. *It can work*, Tracy thought. *If only Jeff Stevens were not involved!*

Her feelings about him were such a roiling mixture of emotions that she was confused and angry with herself. He had done what he did in Madrid for the fun of outwitting her. He had betrayed her, cheated her, and now he was secretly laughing at her.

491

The three men were watching her, waiting for her answer. The boat was passing under the Pont Neuf, the oldest bridge in Paris, which the contrary French insisted on calling the New Bridge. Across the river, two lovers embraced on the edge of the embankment, and Tracy could see the blissful look on the face of the girl. *She's a fool*, Tracy thought. She made her decision. She looked straight into Jeff's eyes as she said, 'All right. I'll go along with it,' and she could feel the tension at the table dissipate.

'We don't have much time,' Vauban was saying. His dead eyes turned to Tracy. 'My brother works for a shipping agent, and he will let us load the soft container with you in it at his warehouse. I hope mademoiselle does not have claustrophobia.'

'Don't worry about me . . . How long will the trip take?'

'You will spend a few minutes in the loading area and one hour flying to Amsterdam.'

'How large is the container?'

'Large enough for you to sit down. There will be other things in it to conceal you – just in case.'

Nothing can go wrong, they had promised. *But just in case . . .*

'I have a list of the things you'll need,' Jeff told her. 'I've already arranged for them.'

The smug bastard. He had been so sure she would say yes.

'Vauban, here, will see to it that your passport has the proper exit and entrance stamps, so you can leave Holland without any problem.'

The boat began docking at its quay.

'We can go over the final plans in the morning,' Ramon Vauban said. 'Now I have to get back to work. *Au revoir*.' And he left.

Jeff asked, 'Why don't we all have dinner together to celebrate?'

'I'm sorry,' Gunther apologized, 'but I have a previous engagement.'

Jeff turned to Tracy. 'Would –'

'No, thanks. I'm tired,' she said quickly.

It was an excuse to avoid being with Jeff, but even as Tracy said it, she realized she really was exhausted. It was probably the strain of the excitement she had been going through for so long. She was feeling light-headed. *When this is over*, she promised herself, *I'm going back to London for a long rest*. Her head was beginning to throb. *I really must*.

'I brought you a little present,' Jeff told her. He handed her a gaily wrapped box. In it was an exquisite silk scarf with the initials TW switched in one corner.

'Thank you.' *He can afford it*, Tracy thought angrily. *He bought it with my half million dollars.*

'Sure you won't change your mind about dinner?'

'I'm positive.'

In Paris, Tracy stayed at the classic Plaza Athénée, in a lovely old suite that overlooked the garden restaurant. There was an elegant restaurant inside the hotel, with soft piano music, but on this evening

Tracy was too tired to change into a more formal dress. She went into the Relais, the hotel's small café, and ordered a bowl of soup. She pushed the plate away, half-finished, and left for her suite.

Daniel Cooper, seated at the other end of the room, noted the time.

Daniel Cooper had a problem. Upon his return to Paris, he had asked for a meeting with Inspector Trignant. The head of Interpol had been less than cordial. He had just spent an hour on the telephone listening to Commandant Ramiro's complaints about the American.

'He is loco!' the commandant had exploded. 'I wasted men and money and time following this Tracy Whitney, who he insisted was going to rob the Prado, and she turned out to be a harmless tourist – just as I said she was.'

The conversation had led Inspector Trignant to believe that Daniel Cooper could have been wrong about Tracy in the first place. There was not one shred of evidence against the woman. The fact that she had been in various cities at the times the crimes were committed was not evidence.

And so, when Daniel Cooper had gone to see the inspector and said, 'Tracy Whitney is in Paris. I would like her placed on twenty-four-hour surveillance,' the inspector had replied. 'Unless you can present me with some proof that this woman is planning to commit a specific crime, there is nothing I can do.'

Cooper had fixed him with his blazing brown eyes and said, 'You're a fool,' and had found himself being unceremoniously ushered out of the office.

That was when Cooper had begun his one-man surveillance. He trailed Tracy everywhere: to shops and restaurants, through the streets of Paris. He went without sleep and often without food. Daniel Cooper could not permit Tracy Whitney to defeat him. His assignment would not be finished until he had put her in prison.

Tracy lay in bed that night, reviewing the next day's plan. She wished her head felt better. She had taken aspirin, but the throbbing was worse. She was perspiring, and the room seemed unbearably hot. *Tomorrow it will be over. Switzerland. That's where I'll go. To the cool mountains of Switzerland. To the château.*

She set the alarm for 5:00 A.M., and when the bell rang she was in her prison cell and Old Iron Pants was yelling, 'Time to get dressed. Move it', and the corridor echoed with the clanging of the bell. Tracy awakened. Her chest felt tight, and the light hurt her eyes. She forced herself into the bathroom. Her face looked blotchy and flushed in the mirror. *I can't get sick now*, Tracy thought. *Not today. There's too much to do.*

She dressed slowly, trying to ignore the throbbing of her head. She put on black overalls with deep pockets, rubber-soled shoes, and a Basque beret. Her heart seemed to beat erratically, but she was not sure whether it was from excitement or the malaise that gripped her. She was dizzy and weak. Her throat felt sore and scratchy. On her table she saw the scarf Jeff had given her. She picked it up and wrapped it around her neck.

The main entrance to the Hôtel Plaza Athénée is on Avenue Montaigne, but the service entrance is on Rue du Boccador, around the corner. A discreet sign reads ENTRÉE DE SERVICE, and the passageway goes from a back hallway of the lobby through a narrow corridor lined with rubbish bins leading to the street. Daniel Cooper, who had taken up an observation post near the main entrance, did not see Tracy leave through the service door, but inexplicably, the moment she was gone, he sensed it. He hurried out to the avenue and looked up and down the street. Tracy was nowhere in sight.

The grey Renault that picked up Tracy at the side entrance to the hotel headed for the Étoile. There was little traffic at that hour, and the driver, a pimply-faced youth who apparently spoke no English, raced into one of the twelve avenues that form the spokes of the Étoile. *I wish he would slow down*, Tracy thought. The motion was making her carsick.

Thirty minutes later the car slammed to a stop in front of a warehouse. The sign over the door read BRUCERE ET CIE. Tracy remembered that this was where Ramon Vauban's brother worked.

The youth opened the car door and murmured, '*Vite!*'

A middle-aged man with a quick, furtive manner appeared as Tracy stepped out of the car. 'Follow me,' he said. 'Hurry.'

Tracy stumbled after him to the back of the warehouse, where there were half a dozen containers, most of them filled and sealed, ready to be taken to the airport. There was one soft container with a canvas side, half-filled with furniture.

'Get in. Quick! We have no time.'

Tracy felt faint. She looked at the box and thought, *I can't get in there. I'll die.*

The man was looking at her strangely. '*Avez vous mal?*'

Now was the time to back out, to put a stop to this. 'I'm all right,' Tracy mumbled. It would be over soon. In a few hours she would be on her way to Switzerland.

'*Bon.* Take this.' He handed her a double-edged knife, a long coil of heavy rope, a flashlight, and a small blue jewel box with a red ribbon around it.

'This is the duplicate of the jewel box you will exchange.'

Tracy took a deep breath, stepped into the container, and sat down. Seconds later a large piece of canvas dropped down over the opening. She could hear ropes being tied around the canvas to hold it in place.

She barely heard his voice through the canvas.

'From now on, no talking, no moving, no smoking.'

'I don't smoke,' Tracy tried to say, but she did not have the energy.

'*Bonne chance*. I've cut some holes in the side of the box so you can breathe. Don't forget to breathe.' He laughed at his joke, and she heard his footsteps fading away. She was alone in the dark.

The box was narrow and cramped, and a set of dining-room chairs took up most of the space. Tracy felt as though she were on fire. Her skin was hot to the touch, and she had difficulty breathing. *I've caught some kind of virus*, she thought, *but it's going to have to wait. I have work to do. Think about something else.*

Gunther's voice: *You've nothing to worry about, Tracy. When they unload the cargo in Amsterdam, your pallet will be taken to a private garage near the airport. Jeff will meet you there. Give him the jewels and return to the airport. There will be a plane ticket for Geneva waiting for you at the Swissair counter. Get out of Amsterdam as fast as you can. As soon as the police learn of the robbery, they'll close up the city tight. Nothing will go wrong, but just in case, here is the address and the key to a safe house in Amsterdam. It is unoccupied.*

She must have dozed, for she awakened with a start as the container was jerked into the air. Tracy felt herself swinging through space, and she clung to the sides for support. The container settled down on something hard. There was a slam of a car door, an engine roared into life, and a moment later the truck was moving.

They were on their way to the airport.

The scheme had been worked out on a split-second schedule. The container with Tracy inside was due to reach the cargo shipping area within a few minutes of the time the De Beers pallet was to arrive. The driver of the truck carrying Tracy had his instructions: *Keep it at a steady fifty miles an hour.*

Traffic on the road to the airport seemed heavier than usual that morning, but the driver was not worried. The pallet would make the plane in time, and he would be in possession of a bonus of 50,000 francs, enough to take his wife and two children on a vacation. *America*, he thought. *We'll go to Disney World.*

He looked at the dashboard clock and grinned to himself. No problem. The airport was only three miles away, and he had ten minutes to get there.

Exactly on schedule, he reached the turnoff for Air France Cargo headquarters at the Fertnord sign and drove past the low grey building at Roissy-Charles de Gaulle Airport, away from the passenger entrance, where barbed-wire fences separated the roadway from the cargo area. As he headed towards the enclosure holding the enormous warehouse, which occupied three blocks and was filled with boxes and packages and containers piled on dollies, there was a sudden explosive sound as the wheel jerked in his hand and the truck began to vibrate. *Foutre!* he thought. A *fucking blowout*.

The giant 747 Air France cargo plane was in the process of being loaded. The nose had been raised, revealing rows of tracks. The cargo containers were on a platform level with the opening, ready to slide across a bridge into the hold of the plane. There were thirty-eight pallets, twenty-eight of them on the main deck and ten of them in the belly holds. On the ceiling an exposed heating pipe ran from one end of the huge cabin to the other, and the wires and cables that controlled the transport were visible on the ceiling. There were no frills on this plane.

The loading had almost been completed. Ramon Vauban looked at his watch again and cursed. The truck was late. The De Beers consignment had already been loaded into its pallet, and the canvas sides fastened down with a crisscross of ropes. Vauban had daubed the side of it with red paint so the woman would have no trouble identifying it. He watched now as the pallet moved along the tracks into the plane and was locked into place. There was room next to it for one more pallet, before the plane took off. There were three more containers on the dock waiting to be loaded. *Where in God's name was the woman?*

The loadmaster inside the plane called, 'Let's go, Ramon. What's holding us up?'

'A minute,' Vauban answered. He hurried

towards the entrance to the loading area. No sign of the truck.

'Vauban! What's the problem?' He turned. A senior supervisor was approaching. 'Finish loading and get this cargo in the air.'

'Yes, sir. I was just waiting for –'

At that moment the truck from Brucere et Cie raced into the warehouse and came to a screaming halt in front of Vauban.

'Here's the last of the cargo,' Vauban announced.

'Well, get it aboard,' the supervisor snapped.

Vauban supervised the unloading of the container from the truck and sent it onto the bridge leading to the plane.

He waved to the loadmaster. 'It's all yours.'

Moments later the cargo was aboard, and the nose of the plane was lowered into place. Vauban watched as the jets were fired up and the giant plane started rolling towards the runway, and he thought, *Now it's up to the woman.*

There was a fierce storm. A giant wave had struck the ship and it was sinking. *I'm drowning*, Tracy thought. *I've got to get out of here.*

She flung out her arms and hit something. It was the side of a lifeboat, rocking and swaying. She tried to stand up and cracked her head on the leg of a table. In a moment of clarity she remembered where she was. Her face and hair dripped with perspiration. She felt giddy, and her body was burning up. How long had she been unconscious?

It was only an hour's flight. Was the plane about to land? *No*, she thought. *It's all right. I'm having a nightmare. I'm in my bed in London, asleep. I'll call for a doctor.* She could not breathe. She struggled upwards to reach for a telephone, then immediately sank down, her body leaden. The plane hit a pocket of turbulence, and Tracy was thrown against the side of the box. She lay there, dazed, desperately trying to concentrate. *How much time do I have?* She wavered between a hellish dream and painful reality. *The diamonds.* Somehow she had to get the diamonds. But first . . . first, she had to cut herself out of the pallet.

She touched the knife in her overalls and found that it was a terrible effort to lift it. *Not enough air*, Tracy thought. *I must have air.* She reached around the edge of the canvas, fumbled for one of the outside ropes, found it, and cut it. It seemed to take an eternity. The canvas opened wider. She cut another rope, and there was room enough to slip outside of the container into the belly of the cargo plane. The air outside the box was cold. She was freezing. Her body began to shake, and the constant jolting of the plane increased her nausea. *I've got to hold on*, Tracy thought. She forced herself to concentrate. *What am I doing here? Something important . . . Yes . . . Diamonds.*

Tracy's vision was blurred, and everything was moving in and out of focus. *I'm not going to make it.*

The plane dipped suddenly, and Tracy was

hurled to the floor, scraping her hands on the sharp metal tracks. She held on while the plane bucked, and when it had settled down, she forced herself to her feet again. The roaring of the jet engines was mixed with the roaring in her head. *The diamonds. I must find the diamonds.*

She stumbled among the containers, squinting at each one, looking for the red paint. Thank God! There it was, on the third container. She stood there, trying to remember what to do next. It was such an effort to concentrate. *If I could just lie down and sleep for a few minutes, I'd be fine. All I need is some sleep.* But there was no time. They could be landing in Amsterdam at any moment. Tracy took the knife and slashed at the ropes of the container. 'One good cut will do it,' they had told her.

She barely had the strength to hold the knife in her grasp. *I can't fail now*, Tracy thought. She began shivering again, and shook so hard that she dropped the knife. *It's not going to work. They're going to catch me and put me back in prison.*

She hesitated indecisively, clinging to the rope, wanting desperately to crawl back into her box where she could sleep, safely hidden until it was all over. It would be so easy. Then, slowly, moving carefully against the fierce pounding in her head, Tracy reached for the knife and picked it up. She began to slash at the heavy rope.

It finally gave way. Tracy pulled back the canvas and stared into the gloomy interior of the container.

She could see nothing. She pulled out the flash-light and, at that moment, she felt a sudden change of pressure in her ears.

The plane was coming down for a landing.

Tracy thought, *I've got to hurry*. But her body refused to respond. She stood there, dazed. *Move*, her mind said.

She shone the flashlight into the interior of the box. It was crammed with packages and envelopes and small cases, and on top of a crate were two little blue boxes with red ribbons around them. *Two of them! There was only supposed to be –* She blinked, and the two boxes merged into one. Everything seemed to have a bright aura around it.

She reached for the box and took the dupli-cate out of her pocket. Holding the two of them in her hand, an overwhelming nausea swept over her, racking her body. She squeezed her eyes together, fighting against it. She started to place the substitute box on top of the case and sud-denly realized that she was no longer sure which box was which. She stared at the two identical boxes. Was it the one in her left hand or her right hand?

The plane began a steeper angle of descent. It would touch down at any moment. She had to make a decision. She set down one of the boxes, prayed that it was the right one, and moved away from the container. She fumbled an uncut coil of rope out of her overalls. *There's something I must do with the rope*. The roaring in her head made it impossible to think. She remembered: *After you cut the rope, put it in your pocket, replace it with the new rope. Don't leave anything around that will make them suspicious.*

It had sounded so easy then, sitting in the warm sun on the deck of the *Bateau Mouche*. Now it was impossible. She had no more strength left. The guards would find the cut rope and the cargo would be searched, and she would be caught. Something deep inside her screamed, *No! No! No!*

With a herculean effort, Tracy began to wind the uncut rope around the container. She felt a jolt beneath her feet as the plane touched the ground, and then another, and she was slammed backwards as the jets were thrust into reverse. Her head smashed against the floor and she blacked out.

The 747 was picking up speed now, taxiing along the runway towards the terminal. Tracy lay crumpled on the floor of the plane with her hair fanning over her white, white face. It was the silence of the engines that brought her back to consciousness. The plane had stopped. She propped herself up on an elbow and slowly forced herself to her knees. She stood up, reeling, hanging on to the container to keep from falling. The new rope was in place. She clasped the jewel box to her chest and began to weave her way back to her pallet. She pushed her body through the canvas opening and flopped down, panting, her body beaded with perspiration. *I've done it*. But there was something more she had to do. Something important. *What? Tape up the rope on your pallet*.

She reached into the pocket of her overalls for the roll of masking tape. It was gone. Her breath was coming in shallow, ragged gasps, and the sound deafened her. She thought she heard voices and forced herself to stop breathing and listen. Yes. There they were again. Someone laughed. Any second now the cargo door would open, and the men would begin unloading. They would see the cut rope, look inside the pallet, and discover her. She had to find a way to hold the rope together. She got to her knees, and as she did she felt the hard roll of masking tape, which had fallen from her pocket sometime during the turbulence of the flight. She lifted the canvas and fumbled around to find the two ends of cut rope, and held them together while she clumsily tried to wrap the tape around them.

She could not see. The perspiration pouring down her face was blinding her. She pulled the scarf from her throat and wiped her face. Better. She finished taping the rope and dropped the canvas back in place; there was nothing to do now but wait. She felt her forehead again, and it seemed hotter than before.

I must get out of the sun, Tracy thought. *Tropical suns can be dangerous*.

She was on holiday somewhere in the Caribbean. Jeff had come here to bring her some diamonds, but he had jumped into the sea and disappeared. She reached out to save him, but he slipped from her grasp. The water was over her head. She was choking, drowning.

She heard the sound of workmen entering the plane.

'Help!' she screamed. 'Please help me.'

But her scream was a whisper, and no one heard.

The giant containers began rolling out of the plane.

Tracy was unconscious when they loaded her container onto a Brucere et Cie truck. Left behind, on the floor of the cargo plane, was the scarf Jeff had given her.

Tracy was awakened by the slash of light hitting the inside of the truck as someone raised the canvas. Slowly, she opened her eyes. The truck was in the warehouse.

Jeff was standing there, grinning at her. 'You made it!' he said. 'You're a marvel. Let's have the box.'

She watched, dully, as he picked up the box from her side. 'See you in Lisbon.' He turned to leave, then stopped and looked down at her. 'You look terrible, Tracy. You all right?'

She could hardly speak. 'Jeff, I –'

But he was gone.

Tracy had only the haziest recollection of what

happened next. There was a change of clothes for her in the back of the warehouse, and some woman said, 'You look ill, mademoiselle. Do you wish me to call a doctor?'

'No doctors,' Tracy whispered.

There will be a plane ticket for Geneva waiting for you at the Swissair counter. Get out of Amsterdam as fast as you can. As soon as the police learn of the robbery, they'll close up the city tight. Nothing will go wrong, but just in case, here is the address and the key to a safe house in Amsterdam. It is unoccupied.

The airport. She had to get to the airport. 'Taxi,' she mumbled. 'Taxi.'

The woman hesitated a moment, then shrugged. 'All right. I will call one. Wait here.'

She was floating higher and higher now, ever closer to the sun.

'Your taxi is here,' a man was saying.

She wished people would stop bothering her. She wanted only to sleep.

The driver said, 'Where do you wish to go, mademoiselle?'

There will be a plane ticket for Geneva waiting for you at the Swissair counter.

She was too ill to board a plane. They would stop her, summon a doctor. She would be questioned. All she needed was to sleep for a few minutes, then she would be fine.

The voice was getting impatient. 'Where to, please?'

She had no place to go. She gave the taxi driver the address of the safe house.

The police were cross-examining her about the diamonds, and when she refused to answer them, they became very angry and put her in a room by herself and turned up the heat until the room was boiling hot. When it became unbearable, they dropped the temperature down, until icicles began to form on the walls.

Tracy pushed her way up through the cold and opened her eyes. She was on a bed, shivering uncontrollably. There was a blanket beneath her, but she did not have the strength to get under it. Her dress was soaked through, and her face and neck were wet.

I'm going to die here. Where was here?

The safe house. I'm in the safe house. And the phrase struck her as so funny that she started to laugh, and the laughter turned into a paroxysm of coughing. It had all gone wrong. She had not got away after all. By now the police would be combing Amsterdam for her: *Mademoiselle Whitney had a ticket on Swissair and did not use it? Then she still must be in Amsterdam.*

She wondered how long she had been in this bed. She lifted her wrist to look at her watch, but the numbers were blurred. She was seeing everything double. There were two beds in the small room and two dressers and four chairs. The shivering stopped, and her body was burning up. She needed to open a window, but she was too weak to move. The room was freezing again.

She was back on the airplane, locked in the crate, screaming for help.

You've made it! You're a marvel. Let's have the box.

Jeff had taken the diamonds, and he was probably on his way to Brazil with her share of the money. He would be enjoying himself with one of his women, laughing at her. He had beaten her once more. She hated him. No. She didn't. Yes, she did. She despised him.

She was in and out of delirium. The hard pelota ball was hurtling towards her, and Jeff grabbed her in his arms and pushed her to the ground, and his lips were very close to hers, and then they were having dinner at Zalacaín. *Do you know how special you are, Tracy?*

I offer you a draw, Boris Melnikov said.

Her body was trembling again, out of control, and she was on an express train whirling through a dark tunnel, and at the end of the tunnel she knew she was going to die. All the other passengers had got off except Alberto Fornati. He was angry with her, shaking her and screaming at her.

'For Christ's sake!' he yelled. 'Open your eyes! Look at me!'

With a superhuman effort, Tracy opened her eyes, and Jeff was standing over her. His face was white, and there was fury in his voice. Of course, it was all a part of her dream.

'How long have you been like this?'

'You're in Brazil,' Tracy mumbled.

After that, she remembered nothing more.

When Inspector Trignant was given the scarf with the initials TW on it, found on the floor of the Air France cargo plane, he stared at it for a long time.

Then he said, 'Get me Daniel Cooper.'

THIRTY-TWO

The picturesque village of Alkmaar, on the north-west coast of Holland facing the North Sea, is a popular tourist attraction, but there is a quarter in the eastern section that tourists seldom visit. Jeff Stevens had been on holiday there several times with a stewardess from KLM who had taught him the language. He remembered the area well, a place where residents minded their own business and were not unduly curious about visitors. It was a perfect place to hide out.

Jeff's first impulse had been to rush Tracy to a hospital, but that was too dangerous. It was also risky for her to remain in Amsterdam a minute longer. He had wrapped her in blankets and carried her out to the car, where she had remained unconscious during the drive to Alkmaar. Her pulse was erratic and her breathing shallow.

In Alkmaar, Jeff checked into a small inn. The inn-keeper watched curiously as Jeff carried Tracy upstairs to her room.

'We're honeymooners,' Jeff explained. 'My wife became ill – a slight respiratory disturbance. She needs rest.'

'Would you like a doctor?'

Jeff was not certain of the answer himself. 'I'll let you know.'

The first thing he had to do was to bring down Tracy's fever. Jeff lowered her onto the large double bed in the room and began to strip off her clothes, sodden with perspiration. He held her up in a sitting position and lifted her dress over her head. Shoes next, then pantyhose. Her body was hot to the touch. Jeff wet a towel with cool water and gently bathed her from head to foot. He covered her with a blanket and sat at the bedside listening to her uneven breathing.

If she's not better by morning, Jeff decided, *I'll have to bring in a doctor.*

In the morning the bedclothes were soaked again. Tracy was still unconscious, but it seemed to Jeff that her breathing was a little easier. He was afraid to let the maid see Tracy; it would lead to too many questions. Instead, he asked the housekeeper for a change of linens and took them inside the room. He washed Tracy's body with a moist towel, changed the sheets on the bed the way he had seen nurses do in hospitals, without disturbing the patient, and covered her up again.

Jeff put a DO NOT DISTURB sign on the door and went looking for the nearest pharmacy. He bought aspirin, a thermometer, a sponge and rubbing alcohol. When he returned to the room, Tracy was still not awake. Jeff took her temperature: 104 degrees. He sponged her body with the cool alcohol, and her fever dropped.

An hour later her temperature was up again. He was going to have to call a doctor. The problem was that the doctor would insist Tracy be taken to a hospital. Questions would be asked. Jeff had no idea whether the police were looking for them, but if they were, they would both be taken into custody. He had to do something. He mashed up four aspirins, placed the powder between Tracy's lips, and gently spooned water into her mouth until she finally swallowed. Once again he bathed her body. After he had finished drying her, it seemed to him that her skin was not as hot as it had been. He checked her pulse once more. It seemed steadier. He put his head to her chest and listened. Was her breathing less congested? He could not be certain. He was sure of only one thing, and he repeated it over and over until it became a litany: 'You're going to get well.' He kissed her gently on the forehead.

Jeff had not slept in forty-eight hours, and he was exhausted and hollow-eyed. *I'll sleep later*, he promised himself. *I'll close my eyes to rest them a moment*.

He slept.

When Tracy opened her eyes and watched the ceiling slowly come into focus, she had no idea where she was. It took long minutes for awareness to seep into her consciousness. Her body felt battered and sore, and she had the feeling that she had returned from a long, wearying journey. Drowsily, she looked around the unfamiliar room, and her heart suddenly skipped a beat. Jeff was slumped in an armchair near the window, asleep. It was impossible. The last time she had seen him, he had taken the diamonds and left. What was he doing here? And with a sudden, sinking sensation, Tracy knew the answer. She had given him the wrong box – the box with the fake diamonds – and Jeff thought she had cheated him. He must have picked her up at the safe house and taken her to wherever this place was.

As she sat up, Jeff stirred and opened his eyes. When he saw Tracy looking at him, a slow, happy grin lit his face.

'Welcome back.' There was a note of such intense relief in his voice that Tracy was confused.

'I'm sorry,' Tracy said. Her voice was a hoarse whisper. 'I gave you the wrong box.'

'What?'

'I mixed up the boxes.'

He walked over to her and said gently, 'No, Tracy. You gave me the real diamonds. They're on their way to Gunther.' She looked at him in bewilderment. 'Then – why – why are you here?'

He sat on the edge of the bed. 'When you handed me the diamonds, you looked like death. I decided I'd better wait at the airport to make sure you caught your flight. You didn't show up, and I knew you were in trouble. I went to the safe house and found you. I couldn't let you die there,' he said lightly. 'It would have been a clue for the police.'

She was watching him, puzzled. 'Tell me the real reason you came back for me.'

'Time to take your temperature,' he said briskly.

'Not bad,' he told her a few minutes later. 'Little over a hundred. You're a wonderful patient.'

'Jeff –'

'Trust me,' he said. 'Hungry?'

Tracy was suddenly ravenous. 'Starved.'

'Good. I'll bring something in.'

He returned from shopping with a bag full of orange juice, milk, and fresh fruit, and large Dutch *broodjes*, rolls filled with different kinds of cheese, meat and fish.

'This seems to be the Dutch version of chicken soup, but it should do the trick. Now, eat slowly.'

He helped her sit up, and fed her. He was careful and tender, and Tracy thought, warily, he's after something.

As they were eating, Jeff said. 'While I was out, I telephoned Gunther. He received the diamonds. He deposited your share of the money in your Swiss bank account.'

She could not keep herself from asking, 'Why didn't you keep it all?'

When Jeff answered, his tone was serious. 'Because it's time we stopped playing games with each other, Tracy. Okay?'

It was another one of his tricks, of course, but she was too tired to worry about it. 'Okay.'

'If you'll tell me your sizes,' Jeff said, 'I'll go out and buy some clothes for you. The Dutch are liberal, but I think if you walked around like that they might be shocked.'

Tracy pulled the covers up closer around her, suddenly aware of her nakedness. She had a vague impression of Jeff's undressing her and bathing her. He had risked his own safety to nurse her. Why? She had believed she understood him. *I don't understand him at all*, Tracy thought. *Not at all*.

She slept.

In the afternoon Jeff brought back two suitcases filled with robes and nightgowns, underwear, dresses, and shoes, and a makeup kit and a comb and brush and hair dryer, toothbrushes and toothpaste. He also had purchased several changes of clothes for himself and brought back the *International Herald Tribune*. On the front page was a story about the diamond hijacking; the police had figured out how it had been committed, but according to the newspaper, the thieves had left no clues.

Jeff said cheerfully, 'We're home free! Now all we have to do is get you well.'

It was Daniel Cooper who had suggested that the scarf with the initials TW be kept from the press. 'We know,' he had told Inspector Trignant, 'who

517

it belongs to, but it's not enough evidence for an indictment. Her lawyers would produce every woman in Europe with the same initials and make fools of you.'

In Cooper's opinion, the police had already made fools of themselves. *God will give her to me.*

He sat in the darkness of the small church, on a hard wooden bench, and he prayed: *Oh, make her mine, Father. Give her to me to punish so that I may wash myself of my sins. The evil in her spirit shall be exorcized, and her naked body shall be flagellated* . . . And he thought about Tracy's naked body in his power and felt himself getting an erection. He hurried from the church in terror that God would see and inflict further punishment on him.

When Tracy awoke, it was dark. She sat up and turned on the lamp on the bedside table. She was alone. He had gone. A feeling of panic washed over her. She had allowed herself to grow dependent on Jeff, and that had been a stupid mistake. *It serves me right*, Tracy thought bitterly. 'Trust me,' Jeff had said, and she had. He had taken care of her only to protect himself, not for any other reason. She had come to believe that he felt something for her. She had *wanted* to trust him, *wanted* to feel that she meant something to him. She lay back on her pillow and closed her eyes, thinking, *I'm going to miss him. Heaven help me, I'm going to miss him.*

God had played a cosmic joke on her. Why did it have to be *him*? she wondered, but the reason did not matter. She would have to make plans to leave this place as soon as possible, find somewhere where she could get well, where she could feel safe. *Oh, you bloody fool*, she thought. *You* –

There was the sound of the door opening, and Jeff's voice called out, 'Tracy, are you awake? I brought you some books and magazines. I thought you might –' He stopped as he saw the expression on her face. 'Hey! Is something wrong?'

'Not now,' Tracy whispered. 'Not now.'

The following morning Tracy's fever was gone.

'I'd like to get out,' she said. 'Do you think we could go for a walk, Jeff?'

They were a curiosity in the lobby. The couple who owned the hotel were delighted by Tracy's recovery. 'Your husband was so wonderful. He insisted on doing everything for you himself. He was so worried. A woman is lucky to have a man who loves her so much.'

Tracy looked at Jeff, and she could have sworn he was blushing.

Outside, Tracy said, 'They're very sweet.'

'Sentimentalists,' Jeff retorted.

Jeff had arranged for a cot to sleep on, placed next to Tracy's bed. As Tracy lay in bed that night, she remembered again how Jeff had taken care of her, tended to her needs, and nursed her and bathed her naked body. She was powerfully aware of his presence. It made her feel protected.

It made her feel nervous.

Slowly, as Tracy grew stronger, she and Jeff spent more time exploring the quaint little town. They walked to the Alkmaarder Meer, along winding, cobblestoned streets that dated from the Middle Ages, and spent hours at the tulip fields on the outskirts of the city. They visited the cheese market and the old weighing house, and went through the municipal museum. To Tracy's surprise, Jeff spoke to the townspeople in Dutch.

'Where did you learn that?' Tracy asked.

'I used to know a Dutch girl.'

She was sorry she had asked.

As the days passed Tracy's healthy young body gradually healed itself. When Jeff felt that Tracy was strong enough, he rented bicycles, and they visited the windmills that dotted the countryside. Each day was a lovely holiday, and Tracy wanted it never to end.

Jeff was a constant surprise. He treated Tracy with a concern and tenderness that melted her defences against him, yet he made no sexual advances. He was an enigma to Tracy. She thought of the beautiful women with whom she had seen him, and she was sure he could have had any of them. Why was he staying by her side in this tiny backwater of the world?

Tracy found herself talking about things she had

thought she would never discuss with anyone. She told Jeff about Joe Romano and Tony Orsatti, and about Ernestine Littlechap and Big Bertha and little Amy Brannigan. Jeff was by turns outraged and distressed and sympathetic. Jeff told her about his stepmother and his Uncle Willie and about his carnival days and his marriage to Louise. Tracy had never felt so close to anyone.

Suddenly it was time to leave.

One morning Jeff said, 'The police aren't looking for us, Tracy. I think we should be moving on.'

Tracy felt a stab of disappointment. 'All right. When?'

'Tomorrow.'

She nodded. 'I'll pack in the morning.'

That night Tracy lay awake, unable to sleep. Jeff's presence seemed to fill the room as never before. This had been an unforgettable period in her life, and it was coming to an end. She looked over at the cot where Jeff lay.

'Are you asleep?' Tracy whispered.

'No . . .'

'What are you thinking about?'

'Tomorrow. Leaving this place. I'll miss it.'

'I'm going to miss you, Jeff.' The words were out before she could stop herself.

Jeff sat up slowly and looked at her. 'How much?' he asked.

'Terribly.'

A moment later he was at her bedside. 'Tracy –'

'Shhh. Don't talk. Just put your arms around me. Hold me.'

It started slowly, a velvet touching and stroking and feeling, a caressing and gentle exploring of the senses. And it began to build and swell in a frenzied, frantic rhythm, until it became a bacchanal, an orgy of pleasure, wild and savage. His hard organ stroked her and pounded her and filled her until she wanted to scream with the unbearable joy. She was at the centre of a rainbow. She felt herself being swept up on a tidal wave that lifted her higher and higher, and there was a sudden molten explosion within her, and her whole body began to shudder. Gradually, the tempest subsided. She closed her eyes. She felt Jeff's lips move down her body, down, down to the centre of her being, and she was caught up in another fierce wave of blissful sensation.

She pulled Jeff to her and held him close, feeling his heart beat against hers. She strained against him, but still she could not get close enough. She crept to the foot of the bed and touched her lips to his body with soft, tender kisses, moving upwards until she felt his hard maleness in her hand. She stroked it softly and slid it into her mouth, and listened to his moans of pleasure. Then Jeff rolled on top of her and was inside her and it began again, more exciting than before, a fountain spilling over with unbearable pleasure, and Tracy thought, *Now I know. For the first time, I know. But I must remember that this is just for tonight, a lovely farewell present.*

All through the night they made love and talked

about everything and nothing, and it was as though some long-locked floodgates had opened for both of them. At dawn, as the canals began to sparkle with the beginning day, Jeff said, 'Marry me, Tracy.'

She was sure she had misunderstood him, but the words came again, and Tracy knew that it was crazy and impossible, and it could never work, and it was deliriously wonderful, and of course it would work. And she whispered, 'Yes. Oh, yes!'

She began to cry, gripped tightly in the safety of his arms. *I'll never be lonely again*, Tracy thought. *We belong to each other. Jeff is a part of all my tomorrows.*

Tomorrow had come.

A long time later Tracy asked, 'When did you know, Jeff?'

'When I saw you in that house and I thought you were dying. I was half out of my mind.'

'I thought you had run away with the diamonds,' Tracy confessed.

He took her in his arms again. 'Tracy, what I did in Madrid wasn't for the money. It was for the game – the challenge. That's why we're both in the business we're in, isn't it? You're given a puzzle that can't possibly be solved, and then you begin to wonder if there isn't some way.'

Tracy nodded. 'I know. At first it was because I needed the money. And then it became something else; I've given away quite a bit of money. I love matching wits against people who are successful and bright and unscrupulous. I love living on the cutting edge of danger.'

After a long silence, Jeff said, 'Tracy . . . how would you feel about giving it up?'

She looked at him, puzzled. 'Giving it up? Why?'

'We were each on our own before. Now, everything has changed. I couldn't bear it if anything happened. Why take any more risks? We have all the money we'll ever need. Why don't we consider ourselves retired?'

'What would we do, Jeff?'

He grinned. 'We'll think of something.'

'Seriously, darling, how would we spend our lives?'

'Doing anything we like, my love. We'll travel, indulge ourselves in hobbies. I've always been fascinated by archaeology. I'd like to go on a dig in Tunisia. I made a promise once to an old friend. We can finance our own digs. We'll travel all over the world.'

'It sounds exciting.'

'Then what do you say?'

She looked at him for a long moment. 'If that's what you want,' Tracy said softly.

He hugged her and began laughing. 'I wonder if we should send a formal announcement to the police?'

Tracy joined in his laughter.

The churches were older than any Cooper had ever known before. Some dated back to the pagan days, and at times he was not certain whether he was praying to the devil or to God. He sat with bowed head in the ancient Beguine Court Church and in St Bavokerk and Pieterskerk and the Nieuwekerk at Delft, and each time his prayer was the same: *Let me make her suffer as I suffer.*

The telephone call from Gunther Hartog came the next day, while Jeff was out.

'How are you feeling?' Gunther asked.

'I feel wonderful,' Tracy assured him.

Gunther had telephoned every day after he had heard what had happened to her. Tracy decided not to tell him the news about Jeff and herself, not yet. She wanted to hug it to herself for a while, take it out and examine it, cherish it.

'Are you and Jeff getting along all right together?'

She smiled. 'We're getting along splendidly.'

'Would you consider working together again?'

Now she had to tell him. 'Gunther . . . we're . . . quitting.'

There was a momentary silence. 'I don't understand.'

'Jeff and I are – as they used to say in the old James Cagney movies – going straight.'

'What? But . . . why?'

'It was Jeff's idea, and I agreed to it. No more risks.'

'Supposing I told you that the job I have in mind is worth two million dollars to you and there are no risks?'

'I'd laugh a lot, Gunther.'

'I'm serious, my dear. You would travel to Amsterdam, which is only an hour from where you are now, and –'

'You'll have to find someone else.'

He sighed. 'I'm afraid there is no one else who could handle this. Will you at least discuss the possibility with Jeff?'

'All right, but it won't do any good.'

'I will call back this evening.'

When Jeff returned, Tracy reported the conversation.

'Didn't you tell him we've become law-abiding citizens?'

'Of course, darling, I told him to find someone else.'

'But he doesn't want to,' Jeff guessed.

'He insisted he needed us. He said there's no risk and that we could pick up two million dollars for a little bit of effort.'

'Which means that whatever he has in mind must be guarded like Fort Knox.'

'Or the Prado,' Tracy said mischievously.

Jeff grinned. 'That was really a neat plan, sweetheart. You know, I think *that's* when I started to fall in love with you.'

'I think when you stole my Goya is when I began to hate you.'

'Be fair,' Jeff admonished. 'You started to hate me before that.'

'True. What do we tell Gunther?'

'You've already told him. We're not in that line of work any more.'

'Shouldn't we at least find out what he's thinking?'

'Tracy, we agreed that –'

'We're going to Amsterdam anyway, aren't we?'

'Yes, but –'

'Well, while we're there darling, why don't we just listen to what he has to say?'

Jeff studied her suspiciously. 'You *want* to do it, don't you?'

'Certainly not! But it can't hurt to hear what he has to say . . .'

They drove to Amsterdam the following day and checked into the Amstel Hotel. Gunther Hartog flew in from London to meet them.

They managed to sit together, as casual tourists, on a Plas Motor launch cruising the Amstel River.

'I'm delighted that you two are getting married,' Gunther said. 'My warmest congratulations.'

'Thank you, Gunther.' Tracy knew that he was sincere.

'I respect your wishes about retiring, but I have come across a situation so unique that I felt I had to call it to your attention. It could be a very rewarding swan song.'

'We're listening,' Tracy said.

Gunther leaned forward and began talking, his voice low. When he had finished, he said, 'Two million dollars if you can pull it off.'

'It's impossible,' Jeff declared flatly. 'Tracy –'

But Tracy was not listening. She was busily figuring out how it could be done.

Amsterdam's police headquarters, at the corner of Marnix Straat and Elandsgracht, is a gracious old five-storey, brown-brick building with a long white-stucco corridor on the ground floor and a marble staircase leading to the upper floors. In a meeting room upstairs, the Gemeentepolitie were in conference. There were six Dutch detectives in the room. The lone foreigner was Daniel Cooper.

Inspector Joop van Duren was a giant of a man, larger than life, with a beefy face adorned by a flowing moustache, and a roaring basso voice. He was addressing Toon Willems, the neat, crisp, efficient chief commissioner, head of the city's police force.

'Tracy Whitney arrived in Amsterdam this morning, Chief Commissioner. Interpol is certain she was responsible for the De Beers hijacking. Mr Cooper, here, feels she has come to Holland to commit another felony.'

Chief Commissioner Willems turned to Cooper. 'Do you have any proof of this, Mr Cooper?'

Daniel Cooper did not need proof. He knew Tracy Whitney, body and soul. *Of course* she was here to carry out a crime, something beyond the scope of their tiny imaginations. He forced himself to remain calm.

'No proof. That's why she must be caught red-handed.'

'And just how do you propose that we do that?'

'By not letting the woman out of our sight.'

The use of the pronoun *our* disturbed the chief commissioner. He had spoken with Inspector Trignant in Paris about Cooper. *He's obnoxious, but he knows what he's about. If we had listened to him, we would have caught the Whitney woman red-handed.* It was the same phrase Cooper had used.

Toon Willems made his decision, and it was based partly on the well-publicized failure of the French police to apprehend the hijackers of the De Beers diamonds. Where the French police had failed, the Dutch police would succeed.

'Very well,' the chief commissioner said. 'If the lady has come to Holland to test the efficiency of our police force, we shall accommodate her.' He turned to Inspector van Duren. 'Take whatever measures you think necessary.'

The city of Amsterdam is divided into six police districts, with each district responsible for its own territory. On orders from Inspector Joop van Duren, the boundaries were ignored, and detectives from different districts were assigned to surveillance teams. 'I want her watched twenty-four hours a day. Don't let her out of your sight.'

Inspector van Duren turned to Daniel Cooper. 'Well, Mr Cooper, are you satisfied?'

'Not until we have her.'

'We will,' the inspector assured him. 'You see, Mr Cooper, we pride ourselves on having the best police force in the world.'

Amsterdam is a tourist's paradise, a city of windmills and dams and row upon row of gabled houses leaning crazily against one another along a network of tree-lined canals filled with houseboats decorated by boxes of geraniums and plants, and laundry flying in the breeze. The Dutch were the friendliest people Tracy had ever met.

'They all seem so happy,' Tracy said.

'Remember, they're the original flower people. Tulips.'

Tracy laughed and took Jeff's arm. She felt such joy in being with him. *He's so wonderful.* And Jeff was looking at her and thinking, *I'm the luckiest fellow in the world.*

Tracy and Jeff did all the usual sightseeing things tourists do. They strolled along Albert Cuyp Straat, the open-air market that stretches block after block and is filled with stands of antiques, fruits and vegetables, flowers, and clothing, and wandered through Dam Square, where young people gathered to listen to itinerant singers and punk bands. They visited Volendam, the old picturesque fishing village on the Zuider Zee, and Madurodam, Holland in miniature. As they drove past the bustling Schiphol Airport, Jeff said, 'Not long ago, all that land the airport stands on was the North

Sea. *Schiphol* means "cemetery of ships".'

Tracy nestled closer to him. 'I'm impressed. It's nice to be in love with such a smart fellow.'

'You ain't heard nothin' yet. Twenty-five percent of the Netherlands is reclaimed land. The whole country is sixteen feet below sea level.'

'Sounds scary.'

'Not to worry. We're perfectly safe as long as that little kid keeps his finger in the dyke.'

Everywhere Tracy and Jeff went, they were followed by the Gemeetepolitie, and each evening Daniel Cooper studied the written reports submitted to Inspector van Duren. There was nothing unusual in them, but Cooper's suspicions were not allayed. *She's up to something,* he told himself, *something big. I wonder if she knows she's being followed? I wonder if she knows I'm going to destroy her?*

As far as the detectives could see, Tracy Whitney and Jeff Stevens were merely tourists.

Inspector van Duren said to Cooper, 'Isn't it possible you're wrong? They could be in Holland just to have a good time.'

'No,' Cooper said stubbornly. 'I'm not wrong. Stay with her.' He had an ominous feeling that time was running out, that if Tracy Whitney did not make a move soon, the police surveillance would be called off again. That could not be allowed to happen. He joined the detectives who were keeping Tracy under observation.

* * *

Tracy and Jeff had connecting rooms at the Amstel. 'For the sake of respectability,' Jeff told Tracy, 'but I won't let you get far from me.'

'Promise?'

Each night Jeff stayed with her until early dawn, and they made love far into the night. He was a protean lover, by turns tender and considerate, wild and feral.

'It's the first time,' Tracy whispered, 'that I've really known what my body was for. Thank you, my love.'

'The pleasure's all mine.'

'Only half.'

They roamed the city in an apparently aimless manner. They had lunch at the Excelsior in the Hôtel de l'Europe and dinner at the Bowedery, and ate all twenty-two courses served at the Indonesian Bali. They had *erwtensoep*, Holland's famous pea soup; sampled *hutsput*, potatoes, carrots, and onions; and *boerenkool met worst*, made from thirteen vegetables and smoked sausage. They walked through the *walletjes*, the red-light district of Amsterdam, where fat, kimono-clad whores sat on the street windows displaying their ample wares; each evening the written report submitted to Inspector Joop van Duren ended with the same note: *Nothing suspicious*.

Patience, Daniel Cooper told himself. *Patience*.

At the urging of Cooper, Inspector van Duren went to Chief Commissioner Willems to ask permission to place electronic eavesdropping devices in the hotel rooms of the two suspects. Permission was denied.

'When you have more substantial grounds for your suspicions,' the chief commissioner said, 'come back to me. Until then, I cannot permit you to eavesdrop on people who are so far guilty only of touring Holland.'

That conversation had taken place on Friday. On Monday morning Tracy and Jeff went to Paulus Potter Straat in Coster, the diamond centre of Amsterdam, to visit the Nederlands Diamond-Cutting Factory. Daniel Cooper was a part of the surveillance team. The factory was crowded with tourists. An English-speaking guide conducted them around the factory, explaining each operation in the cutting process, and at the end of the tour led the group to a large display room, where showcases filled with a variety of diamonds for sale lined the walls. This of course was the ultimate reason visitors were given a tour of the factory. In the centre of the room stood a glass case dramatically mounted on a tall, black pedestal, and inside the case was the most exquisite diamond Tracy had ever seen.

The guide announced proudly, 'And here, ladies and gentlemen, is the famous Lucullan diamond you have all read about. It was once purchased by a stage actor for his film-star wife and is valued at ten million dollars. It is a perfect stone, one of the finest diamonds in the world.'

'That must be quite a target for thieves,' Jeff said aloud.

Daniel Cooper moved forward so he could hear better.

The guide smiled indulgently, '*Nee, mijnheer.*' He nodded towards the armed guard standing near the exhibit. 'This stone is more closely guarded than the jewels in the Tower of London. There is no danger. If anyone touches the glass case, an alarm rings – *vlug!* – and every window and door in this room is instantly sealed off. At night electronic beams are on, and if someone enters the room, an alarm sounds at police headquarters.'

Jeff looked at Tracy and said, 'I guess no one's ever going to steal that diamond.'

Cooper exchanged a look with one of the detectives. That afternoon Inspector van Duren was given a report of the conversation.

The following day Tracy and Jeff visited the Rijksmuseum. At the entrance, Jeff purchased a directory plan of the museum, and he and Tracy passed through the main hall to the Gallery of Honour, filled with Fra Angelicos, Murillos, Rubenses, Van Dycks and Tiepolos. They moved slowly, pausing in front of each painting, and then walked into the Night Watch Room, where Rembrandt's most famous painting hung. There they stayed. And the attractive Constable First-Class Fien Hauer, who was following them, thought to herself, *Oh, my God!*

The official title of the painting is *The Company*

of Captain Frans Banning Cocq and Lieutenant Willem van Ruytenburch, and it portrays, with extraordinary clarity and composition, a group of soldiers preparing to go on their watch, under the command of their colourfully uniformed captain. The area around the portrait was roped off with velvet cords, and a guard stood nearby.

'It's hard to believe,' Jeff told Tracy, 'but Rembrandt caught hell for this painting.'

'But why? It's fantastic.'

'His patron – the captain in the painting – didn't like the attention Rembrandt paid to the other figures.' Jeff turned to the guard. 'I hope this is well protected.'

'*Ja, mijnheer.* Anyone who tries to steal anything from this museum would have to get by electronic beams, security cameras, and, at night, two guards with patrol dogs.'

Jeff smiled easily. 'I guess this painting is going to stay here forever.'

Late that afternoon the exchange was reported to Van Duren. '*The Night Watch!*' he exclaimed. '*Alstublieft, impossible!*'

Daniel Cooper merely blinked at him with his wild, myopic eyes.

At the Amsterdam Convention Centre, there was a meeting of philatelists, and Tracy and Jeff were among the first to arrive. The hall was heavily guarded, for many of the stamps were priceless. Cooper and a Dutch detective watched as the two visitors wandered through the rare-stamp collection. Tracy and Jeff paused in front of the British Guiana, an unattractive magenta, six-sided stamp.

'What an ugly stamp,' Tracy observed.

'Don't knock it, darling. It's the only stamp of its kind in the world.'

'What's it worth?'

'One million dollars.'

The attendant nodded. 'That is correct, sir. Most people would have no idea, just looking at it. But I see that you, sir, love these stamps, as I do. The history of the world is in them.'

Tracy and Jeff moved on to the next case and looked at an Inverted Jenny stamp that portrayed an airplane flying upside down.

'That's an interesting one,' Tracy said.

The attendant guarding the stamp case said, 'It's worth –'

'Seventy-five thousand dollars,' Jeff remarked.

'Yes, sir. Exactly.'

They moved on to a Hawaiian Missionary two-cent blue.

'That's worth a quarter of a million dollars,' Jeff told Tracy.

Cooper was following closely behind them now, mingling with the crowd.

Jeff pointed to another stamp. 'Here's a rare one. The one-pence Mauritius Post Office. Instead of "post-paid", some daydreaming engraver printed "post *office*". It's worth a lot of pence today.'

'They all seem so small and vulnerable,' Tracy

said, 'and so easy to walk away with.'

The guard at the counter smiled. 'A thief wouldn't get very far, miss. The cases are all electronically wired, and armed guards patrol the convention centre day and night.'

'That's a great relief,' Jeff said earnestly. 'One can't be too careful these days, can one?'

That afternoon Daniel Cooper and Inspector Joop van Duren called on Chief Commissioner Willems together. Van Duren placed the surveillance reports on the commissioner's desk and waited.

'There's nothing definite here,' the chief commissioner finally said, 'but I'll admit that your suspects seem to be sniffing around some very lucrative targets. All right, Inspector. Go ahead. You have official permission to place listening devices in their hotel rooms.'

Daniel Cooper was elated. There would be no more privacy for Tracy Whitney. From this point on he would know everything she was thinking, saying, and doing. He thought about Tracy and Jeff together in bed, and remembered the feel of Tracy's underwear against his cheek. So soft, so sweet-smelling.

That afternoon he went to church.

When Tracy and Jeff left the hotel for dinner that evening, a team of police technicians went to work, planting tiny wireless transmitters in Tracy's and Jeff's suites, concealing them behind pictures, in lamps, and under bedside tables.

Inspector Joop van Duren had commandeered the suite on the floor directly above, and there a technician installed a radio receiver with an antenna and plugged in a recorder.

'It's voice activated,' the technician explained. 'No one has to be here to monitor it. When someone speaks, it will automatically begin to record.'

But Daniel Cooper *wanted* to be there. He *had* to be there. It was God's will.

THIRTY-THREE

Early the following morning Daniel Cooper, Inspector Joop van Duren, and his young assistant, Detective Constable Witkamp, were in the upstairs suite listening to the conversation below.

'More coffee?' Jeff's voice.

'No, thank you, darling.' Tracy's voice. 'Try this cheese that room service sent up. It's really wonderful.'

A short silence. 'Mmmm. Delicious. What would you like to do today, Tracy? We could take a drive to Rotterdam.'

'Why don't we just stay in and relax?'

'Sounds good.'

Daniel Cooper knew what they meant by 'relax', and his mouth tightened.

'The queen is dedicating a new home for orphans.'

'Nice. I think the Dutch are the most hospitable, generous people in the world. They're iconoclasts. They hate rules and regulations.'

A laugh. 'Of course. That's why we both like them so much.'

Ordinary morning conversation between lovers. *They're so free and easy with each other*, Cooper thought. *But how she would pay!*

'Speaking of generous' – Jeff's voice – 'guess who's staying at this hotel? The elusive Maximilian Pierpont. I missed him on the *QE Two*.'

'And I missed him on the *Orient Express*.'

'He's probably here to rape another company. Now that we've found him again, Tracy, we really should do something about him. I mean, as long as he's in the neighbourhood . . .'

Tracy's laughter. 'I couldn't agree more, darling.'

'I understand our friend is in the habit of carrying priceless artifacts with him. I have an idea that –'

Another voice, female. '*Dag, mijnheer, dag, mevrouw*. Would you care for your room to be made up now?'

Van Duren turned to Detective Constable Witkamp. 'I want a surveillance team on Maximilian Pierpont. The moment Whitney or Stevens makes any kind of contact with him, I want to know it.'

Inspector van Duren was reporting to Chief Commissioner Toon Willems.

'They could be after any number of targets, Chief Commissioner. They're showing a great deal of interest in a wealthy American here named Maximilian Pierpont, they attended the philatelist convention, they visited the Lucullan diamond at the Nederlands Diamond-Cutting Factory, and spent two hours at *The Night Watch* –'

'*Ein diefstal van de Nachtwacht? Nee!* Impossible!'

The chief commissioner sat back in his chair and wondered whether he was recklessly wasting valuable time and manpower. There was too much speculation and not enough facts. 'So at the moment you have no idea what their target is.'

'No, Chief Commissioner. I'm not certain they themselves have decided. But the moment they do, they will inform us.'

Willems frowned. 'Inform you?'

'The bugs,' Van Duren explained. 'They have no idea they are being bugged.'

The breakthrough for the police came at 9:00 A.M. the following morning. Tracy and Jeff were finishing breakfast in Tracy's suite. At the listening post upstairs were Daniel Cooper, Inspector Joop van Duren and Detective Constable Witkamp. They heard the sound of coffee being poured.

'Here's an interesting item, Tracy. Our friend was right. Listen to this: "Amro Bank is shipping five million dollars in gold bullion to the Dutch West Indies."'

In the suite on the floor above, Detective Constable Witkamp said, 'There's no way –'

'Shh!'

They listened.

'I wonder how much five million dollars in gold would weigh?' Tracy's voice.

'I can tell you exactly, my darling. One thousand six hundred and seventy-two pounds, about sixty-seven gold bars. The wonderful thing about gold is that it's so beautifully anonymous. You melt it down and it could belong to anybody. Of course, it wouldn't be easy to get those bars out of Holland.'

'Even if we could, how would we get hold of them in the first place? Just walk into the bank and pick them up?'

'Something like that.'

'You're joking.'

'I never joke about that kind of money. Why don't we just stroll by the Amro Bank, Tracy, and have a little look?'

'What do you have in mind?'

'I'll tell you all about it on the way.'

There was the sound of a door closing, and the voices ended.

Inspector van Duren was fiercely twisting his moustache. '*Nee!* There is no way they could get their hands on that gold. I, myself, approved those security arrangements.'

Daniel Cooper announced flatly, 'If there's a flaw in the bank's security system, Tracy Whitney will find it.'

It was all Inspector van Duren could do to control his hair-trigger temper. The odd-looking American had been an abomination ever since his arrival. It was his God-given sense of superiority that was so difficult to tolerate. But Inspector van Duren was a policeman first and last; and he had been ordered to cooperate with the weird little man.

The inspector turned to Witkamp. 'I want you to increase the surveillance unit. *Immediately*. I want every contact photographed and questioned. Clear?'

'Yes, Inspector.'

'And very discreetly, mind you. They must not know they are being watched.'

'Yes, Inspector.'

Van Duren looked at Cooper. 'There. Does that make you feel better?'

Cooper did not bother to reply.

During the next five days Tracy and Jeff kept Inspector van Duren's men busy, and Daniel Cooper carefully examined all the daily reports. At night, when the other detectives left the listening post, Cooper lingered. He listened for the sounds of lovemaking that he knew was going on below. He could hear nothing, but in his mind Tracy was moaning, 'Oh, yes, darling, yes, yes. Oh, God, I can't stand it . . . it's so wonderful . . . Now, oh, now . . .'

Then the long, shuddering sigh and the soft, velvety silence. And it was all for him.

Soon you'll belong to me, Cooper thought. *No one else will have you.*

During the day, Tracy and Jeff went their separate ways, and wherever they went they were followed. Jeff visited a printing shop near Leidseplein, and two detectives watched from the street as he held an earnest conversation with the printer. When Jeff left, one of the detectives followed him. The other went into the shop and showed the printer his plastic-coated police identity card with the official stamp, photograph, and the diagonal red, white and blue stripes.

'The man who just left here. What did he want?'

'He's run out of business cards. He wants me to print some more for him.'

'Let me see.'

The printer showed him a handwritten form:

Amsterdam Security Services
Cornelius Wilson, Chief Investigator

The following day Constable First-Class Fien Hauer waited outside a pet shop on Leidseplein as Tracy went in. When she emerged fifteen minutes later, Fien Hauer entered the shop and showed her identification.

'That lady who just left, what did she want?'

'She purchased a bowl of goldfish, two love-birds, a canary and a pigeon.'

A strange combination. 'A pigeon, you said? You mean an ordinary pigeon?'

'Yes, but no pet store stocks them. I told her we would have to locate one for her.'

'Where are you sending these pets?'

'To her hotel, the Amstel.'

On the other side of town, Jeff was speaking to the vice-president of the Amro Bank. They were closeted together for thirty minutes, and when Jeff left the bank, a detective went into the manager's office.

'The man who just walked out. Please tell me why he was here.'

'Mr Wilson? He's chief investigator for the security company our bank uses. They're revising the security system.'

'Did he ask you to discuss the present security arrangements with him?'

'Why, yes, as a matter of fact, he did.'

'And you told him?'

'Of course. But naturally I first took the precaution of telephoning to make sure his credentials were in order.'

'Whom did you telephone?'

'The security service – the number was printed on his identification card.'

At 3:00 that afternoon an armoured truck pulled up outside the Amro Bank. From across the street, Jeff snapped a picture of the truck, while in a doorway a few yards away a detective photographed Jeff.

At police headquarters at Elandsgracht Inspector van Duren was spreading out the rapidly accumulating evidence on the desk of Chief Commissioner Toon Willems.

'What does all this signify?' the chief commissioner asked in his dry, thin voice.

Daniel Cooper spoke. 'I'll tell you what she's planning.' His voice was heavy with conviction. 'She's planning to hijack the gold shipment.'

They were all staring at him.

Commissioner Willems said, 'And I suppose you know how she intends to accomplish this miracle?'

'Yes.' He knew something they did not know. He knew Tracy Whitney's heart and soul and mind. He had put himself inside her, so that he could think like her, plan like her . . . and anticipate her every move.

'By using a fake security truck and getting to the bank before the real truck, and driving off with the bullion.'

'That sounds rather farfetched, Mr Cooper.'

Inspector van Duren broke in. 'I don't know what their scheme is, but they are planning *something*, Chief Commissioner. We have their voices on tape.'

Daniel Cooper remembered the other sounds he had imagined: the night whispers, the cries and moans. She was behaving like a bitch in heat. Well, where he would put her, no man would ever touch her again.

The inspector was saying, 'They learned the security routine of the bank. They know what time the armoured truck makes its pickup and –'

The chief commissioner was studying the report in front of him. 'Lovebirds, a pigeon, goldfish, a canary – do you think any of this nonsense has anything to do with the robbery?'

'No,' Van Duren said.

'Yes,' Cooper said.

* * *

Constable First-Class Fien Hauer, dressed in an aqua polyester trouser suit, trailed Tracy Whitney down Prinsengracht, across the Magere Bridge, and when Tracy reached the other side of the canal, Fien Hauer looked on in frustration as Tracy stepped into a public telephone booth and spoke into the phone for five minutes. The constable would have been just as unenlightened if she could have heard the conversation.

Gunther Hartog, in London, was saying, 'We can depend on Margo, but she'll need time – at least two more weeks.' He listened a moment. 'I understand. When everything is ready, I will get in touch with you. Be careful. And give my regards to Jeff.'

Tracy replaced the receiver and stepped out of the booth. She gave a friendly nod to the woman in the aqua trouser suit who stood waiting to use the telephone.

At 11:00 the following morning a detective reported to Inspector van Duren, 'I'm at the Wolters Truck Rental Company, Inspector. Jeff Stevens has just rented a truck from them.'

'What kind of truck?'

'A service truck, Inspector.'

'Get the dimensions. I'll hold on.'

A few minutes later the detective was back on the phone. 'I have them. The truck is –'

Inspector van Duren said, 'A step van, twenty feet long, seven feet wide, six feet high, dual axles.'

There was an astonished pause. 'Yes, Inspector. How did you know?'

'Never mind. What colour is it?'

'Blue.'

'Who's following Stevens?'

'Jacobs.'

'Good. Report back here.'

Joop van Duren replaced the receiver. He looked up at Daniel Cooper. 'You were right. Except that the van is blue.'

'He'll take it to a car paint shop.'

The paint shop was located in a garage on the Damrak. Two men sprayed the truck a gun-metal grey, while Jeff stood by. On the roof of the garage a detective shot photographs through the skylight.

The pictures were on Inspector van Duren's desk one hour later.

He shoved them towards Daniel Cooper. 'It's being painted the identical colour of the real security truck. We could pick them up now, you know.'

'On what charges? Having some false business cards printed and painting a truck? The only way to make the charge stick is to catch them when they pick up the bullion.'

The little prick acts like he's running the department. 'What do you think he'll do next?'

Cooper was carefully studying the photograph. 'This truck won't take the weight of the gold. They'll have to reinforce the floorboards.'

*   *   *

It was a small, out-of-the-way garage on Muider Straat.

'*Goede morgen, mijnheer*. How may I serve you?'

'I'm going to be carrying some scrap iron in this truck,' Jeff explained, 'and I'm not sure the floorboards are strong enough to take the weight. I'd like them reinforced with metal braces. Can you do that?'

The mechanic walked over to the truck and examined it. '*Ja.* No problem.'

'Good.'

'I can have it ready *vrijdag* – Friday.'

'I was hoping to have it tomorrow.'

'*Morgen? Nee. Ik* –'

'I'll pay you double.'

'*Donderdag* – Thursday.'

'Tomorrow. I'll pay you triple.'

The mechanic scratched his chin thoughtfully. 'What time tomorrow?'

'Noon.'

'*Ja.* Okay.'

'*Dank wel.*'

'*Tot uw dienst.*'

Moments after Jeff left the garage a detective was interrogating the mechanic.

On the same morning the team of surveillance experts assigned to Tracy followed her to the Oude Schans Canal, where she spent half an hour in conversation with the owner of a barge. When Tracy left, one of the detectives stepped aboard the barge.

He identified himself to the owner, who was sipping a large *bessen-jenever*, the potent redcurrant gin. 'What did the young lady want?'

'She and her husband are going to take a tour of the canals. She's rented my barge for a week.'

'Beginning when?'

'Friday. It's a beautiful vacation, *mijnheer*. If you and your wife would be interested in –'

The detective was gone.

The pigeon Tracy had ordered from the pet shop was delivered to her hotel in a birdcage. Daniel Cooper returned to the pet shop and questioned the owner.

'What kind of pigeon did you send her?'

'Oh, you know, an ordinary pigeon.'

'Are you sure it's not a homing pigeon?'

'No.' The man giggled. 'The reason I know it's not a homing pigeon is because I caught it last night in Vondelpark.'

A thousand pounds of gold and an ordinary pigeon? *Why?* Daniel Cooper wondered.

Five days before the transfer of bullion from the Amro Bank was to take place, a large pile of photographs had accumulated on Inspector Joop van Duren's desk.

Each picture is a link in the chain that is going to trap her, Daniel Cooper thought. The Amsterdam police had no imagination, but Cooper had to give them credit for being thorough. Every step

leading to the forthcoming crime was photographed and documented. There was no way Tracy
Whitney could escape justice.

Her punishment will be my redemption.

On the day Jeff picked up the newly painted truck
he drove it to a small garage he had rented near
the Oude Zijds Kolk, the oldest part of Amsterdam.
Six empty wooden boxes stamped MACHINERY
were also delivered to the garage. A photograph
of the boxes lay on Inspector van Duren's desk as
he listened to the latest tape.

Jeff's voice: 'When you drive the truck from the
bank to the barge, stay within the speed limit. I
want to know exactly how long the trip takes.
Here's a stopwatch.'

'Aren't you coming with me, darling?'

'No. I'm going to be busy.'

'What about Monty?'

'He'll arrive Thursday night.'

'Who is this Monty?' Inspector van Duren asked.

'He's probably the man who's going to pose as
the second security guard,' Cooper said. 'They're
going to need uniforms.'

The costume store was on Pieter Cornelisz Hooft
Straat, in a shopping centre.

'I need two uniforms for a costume party,' Jeff
explained to the clerk. 'Similar to the one you have
in the window.'

One hour later Inspector van Duren was looking

at a photograph of a guard's uniform.

'He ordered two of these. He told the clerk he would pick them up Thursday.'

The size of the second uniform indicated that it was for a man much larger than Jeff Stevens. The inspector said, 'Our friend Monty would be about six-feet three and weigh around fifteen stone. We'll have Interpol put that through their computers,' he assured Daniel Cooper, 'and we'll get an identification on him.'

In the private garage Jeff had rented, he was perched on top of the truck, and Tracy was in the driver's seat.

'Are you ready?' Jeff called. '*Now.*'

Tracy pressed a button on the dashboard. A large piece of canvas rolled down each side of the truck, spelling out HEINEKEN HOLLAND BEER.

'It works!' Jeff cheered.

'Heineken beer? *Alstublieft!*' Van Duren looked around at the detectives gathered in his office. A series of blown-up photographs and memos were tacked all around the walls.

Daniel Cooper sat in the back of the room, silent. As far as Cooper was concerned, this meeting was a waste of time. He had long since anticipated every move Tracy Whitney and her lover would make. They had walked into a trap, and the trap was closing in on them. While the detectives in the office were filled with a growing excitement, Cooper felt an odd sense of anticlimax.

'All the pieces have fallen into place,' Inspector van Duren was saying. 'The suspects know what time the real armoured truck is due at the bank. They plan to arrive about half an hour earlier, posing as security guards. By the time the real truck arrives, they'll be gone.' Van Duren pointed to the photograph of an armoured car. 'They will drive away from the bank looking like this, but a block away, on some side street' – he indicated the Heineken beer truck photograph – 'the truck will suddenly look like *this*.'

A detective from the back of the room spoke up. 'Do you know how they plan to get the gold out of the country, Inspector?'

Van Duren pointed to a picture of Tracy stepping onto the barge. 'First, by barge. Holland is so criss-crossed with canals and waterways that they could lose themselves indefinitely.' He indicated an aerial photograph of the truck speeding along the edge of the canal. 'They've timed the run to see how long it takes to get from the bank to their barge. Plenty of time to load the gold onto the barge and be on their way before anyone suspects anything is wrong.' Van Duren walked over to the last photograph on the wall, an enlarged picture of a freighter. 'Two days ago Jeff Stevens reserved cargo space on the *Oresta*, sailing from Rotterdam next week. The cargo was listed as machinery, destination Hong Kong.'

He turned to face the men in the room. 'Well, gentlemen, we're making a slight change in their plans. We're going to let them remove the gold bullion from the bank and load it into the truck.' He looked at Daniel Cooper and smiled. 'Red-handed. We're going to catch these clever people red-handed.'

A detective followed Tracy into the American Express office, where she picked up a medium-sized package; she returned immediately to her hotel.

'No way of knowing what was in the package,' Inspector van Duren told Cooper. 'We searched both their suites when they left, and there was nothing new in either of them.'

Interpol's computers were unable to furnish any information on the fifteen-stone Monty.

At the Amstel late Thursday evening, Daniel Cooper, Inspector van Duren, and Detective Constable Witkamp were in the room above Tracy's, listening to the voices below.

Jeff's voice: 'If we get to the bank exactly thirty minutes before the guards are due, that will give us plenty of time to load the gold and move out. By the time the real truck arrives, we'll be stowing the gold onto the barge.'

Tracy's voice: 'I've had the mechanic check the truck and fill it with petrol. It's ready.'

Detective Constable Witkamp said, 'One must almost admire them. They don't leave a thing to chance.'

'They all slip up sooner or later,' Inspector van Duren said curtly.

Daniel Cooper was silent, listening.

'Tracy, when this is over, how would you like to go on that dig we talked about?'

'Tunisia? Sounds like heaven, darling.'

'Good. I'll arrange it. From now on we'll do nothing but relax and enjoy life.'

Inspector van Duren murmured, 'I'd say their next twenty years are pretty well taken care of.' He rose and stretched. 'Well, I think we can go to bed. Everything is set for tomorrow morning, and we can all use a good night's sleep.'

Daniel Cooper was unable to sleep. He visualized Tracy being grabbed and manhandled by the police, and he could see the terror on her face. It excited him. He went into the bathroom and ran a very hot bath. He removed his glasses, took off his pyjamas, and lay back in the steaming water. It was almost over, and she would pay, as he had made other whores pay. By this time tomorrow he would be on his way home. *No, not home*, Daniel Cooper corrected himself. *To my flat. Home* was a warm safe place where his mother loved him more than she loved anyone else in the world.

'You're my little man,' she said. 'I don't know what I would do without you.'

Daniel's father disappeared when Daniel was four years old, and at first he blamed himself, but his mother explained that it was because of another woman. He hated that other woman, because she made his mother cry. He had never seen her, but he knew she was a whore because he had heard his mother call her that. Later, he was happy that the woman had taken his father away, for now he had his mother all to himself. The Minnesota winters were cold, and Daniel's mother allowed him to crawl into bed with her and snuggle under the warm blankets.

'I'm going to marry you one day,' Daniel promised, and his mother laughed and stroked his hair.

Daniel was always at the head of his class in school. He wanted his mother to be proud of him.

What a brilliant little boy you have, Mrs Cooper. I know. No one is as clever as my little man.

When Daniel was seven years old, his mother started inviting their neighbour, a huge, hairy man, over to their house for dinner, and Daniel became ill. He was in bed for a week with a dangerously high fever, and his mother promised she would never do that again. *I don't need anyone in the world but you, Daniel.*

No one could have been as happy as Daniel. His mother was the most beautiful woman in the whole world. When she was out of the house, Daniel would go into her bedroom and open the drawers of her dresser. He would take out her lingerie and rub the soft material against his cheek. They smelled oh, so wonderful.

He lay back in the warm bath in the Amsterdam hotel, his eyes closed, remembering the terrible day of his mother's murder. It was on his twelfth birthday. He was sent home from school early because he had an earache. He pretended it was worse than it was, because he wanted to be home where his mother would soothe him and put him into her bed and fuss over him. Daniel walked into the house and went to his mother's bedroom, and she was lying naked in their bed, but she was not alone. She was doing unspeakable things to the man who lived next door. Daniel watched as she began to kiss the matted chest and the bloated stomach, and her kisses trailed downward towards the huge red weapon between the man's legs. Before she took it into her mouth, Daniel heard his mother moan, 'Oh, I love you!'

And that was the most unspeakable thing of all. Daniel ran to his bathroom and vomited all over himself. He carefully undressed and cleaned himself up because his mother had taught him to be neat. His earache was really bad now. He heard voices from the hallway and listened.

His mother was saying, 'You'd better go now, darling. I've got to bathe and get dressed. Daniel will be home from school soon. I'm giving him a birthday party. I'll see you tomorrow, sweetheart.'

There was the noise of the front door closing, and then the sound of running water from his mother's bathroom. Except that she was no longer his mother. She was a whore who did dirty things in bed with men, things she had never done with him.

He walked into her bathroom, naked, and she was in the bath, her whore's face smiling. She turned her head and saw him and said, 'Daniel, darling! What are you –?'

He carried a pair of heavy dressmaker's shears in his hand.

'Daniel –' Her mouth was opened into a pink-lined O, but there was no sound until he made the first stab into the breast of the stranger in the bath. He accompanied her screams with his own. 'Whore! Whore! Whore!'

They sang a deadly duet together, until finally there was his voice alone. 'Whore . . . whore . . .'

He was spattered all over with her blood. He stepped into her shower and scrubbed himself until his skin felt raw.

That man next door had killed his mother, and that man would have to pay.

After that, everything seemed to happen with a supernal clarity, in a curious kind of slow motion. Daniel wiped the fingerprints off the shears with a flannel and threw them into the bath. They clanked dully against the enamel. He dressed and telephoned the police. Two police cars arrived, with sirens screaming, and then another car filled with detectives, and they asked Daniel questions, and he told them how he had been sent home from school early and about seeing their next-door neighbour, Fred Zimmer, leaving through the side door. When they questioned the man, he admitted being the lover of Daniel's mother, but denied killing her. It was Daniel's testimony in court that convicted Zimmer.

'When you arrived home from school, you saw your neighbour, Fred Zimmer, running out the side door?'

'Yes, sir.'

'Could you see him clearly?'

'Yes, sir. There was blood all over his hands.'

'What did you do then, Daniel?'

'I – I was so scared. I knew something awful had happened to my mother.'

'Then did you go into the house?'

'Yes, sir.'

'And what happened?'

'I called out, "Mother!" And she didn't answer, so I went into her bathroom and –'

At this point the young boy broke into hysterical sobs and had to be led from the stand.

Fred Zimmer was executed thirteen months later.

In the meantime young Daniel had been sent to live with a distant relative in Texas, Aunt Mattie, whom he had never met. She was a stern woman, a hard-shelled Baptist filled with a vehement righteousness and the conviction that hell's fire awaited all sinners. It was a house without love or joy or pity, and Daniel grew up in that atmosphere, terrified by the secret knowledge of his guilt and the damnation that awaited him. Shortly after his mother's murder Daniel began to have trouble with his vision. The doctors called the problem psy-chosomatic.

'He's blocking out something he doesn't want to see,' the doctors said.

The lenses on his glasses grew thicker.

At seventeen Daniel ran away from Aunt Mattie and Texas forever. He hitchhiked to New York, where he was hired as a messenger boy by the International Insurance Protection Association. Within three years he was promoted to an inves-tigator. He became the best they had. He never demanded a raise in salary or better working con-ditions. He was oblivious to those things. He was the Lord's right arm, his scourge, punishing the wicked. Daniel Cooper rose from his bath and pre-pared for bed. *Tomorrow*, he thought. *Tomorrow will be the whore's day of retribution.*

He wished his mother could be there to see it.

THIRTY-FOUR

Amsterdam
Friday, 22 August – 8:00 A.M.

Daniel Cooper and the two detectives assigned to the listening post heard Tracy and Jeff at breakfast.

'Sweet roll, Jeff? Coffee?'

'No, thanks.'

Daniel Cooper thought, *It's the last breakfast they'll ever have together*.

'Do you know what I'm getting excited about? Our barge trip.'

'This is the big day, and you're excited about a trip on a *barge*? Why?'

'Because it will be just the two of us. Do you think I'm crazy?'

'Absolutely. But you're *my* crazy.'

'Kiss.'

The sound of a kiss.

She should be more nervous, Cooper thought. *I want her to be nervous.*

'In a way, I'll be sorry to leave here, Jeff.'

'Look at it this way, darling. We won't be any the poorer for the experience.'

Tracy's laughter. 'You're right.'

At 9:00 A.M. the conversation was still going on, and Cooper thought, *They should be getting ready. They should be making their last-minute plans. What about Monty? Where are they meeting him?*

Jeff was saying, 'Darling, would you take care of the concierge before you check us out? I'm going to be rather busy.'

'Of course. He's been wonderful. Why don't they have concierges in the States?'

'I guess it's just a European custom. Do you know how it started?'

'No.'

'In France, in 1627, King Hugh built a prison in Paris and put a nobleman in charge of it. He gave him the title of *comte des cierges*, or concierge, meaning "count of the candles". His pay was two pounds and the ashes from the king's fireplace. Later, anyone in charge of a prison or a castle became known as a concierge, and finally, this included those working in hotels.'

What the hell are they talking about? Cooper wondered. *It's nine-thirty. Time for them to be leaving.*

Tracy's voice: 'Don't tell me where you learned that – you used to go with a beautiful concierge.'

A strange female voice: '*Goede morgen, mevrouw, mijnheer.*'

Jeff's voice: 'There are no beautiful concierges.'

The female voice, puzzled: '*Ik begrijp het niet.*'

Tracy's voice: 'I'll bet if there were, you'd find them.'

'What the hell is going on down there?' Cooper demanded.

The detectives looked baffled. 'I don't know. The maid's on the phone calling the housekeeper. She came in to clean, but she says she doesn't understand – she hears voices, but she doesn't see anybody.'

'*What?*' Cooper was on his feet, racing towards the floor, flying down the stairs. Moments later he and the other detectives burst into Tracy's suite. Except for the confused maid, it was empty. On a coffee table in front of a couch a tape recorder was playing.

Jeff's voice: 'I think I'll change my mind about that coffee. Is it still hot?'

Tracy's voice: 'Uh-huh.'

Cooper and the detectives stared in disbelief.

'I – I don't understand,' one of the detectives stammered.

Cooper snapped, 'What's the police emergency number?'

'Twenty-two-twenty-two-twenty-two.'

Cooper hurried over to the phone and dialled.

Jeff's voice on the tape recorder was saying, 'You know, I really think their coffee is better than ours. I wonder how they do it.'

Cooper screamed into the phone, 'This is Daniel

Cooper. Get hold of Inspector van Duren. Tell him Whitney and Stevens have disappeared. Have him check the garage and see if their truck is gone. I'm on my way to the bank!' He slammed down the receiver.

Tracy's voice was saying, 'Have you ever had coffee brewed with eggshells in it? It's really quite –'

Cooper was out the door.

Inspector van Duren said, 'It's all right. The truck has left their garage. They're on their way here.'

Van Duren, Cooper, and two detectives were at a police command post on the roof of a building across from the Amro Bank.

The inspector said, 'They probably decided to move up their plans when they learned they were being bugged, but relax, my friend. Look.' He pushed Cooper towards the wideangle telescope on the roof. On the street below, a man dressed in janitor's clothes was meticulously polishing the brass nameplate of the bank . . . a street cleaner was sweeping the streets . . . a newspaper vendor stood on a corner . . . three repairmen were at work. All were equipped with miniature walkie-talkies.

Van Duren spoke into his walkie-talkie. 'Point A?'

The janitor said, 'I read you, Inspector.'

'Point B?'

'You're coming in, sir.' This from the street cleaner.

'Point C?'

The news vendor looked up and nodded.

'Point D?'

The repairmen stopped their work, and one of them spoke into the walkie-talkie. 'Everything's ready here, sir.'

The inspector turned to Cooper. 'Don't worry. The gold is still safely in the bank. The only way they can get their hands on it is to come for it. The moment they enter the bank, both ends of the street will be barricaded. There's no way they can escape.' He consulted his watch. 'The truck should be in sight any moment now.'

Inside the bank, the tension was growing. The employees had been briefed, and the guards ordered to help load the gold into the armoured truck when it arrived. Everyone was to cooperate fully.

The disguised detectives outside the bank kept working, surreptitiously watching the street for a sign of the truck.

On the roof, Inspector van Duren asked, for the tenth time, 'Any sign of the damned truck yet?'

'*Nee.*'

Detective Constable Witkamp looked at his watch. 'They're thirteen goddamn minutes overdue. If they –'

The walkie-talkie crackled into life. 'Inspector! The truck just came into sight! It's crossing Rozengracht, heading for the bank. You should be able to see it from the roof in a minute.'

The air was suddenly charged with electricity.

Inspector van Duren spoke rapidly into the walkie-talkie. 'Attention, all units. The fish are in the net. Let them swim in.'

A grey armoured truck moved to the entrance of the bank and stopped. As Cooper and Van Duren watched, two men wearing the uniforms of the security guards got out of the truck and walked into the bank.

'Where is she? Where's Tracy Whitney?' Daniel Cooper spoke aloud.

'It doesn't matter,' Inspector van Duren assured him. 'She won't be far from the gold.'

And even if she is, Daniel Cooper thought, *it's not important. The tapes are going to convict her.*

Nervous employees helped the two uniformed men load the gold bullion from the vault onto dollies and wheel them out to the armoured truck. Cooper and van Duren watched the distant figures from the roof across the street.

The loading took eight minutes. When the back of the truck was locked, and the two men started to climb into the front seat, Inspector van Duren yelled into his walkie-talkie, '*Vlug! Pas op!* All units close in! *Close in!*'

Pandemonium erupted. The janitor, the news vendor, the workers in overalls, and a swarm of other detectives raced to the armoured truck and surrounded it, guns drawn. The street was cordoned off from all traffic in either direction.

Inspector van Duren turned to Daniel Cooper

and grinned. 'Is this red-handed enough for you?
Let's wrap it up.'

It's over at last, Cooper thought.

They hurried down to the street. The two uniformed men were facing the wall, hands raised,
surrounded by a circle of armed detectives. Daniel
Cooper and Inspector van Duren pushed their way
through.

Van Duren said, 'You can turn around now.
You're under arrest.'

The two men, ashen-faced, turned to face the
group. Daniel Cooper and Inspector van Duren
stared at them in shock. They were total strangers.

'Who – who are you?' Inspector van Duren
demanded.

'We – we're the guards for the security company,' one of them stammered. 'Don't shoot. Please
don't shoot.'

Inspector van Duren turned to Cooper. 'Their
plan went wrong.' His voice held a note of hysteria. 'They called it off.'

There was a green bile in the pit of Daniel
Cooper's stomach, and it slowly began to rise up
into his chest and throat, so that when he could
finally speak, his voice was choked. 'No. Nothing
went wrong.'

'What are you talking about?'

'They were never after the gold. This whole
setup was a decoy.'

'That's impossible! I mean, the truck, the barge,
the uniforms – we have photographs . . .'

'Don't you understand? They *knew* it. They knew we were on to them all the time!'

Inspector van Duren's face went white. 'Oh, my God! *Waar zijnze – where are they?*'

On Paulus Potter Straat in Coster, Tracy and Jeff were approaching the Nederlands Diamond-Cutting Factory. Jeff wore a beard and moustache, and had altered the shape of his cheeks and nose with foam sponges. He was dressed in a sports outfit and carried a rucksack. Tracy wore a black wig, a maternity dress and padding, heavy makeup, and dark sunglasses. She carried a large briefcase and a round package wrapped in brown paper. The two of them entered the reception room and joined a busload of tourists listening to a guide. '. . . And now, if you will follow me, ladies and gentlemen, you will see our diamond cutters at work and have an opportunity to purchase some of our fine diamonds.'

With the guide leading the way, the crowd entered the doors that led inside the factory. Tracy moved along with them, while Jeff lingered behind. When the others had gone, Jeff turned and hurried down a flight of stairs that led to a basement. He opened his rucksack and took out a pair of oil-stained overalls and a small box of tools. He donned the overalls, walked over to the fuse box, and looked at his watch.

Upstairs, Tracy stayed with the group as it moved from room to room while the guide showed them the various processes that went into making polished gems out of raw diamonds. From time to time Tracy glanced at her watch. The tour was five minutes behind schedule. She wished the guide would move faster.

At last, as the tour ended, they reached the display room. The guide walked over to the roped-off pedestal.

'In this glass case,' he announced proudly, 'is the Lucullan diamond, one of the most valuable diamonds in the world. It was once purchased by a famous stage actor for his film-star wife. It is valued at ten million dollars and is protected by the most modern –'

The lights went out. Instantly, an alarm sounded and steel shutters slammed down in front of the windows and doors, sealing all the exits. Some of the tourists began to scream.

'Please!' the guide shouted above the noise. 'There is no need for concern. It is a simple electrical failure. In a moment the emergency generator will –' The lights came on again.

'You see?' the guide reassured them. 'There is nothing to worry about.'

A German tourist in lederhosen pointed to the steel shutters. 'What are those?'

'A safety precaution,' the guide explained. He took out an odd-shaped key, inserted it in a slot in the wall, and turned it. The steel shutters over the doors and windows retracted. The telephone on the desk rang, and the guide picked it up.

'Hendrik, here. Thank you, Captain. No, every-thing is fine. It was a false alarm. Probably an elec-trical short. I will have it checked out at once. Yes, sir.' He replaced the receiver and turned to the group. 'My apologies, ladies and gentlemen. With something as valuable as this stone, one can't be too careful. Now, for those of you who would like to purchase some of our very fine diamonds –'

The lights went out again. The alarm bell rang, and the steel shutters slammed down once more.

A woman in the crowd cried, 'Let's get out of here, Harry.'

'Will you just shut up, Diane?' her husband growled.

In the basement downstairs, Jeff stood in front of the fuse box, listening to the cries of the tourists upstairs. He waited a few moments, then recon-nected the switch. The lights upstairs flickered on.

'Ladies and gentlemen,' the guide yelled over the uproar. 'It is just a technical difficulty.' He took out the key again and inserted it into the wall slot. The steel shutters rose.

The telephone rang. The guide hurried over and picked it up. 'Hendrik, here. No, Captain. Yes. We will have it fixed as quickly as possible. Thank you.'

A door to the room opened and Jeff came in carrying the tool case, his worker's cap pushed back on his head.

He singled out the guide.

'What's the problem? Someone reported trouble with the electrical circuits.'

'The lights keep flashing off and on,' the guide explained. 'See if you can fix it quickly, please.' He turned to the tourists and forced a smile on his lips. 'Why don't we step over here where you can select some fine diamonds at very reasonable prices?'

The group of tourists began to move towards the showcases. Jeff, unobserved in the press of the crowd, slipped a small cylindrical object from his overalls, pulled the pin, and tossed the device behind the pedestal that held the Lucullan diamond. The contrivance began to emit smoke and sparks.

Jeff called out to the guide, 'Hey! There's your problem. There's a short in the wire under the floor.'

A woman tourist screamed, 'Fire!'

'Please, everybody!' the guide yelled. 'No need to panic. Just keep calm.' He turned to Jeff and hissed, 'Fix it! Fix it!'

'No problem,' Jeff said easily. He moved towards the velvet ropes around the pedestal.

'*Nee!*' the guard urged. 'You can't go near that!'

Jeff shrugged. 'Fine with me. *You* fix it.' He turned to leave.

Smoke was pouring out faster now. The people were beginning to panic again.

'Wait!' the guide pleaded. 'Just a minute.' He hurried over to the telephone and dialled a number. 'Captain? Hendrik, here. I'll have to ask you to shut off all the alarms; we're having a little problem. Yes, sir.' He looked over at Jeff. 'How long will you need them off?'

'Five minutes,' Jeff said.

'Five minutes,' the guide repeated into the phone. '*Dank wel.*' He replaced the receiver. 'The alarms will be off in ten seconds. For God's sake, hurry! We *never* shut off the alarm!'

'I've only got two hands, friend.' Jeff waited ten seconds, then moved inside the ropes and walked up to the pedestal. Hendrik signalled to the armed guard, and the guard nodded and fixed his eyes on Jeff.

Jeff was working behind the pedestal. The frustrated guide turned to the group. 'Now, ladies and gentlemen, as I was saying, over here we have a selection of fine diamonds at bargain prices. We accept credit cards, traveller's cheques' – he gave a little chuckle – 'and even cash.'

Tracy was standing in front of the counter. 'Do you buy diamonds?' she asked in a loud voice.

The guide stared at her. 'What?'

'My husband is a prospector. He just returned from South Africa, and he wants me to sell these.'

As she spoke, she opened the briefcase she carried, but she was holding it upside down, and a torrent of flashing diamonds cascaded down and danced all over the floor.

'My diamonds!' Tracy cried. 'Help me!'

There was one frozen moment of silence, and then all hell broke loose. The polite crowd became a mob. They scrambled for the diamonds on their hands and knees, knocking one another out of the way.

'I've got some . . .'

'Grab a handful, John . . .'

'Let go of that, it's mine . . .'

The guide and the guard were beyond speech. They were hurled aside in a sea of scrambling, greedy human beings, filling their pockets and handbags with the diamonds.

The guard screamed, 'Stand back! Stop that!' and was knocked to the floor.

A busload of Italian tourists entered, and when they saw what was happening, they joined in the frantic scramble.

The guard tried to get to his feet to sound the alarm, but the human tide made it impossible. They were trampling over him. The world had suddenly gone mad. It was a nightmare that seemed to have no end.

When the dazed guard finally managed to stagger to his feet, he pushed his way through the bedlam, reached the pedestal, and stood there, staring in disbelief.

The Lucullan diamond had disappeared.

So had the pregnant lady and the electrician.

Tracy removed her disguise in a stall in the public washroom in Oosterpark, a long away from the factory. Carrying the package wrapped in brown paper, she headed for a park bench. Everything was moving perfectly. She thought about the mob of people scrambling for the worthless zircons and laughed aloud. She saw Jeff approaching, wearing a dark grey suit; the beard and moustache had vanished. Tracy leapt to her feet. Jeff walked up to her and grinned. 'I love you,' he said. He slipped the Lucullan diamond out of his jacket pocket and handed it to Tracy. 'Feed this to your friend, darling. See you later.'

Tracy watched him as he strolled away. Her eyes were shining. They belonged to each other. They would take separate planes and meet in Brazil, and after that, they would be together for the rest of their lives.

Tracy looked around to make sure no one was observing, then she unwrapped the package she held. Inside was a small cage holding a slate-grey pigeon. When it had arrived at the American Express office three days earlier, Tracy had taken it to her suite and released the other pigeon out the window and watched it clumsily flutter away. Now, Tracy took a small chamois sack from her handbag and placed the diamond in it. She removed the pigeon from its cage and held it while she carefully tied the sack to the bird's leg.

'Good girl, Margo. Take it home.'

A uniformed policeman appeared from nowhere. 'Hold it! What do you think you're doing?'

Tracy's heart skipped a beat. 'What's – what's the trouble, officer?'

His eyes were on the cage, and he was angry. 'You *know* what the trouble is. It's one thing to feed these pigeons, but it's against the law to trap them and put them in cages. Now, you just let it go before I place you under arrest.'

Tracy swallowed and took a deep breath. 'If you say so, officer.' She lifted her arms and tossed the pigeon into the air. A lovely smile lit her face as she watched the pigeon soar, higher and higher. It circled once, then headed in the direction of London, 230 miles to the west. A homing pigeon averaged forty miles an hour, Gunther had told her, so Margo would reach him within six hours.

'Don't ever try that again,' the officer warned Tracy.

'I won't,' Tracy promised solemnly. 'Never again.'

Late that afternoon, Tracy was at Schiphol Airport, moving towards the gate from which she would board a plane bound for Brazil. Daniel Cooper stood off in a corner, watching her, his eyes bitter. Tracy Whitney had stolen the Lucullan diamond. Cooper had known it the moment he heard the report. It was her style, daring and imaginative. Yet, there was nothing that could be done about it. Inspector van Duren had shown photographs of Tracy and Jeff to the museum guard. '*Nee*. Never seen either of them. The thief had a beard and a moustache and his cheeks and nose were much fatter, and the lady with the diamonds was dark-haired and pregnant.'

Nor was there any trace of the diamond. Jeff's and Tracy's persons and baggage had been thoroughly searched.

'The diamond is still in Amsterdam,' Inspector van Duren swore to Cooper. 'We'll find it.'

No, you won't, Cooper thought angrily. She had switched pigeons. The diamond had been carried out of the country by a homing pigeon.

Cooper watched helplessly as Tracy Whitney made her way across the concourse. She was the first person who had ever defeated him. He would go to hell because of her.

As Tracy reached the boarding gate, she hesitated a moment, then turned and looked straight into Cooper's eyes. She had been aware that he had been following her all over Europe, like some kind of nemesis. There was something bizarre about him, frightening and at the same time pathetic. Inexplicably, Tracy felt sorry for him. She gave him a small farewell wave, then turned and boarded her plane.

Daniel Cooper touched the letter of resignation in his pocket.

It was a luxurious Pan American 747, and Tracy was seated in Seat 4B on the aisle in first class. She was excited. In a few hours she would be with Jeff. They would be married in Brazil. *No more capers,* Tracy thought, *but I won't miss them. I know I won't. Life will be thrilling enough just being Mrs Jeff Stevens.*

'Excuse me.'

Tracy looked up. A puffy, dissipated-looking middle-aged man was standing over her. He indicated the window seat. 'That's my seat, honey.'

Tracy twisted aside so he could get past her. As

her skirt slid up, he eyed her legs appreciatively.

'Great day for a flight, huh?' There was a leer in his voice.

Tracy turned away. She had no interest in getting into a conversation with a fellow passenger. She had too much to think about. *A whole new life. They would settle down somewhere and be model citizens. The ultrarespectable Mr and Mrs Jeff Stevens.*

Her companion nudged her. 'Since we're gonna be seat mates on this flight, little lady, why don't you and I get acquainted? My name is Maximilian Pierpont.'

Bloodline

Sidney Sheldon

The daughter of a rich and powerful father, Elizabeth Roffe is young, beautiful – and sole heir to a billion dollar fortune.

Then tragedy strikes. Her father is killed in a freak accident and Elizabeth must take command of his mighty global empire, the pharmaceutical company Roffe and Sons. It makes Elizabeth the richest girl in the world. But someone, somewhere, is determined that she must die.

From the backstreets of Istanbul to the upmarket offices of New York, *Bloodline* is a hypnotic tale of love and ambition, danger, intrigue and death.

'Absorbing and eminently well-crafted.'   *New York Times*

'Contains the three basic Sheldon ingredients – glamour, intrigue and sex.'   *Daily Mail*

ISBN 0 00 617501 5

The Other Side of Midnight

Sidney Sheldon

A gripping, glamorous novel of scorching sensuality and heart-stopping evil.

A beautiful French actress whose craving for passion and vengeance takes her from the gutters of Paris to the bedroom of a powerful billionaire; a dynamic Greek tycoon who never forgets an insult, never forgives an injury; and a handsome war hero lured from his wife by another woman.

From Paris to Washington, Hollywood to the islands of Greece, *The Other Side of Midnight* is the story of four star-crossed lives enmeshed in a deadly ritual of passion, intrigue and corruption.

'A master storyteller'   *Daily Mail*

'Sheldon is a writer working at the height of his power'
New York Times

ISBN 0 00 617931 2

Are You Afraid of the Dark?

Sidney Sheldon

In New York, Denver, Paris and Berlin, four people have died in what appear to be random accidents.

When two women – widows of the dead – find themselves under merciless attack, their fear and confusion help them to form an unlikely alliance. But why are they being targeted? Is there a connection to their husbands' mysterious deaths?

Meanwhile, the Chief Executive of an international Think Tank is on the cusp of a discovery which could change the world – and deliver unbelievable power into the company's hands. Could the mysterious deaths be connected to this volatile secret?

Taut with suspense and vivid characterization, and with an unnervingly realistic premise, *Are You Afraid of the Dark?* is a *tour de force* from a master storyteller.

ISBN 0 00 716516 1